D0998617

Complete Stories of Henry James

HENRY JAMES

HENRY JAMES

COMPLETE STORIES
1884–1891

THE LIBRARY OF AMERICA

The paper used in this publication meets the
minimum requirements of the American National Standard for
Information Sciences—Permanence of Paper for Printed
Library Materials, ANSI Z39.48—1984.

Distributed to the trade in the United States
by Penguin Putnam Inc.
and in Canada by Penguin Books Canada Ltd.

Library of Congress Catalog Number: 98–19250
For cataloging information, see end of Notes.
ISBN 1–883011–64–7

First Printing
The Library of America—107

Manufactured in the United States of America

Contents

Georgina's Reasons

S HE WAS certainly a singular girl, and if he felt at the end
that he didn't know her nor understand her, it is not surprising that he should have felt it at the beginning. But he
felt at the beginning what he did not feel at the end, that her
singularity took the form of a charm which—once circumstances had made them so intimate—it was impossible to resist
or conjure away. He had a strange impression (it amounted
at times to a positive distress, and shot through the sense of
pleasure, morally speaking, with the acuteness of a sudden
twinge of neuralgia) that it would be better for each of them
that they should break off short and never see each other
again. In later years he called this feeling a foreboding, and
remembered two or three occasions when he had been on the
point of expressing it to Georgina. Of course, in fact, he never
expressed it; there were plenty of good reasons for that.
Happy love is not disposed to assume disagreeable duties; and
Raymond Benyon's love was happy, in spite of grave presen-
timents, in spite of the singularity of his mistress and the insufferable rudeness of her parents. She was a tall, fair girl, with
a beautiful cold eye, and a smile of which the perfect sweetness, proceeding from the lips, was full of compensation; she
had auburn hair, of a hue that could be qualified as nothing
less than gorgeous, and she seemed to move through life with
a stately grace, as she would have walked through an old-
fashioned minuet. Gentlemen connected with the navy have
the advantage of seeing many types of women; they are able
to compare the ladies of New York with those of Valparaiso,
and those of Halifax with those of the Cape of Good Hope.
Raymond Benyon had had these opportunities, and, being
fond of women, he had learned his lesson; he was in a position
to appreciate Georgina Gressie's fine points. She looked like
a duchess—I don't mean that in foreign ports Benyon had
associated with duchesses—and she took everything so seriously. That was flattering for the young man, who was only a
lieutenant, detailed for duty at the Brooklyn navy-yard, without a penny in the world but his pay; with a set of plain,

I

numerous, seafaring, God-fearing relations in New Hamp-shire, a considerable appearance of talent, a feverish, disguised ambition, and a slight impediment in his speech. He was a spare, tough young man; his dark hair was straight and fine, and his face, a trifle pale, smooth and carefully drawn. He stammered a little, blushing when he did so, at long intervals. I scarcely know how he appeared on shipboard, but on shore, in his civilian's garb, which was of the neatest, he had as little as possible an aroma of winds and waves. He was neither salt nor brown nor red nor particularly "hearty." He never twitched up his trousers, nor, so far as one could see, did he, with his modest, attentive manner, carry himself as a person accustomed to command. Of course, as a subaltern, he had more to do in the way of obeying. He looked as if he followed some sedentary calling, and was indeed supposed to be decid-edly intellectual. He was a lamb with women, to whose charms he was, as I have hinted, susceptible; but with men he was different, and, I believe, as much of a wolf as was neces-sary. He had a manner of adoring the handsome, insolent queen of his affections (I will explain in a moment why I call her insolent); indeed, he looked up to her literally, as well as sentimentally, for she was the least bit the taller of the two.

He had met her the summer before on the piazza of an hotel at Fort Hamilton, to which, with a brother-officer, in a dusty buggy, he had driven over from Brooklyn to spend a tremendously hot Sunday—the kind of day when the navy-yard was loathsome; and the acquaintance had been renewed by his calling in Twelfth Street on New Year's day—a consid-erable time to wait for a pretext, but which proved the im-pression had not been transitory. The acquaintance ripened, thanks to a zealous cultivation (on his part) of occasions which Providence, it must be confessed, placed at his disposal none too liberally; so that now Georgina took up all his thoughts and a considerable part of his time. He was in love with her beyond a doubt; but he could not flatter himself that she was smitten with him, though she seemed willing (what was so strange) to quarrel with her family about him. He didn't see how she could really care for him—she was marked out by nature for so much greater a fortune; and he used to say to her, "Ah, you don't—there's no use talking, you don't—really care for me at all!" To which she answered, "Really? You are very particular. It seems to me it's real enough if I let you touch one of my finger-tips!" That was one of her ways of being insolent. Another was simply her manner of looking at him, or at other people, when they spoke to her, with her hard, divine blue eye—looking quietly, amusedly, with the air of considering, wholly from her own point of view, what they might have said, and then turning her head or her back, while, without taking the trouble to answer them, she broke into a short, liquid, irrelevant laugh. This may seem to contradict what I said just now about her taking the young lieutenant in the navy seriously. What I mean is that she appeared to take him more seriously than she took anything else. She said to him once, "At any rate you have the merit of not being a shop-keeper;" and it was by this epithet she was pleased to designate most of the young men who at that time flourished in the best society of New York. Even if she had rather a free way of expressing general indifference, a young lady is supposed to be serious enough when she consents to marry you. For the rest, as regards a certain haughtiness that might be observed in Georgina Gressie, my story will probably throw sufficient light upon it. She remarked to Benyon once that it was none of his business why she liked him, but that, to please herself, she didn't mind telling him she thought the great Napoleon, before he was celebrated, before he had command of the army of Italy, must have looked something like him; and she sketched in a few words the sort of figure she imagined the incipient Bonaparte to have been—short, lean, pale, poor, intellectual, and with a tremendous future under his hat. Benyon asked himself whether he had a tremendous future, and what in the world Georgina expected of him in the coming years. He was flattered at the comparison, he was ambitious enough not to be frightened at it, and he guessed that she perceived a certain analogy between herself and the Empress Josephine. She would make a very good empress—that was true; Georgina was remarkably imperial. This may not at first seem to make it more clear why she should take into her favour an aspirant who, on the face of the matter, was not original, and whose Corsica was a flat New England seaport; but it afterwards became plain that he owed his brief

happiness—it was very brief—to her father's opposition; her
father's and her mother's, and even her uncles' and her aunts'.
In those days, in New York, the different members of a family
took an interest in its alliances; and the house of Gressie
looked askance at an engagement between the most beautiful
of its daughters and a young man who was not in a paying
business. Georgina declared that they were meddlesome and
vulgar; she could sacrifice her own people, in that way, without a scruple; and Benyon's position improved from the moment that Mr. Gressie—ill-advised Mr. Gressie—ordered the
girl to have nothing to do with him. Georgina was imperial
in this—that she wouldn't put up with an order. When, in the
house in Twelfth Street, it began to be talked about that she
had better be sent to Europe with some eligible friend, Mrs.
Portico for instance, who was always planning to go and who
wanted as a companion some young mind, fresh from manuals
and extracts, to serve as a fountain of history and geogra-
phy—when this scheme for getting Georgina out of the way
began to be aired, she immediately said to Raymond Benyon,
"Oh yes, I'll marry you!" She said it in such an off-hand way
that, deeply as he desired her, he was almost tempted to answer, "But, my dear, have you really thought about it?"

II.

This little drama went on, in New York, in the ancient days,
when Twelfth Street had but lately ceased to be suburban,
when the squares had wooden palings, which were not often
painted, when there were poplars in important thoroughfares
and pigs in the lateral ways, when the theatres were miles
distant from Madison Square, and the battered rotunda of
Castle Garden echoed with expensive vocal music, when "the
park" meant the grass-plats of the City Hall, and the Bloom-
ingdale road was an eligible drive, when Hoboken, of a summer afternoon, was a genteel resort, and the handsomest
house in town was on the corner of Fifth Avenue and Fifteenth Street. This will strike the modern reader, I fear, as
rather a primitive epoch; but I am not sure that the strength
of human passions is in proportion to the elongation of a city.
Several of them, at any rate, the most robust and most familiar

—love, ambition, jealousy, resentment, greed—subsisted in considerable force in the little circle at which we have glanced, where a view by no means favourable was taken of Raymond Benyon's attentions to Miss Gressie. Unanimity was a family trait among these people (Georgina was an exception), especially in regard to the important concerns of life, such as marriages and closing scenes. The Gressies hung together; they were accustomed to do well for themselves and for each other. They did everything well: got themselves born well (they thought it excellent to be born a Gressie), lived well, married well, died well, and managed to be well spoken of afterwards. In deference to this last-mentioned habit, I must be careful what I say of them. They took an interest in each other's concerns, an interest that could never be regarded as of a meddlesome nature, inasmuch as they all thought alike about all their affairs, and interference took the happy form of congratulation and encouragement. These affairs were invariably lucky, and, as a general thing, no Gressie had anything to do but feel that another Gressie had been almost as shrewd and decided as he himself would have been. The great exception to that, as I have said, was this case of Georgina, who struck such a false note, a note that startled them all, when she told her father that she should like to unite herself to a young man engaged in the least paying business that any Gressie had ever heard of. Her two sisters had married into the most flourishing firms, and it was not to be thought of that—with twenty cousins growing up around her—she should put down the standard of success. Her mother had told her a fortnight before this that she must request Mr. Benyon to cease coming to the house; for hitherto his suit had been of the most public and resolute character. He had been conveyed up-town, from the Brooklyn ferry, in the "stage," on certain evenings, had asked for Miss Georgina at the door of the house in Twelfth Street, and had sat with her in the front parlour if her parents happened to occupy the back, or in the back if the family had disposed itself in the front. Georgina, in her way, was a dutiful girl, and she immediately repeated her mother's admonition to Benyon. He was not surprised, for, though he was aware that he had not, as yet, a great knowledge of society, he flattered himself he could tell when and where a polite young man was not wanted. There were houses in Brooklyn where such an animal was much appreciated, and there the signs were quite different.

They had been discouraging, except on Georgina's part, from the first of his calling in Twelfth Street. Mr. and Mrs. Gressie used to look at each other in silence when he came in, and indulge in strange perpendicular salutations, without any shaking of hands. People did that at Portsmouth, N.H., when they were glad to see you; but in New York there was more luxuriance, and gesture had a different value. He had never, in Twelfth Street, been asked to "take anything," though the house had a delightful suggestion, a positive aroma, of sideboards, as if there were mahogany "cellarettes" under every table. The old people, moreover, had repeatedly expressed surprise at the quantity of leisure that officers in the navy seemed to enjoy. The only way in which they had not made themselves offensive was by always remaining in the other room; though at times even this detachment, to which he owed some delightful moments, presented itself to Benyon as a form of disapprobation. Of course, after Mrs. Gressie's message, his visits were practically at an end: he wouldn't give the girl up, but he wouldn't be beholden to her father for the opportunity to converse with her. Nothing was left for the tender couple—there was a curious mutual mistrust in their tenderness—but to meet in the squares, or in the topmost streets, or in the sidemost avenues, on the spring afternoons. It was especially during this phase of their relations that Georgina struck Benyon as imperial. Her whole person seemed to exhale a tranquil, happy consciousness of having broken a law. She never told him how she arranged the matter at home, how she found it possible always to keep the appointments (to meet him out of the house) that she so boldly made, in what degree she dissimulated to her parents, and how much, in regard to their continued acquaintance, the old people suspected and accepted. If Mr. and Mrs. Gressie had forbidden him the house, it was not, apparently, because they wished her to walk with him in the Tenth Avenue or to sit at his side under the blossoming lilacs in Stuyvesant Square. He didn't believe that she told lies in Twelfth Street; he thought she was too imperial to lie; and he wondered what she said to her mother when, at the end of nearly a whole afternoon of vague peregrination with her lover, this rustling, bristling matron asked her where she had been. Georgina was capable of simply telling the truth; and yet if she simply told the truth it was a wonder that she had not been still more simply packed off to Europe. Benyon's ignorance of her pretexts is a proof that this rather oddly-mated couple never arrived at perfect intimacy, in spite of a fact which remains to be related. He thought of this afterwards, and thought how strange it was that he had not felt more at liberty to ask her what she did for him, and how she did it, and how much she suffered for him. She would probably not have admitted that she suffered at all, and she had no wish to pose for a martyr.

Benyon remembered this, as I say, in the after years, when he tried to explain to himself certain things which simply puzzled him; it came back to him with the vision, already faded, of shabby cross-streets, straggling toward rivers, with red sunsets, seen through a haze of dust, at the end; a vista through which the figures of a young man and a girl slowly receded and disappeared, strolling side by side, with the relaxed pace of desultory talk, but more closely linked as they passed into the distance, linked by its at last appearing safe to them—in the Tenth Avenue—that the young lady should take his arm. They were always approaching that inferior thoroughfare; but he could scarcely have told you, in those days, what else they were approaching. He had nothing in the world but his pay, and he felt that this was rather a "mean" income to offer Miss Gressie. Therefore he didn't put it forward; what he offered, instead, was the expression—crude often, and almost boyishly extravagant—of a delighted admiration of her beauty, the tenderest tones of his voice, the softest assurances of his eye, and the most insinuating pressure of her hand at those moments when she consented to place it in his arm. All this was an eloquence which, if necessary, might have been condensed into a single sentence; but those few words were scarcely needed when it was as plain that he expected, in general, she would marry him, as it was indefinite that he counted upon her for living on a few hundred a year. If she had been a different girl he might have asked her to wait, might have talked to her of the coming of better days, of his prospective

promotion, of its being wiser, perhaps, that he should leave
the navy and look about for a more lucrative career. With
Georgina it was difficult to go into such questions; she had
no taste whatever for detail. She was delightful as a woman to
love, because when a young man is in love he discovers that;
but she could not be called helpful, for she never suggested
anything. That is, she never had done so till the day she really
proposed—for that was the form it took—to become his wife
without more delay. "Oh yes, I will marry you:" these words,
which I quoted a little way back, were not so much the answer
to something he had said at the moment as the light conclusion of a report she had just made (for the first time) of her
actual situation in her father's house.

III.

"I am afraid I shall have to see less of you," she had begun
by saying. "They watch me so much."

"It is very little already," he answered. "What is once or
twice a week?"

"That's easy for you to say. You are your own master, but
you don't know what I go through."

"Do they make it very bad for you, dearest? Do they make
scenes?" Benyon asked.

"No, of course not. Don't you know us enough to know
how we behave? No scenes; that would be a relief. However,
I never make them myself, and I never will—that's one comfort for you, for the future, if you want to know. Father and
mother keep very quiet, looking at me as if I were one of the
lost, with little hard, piercing eyes, like gimlets. To me they
scarcely say anything, but they talk it all over with each other,
and try and decide what is to be done. It's my belief that my
father has written to the people in Washington—what do you
call it?—the Department—to have you moved away from
Brooklyn—to have you sent to sea."

"I guess that won't do much good. They want me in
Brooklyn; they don't want me at sea."

"Well, they are capable of going to Europe for a year, on
purpose to take me," Georgina said.

"How can they take you if you won't go? And if you should

go, what good would it do if you were only to find me here when you came back, just the same as you left me?"

"Oh, well!" said Georgina, with her lovely smile, "of course they think that absence would cure me of——cure me of——" And she paused, with a kind of cynical modesty, not saying exactly of what.

"Cure you of what, darling? Say it, please say it," the young man murmured, drawing her hand surreptitiously into his arm.

"Of my absurd infatuation!"

"And would it, dearest?"

"Yes, very likely. But I don't mean to try. I shall not go to Europe—not when I don't want to. But it's better I should see less of you—even that I should appear—a little—to give you up."

"A little? What do you call a little?"

Georgina said nothing for a moment. "Well, that, for instance, you shouldn't hold my hand quite so tight!" And she disengaged this conscious member from the pressure of his arm.

"What good will that do?" Benyon asked.

"It will make them think it's all over—that we have agreed to part."

"And as we have done nothing of the kind, how will that help us?"

They had stopped at the crossing of a street; a heavy dray was lumbering slowly past them. Georgina, as she stood there, turned her face to her lover and rested her eyes for some moments on his own. At last, "Nothing will help us; I don't think we are very happy," she answered, while her strange, ironical, inconsequent smile played about her beautiful lips.

"I don't understand how you see things. I thought you were going to say you would marry me," Benyon rejoined, standing there still, though the dray had passed.

"Oh yes, I will marry you!" And she moved away across the street. That was the way she had said it, and it was very characteristic of her. When he saw that she really meant it, he wished they were somewhere else—he hardly knew where the proper place would be—so that he might take her in his arms. Nevertheless, before they separated that day he had said to her he hoped she remembered they would be very poor, reminding her how great a change she would find it. She answered that she shouldn't mind, and presently she said that if this was all that prevented them the sooner they were married the better. The next time he saw her she was quite of the same opinion; but he found, to his surprise, it was now her conviction that she had better not leave her father's house. The ceremony should take place secretly, of course; but they would wait awhile to let their union be known.

"What good will it do us, then?" Raymond Benyon asked.

Georgina coloured. "Well, if you don't know, I can't tell you!"

Then it seemed to him that he did know. Yet, at the same time, he could not see why, once the knot was tied, secrecy should be required. When he asked what especial event they were to wait for, and what should give them the signal to appear as man and wife, she answered that her parents would probably forgive her if they were to discover, not too abruptly, after six months, that she had taken the great step. Benyon supposed that she had ceased to care whether they forgave her or not; but he had already perceived that the nature of women is a queer mosaic. He had believed her capable of marrying him out of bravado, but the pleasure of defiance was absent if the marriage was kept to themselves. It now appeared that she was not especially anxious to defy; she was disposed rather to manage and temporise.

"Leave it to me; leave it to me. You are only a blundering man," Georgina said. "I shall know much better than you the right moment for saying, 'Well, you may as well make the best of it, because we have already done it!' "

That might very well be, but Benyon didn't quite understand, and he was awkwardly anxious (for a lover) till it came over him afresh that there was one thing at any rate in his favour, which was simply that the finest girl he had ever seen was ready to throw herself into his arms. When he said to her, "There is one thing I hate in this plan of yours—that, for ever so few weeks, so few days, your father should support my wife"—when he made this homely remark, with a little flush of sincerity in his face, she gave him a specimen of that unanswerable laugh of hers, and declared that it would serve Mr.

Gressie right for being so barbarous and so horrid. It was
Benyon's view that from the moment she disobeyed her father
she ought to cease to avail herself of his protection; but I am
bound to add that he was not particularly surprised at finding
this a kind of honour in which her feminine nature was little
versed. To make her his wife first—at the earliest moment—
whenever she would, and trust to fortune and the new influence he should have, to give him, as soon thereafter as possible, complete possession of her: this finally presented itself
to the young officer as the course most worthy of a lover and
a gentleman. He would be only a pedant who would take
nothing because he could not get everything at once. They
wandered further than usual this afternoon, and the dusk was
thick by the time he brought her back to her father's door. It
was not his habit to come so near it, but to-day they had so
much to talk about that he actually stood with her for ten
minutes at the foot of the steps. He was keeping her hand in
his, and she let it rest there while she said—by way of a remark that should sum up all their reasons and reconcile their
differences—

"There's one great thing it will do, you know: it will make
me safe."

"Safe from what?"

"From marrying any one else."

"Ah, my girl, if you were to do that——!" Benyon exclaimed; but he didn't mention the other branch of the contingency. Instead of this, he looked aloft at the blind face of
the house (there were only dim lights in two or three windows, and no apparent eyes) and up and down the empty
street, vague in the friendly twilight; after which he drew
Georgina Gressie to his breast and gave her a long, passionate
kiss. Yes, decidedly, he felt they had better be married. She
had run quickly up the steps, and while she stood there, with
her hand on the bell, she almost hissed at him, under her
breath, "Go away, go away; Amanda's coming!" Amanda was
the parlour-maid; and it was in those terms that the Twelfth
Street Juliet dismissed her Brooklyn Romeo. As he wandered
back into the Fifth Avenue, where the evening air was conscious of a vernal fragrance from the shrubs in the little precinct of the pretty Gothic church ornamenting that pleasant

part of the street, he was too absorbed in the impression of
the delightful contact from which the girl had violently released herself to reflect that the great reason she had mentioned a moment before was a reason for their marrying, of
course, but not in the least a reason for their not making it
public. But, as I said in the opening lines of this chapter, if
he did not understand his mistress's motives at the end, he
cannot be expected to have understood them at the beginning.

IV.

Mrs. Portico, as we know, was always talking about going to
Europe; but she had not yet—I mean a year after the incident
I have just related—put her hand upon a youthful cicerone.
Petticoats, of course, were required; it was necessary that her
companion should be of the sex which sinks most naturally
upon benches, in galleries and cathedrals, and pauses most
frequently upon staircases that ascend to celebrated views. She
was a widow with a good fortune and several sons, all of
whom were in Wall Street, and none of them capable of the
relaxed pace at which she expected to take her foreign tour.
They were all in a state of tension; they went through life
standing. She was a short, broad, high-coloured woman, with
a loud voice and superabundant black hair, arranged in a way
peculiar to herself, with so many combs and bands that it had
the appearance of a national coiffure. There was an impression
in New York, about 1845, that the style was Danish; some
one had said something about having seen it in Schleswig-
Holstein. Mrs. Portico had a bold, humorous, slightly flam-
boyant look; people who saw her for the first time received
an impression that her late husband had married the daughter
of a bar-keeper or the proprietress of a menagerie. Her high,
hoarse, good-natured voice seemed to connect her in some
way with public life; it was not pretty enough to suggest that
she might have been an actress. These ideas quickly passed
away, however, even if you were not sufficiently initiated to
know—as all the Gressies, for instance, knew so well—that her
origin, so far from being enveloped in mystery, was almost the
sort of thing she might have boasted of. But, in spite of the

high pitch of her appearance she didn't boast of anything; she was a genial, easy, comical, irreverent person, with a large charity, a democratic, fraternising turn of mind, and a contempt for many worldly standards, which she expressed not in the least in general axioms (for she had a mortal horror of philosophy), but in violent ejaculations on particular occasions. She had not a grain of moral timidity, and she fronted a delicate social problem as sturdily as she would have barred the way of a gentleman she might have met in her vestibule with the plate-chest. The only thing which prevented her being a bore in orthodox circles was that she was incapable of discussion. She never lost her temper, but she lost her vocabulary, and ended quickly by praying that heaven would give her an opportunity to act out what she believed. She was an old friend of Mr. and Mrs. Gressie, who esteemed her for the antiquity of her lineage and the frequency of her subscriptions, and to whom she rendered the service of making them feel liberal—like people too sure of their own position to be frightened. She was their indulgence, their dissipation, their point of contact with dangerous heresies; so long as they continued to see her they could not be accused of being narrow-minded—a matter as to which they were perhaps vaguely conscious of the necessity of taking their precautions. Mrs. Portico never asked herself whether she liked the Gressies; she had no disposition for morbid analysis, she accepted transmitted associations, and found, somehow, that her acquaintance with these people helped her to relieve herself. She was always making scenes in their drawing-room, scenes half indignant, half jocose, like all her manifestations, to which it must be confessed that they adapted themselves beautifully. They never "met" her, in the language of controversy; but always collected to watch her, with smiles and comfortable platitudes, as if they envied her superior richness of temperament. She took an interest in Georgina, who seemed to her different from the others, with suggestions about her of being likely not to marry so unrefreshingly as her sisters had done, and of a high, bold standard of duty. Her sisters had married from duty, but Mrs. Portico would rather have chopped off one of her large plump hands than behave herself so well as that. She had, in her daughterless condition, a certain ideal of a girl who should be beautiful and romantic, with wistful eyes, and a little persecuted, so that she, Mrs. Portico, might get her out of her troubles. She looked to Georgina, to a considerable degree, to give actuality to this vision; but she had really never understood Georgina at all. She ought to have been shrewd, but she lacked this refinement, and she never understood anything until after many disappointments and vexations. It was difficult to startle her, but she was much startled by a communication that this young lady made her one fine spring morning. With her florid appearance and her speculative mind, she was probably the most innocent woman in New York.

Georgina came very early, earlier even than visits were paid in New York thirty years ago; and instantly, without any preface, looking her straight in the face, told Mrs. Portico that she was in great trouble and must appeal to her for assistance. Georgina had in her aspect no symptom of distress; she was as fresh and beautiful as the April day itself; she held up her head and smiled, with a sort of familiar challenge, looking like a young woman who would naturally be on good terms with fortune. It was not in the least in the tone of a person making a confession or relating a misadventure that she presently said, "Well, you must know, to begin with—of course, it will surprise you—that I am married."

"Married, Georgina Gressie!" Mrs. Portico repeated, in her most resonant tones.

Georgina got up, walked with her majestic step across the room, and closed the door. Then she stood there, her back pressed against the mahogany panels, indicating only by the distance she had placed between herself and her hostess the consciousness of an irregular position. "I am not Georgina Gressie—I am Georgina Benyon; and it has become plain, within a short time, that the natural consequence will take place."

Mrs. Portico was altogether bewildered. "The natural consequence?" she exclaimed, staring.

"Of one's being married, of course; I suppose you know what that is. No one must know anything about it. I want you to take me to Europe."

Mrs. Portico now slowly rose from her place and approached her visitor, looking at her from head to foot as she did so, as if to measure the truth of her remarkable announcement. She rested her hands on Georgina's shoulders a moment, gazing into her blooming face, and then she drew her closer and kissed her. In this way the girl was conducted back to the sofa, where, in a conversation of extreme intimacy, she opened Mrs. Portico's eyes wider than they had ever been opened before. She was Raymond Benyon's wife; they had been married a year, but no one knew anything about it. She had kept it from every one, and she meant to go on keeping it. The ceremony had taken place in a little Episcopal church at Haarlem, one Sunday afternoon, after the service. There was no one in that dusty suburb who knew them; the clergyman, vexed at being detained, and wanting to go home to tea, had made no trouble; he tied the knot before they could turn round. It was ridiculous how easy it had been. Raymond had told him frankly that it must all be under the rose, as the young lady's family disapproved of what she was doing. But she was of legal age, and perfectly free; he could see that for himself. The parson had given a grunt as he looked at her over his spectacles; it was not very complimentary, it seemed to say that she was indeed no chicken. Of course she looked old for a girl; but she was not a girl now, was she? Raymond had certified his own identity as an officer in the United States navy (he had papers, besides his uniform, which he wore), and introduced the clergyman to a friend he had brought with him, who was also in the navy, a venerable paymaster. It was he who gave Georgina away, as it were; he was a dear old man, a regular grandmother, and perfectly safe. He had been married three times himself, and the first time in the same way. After the ceremony she went back to her father's; but she saw Mr. Benyon the next day. After that she saw him— for a little while—pretty often. He was always begging her to come to him altogether; she must do him that justice. But she wouldn't—she wouldn't now—perhaps she wouldn't ever. She had her reasons, which seemed to her very good but were very difficult to explain. She would tell Mrs. Portico in plenty of time what they were. But that was not the question now, whether they were good or bad; the question was for her to get away from the country for several months—far away from any one who had ever known her. She should like to go to some little place in Spain or Italy, where she should be out of the world until everything was over.

Mrs. Portico's heart gave a jump as this serene, handsome, domestic girl, sitting there with a hand in hers and pouring forth her extraordinary tale, spoke of everything being over. There was a glossy coldness in it, an unnatural lightness, which suggested—poor Mrs. Portico scarcely knew what. If Georgina was to become a mother it was to be supposed she would remain a mother. She said there was a beautiful place in Italy— Genoa—of which Raymond had often spoken, and where he had been more than once, he admired it so much; couldn't they go there and be quiet for a little while? She was asking a great favour, that she knew very well; but if Mrs. Portico wouldn't take her she would find some one who would. They had talked of such a journey so often; and, certainly, if Mrs. Portico had been willing before, she ought to be much more willing now. The girl declared that she *would* do something, go somewhere, keep, in one way or another, her situation unperceived. There was no use talking to her about telling; she would rather die than tell. No doubt it seemed strange, but she knew what she was about. No one had guessed any-thing yet—she had succeeded perfectly in doing what she wished—and her father and mother believed—as Mrs. Portico had believed, hadn't she?—that, any time the last year, Raymond Benyon was less to her than he had been before. Well, so he was; yes, he was. He had gone away—he was off, goodness knew where—in the Pacific; she was alone, and now she would remain alone. The family believed it was all over, with his going back to his ship, and other things, and they were right; for it was over, or it would be soon.

v.

Mrs. Portico, by this time, had grown almost afraid of her young friend; she had so little fear, she had even, as it were, so little shame. If the good lady had been accustomed to an-alysing things a little more, she would have said she had so little conscience. She looked at Georgina with dilated eyes —her visitor was so much the calmer of the two—and exclaimed, and murmured, and sank back, and sprang forward, and wiped her forehead with her pocket-handkerchief. There were things she didn't understand; that they should all have been so deceived, that they should have thought Georgina was giving her lover up (they flattered themselves she was discouraged or had grown tired of him) when she was really only making it impossible she should belong to any one else. And with this, her inconsequence, her capriciousness, her absence of motive, the way she contradicted herself, her apparent belief that she could hush up such a situation for ever! There was nothing shameful in having married poor Mr. Benyon, even in a little church at Haarlem, and being given away by a paymaster; it was much more shameful to be in such a state without being prepared to make the proper explanations. And she must have seen very little of her husband; she must have given him up, so far as meeting him went, almost as soon as she had taken him. Had not Mrs. Gressie herself told Mrs. Portico, in the preceding October it must have been, that there now would be no need of sending Georgina away, inasmuch as the affair with the little navy-man—a project in every way so unsuitable—had quite blown over?

"After our marriage I saw him less—I saw him a great deal less," Georgina explained; but her explanation only appeared to make the mystery more dense.

"I don't see, in that case, what on earth you married him for!"

"We had to be more careful; I wished to appear to have given him up. Of course we were really more intimate; I saw him differently," Georgina said, smiling.

"I should think so! I can't for the life of me see why you weren't discovered."

"All I can say is we weren't. No doubt it's remarkable. We managed very well—that is, I managed; he didn't want to manage at all. And then father and mother are incredibly stupid!"

Mrs. Portico exhaled a comprehensive moan, feeling glad, on the whole, that she hadn't a daughter, while Georgina went on to furnish a few more details. Raymond Benyon, in the summer, had been ordered from Brooklyn to Charlestown, near Boston, where, as Mrs. Portico perhaps knew, there was another navy-yard, in which there was a temporary press of work, requiring more oversight. He had remained there several months, during which he had written to her urgently to come to him, and during which, as well, he had received notice that he was to rejoin his ship a little later. Before doing so he came back to Brooklyn for a few weeks, to wind up his work there, and then she had seen him—well, pretty often. That was the best time of all the year that had elapsed since their marriage. It was a wonder at home that nothing had then been guessed, because she had really been reckless, and Benyon had even tried to force on a disclosure. But they were dense, that was very certain. He had besought her again and again to put an end to their false position, but she didn't want it any more than she had wanted it before. They had had rather a bad parting; in fact, for a pair of lovers, it was a very queer parting indeed. He didn't know, now, the thing she had come to tell Mrs. Portico. She had not written to him. He was on a very long cruise. It might be two years before he returned to the United States. "I don't care how long he stays away," Georgina said, very simply.

"You haven't mentioned why you married him. Perhaps you don't remember!" Mrs. Portico broke out, with her masculine laugh.

"Oh yes; I loved him."

"And you have got over that?"

Georgina hesitated a moment. "Why, no, Mrs. Portico, of course I haven't. Raymond's a splendid fellow."

"Then why don't you live with him? You don't explain that."

"What would be the use when he's always away? How can one live with a man who spends half his life in the South Seas? If he wasn't in the navy it would be different; but to go through everything—I mean everything that making our marriage known would bring upon me: the scolding and the exposure and the ridicule, the scenes at home—to go through it all just for the idea, and yet to be alone here, just as I was before, without my husband after all, with none of the good of him"—and here Georgina looked at her hostess as if with the certitude that such an enumeration of inconveniences would touch her effectually—"really, Mrs. Portico, I am

bound to say I don't think that would be worth while; I
haven't the courage for it."

"I never thought you were a coward," said Mrs. Portico.

"Well, I am not, if you will give me time. I am very patient."

"I never thought that either."

"Marrying changes one," said Georgina, still smiling.

"It certainly seems to have had a very odd effect upon you.
Why don't you make him leave the navy and arrange your life
comfortably, like every one else?"

"I wouldn't for the world interfere with his prospects—
with his promotion. That is sure to come for him, and to
come immediately, he has such talents. He is devoted to his
profession; it would ruin him to leave it."

"My dear young woman, you are a living wonder!" Mrs.
Portico exclaimed, looking at her companion as if she had
been in a glass case.

"So poor Raymond says," Georgina answered, smiling
more than ever.

"Certainly, I should have been very sorry to marry a
navy-man; but if I had married him I would stick to him, in
the face of all the scoldings in the universe!"

"I don't know what your parents may have been; I know
what mine are," Georgina replied, with some dignity. "When
he's a captain we shall come out of hiding."

"And what shall you do meanwhile? What will you do with
your children? Where will you hide them? What will you do
with this one?"

Georgina rested her eyes on her lap for a minute; then,
raising them, she met those of Mrs. Portico. "Somewhere in
Europe," she said, in her sweet tone.

"Georgina Gressie, you're a monster!" the elder lady cried.

"I know what I am about, and you will help me," the girl
went on.

"I will go and tell your father and mother the whole story—
that's what I will do!"

"I am not in the least afraid of that—not in the least. You
will help me; I assure you that you will."

"Do you mean I will support the child?"

Georgina broke into a laugh. "I do believe you would, if I

were to ask you! But I won't go so far as that; I have something of my own. All I want you to do is to be with me."

"At Genoa; yes, you have got it all fixed! You say Mr. Benyon is so fond of the place. That's all very well; but how will
he like his baby being deposited there?"

"He won't like it at all. You see I tell you the whole truth,"
said Georgina, gently.

"Much obliged; it's a pity you keep it all for me! It is in
his power, then, to make you behave properly. *He* can publish
your marriage, if you won't; and if he does you will have to
acknowledge your child."

"Publish, Mrs. Portico? How little you know my Raymond!
He will never break a promise; he will go through fire first."

"And what have you got him to promise?"

"Never to insist on a disclosure against my will; never to
claim me openly as his wife till I think it is time; never to let
any one know what has passed between us if I choose to keep
it still a secret—to keep it for years—to keep it for ever. Never
do anything in the matter himself, but to leave it to me. For
this he has given me his solemn word of honour, and I know
what that means!"

Mrs. Portico, on the sofa, fairly bounced.

"You do know what you are about! And Mr. Benyon strikes
me as more demented even than yourself. I never heard of a
man putting his head into such a noose. What good can it do
him?"

"What good? The good it did him was that it gratified me.
At the time he took it he would have made any promise under
the sun. It was a condition I exacted just at the very last,
before the marriage took place. There was nothing at that
moment he would have refused me; there was nothing I
couldn't have made him do. He was in love to that degree—but I don't want to boast," said Georgina, with quiet
grandeur. He wanted—he wanted——" she added; but then
she paused.

"He doesn't seem to have wanted much!" Mrs. Portico
cried, in a tone which made Georgina turn to the window, as
if it might have reached the street. Her hostess noticed the
movement and went on, "Oh, my dear, if I ever do tell your
story I will tell it so that people will hear it!"

"You never will tell it. What I mean is that Raymond wanted the sanction—of the affair at the church—because he saw that I would never do without it. Therefore, for him, the sooner we had it the better, and, to hurry it on, he was ready to take any pledge."

"You have got it pat enough," said Mrs. Portico, in homely phrase. "I don't know what you mean by sanctions, or what you wanted of 'em."

Georgina got up, holding rather higher than before that beautiful head which, in spite of the embarrassments of this interview, had not yet perceptibly abated its elevation. "Would you have liked me to—to not marry?"

Mrs. Portico rose also, and, flushed with the agitation of unwonted knowledge—it was as if she had discovered a skeleton in her favourite cupboard—faced her young friend for a moment. Then her conflicting sentiments resolved themselves into an abrupt question, implying, for Mrs. Portico, much subtlety: "Georgina Gressie, were you really in love with him?"

The question suddenly dissipated the girl's strange, studied, wilful coldness; she broke out, with a quick flash of passion—a passion that, for the moment, was predominately anger, "Why else, in heaven's name, should I have done what I have done? Why else should I have married him? What under the sun had I to gain?"

A certain quiver in Georgina's voice, a light in her eye which seemed to Mrs. Portico more spontaneous, more human, as she uttered these words, caused them to affect her hostess rather less painfully than anything she had yet said. She took the girl's hand and emitted indefinite admonitory sounds. "Help me, my dear old friend, help me," Georgina continued, in a low, pleading tone; and in a moment Mrs. Portico saw that the tears were in her eyes.

"You are a precious mixture, my child!" she exclaimed. "Go straight home to your own mother and tell her everything; that is your best help."

"You are kinder than my mother. You mustn't judge her by yourself."

"What can she do to you? How can she hurt you? We are not living in pagan times," said Mrs. Portico, who was seldom so historical. "Besides, you have no reason to speak of your mother—to think of her even—so! She would have liked you to marry a man of some property; but she has always been a good mother to you."

At this rebuke Georgina suddenly kindled again; she was, indeed, as Mrs. Portico had said, a precious mixture. Conscious, evidently, that she could not satisfactorily justify her present stiffness, she wheeled round upon a grievance which absolved her from self-defence. "Why, then, did he make that promise, if he loved me? No man who really loved me would have made it, and no man that was a man as I understand being a man! He might have seen that I only did it to test him—to see if he wanted to take advantage of being left free himself. It is a proof that he doesn't love me—not as he ought to have done; and in such a case as that a woman isn't bound to make sacrifices!"

Mrs. Portico was not a person of a nimble intellect; her mind moved vigorously, but heavily; yet she sometimes made happy guesses. She saw that Georgina's emotions were partly real and partly fictitious, that, as regards this last matter especially, she was trying to "get up" a resentment, in order to excuse herself. The pretext was absurd, and the good lady was struck with its being heartless on the part of her young visitor to reproach poor Benyon with a concession on which she had insisted, and which could only be a proof of his devotion, inasmuch as he left her free while he bound himself. Altogether, Mrs. Portico was shocked and dismayed at such a want of simplicity in the behaviour of a young person whom she had hitherto believed to be as candid as she was stylish, and her appreciation of this discovery expressed itself in the uncompromising remark, "You strike me as a very bad girl, my dear; you strike me as a very bad girl!"

VI.

It will doubtless seem to the reader very singular that, in spite of this reflection, which appeared to sum up her judgment of the matter, Mrs. Portico should in the course of a very few days have consented to everything that Georgina asked of her. I have thought it well to narrate at length the first conversa-

tion that took place between them, but I shall not trace further the successive phases of the girl's appeal, or the steps by
which—in the face of a hundred robust and salutary convictions—the loud, kind, sharp, simple, sceptical, credulous
woman took under her protection a damsel whose obstinacy
she could not speak of without getting red with anger. It was
the simple fact of Georgina's personal condition that moved
her; this young lady's greatest eloquence was the seriousness
of her predicament. She might be bad, and she had a splendid,
careless, insolent, fair-faced way of admitting it, which at moments, incoherently, inconsistently, irresistibly, transmuted the
cynical confession into tears of weakness; but Mrs. Portico had
known her from her rosiest years, and when Georgina declared that she couldn't go home, that she wished to be with
her and not with her mother, that she couldn't expose herself—she absolutely couldn't—and that she must remain with
her and her only till the day they should sail, the poor lady
was forced to make that day a reality. She was over-mastered,
she was cajoled, she was, to a certain extent, fascinated. She
had to accept Georgina's rigidity (she had none of her own
to oppose to it—she was only violent, she was not continuous), and once she did this it was plain, after all, that to take
her young friend to Europe was to help her, and to leave her
alone was not to help her. Georgina literally frightened Mrs.
Portico into compliance. She was evidently capable of strange
things if thrown upon her own devices. So, from one day to
another, Mrs. Portico announced that she was really at last
about to sail for foreign lands (her doctor having told her that
if she didn't look out she would get too old to enjoy them),
and that she had invited that robust Miss Gressie, who could
stand so long on her feet, to accompany her. There was joy
in the house of Gressie at this announcement, for, though the
danger was over, it was a great general advantage to Georgina
to go, and the Gressies were always elated at the prospect of
an advantage. There was a danger that she might meet Mr.
Benyon on the other side of the world; but it didn't seem
likely that Mrs. Portico would lend herself to a plot of that
kind. If she had taken it into her head to favour their love-
affair she would have done it openly, and Georgina would
have been married by this time. Her arrangements were made

as quickly as her decision had been—or rather had appeared—slow; for this concerned those mercurial young men
down town. Georgina was perpetually at her house; it was
understood in Twelfth Street that she was talking over her
future travels with her kind friend. Talk there was, of course,
to a considerable degree; but after it was settled they should
start nothing more was said about the motive of the journey.
Nothing was said, that is, till the night before they sailed; then
a few plain words passed between them. Georgina had already
taken leave of her relations in Twelfth Street, and was to sleep
at Mrs. Portico's in order to go down to the ship at an early
hour. The two ladies were sitting together in the firelight,
silent with the consciousness of corded luggage, when the
elder one suddenly remarked to her companion that she
seemed to be taking a great deal upon herself in assuming that
Raymond Benyon wouldn't force her hand. He might choose
to acknowledge his child, if she didn't; there were promises
and promises, and many people would consider they had been
let off when circumstances were so altered. She would have
to reckon with Mr. Benyon more than she thought.

"I know what I am about," Georgina answered. "There is
only one promise for him. I don't know what you mean by
circumstances being altered."

"Everything seems to me to be altered," poor Mrs. Portico
murmured, rather tragically.

"Well, he isn't, and he never will! I am sure of him, as sure
as that I sit here. Do you think I would have looked at him
if I hadn't known he was a man of his word?"

"You have chosen him well, my dear," said Mrs. Portico,
who by this time was reduced to a kind of bewildered acqui-
escence.

"Of course I have chosen him well. In such a matter as this
he will be perfectly splendid." Then suddenly, "Perfectly
splendid, that's why I cared for him," she repeated, with a
flash of incongruous passion.

This seemed to Mrs. Portico audacious to the point of being sublime; but she had given up trying to understand anything that the girl might say or do. She understood less and
less after they had disembarked in England and begun to
travel southward; and she understood least of all when, in the

middle of the winter, the event came off with which in imagination she had tried to familiarise herself, but which, when it occurred, seemed to her beyond measure strange and dreadful. It took place at Genoa; for Georgina had made up her mind that there would be more privacy in a big town than in a little; and she wrote to America that both Mrs. Portico and she had fallen in love with the place and would spend two or three months there. At that time people in the United States knew much less than to-day about the comparative attractions of foreign cities; and it was not thought surprising that absent New Yorkers should wish to linger in a seaport where they might find apartments, according to Georgina's report, in a palace painted in fresco by Vandyke and Titian. Georgina, in her letters, omitted, it will be seen, no detail that could give colour to Mrs. Portico's long stay at Genoa. In such a palace—where the travellers hired twenty gilded rooms for the most insignificant sum—a remarkably fine boy came into the world. Nothing could have been more successful and comfortable than this transaction—Mrs. Portico was almost appalled at the facility and felicity of it. She was by this time in a pretty bad way; and—what had never happened to her before in her life—she suffered from chronic depression of spirits. She hated to have to lie, and now she was lying all the time. Everything she wrote home, everything that had been said or done in connection with their stay in Genoa, was a lie. The way they remained indoors to avoid meeting chance compatriots was a lie. Compatriots in Genoa, at that period, were very rare; but nothing could exceed the business-like completeness of Georgina's precautions. Her nerve, her self-possession, her apparent want of feeling, excited on Mrs. Portico's part a kind of gloomy suspense; a morbid anxiety to see how far her companion would go took possession of the excellent woman who, a few months before, hated to fix her mind on disagreeable things. Georgina went very far indeed; she did everything in her power to dissimulate the origin of her child. The record of his birth was made under a false name, and he was baptized at the nearest church by a Catholic priest. A magnificent contadina was brought to light by the doctor in a village in the hills, and this big, brown, barbarous creature, who, to do her justice, was full of handsome, familiar

smiles and coarse tenderness, was constituted nurse to Raymond Benyon's son. She nursed him for a fortnight under the
mother's eye, and she was then sent back to her village with
the baby in her arms and sundry gold coin knotted into a
corner of her pocket-handkerchief. Mr. Gressie had given his
daughter a liberal letter of credit on a London banker, and
she was able, for the present, to make abundant provision for
the little one. She called Mrs. Portico's attention to the fact
that she spent none of her money on futilities; she kept it all
for her small pensioner in the Genoese hills. Mrs. Portico beheld these strange doings with a stupefaction that occasionally
broke into passionate protest; then she relapsed into a brooding sense of having now been an accomplice so far that she
must be an accomplice to the end.

VII.

The two ladies went down to Rome—Georgina was in wonderful trim—to finish the season, and here Mrs. Portico became convinced that she intended to abandon her offspring.
She had not driven into the country to see the nursling before
leaving Genoa; she had said that she couldn't bear to see it in
such a place and among such people. Mrs. Portico, it must be
added, had felt the force of this plea, felt it as regards a plan
of her own, given up after being hotly entertained for a few
hours, of devoting a day, by herself, to a visit to the big contadina. It seemed to her that if she should see the child in the
sordid hands to which Georgina had consigned it, she would
become still more of a participant than she was already. This
young woman's blooming hardness, after they got to Rome,
acted upon her like a kind of Medusa-mask. She had seen a
horrible thing, she had been mixed up with it, and her motherly heart had received a mortal chill. It became more clear
to her every day that, though Georgina would continue to
send the infant money in considerable quantities, she had dis-
possessed herself of it for ever. Together with this induction
a fixed idea settled in her mind—the project of taking the
baby herself, of making him her own, of arranging that matter
with the father. The countenance she had given Georgina up
to this point was an effective pledge that she would not expose

her; but she could adopt the poor little mortal without exposing her, she could say that he was a lovely baby—he was
lovely, fortunately—whom she had picked up in a wretched
village in Italy, a village that had been devastated by brigands.
She could pretend—she could pretend; oh, yes, of course, she
could pretend! Everything was imposture now, and she could
go on to lie as she had begun. The falsity of the whole business sickened her; it made her so yellow that she scarcely knew
herself in her glass. None the less, to rescue the child, even if
she had to become falser still, would be in some measure an
atonement for the treachery to which she had already surrendered herself. She began to hate Georgina, who had dragged
her into such an abyss, and if it had not been for two considerations she would have insisted on their separating. One was
the deference she owed to Mr. and Mrs. Gressie, who had
reposed such a trust in her; the other was that she must keep
hold of the mother till she had got possession of the infant.
Meanwhile, in this forced communion, her detestation of her
companion increased; Georgina came to appear to her a creature of clay and iron. She was exceedingly afraid of her, and
it seemed to her now a wonder of wonders that she should
ever have trusted her enough to come so far. Georgina
showed no consciousness of the change in Mrs. Portico,
though there was, indeed, at present, not even a pretence of
confidence between the two. Miss Gressie—that was another
lie to which Mrs. Portico had to lend herself—was bent on
enjoying Europe, and was especially delighted with Rome. She
certainly had the courage of her undertaking, and she confessed to Mrs. Portico that she had left Raymond Benyon, and
meant to continue to leave him, in ignorance of what had
taken place at Genoa. There was a certain confidence, it must
be said, in that. He was now in Chinese waters, and she probably should not see him for years. Mrs. Portico took counsel
with herself, and the result of her cogitation was that she
wrote to Mr. Benyon that a charming little boy had been born
to him, and that Georgina had put him to nurse with Italian
peasants; but that, if he would kindly consent to it, she, Mrs.
Portico, would bring him up much better than that. She knew
not how to address her letter, and Georgina, even if she
should know, which was doubtful, would never tell her; so she

sent the missive to the care of the Secretary of the Navy, at
Washington, with an earnest request that it might immediately
be forwarded. Such was Mrs. Portico's last effort in this
strange business of Georgina's. I relate rather a complicated
fact in a very few words when I say that the poor lady's anxieties, indignations, repentances, preyed upon her until they
fairly broke her down. Various persons whom she knew in
Rome notified her that the air of the Seven Hills was plainly
unfavourable to her; and she had made up her mind to return
to her native land when she found that, in her depressed condition, malarial fever had laid its hand upon her. She was unable to move, and the matter was settled for her in the course
of an illness which, happily, was not prolonged. I have said
that she was not obstinate, and the resistance she made on
the present occasion was not worthy even of her spasmodic
energy. Brain-fever made its appearance, and she died at the
end of three weeks, during which Georgina's attentions to her
patient and protectress had been unremitting. There were
other Americans in Rome who, after this sad event, extended
to the bereaved young lady every comfort and hospitality. She
had no lack of opportunities for returning under a proper
escort to New York. She selected, you may be sure, the best,
and re-entered her father's house, where she took to plain
dressing; for she sent all her pocket-money, with the utmost
secrecy, to the little boy in the Genoese hills.

VIII.

"Why should he come if he doesn't like you? He is under no
obligation, and he has his ship to look after. Why should he
sit for an hour at a time, and why should he be so pleasant?"

"Do you think he is very pleasant?" Kate Theory asked,
turning away her face from her sister. It was important that
Mildred should not see how little the expression of that
charming countenance corresponded with the inquiry.

This precaution was useless, however, for in a moment
Mildred said, from the delicately draped couch on which she
lay at the open window, "Kate Theory, don't be affected."

"Perhaps it's for you he comes. I don't see why he
shouldn't; you are far more attractive than I, and you have a

great deal more to say. How can he help seeing that you are
the cleverest of the clever? You can talk to him of everything:
of the dates of the different eruptions, of the statues and
bronzes in the museum, which you have never seen, *poverina*,
but which you know more about than he does, than any one
does. What was it you began on last time? Oh yes, you poured
forth floods about Magna Græcia. And then—and then——"

But with this Kate Theory paused; she felt it wouldn't do
to speak the words that had risen to her lips. That her sister
was as beautiful as a saint, and as delicate and refined as an
angel—she had been on the point of saying something of that
sort. But Mildred's beauty and delicacy were the fairness of
mortal disease, and to praise her for her refinement was just
to remind her that she had the tenuity of a consumptive. So,
after she had checked herself, the younger girl—she was
younger only by a year or two—simply kissed her tenderly and
settled the knot of the lace handkerchief that was tied over
her head. Mildred knew what she had been going to say, knew
why she had stopped. Mildred knew everything, without ever
leaving her room, or leaving, at least, that little *salon* of their
own, at the pension, which she had made so pretty by simply
lying there, at the window that had the view of the bay and
of Vesuvius, and telling Kate how to arrange and how to re-
arrange everything. Since it began to be plain that Mildred
must spend her small remnant of years altogether in warm
climates, the lot of the two sisters had been cast in the ungarnished hostelries of southern Europe. Their little sitting-
room was sure to be very ugly, and Mildred was never happy
till it was remodelled. Her sister fell to work, as a matter of
course, the first day, and changed the place of all the tables,
sofas, chairs, till every combination had been tried and the
invalid thought at last that there was a little effect.

Kate Theory had a taste of her own, and her ideas were not
always the same as her sister's; but she did whatever Mildred
liked, and if the poor girl had told her to put the door-mat
on the dining-table, or the clock under the sofa, she would
have obeyed without a murmur. Her own ideas, her personal
tastes, had been folded up and put away, like garments out of
season, in drawers and trunks, with camphor and lavender.
They were not, as a general thing, for southern wear, however

indispensable to comfort in the climate of New England, where poor Mildred had lost her health. Kate Theory, ever since this event, had lived for her companion, and it was almost an inconvenience for her to think that she was attractive to Captain Benyon. It was as if she had shut up her house and was not in a position to entertain. So long as Mildred should live, her own life was suspended; if there should be any time afterwards, perhaps she would take it up again; but for the present, in answer to any knock at her door, she could only call down from one of her dusty windows that she was not at home. Was it really in these terms she should have to dismiss Captain Benyon? If Mildred said it was for her he came she must perhaps take upon herself such a duty; for, as we have seen, Mildred knew everything, and she must therefore be right. She knew about the statues in the museum, about the excavations at Pompeii, about the antique splendour of Magna Græcia. She always had some instructive volume on the table beside her sofa, and she had strength enough to hold the book for half-an-hour at a time. That was about the only strength she had now. The Neapolitan winter had been remarkably soft, but after the first month or two she had been obliged to give up her little walks in the garden. It lay beneath her window like a single enormous bouquet; as early as May, that year, the flowers were so dense. None of them, however, had a colour so intense as the splendid blue of the bay, which filled up all the rest of the view. It would have looked painted if you had not been able to see the little movement of the waves. Mildred Theory watched them by the hour, and the breathing crest of the volcano, on the other side of Naples, and the great sea-vision of Capri, on the horizon, changing its tint while her eyes rested there, and wondered what would become of her sister after she was gone. Now that Percival was married—he was their only brother, and from one day to the other was to come down to Naples to show them his new wife, as yet a complete stranger, or revealed only in the few letters she had written them during her wedding-tour—now that Percival was to be quite taken up, poor Kate's situation would be much more grave. Mildred felt that she should be able to judge better after she should have seen her sister-in-law how much of a home Kate might expect to find with the pair; but even

if Agnes should prove—well, more satisfactory than her letters, it was a wretched prospect for Kate—this living as a mere
appendage to happier people. Maiden-aunts were very well,
but being a maiden-aunt was only a last resource, and Kate's
first resources had not even been tried.

Meanwhile the latter young lady wondered as well, wondered in what book Mildred had read that Captain Benyon
was in love with her. She admired him, she thought, but he
didn't seem a man that would fall in love with one like that.
She could see that he was on his guard: he wouldn't throw
himself away. He thought too much of himself, or at any rate
he took too good care of himself, in the manner of a man to
whom something had happened which had given him a lesson. Of course what had happened was that his heart was
buried somewhere, in some woman's grave; he had loved
some beautiful girl—much more beautiful, Kate was sure,
than she, who thought herself meagre and dusky—and the
maiden had died, and his capacity to love had died with her.
He loved her memory; that was the only thing he would care
for now. He was quiet, gentle, clever, humorous, and very
kind in his manner; but if any one save Mildred had said to
her that if he came three times a week to Posilippo, it was for
anything but to pass his time (he had told them he didn't
know another lady in Naples), she would have felt that this
was simply the kind of thing—usually so idiotic—that people
always thought it necessary to say. It was very easy for him to
come; he had the big ship's boat, with nothing else to do;
and what could be more delightful than to be rowed across
the bay, under a bright awning, by four brown sailors with
Louisiana in blue letters on their immaculate white shirts and
in gilt letters on their fluttering hat-ribbons? The boat came
to the steps of the garden of the pension, where the orange-
trees hung over and made vague yellow balls shine back out
of the water. Kate Theory knew all about that, for Captain
Benyon had persuaded her to take a turn in the boat, and if
they had only had another lady to go with them he could
have conveyed her to the ship and shown her all over it. It
looked beautiful, just a little way off, with the American flag
hanging loose in the Italian air. They would have another lady
when Agnes should arrive; then Percival would remain with

Mildred while they took this excursion. Mildred had stayed alone the day she went in the boat; she had insisted on it, and, of course it was really Mildred who had persuaded her; though now that Kate came to think of it, Captain Benyon had, in his quiet, waiting way—he turned out to be waiting long after you thought he had let a thing pass—said a good deal about the pleasure it would give him. Of course, everything would give pleasure to a man who was so bored. He was keeping the *Louisiana* at Naples, week after week, simply because these were the commodore's orders. There was no work to be done there, and his time was on his hands; but of course the commodore, who had gone to Constantinople with the two other ships, had to be obeyed to the letter, however mysterious his motives. It made no difference that he was a fantastic, grumbling, arbitrary old commodore; only a good while afterwards it occurred to Kate Theory that, for a reserved, correct man, Captain Benyon had given her a considerable proof of confidence in speaking to her in these terms of his superior officer. If he looked at all hot when he arrived at the pension she offered him a glass of cold "orangeade." Mildred thought this an unpleasant drink—she called it messy; but Kate adored it and Captain Benyon always accepted it.

IX.

The day I speak of, to change the subject, she called her sister's attention to the extraordinary sharpness of a zigzaging cloud-shadow on the tinted slope of Vesuvius; but Mildred remarked in answer only that she wished her sister would marry the Captain. It was in this familiar way that constant meditation led Miss Theory to speak of him; it shows how constantly she thought of him, for, in general, no one was more ceremonious than she, and the failure of her health had not caused her to relax any form that it was possible to keep up. There was a kind of slim erectness even in the way she lay on her sofa; and she always received the doctor as if he were calling for the first time.

"I had better wait till he asks me," Kate Theory said. "Dear Milly, if I were to do some of the things you wish me to do, I should shock you very much."

"I wish he would marry you, then. You know there is very little time, if I wish to see it."

"You will never see it, Mildred. I don't see why you should take so for granted that I would accept him."

"You will never meet a man who has so few disagreeable qualities. He is probably not very well off. I don't know what is the pay of a captain in the navy——"

"It's a relief to find there is something you don't know," Kate Theory broke in.

"But when I am gone," her sister went on, calmly, "when I am gone there will be plenty for both of you."

The younger girl, at this, was silent for a moment; then she exclaimed, "Mildred, you may be out of health, but I don't see why you should be dreadful!"

"You know that since we have been leading this life we have seen no one we liked better," said Milly. When she spoke of the life they were leading—there was always a soft resignation of regret and contempt in the allusion—she meant the southern winters, the foreign climates, the vain experiments, the lonely waitings, the wasted hours, the interminable rains, the bad food, the pottering, humbugging doctors, the damp pensions, the chance encounters, the fitful apparitions of fellow-travellers.

"Why shouldn't you speak for yourself alone? I am glad you like him, Mildred."

"If you don't like him, why do you give him orangeade?"

At this inquiry Kate began to laugh, and her sister continued—

"Of course you are glad I like him, my dear. If I didn't like him, and you did, it wouldn't be satisfactory at all. I can imagine nothing more miserable; I shouldn't die in any sort of comfort."

Kate Theory usually checked this sort of allusion—she was always too late—with a kiss; but on this occasion she added that it was a long time since Mildred had tormented her so much as she had done to-day. "You will make me hate him," she added.

"Well, that proves you don't already," Milly rejoined; and it happened that almost at this moment they saw, in the golden afternoon, Captain Benyon's boat approaching the steps at the end of the garden. He came that day, and he came two days later, and he came yet once again after an interval equally brief, before Percival Theory arrived with Mrs. Theory from Rome. He seemed anxious to crowd into these few days, as he would have said, a good deal of intercourse with the two remarkably nice girls—or nice women, he hardly knew which to call them—whom in the course of a long, idle, rather tedious detention at Naples, he had discovered in the lovely suburb of Posilippo. It was the American consul who had put him into relation with them. The sisters had had to sign in the consul's presence some law-papers, transmitted to them by the man of business who looked after their little property in America, and the kindly functionary, taking advantage of the pretext (Captain Benyon happened to come into the consulate as he was starting, indulgently, to wait upon the ladies) to bring together "two parties" who, as he said, ought to appreciate each other, proposed to his fellow-officer in the service of the United States that he should go with him as witness of the little ceremony. He might, of course, take his clerk, but the Captain would do much better; and he represented to Benyon that the Miss Theorys (singular name, wasn't it?) suffered, he was sure, from a lack of society; also that one of them was very sick, that they were real pleasant and extraordinarily refined, and that the sight of a compatriot literally draped, as it were, in the national banner would cheer them up more than most anything, and give them a sense of protection. They had talked to the consul about Benyon's ship, which they could see from their windows, in the distance, at its anchorage. They were the only American ladies then at Naples—the only residents, at least—and the Captain wouldn't be doing the polite thing unless he went to pay them his respects. Benyon felt afresh how little it was in his line to call upon strange women; he was not in the habit of hunting up female acquaintance, or of looking out for the particular emotions which the sex only can inspire. He had his reasons for this abstention, and he seldom relaxed it; but the consul appealed to him on rather strong grounds. And he suffered himself to be persuaded. He was far from regretting, during the first weeks at least, an act which was distinctly inconsistent with his great rule—that of never exposing himself to the danger of becoming entangled with an unmarried woman. He had been obliged to make this rule, and had adhered to it with some success. He was fond of women, but he was forced to restrict himself to superficial sentiments. There was no use tumbling into situations from which the only possible issue was a retreat. The step he had taken with regard to poor Miss Theory and her delightful little sister was an exception on which at first he could only congratulate himself. That had been a happy idea of the ruminating old consul; it made Captain Benyon forgive him his hat, his boots, his shirt-front—a costume which might be considered representative, and the effect of which was to make the observer turn with rapture to a half-naked lazzarone. On either side the acquaintance had helped the time to pass, and the hours he spent at the little pension at Posilippo left a sweet, and by no means innutritive, taste behind.

As the weeks went by his exception had grown to look a good deal like a rule; but he was able to remind himself that the path of retreat was always open to him. Moreover, if he should fall in love with the younger girl there would be no great harm, for Kate Theory was in love with her sister, and it would matter very little to her whether he advanced or retreated. She was very attractive, or rather she was very attracting. Small, pale, attentive without rigidity, full of pretty curves and quick movements, she looked as if the habit of watching and serving had taken complete possession of her, and was literally a little sister of charity. Her thick black hair was pushed behind her ears, as if to help her to listen, and her clear brown eyes had the smile of a person too full of tact to carry a sad face to a sick-bed. She spoke in an encouraging voice, and had soothing and unselfish habits. She was very pretty, producing a cheerful effect of contrasted black and white, and dressed herself daintily, so that Mildred might have something agreeable to look at. Benyon very soon perceived that there was a fund of good service in her. Her sister had it all now; but poor Miss Theory was fading fast, and then what would become of this precious little force? The answer to such a question that seemed most to the point was that it was none of his business. He was not sick—at least not physically—and he was not looking out for a nurse. Such a companion might

be a luxury, but was not, as yet, a necessity. The welcome of
the two ladies, at first, had been simple, and he scarcely knew
what to call it but sweet; a bright, gentle, jocular friendliness
remained the tone of their intercourse. They evidently liked
him to come; they liked to see his big transatlantic ship hover
about those gleaming coasts of exile. The fact of Miss Mildred
being always stretched on her couch—in his successive visits
to foreign waters Benyon had not unlearned (as why should
he?) the pleasant American habit of using the lady's personal
name—made their intimacy seem greater, their differences
less; it was as if his hostesses had taken him into their confidence and he had been—as the consul would have said—of
the same party. Knocking about the salt parts of the globe,
with a few feet square on a rolling frigate for his only home,
the pretty flower-decked sitting-room of the quiet American
sisters became, more than anything he had hitherto known,
his interior. He had dreamed once of having an interior, but
the dream had vanished in lurid smoke, and no such vision
had come to him again. He had a feeling that the end of this
was drawing nigh; he was sure that the advent of the strange
brother, whose wife was certain to be disagreeable, would
make a difference. That is why, as I have said, he came as
often as possible the last week, after he had learned the day
on which Percival Theory would arrive. The limits of the exception had been reached.

He had been new to the young ladies at Posilippo, and
there was no reason why they should say to each other that
he was a very different man from the ingenuous youth who,
ten years before, used to wander with Georgina Gressie down
vistas of plank-fences brushed over with advertisements of
quack medicines. It was natural he should be, and we, who
know him, would have found that he had traversed the whole
scale of alteration. There was nothing ingenuous in him now;
he had the look of experience, of having been seasoned and
hardened by the years. His face, his complexion, were the
same; still smooth-shaven and slim, he always passed, at first,
for a decidedly youthful mariner. But his expression was old,
and his talk was older still—the talk of a man who had seen
much of the world (as indeed he had to-day) and judged most
things for himself, with a humorous scepticism which, what-

ever concessions it might make, superficially, for the sake of
not offending, for instance, two remarkably nice American
women who had kept most of their illusions, left you with the
conviction that the next minute it would go quickly back to
its own stand-point. There was a curious contradiction in him;
he struck you as serious, and yet he could not be said to take
things seriously. This was what made Kate Theory feel so sure
that he had lost the object of his affections; and she said to
herself that it must have been under circumstances of peculiar
sadness, for that was, after all, a frequent accident, and was
not usually thought, in itself, a sufficient stroke to make a man
a cynic. This reflection, it may be added, was, on the young
lady's part, just the least bit acrimonious. Captain Benyon was
not a cynic in any sense in which he might have shocked an
innocent mind; he kept his cynicism to himself, and was a very
clever, courteous, attentive gentleman. If he was melancholy,
you knew it chiefly by his jokes, for they were usually at his
own expense; and if he was indifferent, it was all the more to
his credit that he should have exerted himself to entertain his
countrywomen.

X.

The last time he called before the arrival of the expected
brother he found Miss Theory alone, and sitting up, for a
wonder, at her window. Kate had driven into Naples to give
orders at the hotel for the reception of the travellers, who
required accommodation more spacious than the villa at Posilippo (where the two sisters had the best rooms) could offer
them; and the sick girl had taken advantage of her absence,
and of the pretext afforded by a day of delicious warmth, to
transfer herself for the first time in six months to an arm-chair.
She was practising, as she said, for the long carriage-journey
to the north, where, in a quiet corner they knew of, on the
Lago Maggiore, her summer was to be spent. Raymond Benyon remarked to her that she had evidently turned the corner
and was going to get well, and this gave her a chance to say
various things that were in her mind. She had various things
on her mind, poor Mildred Theory, so caged and restless, and
yet so resigned and patient as she was; with a clear, quick

spirit, in the most perfect health, ever reaching forward, to
the end of its tense little chain, from her wasted and suffering
body; and, in the course of the perfect summer afternoon, as
she sat there, exhilarated by the success of her effort to get
up and by her comfortable opportunity, she took her friendly
visitor into the confidence of most of her anxieties. She told
him, very promptly and positively, that she was not going to
get well at all, that she had probably not more than a twelve-
month yet to live, and that he would oblige her very much
by not forcing her to waste any more breath in contradicting
him on that head. Of course she couldn't talk much; therefore
she wished to say to him only things that he would not hear
from any one else. Such for instance was her present secret—Katie's and hers—the secret of their fearing so much
that they shouldn't like Percival's wife, who was not from Boston but from New York. Naturally, that by itself would be
nothing, but from what they had heard of her set—this subject had been explored by their correspondents—they were
rather nervous, nervous to the point of not being in the least
reassured by the fact that the young lady would bring Percival
a fortune. The fortune was a matter of course, for that was
just what they had heard about Agnes's circle—that the stamp
of money was on all their thoughts and doings. They were
very rich and very new and very splashing, and evidently had
very little in common with the two Miss Theorys, who, moreover, if the truth must be told (and this was a great secret),
did not care much for the letters their sister-in-law had hitherto addressed them. She had been at a French boarding-
school in New York, and yet (and this was the greatest secret
of all) she wrote to them that she had performed a part of
the journey through France in a "diligance"! Of course, they
would see the next day; Miss Mildred was sure she should
know in a moment whether Agnes would like them. She could
never have told him all this if her sister had been there, and
Captain Benyon must promise never to tell Kate how she had
chattered. Kate thought always that they must hide everything, and that even if Agnes should be a dreadful disappointment they must never let any one guess it. And yet Kate was
just the one who would suffer, in the coming years, after she
herself had gone. Their brother had been everything to them,

but now it would all be different. Of course it was not to be
expected that he should have remained a bachelor for their
sake: she only wished he had waited till she was dead and Kate
was married. One of these events, it was true, was much less
sure than the other; Kate might never marry, much as she
wished she would. She was quite morbidly unselfish, and
didn't think she had a right to have anything of her own—
not even a husband.

Miss Mildred talked a good while about Kate, and it never
occurred to her that she might bore Captain Benyon. She
didn't, in point of fact; he had none of the trouble of wondering why this poor, sick, worried lady was trying to push
her sister down his throat. Their peculiar situation made
everything natural, and the tone she took with him now
seemed only what their pleasant relations for the last three
months led up to. Moreover, he had an excellent reason for
not being bored: the fact, namely, that, after all, with regard
to her sister, Miss Mildred appeared to him to keep back more
than she uttered. She didn't tell him the great thing—she
had nothing to say as to what that charming girl thought of
Raymond Benyon. The effect of their interview, indeed, was
to make him shrink from knowing, and he felt that the right
thing for him would be to get back into his boat, which was
waiting at the garden-steps, before Kate Theory should return
from Naples. It came over him, as he sat there, that he was
far too interested in knowing what this young lady thought
of him. She might think what she pleased; it could make no
difference to him. The best opinion in the world—if it looked
out at him from her tender eyes—would not make him a whit
more free or more happy. Women of that sort were not for
him, women whom one could not see familiarly without falling in love with them, and whom it was no use to fall in love
with unless one was ready to marry them. The light of the
summer-afternoon, and of Miss Mildred's pure spirit, seemed
suddenly to flood the whole subject. He saw that he was in
danger, and he had long since made up his mind that from
this particular peril it was not only necessary but honourable
to flee. He took leave of his hostess before her sister reappeared, and had the courage even to say to her that he should
not come back often after that; they would be so much oc-

cupied by their brother and his wife! As he moved across the glassy bay, to the rhythm of the oars, he wished either that the sisters would leave Naples or that his confounded commodore would send for him.

When Kate returned from her errand, ten minutes later, Milly told her of the Captain's visit, and added that she had never seen anything so sudden as the way he left her. "He wouldn't wait for you, my dear, and he said he thought it more than likely that he should never see us again. It is as if he thought you were going to die too!"

"Is his ship called away?" Kate Theory asked.

"He didn't tell me so; he said we should be so busy with Percival and Agnes."

"He has got tired of us; that is all. There is nothing wonderful in that; I knew he would."

Mildred said nothing for a moment; she was watching her sister, who was very attentively arranging some flowers. "Yes, of course, we are very dull, and he is like everybody else."

"I thought you thought he was so wonderful," said Kate—"and so fond of us."

"So he is; I am surer of that than ever. That's why he went away so abruptly."

Kate looked at her sister now. "I don't understand."

"Neither do I, *cara*. But you will, one of these days."

"How, if he never comes back?"

"Oh, he will—after a while—when I am gone. Then he will explain; that, at least, is clear to me."

"My poor precious, as if I cared!" Kate Theory exclaimed, smiling as she distributed her flowers. She carried them to the window, to place them near her sister, and here she paused a moment, her eye caught by an object, far out in the bay, with which she was not unfamiliar. Mildred noticed its momentary look, and followed its direction.

"It's the Captain's gig going back to the ship," Milly said. "It's so still one can almost hear the oars."

Kate Theory turned away, with a sudden, strange violence, a movement and exclamation which, the very next minute, as she became conscious of what she had said—and, still more, of what she felt—smote her own heart (as it flushed her face) with surprise and with the force of a revelation. "I wish it would sink him to the bottom of the sea!"

Her sister stared, then caught her by the dress, as she passed from her, drawing her back with a weak hand. "Oh, my darling dear!" And she drew Kate down and down toward her, so that the girl had nothing for it but to sink on her knees and bury her face in Mildred's lap. If that ingenious invalid did not know everything now, she knew a great deal.

XI.

Mrs. Percival proved very pretty; it is more gracious to begin with this declaration, instead of saying, in the first place, that she proved very vapid. It took a long day to arrive at the end of her silliness, and the two ladies at Posilippo, even after a week had passed, suspected that they had only skirted its edges. Kate Theory had not spent half an hour in her company before she gave a little private sigh of relief; she felt that a situation which had promised to be embarrassing was now quite clear, was even of a primitive simplicity. She would spend with her sister-in-law, in the coming time, one week in the year; that was all that would be mortally possible. It was a blessing that one could see exactly what she was, for in that way the question settled itself. It would have been much more tiresome if Agnes had been a little less obvious; then one would have had to hesitate and consider and weigh one thing against another. She was pretty and silly, as distinctly as an orange is yellow and round; and Kate Theory would as soon have thought of looking to her to give interest to the future as she would have thought of looking to an orange to impart solidity to the prospect of dinner. Mrs. Percival travelled in the hope of meeting her American acquaintance, or of making acquaintance with such Americans as she did meet, and for the purpose of buying mementos for her relations. She was perpetually adding to her store of articles in tortoise-shell, in mother-of-pearl, in olive-wood, in ivory, in filigree, in tartan lacquer, in mosaic; and she had a collection of Roman scarfs and Venetian beads which she looked over exhaustively every night before she went to bed. Her conversation bore mainly upon the manner in which she intended to dispose of these accumulations. She was constantly changing about, among each other, the persons to whom they were respectively to be offered. At Rome one of the first things she said to her husband after entering the Coliseum had been, "I guess I will give the ivory work-box to Bessie and the Roman pearls to Aunt Harriet!" She was always hanging over the travellers' book at the hotel; she had it brought up to her, with a cup of chocolate, as soon as she arrived. She searched its pages for the magical name of New York, and she indulged in infinite conjecture as to who the people were—the name was sometimes only a partial cue—who had inscribed it there. What she most missed in Europe, and what she most enjoyed, was the New Yorkers; when she met them she talked about the people in their native city who had "moved" and the streets they had moved to. "Oh yes, the Drapers are going up town, to Twenty-fourth Street, and the Vanderdeckens are going to be in Twenty-third Street, right back of them. My uncle, Mr. Henry Platt, thinks of building round there." Mrs. Percival Theory was capable of repeating statements like these thirty times over—of lingering on them for hours. She talked largely of herself, of her uncles and aunts, of her clothes—past, present and future. These articles, in especial, filled her horizon; she considered them with a complacency which might have led you to suppose that she had invented the custom of draping the human form. Her main point of contact with Naples was the purchase of coral; and all the while she was there the word "set"—she used it as if every one would understand—fell with its little flat, common sound upon the ears of her sisters-in-law, who had no sets of anything. She cared little for pictures and mountains; Alps and Apennines were not productive of New Yorkers, and it was difficult to take an interest in Madonnas who flourished at periods when apparently there were no fashions, or at any rate no trimmings.

I speak here not only of the impression she made upon her husband's anxious sisters, but of the judgment passed on her (he went so far as that, though it was not obvious how it mattered to him) by Raymond Benyon. And this brings me at a jump (I confess it's a very small one) to the fact that he did, after all, go back to Posilippo. He stayed away for nine

days, and at the end of this time Percival Theory called upon
him to thank him for the civility he had shown his kinswomen.
He went to this gentleman's hotel, to return his visit, and
there he found Miss Kate, in her brother's sitting-room. She
had come in by appointment from the villa, and was going
with the others to look at the royal palace, which she had not
yet had an opportunity to inspect. It was proposed (not by
Kate), and presently arranged, that Captain Benyon should go
with them; and he accordingly walked over marble floors for
half an hour, exchanging conscious commonplaces with the
woman he loved. For this truth had rounded itself during
those nine days of absence; he discovered that there was nothing particularly sweet in his life when once Kate Theory had
been excluded from it. He had stayed away to keep himself
from falling in love with her; but this expedient was in itself
illuminating, for he perceived that, according to the vulgar
adage, he was locking the stable-door after the horse had been
stolen. As he paced the deck of his ship and looked toward
Posilippo his tenderness crystallised; the thick, smoky flame of
a sentiment that knew itself forbidden, and was angry at the
knowledge, now danced upon the fuel of his good resolu-
tions. The latter, it must be said, resisted, declined to be
consumed. He determined that he would see Kate Theory
again, for a time just sufficient to bid her good-bye and to
add a little explanation. He thought of his explanation very
lovingly, but it may not strike the reader as a happy inspiration. To part from her dryly, abruptly, without an allusion
to what he might have said if everything had been different
—that would be wisdom, of course, that would be virtue, that
would be the line of a practical man, of a man who kept himself well in hand. But it would be virtue terribly unre-
warded—it would be virtue too austere even for a person who
flattered himself that he had taught himself stoicism. The minor luxury tempted him irresistibly, since the larger—that of
happy love—was denied him; the luxury of letting the girl
know that it would not be an accident—oh, not at all—that
they should never meet again. She might easily think it was,
and thinking it was would doubtless do her no harm. But this
wouldn't give him his pleasure—the platonic satisfaction of
expressing to her at the same time his belief that they might

have made each other happy and the necessity of his renunciation. That, probably, wouldn't hurt her either, for she had
given him no proof whatever that she cared for him. The nearest approach to it was the way she walked beside him now,
sweet and silent, without the least reference to his not having
come back to the villa. The place was cool and dusky, the
blinds were drawn to keep out the light and noise, and the
little party wandered through the high saloons, where precious marbles and the gleam of gilding and satin made reflections in the rich dimness. Here and there the cicerone, in
slippers, with Neapolitan familiarity, threw open a shutter to
show off a picture or a tapestry. He strolled in front with
Percival Theory and his wife, while this lady, drooping silently
from her husband's arm as they passed, felt the stuff of
the curtains and the sofas. When he caught her in these experiments the cicerone, in expressive deprecation, clasped his
hands and lifted his eyebrows; whereupon Mrs. Theory exclaimed to her husband, "Oh, bother his old king!" It
was not striking to Captain Benyon why Percival Theory
had married the niece of Mr. Henry Platt. He was less interesting than his sisters—a smooth, cool, correct young man,
who frequently took out a pencil and did a little arithmetic
on the back of a letter. He sometimes, in spite of his correctness, chewed a toothpick, and he missed the American
papers, which he used to ask for in the most unlikely places.
He was a Bostonian converted to New York; a very special
type.

"Is it settled when you leave Naples?" Benyon asked of
Kate Theory.

"I think so; on the twenty-fourth. My brother has been
very kind; he has lent us his carriage, which is a large one, so
that Mildred can lie down. He and Agnes will take another;
but of course we shall travel together."

"I wish to heaven I were going with you!" Captain Benyon
said. He had given her the opportunity to respond, but she
did not take it; she merely remarked, with a vague laugh, that
of course he couldn't take his ship over the Apennines. "Yes,
there is always my ship," he went on. "I am afraid that in
future it will carry me far away from you."

They were alone in one of the royal apartments; their companions had passed, in advance of them, into the adjoining room. Benyon and his fellow-visitor had paused beneath one of the immense chandeliers of glass, which in the clear, coloured gloom, through which one felt the strong outer light of Italy beating in, suspended its twinkling drops from the decorated vault. They looked round them confusedly, made shy for the moment by Benyon's having struck a note more serious than any that had hitherto sounded between them, looked at the sparse furniture, draped in white overalls, at the scagliola floor, in which the great cluster of crystal pendants seemed to shine again.

"You are master of your ship—can't you sail it as you like?" Kate Theory asked, with a smile.

"I am not master of anything. There is not a man in the world less free. I am a slave. I am a victim."

She looked at him with kind eyes; something in his voice suddenly made her put away all thought of the defensive airs that a girl, in certain situations, is expected to assume. She perceived that he wanted to make her understand something, and now her only wish was to help him to say it. "You are not happy," she murmured simply, her voice dying away in a kind of wonderment at this reality.

The gentle touch of her words—it was as if her hand had stroked his cheek—seemed to him the sweetest thing he had ever known. "No, I am not happy, because I am not free. If I were—if I were, I would give up my ship, I would give up everything, to follow you. I can't explain; that is part of the hardness of it. I only want you to know it, that if certain things were different, if everything was different, I might tell you that I believe I should have a right to speak to you. Perhaps some day it will change; but probably then it will be too late. Meanwhile, I have no right of any kind. I don't want to trouble you, and I don't ask of you—anything! It is only to have spoken just once. I don't make you understand, of course. I am afraid I seem to you rather a brute, perhaps even a humbug. Don't think of it now; don't try to understand. But some day, in the future, remember what I have said to you, and how we stood here, in this strange old place, alone! Perhaps it will give you a little pleasure."

Kate Theory began by listening to him with visible eagerness; but in a moment she turned away her eyes. "I am very sorry for you," she said, gravely.

"Then you do understand enough?"

"I shall think of what you have said—in the future."

Benyon's lips formed the beginning of a word of tenderness, which he instantly suppressed; and in a different tone, with a bitter smile and a sad shake of the head, raising his arms a moment and letting them fall, he rejoined, "It won't hurt any one, your remembering this!"

"I don't know whom you mean." And the girl, abruptly, began to walk to the end of the room. He made no attempt to tell her whom he meant, and they proceeded together in silence till they overtook their companions.

XII.

There were several pictures in the neighbouring room, and Percival Theory and his wife had stopped to look at one of them, of which the cicerone announced the title and the authorship as Benyon came up. It was a modern portrait of a Bourbon princess, a woman young, fair, handsome, covered with jewels. Mrs. Percival appeared to be more struck with it than with anything the palace had yet offered to her sight, while her sister-in-law walked to the window, which the custodian had opened, to look out into the garden. Benyon noticed this; he was conscious that he had given the girl something to reflect upon, and his ears burned a little as he stood beside Mrs. Percival and looked up, mechanically, at the royal lady. He already repented a little of what he had said; for, after all, what was the use? And he hoped the others wouldn't observe that he had been making love.

"Gracious, Percival! Do you see who she looks like?" Mrs. Theory said to her husband.

"She looks like a lady who has a big bill at Tiffany's," this gentleman answered.

"She looks like my sister-in-law; the eyes, the mouth, the way the hair's done—the whole thing."

"Which do you mean? You have got about a dozen."

"Why, Georgina, of course—Georgina Roy. She's awfully like."

"Do you call her your sister-in-law?" Percival Theory asked. "You must want very much to claim her."

"Well, she's handsome enough. You have got to invent some new name, then. Captain Benyon, what do you call your brother-in-law's second wife?" Mrs. Percival continued, turning to her neighbour, who still stood staring at the portrait. At first he had looked without seeing; then sight, and hearing as well, became quick. They were suddenly peopled with thrilling recognitions. The Bourbon princess—the eyes, the mouth, the way the hair was done, these things took on an identity, and the gaze of the painted face seemed to fasten itself to his own. But who in the world was Georgina Roy, and what was this talk about sisters-in-law? He turned to the little lady at his side a countenance unexpectedly puzzled by the problem she had lightly presented to him.

"Your brother-in-law's second wife? That's rather complicated."

"Well, of course, he needn't have married again," said Mrs. Percival, with a small sigh.

"Whom did he marry?" asked Benyon, staring. Percival Theory had turned away. "Oh, if you are going into her relationships," he murmured, and joined his sister at the brilliant window, through which, from the distance, the many-voiced uproar of Naples came in.

"He married first my sister Cora, and she died five years ago. Then he married *her*;" and Mrs. Percival nodded at the princess.

Benyon's eyes went back to the portrait; he could see what she meant—it stared out at him. "Her? Georgina?"

"Georgina Gressie! Gracious, do you know her?"

It was very distinct—that answer of Mrs. Percival's, and the question that followed it as well. But he had the resource of the picture; he could look at it, seem to take it very seriously, though it danced up and down before him. He felt that he was turning red, then he felt that he was turning pale. "The brazen impudence!" That was the way he could speak to himself now of the woman he had once loved, and whom he afterwards hated, till this had died out too. Then the wonder of it was lost in the quickly growing sense that it would make a difference for him—a great difference. Exactly what, he didn't see yet; only a difference that swelled and swelled as he thought of it, and caught up, in its expansion, the girl who stood behind him so quietly, looking into the Italian garden.

The custodian drew Mrs. Percival away to show her another princess, before Benyon answered her last inquiry. This gave him time to recover from his first impulse, which had been to answer it with a negative; he saw in a moment that an admission of his acquaintance with Mrs. Roy (Mrs. Roy!—it was prodigious!) was necessarily helping him to learn more. Besides, it needn't be compromising. Very likely Mrs. Percival would hear one day that he had once wanted to marry her. So, when he joined his companions a minute later he remarked that he had known Miss Gressie years before, and had even admired her considerably, but had lost sight of her entirely in later days. She had been a great beauty, and it was a wonder that she had not married earlier. Five years ago, was it? No, it was only two. He had been going to say that in so long a time it would have been singular he should not have heard of it. He had been away from New York for ages; but one always heard of marriages and deaths. This was a proof, though two years was rather long. He led Mrs. Percival insidiously into a further room, in advance of the others, to whom the cicerone returned. She was delighted to talk about her "connections," and she supplied him with every detail. He could trust himself now; his self-possession was complete, or, so far as it was wanting, the fault was that of a sudden gaiety which he could not, on the spot, have accounted for. Of course it was not very flattering to them—Mrs. Percival's own people—that poor Cora's husband should have consoled himself; but men always did it (talk of widows!) and he had chosen a girl who was—well, very fine-looking, and the sort of successor to Cora that they needn't be ashamed of. She had been awfully admired, and no one had understood why she had waited so long to marry. She had had some affair as a girl—an engagement to an officer in the army—and the man had jilted her, or they had quarrelled, or something or other. She was almost an old maid—well, she was thirty, or very nearly—but she had done something good now. She was handsomer than ever, and tremendously striking. William Roy had one of the biggest incomes in the city, and he was quite

deepened in the east before he had discovered in what the change consisted. By that time he saw it clearly—it consisted in Georgina's being in his power now, in place of his being in hers. He laughed as he sat alone in the darkness at the thought of what she had done. It had occurred to him more than once that she would do it; he believed her capable of anything; but the accomplished fact had a freshness of comicality. He thought of William Roy, of his big income, of his being "quite affectionate," of his blooming son and heir, of his having found such a worthy successor to poor Mrs. Cora. He wondered whether Georgina had mentioned to him that she had a husband living, but was strongly of the belief that she had not. Why should she, after all? She had neglected to mention it to so many others. He had thought he knew her, in so many years, that he had nothing more to learn about her, but this ripe stroke revived his sense of her audacity. Of course it was what she had been waiting for, and if she had not done it sooner it was because she had hoped he would be lost at sea in one of his long cruises and relieve her of the necessity of a crime. How she must hate him to-day for not having been lost, for being alive, for continuing to put her in the wrong! Much as she hated him, however, his own loathing was at least a match for hers. She had done him the foulest of wrongs— she had ravaged his life. That he should ever detest in this degree a woman whom he had once loved as he loved her he would not have thought possible in his innocent younger years. But neither would he have thought it possible then that a woman should be such a cold-blooded devil as she had been. His love had perished in his rage, his blinding, impotent rage, at finding that he had been duped and measuring his impotence. When he learned, years before, from Mrs. Portico, what she had done with her baby, of whose entrance into life she herself had given him no intimation, he felt that he was face to face with a full revelation of her nature. Before that it had puzzled him, it had mocked him; his relations with her were bewildering, stupefying. But when, after obtaining, with difficulty and delay, a leave of absence from Government, and betaking himself to Italy to look for the child and assume possession of it, he had encountered absolute failure and defeat, then the case presented itself to him more simply. He perceived that he had mated himself with a creature who just happened to be a monster, a human exception altogether. That was what he couldn't pardon—her conduct about the child; never, never, never! To him she might have done what she chose—dropped him, pushed him out into eternal cold, with his hands fast tied—and he would have accepted it, excused her almost, admitted that it had been his business to mind better what he was about. But she had tortured him through the poor little irrecoverable son whom he had never seen, through the heart and the human vitals that she had not herself, and that he had to have, poor wretch, for both of them.

All his effort, for years, had been to forget those horrible months, and he had cut himself off from them so that they seemed at times to belong to the life of another person. But to-night he lived them over again; he retraced the different gradations of darkness through which he had passed, from the moment, so soon after his extraordinary marriage, when it came over him that she already repented and meant, if possible, to elude all her obligations. This was the moment when he saw why she had reserved herself—in the strange vow she extracted from him—an open door for retreat; the moment, too, when her having had such an inspiration (in the midst of her momentary good faith, if good faith it had ever been) struck him as a proof of her essential depravity. What he had tried to forget came back to him: the child that was not his child produced for him when he fell upon that squalid nest of peasants in the Genoese country, and then the confessions, retractations, contradictions, lies, terrors, threats, and general bottomless, baffling mendacity and idiocy of every one in the place. The child was gone; that had been the only definite thing. The woman who had taken it to nurse had a dozen different stories, her husband had as many, and every one in the village had a hundred more. Georgina had been sending money—she had managed, apparently, to send a good deal—and the whole country seemed to have been living on it and making merry. At one moment, the baby had died and received a most expensive burial; at another, he had been entrusted (for more healthy air, Santissima Madonna!) to the woman's cousin, in another village. According to a version which for a day or two Benyon had inclined to think the least false, he had been taken by the cousin (for his beauty's sake) to Genoa, when she went for the first time in her life to the town to see her daughter in service there, and had been confided for a few hours to a third woman, who was to keep him while the cousin walked about the streets, but who, having no child of her own, took such a fancy to him that she refused to give him up, and a few days later left the place (she was a Pisana) never to be heard of more. The cousin had forgotten her name—it had happened six months before. Benyon spent a year looking up and down Italy for his child, and inspecting hundreds of swaddled infants, inscrutable candidates for recognition. Of course he could only get further and further from real knowledge, and his search was arrested by the conviction that it was making him mad. He set his teeth and made up his mind, or tried to, that the baby had died in the hands of its nurse. This was, after all, much the likeliest supposition, and the woman had maintained it, in the hope of being rewarded for her candour, quite as often as she had asseverated that it was still somewhere, alive, in the hope of being remunerated for her good news. It may be imagined with what sentiments toward his wife Benyon had emerged from this episode. To-night his memory went further back—back to the beginning and to the days when he had had to ask himself, with all the crudity of his first surprise, what in the name of perversity she had wished to do with him. The answer to this speculation was so old, it had dropped so out of the line of recurrence, that it was now almost new again. Moreover, it was only approximate, for, as I have already said, he could comprehend such baseness as little at the end as at the beginning. She had found herself on a slope which her nature forced her to descend to the bottom. She did him the honour of wishing to enjoy his society, and she did herself the honour of thinking that their intimacy, however brief, must have a certain consecration. She felt that with him, after his promise (he would have made any promise to lead her on), she was secure, secure as she had proved to be, secure as she must think herself. That security had helped her to ask herself, after the first flush of passion was over, and her native, her twice-inherited worldliness had had time to open its eyes again, why she should keep faith with a man whose deficiencies (as a husband before the world—another affair) had been so scientifically exposed to her by her parents. So she had simply determined *not* to keep faith; and her determination, at least, she did keep.

By the time Benyon turned in he had satisfied himself, as I say, that Georgina was now in his power; and this seemed to him such an improvement in his situation that he allowed himself, for the next ten days, a license which made Kate Theory almost as happy as it made her sister, though she pretended to understand it far less. Mildred sank to her rest, or rose to fuller comprehensions, within the year, in the Isle of Wight; and Captain Benyon, who had never written so many letters as since they left Naples, sailed westward about the same time as the sweet survivor. For the *Louisiana* at last was ordered home.

XIV.

Certainly, I will see you if you come, and you may appoint any day or hour you like. I should have seen you with pleasure any time these last years. Why should we not be friends, as we used to be? Perhaps we shall be yet. I say "perhaps" only, on purpose, because your note is rather vague about your state of mind. Don't come with any idea about making me nervous or uncomfortable. I am not nervous by nature, thank heaven, and I won't, I positively won't (do you hear, dear Captain Benyon?) be uncomfortable. I have been so (it served me right) for years and years; but I am very happy now. To remain so is the very definite intention of yours ever.

GEORGINA ROY.

This was the answer Benyon received to a short letter that he despatched to Mrs. Roy after his return to America. It was not till he had been there some weeks that he wrote to her. He had been occupied in various ways: he had had to look after his ship; he had had to report at Washington; he had spent a fortnight with his mother at Portsmouth, N.H.; and he had paid a visit to Kate Theory in Boston. She herself was paying visits; she was staying with various relatives and friends. She had more colour—it was very delicately rosy—than she had had of old, in spite of her black dress; and the effect of her looking at him seemed to him to make her eyes grow still prettier. Though sisterless now, she was not without duties, and Benyon could easily see that life would press hard on her unless some one should interfere. Every one regarded her as just the person to do certain things. Every one thought she could do everything, because she had nothing else to do. She used to read to the blind, and, more onerously, to the deaf. She looked after other people's children while the parents attended anti-slavery conventions.

She was coming to New York, later, to spend a week at her brother's, but beyond this she had no idea what she should do. Benyon felt it to be awkward that he should not be able just now to tell her; and this had much to do with his coming to the point, for he accused himself of having rather hung fire. Coming to the point, for Benyon, meant writing a note to Mrs. Roy (as he must call her), in which he asked whether she would see him if he should present himself. The missive was short; it contained, in addition to what I have hinted, little more than the remark that he had something of importance to say to her. Her reply, which we have just read, was prompt. Benyon designated an hour, and rang the door-bell of her big modern house, whose polished windows seemed to shine defiance at him.

As he stood on the steps, looking up and down the straight vista of the Fifth Avenue, he perceived that he was trembling a little, that he was nervous, if she were not. He was ashamed of his agitation, and he pulled himself vigorously together. Afterwards he saw that what had made him nervous was not any doubt of the goodness of his cause, but his revived sense (as he drew near her) of his wife's hardness, her capacity for insolence. He might only break himself against that, and the prospect made him feel helpless. She kept him waiting for a long time after he had been introduced; and as he walked up and down her drawing-room, an immense, florid, expensive apartment, covered with blue satin, gilding, mirrors and bad frescoes, it came over him as a certainty that her delay was calculated. She wished to annoy him, to weary him; she was as ungenerous as she was unscrupulous. It never occurred to him that, in spite of the bold words of her note, she, too, might be in a tremor, and if any one in their secret had suggested that she was afraid to meet him, he would have laughed at this idea. This was of bad omen for the success of his errand; for it showed that he recognised the ground of her presumption—his having the superstition of old promises. By the time she appeared he was flushed, very angry. She closed the door behind her, and stood there looking at him, with the width of the room between them.

The first emotion her presence excited was a quick sense of the strange fact that, after all these years of loneliness, such a magnificent person should be his wife. For she was magnificent, in the maturity of her beauty, her head erect, her complexion splendid, her auburn tresses undimmed, a certain plenitude in her very glance. He saw in a moment that she wished to seem to him beautiful, she had endeavoured to dress herself to the best effect. Perhaps, after all, it was only for this she had delayed; she wished to give herself every possible touch. For some moments they said nothing; they had not stood face to face for nearly ten years, and they met now as adversaries. No two persons could possibly be more interested in taking each other's measure. It scarcely belonged to Georgina, however, to have too much the air of timidity, and after a moment, satisfied, apparently, that she was not to receive a broadside, she advanced, slowly, rubbing her jewelled hands and smiling. He wondered why she should smile, what thought was in her mind. His impressions followed each other with extraordinary quickness of pulse, and now he saw, in addition to what he had already perceived, that she was waiting to take her cue: she had determined on no definite line. There was nothing definite about her but her courage; the rest would depend upon him. As for her courage, it seemed to glow in the beauty which grew greater as she came nearer, with her eyes on his and her fixed smile; to be expressed in the very perfume that accompanied her steps. By this time he had got a still further impression, and it was the strangest of all. She was ready for anything, she was capable of anything, she wished to surprise him with her beauty, to remind him that it belonged, after all, at the bottom of everything, to him. She was ready to bribe him, if bribing should be necessary. She had carried on an intrigue before she was twenty; it would be more, rather than less, easy for her now that she was thirty. All this and more was in her cold, living eyes, as, in the prolonged silence, they engaged themselves with his; but I must not dwell upon it, for reasons extraneous to the remarkable fact. She was a truly amazing creature.

"Raymond!" she said, in a low voice—a voice which might represent either a vague greeting or an appeal.

He took no heed of the exclamation, but asked her why she had deliberately kept him waiting, as if she had not made a fool enough of him already. She couldn't suppose it was for his pleasure he had come into the house.

She hesitated a moment, still with her smile. "I must tell you I have a son, the dearest little boy. His nurse happened to be engaged for the moment, and I had to watch him. I am more devoted to him than you might suppose."

He fell back from her a few steps. "I wonder if you are insane," he murmured.

"To allude to my child? Why do you ask me such questions then? I tell you the simple truth. I take every care of this one. I am older and wiser. The other one was a complete mistake; he had no right to exist."

"Why didn't you kill him then with your own hands, instead of that torture?"

"Why didn't I kill myself? That question would be more to the point. You are looking wonderfully well," she broke off, in another tone; "hadn't we better sit down?"

"I didn't come here for the advantage of conversation," Benyon answered. And he was going on, but she interrupted him.

"You came to say something dreadful, very likely; though I hoped you would see it was better not. But just tell me this, before you begin. Are you successful, are you happy? It has been so provoking, not knowing more about you."

There was something in the manner in which this was said that caused him to break into a loud laugh; whereupon she added—

"Your laugh is just what it used to be. How it comes back to me! You *have* improved in appearance," she continued.

She had seated herself, though he remained standing; and she leaned back in a low, deep chair, looking up at him, with her arms folded. He stood near her and over her, as it were, dropping his baffled eyes on her, with his hand resting on the corner of the chimney-piece. "Has it never occurred to you that I may deem myself absolved from the promise I made you before I married you?"

"Very often, of course. But I have instantly dismissed the idea. How can you be 'absolved'? One promises, or one doesn't. I attach no meaning to that, and neither do you." And she glanced down at the front of her dress.

Benyon listened, but he went on as if he had not heard her. "What I came to say to you is this: that I should like your consent to my bringing a suit for divorce against you."

"A suit for divorce? I never thought of that."

"So that I may marry another woman. I can easily obtain a divorce on the ground of your desertion. It will simplify our situation."

She stared a moment, then her smile solidified, as it were, and she looked grave; but he could see that her gravity, with her lifted eyebrows, was partly assumed. "Ah, you want to marry another woman!" she exclaimed, slowly, thoughtfully. He said nothing, and she went on, "Why don't you do as I have done?"

"Because I don't want my children to be——"

Before he could say the words she sprang up, checking him with a cry. "Don't say it; it isn't necessary! Of course I know what you mean; but they won't be if no one knows it."

"I should object to knowing it myself; it's enough for me to know it of yours."

"Of course I have been prepared for your saying that."

"I should hope so!" Benyon exclaimed. "You may be a bigamist, if it suits you, but to me the idea is not attractive. I wish to marry——" and, hesitating a moment, with his slight stammer, he repeated, "I wish to marry——"

"Marry, then, and have done with it!" cried Mrs. Roy.

He could already see that he should be able to extract no consent from her; he felt rather sick. "It's extraordinary to me that you shouldn't be more afraid of being found out," he said, after a moment's reflection. "There are two or three possible accidents."

"How do you know how much afraid I am? I have thought of every accident, in dreadful nights. How do you know what my life is, or what it has been all these horrid years? But every one is dead."

"You look wasted and worn, certainly."

"Ah, don't compliment me!" Georgina exclaimed. "If I had never known you—if I had not been through all this—I believe I should have been handsome. When did you hear of my marriage? Where were you at the time?"

"At Naples, more than six months ago, by a mere chance."

"How strange that it should have taken you so long! Is the lady a Neapolitan? They don't mind what they do over there."

"I have no information to give you beyond what I have just said," Benyon rejoined. "My life doesn't in the least regard you."

"Ah, but it does from the moment I refuse to let you divorce me."

"You refuse?" Benyon said, softly.

"Don't look at me that way! You haven't advanced so rapidly as I used to think you would; you haven't distinguished yourself so much," she went on, irrelevantly.

"I shall be promoted commodore one of these days," Benyon answered. "You don't know much about it, for my advancement has already been extraordinary rapid." He blushed as soon as the words were out of his mouth. She gave a light laugh on seeing it; but he took up his hat and added, "Think over a day or two what I have proposed to you. It's a perfectly possible proceeding. Think of the temper in which I ask it."

"The temper?" she stared. "Pray, what have you to do with temper?" And as he made no reply, smoothing his hat with his glove, she went on, "Years ago, as much as you please! you had a good right, I don't deny, and you raved, in your letters, to your heart's content. That's why I wouldn't see you; I didn't wish to take it full in the face. But that's all over now; time is a healer; you have cooled off, and by your own admission you have consoled yourself. Why do you talk to me about temper? What in the world have I done to you but let you alone?"

"What do you call this business?" Benyon asked, with his eye flashing all over the room.

"Ah, excuse me, that doesn't touch you; it's my affair. I leave you your liberty, and I can live as I like. If I choose to live in this way, it may be queer (I admit it is, tremendously), but you have nothing to say to it. If I am willing to take the risk, you may be. If I am willing to play such an infernal trick upon a confiding gentleman (I will put it as strongly as you possibly could), I don't see what you have to say to it except that you are exceedingly glad such a woman as that isn't known to be your wife!" She had been cool and deliberate up to this time, but with these words her latent agitation broke out. "Do you think I have been happy? Do you think I have enjoyed existence? Do you see me freezing up into a stark old maid?"

"I wonder you stood out so long," said Benyon.

"I wonder I did! They were bad years."

"I have no doubt they were!"

"You could do as you pleased," Georgina went on. "You roamed about the world, you formed charming relations. I am delighted to hear it from your own lips. Think of my going back to my father's house—that family vault—and living there, year after year, as Miss Gressie! If you remember my father and mother—they are round in Twelfth Street, just the same—you must admit that I paid for my folly!"

"I have never understood you; I don't understand you now," said Benyon.

She looked at him a moment. "I adored you."

"I could damn you with a word!" he exclaimed.

XV.

The moment he had spoken she grasped his arm and held up her other hand, as if she were listening to a sound outside the room. She had evidently had an inspiration, and she carried it into instant effect. She swept away to the door, flung it open, and passed into the hall, whence her voice came back to Benyon as she addressed a person who apparently was her husband. She had heard him enter the house at his habitual hour, after his long morning at business; the closing of the door of the vestibule had struck her ear. The parlour was on a level with the hall, and she greeted him without impediment. She asked him to come in and be introduced to Captain Benyon, and he responded with due solemnity. She returned in advance of him, her eyes fixed upon Benyon and lighted with defiance, her whole face saying to him vividly, "Here is your opportunity; I give it to you with my own hands. Break your promise and betray me if you dare! You say you can damn me with a word; speak the word and let us see!"

Benyon's heart beat faster, as he felt that it was indeed a chance; but half his emotion came from the spectacle, magnificent in its way, of her unparalleled impudence. A sense of all that he had escaped in not having had to live with her rolled over him like a wave, while he looked strangely at Mr. Roy, to whom this privilege had been vouchsafed. He saw in a moment his successor had a constitution that would carry it. Mr. Roy suggested squareness and solidity; he was a broad-based, comfortable, polished man, with a surface in which the rank tendrils of irritation would not easily obtain a foothold. He had a broad, blank face, a capacious mouth, and a small, light eye, to which, as he entered, he was engaged in adjusting a double gold-rimmed glass. He approached Benyon with a prudent, civil, punctual air, as if he habitually met a good many gentlemen in the course of business, and though, naturally, this was not that sort of occasion, he was not a man to waste time in preliminaries. Benyon had immediately the impression of having seen him, or his equivalent, a thousand times before. He was middle-aged, fresh-coloured, whiskered, prosperous, indefinite. Georgina introduced them to each other—she spoke of Benyon as an old friend, whom she had known long before she had known Mr. Roy, who had been very kind to her years ago, when she was a girl.

"He is in the navy. He has just come back from a long cruise."

Mr. Roy shook hands—Benyon gave him his before he knew it—said he was very happy, smiled, looked at Benyon from head to foot, then at Georgina, then round the room, then back at Benyon again—at Benyon, who stood there, without sound or movement, with a dilated eye and a pulse quickened to a degree of which Mr. Roy could have little idea. Georgina made some remark about their sitting down, but William Roy replied that he hadn't time for that, if Captain Benyon would excuse him. He should have to go straight into the library and write a note to send back to his office, where, as he just remembered, he had neglected to give, in leaving the place, an important direction.

"You can wait a moment, surely," Georgina said. "Captain Benyon wants so much to see you."

"Oh yes, my dear; I can wait a minute, and I can come back."

Benyon saw, accordingly, that he was waiting, and that Georgina was waiting too. Each was waiting for him to say something, though they were waiting for different things. Mr. Roy put his hands behind him, balanced himself on his toes, hoped that Captain Benyon had enjoyed his cruise—though he shouldn't care much for the navy himself—and evidently wondered at the vacuity of his wife's visitor. Benyon knew he was speaking, for he indulged in two or three more observations, after which he stopped. But his meaning was not present to our hero. This personage was conscious of only one thing, of his own momentary power, of everything that hung on his lips; all the rest swam before him; there was vagueness in his ears and eyes. Mr. Roy stopped, as I say, and there was a pause, which seemed to Benyon of tremendous length. He knew, while it lasted, that Georgina was as conscious as himself that he felt his opportunity, that he held it there in his hand, weighing it noiselessly in the palm, and that she braved and scorned, or rather that she enjoyed, the danger. He asked himself whether he should be able to speak if he were to try, and then he knew that he should not, that the words would stick in his throat, that he should make sounds which would dishonour his cause. There was no real choice nor decision, then, on Benyon's part; his silence was after all the same old silence, the fruit of other hours and places, the stillness to which Georgina listened while he felt her eager eyes fairly eat into his face, so that his cheeks burned with the touch of them. The moments stood before him in their turn; each one was distinct. "Ah, well," said Mr. Roy, "perhaps I interrupt; I will just dash off my note." Benyon knew that he was rather bewildered, that he was making a protest, that he was leaving the room; knew presently that Georgina again stood before him alone.

"You are exactly the man I thought you!" she announced, as joyously as if she had won a bet.

"You are the most horrible woman I can imagine. Good God, if I had to live with you!" That is what he said to her in answer.

Even at this she never flinched; she continued to smile in triumph. "He adores me—but what's that to you? Of course you have all the future," she went on; "but I know you as if I had made you!"

Benyon considered a moment. "If he adores you, you are all right. If our divorce is pronounced you will be free, and then he can marry you properly, which he would like ever so much better."

"It's too touching to hear you reason about it. Fancy me telling such a hideous story—about myself—me—me!" And she touched her breasts with her white fingers.

Benyon gave her a look that was charged with all the sickness of his helpless rage. "You—you!" he repeated, as he turned away from her and passed through the door which Mr. Roy had left open.

She followed him into the hall, she was close behind him; he moved before her as she pressed. "There was one more reason," she said. "I wouldn't be forbidden. It was my hideous pride. That's what prevents me now."

"I don't care what it is," Benyon answered, wearily, with his hand on the knob of the door.

She laid hers on his shoulder; he stood there an instant, feeling it, wishing that her loathsome touch gave him the right to strike her to the earth, to strike her so that she should never rise again.

"How clever you are, and intelligent always, as you used to be; to feel so perfectly and know so well—without more scenes—that it's hopeless—my ever consenting! If I have, with you, the shame of having made you promise, let me at least have the profit!"

His back had been turned to her, but at this he glanced round. "To hear you talk of shame——!"

"You don't know what I have gone through; but, of course, I don't ask any pity from you. Only I should like to say something kind to you before we part. I admire you so much. Who will ever tell her, if you don't? How will she ever know, then?

She will be as safe as I am. You know what that is," said Georgina, smiling.

He had opened the door wide while she spoke, apparently not heeding her, thinking only of getting away from her for ever. In reality he heard every word she said, and felt to his marrow the lowered, suggestive tone in which she made him that last recommendation. Outside, on the steps—she stood there in the doorway—he gave her his last look. "I only hope you will die. I shall pray for that!" And he descended into the street and took his way.

It was after this that his real temptation came. Not the temptation to return betrayal for betrayal; that passed away even in a few days, for he simply knew that he couldn't break his promise, that it imposed itself on him as stubbornly as the colour of his eyes or the stammer of his lips; it had gone forth into the world to live for itself, and was far beyond his reach or his authority. But the temptation to go through the form of a marriage with Kate Theory, to let her suppose that he was as free as herself and that their children, if they should have any, would, before the law, have a right to exist—this attractive idea held him fast for many weeks, and caused him to pass some haggard nights and days. It was perfectly possible she might never learn his secret, and that, as no one could either suspect it or have an interest in bringing it to light, they both might live and die in security and honour. This vision fascinated him; it was, I say, a real temptation. He thought of other solutions—of telling her that he was married (without telling her to whom), and inducing her to overlook such an accident and content herself with a ceremony in which the world would see no flaw. But after all the contortions of his spirit it remained as clear to him as before that dishonour was in everything but renunciation. So, at last, he renounced. He took two steps which attested this act to himself. He addressed an urgent request to the Secretary of the Navy that he might, with as little delay as possible, be despatched on another long voyage; and he returned to Boston to tell Kate Theory that they must wait. He could explain so little that, say what he would, he was aware that he could not make his conduct seem natural, and he saw that the girl only trusted him, that she never understood. She trusted without understanding, and she agreed to wait. When the writer of these pages last heard of the pair they were waiting still.

A New England Winter

MRS. DAINTRY stood on her steps a moment, to address a parting injunction to her little domestic, whom she had induced a few days before, by earnest and friendly argument—the only coercion or persuasion this enlightened mistress was ever known to use—to crown her ruffled tresses with a cap; and then, slowly and with deliberation, she descended to the street. As soon as her back was turned, her maid-servant closed the door, not with violence, but inaudibly, quickly, and firmly; so that when she reached the bottom of the steps and looked up again at the front—as she always did before leaving it, to assure herself that everything was well—the folded wings of her portal were presented to her, smooth and shining, as wings should be, and ornamented with the large silver plate on which the name of her late husband was inscribed—which she had brought with her when, taking the inevitable course of good Bostonians, she had transferred her household goods from the "hill" to the "new land," and the exhibition of which, as an act of conjugal fidelity, she preferred—how much, those who knew her could easily understand—to the more distinguished modern fashion of suppressing the domiciliary label. She stood still for a minute on the pavement, looking at the closed aperture of her dwelling and asking herself a question; not that there was anything extraordinary in that, for she never spared herself in this respect. She would greatly have preferred that her servant should not shut the door till she had reached the sidewalk and dismissed her, as it were, with that benevolent, that almost maternal, smile with which it was a part of Mrs. Daintry's religion to encourage and reward her domestics. She liked to know that her door was being held open behind her until she should pass out of sight of the young woman standing in the hall. There was a want of respect in shutting her out so precipitately; it was almost like giving her a push down the steps. What Mrs. Daintry asked herself was, whether she should not do right to ascend the steps again, ring the bell, and request Beatrice, the parlour-maid, to be so good as to wait a little longer. She felt that this would have been a proceeding of some importance, and she presently decided against it. There were a good many reasons, and she thought them over as she took her way slowly up Newbury Street, turning as soon as possible into Commonwealth Avenue; for she was very fond of the south side of this beautiful prospect, and the autumn sunshine to-day was delightful. During the moment that she paused, looking up at her house, she had had time to see that everything was as fresh and bright as she could desire. It looked a little too new, perhaps, and Florimond would not like that; for of course his great fondness was for the antique, which was the reason for his remaining year after year in Europe, where, as a young painter of considerable, if not of the highest, promise, he had opportunities to study the most dilapidated buildings. It was a comfort to Mrs. Daintry, however, to be able to say to herself that he would be struck with her living really very nicely—more nicely, in many ways, than he could possibly be accommodated—that she was sure of—in a small dark *appartement de garçon* in Paris, on the uncomfortable side of the Seine. Her state of mind at present was such that she set the highest value on anything that could possibly help to give Florimond a pleasant impression. Nothing could be too small to count, she said to herself; for she knew that Florimond was both fastidious and observant. Everything that would strike him agreeably would contribute to detain him, so that if there were only enough agreeable things he would perhaps stay four or five months, instead of three, as he had promised—the three that were to date from the day of his arrival in Boston, not from that (an important difference) of his departure from Liverpool, which was about to take place.

It was Florimond that Mrs. Daintry had had in mind when, on emerging from the little vestibule, she gave the direction to Beatrice about the position of the door-mat—in which the young woman, so carefully selected, as a Protestant, from the British Provinces, had never yet taken the interest that her mistress expected from such antecedents. It was Florimond also that she had thought of in putting before her parlour-maid the question of donning a badge of servitude in the shape of a neat little muslin coif, adorned with pink ribbon and stitched together by Mrs. Daintry's own beneficent fingers. Naturally there was no obvious connection between the parlour-maid's coiffure and the length of Florimond's stay; that detail was to be only a part of the general effect of American life. It was still Florimond that was uppermost as his mother, on her way up the hill, turned over in her mind that question of the ceremony of the front-door. He had been living in a country in which servants observed more forms, and he would doubtless be shocked at Beatrice's want of patience. An accumulation of such anomalies would at last undermine his loyalty. He would not care for them for himself, of course, but he would care about them for her; coming from France, where, as she knew by his letters, and indeed by her own reading—for she made a remarkably free use of the Athenæum—that the position of a mother was one of the most exalted, he could not fail to be *froissé* at any want of consideration for his surviving parent. As an artist, he could not make up his mind to live in Boston; but he was a good son for all that. He had told her frequently that they might easily live together if she would only come to Paris; but of course she could not do that, with Joanna and her six children round in Clarendon Street, and her responsibilities to her daughter multiplied in the highest degree. Besides, during that winter she spent in Paris, when Florimond was definitely making up his mind, and they had in the evening the most charming conversations, interrupted only by the repeated care of winding-up the lamp, or applying the bellows to the obstinate little fire—during that winter she had felt that Paris was not her element. She had gone to the lectures at the Sorbonne, and she had visited the Louvre as few people did it, catalogue in hand, taking the catalogue volume by volume; but all the while she was thinking of Joanna and her new baby, and how the other three (that was the number then) were getting on while their mother was so much absorbed with the last. Mrs. Daintry, familiar as she was with these anxieties, had not the step of a grandmother; for a mind that was always intent had the effect of refreshing and brightening her years. Responsibility with her was not a weariness, but a joy—at least it was the nearest approach to a joy that she knew, and she did not regard her life as especially cheerless; there were many others that were more denuded. She moved with circum-

spection, but without reluctance, holding up her head and looking at every one she met with a clear, unaccusing gaze. This
expression showed that she took an interest, as she ought, in
everything that concerned her fellow-creatures; but there was
that also in her whole person which indicated that she went
no farther than Christian charity required. It was only with
regard to Joanna and that vociferous houseful—so fertile
in problems, in opportunities for devotion—that she went
really very far. And now to-day, of course, in this matter of
Florimond's visit, after an absence of six years; which was perhaps more on her mind than anything had ever been. People
who met Mrs. Daintry after she had traversed the Public Garden—she always took that way—and begun to ascend the
charming slope of Beacon Street, would never, in spite of the
relaxation of her pace as she measured this eminence, have
mistaken her for a little old lady who should have crept out,
vaguely and timidly, to inhale one of the last mild days. It was
easy to see that she was not without a duty, or at least a reason—and indeed Mrs. Daintry had never in her life been left
in this predicament. People who knew her ever so little would
have felt that she was going to call on a relation; and if they
had been to the manner born they would have added a mental
hope that her relation was prepared for her visit. No one
would have doubted this, however, who had been aware that
her steps were directed to the habitation of Miss Lucretia
Daintry. Her sister-in-law, her husband's only sister, lived in
that commodious nook which is known as Mount Vernon
Place; and Mrs. Daintry therefore turned off at Joy Street. By
the time she did so, she had quite settled in her mind the
question of Beatrice's behaviour in connection with the front-
door. She had decided that it would never do to make a formal
remonstrance, for it was plain that, in spite of the Old-World
training which she hoped the girl might have imbibed in Nova
Scotia (where, until lately, she learned, there had been an English garrison), she would in such a case expose herself to the
danger of desertion; Beatrice would not consent to stand
there holding the door open for nothing. And after all, in the
depths of her conscience Mrs. Daintry was not sure that she
ought to; she was not sure that this was an act of homage
that one human being had a right to exact of another, simply

because this other happened to wear a little muslin cap with pink ribbons. It was a service that ministered to her importance, to her dignity, not to her hunger or thirst; and Mrs. Daintry, who had had other foreign advantages besides her winter in Paris, was quite aware that in the United States the machinery for that former kind of tribute was very undeveloped. It was a luxury that one ought not to pretend to enjoy—it was a luxury, indeed, that she probably ought not to presume to desire. At the bottom of her heart Mrs. Daintry suspected that such hankerings were criminal. And yet, turning the thing over, as she turned everything, she could not help coming back to the idea that it would be very pleasant, it would be really delightful, if Beatrice herself, as a result of the growing refinement of her taste, her transplantation to a society after all more elaborate than that of Nova Scotia, should perceive the fitness, the felicity, of such an attitude. This perhaps was too much to hope; but it did not much matter, for before she had turned into Mount Vernon Place Mrs. Daintry had invented a compromise. She would continue to talk to her parlour-maid until she should reach the bottom of her steps, making earnestly one remark after the other over her shoulder, so that Beatrice would be obliged to remain on the threshold. It is true that it occurred to her that the girl might not attach much importance to these Parthian observations, and would perhaps not trouble herself to wait for their natural term; but this idea was too fraught with embarrassment to be long entertained. It must be added that this was scarcely a moment for Mrs. Daintry to go much into the ethics of the matter, for she felt that her call upon her sister-in-law was the consequence of a tolerably unscrupulous determination.

II.

Lucretia Daintry was at home, for a wonder; but she kept her visitor waiting a quarter of an hour, during which this lady had plenty of time to consider her errand afresh. She was a little ashamed of it; but she did not so much mind being put to shame by Lucretia, for Lucretia did things that were much more ambiguous than any she should have thought of doing.

It was even for this that Mrs. Daintry had picked her out, among so many relations, as the object of an appeal in its nature somewhat ambiguous. Nevertheless, her heart beat a little faster than usual as she sat in the quiet parlour, looking about her for the thousandth time at Lucretia's "things," and observing that she was faithful to her old habit of not having her furnace lighted until long after every one else. Miss Daintry had her own habits, and she was the only person her sister-in-law knew who had more reasons than herself. Her taste was of the old fashion, and her drawing-room embraced neither festoons nor Persian rugs, nor plates and *plaques* upon the wall, nor faded stuffs suspended from unexpected projections. Most of the articles it contained dated from the year 1830; and a sensible, reasonable, rectangular arrangement of them abundantly answered to their owner's conception of the decorative. A rosewood sofa against the wall, surmounted by an engraving from Kaulbach; a neatly drawn carpet, faded, but little worn, and sprigged with a floral figure; a chimney-piece of black marble, veined with yellow, garnished with an empire clock and antiquated lamps; half a dozen large mirrors, with very narrow frames; and an immense glazed screen representing, in the livid tints of early worsted-work, a ruined temple overhanging a river—these were some of the more obvious of Miss Daintry's treasures. Her sister-in-law was a votary of the newer school, and had made sacrifices to have everything in black and gilt; but she could not fail to see that Lucretia had some very good pieces. It was a wonder how she made them last, for Lucretia had never been supposed to know much about the keeping of a house, and no one would have thought of asking her how she treated the marble floor of her vestibule, or what measures she took in the spring with regard to her curtains. Her work in life lay outside. She took an interest in questions and institutions, sat on committees, and had views on Female Suffrage—a movement which she strongly opposed. She even wrote letters sometimes to the *Transcript*, not "chatty" and jocular, and signed with a fancy name, but "over" her initials, as the phrase was—every one recognised them—and bearing on some important topic. She was not, however, in the faintest degree slipshod or dishevelled, like some of the ladies of the newspaper and the forum; she had no ink on her fingers, and she wore her bonnet as scientifically poised as the dome of the State House. When you rang at her door-bell you were never kept waiting, and when you entered her dwelling you were not greeted with those culinary odours which, pervading halls and parlours, had in certain other cases been described as the right smell in the wrong place. If Mrs. Daintry was made to wait some time before her hostess appeared, there was nothing extraordinary in this, for none of her friends came down directly, and she never did herself. To come down directly would have seemed to her to betray a frivolous eagerness for the social act. The delay, moreover, not only gave her, as I have said, opportunity to turn over her errand afresh, but enabled her to say to herself, as she had often said before, that though Lucretia had no taste, she had some very good things, and to wonder both how she had kept them so well, and how she had originally got them. Mrs. Daintry knew that they proceeded from her mother and her aunts, who had been supposed to distribute among the children of the second generation the accumulations of the old house in Federal Street, where many Daintrys had been born in the early part of the century. Of course she knew nothing of the principles on which the distribution had been made, but all she could say was that Lucretia had evidently been first in the field. There was apparently no limit to what had come to her. Mrs. Daintry was not obliged to look, to assure herself that there was another clock in the back parlour—which would seem to indicate that all the clocks had fallen to Lucretia. She knew of four other timepieces in other parts of the house, for of course in former years she had often been upstairs; it was only in comparatively recent times that she had renounced that practice. There had been a period when she ascended to the second story as a matter of course, without asking leave. On seeing that her sister-in-law was in neither of the parlours, she mounted and talked with Lucretia at the door of her bedroom, if it happened to be closed. And there had been another season when she stood at the foot of the staircase, and, lifting her voice, inquired of Miss Daintry— who called down with some shrillness in return—whether she might climb, while the maid-servant, wandering away with a vague cachinnation, left her to her own devices. But both of these phases belonged to the past. Lucretia never came into *her* bedroom to-day, nor did she presume to penetrate into Lucretia's; so that she did not know for a long time whether she had renewed her chintz nor whether she had hung in that bower the large photograph of Florimond, presented by Mrs. Daintry herself to his aunt, which had been placed in neither of the parlours. Mrs. Daintry would have given a good deal to know whether this memento had been honoured with a place in her sister-in-law's "chamber"—it was by this name, on each side, that these ladies designated their sleeping-apartment; but she could not bring herself to ask directly, for it would be embarrassing to learn—what was possible—that Lucretia had not paid the highest respect to Florimond's portrait. The point was cleared up by its being revealed to her accidentally that the photograph—an expensive and very artistic one, taken in Paris—had been relegated to the spare-room, or guest-chamber. Miss Daintry was very hospitable, and constantly had friends of her own sex staying with her. They were very apt to be young women in their twenties; and one of them had remarked to Mrs. Daintry that her son's portrait—he must be wonderfully handsome—was the first thing she saw when she woke up in the morning. Certainly Florimond was handsome; but his mother had a lurking suspicion that, in spite of his beauty, his aunt was not fond of him. She doubtless thought he ought to come back and settle down in Boston; he was the first of the Daintrys who had had so much in common with Paris. Mrs. Daintry knew as a fact that, twenty-eight years before, Lucretia, whose opinions even at that period were already wonderfully formed, had not approved of the romantic name which, in a moment of pardonable weakness, she had conferred upon her rosy babe. The spinster (she had been as much of a spinster at twenty as she was to-day) had accused her of making a fool of the child. Every one was reading old ballads in Boston then, and Mrs. Daintry had found the name in a ballad. It doubled any anxiety she might feel with regard to her present business to think that, as certain foreign newspapers which her son sent her used to say about ambassadors, Florimond was perhaps not a *persona grata* to his aunt. She reflected, however, that if his fault were in his absenting himself, there was nothing that would remedy it so effectively as his coming home. She reflected, too, that if she and Lucretia no longer took liberties with each other, there was still something a little indiscreet in her purpose this morning. But it fortified and consoled her for everything to remember, as she sat looking at the empire clock, which was a very handsome one, that her husband at least had been disinterested.

Miss Daintry found her visitor in this attitude, and thought it was an expression of impatience; which led her to explain that she had been on the roof of her house with a man who had come to see about repairing it. She had walked all over it, and peeped over the cornice, and not been in the least dizzy; and had come to the conclusion that one ought to know a great deal more about one's roof than was usual.

"I am sure you have never been over yours," she said to her sister-in-law.

Mrs. Daintry confessed with some embarrassment that she had not, and felt, as she did so, that she was superficial and slothful. It annoyed her to reflect that while she supposed, in her new house, she had thought of everything, she had not thought of this important feature. There was no one like Lucretia for giving one such reminders.

"I will send Florimond up when he comes," she said; "he will tell me all about it."

"Do you suppose he knows about roofs, except tumble-down ones, in his little pictures? I am afraid it will make him giddy." This had been Miss Daintry's rejoinder, and the tone of it was not altogether reassuring. She was nearly fifty years old; she had a plain, fresh, delightful face, and in whatever part of the world she might have been met, an attentive observer of American life would not have had the least difficulty in guessing what phase of it she represented. She represented the various and enlightened activities which cast their rapid shuttle—in the comings and goings of eager workers—from one side to the other of Boston Common. She had in an eminent degree the physiognomy, the accent, the costume, the conscience, and the little eyeglass, of her native place. She had never sacrificed to the graces, but she inspired unlimited confidence. Moreover, if she was thoroughly in sympathy with the New England capital, she reserved her liberty; she had a great charity, but she was independent and witty; and if she was as earnest as other people, she was not quite so serious. Her voice was a little masculine; and it had been said of her that she didn't care in the least how she looked. This was far from true, for she would not for the world have looked better than she thought was right for so plain a woman.

Mrs. Daintry was fond of calculating consequences; but she was not a coward, and she arrived at her business as soon as possible.

"You know that Florimond sails on the 20th of this month. He will get home by the 1st of December."

"Oh yes, my dear, I know it; everybody is talking about it. I have heard it thirty times. That's where Boston is so small," Lucretia Daintry remarked.

"Well, it's big enough for me," said her sister-in-law. "And of course people notice his coming back; it shows that everything that has been said is false, and that he really does like us."

"He likes his mother, I hope; about the rest I don't know that it matters."

"Well, it certainly will be pleasant to have him," said Mrs. Daintry, who was not content with her companion's tone, and wished to extract from her some recognition of the importance of Florimond's advent. "It will prove how unjust so much of the talk has been."

"My dear woman, I don't know anything about the talk. We make too much fuss about everything. Florimond was an infant when I last saw him."

This was open to the interpretation that too much fuss had been made about Florimond—an idea that accorded ill with the project that had kept Mrs. Daintry waiting a quarter of an hour while her hostess walked about on the roof. But Miss Daintry continued, and in a moment gave her sister-in-law the best opportunity she could have hoped for. "I don't suppose he will bring with him either salvation or the other thing; and if he has decided to winter among the bears, it will matter much more to him than to any one else. But I shall be very glad to see him if he behaves himself; and I needn't tell you that if there is anything I can do for him——" and Miss Daintry, tightening her lips together a little, paused, suiting her action to the idea that professions were usually humbug.

"There is indeed something you can do for him," her sister-in-law hastened to respond; "or something you can do for me, at least," she added, more discreetly.

"Call it for both of you. What is it?" and Miss Daintry put on her eyeglass.

"I know you like to do kindnesses, when they are *real* ones; and you almost always have some one staying with you for the winter."

Miss Daintry stared. "Do you want to put him to live with me?"

"No, indeed! Do you think I could part with him? It's another person—a lady!"

"A lady! Is he going to bring a woman with him?"

"My dear Lucretia, you won't wait. I want to make it as pleasant for him as possible. In that case he may stay longer. He has promised three months; but I should so like to keep him till the summer. It would make me very happy."

"Well, my dear, keep him, then, if you can."

"But I can't, unless I am helped."

"And you want me to help you? Tell me what I must do. Should you wish me to make love to him?"

Mrs. Daintry's hesitation at this point was almost as great as if she had found herself obliged to say yes. She was well aware that what she had come to suggest was very delicate; but it seemed to her at the present moment more delicate than ever. Still, her cause was good, because it was the cause of maternal devotion. "What I should like you to do would be to ask Rachel Torrance to spend the winter with you."

Miss Daintry had not sat so much on committees without getting used to queer proposals, and she had long since ceased to waste time in expressing a vain surprise. Her method was Socratic; she usually entangled her interlocutor in a net of questions.

"Ah, do you want *her* to make love to him?"

"No, I don't want any love at all. In such a matter as that I want Florimond to be perfectly free. But Rachel is such an attractive girl; she is so artistic and so bright."

"I don't doubt it; but I can't invite all the attractive girls in the country. Why don't you ask her yourself?"

"It would be too marked. And then Florimond might not like her in the same house; he would have too much of her. Besides, she is no relation of mine, you know; the cousin-ship—such as it is, it is not very close—is on your side. I have reason to believe she would like to come; she knows so little of Boston, and admires it so much. It is astonishing how little idea the New York people have. She would be different from any one here, and that would make a pleasant change for Florimond. She was in Europe so much when she was young. She speaks French perfectly, and Italian, I think, too; and she was brought up in a kind of artistic way. Her father never did anything; but even when he hadn't bread to give his children, he always arranged to have a studio, and they gave musical parties. That's the way Rachel was brought up. But they tell me that it hasn't in the least spoiled her; it has only made her very familiar with life."

"Familiar with rubbish!" Miss Daintry ejaculated.

"My dear Lucretia, I assure you she is a very good girl, or I never would have proposed such a plan as this. She paints very well herself, and tries to sell her pictures. They are dread-fully poor—I don't mean the pictures, but Mrs. Torrance and the rest—and they live in Brooklyn, in some second-rate boarding-house. With that, Rachel has everything about her that would enable her to appreciate Boston. Of course it would be a real kindness, because there would be one less to pay for at the boarding-house. You haven't a son, so you can't understand how a mother feels. I want to prepare everything, to have everything pleasantly arranged. I want to deprive him of every pretext for going away before the summer; because in August—I don't know whether I have told you—I have a kind of idea of going back with him myself. I am so afraid he will miss the artistic side. I don't mind saying that to you, Lucretia, for I have heard you say yourself that you thought it had been left out here. Florimond might go and see Rachel Torrance every day if he liked; of course, being his cousin, and calling her Rachel, it couldn't attract any particular atten-tion. I shouldn't much care if it did," Mrs. Daintry went on, borrowing a certain bravado that in calmer moments was eminently foreign to her nature from the impunity with which she had hitherto proceeded. Her project, as she heard herself unfold it, seemed to hang together so well that she felt something of the intoxication of success. "I shouldn't care if it did," she repeated, "so long as Florimond had a little of the conversation that he is accustomed to, and I was not in perpetual fear of his starting off."

Miss Daintry had listened attentively while her sister-in-law spoke, with eager softness, passing from point to point with a *crescendo* of lucidity, like a woman who had thought it all out and had the consciousness of many reasons on her side. There had been momentary pauses, of which Lucretia had not taken advantage, so that Mrs. Daintry rested at last in the enjoyment of a security that was almost complete and that her companion's first question was not of a nature to dispel.

"It's so long since I have seen her. Is she pretty?" Miss Daintry inquired.

"She is decidedly striking; she has magnificent hair!" her visitor answered, almost with enthusiasm.

"Do you want Florimond to marry her?"

This, somehow, was less pertinent. "Ah, no, my dear," Mrs. Daintry rejoined, very judicially. "That is not the kind of education—the kind of *milieu*—one would wish for the wife of one's son." She knew, moreover, that her sister-in-law knew her opinion about the marriage of young people. It was a sacrament more high and holy than any words could express, the propriety and timeliness of which lay deep in the hearts of the contracting parties, below all interference from parents and friends; it was an inspiration from above, and she would no more have thought of laying a train to marry her son than she would have thought of breaking open his letters. More relevant even than this, however, was the fact that she did not believe he would wish to make a wife of a girl from a slipshod family in Brooklyn, however little he might care to lose sight of the artistic side. It will be observed that she gave Florimond the credit of being a very discriminating young man; and she indeed discriminated for him in cases in which she would not have presumed to discriminate for herself.

"My dear Susan, you are simply the most immoral woman

in Boston!" These were the words of which, after a moment, her sister-in-law delivered herself.

Mrs. Daintry turned a little pale. "Don't you think it would be right?" she asked quickly.

"To sacrifice the poor girl to Florimond's amusement? What has she done that you should wish to play her such a trick?" Miss Daintry did not look shocked: she never looked shocked, for even when she was annoyed she was never frightened; but after a moment she broke into a loud, uncompromising laugh—a laugh which her sister-in-law knew of old and regarded as a peculiarly dangerous form of criticism.

"I don't see why she should be sacrificed. She would have a lovely time if she were to come on. She would consider it the greatest kindness to be asked."

"To be asked to come and amuse Florimond."

Mrs. Daintry hesitated a moment. "I don't see why she should object to that. Florimond is certainly not beneath a person's notice. Why, Lucretia, you speak as if there were something disagreeable about Florimond."

"My dear Susan," said Miss Daintry, "I am willing to believe that he is the first young man of his time; but, all the same, it isn't a thing to do."

"Well, I have thought of it in every possible way, and I haven't seen any harm in it. It isn't as if she were giving up anything to come."

"You have thought of it too much, perhaps. Stop thinking for a while. I should have imagined you were more scrupulous."

Mrs. Daintry was silent a moment; she took her sister-in-law's asperity very meekly, for she felt that if she had been wrong in what she proposed she deserved a severe judgment. But why was she wrong? She clasped her hands in her lap and rested her eyes with extreme seriousness upon Lucretia's little *pince-nez*, inviting her to judge her, and too much interested in having the question of her culpability settled to care whether or no she were hurt. "It is very hard to know what is right," she said presently. "Of course it is only a plan; I wondered how it would strike you."

"You had better leave Florimond alone," Miss Daintry answered. "I don't see why you should spread so many carpets for him. Let him shift for himself. If he doesn't like Boston, Boston can spare him."

"You are not nice about him; no, you are not, Lucretia!" Mrs. Daintry cried, with a slight tremor in her voice.

"Of course I am not as nice as you—he is not my son; but I am trying to be nice about Rachel Torrance."

"I am sure she would like him—she would delight in him!" Mrs. Daintry broke out.

"That's just what I'm afraid of; I couldn't stand that."

"Well, Lucretia, I am not convinced," Mrs. Daintry said, rising, with perceptible coldness. "It is very hard to be sure one is not unjust. Of course I shall not expect you to send for her; but I shall think of her with a good deal of compassion, all winter, in that dingy place in Brooklyn. And if you have some one else with you—and I am sure you will, because you always do, unless you remain alone on purpose this year, to put me in the wrong—if you have some one else I shall keep saying to myself: 'Well, after all, it might have been Rachel!'"

Miss Daintry gave another of her loud laughs at the idea that she might remain alone "on purpose." "I shall have a visitor, but it will be some one who will not amuse Florimond in the least. If he wants to go away, it won't be for anything in this house that he will stay."

"I really don't see why you should hate him," said poor Mrs. Daintry.

"Where do you find that? On the contrary, I appreciate him very highly. That's just why I think it very possible that a girl like Rachel Torrance—an odd, uninstructed girl, who hasn't had great advantages—may fall in love with him and break her heart."

Mrs. Daintry's clear eyes expanded. "Is *that* what you are afraid of?"

"Do you suppose my solicitude is for Florimond? An accident of that sort—if she were to show him her heels at the end—might perhaps do him good. But I am thinking of the girl, since you say you don't want him to marry her."

"It was not for that that I suggested what I did. I don't want him to marry any one—I have no plans for that," Mrs. Daintry said, as if she were resenting an imputation.

"Rachel Torrance least of all!" And Miss Daintry indulged still again in that hilarity, so personal to herself, which sometimes made the subject look so little jocular to others. "My dear Susan, I don't blame you," she said; "for I suppose mothers are necessarily unscrupulous. But that is why the rest of us should hold them in check."

"It's merely an assumption, that she would fall in love with him," Mrs. Daintry continued, with a certain majesty; "there is nothing to prove it, and I am not bound to take it for granted."

"In other words, you don't care if she should! Precisely; that, I suppose, is your *rôle*. I am glad I haven't any children; it is very sophisticating. For so good a woman, you are very bad. Yes, you *are* good, Susan; and you *are* bad."

"I don't know that I pretend to be particularly good," Susan remarked, with the warmth of one who had known something of the burden of such a reputation, as she moved toward the door.

"You have a conscience, and it will wake up," her companion returned. "It will come over you in the watches of the night that your idea was—as I have said—immoral."

Mrs. Daintry paused in the hall, and stood there looking at Lucretia. It was just possible that she was being laughed at, for Lucretia's deepest mirth was sometimes silent—that is, one heard the laughter several days later. Suddenly she coloured to the roots of her hair, as if the conviction of her error had come over her. Was it possible she had been corrupted by an affection in itself so pure? "I only want to do right," she said softly. "I would rather he should never come home than that I should go too far."

She was turning away, but her sister-in-law held her a moment and kissed her. "You are a delightful woman, but I won't ask Rachel Torrance!" This was the understanding on which they separated.

III.

Miss Daintry, after her visitor had left her, recognised that she had been a little brutal; for Susan's proposition did not really strike her as so heinous. Her eagerness to protect the poor girl in Brooklyn was not a very positive quantity, inasmuch as she had an impression that this young lady was on the whole very well able to take care of herself. What her talk with Mrs. Daintry had really expressed was the lukewarmness of her sentiment with regard to Florimond. She had no wish to help his mother lay carpets for him, as she said. Rightly or wrongly, she had a conviction that he was selfish, that he was spoiled, that he was conceited; and she thought Lucretia Daintry meant for better things than the service of sugaring for the young man's lips the pill of a long-deferred visit to Boston. It was quite indifferent to her that he should be conscious, in that city, of unsatisfied needs. At bottom, she had never forgiven him for having sought another way of salvation. Moreover, she had a strong sense of humour, and it amused her more than a little that her sister-in-law—of all women in Boston—should have come to her on that particular errand. It completed the irony of the situation that one should frighten Mrs. Daintry—just a little—about what she had undertaken; and more than once that day Lucretia had, with a smile, the vision of Susan's countenance as she remarked to her that she was immoral. In reality, and speaking seriously, she did not consider Mrs. Daintry's inspiration unpardonable; what was very positive was simply that she had no wish to invite Rachel Torrance for the benefit of her nephew. She was by no means sure that she should like the girl for her own sake, and it was still less apparent that she should like her for that of Florimond. With all this, however, Miss Daintry had a high love of justice; she revised her social accounts from time to time to see that she had not cheated any one. She thought over her interview with Mrs. Daintry the next day, and it occurred to her that she had been a little unfair. But she scarcely knew what to do to repair her mistake, by which Rachel Torrance also had suffered, perhaps; for after all, if it had not been wicked of her sister-in-law to ask such a favour, it had at least been cool; and the penance that presented itself to Lucretia Daintry did not take the form of despatching a letter to Brooklyn. An accident came to her help, and four days after the conversation I have narrated she wrote her a note which explains itself and which I will presently transcribe. Meanwhile Mrs. Daintry, on her side, had held an examination of her heart; and though she did not think she had been very civilly treated, the result of her reflections was to give her a fit of remorse. Lucretia was right: she had been anything but scrupulous; she had skirted the edge of an abyss. Questions of conduct had long been familiar to her; and the cardinal rule of life in her eyes was, that before one did anything which involved in any degree the happiness or the interest of another, one should take one's motives out of the closet in which they are usually laid away and give them a thorough airing. This operation, undertaken before her visit to Lucretia, had been cursory and superficial; for now that she repeated it, she discovered among the recesses of her spirit a number of nut-like scruples which she was astonished to think she should have overlooked. She had really been very wicked, and there was no doubt about *her* proper penance. It consisted of a letter to her sister-in-law, in which she completely disavowed her little project, attributing it to momentary intermission of her reason. She saw it would never do, and she was quite ashamed of herself. She did not exactly thank Miss Daintry for the manner in which she had admonished her, but she spoke as one saved from a great danger, and assured her relative of Mount Vernon Place that she should not soon again expose herself. This letter crossed with Miss Daintry's missive, which ran as follows:—

"MY DEAR SUSAN—I have been thinking over our conversation of last Tuesday, and I am afraid I went rather too far in my condemnation of your idea with regard to Rachel Torrance. If I expressed myself in a manner to wound your feelings, I can assure you of my great regret. Nothing could have been further from my thoughts than the belief that you are wanting in delicacy. I know very well that you were prompted by the highest sense of duty. It is possible, however, I think, that your sense of duty to poor Florimond is a little too high. You think of him too much as that famous dragon of antiquity—wasn't it in Crete, or somewhere?—to whom young virgins had to be sacrificed. It may relieve your mind, however, to hear that this particular virgin will probably, during the coming winter, be provided for. Yesterday, at Doll's, where I had gone in to look at the new pictures (there is a striking

Appleton Brown), I met Pauline Mesh, whom I had not seen for ages, and had half an hour's talk with her. She seems to me to have come out very much this winter, and to have altogether a higher tone. In short, she is much enlarged, and seems to want to take an interest in something. Of course you will say: Has she not her children? But, somehow, they don't seem to fill her life. You must remember that they are very small as yet to fill anything. Anyway, she mentioned to me her great disappointment in having had to give up her sister, who was to have come on from Baltimore to spend the greater part of the winter. Rosalie is very pretty, and Pauline expected to give a lot of Germans, and make things generally pleasant. I shouldn't wonder if she thought something might happen that would make Rosalie a fixture in our city. She would have liked this immensely; for, whatever Pauline's faults may be, she has plenty of family feeling. But her sister has suddenly got engaged in Baltimore (I believe it's much easier than here), so that the visit has fallen through. Pauline seemed to be quite in despair, for she had made all sorts of beautifications in one of her rooms, on purpose for Rosalie; and not only had she wasted her labour (you know how she goes into those things, whatever we may think, sometimes, of her taste), but she spoke as if it would make a great difference in her winter; said she should suffer a great deal from loneliness. She says Boston is no place for a married woman, standing on her own merits; she can't have any sort of time unless she hitches herself to some attractive girl who will help her to pull the social car. You know that isn't what every one says, and how much talk there has been the last two or three winters about the frisky young matrons. Well, however that may be, I don't pretend to know much about it, not being in the married set. Pauline spoke as if she were really quite high and dry, and I felt so sorry for her that it suddenly occurred to me to say something about Rachel Torrance. I remembered that she is related to Donald Mesh in about the same degree as she is to me—a degree nearer, therefore, than to Florimond. Pauline didn't seem to think much of the relationship—it's so remote; but when I told her that Rachel (strange as it might appear) would probably be thankful for a season in Boston, and might be a good substitute for Rosalie, why she quite jumped at the idea. She has never seen her, but she knows who she is—fortunately, for I could never begin to explain. She seems to think such a girl will be quite a novelty in this place. I don't suppose Pauline can do her any particular harm, from what you tell me of Miss Torrance; and, on the other hand, I don't know that she could injure Pauline. She is certainly very kind (Pauline, of course), and I have no doubt she will immediately write to Brooklyn, and that Rachel will come on. Florimond won't, of course, see as much of her as if she were staying with me, and I don't know that he will particularly care about Pauline Mesh, who, you know, is intensely American; but they will go out a great deal, and he will meet them (if he takes the trouble), and I have no doubt that Rachel will take the edge off the east wind for him. At any rate I have perhaps done her a good turn. I must confess to you—and it won't surprise you—that I was thinking of her, and not of him, when I spoke to Pauline. Therefore I don't feel that I have taken a risk, but I don't much care if I have. I have my views, but I never worry. I recommend you not to do so either—for you go, I know, from one extreme to the other. I have told you my little story; it was on my mind. Aren't you glad to see the lovely snow?—Ever affectionately yours,   L. D.

"*P.S.*—The more I think of it, the more convinced I am that you *will* worry now about the danger for Rachel. Why did I drop the poison into your mind? Of course I didn't say a word about you or Florimond."

This epistle reached Mrs. Daintry, as I have intimated, about an hour after her letter to her sister-in-law had been posted; but it is characteristic of her that she did not for a moment regret having made a retractation rather humble in form, and which proved after all, scarcely to have been needed. The delight of having done that duty carried her over the sense of having given herself away. Her sister-in-law spoke from knowledge when she wrote that phrase about Susan's now beginning to worry from the opposite point of view. Her conscience, like the good Homer, might sometimes nod; but when it woke, it woke with a start; and for many a day afterward its vigilance was feverish. For the moment her emotions were mingled. She thought Lucretia very strange, and that *she* was scarcely in a position to talk about one's going from one extreme to the other. It was good news to her that Rachel Torrance would probably be on the ground after all, and she was delighted that on Lucretia the responsibility of such a fact should rest. This responsibility, even after her revulsion, as we know, she regarded as grave; she exhaled an almost voluptuous sigh when she thought of having herself escaped from it. What she did not quite understand was Lucretia's apology, and her having, even if Florimond's happiness were not her motive, taken almost the very step which three days before she had so severely criticised. This was puzzling, for Lucretia was usually so consistent. But all the same Mrs. Daintry did not repent of her own penance; on the contrary, she took more and more comfort in it. If, with that, Rachel Torrance should be really useful, it would be delightful.

IV.

Florimond Daintry had stayed at home for three days after his arrival; he had sat close to the fire, in his slippers, every now and then casting a glance over his shoulders at the hard white world which seemed to glare at him from the other side of the window-panes. He was very much afraid of the cold, and he was not in a hurry to go out and meet it. He had met it, on disembarking in New York, in the shape of a wave of frozen air, which had travelled from some remote point in the West (he was told), on purpose, apparently, to smite him in the face. That portion of his organism tingled yet with it, though the gasping, bewildered look which sat upon his features during the first few hours had quite left it. I am afraid it will be thought he was a young man of small courage; and on a point so delicate I do not hold myself obliged to pronounce. It is only fair to add that it was delightful to him to be with his mother and that they easily spent three days in talking. Moreover he had the company of Joanna and her children, who, after a little delay, occasioned apparently by their waiting to see whether he would not first come to them, had arrived in a body and had spent several hours. As regards the majority of them, they had repeated this visit several times in the three days, Joanna being obliged to remain at home with the two

younger ones. There were four older ones, and their grandmother's house was open to them as a second nursery. The
first day, their Uncle Florimond thought them charming; and,
as he had brought a French toy for each, it is probable that
this impression was mutual. The second day, their little ruddy
bodies and woollen clothes seemed to him to have a positive
odour of the cold—it was disagreeable to him, and he spoke
to his mother about their "wintry smell." The third day they
had become very familiar; they called him "Florry;" and he
had made up his mind that, to let them loose in that way on
his mother, Joanna must be rather wanting in delicacy—not
mentioning this deficiency, however, as yet, for he saw that
his mother was not prepared for it. She evidently thought it
proper, or at least it seemed inevitable, that either she should
be round at Joanna's or the children should be round in Newbury Street; for "Joanna's" evidently represented primarily
the sound of small, loud voices, and the hard breathing that
signalised the intervals of romps. Florimond was rather disappointed in his sister, seeing her after a long separation; he
remarked to his mother that she seemed completely sub-
merged. As Mrs. Daintry spent most of her time under the
waves with her daughter, she had grown to regard this element as sufficiently favourable to life, and was rather surprised
when Florimond said to her that he was sorry to see she and
his sister appeared to have been converted into a pair of *bonnes
d'enfants*. Afterward, however, she perceived what he meant;
she was not aware, until he called her attention to it, that the
little Merrimans took up an enormous place in the intellectual
economy of two households. "You ought to remember that
they exist for you, and not you for them," Florimond said to
her in a tone of friendly admonition; and he remarked on
another occasion that the perpetual presence of children was
a great injury to conversation—it kept it down so much; and
that in Boston they seemed to be present even when they were
absent, inasmuch as most of the talk was about them. Mrs.
Daintry did not stop to ask herself what her son knew of
Boston, leaving it years before, as a boy, and not having so
much as looked out of the window since his return; she was
taken up mainly with noting certain little habits of speech
which he evidently had formed, and in wondering how they

would strike his fellow-citizens. He was very definite and trenchant; he evidently knew perfectly what he thought; and though his manner was not defiant—he had, perhaps, even too many of the forms of politeness, as if sometimes, for mysterious reasons, he were playing upon you—the tone in which he uttered his opinions did not appear exactly to give you the choice. And then apparently he had a great many; there was a moment when Mrs. Daintry vaguely foresaw that the little house in Newbury Street would be more crowded with Florimond's views than it had ever been with Joanna's children. She hoped very much people would like him, and she hardly could see why they should fail to find him agreeable. To herself he was sweeter than any grandchild; he was as kind as if he had been a devoted parent. Florimond had but a small acquaintance with his brother-in-law; but after he had been at home forty-eight hours he found that he bore Arthur Merriman a grudge, and was ready to think rather ill of him—having a theory that he ought to have held up Joanna and interposed to save her mother. Arthur Merriman was a young and brilliant commission-merchant, who had not married Joanna Daintry for the sake of Florimond, and, doing an active business all day in East Boston, had a perfectly good conscience in leaving his children's mother and grandmother to establish their terms of intercourse.

Florimond, however, did not particularly wonder why his brother-in-law had not been round to bid him welcome. It was for Mrs. Daintry that this anxiety was reserved; and what made it worse was her uncertainty as to whether she should be justified in mentioning the subject to Joanna. It might wound Joanna to suggest to her that her husband was derelict—especially if she did not think so, and she certainly gave her mother no opening; and on the other hand Florimond might have ground for complaint if Arthur should continue not to notice him. Mrs. Daintry earnestly desired that nothing of this sort should happen, and took refuge in the hope that Florimond would have adopted the foreign theory of visiting, in accordance with which the newcomer was to present himself first. Meanwhile the young man, who had looked upon a meeting with his brother-in-law as a necessity rather than a privilege, was simply conscious of a reprieve; and up in

Clarendon Street, as Mrs. Daintry said, it never occurred to
Arthur Merriman to take this social step, nor to his wife to
propose it to him. Mrs. Merriman simply took for granted
that her brother would be round early some morning to see
the children. A day or two later the couple dined at her
mother's, and that virtually settled the question. It is true
that Mrs. Daintry, in later days, occasionally recalled the
fact that, after all, Joanna's husband never had called upon
Florimond; and she even wondered why Florimond, who
sometimes said bitter things, had not made more of it. The
matter came back at moments when, under the pressure of
circumstances which, it must be confessed, were rare, she
found herself giving assent to an axiom that sometimes
reached her ears. This axiom, it must be added, did not justify
her in the particular case I have mentioned, for the full pur-
port of it was that the queerness of Bostonians was collective,
not individual.

There was no doubt, however, that it was Florimond's place
to call first upon his aunt, and this was a duty of which she
could not hesitate to remind him. By the time he took his
way across the long expanse of the new land and up the
charming hill which constitutes, as it were, the speaking face
of Boston, the temperature either had relaxed, or he had got
used, even in his mother's hot little house, to his native air.
He breathed the bright cold sunshine with pleasure; he raised
his eyes to the arching blueness, and thought he had never
seen a dome so magnificently painted. He turned his head this
way and that, as he walked (now that he had recovered his
legs, he foresaw that he should walk a good deal), and freely
indulged his most valued organ, the organ that had won him
such reputation as he already enjoyed. In the little artistic
circle in which he moved in Paris, Florimond Daintry was
thought to have a great deal of eye. His power of rendering
was questioned, his execution had been called pretentious and
feeble; but a conviction had somehow been diffused that he
saw things with extraordinary intensity. No one could tell better than he what to paint, and what not to paint, even though
his interpretation were sometimes rather too sketchy. It will
have been guessed that he was an impressionist; and it must
be admitted that this was the character in which he proceeded

on his visit to Miss Daintry. He was constantly shutting one
eye, to see the better with the other, making a little telescope
by curving one of his hands together, waving these members
in the air with vague pictorial gestures, pointing at things
which, when people turned to follow his direction, seemed to
mock the vulgar vision by eluding it. I do not mean that he
practised these devices as he walked along Beacon Street, into
which he had crossed shortly after leaving his mother's house;
but now that he had broken the ice he acted quite in the spirit
of the reply he had made to a friend in Paris, shortly before
his departure, who asked him why he was going back to
America—"I am going to see how it looks." He was of course
very conscious of his eye; and his effort to cultivate it was
both intuitive and deliberate. He spoke of it freely, as he might
have done of a valuable watch or a horse. He was always trying
to get the visual impression; asking himself, with regard to
such and such an object or a place, of what its "character"
would consist. There is no doubt he really saw with great
intensity; and the reader will probably feel that he was welcome to this ambiguous privilege. It was not important for
him that things should be beautiful; what he sought to discover was their identity—the signs by which he should know
them. He began this inquiry as soon as he stepped into Newbury Street from his mother's door, and he was destined to
continue it for the first few weeks of his stay in Boston. As
time went on, his attention relaxed; for one couldn't do more
than see, as he said to his mother and another person; and he
had seen. Then the novelty wore off—the novelty which is
often so absurdly great in the eyes of the American who returns to his native land after a few years spent in the foreign
element—an effect to be accounted for only on the supposition that in the secret parts of his mind he recognises the
aspect of life in Europe as, through long heredity, the more
familiar; so that superficially, having no interest to oppose it,
it quickly supplants the domestic type, which, upon his return,
becomes supreme, but with its credit in many cases appreciably and permanently diminished. Florimond painted a few
things while he was in America, though he had told his
mother he had come home to rest; but when, several months
later, in Paris, he showed his "notes," as he called them, to a

friend, the young Frenchman asked him if Massachusetts were really so much like Andalusia.

There was certainly nothing Andalusian in the prospect as Florimond traversed the artificial bosom of the Back Bay. He had made his way promptly into Beacon Street, and he greatly admired that vista. The long straight avenue lay airing its new-ness in the frosty day, and all its individual façades, with their neat, sharp ornaments, seemed to have been scoured, with a kind of friction, by the hard, salutary light. Their brilliant browns and drabs, their rosy surfaces of brick, made a variety of fresh, violent tones, such as Florimond liked to memorise, and the large clear windows of their curved fronts faced each other, across the street, like candid, inevitable eyes. There was something almost terrible in the windows; Florimond had for-gotten how vast and clean they were, and how, in their sculp-tured frames, the New England air seemed, like a zealous housewife, to polish and preserve them. A great many ladies were looking out, and groups of children, in the drawing-rooms, were flattening their noses against the transparent plate. Here and there, behind it, the back of a statuette or the symmetry of a painted vase, erect on a pedestal, presented itself to the street, and enabled the passer to construct, more or less, the room within—its frescoed ceilings, its new silk sofas, its untarnished fixtures. This continuity of glass consti-tuted a kind of exposure, within and without, and gave the street the appearance of an enormous corridor, in which the public and the private were familiar and intermingled. But it was all very cheerful and commodious, and seemed to speak of diffused wealth, of intimate family life, of comfort con-stantly renewed. All sorts of things in the region of the tem-perature had happened during the few days that Florimond had been in the country. The cold wave had spent itself, a snowstorm had come and gone, and the air, after this tem-porary relaxation, had renewed its keenness. The snow, which had fallen in but moderate abundance, was heaped along the side of the pavement; it formed a radiant cornice on the housetops and crowned the windows with a plain white cap. It deepened the colour of everything else, made all surfaces look ruddy, and at a distance sent into the air a thin, delicate mist—a vaporous blur—which occasionally softened an edge.

The upper part of Beacon Street seemed to Florimond charming—the long, wide, sunny slope, the uneven line of the older houses, the contrasted, differing, bulging fronts, the painted bricks, the tidy facings, the immaculate doors, the burnished silver plates, the denuded twigs of the far extent of the Common, on the other side; and to crown the eminence and complete the picture, high in the air, poised in the right place, over everything that clustered below, the most felicitous object in Boston—the gilded dome of the State House. It was in the shadow of this monument, as we know, that Miss Daintry lived; and Florimond, who was always lucky, had the good fortune to find her at home.

V.

It may seem that I have assumed on the part of the reader too great a curiosity about the impressions of this young man, who was not very remarkable, and who has not even the recommendation of being the hero of our perhaps too descriptive tale. The reader will already have discovered that a hero fails us here; but if I go on at all risks to say a few words about Florimond, he will perhaps understand the better why this part has not been filled. Miss Daintry's nephew was not very original; it was his own illusion that he had in a considerable degree the value of rareness. Even this youthful conceit was not rare, for it was not of heroic proportions, and was liable to lapses and discouragements. He was a fair, slim, civil young man, and you would never have guessed from his appearance that he was an impressionist. He was neat and sleek and quite anti-Bohemian, and in spite of his looking about him as he walked, his figure was much more in harmony with the Boston landscape than he supposed. He was a little vain, a little affected, a little pretentious, a little good-looking, a little amusing, a little spoiled, and at times a little tiresome. If he was disagreeable, however, it was also only a little; he did not carry anything to a very high pitch; he was accomplished, industrious, successful—all in the minor degree. He was fond of his mother and fond of himself; he also liked the people who liked him. Such people could belong only to the class of good listeners, for Florimond, with the least encouragement (he was very susceptible to that), would chatter by the hour. As he was very observant, and knew a great many stories, his talk was often entertaining, especially to women, many of whom thought him wonderfully sympathetic. It may be added that he was still very young and fluid, and neither his defects nor his virtues had a great consistency. He was fond of the society of women, and had an idea that he knew a great deal about that element of humanity. He believed himself to know everything about art, and almost everything about life, and he expressed himself as much as possible in the phrases that are current in studios. He spoke French very well, and it had rubbed off on his English.

His aunt listened to him attentively, with her nippers on her nose. She had been a little restless at first, and, to relieve herself, had vaguely punched the sofa-cushion which lay beside her—a gesture that her friends always recognised; they knew it to express a particular emotion. Florimond, whose egotism was candid and confiding, talked for an hour about himself—about what he had done, and what he intended to do, what he had said and what had been said to him; about his habits, tastes, achievements, peculiarities, which were apparently so numerous; about the decorations of his studio in Paris; about the character of the French, the works of Zola, the theory of art for art, the American type, the "stupidity" of his mother's new house—though of course it had some things that were knowing—the pronunciation of Joanna's children, the effect of the commission-business on Arthur Merriman's conversation, the effect of everything on his mother, Mrs. Daintry, and the effect of Mrs. Daintry on her son Florimond. The young man had an epithet which he constantly introduced to express disapproval; when he spoke of the architecture of his mother's house, over which she had taken great pains (she remembered the gabled fronts of Nuremberg), he said that a certain effect had been dreadfully missed, that the character of the doorway was simply "crass." He expressed, however, a lively sense of the bright cleanness of American interiors. "Oh, as for that," he said, "the place is kept—it's kept;" and, to give an image of this idea, he put his gathered fingers to his lips an instant, seemed to kiss them or blow upon them, and then opened them into the air. Miss

Daintry had never encountered this gesture before; she had heard it described by travelled persons; but to see her own nephew in the very act of it led her to administer another thump to the sofa-cushion. She finally got this article under control, and sat more quiet, with her hands clasped upon it, while her visitor continued to discourse. In pursuance of his character as an impressionist, he gave her a great many impressions; but it seemed to her that as he talked, he simply exposed himself—exposed his egotism, his little pretensions. Lucretia Daintry, as we know, had a love of justice, and though her opinions were apt to be very positive, her charity was great and her judgments were not harsh; moreover, there was in her composition not a drop of acrimony. Nevertheless, she was, as the phrase is, rather hard on poor little Florimond; and to explain her severity we are bound to assume that in the past he had in some way offended her. To-day, at any rate, it seemed to her that he patronised his maiden-aunt. He scarcely asked about her health, but took for granted on her part an unlimited interest in his own sensations. It came over her afresh that his mother had been absurd in thinking that the usual resources of Boston would not have sufficed to maintain him; and she smiled a little grimly at the idea that a special provision should have been made. This idea presently melted into another, over which she was free to regale herself only after her nephew had departed. For the moment she contented herself with saying to him, when a pause in his young eloquence gave her a chance—"You will have a great many people to go and see. You pay the penalty of being a Bostonian; you have several hundred cousins. One pays for everything."

Florimond lifted his eyebrows. "I pay for that every day of my life. Have I got to go and see them all?"

"All—every one," said his aunt, who in reality did not hold this obligation in the least sacred.

"And to say something agreeable to them all?" the young man went on.

"Oh no, that is not necessary," Miss Daintry rejoined, with more exactness. "There are one or two, however, who always appreciate a pretty speech." She added in an instant, "Do you remember Mrs. Mesh?"

"Mrs. Mesh?" Florimond apparently did not remember.

"The wife of Donald Mesh; your grandfathers were first cousins. I don't mean her grandfather, but her husband's. If you don't remember her, I suppose he married her after you went away."

"I remember Donald; but I never knew he was a relation. He was single then, I think."

"Well, he's double now," said Miss Daintry; "he's triple, I may say, for there are two ladies in the house."

"If you mean he's a polygamist—are there Mormons even here?" Florimond, leaning back in his chair, with his elbow on the arm, and twisting with his gloved fingers the point of a small fair moustache, did not appear to have been arrested by this account of Mr. Mesh's household; for he almost immediately asked, in a large, detached way—"Are there any nice women here?"

"It depends on what you mean by nice women; there are some very sharp ones."

"Oh, I don't like sharp ones," Florimond remarked, in a tone which made his aunt long to throw her sofa-cushion at his head. "Are there any pretty ones?"

She looked at him a moment, hesitating. "Rachel Torrance is pretty, in a strange, unusual way—black hair and blue eyes, a serpentine figure, old coins in her tresses; that sort of thing."

"I have seen a good deal of that sort of thing," said Florimond, abstractedly.

"That I know nothing about. I mention Pauline Mesh's as one of the houses that you ought to go to, and where I know you are expected."

"I remember now that my mother has said something about that. But who is the woman with coins in her hair?— what has she to do with Pauline Mesh?"

"Rachel is staying with her; she came from New York a week ago, and I believe she means to spend the winter. She isn't a woman, she's a girl."

"My mother didn't speak of her," said Florimond; "but I don't think she would recommend me a girl with a serpentine figure."

"Very likely not," Miss Daintry answered, dryly. "Rachel Torrance is a far-away cousin of Donald Mesh, and consequently of mine and of yours. She's an artist, like yourself; she paints flowers on little panels and *plaques*."

"Like myself?—I never painted a *plaque* in my life!" exclaimed Florimond, staring.

"Well, she's a model also; you can paint her if you like; she has often been painted, I believe."

Florimond had begun to caress the other tip of his moustache. "I don't care for women who have been painted before. I like to find them out. Besides, I want to rest this winter."

His aunt was disappointed; she wished to put him into relation with Rachel Torrance, and his indifference was an obstacle. The meeting was sure to take place sooner or later, but she would have him glad to precipitate it, and, above all, to quicken her nephew's susceptibilities. "Take care you are not found out yourself!" she exclaimed, tossing away her sofa-cushion and getting up.

Florimond did not see what she meant, and he accordingly bore her no rancour; but when, before he took his leave, he said to her, rather irrelevantly, that if he should find himself in the mood during his stay in Boston, he should like to do her portrait—she had such a delightful face—she almost thought the speech a deliberate impertinence. "Do you mean that you have discovered me—that no one has suspected it before?" she inquired with a laugh, and a little flush in the countenance that he was so good as to appreciate.

Florimond replied, with perfect coolness and good-nature, that he didn't know about this, but that he was sure no one had seen her in just the way he saw her; and he waved his hand in the air with strange circular motions, as if to evoke before him the image of a canvas, with a figure just rubbed in. He repeated this gesture, or something very like it, by way of farewell, when he quitted his aunt, and she thought him insufferably patronising.

This is why she wished him, without loss of time, to make the acquaintance of Rachel Torrance, whose treatment of his pretensions she thought would be salutary. It may now be communicated to the reader—after a delay proportionate to the momentousness of the fact—that this had been the idea which suddenly flowered in her brain, as she sat face to face with her irritating young visitor. It had vaguely shaped itself

after her meeting with that strange girl from Brooklyn, whom
Mrs. Mesh, all gratitude—for she liked strangeness—promptly
brought to see her; and her present impression of her nephew
rapidly completed it. She had not expected to take an interest
in Rachel Torrance, and could not see why, through a freak
of Susan's, she should have been called upon to think so much
about her; but, to her surprise, she perceived that Mrs. Daintry's proposed victim was not the usual forward girl. She perceived at the same time that it had been ridiculous to think
of Rachel as a victim—to suppose that she was in danger of
vainly fixing her affections upon Florimond. She was much
more likely to triumph than to suffer; and if her visit to Boston
were to produce bitter fruits, it would not be she who should
taste them. She had a striking, oriental head, a beautiful smile,
a manner of dressing which carried out her exotic type, and a
great deal of experience and wit. She evidently knew the
world, as one knows it when one has to live by its help. If she
had an aim in life, she would draw her bow well above the
tender breast of Florimond Daintry. With all this, she certainly
was an honest, obliging girl, and had a sense of humour which
was a fortunate obstacle to her falling into a pose. Her coins
and amulets and seamless garments were, for her, a part of
the general joke of one's looking like a Circassian or a Smyr-
niote—an accident for which nature was responsible; and it
may be said of her that she took herself much less seriously
than other people took her. This was a defect for which
Lucretia Daintry had a great kindness; especially as she quickly
saw that Rachel was not of an insipid paste, as even triumphant coquettes sometimes are. In spite of her poverty and
the opportunities her beauty must have brought her, she had
not yet seen fit to marry—which was a proof that she was
clever as well as disinterested. It looks dreadfully cold-blooded
as I write it here, but the notion that this capable creature
might administer poetic justice to Florimond gave a measur-
able satisfaction to Miss Daintry. He was in distinct need of a
snub, for down in Newbury Street his mother was perpetually
swinging the censer; and no young nature could stand that
sort of thing—least of all such a nature as Florimond's. She
said to herself that such a "putting in his place" as he might
receive from Rachel Torrance would probably be a permanent

correction. She wished his good, as she wished the good of every one; and that desire was at the bottom of her vision. She knew perfectly what she should like: she should like him to fall in love with Rachel, as he probably would, and to have no doubt of her feeling immensely honoured. She should like Rachel to encourage him just enough—just so far as she might, without being false. A little would do, for Florimond would always take his success for granted. To this point did the study of her nephew's moral regeneration bring the excellent woman who a few days before had accused his mother of a lack of morality. His mother was thinking only of his pleasure; *she* was thinking of his immortal spirit. She should like Rachel to tell him at the end that he was a presumptuous little boy, and that since it was his business to render "impressions," he might see what he could do with that of having been jilted. This extraordinary flight of fancy on Miss Daintry's part was caused in some degree by the high spirits which sprang from her conviction, after she met the young lady, that Mrs. Mesh's companion was not in danger; for even when she wrote to her sister-in-law in the manner the reader knows, her conscience was not wholly at rest. There was still a risk, and she knew not why she should take risks for Florimond. Now, however, she was prepared to be perfectly happy when she should hear that the young man was constantly in Arlington Street; and at the end of a little month she enjoyed this felicity.

VI.

Mrs. Mesh sat on one side of the fire, and Florimond on the other; he had by this time acquired the privilege of a customary seat. He had taken a general view of Boston. It was like a first introduction, for before his going to live in Paris he had been too young to judge; and the result of this survey was the conviction that there was nothing better than Mrs. Mesh's drawing-room. She was one of the few persons whom one was certain to find at home after five o'clock; and the place itself was agreeable to Florimond, who was very fastidious about furniture and decorations. He was willing to concede that Mrs. Mesh (the relationship had not yet seemed close enough to justify him in calling her Pauline) knew a great deal

about such matters; though it was clear that she was indebted
for some of her illumination to Rachel Torrance, who had
induced her to make several changes. These two ladies, between them, represented a great fund of taste; with a difference that was a result of Rachel's knowing clearly beforehand
what she liked (Florimond called her, at least, by her baptismal
name), and Mrs. Mesh's only knowing it after a succession of
experiments, of transposings and drapings, all more or less
ingenious and expensive. If Florimond liked Mrs. Mesh's
drawing-room better than any other corner of Boston, he also
had his preference in regard to its phases and hours. It was
most charming in the winter twilight, by the glow of the fire,
before the lamps had been brought in. The ruddy flicker
played over many objects, making them look more mysterious
than Florimond had supposed anything could look in Boston,
and, among others, upon Rachel Torrance, who, when she
moved about the room in a desultory way (never so much
enfoncée, as Florimond said, in a chair as Mrs. Mesh was)
certainly attracted and detained the eye. The young man from
his corner (he was almost as much *enfoncé* as Mrs. Mesh) used
to watch her; and he could easily see what his aunt had meant
by saying she had a serpentine figure. She was slim and flexible, she took attitudes which would have been awkward in
other women, but which her charming pliancy made natural.
She reminded him of a celebrated actress in Paris who was the
ideal of tortuous thinness. Miss Torrance used often to seat
herself for a short time at the piano; and though she never
had been taught this art (she played only by ear), her musical
feeling was such that she charmed the twilight hour. Mrs.
Mesh sat on one side of the fire, as I have said, and Florimond
on the other; the two might have been found in this relation—
listening, face to face—almost any day in the week. Mrs. Mesh
raved about her new friend, as they said in Boston—I mean
about Rachel Torrance, not about Florimond Daintry. She
had at last got hold of a mind that understood her own (Mrs.
Mesh's mind contained depths of mystery), and she sacrificed
herself, generally, to throw her companion into relief. Her
sacrifice was rewarded, for the girl was universally liked and
admired; she was a new type altogether; she was the lioness
of the winter. Florimond had an opportunity to see his native

town in one of its fits of enthusiasm. He had heard of the
infatuations of Boston, literary and social; of its capacity for
giving itself with intensity to a temporary topic; and he was
now conscious, on all sides, of the breath of New England
discussion. Some one had said to him—or had said to some
one, who repeated it—that there was no place like Boston for
taking up with such seriousness a second-rate spinster from
Brooklyn. But Florimond himself made no criticism; for, as
we know, he speedily fell under the charm of Rachel Torrance's personality. He was perpetually talking with Mrs. Mesh
about it; and when Mrs. Mesh herself descanted on the subject, he listened with the utmost attention. At first, on his
return, he rather feared the want of topics; he foresaw that he
should miss the talk of the studios, of the theatres, of the
boulevard, of a little circle of "naturalists" (in literature and
art) to which he belonged, without sharing all its views. But
he presently perceived that Boston, too, had its actualities, and
that it even had this in common with Paris—that it gave its
attention most willingly to a female celebrity. If he had had
any hope of being himself the lion of the winter, it had been
dissipated by the spectacle of his cousin's success. He saw that
while she was there he could only be a subject of secondary
reference. He bore her no grudge for this. I must hasten to
declare that from the pettiness of this particular jealousy poor
Florimond was quite exempt. Moreover, he was swept along
by the general chorus; and he perceived that when one
changes one's sky, one inevitably changes, more or less, one's
standard. Rachel Torrance was neither an actress, nor a singer,
nor a beauty, nor one of the ladies who were chronicled in
the *Figaro*, nor the author of a successful book, nor a person
of the great world; she had neither a future, nor a past, nor a
position, nor even a husband, to make her identity more solid;
she was a simple American girl, of the class that lived in *pensions* (a class of which Florimond had ever entertained a
theoretic horror); and yet she had profited to the degree of
which our young man was witness, by those treasures of sympathy constantly in reserve in the American public (as has already been intimated) for the youthful-feminine. If Florimond
was struck with all this, it may be imagined whether or not
his mother thought she had been clever when it occurred to

her (before any one else) that Rachel would be a resource for the term of hibernation. She had forgotten all her scruples and hesitations; she only knew she had seen very far. She was proud of her prescience, she was even amused with it; and for the moment she held her head rather high. No one knew of it but Lucretia—for she had never confided it to Joanna, of whom she would have been more afraid in such a connection even than of her sister-in-law; but Mr. and Mrs. Merriman perceived an unusual lightness in her step, a fitful sparkle in her eye. It was of course easy for them to make up their mind that she was exhilarated to this degree by the presence of her son; especially as he seemed to be getting on beautifully in Boston.

"She stays out longer every day; she is scarcely ever home to tea," Mrs. Mesh remarked, looking up at the clock on the chimney-piece.

Florimond could not fail to know to whom she alluded, for it has been intimated that between these two there was much conversation about Rachel Torrance. "It's funny, the way the girls run about alone here," he said, in the amused, contemplative tone in which he frequently expressed himself on the subject of American life. "Rachel stays out after dark, and no one thinks any the worse of her."

"Oh, well, she's old enough," Mrs. Mesh rejoined, with a little sigh, which seemed to suggest that Rachel's age was really affecting. Her eyes had been opened by Florimond to many of the peculiarities of the society that surrounded her; and though she had spent only as many months in Europe as her visitor had spent years, she now sometimes spoke as if she thought the manners of Boston more odd even than he could pretend to do. She was very quick at picking up an idea, and there was nothing she desired more than to have the last on every subject. This winter, from her two new friends, Florimond and Rachel, she had extracted a great many that were new to her; the only trouble was that, coming from different sources, they sometimes contradicted each other. Many of them, however, were very vivifying; they added a new zest to that prospect of life which had always, in winter, the denuded bushes, the solid pond, the plank-covered walks, the exaggerated bridge, the patriotic statues, the dry, hard texture, of the Public Garden for its foreground, and for its middle distance the pale, frozen twigs, stiff in the windy sky that whistled over the Common, the domestic dome of the State House, familiar in the untinted air, and the competitive spires of a liberal faith. Mrs. Mesh had an active imagination, and plenty of time on her hands. Her two children were young, and they slept a good deal; she had explained to Florimond, who observed that she was a great deal less in the nursery than his sister, that she pretended only to give her attention to their waking hours. "I have people for the rest of the time," she said; and the rest of the time was considerable; so that there were very few obstacles to her cultivation of ideas. There was one in her mind now, and I may as well impart it to the reader without delay. She was not quite so delighted with Rachel Torrance as she had been a month ago; it seemed to her that the young lady took up—socially speaking—too much room in the house; and she wondered how long she intended to remain, and whether it would be possible, without a direct request, to induce her to take her way back to Brooklyn. This last was the conception with which she was at present engaged; she was at moments much pressed by it, and she had thoughts of taking Florimond Daintry into her confidence. This, however, she determined not to do, lest he should regard it as a sign that she was jealous of her companion. I know not whether she was, but this I know—that Mrs. Mesh was a woman of a high ideal and would not for the world have appeared so. If she was jealous, this would imply that she thought Florimond was in love with Rachel; and she could only object to that on the ground of being in love with him herself. She was not in love with him, and had no intention of being; of this the reader, possibly alarmed, may definitely rest assured. Moreover, she did not think him in love with Rachel; as to her reason for this reserve, I need not, perhaps, be absolutely outspoken. She was not jealous, she would have said; she was only oppressed—she was a little over-ridden. Rachel pervaded her house, pervaded her life, pervaded Boston; every one thought it necessary to talk to her about Rachel, to rave about her in the Boston manner, which seemed to Mrs. Mesh, in spite of the Puritan tradition, very much more unbridled than that of Baltimore. They thought it would give her pleasure; but by this time she knew everything about Rachel. The girl had proved rather more of a figure than she expected; and though she could not be called pretentious, she had the air, in staying with Pauline Mesh, of conferring rather more of a favour than she received. This was absurd for a person who was, after all, though not in her first youth, only a girl, and who, as Mrs. Mesh was sure from her biography—for Rachel had related every item—had never before had such unrestricted access to the fleshpots. The fleshpots were full, under Donald Mesh's roof, and his wife could easily believe that the poor girl would not be in a hurry to return to her boarding-house in Brooklyn. For that matter there were lots of people in Boston who would be delighted that she should come to them. It was doubtless an inconsistency on Mrs. Mesh's part that if she was overdone with the praises of Rachel Torrance which fell from every lip, she should not herself have forborne to broach the topic. But I have sufficiently intimated that it had a perverse fascination for her; it is true she did not speak of Rachel only to praise her. Florimond, in truth, was a little weary of the young lady's name; he had plenty of topics of his own, and he had his own opinion about Rachel Torrance. He did not take up Mrs. Mesh's remark as to her being old enough.

"You must wait till she comes in. Please ring for tea," said Mrs. Mesh, after a pause. She had noticed that Florimond was comparing his watch with her clock; it occurred to her that he might be going.

"Oh, I always wait, you know; I like to see her when she has been anywhere. She tells one all about it, and describes everything so well."

Mrs. Mesh looked at him a moment. "She sees a great deal more in things than I am usually able to discover. She sees the most extraordinary things in Boston."

"Well, so do I," said Florimond, placidly.

"Well, I don't, I must say!" She asked him to ring again; and then, with a slight irritation, accused him of not ringing hard enough; but before he could repeat the operation she left her chair and went herself to the bell. After this she stood before the fire a moment, gazing into it; then suggested to Florimond that he should put on a log.

"Is it necessary—when your servant is coming in a moment?" the young man asked, unexpectedly, without moving. In an instant, however, he rose; and then he explained that this was only his little joke.

"Servants are too stupid," said Mrs. Mesh. "But I spoil you. What would your mother say?" She watched him while he placed the log. She was plump, and she was not tall; but she was a very pretty woman. She had round brown eyes, which looked as if she had been crying a little—she had nothing in life to cry about; and dark, wavy hair, which here and there, in short, crisp tendrils, escaped artfully from the form in which it was dressed. When she smiled, she showed very pretty teeth; and the combination of her touching eyes and her parted lips was at such moments almost bewitching. She was accustomed to express herself in humorous superlatives, in pictorial circumlocutions; and had acquired in Boston the rudiments of a social dialect which, to be heard in perfection, should be heard on the lips of a native. Mrs. Mesh had picked it up; but it must be confessed that she used it without originality. It was an accident that on this occasion she had not expressed her wish for her tea by saying that she should like a pint or two of that Chinese fluid.

"My mother believes I can't be spoiled," said Florimond, giving a little push with his toe to the stick that he had placed in the embers; after which he sank back into his chair, while Mrs. Mesh resumed possession of her own. "I am ever fresh—ever pure."

"You are ever conceited. I don't see what you find so extraordinary in Boston," Mrs. Mesh added, reverting to his remark of a moment before.

"Oh, everything! the ways of the people, their ideas, their peculiar *cachet*. The very expression of their faces amuses me."

"Most of them have no expression at all."

"Oh, you are used to it," Florimond said. "You have become one of themselves; you have ceased to notice."

"I am more of a stranger than you; I was born beneath other skies. Is it possible that you don't know yet that I am a native of Baltimore? 'Maryland, my Maryland!'"

"Have they got so much expression in Maryland? No, I thank you; no tea. Is it possible," Florimond went on, with the familiarity of pretended irritation, "is it possible that you haven't noticed yet that I never take it? *Boisson fade, écœurante*, as Balzac calls it."

"Ah, well, if you don't take it on account of Balzac!" said Mrs. Mesh. "I never saw a man who had such fantastic reasons. Where, by the way, is the volume of that depraved old author you promised to bring me?"

"When do you think he flourished? You call everything old, in this country, that isn't in the morning paper. I haven't brought you the volume, because I don't want to bring you presents," Florimond said; "I want you to love me for myself, as they say in Paris."

"Don't quote what they say in Paris! Don't profane this innocent bower with those fearful words!" Mrs. Mesh rejoined, with a jocose intention. "Dear lady, your son is not everything we could wish!" she added in the same mock-dramatic tone, as the curtain of the door was lifted, and Mrs. Daintry rather timidly advanced. Mrs. Daintry had come to satisfy a curiosity, after all quite legitimate; she could no longer resist the impulse to ascertain for herself, so far as she might, how Rachel Torrance and Florimond were getting on. She had had no definite expectation of finding Florimond at Mrs. Mesh's; but she supposed that at this hour of the afternoon —it was already dark, and the ice, in many parts of Beacon Street, had a polish which gleamed through the dusk—she should find Rachel. "Your son has lived too long in far-off lands; he has dwelt among outworn things," Mrs. Mesh went on, as she conducted her visitor to a chair. "Dear lady, you are not as Balzac was; do you start at the mention of his name? —therefore you will have some tea in a little painted cup."

Mrs. Daintry was not bewildered, though it may occur to the reader that she might have been; she was only a little disappointed. She had hoped she might have occasion to talk about Florimond; but the young man's presence was a denial of this privilege. "I am afraid Rachel is not at home," she remarked. "I am afraid she will think I have not been very attentive."

"She will be in in a moment; we are waiting for her," Florimond said. "It's impossible she should think any harm of you. I have told her too much good."

"Ah, Mrs. Daintry, don't build too much on what he has told her! He's a false and faithless man!" Pauline Mesh interposed; while the good lady from Newbury Street, smiling at this adjuration, but looking a little grave, turned from one of her companions to the other. Florimond had relapsed into his chair by the fireplace; he sat contemplating the embers, and fingering the tip of his moustache. Mrs. Daintry imbibed her tea, and told how often she had slipped coming down the hill. These expedients helped her to wear a quiet face; but in reality she was nervous, and she felt rather foolish. It came over her that she was rather dishonest; she had presented herself at Mrs. Mesh's in the capacity of a spy. The reader already knows she was subject to sudden revulsions of feeling. There is an adage about repenting at leisure; but Mrs. Daintry always repented in a hurry. There was something in the air—something impalpable, magnetic—that told her she had better not have come; and even while she conversed with Mrs. Mesh she wondered what this mystic element could be. Of course she had been greatly preoccupied, these last weeks; for it had seemed to her that her plan with regard to Rachel Torrance was succeeding only too well. Florimond had frankly accepted her in the spirit in which she had been offered, and it was very plain that she was helping him to pass his winter. He was constantly at the house—Mrs. Daintry could not tell exactly how often; but she knew very well that in Boston, if one saw anything of a person, one saw a good deal. At first he used to speak of it; for two or three weeks he had talked a good deal about Rachel Torrance. More lately, his allusions had become few; yet to the best of Mrs. Daintry's belief his step was often in Arlington Street. This aroused her suspicions, and at times it troubled her conscience; there were moments when she wondered whether, in arranging a genial winter for Florimond, she had also prepared a season of torment for herself. Was he in love with the girl, or had he already discovered that the girl was in love with him? The delicacy of either situation would account for his silence. Mrs. Daintry said to herself that it would be a grim joke if she should prove to have plotted only too well. It was her sister-in-law's warning in especial that haunted her imagination, and she scarcely knew, at times, whether more to hope that Florimond might have been smitten, or to

pray that Rachel might remain indifferent. It was impossible
for Mrs. Daintry to shake off the sense of responsibility; she
could not shut her eyes to the fact that she had been the prime
mover. It was all very well to say that the situation, as it stood,
was of Lucretia's making; the thing never would have come
into Lucretia's head if she had not laid it before her. Unfortunately, with the quiet life she led, she had very little chance
to observe; she went out so little, that she was reduced to
guessing what the manner of the two young persons might
be to each other when they met in society, and she should
have thought herself wanting in delicacy if she had sought to
be intimate with Rachel Torrance. Now that her plan was in
operation, she could make no attempt to foster it, to acknowledge it in the face of Heaven. Fortunately, Rachel had so many
attentions, that there was no fear of her missing those of Newbury Street. She had dined there once, in the first days of her
sojourn, without Pauline and Donald, who had declined, and
with Joanna and Joanna's husband for all "company." Mrs.
Daintry had noticed nothing particular then, save that Arthur
Merriman talked rather more than usual—though he was always a free talker—and had bantered Rachel rather more familiarly than was perhaps necessary (considering that *he*, after
all, was not her cousin) on her ignorance of Boston, and her
thinking that Pauline Mesh could tell her anything about it.
On this occasion Florimond talked very little; of course he
could not say much when Arthur was in such extraordinary
spirits. She knew by this time all that Florimond thought of
his brother-in-law, and she herself had to confess that she liked
Arthur better in his jaded hours, even though then he was a
little cynical. Mrs. Daintry had been perhaps a little disappointed in Rachel, whom she saw for the first time in several
years. The girl was less peculiar than she remembered her being, savoured less of the old studio, the musical parties, the
creditors waiting at the door. However, people in Boston
found her unusual, and Mrs. Daintry reflected, with a twinge
at her depravity, that perhaps she had expected something too
dishevelled. At any rate, several weeks had elapsed since then,
and there had been plenty of time for Miss Torrance to attach
herself to Florimond. It was less than ever Mrs. Daintry's wish

that he should (even in this case) ask her to be his wife. It seemed to her less than ever the way her son should marry—because he had got entangled with a girl in consequence of his mother's rashness. It occurred to her, of course, that she might warn the young man; but when it came to the point she could not bring herself to speak. She had never discussed the question of love with him, and she didn't know what ideas he might have brought with him from Paris. It was too delicate; it might put notions into his head. He might say something strange and French, which she shouldn't like; and then perhaps she should feel bound to warn Rachel herself—a complication from which she absolutely shrank. It was part of her embarrassment now, as she sat in Mrs. Mesh's drawing-room, that she should probably spoil Florimond's entertainment for this afternoon, and that such a crossing of his inclination would make him the more dangerous. He had told her that he was waiting for Rachel to come in; and at the same time, in view of the lateness of the hour and her being on foot, when she herself should take her leave he would be bound in decency to accompany her. As for remaining after Rachel should come in, that was an indiscretion which scarcely seemed to her possible. Mrs. Daintry was an American mother, and she knew what the elder generation owes to the younger. If Florimond had come there to call on a young lady, he didn't, as they used to say, want any mothers round. She glanced covertly at her son, to try and find some comfort in his countenance; for her perplexity was heavy. But she was struck only with his looking very handsome, as he lounged there in the firelight, and with his being very much at home. This did not lighten her burden, and she expressed all the weight of it—in the midst of Mrs. Mesh's flights of comparison—in an irrelevant little sigh. At such a time her only comfort could be the thought that at all events she had not betrayed herself to Lucretia. She had scarcely exchanged a word with Lucretia about Rachel since that young lady's arrival; and she had observed in silence that Miss Daintry now had a guest in the person of a young woman who had lately opened a kindergarten. This reticence might surely pass for natural.

Rachel came in before long, but even then Mrs. Daintry

ventured to stay a little. The visitor from Brooklyn embraced
Mrs. Mesh, who told her that, prodigal as she was, there was
no fatted calf for her return; she must content herself with
cold tea. Nothing could be more charming than her manner,
which was full of native archness; and it seemed to Mrs. Daintry that she directed her pleasantries at Florimond with a grace
that was intended to be irresistible. The relation between
them was a relation of "chaff," and consisted, on one side
and the other, in alternations of attack and defence. Mrs.
Daintry reflected that she should not wish her son to have a
wife who should be perpetually turning him into a joke; for
it seemed to her, perhaps, that Rachel Torrance put in her
thrusts rather faster than Florimond could parry them. She
was evidently rather wanting in the faculty of reverence, and
Florimond panted a little. They presently went into an adjoining room, where the lamplight was brighter; Rachel
wished to show the young man an old painted fan, which she
had brought back from the repairer's. They remained there
ten minutes. Mrs. Daintry, as she sat with Mrs. Mesh, heard
their voices much intermingled. She wished very much to confide herself a little to Pauline—to ask her whether she thought
Rachel was in love with Florimond. But she had a foreboding
that this would not be safe; Pauline was capable of repeating
her question to the others, of calling out to Rachel to come
back and answer it. She contented herself, therefore, with asking her hostess about the little Meshes, and regaling her with
anecdotes of Joanna's progeny.

"Don't you ever have your little ones with you at this
hour?" she inquired. "You know this is what Longfellow calls
the children's hour."

Mrs. Mesh hesitated a moment. "Well, you know, one can't
have everything at once. I have my social duties now; I have
my guests. I have Miss Torrance—you see she is not a person
one can overlook."

"I suppose not," said poor Mrs. Daintry, remembering how
little she herself had overlooked her.

"Have you done brandishing that superannuated relic?"
Mrs. Mesh asked of Rachel and Florimond, as they returned
to the fireside. "I should as soon think of fanning myself with
the fire-shovel!"

"He has broken my heart," Rachel said. "He tells me it is not a Watteau."

"Do you believe everything he tells you, my dear? His word is the word of the betrayer."

"Well, I know Watteau didn't paint fans," Florimond remarked, "any more than Michael Angelo."

"I suppose you think he painted ceilings," said Rachel Torrance. "I have painted a great many myself."

"A great many ceilings? I should like to see that!" Florimond exclaimed.

Rachel Torrance, with her usual promptness, adopted this fantasy. "Yes, I have decorated half the churches in Brooklyn; you know how many there are."

"If you mean fans, I wish men carried them," the young man went on; "I should like to have one *de votre façon*."

"You're cool enough as you are; I should be sorry to give you anything that would make you cooler!"

This retort, which may not strike the reader by its originality, was pregnant enough for Mrs. Daintry; it seemed to her to denote that the situation was critical; and she proposed to retire. Florimond walked home with her; but it was only as they reached their door that she ventured to say to him what had been on her tongue's end since they left Arlington Street.

"Florimond, I want to ask you something. I think it is important, and you mustn't be surprised. Are you in love with Rachel Torrance?"

Florimond stared, in the light of the street-lamp. The collar of his overcoat was turned up; he stamped a little as he stood still; the breath of the February evening pervaded the empty vistas of the "new land." "In love with Rachel Torrance? *Jamais de la vie!* What put that into your head?"

"Seeing you with her, that way, this evening. You know you are very attentive."

"How do you mean, attentive?"

"You go there very often. Isn't it almost every day?"

Florimond hesitated, and, in spite of the frigid dusk, his mother could see that there was irritation in his eye. "Where else can I go, in this precious place? It's the pleasantest house here."

"Yes, I suppose it's very pleasant," Mrs. Daintry murmured. "But I would rather have you return to Paris than go there too often," she added, with sudden energy.

"How do you mean, too often? *Qu'est-ce qui vous prend, ma mère?*" said Florimond.

"Is Rachel—Rachel in love with *you?*" she inquired solemnly. She felt that this question, though her heart beat as she uttered it, should not be mitigated by a circumlocution.

"Good heavens! mother, fancy talking about love in this temperature!" Florimond exclaimed. "Let one at least get into the house."

Mrs. Daintry followed him reluctantly; for she always had a feeling that if anything disagreeable were to be done one should not make it less drastic by selecting agreeable conditions. In the drawing-room, before the fire, she returned to her inquiry. "My son, you have not answered me about Rachel."

"Is she in love with me? Why, very possibly!"

"Are you serious, Florimond?"

"Why shouldn't I be? I have seen the way women go off."

Mrs. Daintry was silent a moment. "Florimond, is it true?" she said presently.

"Is what true? I don't see where you want to come out."

"Is it true that that girl has fixed her affections——" and Mrs. Daintry's voice dropped.

"Upon me, *ma mère?* I don't say it's true, but I say it's possible. You ask me, and I can only answer you. I am not swaggering, I am simply giving you decent satisfaction. You wouldn't have me think it impossible that a woman should fall in love with me? You know what women are, and how there is nothing, in that way, too queer for them to do."

Mrs. Daintry, in spite of the knowledge of her sex that she might be supposed to possess, was not prepared to rank herself on the side of this axiom. "I wished to warn you," she simply said; "do be very careful."

"Yes, I'll be careful; but I can't give up the house."

"There are other houses, Florimond."

"Yes, but there is a special charm there."

"I would rather you should return to Paris than do any harm."

"Oh, I shan't do any harm; don't worry, *ma mère*," said Florimond.

It was a relief to Mrs. Daintry to have spoken, and she endeavoured not to worry. It was doubtless this effort that, for the rest of the winter, gave her a somewhat rigid, anxious look. People who met her in Beacon Street missed something from her face. It was her usual confidence in the clearness of human duty; and some of her friends explained the change by saying that she was disappointed about Florimond—she was afraid he was not particularly liked.

VII.

By the first of March this young man had received a good many optical impressions, and had noted in water-colours several characteristic winter effects. He had perambulated Boston in every direction, he had even extended his researches to the suburbs; and if his eye had been curious, his eye was now almost satisfied. He perceived that even amid the simple civilisation of New England there was material for the naturalist; and in Washington Street of a winter's afternoon, it came home to him that it was a fortunate thing the impressionist was not exclusively preoccupied with the beautiful. He became familiar with the slushy streets, crowded with thronging pedestrians and obstructed horse-cars, bordered with strange, promiscuous shops, which seemed at once violent and indifferent, overhung with snowbanks from the housetops; the avalanche that detached itself at intervals, fell with an enormous thud amid the dense processions of women, made for a moment a clear space, splashed with whiter snow, on the pavement, and contributed to the gaiety of the Puritan capital. Supreme in the thoroughfare was the rigid groove of the railway, where oblong receptacles, of fabulous capacity, governed by familiar citizens, jolted and jingled eternally, close on each other's rear, absorbing and emitting innumerable specimens of a single type. The road on either side, buried in mounds of pulverised, mud-coloured ice, was ploughed across by labouring vehicles, and traversed periodically by the sisterhood of "shoppers," laden with satchels and parcels, and protected by a round-backed policeman. Florimond looked at the shops,

saw the women disgorged, surging, ebbing, dodged the ava-
lanches, squeezed in and out of the horse-cars, made himself,
on their little platforms, where flatness was enforced, as perpendicular as possible. The horses steamed in the sunny air,
the conductor punched the tickets and poked the passengers,
some of whom were under and some above, and all alike sta-
bled in trampled straw. They were precipitated, collectively, by
stoppages and starts; the tight, silent interior stuffed itself
more and more, and the whole machine heaved and reeled in
its interrupted course. Florimond had forgotten the look of
many things, the details of American publicity; in some cases,
indeed, he only pretended to himself that he had forgotten
them, because it helped to entertain him. The houses—a bristling, jagged line of talls and shorts, a parti-coloured surface,
expressively commercial—were spotted with staring signs,
with labels and pictures, with advertisements familiar, colloquial, vulgar; the air was traversed with the tangle of the telegraph, with festoons of bunting, with banners not of war,
with inexplicable loops and ropes; the shops, many of them
enormous, had heterogeneous fronts, with queer juxtaposi-
tions in the articles that peopled them, an incompleteness of
array, the stamp of the latest modern ugliness. They had pen-
dant stuffs in the doorways, and flapping tickets outside.
Every fifty yards there was a "candy store;" in the intervals
was the painted panel of a chiropodist, representing him in
his professional attitude. Behind the plates of glass, in the hot
interiors, behind the counters, were pale, familiar, delicate,
tired faces of women, with polished hair and glazed complexions. Florimond knew their voices; he knew how women
would speak when their hair was "treated," as they said in the
studios, like that. But the women that passed through the
streets were the main spectacle. Florimond had forgotten their
extraordinary numerosity, and the impression that they produced of a deluge of petticoats. He could see that they were
perfectly at home on the road; they had an air of possession,
of perpetual equipment, a look, in the eyes, of always meeting
the gaze of crowds, always seeing people pass, noting things
in shop-windows, and being on the watch at crossings; many
of them evidently passed most of their time in these conditions, and Florimond wondered what sort of *intérieurs* they

could have. He felt at moments that he was in a city of women, in a country of women. The same impression came to him *dans le monde*, as he used to say, for he made the most incongruous application of his little French phrases to Boston. The talk, the social life, were so completely in the hands of the ladies, the masculine note was so subordinate, that on certain occasions he could have believed himself (putting the brightness aside) in a country stricken by a war, where the men had all gone to the army, or in a seaport half depopulated by the absence of its vessels. This idea had intermissions; for instance, when he walked out to Cambridge. In this little excursion he often indulged; he used to go and see one of his college-mates, who was now a tutor at Harvard. He stretched away across the long, mean bridge that spans the mouth of the Charles—a mile of wooden piles, supporting a brick pavement, a roadway deep in mire, and a rough timber fence, over which the pedestrian enjoys a view of the frozen bay, the backs of many new houses, and a big brown marsh. The horse-cars bore him company, relieved here of the press of the streets, though not of their internal congestion, and constituting the principal feature of the wide, blank avenue, where the puddles lay large across the bounding rails. He followed their direction through a middle region, in which the small wooden houses had an air of tent-like impermanence, and the February mornings, splendid and indiscreet, stared into bare windows and seemed to make civilisation transparent. Further, the suburb remained wooden, but grew neat, and the painted houses looked out on the car-track with an expression almost of superiority. At Harvard, the buildings were square and fresh; they stood in a yard planted with slender elms, which the winter had reduced to spindles; the town stretched away from the horizontal palings of the collegiate precinct, low, flat and immense, with vague, featureless spaces and the air of a clean encampment. Florimond remembered that when the summer came in, the whole place was transformed. It was pervaded by verdure and dust, the slender elms became profuse, arching over the unpaved streets, the green shutters bowed themselves before the windows, the flowers and creeping-plants bloomed in the small gardens, and on the piazzas, in the gaps of dropped awnings, light dresses arrested the eye. At night, in the warm darkness—for Cambridge is not festooned with lamps—the bosom of nature would seem to palpitate, there would be a smell of earth and vegetation—a smell more primitive than the odour of Europe—and the air would vibrate with the sound of insects. All this was in reserve, if one would have patience, especially from March to June; but for the present the seat of the University struck our poor little critical Florimond as rather hard and bare. As the winter went on, and the days grew longer, he knew that Mrs. Daintry often believed him to be in Arlington Street when he was walking out to see his friend the tutor, who had once spent a winter in Paris and never tired of talking about it. It is to be feared that he did not undeceive her so punctually as he might; for, in the first place, he was at Mrs. Mesh's very often; in the second, he failed to understand how worried his mother was; and in the third, the idea that he should be thought to have the peace of mind of a brilliant girl in his keeping was not disagreeable to him.

One day his Aunt Lucretia found him in Arlington Street; it occurred to her about the middle of the winter that, considering she liked Rachel Torrance so much, she had not been to see her very often. She had little time for such indulgences; but she caught a moment in its flight, and was told at Mrs. Mesh's door that this lady had not yet come in, but that her companion was accessible. Florimond was in his customary chair by the chimney-corner (his aunt perhaps did not know quite how customary it was), and Rachel, at the piano, was regaling him with a composition of Schubert. Florimond, up to this time, had not become very intimate with his aunt, who had not, as it were, given him the key of her house, and in whom he detected a certain want of interest in his affairs. He had a limited sympathy with people who were interested only in their own, and perceived that Miss Daintry belonged to this preoccupied and ungraceful class. It seemed to him that it would have been more becoming in her to feign at least a certain attention to the professional and social prospects of the most promising of her nephews. If there was one thing that Florimond disliked more than another, it was an eager self-absorption; and he could not see that it was any better for people to impose their personality upon committees and charities than upon general society. He would have modified this judgment of his kinswoman, with whom he had dined but once, if he could have guessed with what anxiety she watched for the symptoms of that salutary change which she expected to see wrought in him by the fascinating independence of Rachel Torrance. If she had dared, she would have prompted the girl a little; she would have confided to her this secret desire. But the matter was delicate; and Miss Daintry was shrewd enough to see that everything must be spontaneous. When she paused at the threshold of Mrs. Mesh's drawing-room, looking from one of her young companions to the other, she felt a slight pang, for she feared they were getting on too well. Rachel was pouring sweet music into the young man's ears, and turning to look at him over her shoulder while she played; and he, with his head tipped back and his eyes on the ceiling, hummed an accompaniment which occasionally became an articulate remark. Harmonious intimacy was stamped upon the scene, and poor Miss Daintry was not struck with its being in any degree salutary. She was not re-assured when, after ten minutes, Florimond took his depar-ture; she could see that he was irritated by the presence of a third person; and this was a proof that Rachel had not yet begun to do her duty by him. It is possible that when the two ladies were left together, her disappointment would have led her to betray her views, had not Rachel almost immediately said to her: "My dear cousin, I am so glad you have come; I might not have seen you again. I go away in three days."

"Go away? Where do you go to?"

"Back to Brooklyn," said Rachel, smiling sweetly.

"Why on earth—I thought you had come here to stay for six months?"

"Oh, you know, six months would be a terrible visit for these good people; and of course no time was fixed. That would have been very absurd. I have been here an immense time already. It was to be as things should go."

"And haven't they gone well?"

"Oh yes, they have gone beautifully."

"Then why in the world do you leave?"

"Well, you know, I have duties at home. My mother coughs a good deal, and they write me dismal letters."

"They are ridiculous, selfish people. You are going home because your mother coughs? I don't believe a word of it!" Miss Daintry cried. "You have some other reason. Something has happened here; it has become disagreeable. Be so good as to tell me the whole story."

Rachel answered that there was not any story to tell, and that her reason consisted entirely of conscientious scruples as to absenting herself so long from her domestic circle. Miss Daintry esteemed conscientious scruples when they were well placed, but she thought poorly on the present occasion of those of Mrs. Mesh's visitor; they interfered so much with her own sense of fitness. "Has Florimond been making love to you?" she suddenly inquired. "You mustn't mind that—beyond boxing his ears."

Her question appeared to amuse Miss Torrance exceedingly; and the girl, a little inarticulate with her mirth, answered very positively that the young man had done her no such honour.

"I am very sorry to hear it," said Lucretia; "I was in hopes he would give you a chance to take him down. He needs it very much. He's dreadfully puffed up."

"He's an amusing little man!"

Miss Daintry put on her nippers. "Don't tell me it's you that are in love!"

"Oh, dear no! I like big, serious men; not small Frenchified gentlemen, like Florimond. Excuse me if he's your nephew, but you began it. Though I am fond of art," the girl added, "I don't think I am fond of artists."

"Do you call Florimond an artist?"

Rachel Torrance hesitated a little, smiling. "Yes, when he poses for Pauline Mesh."

This rejoinder for a moment left Miss Daintry in visible perplexity; then a sudden light seemed to come to her. She flushed a little; what she found was more than she was looking for. She thought of many things quickly, and among others she thought that she had accomplished rather more than she intended. "Have you quarrelled with Pauline?" she said presently.

"No, but she is tired of me."

"Everything has not gone well, then, and you *have* another reason for going home than your mother's cough?"

"Yes, if you must know, Pauline wants me to go. I didn't feel free to tell you that; but since you guess it——" said Rachel, with her rancourless smile.

"Has she asked you to decamp?"

"Oh, dear no! for what do you take us? But she absents herself from the house; she stays away all day. I have to play to Florimond to console him."

"So you *have* been fighting about him?" Miss Daintry remarked, perversely.

"Ah, my dear cousin, what have you got in your head? Fighting about sixpence! if you knew how Florimond bores me! I play to him to keep him silent. I have heard everything he has to say, fifty times over!"

Miss Daintry sank back in her chair; she was completely out of her reckoning. "I think he might have made love to you a little!" she exclaimed, incoherently.

"So do I! but he didn't—not a crumb. He is afraid of me—thank heaven!"

"It isn't for you he comes, then?" Miss Daintry appeared to cling to her theory.

"No, my dear cousin, it isn't!"

"Just now, as he sat there, one could easily have supposed it. He didn't at all like my interruption."

"That was because he was waiting for Pauline to come in. He will wait that way an hour. You may imagine whether he likes me for boring her so that, as I tell you, she can't stay in the house. I am out myself as much as possible. But there are days when I drop with fatigue; then I must rest. I can assure you that it's fortunate that I go so soon."

"Is Pauline in love with him?" Miss Daintry asked, gravely.

"Not a grain. She is the best little woman in the world."

"Except for being a goose. Why, then, does she object to your company—after being so enchanted with you?"

"Because even the best little woman in the world must object to something. She has everything in life, and nothing to complain of. Her children sleep all day, and her cook is a jewel. Her husband adores her, and she is perfectly satisfied with Mr. Mesh. I act on her nerves, and I think she believes I regard her as rather silly to care so much for Florimond. Excuse me again!"

"You contradict yourself. She *does* care for him, then?"

"Oh, as she would care for a new *coupé*! She likes to have a young man of her own—fresh from Paris—quite to herself. She has everything else—why shouldn't she have that? She thinks your nephew very original, and he thinks her what she is—the prettiest woman in Boston. They have an idea that they are making a 'celebrated friendship'—like Horace Walpole and Madame du Deffand. They sit there face to face— they are as innocent as the shovel and tongs. But, all the same, I am in the way, and Pauline is provoked that I am not jealous."

Miss Daintry got up with energy. "She's a vain, hollow, silly little creature, and you are quite right to go away; you are worthy of better company. Only you will not go back to Brooklyn, in spite of your mother's cough; you will come straight to Mount Vernon Place."

Rachel hesitated to agree to this. She appeared to think it was her duty to quit Boston altogether; and she gave as a reason that she had already refused other invitations. But Miss Daintry had a better reason than this—a reason that glowed in her indignant breast. It was she who had been the cause of the girl's being drawn into this sorry adventure; it was she who should charge herself with the reparation. The conversation I have related took place on a Tuesday; and it was settled that on the Friday Miss Torrance should take up her abode for the rest of the winter under her Cousin Lucretia's roof. This lady left the house without having seen Mrs. Mesh.

On Thursday she had a visit from her sister-in-law, the motive of which was not long in appearing. All winter Mrs. Daintry had managed to keep silent on the subject of her doubts and fears. Discretion and dignity recommended this course; and the topic was a painful one to discuss with Lucretia, for the bruises of their primary interview still occasionally throbbed. But at the first sign of alleviation the excellent woman overflowed, and she lost no time in announcing to Lucretia, as a heaven-sent piece of news, that Rachel had been called away by the illness of poor Mrs. Torrance and was to leave Boston from one day to the other. Florimond had given her this information the evening before, and it had made her so happy that she couldn't help coming to let Lucretia know that they were safe. Lucretia listened to her announcement in silence, fixing her eyes on her sister-in-law with an expression that the latter thought singular; but when Mrs. Daintry, expanding still further, went on to say that she had spent a winter of misery, that the harm the two together (she and Lucretia) might have done was never out of her mind, for Florimond's assiduity in Arlington Street had become notorious, and she had been told that the most cruel things were said—when Mrs. Daintry, expressing herself to this effect, added that from the present moment she breathed, the danger was over, the sky was clear, and her conscience might take a holiday—her hostess broke into the most prolonged, the most characteristic and most bewildering fit of laughter in which she had ever known her to indulge. They were safe, Mrs. Daintry had said? For Lucretia this was true, now, of herself, at least; she was secure from the dangers of her irritation; her sense of the whole affair had turned to hilarious music. The contrast that rose before her between her visitor's anxieties and the real position of the parties, her quick vision of poor Susan's dismay in case *that* reality should meet her eyes, among the fragments of her squandered scruples—these things smote the chords of mirth in Miss Daintry's spirit, and seemed to her in their high comicality to offer a sufficient reason for everything that had happened. The picture of her sister-in-law sitting all winter with her hands clasped and her eyes fixed on the wrong object was an image that would abide with her always; and it would render her an inestimable service—it would cure her of the tendency to worry. As may be imagined, it was eminently open to Mrs. Daintry to ask her what on earth she was laughing at; and there was a colour in the cheek of Florimond's mother that brought her back to propriety. She suddenly kissed this lady very tenderly—to the latter's great surprise, there having been no kissing since her visit in November—and told her that she would reveal to her some day, later, the cause of so much merriment. She added that Miss Torrance was leaving Arlington Street, yes; but only to go as far as Mount Vernon Place. She was engaged to spend

three months in that very house. Mrs. Daintry's countenance
at this fell several inches, and her joy appeared completely to
desert her. She gave her sister-in-law a glance of ineffable reproach, and in a moment she exclaimed: "Then nothing is
gained! it will all go on here!"

"Nothing will go on here. If you mean that Florimond will
pursue the young lady into this mountain fastness, you may
simply be quiet. He is not fond enough of me to wear out
my threshold."

"Are you very sure?" Mrs. Daintry murmured, dubiously.

"I know what I say. Hasn't he told you he hates me?"

Mrs. Daintry coloured again, and hesitated. "I don't know
how you think we talk," she said.

"Well, he does, and he will leave us alone."

Mrs. Daintry sprang up with an elasticity that was comical.
"That's all I ask!" she exclaimed.

"I believe you hate me too!" Lucretia said, laughing; but
at any risk she kissed her sister-in-law again before they separated.

Three weeks later Mrs. Daintry paid her another visit; and
this time she looked very serious. "It's very strange. I don't
know what to think. But perhaps you know it already?" This
was her *entrée en matière*, as the French say. "Rachel's leaving
Arlington Street has made no difference. He goes there as
much as ever. I see no change at all. Lucretia, I have not the
peace that I thought had come," said poor Mrs. Daintry,
whose voice had failed, below her breath.

"Do you mean that he goes to see Pauline Mesh?"

"I am afraid so, every day."

"Well, my dear, what's the harm?" Miss Daintry asked. "He
can't hurt *her* by not marrying her."

Mrs. Daintry stared; she was amazed at her sister-in-law's
tone. "But it makes one suppose that all winter, for so many
weeks, it has been for *her* that he has gone!" And the image
of the *tête-à-tête* in which she had found them immersed that
day, rose again before her; she could interpret it now.

"You wanted some one; why may not Pauline have served?"

Mrs. Daintry was silent, with the same expanded eyes.
"Lucretia, it is not right!"

"My dear Susan, you are touching," Lucretia said.

Mrs. Daintry went on, without heeding her. "It appears that people are talking about it; they have noticed it for ever so long. Joanna never hears anything, or she would have told me. The children are too much. I have been the last to know."

"I knew it a month ago," said Miss Daintry, smiling.

"And you never told me?"

"I knew that you wanted to detain him. Pauline will detain him a year."

Mrs. Daintry gathered herself together. "Not a day, not an hour, that I can help! He shall go, if I have to take him."

"My dear Susan," murmured her sister-in-law on the threshold. Miss Daintry scarcely knew what to say; she was almost frightened at the rigidity of her face.

"My dear Lucretia, it is not right!" This ejaculation she solemnly repeated, and she took her departure as if she were decided upon action.

She had found so little sympathy in her sister-in-law that she made no answer to a note Miss Daintry wrote her that evening, to remark that she was really unjust to Pauline, who was silly, vain, and flattered by the development of her ability to monopolise an impressionist, but a perfectly innocent little woman and incapable of a serious flirtation. Miss Daintry had been careful to add to these last words no comment that could possibly shock Florimond's mother. Mrs. Daintry announced, about the 10th of April, that she had made up her mind she needed a change, and had determined to go abroad for the summer; and she looked so tired that people could see there was reason in it. Her summer began early; she embarked on the 20th of the month, accompanied by Florimond. Miss Daintry, who had not been obliged to dismiss the young lady of the kindergarten to make room for Rachel Torrance, never knew what had passed between the mother and the son, and she was disappointed at Mrs. Mesh's coolness in the face of this catastrophe. She disapproved of her flirtation with Florimond, and yet she was vexed at Pauline's pert resignation; it proved her to be so superficial. She disposed of everything with her absurd little phrases, which were half slang and half quotation. Mrs. Daintry was a native of Salem, and this gave Pauline, as a Baltimorean and a descendant of the Cavaliers, an obvious opportunity. Rachel repeated her words to

Miss Daintry, for she had spoken to Rachel of Florimond's departure, the day after he embarked. "Oh yes, he's in the midst of the foam, the cruel, crawling foam! I 'kind of' miss him, afternoons; he was so useful round the fire. It's his mother that charmed him away; she's a most uncanny old party. I don't care for Salem witches, anyway; she has worked on him with philters and spells!" Lucretia was obliged to recognise a grain of truth in this last assertion; she felt that her sister-in-law must indeed have worked upon Florimond, and she smiled to think that the conscientious Susan should have descended, in the last resort, to an artifice, to a pretext. She had probably persuaded him she was out of patience with Joanna's children.

The Path of Duty

I AM GLAD I said to you the other night at Doubleton, inquiring—too inquiring—compatriot, that I wouldn't undertake to tell you the story (about Ambrose Tester), but would write it out for you; inasmuch as, thinking it over since I came back to town, I see that it may really be made interesting. It *is* a story, with a regular development, and for telling it I have the advantage that I happened to know about it from the first, and was more or less in the confidence of every one concerned. Then it will amuse me to write it, and I shall do so as carefully and as cleverly as possible. The first winter days in London are not madly gay, so that I have plenty of time, and if the fog is brown outside the fire is red within. I like the quiet of this season; the glowing chimney-corner, in the midst of the December mirk, makes me think, as I sit by it, of all sorts of things. The idea that is almost always uppermost is the bigness and strangeness of this London world. Long as I have lived here—the sixteenth anniversary of my marriage is only ten days off—there is still a kind of novelty and excitement in it. It is a great pull, as they say here, to have remained sensitive—to have kept one's own point of view. I mean it's more entertaining—it makes you see a thousand things (not that they are all very charming). But the pleasure of observation does not in the least depend on the beauty of what one observes. You see innumerable little dramas; in fact almost everything has acts and scenes, like a comedy. Very often it is a comedy with tears. There have been a good many of them, I am afraid, in the case I am speaking of. It is because this history of Sir Ambrose Tester and Lady Vandeleur struck me, when you asked me about the relations of the parties, as having that kind of progression, that when I was on the point of responding I checked myself, thinking it a pity to tell you a little when I might tell you all. I scarcely know what made you ask, inasmuch as I had said nothing to excite your curiosity. Whatever you suspected you suspected on your own hook, as they say. You had simply noticed the pair together that evening at Doubleton. If you suspected anything in particular, it is a proof that you are rather sharp, because they are very careful about the way they behave in public. At least they think they are; the result, perhaps, doesn't necessarily follow. If I have been in their confidence you may say that I make a strange use of my privilege in serving them up to feed the prejudices of an opinionated American. You think English society very wicked, and my little story will probably not correct the impression. Though, after all, I don't see why it should minister to it; for what I said to you (it was all I did say) remains the truth. They are treading together the path of duty. You would be quite right about its being base in me to betray them. It is very true that they have ceased to confide in me; even Joscelind has said nothing to me for more than a year. That is doubtless a sign that the situation is more serious than before, all round—too serious to be talked about. It is also true that you are remarkably discreet, and that even if you were not it would not make much difference, inasmuch as if you were to repeat my revelations in America no one would know whom you were talking about. But, all the same, I should be base; and, therefore, after I have written out my reminiscences for your delectation, I shall simply keep them for my own. You must content yourself with the explanation I have already given you of Sir Ambrose Tester and Lady Vandeleur: they are following—hand in hand, as it were—the path of duty. This will not prevent me from telling everything; on the contrary, don't you see?

I.

His brilliant prospects dated from the death of his brother, who had no children, had indeed steadily refused to marry. When I say brilliant prospects, I mean the vision of the baronetcy, one of the oldest in England, of a charming seventeenth-century house, with its park, in Dorsetshire, and a property worth some twenty thousand a year. Such a collection of items is still dazzling to me, even after what you would call, I suppose, a familiarity with British grandeur. My husband isn't a baronet (or we probably shouldn't be in London in December), and he is far, alas, from having twenty thousand a year. The full enjoyment of these luxuries, on Ambrose

Tester's part, was dependent naturally on the death of his father, who was still very much to the fore at the time I first knew the young man. The proof of it is the way he kept nagging at his sons, as the younger used to say, on the question of taking a wife. The nagging had been of no avail, as I have mentioned, with regard to Francis, the elder, whose affections were centred (his brother himself told me) on the wine-cup and the faro-table. He was not a person to admire or imitate, and as the heir to an honourable name and a fine estate was very unsatisfactory indeed. It had been possible in those days to put him into the army, but it was not possible to keep him there, and he was still a very young man when it became plain that any parental dream of a "career" for Frank Tester was exceedingly vain. Old Sir Edmund had thought matrimony would perhaps correct him, but a sterner process than this was needed, and it came to him one day at Monaco—he was most of the time abroad—after an illness so short that none of the family arrived in time. He was reformed altogether, he was utterly abolished. The second son, stepping into his shoes, was such an improvement that it was impossible there should be much simulation of mourning. You have seen him, you know what he is, there is very little mystery about him. As I am not going to show this composition to you, there is no harm in my writing here that he is—or, at any rate, he was—a remarkably attractive man. I don't say this because he made love to me, but precisely because he didn't. He was always in love with some one else—generally with Lady Vandeleur. You may say that in England that usually doesn't prevent; but Mr. Tester, though he had almost no intermissions, didn't, as a general thing, have duplicates. He was not provided with a second loved object, "understudying," as they say, the part. It was his practice to keep me accurately informed of the state of his affections—a matter about which he was never in the least vague. When he was in love he knew it and rejoiced in it, and when by a miracle he was not he greatly regretted it. He expatiated to me on the charms of other persons, and this interested me much more than if he had attempted to direct the conversation to my own, as regards which I had no illusions. He has told me some singular things, and I think I may say that for a considerable period my most valued knowledge of English society was extracted from this genial youth. I suppose he usually found me a woman of good counsel, for certain it is that he has appealed to me for the light of wisdom in very extraordinary predicaments. In his earlier years he was perpetually in hot water; he tumbled into scrapes as children tumble into puddles. He invited them, he invented them; and when he came to tell you how his trouble had come about (and he always told the whole truth) it was difficult to believe that a man should have been so idiotic.

And yet he was not an idiot; he was supposed to be very clever, and certainly is very quick and amusing. He was only reckless, and extraordinarily natural, as natural as if he had been an Irishman. In fact, of all the Englishmen that I have known he is the most Irish in temperament (though he has got over it comparatively of late). I used to tell him that it was a great inconvenience that he didn't speak with a brogue, because then we should be forewarned and know with whom we were dealing. He replied that, by analogy, if he were Irish enough to have a brogue he would probably be English; which seemed to me an answer wonderfully in character. Like most young Britons of his class he went to America, to see the great country, before he was twenty, and he took a letter to my father, who had occasion, à propos of some pickle, of course, to render him a considerable service. This led to his coming to see me—I had already been living here three or four years—on his return; and that, in the course of time, led to our becoming fast friends, without, as I tell you, the smallest philandering on either side. But I mustn't protest too much; I shall excite your suspicion. "If he has made love to so many women, why shouldn't he have made love to you?"—some inquiry of that sort you will be likely to make. I have answered it already, "Simply on account of those very engagements." He couldn't make love to every one, and with me it wouldn't have done him the least good. It was a more amiable weakness than his brother's, and he has always behaved very well. How well he behaved on a very important occasion is precisely the subject of my story.

He was supposed to have embraced the diplomatic career, had been secretary of legation at some German capital; but after his brother's death he came home and looked out for a seat in Parliament. He found it with no great trouble, and has kept it ever since. No one would have the heart to turn him out, he is so good-looking. It's a great thing to be represented by one of the handsomest men in England, it creates such a favourable association of ideas. Any one would be amazed to discover that the borough he sits for, and the name of which I am always forgetting, is not a very pretty place. I have never seen it, and have no idea that it isn't, and I am sure he will survive every revolution. The people must feel that if they shouldn't keep him some monster would be returned. You remember his appearance, how tall, and fair, and strong he is, and always laughing, yet without looking silly. He is exactly the young man girls in America figure to themselves—in the place of the hero—when they read English novels and wish to imagine something very aristocratic and Saxon. A "bright Bostonian" who met him once at my house, exclaimed as soon as he had gone out of the room, "At last, at last, I behold it, the moustache of Roland Tremayne!"

"Of Roland Tremayne?"

"Don't you remember in *A Lawless Love*, how often it's mentioned, and how glorious and golden it was? Well, I have never seen it till now, but now I *have* seen it!"

If you hadn't seen Ambrose Tester, the best description I could give of him would be to say that he looked like Roland Tremayne. I don't know whether that hero was a "strong Liberal," but this is what Sir Ambrose is supposed to be. (He succeeded his father two years ago, but I shall come to that.) He is not exactly what I should call thoughtful, but he is interested, or thinks he is, in a lot of things that I don't understand, and that one sees and skips in the newspapers—volunteering, and redistribution, and sanitation, and the representation of minors—minorities—what is it? When I said just now that he is always laughing, I ought to have explained that I didn't mean when he is talking to Lady Vandeleur. She makes him serious, makes him almost solemn; by which I don't mean that she bores him. Far from it; but when he is in her company he is thoughtful; he pulls his golden moustache, and Roland Tremayne looks as if his vision were turned in, and he were meditating on her words. He doesn't say much himself; it is she—she used to be so silent—who does the talking. She has plenty to say to him; she describes to him the charms that she discovers in the path of duty. He seldom speaks in the House, I believe, but when he does it's off-hand, and amusing, and sensible, and every one likes it. He will never be a great statesman, but he will add to the softness of Dorsetshire, and remain, in short, a very gallant, pleasant, prosperous, typical English gentleman, with a name, a fortune, a perfect appearance, a devoted, bewildered little wife, a great many reminiscences, a great many friends (including Lady Vandeleur and myself), and, strange to say, with all these advantages, something that faintly resembles a conscience.

II.

Five years ago he told me his father insisted on his marrying—would not hear of his putting it off any longer. Sir Edmund had been harping on this string ever since he came back from Germany, had made it both a general and a particular request, not only urging him to matrimony in the abstract, but pushing him into the arms of every young woman in the country. Ambrose had promised, procrastinated, temporised; but at last he was at the end of his evasions, and his poor father had taken the tone of supplication. "He thinks immensely of the name, of the place, and all that, and he has got it into his head that if I don't marry before he dies I won't marry after." So much I remember Ambrose Tester said to me. "It's a fixed idea; he has got it on the brain. He wants to see me married with his eyes, and he wants to take his grandson in his arms. Not without that will he be satisfied that the whole thing will go straight. He thinks he is nearing his end, but he isn't—he will live to see a hundred, don't you think so?—and he has made me a solemn appeal to put an end to what he calls his suspense. He has an idea some one will get hold of me—some woman I can't marry. As if I were not old enough to take care of myself!"

"Perhaps he is afraid of me," I suggested, facetiously.

"No, it isn't you," said my visitor, betraying by his tone that it was some one, though he didn't say whom. "That's all rot, of course; one marries sooner or later, and I shall do like every one else. If I marry before I die it's as good as if I marry before he dies, isn't it? I should be delighted to have the governor at my wedding, but it isn't necessary for the legality, is it?"

I asked him what he wished me to do, and how I could help him. He knew already my peculiar views, that I was trying to get husbands for all the girls of my acquaintance and to prevent the men from taking wives. The sight of an unmarried woman afflicted me, and yet when my male friends changed their state I took it as a personal offence. He let me know that, so far as he was concerned, I must prepare myself for this injury, for he had given his father his word that another twelvemonth should not see him a bachelor. The old man had given him *carte blanche*, he made no condition beyond exacting that the lady should have youth and health. Ambrose Tester, at any rate, had taken a vow, and now he was going seriously to look about him. I said to him that what must be must be, and that there were plenty of charming girls about the land, among whom he could suit himself easily enough. There was no better match in England, I said, and he would only have to make his choice. That, however, is not what I thought, for my real reflections were summed up in the silent exclamation, "What a pity Lady Vandeleur isn't a widow!" I hadn't the smallest doubt that if she were he would marry her on the spot; and after he had gone I wondered considerably what *she* thought of this turn in his affairs. If it was disappointing to me, how little it must be to *her* taste! Sir Edmund had not been so much out of the way in fearing there might be obstacles to his son's taking the step he desired. Margaret Vandeleur was an obstacle—I knew it as well as if Mr. Tester had told me.

I don't mean there was anything in their relation he might not freely have alluded to, for Lady Vandeleur, in spite of her beauty and her tiresome husband, was not a woman who could be accused of an indiscretion. Her husband was a pedant about trifles—the shape of his hat-brim, the *pose* of his coachman, and cared for nothing else; but she was as nearly a saint as one may be when one has rubbed shoulders for ten years with the best society in Europe. It is a characteristic of that society that even its saints are suspected, and I go too far

in saying that little pin-pricks were not administered, in
considerable numbers, to her reputation. But she didn't feel
them, for, still more than Ambrose Tester, she was a person
to whose happiness a good conscience was necessary. I should
almost say that for her happiness it was sufficient, and, at any
rate, it was only those who didn't know her that pretended
to speak of her lightly. If one had the honour of her acquaintance one might have thought her rather shut up to her
beauty and her grandeur, but one couldn't but feel there was
something in her composition that would keep her from vulgar aberrations. Her husband was such a feeble type that she
must have felt doubly she had been put upon her honour. To
deceive such a man as that was to make him more ridiculous
than he was already, and from such a result a woman bearing
his name may very well have shrunk. Perhaps it would have
been worse for Lord Vandeleur, who had every pretension of
his order and none of its amiability, if he had been a better
or, at least, a cleverer man. When a woman behaves so well
she is not obliged to be careful, and there is no need of consulting appearances when one is one's self an appearance. Lady
Vandeleur accepted Ambrose Tester's attentions, and heaven
knows they were frequent; but she had such an air of perfect
equilibrium that one couldn't see her, in imagination, bend
responsive. Incense was incense, but one saw her sitting quite
serene among the fumes. That honour of her acquaintance of
which I just now spoke it had been given me to enjoy; that
is to say, I met her a dozen times in the season in a hot crowd,
and we smiled sweetly and murmured a vague question or
two, without hearing, or even trying to hear, each other's
answer. If I knew that Ambrose Tester was perpetually in and
out of her house and always arranging with her that they
should go to the same places, I doubt whether she, on her
side, knew how often he came to see me. I don't think he
would have let her know, and am conscious, in saying this,
that it indicated an advanced state of intimacy (with her, I
mean).

   I also doubt very much whether he asked her to look about,
on his behalf, for a future Lady Tester. This request he was
so good as to make of me; but I told him I would have

nothing to do with the matter. If Joscelind is unhappy, I am
thankful to say the responsibility is not mine. I have found
English husbands for two or three American girls, but providing English wives is a different affair. I know the sort of men
that will suit women, but one would have to be very clever
to know the sort of women that will suit men. I told Ambrose
Tester that he must look out for himself, but, in spite of his
promise, I had very little belief that he would do anything of
the sort. I thought it probable that the old baronet would
pass away without seeing a new generation come in; though
when I intimated as much to Mr. Tester, he made answer in
substance (it was not quite so crudely said) that his father, old
as he was, would hold on till his bidding was done, and if it
should not be done he would hold on out of spite. "Oh, he
will tire me out": that I remember Ambrose Tester did say. I
had done him injustice, for six months later he told me he
was engaged. It had all come about very suddenly. From one
day to the other the right young woman had been found. I
forget who had found her; some aunt or cousin, I think; it
had not been the young man himself. But when she was
found, he rose to the occasion; he took her up seriously, he
approved of her thoroughly, and I am not sure that he didn't
fall a little in love with her, ridiculous (excuse my London
tone) as this accident may appear. He told me that his father
was delighted, and I knew afterwards that he had good reason
to be. It was not till some weeks later that I saw the girl; but
meanwhile I had received the pleasantest impression of her,
and this impression came—must have come—mainly from
what her intended told me. That proves that he spoke with
some positiveness, spoke as if he really believed he was doing
a good thing. I had it on my tongue's end to ask him how
Lady Vandeleur liked her, but I fortunately checked this vulgar
inquiry. He liked her, evidently, as I say; every one liked her,
and when I knew her I liked her better even than the others.
I like her to-day more than ever; it is fair you should know
that, in reading this account of her situation. It doubtless colours my picture, gives a point to my sense of the strangeness
of my little story.

Joscelind Bernardstone came of a military race, and had

been brought up in camps—by which I don't mean she was one of those objectionable young women who are known as garrison-hacks. She was in the flower of her freshness, and had been kept in the tent, receiving, as an only daughter, the most "particular" education from the excellent Lady Emily (General Bernardstone married a daughter of Lord Clanduffy), who looks like a pink-faced rabbit, and is (after Joscelind) one of the nicest women I know. When I met them in a country-house, a few weeks after the marriage was "arranged," as they say here, Joscelind won my affections by saying to me, with her timid directness (the speech made me feel sixty years old), that she must thank me for having been so kind to Mr. Tester. You saw her at Doubleton, and you will remember that, though she has no regular beauty, many a prettier woman would be very glad to look like her. She is as fresh as a new-laid egg, as light as a feather, as strong as a mail-phaeton. She is perfectly mild, yet she is clever enough to be sharp if she would. I don't know that clever women are necessarily thought ill-natured, but it is usually taken for granted that amiable women are very limited. Lady Tester is a refutation of the theory, which must have been invented by a vixenish woman who was *not* clever. She has an adoration for her husband, which absorbs her without in the least making her silly, unless indeed it is silly to be modest, as in this brutal world I sometimes believe. Her modesty is so great that being unhappy has hitherto presented itself to her as a form of egotism—that egotism which she has too much delicacy to cultivate. She is by no means sure that, if being married to her beautiful baronet is not the ideal state she dreamed it, the weak point of the affair is not simply in her own presumption. It doesn't express her condition, at present, to say that she is unhappy or disappointed, or that she has a sense of injury. All this is latent; meanwhile, what is obvious is that she is bewildered—she simply doesn't understand, and her perplexity, to me, is unspeakably touching. She looks about her for some explanation, some light. She fixes her eyes on mine sometimes, and on those of other people, with a kind of searching dumbness, as if there were some chance that I—that they—may explain, may tell her what it is that has happened to her. I can explain very well—but not to her—only to you!

III.

It was a brilliant match for Miss Bernardstone, who had no fortune at all, and all her friends were of the opinion that she had done very well. After Easter she was in London with her people, and I saw a good deal of them—in fact, I rather cultivated them. They might perhaps even have thought me a little patronising, if they had been given to thinking that sort of thing. But they were not; that is not in their line. English people are very apt to attribute motives—some of them attribute much worse ones than we poor simpletons in America recognise, than we have even heard of. But that is only some of them; others don't, but take everything literally and genially. That was the case with the Bernardstones; you could be sure that on their way home, after dining with you, they wouldn't ask each other how in the world any one could call you pretty, or say that many people *did* believe, all the same, that you had poisoned your grandfather.

Lady Emily was exceedingly gratified at her daughter's engagement; of course she was very quiet about it, she didn't clap her hands or drag in Mr. Tester's name; but it was easy to see that she felt a kind of maternal peace, an abiding satisfaction. The young man behaved as well as possible, was constantly seen with Joscelind, and smiled down at her in the kindest, most protecting way. They looked beautiful together—you would have said it was a duty for people whose colour matched so well to marry. Of course he was immensely taken up, and didn't come very often to see me; but he came sometimes, and when he sat there he had a look which I didn't understand at first. Presently I saw what it expressed; in my drawing-room he was off duty, he had no longer to sit up and play a part; he would lean back and rest and draw a long breath, and forget that the day of his execution was fixed. There was to be no indecent haste about the marriage; it was not to take place till after the session, at the end of August. It puzzled me and rather distressed me that his heart shouldn't be a little more in the matter; it seemed strange to be engaged to so charming a girl and yet go through with it as if it were simply a social duty. If one hadn't been in love with her at first, one ought to have been at the end of a week or two. If Ambrose Tester was not (and to me he didn't pretend to be), he carried it off, as I have said, better than I should have expected. He was a gentleman, and he behaved like a gentleman—with the added punctilio, I think, of being sorry for his betrothed. But it was difficult to see what, in the long run, he could expect to make of such a position. If a man marries an ugly, unattractive woman for reasons of state, the thing is comparatively simple; it is understood between them, and he need have no remorse at not offering her a sentiment of which there has been no question. But when he picks out a charming creature to gratify his father and *les convenances*, it is not so easy to be happy in not being able to care for her. It seemed to me that it would have been much better for Ambrose Tester to bestow himself upon a girl who might have given him an excuse for tepidity. His wife should have been healthy but stupid, prolific but morose. Did he expect to continue not to be in love with Joscelind, or to conceal from her the mechanical nature of his attentions? It was difficult to see how he could wish to do the one or succeed in doing the other. Did he expect such a girl as that would be happy if he didn't love her? and did he think himself capable of being happy if it should turn out that she was miserable? If she shouldn't be miserable—that is, if she should be indifferent, and, as they say, console herself, would he like that any better?

I asked myself all these questions and I should have liked to ask them of Mr. Tester; but I didn't, for after all he couldn't have answered them. Poor young man! he didn't pry into things as I do; he was not analytic, like us Americans, as they say in reviews. He thought he was behaving remarkably well, and so he was—for a man; that was the strange part of it. It had been proper that in spite of his reluctance he should take a wife, and he had dutifully set about it. As a good thing is better for being well done, he had taken the best one he could possibly find. He was enchanted with—with his young lady, you might ask? Not in the least; with himself; that is the sort of person a man is! Their virtues are more dangerous than their vices, and heaven preserve you when they want to keep a promise! It is never a promise to *you*, you will notice. A man will sacrifice a woman to live as a gentleman should, and then ask for your sympathy—for *him*! And I don't speak of the bad ones, but of the good. They, after all, are the worst. Ambrose Tester, as I say, didn't go into these details, but, synthetic as he might be, was conscious that his position was false. He felt that sooner or later, and rather sooner than later, he would have to make it true—a process that couldn't possibly be agreeable. He would really have to make up his mind to care for his wife or not to care for her. What would Lady Vandeleur say to one alternative, and what would little Joscelind say to the other? That is what it was to have a pertinacious father and to be an accommodating son. With me it was easy for Ambrose Tester to be superficial, for, as I tell you, if I didn't wish to engage him, I didn't wish to disengage him, and I didn't insist. Lady Vandeleur insisted, I was afraid; to be with her was, of course, very complicated; even more than Miss Bernardstone she must have made him feel that his position was false. I must add that he once mentioned to me that she had told him he ought to marry. At any rate it is an immense thing to be a pleasant fellow. Our young fellow was so universally pleasant that, of course, his *fiancée* came in for her share. So did Lady Emily, suffused with hope, which made her pinker than ever; she told me he sent flowers even to her. One day in the Park, I was riding early; the Row was almost empty. I came up behind a lady and gentleman who were walking their horses, close to each other, side by side. In a moment I recognised her, but not before seeing that nothing could have been more benevolent than the way Ambrose Tester was bending over his future wife. If he struck me as a lover at that moment, of course he struck her so. But that isn't the way they ride to-day.

IV.

One day, about the end of June, he came in to see me when I had two or three other visitors; you know that even at that season I am almost always at home from six to seven. He had not been three minutes in the room before I saw that he was different—different from what he had been the last time, and I guessed that something had happened in relation to his marriage. My visitors didn't, unfortunately, and they stayed and

stayed until I was afraid he would have to go away without
telling me what, I was sure, he had come for. But he sat them
out; I think that, by exception, they didn't find him pleasant.
After we were alone he abused them a little, and then he said,
"Have you heard about Vandeleur? He's very ill. She's awfully
anxious." I hadn't heard, and I told him so, asking a question
or two; then my inquiries ceased, my breath almost failed me,
for I had become aware of something very strange. The way
he looked at me when he told me his news was a full confession—a confession so full that I had needed a moment to
take it in. He was not too strong a man to be taken by surprise—not so strong but that in the presence of an unexpected
occasion his first movement was to look about for a little help.
I venture to call it help, the sort of thing he came to me for
on that summer afternoon. It is always help when a woman
who is not an idiot lets an embarrassed man take up her time.
If he too is not an idiot, that doesn't diminish the service; on
the contrary his superiority to the average helps him to profit.
Ambrose Tester had said to me more than once, in the past,
that he was capable of telling me things, because I was an
American, that he wouldn't confide to his own people. He
had proved it before this, as I have hinted, and I must say
that being an American, with him, was sometimes a questionable honour. I don't know whether he thinks us more discreet
and more sympathetic (if he keeps up the system: he has abandoned it with me), or only more insensible, more proof
against shocks; but it is certain that, like some other Englishmen I have known, he has appeared, in delicate cases, to think
I would take a comprehensive view. When I have inquired into
the grounds of this discrimination in our favour, he has contented himself with saying, in the British-cursory manner,
"Oh, I don't know; you are different!" I remember he remarked once that our impressions were fresher. And I am sure
that now it was because of my nationality, in addition to other
merits, that he treated me to the confession I have just alluded
to. At least I don't suppose he would have gone about saying
to people in general, "Her husband will probably die, you
know; then why shouldn't I marry Lady Vandeleur?"

That was the question which his whole expression and manner asked of me, and of which, after a moment, I decided to

take no notice. Why shouldn't he? There was an excellent reason why he shouldn't. It would just kill Joscelind Bernardstone; that was why he shouldn't! The idea that he should be ready to do it frightened me, and, independent as he might think my point of view, I had no desire to discuss such abominations. It struck me as an abomination at this very first moment, and I have never wavered in my judgment of it. I am always glad when I can take the measure of a thing as soon as I see it; it's a blessing to *feel* what we think, without balancing and comparing. It's a great rest, too, and a great luxury. That, as I say, was the case with the feeling excited in me by this happy idea of Ambrose Tester's. Cruel and wanton I thought it then, cruel and wanton I thought it later, when it was pressed upon me. I knew there were many other people that didn't agree with me, and I can only hope for them that their conviction was as quick and positive as mine; it all depends upon the way a thing strikes one. But I will add to this another remark. I thought I was right then, and I still think I was right; but it strikes me as a pity that I should have wished so much to be right. Why couldn't I be content to be wrong? to renounce my influence (since I appeared to possess the mystic article), and let my young friend do as he liked? As you observed the situation at Doubleton, shouldn't you say it was of a nature to make one wonder whether, after all, one did render a service to the younger lady?

At all events, as I say, I gave no sign to Ambrose Tester that I understood him, that I guessed what he wished to come to. He got no satisfaction out of me that day; it is very true that he made up for it later. I expressed regret at Lord Vandeleur's illness, inquired into its nature and origin, hoped it wouldn't prove as grave as might be feared, said I would call at the house and ask about him, commiserated discreetly her ladyship, and, in short, gave my young man no chance whatever. He knew that I had guessed his *arrière-pensée*, but he let me off for the moment, for which I was thankful; either because he was still ashamed of it, or because he supposed I was reserving myself for the catastrophe—should it occur. Well, my dear, it did occur, at the end of ten days. Mr. Tester came to see me twice in that interval, each time to tell me that poor Vandeleur was worse; he had some internal inflammation

which in nine cases out of ten, is fatal. His wife was all devotion; she was with him night and day. I had the news from
other sources as well; I leave you to imagine whether in London, at the height of the season, such a situation could fail to
be considerably discussed. To the discussion as yet, however,
I contributed little, and with Ambrose Tester nothing at all.
I was still on my guard. I never admitted for a moment that
it was possible there should be any change in his plans. By
this time, I think, he had quite ceased to be ashamed of his
idea, he was in a state almost of exultation about it; but he
was very angry with me for not giving him an opening.

As I look back upon the matter now, there is something
almost amusing in the way we watched each other—he thinking that I evaded his question only to torment him (he believed me, or pretended to believe me, capable of this sort of
perversity), and I determined not to lose ground by betraying
an insight into his state of mind which he might twist into an
expression of sympathy. I wished to leave my sympathy where
I had placed it, with Lady Emily and her daughter, of whom
I continued, bumping against them at parties, to have some
observation. They gave no signal of alarm; of course it would
have been premature. The girl, I am sure, had no idea of the
existence of a rival. How they had kept her in the dark I don't
know; but it was easy to see she was too much in love to
suspect or to criticise. With Lady Emily it was different; she
was a woman of charity, but she touched the world at too
many points not to feel its vibrations. However, the dear little
lady planted herself firmly; to the eye she was still enough. It
was not from Ambrose Tester that I first heard of Lord Vandeleur's death; it was announced, with a quarter of a column
of "padding," in the *Times*. I have always known the *Times*
was a wonderful journal, but this never came home to me so
much as when it produced a quarter of a column about Lord
Vandeleur. It was a triumph of word-spinning. If he had carried out his vocation, if he had been a tailor or a hatter (that's
how I see him), there might have been something to say about
him. But he missed his vocation, he missed everything but
posthumous honours. I was so sure Ambrose Tester would
come in that afternoon, and so sure he knew I should expect
him, that I threw over an engagement on purpose. But he

didn't come in, nor the next day, nor the next. There were
two possible explanations of his absence. One was that he was
giving all his time to consoling Lady Vandeleur; the other was
that he was giving it all, as a blind, to Joscelind Bernardstone.
Both proved incorrect, for when he at last turned up he told
me he had been for a week in the country, at his father's. Sir
Edmund also had been unwell; but he had pulled through
better than poor Lord Vandeleur. I wondered at first whether
his son had been talking over with him the question of a
change of base; but guessed in a moment that he had not
suffered this alarm. I don't think that Ambrose would have
spared him if he had thought it necessary to give him warning;
but he probably held that his father would have no ground
for complaint so long as he should marry some one; would
have no right to remonstrate if he simply transferred his contract. Lady Vandeleur had had two children (whom she had
lost), and might, therefore, have others whom she shouldn't
lose; that would have been a reply to nice discriminations on
Sir Edmund's part.

V.

In reality what the young man had been doing was thinking
it over beneath his ancestral oaks and beeches. His countenance showed this—showed it more than Miss Bernardstone
could have liked. He looked like a man who was crossed, not
like a man who was happy, in love. I was no more disposed
than before to help him out with his plot, but at the end of
ten minutes we were articulately discussing it. When I say *we*
were, I mean he was; for I sat before him quite mute, at first,
and amazed at the clearness with which, before his conscience,
he had argued his case. He had persuaded himself that it was
quite a simple matter to throw over poor Joscelind and keep
himself free for the expiration of Lady Vandeleur's term of
mourning. The deliberations of an impulsive man sometimes
land him in strange countries. Ambrose Tester confided his
plan to me as a tremendous secret. He professed to wish immensely to know how it appeared to me, and whether my
woman's wit couldn't discover for him some loophole big
enough round, some honourable way of not keeping faith.

Yet at the same time he seemed not to foresee that I should, of necessity, be simply horrified. Disconcerted and perplexed (a little), that he was prepared to find me; but if I had refused, as yet, to come to his assistance, he appeared to suppose it was only because of the real difficulty of suggesting to him that perfect pretext of which he was in want. He evidently counted upon me, however, for some illuminating proposal, and I think he would have liked to say to me, "You have always pretended to be a great friend of mine"—I hadn't; the pretension was all on his side—"and now is your chance to show it. Go to Joscelind and make her feel (women have a hundred ways of doing that sort of thing) that through Vandeleur's death the change in my situation is complete. If she is the girl I take her for, she will know what to do in the premises."

I was not prepared to oblige him to this degree, and I lost no time in telling him so, after my first surprise at seeing how definite his purpose had become. His contention, after all, was very simple. He had been in love with Lady Vandeleur for years, and was now more in love with her than ever. There had been no appearance of her being, within a calculable period, liberated by the death of her husband. This nobleman was—he didn't say what just then (it was too soon)—but he was only forty years old, and in such health and preservation as to make such a contingency infinitely remote. Under these circumstances, Ambrose had been driven, for the most worldly reasons—he was ashamed of them, pah!—into an engagement with a girl he didn't love, and didn't pretend to love. Suddenly the unexpected occurred; the woman he did love had become accessible to him, and all the relations of things were altered. Why shouldn't he alter too?—why shouldn't Miss Bernardstone alter, Lady Emily alter, and every one alter? It would be *wrong* in him to marry Joscelind in so changed a world—a moment's consideration would certainly assure me of that. He could no longer carry out his part of the bargain, and the transaction must stop before it went any further. If Joscelind knew, she would be the first to recognise this, and the thing for her now was to know.

"Go and tell her, then, if you are so sure of it," I said. "I wonder you have put it off so many days."

He looked at me with a melancholy eye. "Of course I know it's beastly awkward."

It was beastly awkward certainly; there I could quite agree with him, and this was the only sympathy he extracted from me. It was impossible to be less helpful, less merciful, to an embarrassed young man than I was on that occasion. But other occasions followed very quickly, on which Mr. Tester renewed his appeal with greater eloquence. He assured me that it was torture to be with his intended, and every hour that he didn't break off committed him more deeply and more fatally. I repeated only once my previous question—asked him only once why then he didn't tell her he had changed his mind. The inquiry was idle, was even unkind, for my young man was in a very tight place. He didn't tell her, simply because he couldn't, in spite of the anguish of feeling that his chance to right himself was rapidly passing away. When I asked him if Joscelind appeared to have guessed nothing he broke out, "How in the world can she guess when I am so kind to her? I am so sorry for her, poor little wretch, that I can't help being nice to her. And from the moment I am nice to her she thinks it's all right."

I could see perfectly what he meant by that, and I liked him more for this little generosity than I disliked him for his nefarious scheme. In fact, I didn't dislike him at all when I saw what an influence my judgment would have on him. I very soon gave him the full benefit of it. I had thought over his case with all the advantages of his own presentation of it, and it was impossible for me to see how he could decently get rid of the girl. That, as I have said, had been my original opinion, and quickened reflection only confirmed it. As I have also said, I hadn't in the least recommended him to become engaged; but once he had done so I recommended him to abide by it. It was all very well being in love with Lady Vandeleur; he might be in love with her, but he hadn't promised to marry her. It was all very well not being in love with Miss Bernardstone; but, as it happened, he had promised to marry her, and in my country a gentleman was supposed to keep such promises. If it was a question of keeping them only so long as was convenient where would any of us be? I assure you I became very eloquent and moral—yes, moral, I maintain the word, in spite of your perhaps thinking (as you are very capable of doing) that I ought to have advised him in just the opposite sense. It was not a question of love, but of marriage, for he had never promised to love poor Joscelind. It was useless his saying it was dreadful to marry without love; he knew that he thought it, and the people he lived with thought it, nothing of the kind. Half his friends had married on those terms. "Yes, and a pretty sight their private life presented!" That might be, but it was the first time I had ever heard him say it. A fortnight before he had been quite ready to do like the others. I knew what I thought, and I suppose I expressed it with some clearness, for my arguments made him still more uncomfortable, unable as he was either to accept them or to act in contempt of them. Why he should have cared so much for my opinion is a mystery I can't elucidate; to understand my little story you must simply swallow it. That he did care is proved by the exasperation with which he suddenly broke out, "Well, then, as I understand you, what you recommend me is to marry Miss Bernardstone, and carry on an intrigue with Lady Vandeleur!"

He knew perfectly that I recommended nothing of the sort, and he must have been very angry to indulge in this *boutade*. He told me that other people didn't think as I did—that every one was of the opinion that between a woman he didn't love and a woman he had adored for years it was a plain moral duty not to hesitate. "Don't hesitate then!" I exclaimed; but I didn't get rid of him with this, for he returned to the charge more than once (he came to me so often that I thought he must neglect both his other alternatives), and let me know again that the voice of society was quite against my view. You will doubtless be surprised at such an intimation that he had taken "society" into his confidence, and wonder whether he went about asking people whether they thought he might back out. I can't tell you exactly, but I know that for some weeks his dilemma was a great deal talked about. His friends perceived he was at the parting of the roads, and many of them had no difficulty in saying which one *they* would take. Some observers thought he ought to do nothing, to leave things as they were. Others took very high ground and discoursed upon the sanctity of love and the wickedness of really deceiving the girl, as that would be what it would amount to (if he should lead her to the altar). Some held that it was too late to escape, others maintained that it is never too late. Some thought Miss Bernardstone very much to be pitied; some reserved their compassion for Ambrose Tester; others, still, lavished it upon Lady Vandeleur. The prevailing opinion, I think, was that he ought to obey the promptings of his heart—London cares so much for the heart! Or is it that London is simply ferocious, and always prefers the spectacle that is more entertaining? As it would prolong the drama for the young man to throw over Miss Bernardstone, there was a considerable readiness to see the poor girl sacrificed. She was like a Christian maiden in the Roman arena. That is what Ambrose Tester meant by telling me that public opinion was on his side. I don't think he chattered about his quandary, but people, knowing his situation, guessed what was going on in his mind, and he, on his side, guessed what they said. London discussions might as well go on in the whispering-gallery of St. Paul's.

I could, of course, do only one thing—I could but re affirm my conviction that the Roman attitude, as I may call it, was cruel, was falsely sentimental. This naturally didn't help him as he wished to be helped—didn't remove the obstacle to his marrying in a year or two Lady Vandeleur. Yet he continued to look to me for inspiration—I must say it at the cost of making him appear a very feeble-minded gentleman. There was a moment when I thought him capable of an oblique movement, of temporising with a view to escape. If he succeeded in postponing his marriage long enough, the Bernardstones would throw *him* over, and I suspect that for a day he entertained the idea of fixing this responsibility on them. But he was too honest and too generous to do so for longer, and his destiny was staring him in the face when an accident gave him a momentary relief. General Bernardstone died, after an illness as sudden and short as that which had carried off Lord Vandeleur; his wife and daughter were plunged into mourning and immediately retired into the country. A week later we heard that the girl's marriage would be put off for several months—partly on account of her mourning and partly because her mother, whose only companion she had now

become, could not bear to part with her at the time originally
fixed and actually so near. People of course looked at each
other—said it was the beginning of the end, a "dodge" of
Ambrose Tester's. I wonder they didn't accuse him of poi-
soning the poor old general. I know to a certainty that he had
nothing to do with the delay, that the proposal came from
Lady Emily, who, in her bereavement, wished, very naturally,
to keep a few months longer the child she was going to lose
for ever. It must be said, in justice to her prospective son-in-
law, that he was capable either of resigning himself or of
frankly (with however many blushes) telling Joscelind he
couldn't keep his agreement, but was not capable of trying to
wriggle out of his difficulty. The plan of simply telling
Joscelind he couldn't—this was the one he had fixed upon as
the best, and this was the one of which I remarked to him that
it had a defect which should be counted against its advantages.
The defect was that it would kill Joscelind on the spot.

I think he believed me, and his believing me made this unexpected respite very welcome to him. There was no knowing
what might happen in the interval, and he passed a large part
of it in looking for an issue. And yet, at the same time, he
kept up the usual forms with the girl whom in his heart he
had renounced. I was told more than once (for I had lost
sight of the pair during the summer and autumn) that these
forms were at times very casual, that he neglected Miss Bernardstone most flagrantly, and had quite resumed his old intimacy with Lady Vandeleur. I don't exactly know what was
meant by this, for she spent the first three months of her
widowhood in complete seclusion, in her own old house in
Norfolk, where he certainly was not staying with her. I believe
he stayed some time, for the partridge-shooting, at a place a
few miles off. It came to my ears that if Miss Bernardstone
didn't take the hint it was because she was determined to stick
to him through thick and thin. She never offered to let him
off, and I was sure she never would; but I was equally sure
that, strange as it may appear, he had not ceased to be nice
to her. I have never exactly understood why he didn't hate
her, and I am convinced that he was not a comedian in his
conduct to her—he was only a good fellow. I have spoken of
the satisfaction that Sir Edmund took in his daughter-in-law

that was to be; he delighted in looking at her, longed for her when she was out of his sight, and had her, with her mother, staying with him in the country for weeks together. If Ambrose was not so constantly at her side as he might have been, this deficiency was covered by his father's devotion to her, by her appearance of being already one of the family. Mr. Tester was away as he might be away if they were already married.

VI.

In October I met him at Doubleton; we spent three days there together. He was enjoying his respite, as he didn't scruple to tell me, and he talked to me a great deal—as usual—about Lady Vandeleur. He didn't mention Joscelind, except by implication, in this assurance of how much he valued his weeks of grace.

"Do you mean to say that, under the circumstances, Lady Vandeleur is willing to marry you?"

I made this inquiry more expressively, doubtless, than before; for when we had talked of the matter then he had naturally spoken of her consent as a simple contingency. It was contingent upon the lapse of the first months of her bereavement; it was not a question he could begin to press a few days after her husband's death.

"Not immediately, of course, but if I wait I think so." That, I remember, was his answer.

"If you wait till you get rid of that poor girl, of course."

"She knows nothing about that—it's none of her business."

"Do you mean to say she doesn't know you are engaged?"

"How should she know it, how should she believe it, when she sees how I love her?" the young man exclaimed; but he admitted afterwards that he had not deceived her, and that she rendered full justice to the motives that had determined him. He thought he could answer for it that she would marry him some day or other.

"Then she is a very cruel woman," I said, "and I should like, if you please, to hear no more about her." He protested against this, and, a month later, brought her up again, for a purpose. The purpose, you will see, was a very strange one. I had then come back to town; it was the early part of

December. I supposed he was hunting, with his own hounds; but he appeared one afternoon in my drawing-room and told me I should do him a great favour if I would go and see Lady Vandeleur.

"Go and see her? where do you mean, in Norfolk?"

"She has come up to London—didn't you know it? She has a lot of business. She will be kept here till Christmas; I wish you would go."

"Why should I go?" I asked. "Won't you be kept here till Christmas too, and isn't that company enough for her?"

"Upon my word, you are cruel," he said, "and it's a great shame of you, when a man is trying to do his duty and is behaving like a saint."

"Is that what you call saintly, spending all your time with Lady Vandeleur? I will tell you whom I think a saint, if you would like to know."

"You needn't tell me, I know it better than you. I haven't a word to say against her; only she is stupid and hasn't any perceptions. If I am stopping a bit in London you don't understand why; it's as if you hadn't any perceptions either! If I am here for a few days I know what I am about."

"Why should I understand?" I asked—not very candidly, because I should have been glad to. "It's your own affair, you know what you are about, as you say, and of course you have counted the cost."

"What cost do you mean? It's a pretty cost, I can tell you." And then he tried to explain—if I would only enter into it, and not be so suspicious. He was in London for the express purpose of breaking off.

"Breaking off what—your engagement?"

"No, no, damn my engagement—the other thing. My acquaintance, my relations——"

"Your intimacy with Lady Van——?" It was not very gentle, but I believe I burst out laughing. "If this is the way you break off, pray, what would you do to keep up?"

He flushed, and looked both foolish and angry, for of course it was not very difficult to see my point. But he was—in a very clumsy manner of his own—trying to cultivate a good conscience, and he was getting no credit for it. "I suppose I may be allowed to look at her! It's a matter we have to talk over. One doesn't drop such a friend in half an hour."

"One doesn't drop her at all, unless one has the strength to make a sacrifice."

"It's easy for you to talk of sacrifice. You don't know what she is!" my visitor cried.

"I think I know what she is not. She is not a friend, as you call her, if she encourages you in the wrong, if she doesn't help you. No, I have no patience with her," I declared; "I don't like her, and I won't go to see her!"

Mr. Tester looked at me a moment, as if he were too vexed to trust himself to speak. He had to make an effort not to say something rude. That effort, however, he was capable of making, and though he held his hat as if he were going to walk out of the house, he ended by staying, by putting it down again, by leaning his head, with his elbows on his knees, in his hands, and groaning out that he had never heard of anything so impossible, and that he was the most wretched man in England. I was very sorry for him, and of course I told him so; but privately I didn't think he stood up to his duty as he ought. I said to him, however, that if he would give me his word of honour that he would not abandon Miss Bernardstone, there was no trouble I wouldn't take to be of use to him. I didn't think Lady Vandeleur was behaving well. He must allow me to repeat that; but if going to see her would give him any pleasure (of course there was no question of pleasure for *her*) I would go fifty times. I couldn't imagine how it would help him, but I would do it, as I would do anything else he asked me. He didn't give me his word of honour, but he said quietly, "*I* shall go straight; you needn't be afraid;" and as he spoke there was honour enough in his face. This left an opening, of course, for another catastrophe. There might be further postponements, and poor Lady Emily, indignant for the first time in her life, might declare that her daughter's situation had become intolerable, and that they withdrew from the engagement. But this was too odious a chance, and I accepted Mr. Tester's assurance. He told me that the good I could do by going to see Lady Vandeleur was that it would cheer her up, in that dreary, big house in Upper

Brook Street, where she was absolutely alone, with horrible overalls on the furniture, and newspapers—actually newspapers—on the mirrors. She was seeing no one, there was no one to see; but he knew she would see me. I asked him if she knew, then, he was to speak to me of coming, and whether I might allude to him, whether it was not too delicate. I shall never forget his answer to this, nor the tone in which he made it, blushing a little and looking away. "Allude to me? Rather!" It was not the most fatuous speech I had ever heard; it had the effect of being the most modest; and it gave me an odd idea, and especially a new one, of the condition in which, at any time, one might be destined to find Lady Vandeleur. If she, too, were engaged in a struggle with her conscience (in this light they were an edifying pair!) it had perhaps changed her considerably, made her more approachable; and I reflected, ingeniously, that it probably had a humanising effect upon her. Ambrose Tester didn't go away after I had told him that I would comply with his request. He lingered, fidgeting with his stick and gloves, and I perceived that he had more to tell me, and that the real reason why he wished me to go and see Lady Vandeleur was not that she had newspapers on her mirrors. He came out with it at last, for that "Rather!" of his (with the way I took it) had broken the ice.

"You say you don't think she behaves well" (he naturally wished to defend her). "But I daresay you don't understand her position. Perhaps you wouldn't behave any better in her place."

"It's very good of you to imagine me there!" I remarked, laughing.

"It's awkward for me to say. One doesn't want to dot one's i's to that extent."

"She would be delighted to marry you. That's not such a mystery."

"Well, she likes me awfully," Mr. Tester said, looking like a handsome child. "It's not all on one side, it's on both. That's the difficulty."

"You mean she won't let you go?—she holds you fast?"

But the poor fellow had, in delicacy, said enough, and at this he jumped up. He stood there a moment, smoothing his hat; then he broke out again. "Please do this. Let her know—make her feel. You can bring it in, you know." And here he paused, embarrassed.

"What can I bring in, Mr. Tester? That's the difficulty, as you say."

"What you told me the other day. You know. What you have told me before."

"What I have told you . . . ?"

"That it would put an end to Joscelind! If you can't work round to it, what's the good of being—you?" And with this tribute to my powers he took his departure.

VII.

It was all very well of him to be so flattering, but I really didn't see myself talking in that manner to Lady Vandeleur. I wondered why he didn't give her this information himself, and what particular value it could have as coming from me. Then I said to myself that of course he *had* mentioned to her the truth I had impressed upon him (and which by this time he had evidently taken home), but that to enable it to produce its full effect upon Lady Vandeleur the further testimony of a witness more independent was required. There was nothing for me but to go and see her, and I went the next day, fully conscious that to execute Mr. Tester's commission I should have either to find myself very brave or to find her strangely confidential; and fully prepared, also, not to be admitted. But she received me, and the house in Upper Brook Street was as dismal as Ambrose Tester had represented it. The December fog (the afternoon was very dusky) seemed to pervade the muffled rooms, and her ladyship's pink lamp-light to waste itself in the brown atmosphere. He had mentioned to me that the heir to the title (a cousin of her husband), who had left her unmolested for several months, was now taking possession of everything, so that what kept her in town was the business of her "turning out," and certain formalities connected with her dower. This was very ample, and the large provision made for her included the London house. She was very gracious on this occasion, but she certainly had remarkably little to say. Still, she was different, or, at any rate (having taken that hint), I saw her differently. I saw, indeed, that I had never quite done her justice, that I had exaggerated her stiffness, attrib-uted to her a kind of conscious grandeur which was in reality much more an accident of her appearance, of her figure, than a quality of her character. Her appearance is as grand as you know, and on the day I speak of, in her simplified mourning, under those vaguely-gleaming *lambris*, she looked as beautiful as a great white lily. She is very simple and good-natured; she will never make an advance, but she will always respond to one, and I saw, that evening, that the way to get on with her was to treat her as if she were not too imposing. I saw also that, with her nun-like robes and languid eyes, she was a woman who might be immensely in love. All the same, we hadn't much to say to each other. She remarked that it was very kind of me to come, that she wondered how I could endure London at that season, that she had taken a drive and found the Park too dreadful, that she would ring for some more tea if I didn't like what she had given me. Our conver-sation wandered, stumbling a little, among these platitudes, but no allusion was made on either side to Ambrose Tester. Nevertheless, as I have said, she was different, though it was not till I got home that I phrased to myself what I had de-tected.

Then, recalling her white face, and the deeper, stranger ex-pression of her beautiful eyes, I entertained myself with the idea that she was under the influence of "suppressed exalta-tion." The more I thought of her the more she appeared to me not natural; wound up, as it were, to a calmness beneath which there was a deal of agitation. This would have been nonsense if I had not, two days afterwards, received a note from her which struck me as an absolutely "exalted" produc-tion. Not superficially, of course; to the casual eye it would have been perfectly commonplace. But this was precisely its peculiarity, that Lady Vandeleur should have written me a note which had no apparent point save that she should like to see me again, a desire for which she did succeed in assigning a reason. She reminded me that she was paying no calls, and she hoped I wouldn't stand on ceremony, but come in very soon again, she had enjoyed my visit so much. We had not been on note-writing terms, and there was nothing in that visit to alter our relations; moreover, six months before, she would not have dreamed of addressing me in that way. I was doubly convinced, therefore, that she was passing through a crisis—that she was not in her normal equilibrium. Mr. Tester had not reappeared since the occasion I have described at length, and I thought it possible he had been capable of the bravery of leaving town. I had, however, no fear of meeting him in Upper Brook Street; for, according to my theory of his relations with Lady Vandeleur he regularly spent his evenings with her, it being clear to me that they must dine together. I could answer her note only by going to see her the next day, when I found abundant confirmation of that idea about the crisis. I must confess to you in advance that I have never really understood her behaviour—never understood why she should have taken to me so suddenly—with whatever reserves, and however much by implication merely—into her confidence. All I can say is that this is an accident to which one is exposed with English people, who, in my opinion, and contrary to common report, are the most demonstrative, the most expansive, the most gushing in the world. I think she felt rather isolated at this moment, and she had never had many intimates of her own sex. That sex, as a general thing, disapproved of her proceedings during the last few months, held that she was making Joscelind Bernardstone suffer too cruelly. She possibly felt the weight of this censure, and at all events was not above wishing some one to know that, whatever injury had fallen upon the girl to whom Mr. Tester had so stupidly engaged himself, had not, so far as she was concerned, been wantonly inflicted. I was there, I was more or less aware of her situation, and I would do as well as any one else.

She seemed really glad to see me, but she was very nervous. Nevertheless, nearly half an hour elapsed, and I was still wondering whether she had sent for me only to discuss the question of how a London house whose appointments had the stamp of a debased period (it had been thought very handsome in 1850) could be "done up" without being made æsthetic. I forget what satisfaction I gave her on this point; I was asking myself how I could work round in the manner prescribed by Joscelind's intended. At the last, however, to my extreme surprise, Lady Vandeleur herself relieved me of this effort.

"I think you know Mr. Tester rather well," she remarked abruptly, irrelevantly, and with a face more conscious of the bearings of things than any I had ever seen her wear. On my confessing to such an acquaintance, she mentioned that Mr. Tester (who had been in London a few days—perhaps I had seen him) had left town and wouldn't come back for several weeks. This, for the moment, seemed to be all she had to communicate; but she sat looking at me from the corner of her sofa as if she wished me to profit in some way by the opportunity she had given me. Did she want help from out-side, this proud, inscrutable woman, and was she reduced to throwing out signals of distress? Did she wish to be protected against herself—applauded for such efforts as she had already made? I didn't rush forward, I was not precipitate, for I felt that now, surely, I should be able at my convenience to exe-cute my commission. What concerned me was not to prevent Lady Vandeleur's marrying Mr. Tester, but to prevent Mr. Tester's marrying her. In a few moments—with the same ir-relevance—she announced to me that he wished to, and asked whether I didn't know it. I saw that this was my chance, and instantly with extreme energy, I exclaimed—

"Ah, for heaven's sake, don't listen to him! It would kill Miss Bernardstone!"

The tone of my voice made her colour a little, and she repeated, "Miss Bernardstone?"

"The girl he is engaged to—or has been—don't you know? Excuse me, I thought every one knew."

"Of course I know he is dreadfully entangled. He was fairly hunted down." Lady Vandeleur was silent a moment, and then she added, with a strange smile, "Fancy, in such a situ-ation, his wanting to marry me!"

"Fancy!" I replied. I was so struck with the oddity of her telling me her secrets that for the moment my indignation did not come to a head—my indignation, I mean, at her accusing poor Lady Emily (and even the girl herself) of having "trapped" our friend. Later I said to myself that I supposed she was within her literal right in abusing her rival, if she was trying sincerely to give him up. "I don't know anything about his having been hunted down," I said; "but this I do know, Lady Vandeleur, I assure you, that if he should throw

Joscelind over she would simply go out like that!" And I snapped my fingers.

Lady Vandeleur listened to this serenely enough; she tried at least to take the air of a woman who has no need of new arguments. "Do you know her very well?" she asked, as if she had been struck by my calling Miss Bernardstone by her Christian name.

"Well enough to like her very much." I was going to say "to pity her;" but I thought better of it.

"She must be a person of very little spirit. If a man were to jilt me, I don't think I should go out!" cried her ladyship, with a laugh.

"Nothing is more probable than that she has not your courage or your wisdom. She may be weak, but she is passionately in love with him."

I looked straight into Lady Vandeleur's eyes as I said this, and I was conscious that it was a tolerably good description of my hostess.

"Do you think she would really die?" she asked in a moment.

"Die as if one should stab her with a knife. Some people don't believe in broken hearts," I continued. "I didn't till I knew Joscelind Bernardstone; then I felt that she had one that wouldn't be proof."

"One ought to live—one ought always to live," said Lady Vandeleur; "and always to hold up one's head."

"Ah, I suppose that one oughtn't to feel at all, if one wishes to be a great success."

"What do you call a great success?" she asked.

"Never having occasion to be pitied."

"Being pitied? That must be odious!" she said; and I saw that though she might wish for admiration, she would never wish for sympathy. Then, in a moment, she added that men, in her opinion, were very base—a remark that was deep, but not, I think, very honest; that is, in so far as the purpose of it had been to give me the idea that Ambrose Tester had done nothing but press her, and she had done nothing but resist. They were very odd, the discrepancies in the statements of each of this pair; but it must be said for Lady Vandeleur that now that she had made up her mind (as I believed she had)

to sacrifice herself, she really persuaded herself that she had
not had a moment of weakness. She quite unbosomed herself,
and I fairly assisted at her crisis. It appears that she had a
conscience—very much so, and even a high ideal of duty.
She represented herself as moving heaven and earth to keep
Ambrose Tester up to the mark, and you would never have
guessed from what she told me that she had entertained, ever
so faintly, the idea of marrying him. I am sure this was a
dreadful perversion, but I forgave it on the score of that exaltation of which I have spoken. The things she said, and the
way she said them, come back to me, and I thought that if
she looked as handsome as that when she preached virtue to
Mr. Tester, it was no wonder he liked the sermon to be going
on perpetually.

"I daresay you know what old friends we are; but that
doesn't make any difference, does it? Nothing would induce
me to marry him—I haven't the smallest intention of marrying again. It is not a time for me to think of marrying, before
his lordship has been dead six months. The girl is nothing to
me; I know nothing about her, and I don't wish to know; but
I should be very, very sorry if she were unhappy. He is the
best friend I ever had, but I don't see that that's any reason
I should marry him, do you?" Lady Vandeleur appealed to
me, but without waiting for my answers, asking advice in spite
of herself, and then remembering it was beneath her dignity
to appear to be in need of it. "I have told him that if he
doesn't act properly I shall never speak to him again. She's a
charming girl, every one says, and I have no doubt she will
make him perfectly happy. Men don't feel things like women,
I think, and if they are coddled and flattered they forget the
rest. I have no doubt she is very sufficient for all that. For me,
at any rate, once I see a thing in a certain way, I must abide
by that. I think people are so dreadful—they do such horrible
things. They don't seem to think what one's duty may be. I
don't know whether you think much about that, but really
one must at times, don't you think so? Every one is so selfish,
and then, when they have never made an effort or a sacrifice
themselves, they come to you and talk such a lot of hypocrisy.
I know so much better than any one else whether I should
marry or not. But I don't mind telling you that I don't see

why I should. I am not in such a bad position—with my liberty and a decent maintenance."

In this manner she rambled on, gravely and communicatively, contradicting herself at times; not talking fast (she never did), but dropping one simple sentence, with an interval, after the other, with a certain richness of voice which always was part of the charm of her presence. She wished to be convinced against herself, and it was a comfort to her to hear herself argue. I was quite willing to be part of the audience, though I had to confine myself to very superficial remarks; for when I had said the event I feared would kill Miss Bernardstone I had said everything that was open to me. I had nothing to do with Lady Vandeleur's marrying, apart from that. I probably disappointed her. She had caught a glimpse of the moral beauty of self-sacrifice, of a certain ideal of conduct (I imagine it was rather new to her), and would have been glad to elicit from me, as a person of some experience of life, an assurance that such joys are not unsubstantial. I had no wish to wind her up to a spiritual ecstasy from which she would inevitably descend again, and I let her deliver herself according to her humour, without attempting to answer for it that she would find renunciation the road to bliss. I believed that if she should give up Mr. Tester she would suffer accordingly; but I didn't think that a reason for not giving him up. Before I left her she said to me that nothing would induce her to do anything that she didn't think right. "It would be no pleasure to me, don't you see? I should be always thinking that another way would have been better. Nothing would induce me—nothing, nothing!"

VIII.

She protested too much, perhaps, but the event seemed to show that she was in earnest. I have described these two first visits of mine in some detail, but they were not the only ones I paid her. I saw her several times again, before she left town, and we became intimate, as London intimacies are measured. She ceased to protest (to my relief, for it made me nervous), she was very gentle, and gracious, and reasonable, and there was something in the way she looked and spoke that told me that for the present she found renunciation its own reward. So far, my scepticism was put to shame; her spiritual ecstasy maintained itself. If I could have foreseen then that it would maintain itself till the present hour I should have felt that Lady Vandeleur's moral nature is finer indeed than mine. I heard from her that Mr. Tester remained at his father's, and that Lady Emily and her daughter were also there. The day for the wedding had been fixed, and the preparations were going rapidly forward. Meanwhile—she didn't tell me, but I gathered it from things she dropped—she was in almost daily correspondence with the young man. I thought this a strange concomitant of his bridal arrangements; but apparently, henceforth, they were bent on convincing each other that the torch of virtue lighted their steps, and they couldn't convince each other too much. She intimated to me that she had now effectually persuaded him (always by letter) that he would fail terribly if he should try to found his happiness on an injury done to another, and that of course she could never be happy (in a union with him) with the sight of his wretchedness before her. That a good deal of correspondence should be required to elucidate this is perhaps after all not remarkable. One day, when I was sitting with her (it was just before she left town), she suddenly burst into tears. Before we parted I said to her that there were several women in London I liked very much—that was common enough—but for her I had a positive respect, and that was rare. My respect continues still, and it sometimes makes me furious.

About the middle of January Ambrose Tester reappeared in town. He told me he came to bid me good-bye. He was going to be beheaded. It was no use saying that old relations would be the same after a man was married; they would be different, everything would be different. I had wanted him to marry, and now I should see how I liked it. He didn't mention that I had also wanted him not to marry, and I was sure that if Lady Vandeleur had become his wife she would have been a much greater impediment to our harmless friendship than Joscelind Bernardstone would ever be. It took me but a short time to observe that he was in very much the same condition as Lady Vandeleur. He was finding how sweet it is to renounce, hand in hand with one we love. Upon him, too, the

peace of the Lord had descended. He spoke of his father's
delight at the nuptials being so near at hand; at the festivities
that would take place in Dorsetshire when he should bring
home his bride. The only allusion he made to what we had
talked of the last time we were together was to exclaim suddenly, "How can I tell you how easy she has made it? She is
so sweet, so noble! She really is a perfect creature!" I took
for granted that he was talking of his future wife, but in a
moment, as we were at cross-purposes, perceived that he
meant Lady Vandeleur. This seemed to me really ominous—
it stuck in my mind after he had left me. I was half tempted
to write him a note, to say, "There is, after all, perhaps, something worse than your jilting Miss Bernardstone; and that is
the danger that your rupture with Lady Vandeleur may become more of a bond than your marrying her would have
been. For heaven's sake, let your sacrifice *be* a sacrifice; keep
it in its proper place!"

Of course I didn't write; even the slight responsibility I had
already incurred began to frighten me, and I never saw Mr.
Tester again till he was the husband of Joscelind Bernardstone. They have now been married some four years; they
have two children, the elder of whom is, as he should be, a
boy. Sir Edmund waited till his grandson had made good his
place in the world, and then, feeling it was safe, he quietly,
genially, surrendered his trust. He died, holding the hand of
his daughter-in-law, and giving it doubtless a pressure which
was an injunction to be brave. I don't know what he thought
of the success of his plan for his son; but perhaps, after all, he
saw nothing amiss, for Joscelind is the last woman in the
world to have troubled him with her sorrows. From him, no
doubt, she successfully concealed that bewilderment on which
I have touched. You see I speak of her sorrows as if they were
a matter of common recognition; certain it is that any one
who meets her must see that she doesn't pass her life in joy.
Lady Vandeleur, as you know, has never married again; she is
still the most beautiful widow in England. She enjoys the esteem of every one, as well as the approbation of her conscience, for every one knows the sacrifice she made, knows
that she was even more in love with Sir Ambrose than he was
with her. She goes out again, of course, as of old, and she

constantly meets the baronet and his wife. She is supposed to be even "very nice" to Lady Tester, and she certainly treats her with exceeding civility. But you know (or perhaps you don't know) all the deadly things that, in London, may lie beneath that method. I don't in the least mean that Lady Vandeleur has any deadly intentions; she is a very good woman, and I am sure that in her heart she thinks she lets poor Joscelind off very easily. But the result of the whole situation is that Joscelind is in dreadful fear of her, for how can she help seeing that she has a very peculiar power over her husband? There couldn't have been a better occasion for observing the three together (if together it may be called, when Lady Tester is so completely outside) than those two days of ours at Doubleton. That's a house where they have met more than once before; I think she and Sir Ambrose like it. By "she" I mean, as he used to mean, Lady Vandeleur. You saw how Lady Tester was absolutely white with uneasiness. What can she do when she meets everywhere the implication that if two people in our time have distinguished themselves for their virtue, it is her husband and Lady Vandeleur? It is my impression that this pair are exceedingly happy. His marriage *has* made a difference, and I see him much less frequently and less intimately. But when I meet him I notice in him a kind of emanation of quiet bliss. Yes, they are certainly in felicity, they have trod the clouds together, they have soared into the blue, and they wear in their faces the glory of those altitudes. They encourage, they cheer, inspire, sustain each other; remind each other that they have chosen the better part. Of course they have to meet for this purpose, and their interviews are filled, I am sure, with its sanctity. He holds up his head, as a man may who on a very critical occasion behaved like a perfect gentleman. It is only poor Joscelind that droops. Haven't I explained to you now why she doesn't understand?

Mrs. Temperly

'Why, Cousin Raymond, how can you suppose? Why, she's only sixteen!'

'She told me she was seventeen,' said the young man, as if it made a great difference.

'Well, only *just*!' Mrs. Temperly replied, in the tone of graceful, reasonable concession.

'Well, that's a very good age for me. I'm very young.'

'You are old enough to know better,' the lady remarked, in her soft, pleasant voice, which always drew the sting from a reproach, and enabled you to swallow it as you would a cooked plum, without the stone. 'Why, she hasn't finished her education!'

'That's just what I mean,' said her interlocutor. 'It would finish it beautifully for her to marry me.'

'Have you finished yours, my dear?' Mrs. Temperly inquired. 'The way you young people talk about marrying!' she exclaimed, looking at the itinerant functionary with the long wand who touched into a flame the tall gas-lamp on the other side of the Fifth Avenue. The pair were standing, in the recess of a window, in one of the big public rooms of an immense hotel, and the October day was turning to dusk.

'Well, would you have us leave it to the old?' Raymond asked. 'That's just what I think—she would be such a help to me,' he continued. 'I want to go back to Paris to study more. I have come home too soon. I don't know half enough; they know more here than I thought. So it would be perfectly easy, and we should all be together.'

'Well, my dear, when you do come back to Paris we will talk about it,' said Mrs. Temperly, turning away from the window.

'I should like it better, Cousin Maria, if you trusted me a little more,' Raymond sighed, observing that she was not really giving her thoughts to what he said. She irritated him somehow; she was so full of her impending departure, of her arrangements, her last duties and memoranda. She was not exactly important, any more than she was humble; she was too conciliatory for the one and too positive for the other. But she bustled quietly and gave one the sense of being 'up to' everything; the successive steps of her enterprise were in advance perfectly clear to her, and he could see that her imagination (conventional as she was she had plenty of that faculty) had already taken up its abode on one of those fine *premiers* which she had never seen, but which by instinct she seemed to know all about, in the very best part of the quarter of the Champs Elysées. If she ruffled him envy had perhaps something to do with it: she was to set sail on the morrow for the city of his affection and he was to stop in New York, where the fact that he was but half pleased did not alter the fact that he had his studio on his hands and that it was a bad one (though perhaps as good as any use he should put it to), which no one would be in a hurry to relieve him of.

It was easy for him to talk to Mrs. Temperly in that airy way about going back, but he couldn't go back unless the old gentleman gave him the means. He had already given him a great many things in the past, and with the others coming on (Marian's marriage-outfit, within three months, had cost literally thousands), Raymond had not at present the face to ask for more. He must sell some pictures first, and to sell them he must first paint them. It was his misfortune that he saw what he wanted to do so much better than he could do it. But he must really try and please himself—an effort that appeared more possible now that the idea of following Dora across the ocean had become an incentive. In spite of secret aspirations and even intentions, however, it was not encouraging to feel that he made really no impression at all on Cousin Maria. This certitude was so far from agreeable to him that he almost found it in him to drop the endearing title by which he had hitherto addressed her. It was only that, after all, her husband had been distantly related to his mother. It was not as a cousin that he was interested in Dora, but as something very much more intimate. I know not whether it occurred to him that Mrs. Temperly herself would never give his displeasure the benefit of dropping the affectionate form. She might shut her door to him altogether, but he would always be her kinsman and her dear. She was much addicted to these little embellishments of human intercourse—the friendly apostrophe and even the caressing hand—and there was something homely and cosy, a rustic, motherly *bonhomie*, in her use of them. She was as lavish of them as she was really careful in the selection of her friends.

She stood there with her hand in her pocket, as if she were feeling for something; her little plain, pleasant face was presented to him with a musing smile, and he vaguely wondered whether she were fumbling for a piece of money to buy him off from wishing to marry her daughter. Such an idea would be quite in keeping with the disguised levity with which she treated his state of mind. If her levity was wrapped up in the air of tender solicitude for everything that related to the feelings of her child, that only made her failure to appreciate his suit more deliberate. She struck him almost as impertinent (at the same time that he knew this was never her intention) as she looked up at him—her tiny proportions always made her throw back her head and set something dancing in her cap—and inquired whether he had noticed if she gave two keys, tied together by a blue ribbon, to Susan Winkle, when that faithful but flurried domestic met them in the lobby. She was thinking only of questions of luggage, and the fact that he wished to marry Dora was the smallest incident in their getting off.

'I think you ask me that only to change the subject,' he said. 'I don't believe that ever in your life you have been unconscious of what you have done with your keys.'

'Not often, but you make me nervous,' she answered, with her patient, honest smile.

'Oh, Cousin Maria!' the young man exclaimed, ambiguously, while Mrs. Temperly looked humanely at some totally uninteresting people who came straggling into the great hot, frescoed, velvety drawing-room, where it was as easy to see you were in an hotel as it was to see that, if you were, you were in one of the very best. Mrs. Temperly, since her husband's death, had passed much of her life at hotels, where she flattered herself that she preserved the tone of domestic life free from every taint and promoted the refined development of her children; but she selected them as well as she selected her friends. Somehow they became better from the very fact of her being there, and her children were smuggled in and out in the most extraordinary way; one never met them racing and whooping, as one did hundreds of others, in the lobbies. Her frequentation of hotels, where she paid enormous bills, was part of her expensive but practical way of living, and also of her theory that, from one week to another, she was going to Europe for a series of years as soon as she had wound up certain complicated affairs which had devolved upon her at her husband's death. If these affairs had dragged on it was owing to their inherent troublesomeness and implied no doubt of her capacity to bring them to a solution and to administer the very considerable fortune that Mr. Temperly had left. She used, in a superior, unprejudiced way, every convenience that the civilisation of her time offered her, and would have lived without hesitation in a lighthouse if this had contributed to her general scheme. She was now, in the interest of this scheme, preparing to use Europe, which she had not yet visited and with none of whose foreign tongues she was acquainted. This time she was certainly embarking.

She took no notice of the discredit which her young friend appeared to throw on the idea that she had nerves, and betrayed no suspicion that he believed her to have them in about the same degree as a sound, productive Alderney cow. She only moved toward one of the numerous doors of the room, as if to remind him of all she had still to do before night. They passed together into the long, wide corridor of the hotel—a vista of soft carpet, numbered doors, wandering women and perpetual gaslight—and approached the staircase by which she must ascend again to her domestic duties. She counted over, serenely, for his enlightenment, those that were still to be performed; but he could see that everything would be finished by nine o'clock—the time she had fixed in advance. The heavy luggage was then to go to the steamer; she herself was to be on board, with the children and the smaller things, at eleven o'clock the next morning. They had thirty pieces, but this was less than they had when they came from California five years before. She wouldn't have done that again. It was true that at that time she had had Mr. Temperly to help: he had died, Raymond remembered, six months after the settlement in New York. But, on the other hand, she knew more now. It was one of Mrs. Temperly's amiable qualities that she admitted herself so candidly to be still susceptible of development. She never professed to be in possession of all the knowledge requisite for her career; not only did she let her friends know that she was always learning, but she appealed to them to instruct her, in a manner which was in itself an example.

When Raymond said to her that he took for granted she would let him come down to the steamer for a last good-bye, she not only consented graciously but added that he was free to call again at the hotel in the evening, if he had nothing better to do. He must come between nine and ten, she expected several other friends—those who wished to see the last of them, yet didn't care to come to the ship. Then he would see all of them—she meant all of themselves, Dora and Effie and Tishy, and even Mademoiselle Bourde. She spoke exactly as if he had never approached her on the subject of Dora and as if Tishy, who was ten years of age, and Mademoiselle Bourde, who was the French governess and forty, were objects of no less an interest to him. He felt what a long pull he should have ever to get round her, and the sting of this knowledge was in his consciousness that Dora was really in her mother's hands. In Mrs. Temperly's composition there was not a hint of the bully; but none the less she held her children—she would hold them for ever. It was not simply by tenderness; but what it was by she knew best herself. Raymond appreciated the privilege of seeing Dora again that evening as well as on the morrow; yet he was so vexed with her mother that his vexation betrayed him into something that almost savoured of violence—a fact which I am ashamed to have to chronicle, as Mrs. Temperly's own urbanity deprived such breaches of every excuse. It may perhaps serve partly as an excuse for Raymond Bestwick that he was in love, or at least that he thought he was. Before she parted from him at the foot of the staircase he said to her, 'And of course, if things go as you like over there, Dora will marry some foreign prince.'

She gave no sign of resenting this speech, but she looked at him for the first time as if she were hesitating, as if it were not instantly clear to her what to say. It appeared to him, on his side, for a moment, that there was something strange in

her hesitation, that abruptly, by an inspiration, she was almost
making up her mind to reply that Dora's marriage to a prince
was, considering Dora's peculiarities (he knew that her mother
deemed her peculiar, and so did he, but that was precisely
why he wished to marry her), so little probable that, after all,
once such a union was out of the question, *he* might be no
worse than another plain man. These, however, were not the
words that fell from Mrs. Temperly's lips. Her embarrassment
vanished in her clear smile. 'Do you know what Mr. Temperly
used to say? He used to say that Dora was the pattern of an
old maid—she would never make a choice.'

'I hope—because that would have been too foolish—that
he didn't say she wouldn't have a chance.'

'Oh, a chance! what do you call by that fine name?' Cousin
Maria exclaimed, laughing, as she ascended the stair.

II

When he came back, after dinner, she was again in one of the
public rooms; she explained that a lot of the things for the
ship were spread out in her own parlours: there was no space
to sit down. Raymond was highly gratified by this fact; it offered an opportunity for strolling away a little with Dora, especially as, after he had been there ten minutes, other people
began to come in. They were entertained by the rest, by Effie
and Tishy, who was allowed to sit up a little, and by Mademoiselle Bourde, who besought every visitor to indicate her a
remedy that was *really* effective against the sea—some charm,
some philter, some potion or spell. 'Never mind, ma'm'selle,
I've got a remedy,' said Cousin Maria, with her cheerful decision, each time; but the French instructress always began
afresh.

As the young man was about to be parted for an indefinite
period from the girl whom he was ready to swear that he
adored, it is clear that he ought to have been equally ready to
swear that she was the fairest of her species. In point of fact,
however, it was no less vivid to him than it had been before
that he loved Dora Temperly for qualities which had nothing
to do with straightness of nose or pinkness of complexion.
Her figure was straight, and so was her character, but her nose

was not, and Philistines and other vulgar people would have committed themselves, without a blush on their own flat faces, to the assertion that she was decidedly plain. In his artistic imagination he had analogies for her, drawn from legend and literature; he was perfectly aware that she struck many persons as silent, shy and angular, while his own version of her peculiarities was that she was like a figure on the *predella* of an early Italian painting or a mediæval maiden wandering about a lonely castle, with her lover gone to the Crusades. To his sense, Dora had but one defect—her admiration for her mother was too undiscriminating. An ardent young man may well be slightly vexed when he finds that a young lady will probably never care for him so much as she cares for her parent; and Raymond Bestwick had this added ground for chagrin, that Dora had—if she chose to take it—so good a pretext for discriminating. For she had nothing whatever in common with the others; she was not of the same stuff as Mrs. Temperly and Effie and Tishy.

She was original and generous and uncalculating, besides being full of perception and taste in regard to the things *he* cared about. She knew nothing of conventional signs or estimates, but understood everything that might be said to her from an artistic point of view. She was formed to live in a studio, and not in a stiff drawing-room, amid upholstery horribly new; and moreover her eyes and her voice were both charming. It was only a pity she was so gentle; that is, he liked it for himself, but he deplored it for her mother. He considered that he had virtually given that lady his word that he would not make love to her; but his spirits had risen since his visit of three or four hours before. It seemed to him, after thinking things over more intently, that a way would be opened for him to return to Paris. It was not probable that in the interval Dora would be married off to a prince; for in the first place the foolish race of princes would be sure not to appreciate her, and in the second she would not, in this matter, simply do her mother's bidding—her gentleness would not go so far as that. She might remain single by the maternal decree, but she would not take a husband who was disagreeable to her. In this reasoning Raymond was obliged to shut his eyes very tight to the danger that some particular prince might not be disagreeable to her, as well as to the attraction proceeding from what her mother might announce that she would 'do.' He was perfectly aware that it was in Cousin Maria's power, and would probably be in her pleasure, to settle a handsome marriage-fee upon each of her daughters. He was equally certain that this had nothing to do with the nature of his own interest in the eldest, both because it was clear that Mrs. Temperly would do very little for *him*, and because he didn't care how little she did.

Effie and Tishy sat in the circle, on the edge of rather high chairs, while Mademoiselle Bourde surveyed in them with complacency the results of her own superiority. Tishy was a child, but Effie was fifteen, and they were both very nice little girls, arrayed in fresh travelling dresses and deriving a quaintness from the fact that Tishy was already armed, for foreign adventures, with a smart new reticule, from which she could not be induced to part, and that Effie had her finger in her 'place' in a fat red volume of *Murray*. Raymond knew that in a general way their mother would not have allowed them to appear in the drawing-room with these adjuncts, but something was to be allowed to the fever of anticipation. They were both pretty, with delicate features and blue eyes, and would grow up into worldly, conventional young ladies, just as Dora had not done. They looked at Mademoiselle Bourde for approval whenever they spoke, and, in addressing their mother alternately with that accomplished woman, kept their two languages neatly distinct.

Raymond had but a vague idea of who the people were who had come to bid Cousin Maria farewell, and he had no wish for a sharper one, though she introduced him, very definitely, to the whole group. She might make light of him in her secret soul, but she would never put herself in the wrong by omitting the smallest form. Fortunately, however, he was not obliged to like all her forms, and he foresaw the day when she would abandon this particular one. She was not so well made up in advance about Paris but that it would be in reserve for her to detest the period when she had thought it proper to 'introduce all round.' Raymond detested it already, and tried to make Dora understand that he wished her to take a walk with him in the corridors. There was a gentleman with a curl on his forehead who especially displeased him; he made child-ish jokes, at which the others laughed all at once, as if they had rehearsed for it—jokes *à la portée* of Effie and Tishy and mainly about them. These two joined in the merriment, as if they followed perfectly, as indeed they might, and gave a small sigh afterward, with a little factitious air. Dora remained grave, almost sad; it was when she was different, in this way, that he felt how much he liked her. He hated, in general, a large ring of people who had drawn up chairs in the public room of an hotel: some one was sure to undertake to be funny.

He succeeded at last in drawing Dora away; he endeavoured to give the movement a casual air. There was nothing peculiar, after all, in their walking a little in the passage; a dozen other persons were doing the same. The girl had the air of not sus-pecting in the least that he could have anything particular to say to her—of responding to his appeal simply out of her gen-eral gentleness. It was not in her companion's interest that her mind should be such a blank; nevertheless his conviction that in spite of the ministrations of Mademoiselle Bourde she was not falsely ingenuous made him repeat to himself that he would still make her his own. They took several turns in the hall, during which it might still have appeared to Dora Tem-perly that her cousin Raymond had nothing particular to say to her. He remarked several times that he should certainly turn up in Paris in the spring; but when once she had replied that she was very glad that subject seemed exhausted. The young man cared little, however; it was not a question now of mak-ing any declaration: he only wanted to be with her. Suddenly, when they were at the end of the corridor furthest removed from the room they had left, he said to her: 'Your mother is very strange. Why has she got such an idea about Paris?'

'How do you mean, such an idea?' He had stopped, making the girl stand there before him.

'Well, she thinks so much of it without having ever seen it, or really knowing anything. She appears to have planned out such a great life there.'

'She thinks it's the best place,' Dora rejoined, with the dim smile that always charmed our young man.

'The best place for what?'

'Well, to learn French.' The girl continued to smile.

'Do you mean for her? She'll never learn it; she can't.'

'No; for us. And other things.'

'You know it already. And *you* know other things,' said Raymond.

'She wants us to know them better—better than any girls know them.'

'I don't know what things you mean,' exclaimed the young man, rather impatiently,

'Well, we shall see,' Dora returned, laughing.

He said nothing for a minute, at the end of which he resumed: 'I hope you won't be offended if I say that it seems curious your mother should have such aspirations—such Napoleonic plans. I mean being just a quiet little lady from California, who has never seen any of the kind of thing that she has in her head.'

'That's just why she wants to see it, I suppose; and I don't know why her being from California should prevent. At any rate she wants us to have the best. Isn't the best taste in Paris?'

'Yes; and the worst.' It made him gloomy when she defended the old lady, and to change the subject he asked: 'Aren't you sorry, this last night, to leave your own country for such an indefinite time?'

It didn't cheer him up that the girl should answer: 'Oh, I would go anywhere with mother!'

'And with *her*?' Raymond demanded, sarcastically, as Mademoiselle Bourde came in sight, emerging from the drawing-room. She approached them; they met her in a moment, and she informed Dora that Mrs. Temperly wished her to come back and play a part of that composition of Saint-Saens—the last one she had been learning—for Mr. and Mrs. Parminter: they wanted to judge whether their daughter could manage it.

'I don't believe she can,' said Dora, smiling; but she was moving away to comply when her companion detained her a moment.

'Are you going to bid me good-bye?'

'Won't you come back to the drawing-room?'

'I think not; I don't like it.'

'And to mamma—you'll say nothing?' the girl went on.

'Oh, we have made our farewell; we had a special interview this afternoon.'

'And you won't come to the ship in the morning?'

Raymond hesitated a moment. 'Will Mr. and Mrs. Parminter be there?'

'Oh, surely they will!' Mademoiselle Bourde declared, surveying the young couple with a certain tactful serenity, but standing very close to them, as if it might be her duty to interpose.

'Well then, I won't come.'

'Well, good-bye then,' said the girl gently, holding out her hand.

'Good-bye, Dora.' He took it, while she smiled at him, but he said nothing more—he was so annoyed at the way Mademoiselle Bourde watched them. He only looked at Dora; she seemed to him beautiful.

'My dear child—that poor Madame Parminter,' the governess murmured.

'I shall come over very soon,' said Raymond, as his companion turned away.

'That will be charming.' And she left him quickly, without looking back.

Mademoiselle Bourde lingered—he didn't know why, unless it was to make him feel, with her smooth, finished French assurance, which had the manner of extreme benignity, that she was following him up. He sometimes wondered whether she copied Mrs. Temperly or whether Mrs. Temperly tried to copy her. Presently she said, slowly rubbing her hands and smiling at him:

'You will have plenty of time. We shall be long in Paris.'

'Perhaps you will be disappointed,' Raymond suggested.

'How can we be—unless *you* disappoint us?' asked the governess, sweetly.

He left her without ceremony: the imitation was probably on the part of Cousin Maria.

III

'Only just ourselves,' her note had said; and he arrived, in his natural impatience, a few moments before the hour. He remembered his Cousin Maria's habitual punctuality, but when he entered the splendid *salon* in the quarter of the Parc Monceau—it was there that he had found her established—he saw that he should have it, for a little, to himself. This was pleasing, for he should be able to look round—there were admirable things to look at. Even to-day Raymond Bestwick was not sure that he had learned to paint, but he had no doubt of his judgment of the work of others, and a single glance showed him that Mrs. Temperly had 'known enough' to select, for the adornment of her walls, half a dozen immensely valuable specimens of contemporary French art. Her choice of other objects had been equally enlightened, and he remembered what Dora had said to him five years before—that her mother wished them to have the best. Evidently, now they had got it; if five years was a long time for him to have delayed (with his original plan of getting off so soon) to come to Paris, it was a very short one for Cousin Maria to have taken to arrive at the highest good.

Rather to his surprise the first person to come in was Effie, now so complete a young lady, and such a very pretty girl, that he scarcely would have known her. She was fair, she was graceful, she was lovely, and as she entered the room, blushing and smiling, with a little floating motion which suggested that she was in a liquid element, she brushed down the ribbons of a delicate Parisian *toilette de jeune fille*. She appeared to expect that he would be surprised, and as if to justify herself for being the first she said, 'Mamma told me to come; she knows you are here; she said I was not to wait.' More than once, while they conversed, during the next few moments, before any one else arrived, she repeated that she was acting by her mamma's directions. Raymond perceived that she had not only the costume but several other of the attributes of a *jeune fille*. They talked, I say, but with a certain difficulty, for Effie asked him no questions, and this made him feel a little stiff about thrusting information upon her. Then she was so pretty, so exquisite, that this by itself disconcerted him. It seemed to him almost that she had falsified a prophecy, instead of bringing one to pass. He had foretold that she would be like this; the only difference was that she was so much more like it. She made no inquiries about his arrival, his people in America, his plans; and they exchanged vague remarks about the pictures, quite as if they had met for the first time.

When Cousin Maria came in Effie was standing in front of the fire fastening a bracelet, and he was at a distance gazing in silence at a portrait of his hostess by Bastien-Lepage. One of his apprehensions had been that Cousin Maria would allude ironically to the difference there had been between his threat (because it had been really almost a threat) of following them speedily to Paris and what had in fact occurred; but he saw in a moment how superficial this calculation had been. Besides, when had Cousin Maria ever been ironical? She treated him as if she had seen him last week (which did not preclude kindness), and only expressed her regret at having missed his visit the day before, in consequence of which she had immediately written to him to come and dine. He might have come from round the corner, instead of from New York and across the wintry ocean. This was a part of her 'cosiness,' her friendly, motherly optimism, of which, even of old, the habit had been never to recognise nor allude to disagreeable things; so that to-day, in the midst of so much that was not disagreeable, the custom would of course be immensely confirmed.

Raymond was perfectly aware that it was not a pleasure, even for her, that, for several years past, things should have gone so ill in New York with his family and himself. His father's embarrassments, of which Marian's silly husband had been the cause and which had terminated in general ruin and humiliation, to say nothing of the old man's 'stroke' and the necessity, arising from it, for a renunciation on his own part of all present thoughts of leaving home again and even for a partial relinquishment of present work, the old man requiring so much of his personal attention—all this constituted an episode which could not fail to look sordid and dreary in the light of Mrs. Temperly's high success. The odour of success was in the warm, slightly heavy air, which seemed distilled from rare old fabrics, from brocades and tapestries, from the deep, mingled tones of the pictures, the subdued radiance of cabinets and old porcelain and the jars of winter roses standing in soft circles of lamp-light. Raymond felt himself in the presence of an effect in regard to which he remained in ignorance of the cause—a mystery that required a key. Cousin Maria's success was unexplained so long as she simply stood there with her little familiar, comforting, upward gaze, talking in coaxing cadences, with exactly the same manner she had brought ten years ago from California, to a tall, bald, bending, smiling young man, evidently a foreigner, who had just come in and whose name Raymond had not caught from the lips of the *maître d'hôtel*. Was he just one of themselves—was he there for Effie, or perhaps even for Dora? The unexplained must preponderate till Dora came in; he found he counted upon her, even though in her letters (it was true that for the last couple of years they had come but at long intervals) she had told him so little about their life. She never spoke of people; she talked of the books she read, of the music she had heard or was studying (a whole page sometimes about the last concert at the Conservatoire), the new pictures and the manner of the different artists.

When she entered the room three or four minutes after the arrival of the young foreigner, with whom her mother conversed in just the accents Raymond had last heard at the hotel in the Fifth Avenue (he was obliged to admit that she gave herself no airs; it was clear that her success had not gone in the least to her head); when Dora at last appeared she was accompanied by Mademoiselle Bourde. The presence of this lady—he didn't know she was still in the house—Raymond took as a sign that they were really dining *en famille*, so that the young man was either an actual or a prospective intimate. Dora shook hands first with her cousin, but he watched the manner of her greeting with the other visitor and saw that it indicated extreme friendliness—on the part of the latter. If there was a charming flush in her cheek as he took her hand, that was the remainder of the colour that had risen there as she came toward Raymond. It will be seen that our young man still had an eye for the element of fascination, as he used to regard it, in this quiet, dimly-shining maiden.

He saw that Effie was the only one who had changed (Tishy remained yet to be judged), except that Dora really looked older, quite as much older as the number of years had given her a right to: there was as little difference in her as there was in her mother. Not that she was like her mother, but she was perfectly like herself. Her meeting with Raymond was bright, but very still; their phrases were awkward and commonplace, and the thing was mainly a contact of looks—conscious, embarrassed, indirect, but brightening every moment with old familiarities. Her mother appeared to pay no attention, and neither, to do her justice, did Mademoiselle Bourde, who, after an exchange of expressive salutations with Raymond began to scrutinise Effie with little admiring gestures and smiles. She surveyed her from head to foot; she pulled a ribbon straight; she was evidently a flattering governess. Cousin Maria explained to Cousin Raymond that they were waiting for one more friend—a very dear lady. 'But she lives near, and when people live near they are always late—haven't you noticed that?'

'Your hotel is far away, I know, and yet you were the first,' Dora said, smiling to Raymond.

'Oh, even if it were round the corner I should be the first—to come to *you*!' the young man answered, speaking loud and clear, so that his words might serve as a notification to Cousin Maria that his sentiments were unchanged.

'You are more French than the French,' Dora returned.

'You say that as if you didn't like them: I hope you don't,' said Raymond, still with intentions in regard to his hostess.

'We like them more and more, the more we see of them,' this lady interposed; but gently, impersonally, and with an air of not wishing to put Raymond in the wrong.

'*Mais j'espère bien!*' cried Mademoiselle Bourde, holding up her head and opening her eyes very wide. 'Such friendships as we form, and, I may say, as we inspire! *Je m'en rapporte à Effie,*' the governess continued.

'We have received immense kindness; we have established relations that are so pleasant for us, Cousin Raymond. We have the *entrée* of so many charming homes,' Mrs. Temperly remarked.

'But ours is the most charming of all; that I will say,' exclaimed Mademoiselle Bourde. 'Isn't it so, Effie?'

'Oh yes, I think it is; especially when we are expecting the Marquise,' Effie responded. Then she added, 'But here she comes now; I hear her carriage in the court.'

The Marquise too was just one of themselves; she was a part of their charming home.

'She *is* such a love!' said Mrs. Temperly to the foreign gentleman, with an irrepressible movement of benevolence.

To which Raymond heard the gentleman reply that, Ah, she was the most distinguished woman in France.

'Do you know Madame de Brives?' Effie asked of Raymond, while they were waiting for her to come in.

She came in at that moment, and the girl turned away quickly without an answer.

'How in the world should I know her?' That was the answer he would have been tempted to give. He felt very much out of Cousin Maria's circle. The foreign gentleman fingered his moustache and looked at him sidewise. The Marquise was a very pretty woman, fair and slender, of middle age, with a smile, a complexion, a diamond necklace, of great splendour, and a charming manner. Her greeting to her friends was sweet and familiar, and was accompanied with much kissing, of a sisterly, motherly, daughterly kind; and yet with this expression of simple, almost homely sentiment there was something in her that astonished and dazzled. She might very well have been, as the foreign young man said, the most distinguished woman in France. Dora had not rushed forward to meet her with nearly so much *empressement* as Effie, and this gave him a chance to ask the former who she was. The girl replied that she was her mother's most intimate friend: to which he rejoined that that was not a description; what he wanted to know was her title to this exalted position.

'Why, can't you see it? She is beautiful and she is good.'

'I see that she is beautiful; but how can I see that she is good?'

'Good to mamma, I mean, and to Effie and Tishy.'

'And isn't she good to you?'

'Oh, I don't know her so well. But I delight to look at her.'

'Certainly, that must be a great pleasure,' said Raymond. He enjoyed it during dinner, which was now served, though his enjoyment was diminished by his not finding himself next to Dora. They sat at a small round table and he had at his right his Cousin Maria, whom he had taken in. On his left was Madame de Brives, who had the foreign gentleman for a neighbour. Then came Effie and Mademoiselle Bourde, and Dora was on the other side of her mother. Raymond regarded this as marked—a symbol of the fact that Cousin Maria would continue to separate them. He remained in ignorance of the other gentleman's identity, and remembered how he had prophesied at the hotel in New York that his hostess would give up introducing people. It was a friendly, easy little family repast, as she had said it would be, with just a marquise and a secretary of embassy—Raymond ended by guessing that the stranger was a secretary of embassy—thrown in. So far from interfering with the family tone Madame de Brives directly contributed to it. She eminently justified the affection in which she was held in the house; she was in the highest degree sociable and sympathetic, and at the same time witty (there was no insipidity in Madame de Brives), and was the cause of Raymond's making the reflection—as he had made it often in his earlier years—that an agreeable Frenchwoman is a triumph of civilisation. This did not prevent him from giving the Marquise no more than half of his attention; the rest was dedicated to Dora, who, on her side, though in common with Effie and Mademoiselle Bourde she bent a frequent, interested gaze on the splendid French lady, very often met our young man's eyes with mute, vague but, to his sense, none the less valuable intimations. It was as if she knew what was going on in his mind (it is true that he scarcely knew it himself), and might be trusted to clear things up at some convenient hour.

Madame de Brives talked across Raymond, in excellent English, to Cousin Maria, but this did not prevent her from being gracious, even encouraging, to the young man, who was a little afraid of her and thought her a delightful creature. She asked him more questions about himself than any of them had done. Her conversation with Mrs. Temperly was of an intimate, domestic order, and full of social, personal allusions, which Raymond was unable to follow. It appeared to be concerned considerably with the private affairs of the old French *noblesse*, into whose councils—to judge by the tone of the Marquise—Cousin Maria had been admitted by acclamation. Every now and then Madame de Brives broke into French, and it was in this tongue that she uttered an apostrophe to her hostess: 'Oh, you, *ma toute-bonne*, you who have the genius of good sense!' And she appealed to Raymond to know if his Cousin Maria had not the genius of good sense—the wisdom of the ages. The old lady did not defend herself from the compliment; she let it pass, with her motherly, tolerant smile; nor did Raymond attempt to defend her, for he felt the justice of his neighbour's description: Cousin Maria's good sense was incontestable, magnificent. She took an affectionate, indulgent view of most of the persons mentioned, and yet her tone was far from being vapid or vague. Madame de Brives usually remarked that they were coming very soon again to see her, she did them so much good. 'The freshness of your judgment—the freshness of your judgment!' she repeated, with a kind of glee, and she narrated that Eléonore (a personage unknown to Raymond) had said that she was a woman of Plutarch. Mrs. Temperly talked a great deal about the health of their friends; she seemed to keep the record of the influenzas and neuralgias of a numerous and susceptible circle. He did not find it in him quite to agree—the Marquise dropping the statement into his ear at a moment when their hostess was making some inquiry of Mademoiselle Bourde—that she was a nature absolutely marvellous; but he could easily see that to world-worn Parisians her quiet charities of speech and manner, with something quaint and rustic in their form, might be restorative and salutary. She allowed for everything, yet she was so good, and indeed Madame de Brives summed this up before they left the table in saying to her, 'Oh, you, my dear, your success, more than any other that has ever taken place, has been a *succès de bonté*.' Raymond was greatly amused at this idea of Cousin Maria's *succès de bonté*: it seemed to him delightfully Parisian.

Before dinner was over she inquired of him how he had got on 'in his profession' since they last met, and he was too proud, or so he thought, to tell her anything but the simple truth, that he had not got on very well. If he was to ask her again for Dora it would be just as he was, an honourable but not particularly successful man, making no show of lures and bribes. 'I am not a remarkably good painter,' he said. 'I judge myself perfectly. And then I have been handicapped at home. I have had a great many serious bothers and worries.'

'Ah, we were so sorry to hear about your dear father.'

The tone of these words was kind and sincere; still Raymond thought that in this case her *bonté* might have gone a little further. At any rate this was the only allusion that she made to his bothers and worries. Indeed, she always passed over such things lightly; she was an optimist for others as well as for herself, which doubtless had a great deal to do (Raymond indulged in the reflection) with the headway she made in a society tired of its own pessimism.

After dinner, when they went into the drawing-room, the young man noted with complacency that this apartment, vast in itself, communicated with two or three others into which it would be easy to pass without attracting attention, the doors being replaced by old tapestries, looped up and offering no barrier. With pictures and curiosities all over the place, there were plenty of pretexts for wandering away. He lost no time in asking Dora whether her mother would send Mademoiselle Bourde after them if she were to go with him into one of the other rooms, the same way she had done—didn't she remember?—that last night in New York, at the hotel. Dora didn't admit that she remembered (she was too loyal to her mother for that, and Raymond foresaw that this loyalty would be a source of irritation to him again, as it had been in the past), but he perceived, all the same, that she had not forgotten. She raised no difficulty, and a few moments later, while they stood in an adjacent *salon* (he had stopped to admire a bust of Effie, wonderfully living, slim and juvenile, the work of one of the sculptors who are the pride of contemporary French art), he said to her, looking about him, 'How has she done it so fast?'

'Done what, Raymond?'

'Why, done everything. Collected all these wonderful things; become intimate with Madame de Brives and every one else; organised her life—the life of all of you—so brilliantly.'

'I have never seen mamma in a hurry,' Dora replied.

'Perhaps she will be, now that I have come,' Raymond suggested, laughing.

The girl hesitated a moment 'Yes, she was, to invite you— the moment she knew you were here.'

'She has been most kind, and I talk like a brute. But I am liable to do worse—I give you notice. She won't like it any more than she did before, if she thinks I want to make up to you.'

'Don't, Raymond—don't!' the girl exclaimed, gently, but with a look of sudden pain.

'Don't what, Dora?—don't make up to you?'

'Don't begin to talk of those things. There is no need. We can go on being friends.'

'I will do exactly as you prescribe, and heaven forbid I should annoy you. But would you mind answering me a question? It is very particular, very intimate.' He stopped, and she only looked at him, saying nothing. So he went on: 'Is it an idea of your mother's that you should marry—some person here?' He gave her a chance to reply, but still she was silent, and he continued: 'Do you mind telling me this? Could it ever be an idea of your own?'

'Do you mean some Frenchman?'

Raymond smiled. 'Some protégé of Madame de Brives.'

Then the girl simply gave a slow, sad head-shake which struck him as the sweetest, proudest, most suggestive thing in the world. 'Well, well, that's all right,' he remarked, cheerfully, and looked again a while at the bust, which he thought extraordinarily clever. 'And haven't *you* been done by one of these great fellows?'

'Oh dear no; only mamma and Effie. But Tishy is going to be, in a month or two. The next time you come you must see her. She remembers you vividly.'

'And I remember her that last night, with her reticule. Is she always pretty?'

Dora hesitated a moment. 'She is a very sweet little creature, but she is not so pretty as Effie.'

'And have none of them wished to do you—none of the painters?'

'Oh, it's not a question of me. I only wish them to let me alone.'

'For me it would be a question of you, if you would sit for me. But I daresay your mother wouldn't allow that.'

'No, I think not,' said Dora, smiling.

She smiled, but her companion looked grave. However, not to pursue the subject, he asked, abruptly, 'Who is this Madame de Brives?'

'If you lived in Paris you would know. She is very celebrated.'

'Celebrated for what?'

'For everything.'

'And is she good—is she genuine?' Raymond asked. Then, seeing something in the girl's face, he added: 'I told you I should be brutal again. Has she undertaken to make a great marriage for Effie?'

'I don't know what she has undertaken,' said Dora, impatiently.

'And then for Tishy, when Effie has been disposed of?'

'Poor little Tishy!' the girl continued, rather inscrutably.

'And can she do nothing for you?' the young man inquired.

Her answer surprised him—after a moment. 'She has kindly offered to exert herself, but it's no use.'

'Well, that's good. And who is it the young man comes for—the secretary of embassy?'

'Oh, he comes for all of us,' said Dora, laughing.

'I suppose your mother would prefer a preference,' Raymond suggested.

To this she replied, irrelevantly, that she thought they had better go back; but as Raymond took no notice of the recommendation she mentioned that the secretary was no one in particular. At this moment Effie, looking very rosy and happy, pushed through the *portière* with the news that her sister must come and bid good-bye to the Marquise. She was taking her to the Duchess's—didn't Dora remember? To the *bal blanc*—the *sauterie de jeunes filles*.

'I thought we should be called,' said Raymond, as he followed Effie; and he remarked that perhaps Madame de Brives would find something suitable at the Duchess's.

'I don't know. Mamma would be very particular,' the girl rejoined; and this was said simply, sympathetically, without the least appearance of deflection from that loyalty which Raymond deplored.

IV

'You must come to us on the 17th; we expect to have a few people and some good music,' Cousin Maria said to him before he quitted the house; and he wondered whether, the 17th being still ten days off, this might not be an intimation that

they could abstain from his society until then. He chose, at
any rate, not to take it as such, and called several times in the
interval, late in the afternoon, when the ladies would be sure
to have come in.

They were always there, and Cousin Maria's welcome was,
for each occasion, maternal, though when he took leave she
made no allusion to future meetings—to his coming again;
but there were always other visitors as well, collected at tea
round the great fire of logs, in the friendly, brilliant drawing-room where the luxurious was no enemy to the casual and
Mrs. Temperly's manner of dispensing hospitality recalled to
our young man somehow certain memories of his youthful
time: visits in New England, at old homesteads flanked with
elms, where a talkative, democratic, delightful farmer's wife
pressed upon her company rustic viands in which she herself
had had a hand. Cousin Maria enjoyed the services of a distinguished *chef*, and delicious *petits fours* were served with her
tea; but Raymond had a sense that to complete the impression
hot home-made gingerbread should have been produced.

The atmosphere was suffused with the presence of Madame
de Brives. She was either there or she was just coming or she
was just gone; her name, her voice, her example and encouragement were in the air. Other ladies came and went—sometimes accompanied by gentlemen who looked worn out, had
waxed moustaches and knew how to talk—and they were
sometimes designated in the same manner as Madame de
Brives; but she remained the Marquise *par excellence*, the in-
carnation of brilliancy and renown. The conversation moved
among simple but civilised topics, was not dull and, considering that it consisted largely of personalities, was not ill-natured. Least of all was it scandalous, for the girls were always
there, Cousin Maria not having thought it in the least necessary, in order to put herself in accord with French traditions,
to relegate her daughters to the middle distance. They occupied a considerable part of the foreground, in the prettiest,
most modest, most becoming attitudes.

It was Cousin Maria's theory of her own behaviour that she
did in Paris simply as she had always done; and though this
would not have been a complete account of the matter
Raymond could not fail to notice the good sense and good

taste with which she laid down her lines and the quiet *bon-homie* of the authority with which she caused the tone of the American home to be respected. Scandal stayed outside, not simply because Effie and Tishy were there, but because, even if Cousin Maria had received alone, she never would have received evil-speakers. Indeed, for Raymond, who had been accustomed to think that in a general way he knew pretty well what the French capital was, this was a strange, fresh Paris altogether, destitute of the salt that seasoned it for most palates, and yet not insipid nor innutritive. He marvelled at Cousin Maria's air, in such a city, of knowing, of recognising nothing bad: all the more that it represented an actual state of mind. He used to wonder sometimes what she would do and how she would feel if some day, in consequence of researches made by the Marquise in the *grand monde*, she should find herself in possession of a son-in-law formed according to one of the types of which *he* had impressions. However, it was not credible that Madame de Brives would play her a trick. There were moments when Raymond almost wished she might—to see how Cousin Maria would handle the gentleman.

Dora was almost always taken up by visitors, and he had scarcely any direct conversation with her. She was there, and he was glad she was there, and she knew he was glad (he knew that), but this was almost all the communion he had with her. She was mild, exquisitely mild—this was the term he mentally applied to her now—and it amply sufficed him, with the conviction he had that she was not stupid. She attended to the tea (for Mademoiselle Bourde was not always free), she handed the *petits fours*, she rang the bell when people went out; and it was in connection with these offices that the idea came to him once—he was rather ashamed of it afterward—that she was the Cinderella of the house, the domestic drudge, the one for whom there was no career, as it was useless for the Marquise to take up her case. He was ashamed of this fancy, I say, and yet it came back to him; he was even surprised that it had not occurred to him before. Her sisters were neither ugly nor proud (Tishy, indeed, was almost touchingly delicate and timid, with exceedingly pretty points, yet with a little appealing, old-womanish look, as if, small—very small

—as she was, she was afraid she shouldn't grow any more);
but her mother, like the mother in the fairy-tale, was a *femme
forte*. Madame de Brives could do nothing for Dora, not absolutely because she was too plain, but because she would
never lend herself, and that came to the same thing. Her
mother accepted her as recalcitrant, but Cousin Maria's attitude, at the best, could only be resignation. She would respect
her child's preferences, she would never put on the screw; but
this would not make her love the child any more. So Raymond
interpreted certain signs, which at the same time he felt to
be very slight, while the conversation in Mrs. Temperly's
salon (this was its preponderant tendency) rambled among
questions of bric-à-brac, of where Tishy's portrait should be
placed when it was finished, and the current prices of old
Gobelins. *Ces dames* were not in the least above the discussion
of prices.

On the 17th it was easy to see that more lamps than usual
had been lighted. They streamed through all the windows of
the charming hotel and mingled with the radiance of the car-
riage-lanterns, which followed each other slowly, in couples,
in a close, long rank, into the fine sonorous court, where the
high stepping of valuable horses was sharp on the stones, and
up to the ruddy portico. The night was wet, not with a down-
pour, but with showers interspaced by starry patches, which
only added to the glitter of the handsome, clean Parisian surfaces. The *sergents de ville* were about the place, and seemed
to make the occasion important and official. These night aspects of Paris in the *beaux quartiers* had always for Raymond
a particularly festive association, and as he passed from his cab
under the wide permanent tin canopy, painted in stripes like
an awning, which protected the low steps, it seemed to him
odder than ever that all this established prosperity should be
Cousin Maria's.

If the thought of how well she did it bore him company
from the threshold, it deepened to admiration by the time he
had been half an hour in the place. She stood near the entrance with her two elder daughters, distributing the most
familiar, most encouraging smiles, together with hand-shakes
which were in themselves a whole system of hospitality. If her
party was grand Cousin Maria was not; she indulged in no

assumption of stateliness and no attempt at graduated wel-
comes. It seemed to Raymond that it was only because it
would have taken too much time that she didn't kiss every
one. Effie looked lovely and just a little frightened, which was
exactly what she ought to have done; and he noticed that
among the arriving guests those who were not intimate
(which he could not tell from Mrs. Temperly's manner, but
could from their own) recognised her as a daughter much
more quickly than they recognised Dora, who hung back disinterestedly, as if not to challenge their discernment, while the
current passed her, keeping her little sister in position on its
brink meanwhile by the tenderest small gesture.

'May I talk with you a little, later?' he asked of Dora, with
only a few seconds for the question, as people were pressing
behind him. She answered evasively that there would be very
little talk—they would all have to listen—it was very serious;
and the next moment he had received a programme from the
hand of a monumental yet gracious personage who stood beyond and who had a silver chain round his neck.

The place was arranged for music, and how well arranged
he saw later, when every one was seated, spaciously, luxu-
riously, without pushing or over-peeping, and the finest talents in Paris performed selections at which the best taste had
presided. The singers and players were all stars of the first
magnitude. Raymond was fond of music and he wondered
whose taste it had been. He made up his mind it was
Dora's—it was only she who could have conceived a combination so exquisite; and he said to himself: 'How they all pull
together! She is not in it, she is not of it, and yet she too works
for the common end.' And by 'all' he meant also Mademoiselle
Bourde and the Marquise. This impression made him feel
rather hopeless, as if, *en fin de compte*, Cousin Maria were too
large an adversary. Great as was the pleasure of being present on
an occasion so admirably organised, of sitting there in a beautiful room, in a still, attentive, brilliant company, with all the
questions of temperature, space, light and decoration solved to
the gratification of every sense, and listening to the best artists
doing their best—happily constituted as our young man was
to enjoy such a privilege as this, the total effect was depressing: it made him feel as if the gods were not on his side.

'And does she do it so well without a man? There must be so many details a woman can't tackle,' he said to himself; for even counting in the Marquise and Mademoiselle Bourde this only made a multiplication of petticoats. Then it came over him that she *was* a man as well as a woman—the masculine element was included in her nature. He was sure that she bought her horses without being cheated, and very few men could do that. She had the American national quality—she had 'faculty' in a supreme degree. 'Faculty—faculty,' the voices of the quartette of singers seemed to repeat, in the quick movement of a composition they rendered beautifully, while they swelled and went faster, till the thing became a joyous chant of praise, a glorification of Cousin Maria's practical genius.

During the intermission, in the middle of the concert, people changed places more or less and circulated, so that, walking about at this time, he came upon the Marquise, who, in her sympathetic, demonstrative way, appeared to be on the point of clasping her hostess in her arms. 'Décidément, ma bonne, il n'y a que vous! C'est une perfection——' he heard her say. To which, gratified but unelated, Cousin Maria replied, according to her simple, sociable wont: 'Well, it *does* seem quite a successful occasion. If it will only keep on to the end!'

Raymond, wandering far, found himself in a world that was mainly quite new to him, and explained his ignorance of it by reflecting that the people were probably celebrated: so many of them had decorations and stars and a quiet of manner that could only be accounted for by renown. There were plenty of Americans with no badge but a certain fine negativeness, and *they* were quiet for a reason which by this time had become very familiar to Raymond: he had heard it so often mentioned that his country-people were supremely 'adaptable.' He tried to get hold of Dora, but he saw that her mother had arranged things beautifully to keep her occupied with other people; so at least he interpreted the fact—after all very natural—that she had half a dozen fluttered young girls on her mind, whom she was providing with programmes, seats, ices, occasional murmured remarks and general support and protection. When the concert was over she supplied them with further entertainment in the form of several young men who had pliable backs and flashing breastpins and whom she inarticulately introduced to them, which gave her still more to do, as after this serious step she had to stay and watch all parties. It was strange to Raymond to see her transformed by her mother into a precocious duenna. Him she introduced to no young girl, and he knew not whether to regard this as cold neglect or as high consideration. If he had liked he might have taken it as a sweet intimation that she knew he couldn't care for any girl but her.

On the whole he was glad, because it left him free—free to get hold of her mother, which by this time he had boldly determined to do. The conception was high, inasmuch as Cousin Maria's attention was obviously required by the ambassadors and other grandees who had flocked to do her homage. Nevertheless, while supper was going on (he wanted none, and neither apparently did she), he collared her, as he phrased it to himself, in just the right place—on the threshold of the conservatory. She was flanked on either side with a foreigner of distinction, but he didn't care for her foreigners now. Besides, a conservatory was meant only for couples; it was a sign of her comprehensive sociability that she should have been rambling among the palms and orchids with a double escort. Her friends would wish to quit her but would not wish to appear to give way to each other; and Raymond felt that he was relieving them both (though he didn't care) when he asked her to be so good as to give him a few minutes' conversation. He made her go back with him into the conservatory: it was the only thing he had ever made her do, or probably ever would. She began to talk about the great Gregorini—how it had been too sweet of her to repeat one of her songs, when it had really been understood in advance that repetitions were not expected. Raymond had no interest at present in the great Gregorini. He asked Cousin Maria vehemently if she remembered telling him in New York—that night at the hotel, five years before—that when he should have followed them to Paris he would be free to address her on the subject of Dora. She had given him a promise that she would listen to him in this case, and now he must keep her up to the mark. It was impossible to see her alone, but, at whatever inconvenience to herself, he must insist on her giving him his opportunity.

'About Dora, Cousin Raymond?' she asked, blandly and kindly—almost as if she didn't exactly know who Dora was.

'Surely you haven't forgotten what passed between us the evening before you left America. I was in love with her then and I have been in love with her ever since. I told you so then, and you stopped me off, but you gave me leave to make another appeal to you in the future. I make it now—this is the only way I have—and I think you ought to listen to it. Five years have passed, and I love her more than ever. I have behaved like a saint in the interval: I haven't attempted to practise upon her without your knowledge.'

'I am so glad; but she would have let me know,' said Cousin Maria, looking round the conservatory as if to see if the plants were all there.

'No doubt. I don't know what you do to her. But I trust that to-day your opposition falls—in face of the proof that we have given you of mutual fidelity.'

'Fidelity?' Cousin Maria repeated, smiling.

'Surely—unless you mean to imply that Dora has given me up. I have reason to believe that she hasn't.'

'I think she will like better to remain just as she is.'

'Just as she is?'

'I mean, not to make a choice,' Cousin Maria went on, smiling.

Raymond hesitated a moment. 'Do you mean that you have tried to make her make one?'

At this the good lady broke into a laugh. 'My dear Raymond, how little you must think I know my child!'

'Perhaps, if you haven't tried to make her, you have tried to prevent her. Haven't you told her I am unsuccessful, I am poor?'

She stopped him, laying her hand with unaffected solicitude on his arm. '*Are* you poor, my dear? I should be so sorry!'

'Never mind; I can support a wife,' said the young man.

'It wouldn't matter, because I am happy to say that Dora has something of her own,' Cousin Maria went on, with her imperturbable candour. 'Her father thought that was the best way to arrange it. I had quite forgotten my opposition, as you call it; that was so long ago. Why, she was only a little girl. Wasn't that the ground I took? Well, dear, she's older now, and you can say anything to her you like. But I do think she wants to stay——' And she looked up at him, cheerily.

'Wants to stay?'

'With Effie and Tishy.'

'Ah, Cousin Maria,' the young man exclaimed, 'you are modest about yourself!'

'Well, we are all together. Now is that all? I *must* see if there is enough champagne. Certainly—you can say to her what you like. But twenty years hence she will be just as she is to-day; that's how I see her.'

'Lord, what is it you do to her?' Raymond groaned, as he accompanied his hostess back to the crowded rooms.

He knew exactly what she would have replied if she had been a Frenchwoman; she would have said to him, triumphantly, overwhelmingly: 'Que voulez-vous? Elle adore sa mère!' She was, however, only a Californian, unacquainted with the language of epigram, and her answer consisted simply of the words: 'I am sorry you have ideas that make you unhappy. I guess you are the only person here who hasn't enjoyed himself to-night.'

Raymond repeated to himself, gloomily, for the rest of the evening, 'Elle adore sa mère—elle adore sa mère!' He remained very late, and when but twenty people were left and he had observed that the Marquise, passing her hand into Mrs. Temperly's arm, led her aside as if for some important confabulation (some new light doubtless on what might be hoped for Effie), he persuaded Dora to let the rest of the guests depart in peace (apparently her mother had told her to look out for them to the very last), and come with him into some quiet corner. They found an empty sofa in the outlasting lamp-light, and there the girl sat down with him. Evidently she knew what he was going to say, or rather she thought she did; for in fact, after a little, after he had told her that he had spoken to her mother and she had told him he might speak to *her*, he said things that she could not very well have expected.

'Is it true that you wish to remain with Effie and Tishy?

That's what your mother calls it when she means that you will give me up.'

'How can I give you up?' the girl demanded. 'Why can't we go on being friends, as I asked you the evening you dined here?'

'What do you mean by friends?'

'Well, not making everything impossible.'

'You didn't think anything impossible of old,' Raymond rejoined, bitterly. 'I thought you liked me then, and I have even thought so since.'

'I like you more than I like any one. I like you so much that it's my principal happiness.'

'Then why are there impossibilities?'

'Oh, some day I'll tell you!' said Dora, with a quick sigh. 'Perhaps after Tishy is married. And meanwhile, are you not going to remain in Paris, at any rate? Isn't your work here? You are not here for me only. You can come to the house often. That's what I mean by our being friends.'

Her companion sat looking at her with a gloomy stare, as if he were trying to make up the deficiencies in her logic.

'After Tishy is married? I don't see what that has to do with it. Tishy is little more than a baby; she may not be married for ten years.'

'That is very true.'

'And you dispose of the interval by a simple "meanwhile"? My dear Dora, your talk is strange,' Raymond continued, with his voice passionately lowered. 'And I may come to the house—often? How often do you mean—in ten years? Five times—or even twenty?' He saw that her eyes were filling with tears, but he went on: 'It has been coming over me little by little (I notice things very much if I have a reason), and now I think I understand your mother's system.'

'Don't say anything against my mother,' the girl broke in, beseechingly.

'I shall not say anything unjust. That is if I am unjust you must tell me. This is my idea, and your speaking of Tishy's marriage confirms it. To begin with she has had immense plans for you all; she wanted each of you to be a princess or a duchess—I mean a good one. But she has had to give *you* up.'

'No one has asked for me,' said Dora, with unexpected honesty.

'I don't believe it. Dozens of fellows have asked for you, and you have shaken your head in that divine way (divine for me, I mean) in which you shook it the other night.'

'My mother has never said an unkind word to me in her life,' the girl declared, in answer to this.

'I never said she had, and I don't know why you take the precaution of telling me so. But whatever you tell me or don't tell me,' Raymond pursued, 'there is one thing I see very well—that so long as you won't marry a duke Cousin Maria has found means to prevent you from marrying till your sisters have made rare alliances.'

'Has found means?' Dora repeated, as if she really wondered what was in his thought.

'Of course I mean only through your affection for her. How she works that, you know best yourself.'

'It's delightful to have a mother of whom every one is so fond,' said Dora, smiling.

'She is a most remarkable woman. Don't think for a moment that I don't appreciate her. You don't want to quarrel with her, and I daresay you are right.'

'Why, Raymond, of course I'm right!'

'It proves you are not madly in love with me. It seems to me that for you *I* would have quarrelled——'

'Raymond, Raymond!' she interrupted, with the tears again rising.

He sat looking at her, and then he said, 'Well, when they *are* married?'

'I don't know the future—I don't know what may happen.'

'You mean that Tishy is so small—she doesn't grow—and will therefore be difficult? Yes, she *is* small.' There was bitterness in his heart, but he laughed at his own words. 'However, Effie ought to go off easily,' he went on, as Dora said nothing. 'I really wonder that, with the Marquise and all, she hasn't gone off yet. This thing, to-night, ought to do a great deal for her.'

Dora listened to him with a fascinated gaze; it was as if he expressed things for her and relieved her spirit by making them clear and coherent. Her eyes managed, each time, to be dry again, and now a somewhat wan, ironical smile moved her lips. 'Mamma knows what she wants—she knows what she will take. And she will take only that.'

'Precisely—something tremendous. And she is willing to wait, eh? Well, Effie is very young, and she's charming. But she won't be charming if she has an ugly appendage in the shape of a poor unsuccessful American artist (not even a good one), whose father went bankrupt, for a brother-in-law. That won't smooth the way, of course; and if a prince is to come into the family, the family must be kept tidy to receive him.' Dora got up quickly, as if she could bear his lucidity no longer, but he kept close to her as she walked away. 'And she can sacrifice you like that, without a scruple, without a pang?'

'I might have escaped—if I would marry,' the girl replied.

'Do you call that escaping? She has succeeded with you, but is it a part of what the Marquise calls her *succès de bonté*?'

'Nothing that you can say (and it's far worse than the reality) can prevent her being delightful.'

'Yes, that's your loyalty, and I could shoot you for it!' he exclaimed, making her pause on the threshold of the adjoining room. 'So you think it will take about ten years, considering Tishy's size—or want of size?' He himself again was the only one to laugh at this. 'Your mother is closeted, as much as she can be closeted now, with Madame de Brives, and perhaps this time they are really settling something.'

'I have thought that before and nothing has come. Mamma wants something so good; not only every advantage and every grandeur, but every virtue under heaven, and every guarantee. Oh, she wouldn't expose them!'

'I see; that's where her goodness comes in and where the Marquise is impressed.' He took Dora's hand; he felt that he must go, for she exasperated him with her irony that stopped short and her patience that wouldn't stop. 'You simply propose that I should wait?' he said, as he held her hand.

'It seems to me that you might, if *I* can.' Then the girl remarked, 'Now that you are here, it's far better.'

There was a sweetness in this which made him, after glancing about a moment, raise her hand to his lips. He went away without taking leave of Cousin Maria, who was still out of sight, her conference with the Marquise apparently not having terminated. This looked (he reflected as he passed out) as if something might come of it. However, before he went home he fell again into a gloomy forecast. The weather had changed, the stars were all out, and he walked the empty streets for an hour. Tishy's perverse refusal to grow and Cousin Maria's conscientious exactions promised him a terrible probation. And in those intolerable years what further interference, what meddlesome, effective pressure, might not make itself felt? It may be added that Tishy is decidedly a dwarf and his probation is not yet over.

Louisa Pallant

NEVER SAY you know the last word about any human heart! I was once treated to a revelation which startled and touched me, in the nature of a person with whom I had been acquainted (well, as I supposed) for years, whose character I had had good reasons, heaven knows, to appreciate and in regard to whom I flattered myself that I had nothing more to learn.

It was on the terrace of the Kursaal at Homburg, nearly ten years ago, one lovely night toward the end of July. I had come to the place that day from Frankfort, with vague intentions, and was mainly occupied in waiting for my young nephew, the only son of my sister, who had been intrusted to my care by a very fond mother for the summer (I was expected to show him Europe—only the very best of it), and was on his way from Paris to join me. The excellent band discoursed music not too abstruse, and the air was filled besides with the murmur of different languages, the smoke of many cigars, the creak on the gravel of the gardens of strolling shoes and the thick tinkle of beer-glasses. There were a hundred people walking about, there were some in clusters at little tables and many on benches and rows of chairs, watching the others as if they had paid for the privilege and were rather disappointed. I was among these last; I sat by myself, smoking my cigar and thinking of nothing very particular while families and couples passed and repassed me.

I scarcely know how long I had sat there when I became aware of a recognition which made my meditations definite. It was on my own part, and the object of it was a lady who moved to and fro, unconscious of my observation, with a young girl at her side. I had not seen her for ten years, and what first struck me was the fact not that she was Mrs. Henry Pallant but that the girl who was with her was remarkably pretty—or rather first of all that every one who passed her turned round to look at her. This led me to look at the young lady myself, and her charming face diverted my attention for some time from that of her companion. The latter, moreover, though it was night, wore a thin, light veil which made her features vague. The couple walked and walked, slowly, but though they were very quiet and decorous, and also very well dressed, they seemed to have no friends. Every one looked at them but no one spoke; they appeared even to talk very little to each other. Moreover they bore with extreme composure and as if they were thoroughly used to it the attention they excited. I am afraid it occurred to me to take for granted that they were not altogether honourable and that if they had been the elder lady would have covered the younger up a little more from the public stare and not have been so ashamed to exhibit her own face. Perhaps this question came into my mind too easily just then—in view of my prospective mentorship to my nephew. If I was to show him only the best of Europe I should have to be very careful about the people he should meet—especially the ladies—and the relations he should form. I suspected him of knowing very little of life and I was rather uneasy about my responsibilities. Was I completely relieved and reassured when I perceived that I simply had Louisa Pallant before me and that the girl was her daughter Linda, whom I had known as a child—Linda grown up into a regular beauty?

The question is delicate and the proof that I was not very sure is perhaps that I forbore to speak to the ladies immediately. I watched them awhile—I wondered what they would do. No great harm, assuredly; but I was anxious to see if they were really isolated. Homburg is a great resort of the English—the London season takes up its tale there toward the first of August—and I had an idea that in such a company as that Louisa would naturally know people. It was my impression that she 'cultivated' the English, that she had been much in London and would be likely to have views in regard to a permanent settlement there. This supposition was quickened by the sight of Linda's beauty, for I knew there is no country in which a handsome person is more appreciated. You will see that I took time, and I confess that as I finished my cigar I thought it all over. There was no good reason in fact why I should have rushed into Mrs. Pallant's arms. She had not treated me well and we had never really made it up. Somehow even the circumstance that (after the first soreness) I was glad to have lost her had never put us quite right with each other;

nor, for herself, had it made her less ashamed of her heartless behaviour that poor Pallant after all turned out no great catch. I had forgiven her; I had not felt that it was anything but an escape not to have married a girl who had it in her to take back her given word and break a fellow's heart, for mere flesh-pots—or the shallow promise, as it pitifully proved, of flesh-pots; moreover we had met since then, on the occasion of my former visit to Europe; we had looked each other in the eyes, we had pretended to be free friends and had talked of the wickedness of the world as composedly as if we were the only just, the only pure. I knew then what she had given out—that I had driven her off by my insane jealousy before she ever thought of Henry Pallant, before she had ever seen him. This had not been then and it could not be to-day a ground of real reunion, especially if you add to it that she knew perfectly what I thought of her. It is my belief that it does not often minister to friendship that your friend shall know your real opinion, for he knows it mainly when it is unfavourable, and this is especially the case when (if the solecism may pass) he is a woman. I had not followed Mrs. Pallant's fortunes; the years elapsed, for me, in my own country, whereas she led her life, which I vaguely believed to be difficult after her hus-band's death—virtually that of a bankrupt—in foreign lands. I heard of her from time to time; always as 'established' some-where, but on each occasion in a different place. She drifted from country to country, and if she had been of a hard com-position at the beginning it could never occur to me that her struggle with society, as it might be called, would have soft-ened the paste. Whenever I heard a woman spoken of as 'hor-ribly worldly' I thought immediately of the object of my early passion. I imagined she had debts, and when I now at last made up my mind to recall myself to her it was present to me that she might ask me to lend her money. More than anything else, at this time of day, I was sorry for her, so that such an idea did not operate as a deterrent.

She pretended afterwards that she had not noticed me—expressing great surprise and wishing to know where I had dropped from; but I think the corner of her eye had taken me in and she was waiting to see what I would do. She had ended by sitting down with her girl on the same row of chairs

with myself, and after a little, on the seat next to her becoming
vacant, I went and stood before her. She looked up at me a
moment, staring, as if she could not imagine who I was or
what I wanted; then, smiling and extending her hands, she
broke out, 'Ah, my dear old friend—what a delight!' If she
had waited to see what I would do, in order to choose her
own line, she at least carried out this line with the utmost
grace. She was cordial, friendly, artless, interested, and indeed
I am sure she was very glad to see me. I may as well say
immediately, however, that she gave neither then nor later any
sign of a disposition to borrow money. She had none too
much—that I learned—but for the moment she seemed able
to pay her way. I took the empty chair and we remained talking for an hour. After a while she made me sit on the other
side of her, next to her daughter, whom she wished to know
me—to love me—as one of their oldest friends. 'It goes back,
back, back, doesn't it?' said Mrs. Pallant; 'and of course she
remembers you as a child.' Linda smiled very sweetly and indefinitely, and I saw she remembered me not at all. When her
mother intimated that they had often talked about me she
failed to take it up, though she looked extremely nice. Looking nice was her strong point; she was prettier even than her
mother had been. She was such a little lady that she made me
ashamed of having doubted, however vaguely and for a moment, of her position in the scale of propriety. Her appearance
seemed to say that if she had no acquaintances, it was because
she did not want to—because there was nobody there who
struck her as attractive: there was not the slightest difficulty
about her choosing her friends. Linda Pallant, young as she
was, and fresh and fair and charming and gentle and sufficiently shy, looked somehow exclusive—as if the dust of the
common world had never been meant to settle upon her. She
was simpler than her mother and was evidently not a young
woman of professions—except in so far as she was committed
to an interest in you by her bright, pure, intelligent smile. A
girl who had such a lovely way of showing her teeth could
never pass for heartless.

As I sat between the pair I felt that I had been taken possession of and that for better or worse my stay at Homburg
would be intimately associated with theirs. We gave each other

a great deal of news and expressed unlimited interest in each other's history since our last meeting. I know not what Mrs. Pallant kept back, but for myself I was frank enough. She let me see at any rate that her life had been a good deal what I supposed, though the terms she used to describe it were less crude than those of my thought. She confessed that they had drifted and that they were drifting still. Her narrative rambled and got what is vulgarly called somewhat mixed, as I thought Linda perceived while she sat watching the passers in a manner which betrayed no consciousness of their attention, without coming to her mother's aid. Once or twice Mrs. Pallant made me feel like a cross-questioner, which I had no intention of being. I took it that if the girl never put in a word it was because she had perfect confidence in her mother's ability to come out straight. It was suggested to me, I scarcely knew how, that this confidence between the two ladies went to a great length; that their union of thought, their system of re-ciprocal divination, was remarkable, and that they probably seldom needed to resort to the clumsy and in some cases dan-gerous expedient of putting their ideas into words. I suppose I made this reflection not all at once—it was not wholly the result of that first meeting. I was with them constantly for the next several days and my impressions had time to clarify.

I do remember however that it was on this first evening that Archie's name came up. She attributed her own stay at Homburg to no refined nor exalted motive—did not say that she was there because she always came or because a high med-ical authority had ordered her to drink the waters; she frankly admitted that the reason of her visit had been simply that she did not know where else to turn. But she appeared to assume that my behaviour rested on higher grounds and even that it required explanation, the place being frivolous and modern —devoid of that interest of antiquity which I used to value. 'Don't you remember—ever so long ago—that you wouldn't look at anything in Europe that was not a thousand years old? Well, as we advance in life I suppose we don't think that's quite such a charm.' And when I told her that I had come to Homburg because it was as good a place as another to wait for my nephew, she exclaimed: 'Your nephew—what nephew? He must have come up of late.' I answered that he was a youth named Archer Pringle and very modern indeed; he was coming of age in a few months and was in Europe for the first time. My last news of him had been from Paris and I was expecting to hear from him from one day to the other. His father was dead, and though a selfish bachelor, little versed in the care of children, I was considerably counted on by his mother to see that he did not smoke too much nor fall off an Alp.

Mrs. Pallant immediately guessed that his mother was my sister Charlotte, whom she spoke of familiarly, though I knew she had seen her but once or twice. Then in a moment it came to her which of the Pringles Charlotte had married; she remembered the family perfectly, in the old New York days—'that disgustingly rich lot.' She said it was very nice having the boy come out that way to my care; to which I replied that it was very nice for him. She declared that she meant for me—I ought to have had children; there was something so parental about me and I would have brought them up so well. She could make an allusion like that—to all that might have been and had not been—without a gleam of guilt in her eye; and I foresaw that before I left the place I should have confided to her that though I detested her and was very glad we had fallen out, yet our old relations had left me no heart for marrying another woman. If I was a maundering old bachelor to-day it was no one's fault but hers. She asked me what I meant to do with my nephew and I said it was much more a question of what he would do with me. She inquired whether he were a nice young man and had brothers and sisters and any particular profession. I told her that I had really seen but little of him; I believed him to be six feet high and of tolerable parts. He was an only son, but there was a little sister at home, a delicate, unsuccessful child, demanding all the mother's care.

'So that makes your responsibility greater, as it were, about the boy, doesn't it?' said Mrs. Pallant.

'Greater? I'm sure I don't know.'

'Why, if the girl's life is uncertain he may be, some moment, all the mother has. So that being in your hands——'

'Oh, I shall keep him alive, I suppose, if you mean that,' I rejoined.

'Well, *we* won't kill him, shall we, Linda?' Mrs. Pallant went on, with a laugh.

'I don't know—perhaps we shall!' said the girl, smiling.

II

I called on them the next day at their lodgings, the modesty of which was enhanced by a hundred pretty feminine devices—flowers and photographs and portable knick-knacks and a hired piano and morsels of old brocade flung over angular sofas. I asked them to drive; I met them again at the Kursaal; I arranged that we should dine together, after the Homburg fashion, at the same *table d'hôte*; and during several days this revived familiar intercourse continued, imitating intimacy if it did not quite achieve it. I liked it, for my companions passed my time for me and the conditions of our life were soothing—the feeling of summer and shade and music and leisure, in the German gardens and woods, where we strolled and sat and gossiped; to which may be added a kind of sociable sense that among people whose challenge to the curiosity was mainly not irresistible we kept quite to ourselves. We were on the footing of old friends who, with regard to each other, still had discoveries to make. We knew each other's nature but we did not know each other's experience; so that when Mrs. Pallant related to me what she had been 'up to' (as I called it) for so many years, the former knowledge attached a hundred interpretative footnotes (as if I had been editing an author who presented difficulties) to the interesting page. There was nothing new to me in the fact that I did not esteem her, but there was a sort of refreshment in finding that this was not necessary at Homburg and that I could like her in spite of it. She seemed to me, in the oddest way, both improved and degenerate, as if in her nature the two processes had gone on together. She was battered and world-worn and, spiritually speaking, vulgarised; something fresh had rubbed off her (it even included the vivacity of her early desire to do the best thing for herself), and something very stale had rubbed on. On the other hand she betrayed a scepticism, and that was rather becoming, as it quenched the eagerness of her prime, which had taken a form so unfortunate for me. She had grown weary and indifferent, and as she struck me as having seen more of the evil of the world than of the good, that was a gain; in other words the cynicism that had formed itself in her nature had a softer surface than some of her old ambitions. And then I had to recognise that her devotion to her daughter had been a kind of religion; she had done the very best possible for Linda.

Linda was curious—Linda was interesting; I have seen girls I liked better (charming as she was), but I have never seen one who for the time I was with her (the impression passed, somehow, when she was out of sight) occupied me more. I can best describe the sort of attention that she excited by saying that she struck one above all things as a final product—just as some plant or fruit does, some waxen orchid or some perfect peach. More than any girl I ever saw she was the result of a process of calculation; a process patiently educative; a pressure exerted in order that she should reach a high point. This high point had been the star of her mother's heaven (it hung before her so definitely), and had been the source of the only light—in default of a better—that shone upon the poor lady's path. It stood her in stead of every other religion. The very most and the very best—that was what the girl had been led on to achieve; I mean, of course (for no real miracle had been wrought), the most and the best that she was capable of. She was as pretty, as graceful, as intelligent, as well-bred, as well-informed, as well-dressed, as it would have been possible for her to be; her music, her singing, her German, her French, her English, her step, her tone, her glance, her manner, and everything in her person and movement, from the shade and twist of her hair to the way you saw her finger-nails were pink when she raised her hand, had been carried so far that one found one's self accepting them as a kind of standard. I regarded her as a model, and yet it was a part of her perfection that she had none of the stiffness of a pattern. If she held the observation it was because one wondered where and when she would break down; but she never did, either in her French accent or in her *rôle* of educated angel.

After Archie had come the ladies were manifestly a great resource to him, and all the world knows that a party of four is more convenient than a party of three. My nephew kept me waiting a week, with a placidity all his own; but this same placidity was an element of success in our personal relations—so long, that is, as I did not lose my temper with it. I did not, for the most part, because my young man's unsurprised acceptance of the most various forms of good fortune had more than anything else the effect of amusing me. I had seen little of him for the last three or four years. I knew not what his impending majority would have made of him (he did not look himself in the least as if the wind were rising), and I watched him with a solicitude which usually ended in a joke. He was a tall, fresh-coloured youth, with a candid circular countenance and a love of cigarettes, horses and boats which had not been sacrificed to more transcendent studies. He was refreshingly natural, in a supercivilised age, and I soon made up my mind that the formula of his character was a certain simplifying serenity. After that I had time to meditate on the line which divides the serene from the inane and simplification from death. Archie was not clever—that theory it was not possible to maintain, though Mrs. Pallant tried it once or twice; but on the other hand it seemed to me that his want of wit was a good defensive weapon. It was not the sort of density that would let him in, but the sort that would keep him out. By which I don't mean that he had shortsighted suspicions, but on the contrary that imagination would never be needed to save him, because she would never put him in danger. In short he was a well-grown, well-washed, muscular young American, whose extreme good-nature might have made him pass for conceited. If he looked pleased with himself it was only because he was pleased with life (as well he might be, with the money he was on the point of stepping into), and his big healthy, independent person was an inevitable part of that. I am bound to add that he was accommodating—for which I was grateful. His own habits were active, but he did not insist on my adopting them and he made noteworthy sacrifices for the sake of my society. When I say for the sake of mine I must of course remember that mine and that of Mrs. Pallant and Linda were now very much the same thing. He was willing to sit and smoke for hours under the trees or, regulating his long legs to the pace of his three companions, stroll through the nearer woods of the charming little hill-range of the Taunus to those rustic *Wirthschaften* where coffee might be drunk under a trellis.

Mrs. Pallant took a great interest in him; she talked a great deal about him and thought him a delightful specimen, as a young gentleman of his period and country. She even asked me the sort of 'figure' that his fortune might really amount to and expressed the most hungry envy when I told her what I supposed it to be. While we talked together Archie, on his side, could not do less than converse with Linda, nor to tell the truth did he manifest the least inclination for any different exercise. They strolled away together while their elders rested; two or three times, in the evening, when the ballroom of the Kursaal was lighted and dance-music played, they whirled over the smooth floor in a waltz that made me remember. Whether it had the same effect on Mrs. Pallant I know not, for she held her peace. We had on certain occasions our moments, almost our half-hours, of unembarrassed silence while our young companions disported themselves. But if at other times her inquiries and comments were numerous on the subject of my ingenuous kinsman this might very well have passed for a courteous recognition of the frequent admiration that I expressed for Linda—an admiration to which I noticed that she was apt to give but a small direct response. I was struck with something anomalous in her way of taking my remarks about her daughter—they produced so little of a maternal flutter. Her detachment, her air of having no fatuous illusions and not being blinded by prejudice seemed to me at times to amount to an affectation. Either she answered me with a vague, slightly impatient sigh and changed the subject, or else she said before doing so: 'Oh yes, yes, she's a very brilliant creature. She ought to be; God knows what I have done for her!'

The reader will have perceived that I am fond of looking at the explanations of things, and in regard to this I had my theory that she was disappointed in the girl. What had been her particular disappointment? As she could not possibly have wished her prettier or more pleasing it could only be that Linda had not made a successful use of her gifts. Had she expected her to capture a prince the day after she left the schoolroom? After all there was plenty of time for this, as

Linda was only two and twenty. It did not occur to me to
wonder whether the source of her mother's tepidity was that
the young lady had not turned out so nice a nature as she had
hoped, because in the first place Linda struck me as perfectly
innocent and in the second I was not paid, as the French say,
for thinking that Louisa Pallant would much mind whether
she were or not. The last hypothesis I should have resorted
to was that of private despair at bad moral symptoms. And in
relation to Linda's nature I had before me the daily spectacle
of her manner with my nephew. It was as charming as it could
be, without the smallest indication of a desire to lead him on.
She was as familiar as a cousin, but as a distant one—a cousin
who had been brought up to observe degrees. She was so
much cleverer than Archie that she could not help laughing
at him, but she did not laugh enough to exclude variety, being
well aware, no doubt, that a woman's cleverness most shines
in contrast with a man's stupidity when she pretends to take
that stupidity for wisdom. Linda Pallant moreover was not a
chatter-box; as she knew the value of many things she knew
the value of intervals. There were a good many in the conversation of these young persons; my nephew's own speech,
to say nothing of his thought, being not exempt from periods
of repose; so that I sometimes wondered how their association
was kept at that pitch of friendliness of which it certainly bore
the stamp.

It was friendly enough, evidently, when Archie sat near
her—near enough for low murmurs, if they had risen to his
lips—and watched her with interested eyes and with liberty
not to try too hard to make himself agreeable. She was always
doing something—finishing a flower in a piece of tapestry,
cutting the leaves of a magazine, sewing a button on her glove
(she carried a little work-bag in her pocket and was a person
of the daintiest habits), or plying her pencil in a sketchbook
which she rested on her knee. When we were indoors, at her
mother's house, she had always the resource of her piano, of
which she was of course a perfect mistress. These avocations
enabled her to bear such close inspection with composure (I
ended by rebuking Archie for it—I told him he stared at the
poor girl too much), and she sought further relief in smiling
all over the place. When my young man's eyes shone at her

those of Miss Pallant addressed themselves brightly to the trees and clouds and other surrounding objects, including her mother and me. Sometimes she broke out into a sudden embarrassed, happy, pointless laugh. When she wandered away from us she looked back at us in a manner which said that it was not for long—that she was with us still in spirit. If I was pleased with her it was for a good reason: it was many a day since any pretty girl had had the air of taking me so much into account. Sometimes, when they were so far away as not to disturb us, she read aloud a little to Mr. Archie. I don't know where she got her books—I never provided them, and certainly he did not. He was no reader and I daresay he went to sleep.

III

I remember well the first time—it was at the end of about ten days of this—that Mrs. Pallant remarked to me: 'My dear friend, you are quite amazing! You behave for all the world as if you were perfectly ready to accept certain consequences.' She nodded in the direction of our young companions, but I nevertheless put her at the pains of saying what consequences she meant. 'What consequences?' she repeated. 'Why, the consequences that ensued when you and I first became acquainted.'

I hesitated a moment and then, looking her in the eyes, I said, 'Do you mean that she would throw him over?'

'You are not kind, you are not generous,' she replied, colouring quickly. 'I am giving you a warning.'

'You mean that my boy may fall in love with her?'

'Certainly. It looks even as if the harm might be already done.'

'Then your warning is too late,' I said, smiling. 'But why do you call it a harm?'

'Haven't you any sense of responsibility?' she asked. 'Is that what his mother sent him out to you for—that you should find him a wife—let him put his head into a noose the day after his arrival?'

'Heaven forbid I should do anything of the kind! I know moreover that his mother doesn't want him to marry young.

She thinks it's a mistake and that at that age a man never really chooses. He doesn't choose till he has lived awhile—till he has looked about and compared.'

'And what do you think yourself?'

'I should like to say I consider that love itself, however young, is a sufficient choice. But my being a bachelor at this time of day would contradict me too much.'

'Well then, you're too primitive. You ought to leave this place to-morrow.'

'So as not to see Archie tumble in?'

'You ought to fish him out now and take him with you.'

'Do you think he is in very far?' I inquired.

'If I were his mother I know what I should think. I can put myself in her place—I am not narrow—I know perfectly well how she must regard such a question.'

'And don't you know that in America that's not thought important—the way the mother regards it?'

Mrs. Pallant was silent a moment, as if I partly mystified and partly vexed her. 'Well, we are not in America; we happen to be here.'

'No; my poor sister is up to her neck in New York.'

'I am almost capable of writing to her to come out,' said Mrs. Pallant.

'You *are* warning me,' I exclaimed, 'but I hardly know of what. It seems to me that my responsibility would begin only at the moment when it should appear that your daughter herself was in danger.'

'Oh, you needn't mind that; I'll take care of her.'

'If you think she is in danger already I'll take him away to-morrow,' I went on.

'It would be the best thing you could do.'

'I don't know. I should be very sorry to act on a false alarm. I am very well here; I like the place and the life and your society. Besides, it doesn't strike me that—on her side—there is anything.'

She looked at me with an expression that I had never seen in her face, and if I had puzzled her she repaid me in kind. 'You are very annoying; you don't deserve what I would do for you.'

What she would do for me she did not tell me that day, but we took up the subject again. I said to her that I did not really see why we should assume that a girl like Linda—brilliant enough to make one of the greatest matches—would fall into my nephew's arms. Might I inquire whether her mother had won a confession from her—whether she had stammered out her secret? Mrs. Pallant answered that they did not need to tell each other such things—they had not lived together twenty years in such intimacy for nothing. To this I rejoined that I had guessed as much but that there might be an exception for a great occasion like the present. If Linda had shown nothing it was a sign that for her the occasion was not great; and I mentioned that Archie had not once spoken to me of the young lady, save to remark casually and rather patronisingly, after his first encounter with her, that she was a regular little flower. (The little flower was nearly three years older than himself.) Apart from this he had not alluded to her and had taken up no allusion of mine. Mrs. Pallant informed me again (for which I was prepared) that I was quite too primitive; and then she said: 'We needn't discuss the matter if you don't wish to, but I happen to know—how I obtained my knowledge is not important—that the moment Mr. Pringle should propose to my daughter she would gobble him down. Surely it's a detail worth mentioning to you.'

'Very good. I will sound him. I will look into the matter to-night.'

'Don't, don't; you will spoil everything!' she murmured, in a peculiar tone of discouragement. 'Take him off—that's the only thing.'

I did not at all like the idea of taking him off; it seemed too summary, unnecessarily violent, even if presented to him on specious grounds; and, moreover, as I had told Mrs. Pallant, I really had no wish to move. I did not consider it a part of my bargain with my sister that, with my middle-aged habits, I should duck and dodge about Europe. So I said: 'Should you really object to the boy so much as a son-in-law? After all he's a good fellow and a gentleman.'

'My poor friend, you are too superficial—too frivolous,' Mrs Pallant rejoined, with considerable bitterness.

There was a vibration of contempt in this which nettled me, so that I exclaimed, 'Possibly; but it seems odd that a lesson in consistency should come from you.'

I had no retort from her; but at last she said, quietly: 'I think Linda and I had better go away. We have been here a month—that's enough.'

'Dear me, that will be a bore!' I ejaculated; and for the rest of the evening, until we separated (our conversation had taken place after dinner, at the Kursaal), she remained almost silent, with a subdued, injured air. This, somehow, did not soothe me, as it ought to have done, for it was too absurd that Louisa Pallant, of all women, should propose to put me in the wrong. If ever a woman had been in the wrong herself——! Archie and I usually attended the ladies back to their own door— they lived in a street of minor accommodation, at a certain distance from the Rooms—and we parted for the night late, on the big cobble-stones, in the little sleeping German town, under the closed windows of which, suggesting stuffy interiors, our English farewells sounded gay. On this occasion however they were not gay, for the difficulty that had come up, for me, with Mrs. Pallant appeared to have extended by a mysterious sympathy to the young couple. They too were rather conscious and dumb.

As I walked back to our hotel with my nephew I passed my hand into his arm and asked him, by no roundabout approach to the question, whether he were in serious peril of love.

'I don't know, I don't know—really, uncle, I don't know!'—this was all the satisfaction I could extract from the youth, who had not the smallest vein of introspection. He might not know, but before we reached the inn (we had a few more words on the subject), it seemed to me that I did. His mind was not made to contain many objects at once, but Linda Pallant for the moment certainly constituted its principal furniture. She pervaded his consciousness, she solicited his curiosity, she associated herself, in a manner as yet undefined and unformulated, with his future. I could see that she was the first intensely agreeable impression of his life. I did not betray to him, however, how much I saw, and I slept not particularly well, for thinking that, after all, it had been none of my business to provide him with intensely agreeable impressions. To find him a wife was the last thing that his mother had expected of me or that I had expected of myself. Moreover it was quite my opinion that he himself was too young to be a judge of wives. Mrs. Pallant was right and I had been strangely superficial in regarding her, with her beautiful daughter, as a 'resource.' There were other resources and one of them would be most decidedly to go away. What did I know after all about the girl except that I was very glad to have escaped from marrying her mother? That mother, it was true, was a singular person, and it was strange that her conscience should have begun to fidget before my own did and that she was more anxious on my nephew's behalf than I was. The ways of women were mysterious and it was not a novelty to me that one never knew where one would find them. As I have not hesitated in this narrative to reveal the irritable side of my own nature I will confess that I even wondered whether Mrs. Pallant's solicitude had not been a deeper artifice. Was it not possibly a plan of her own for making sure of my young man—though I did not quite see the logic of it? If she regarded him, as she might in view of his large fortune, as a great catch, might she not have arranged this little comedy, in their personal interest, with the girl?

That possibility at any rate only made it a happier thought that I should carry the boy away to visit other cities. There were many assuredly much more worthy of his attention than Homburg. In the course of the morning (it was after our early luncheon) I walked round to Mrs. Pallant's, to let her know that this truth had come over me with force; and while I did so I again felt the unlikelihood of the part attributed by my fears and by the mother's own, if they were real, to Linda. Certainly if she was such a girl as these fears represented her she would fly at higher game. It was with an eye to high game, Mrs. Pallant had frankly admitted to me, that she had been trained, and such an education, to say nothing of such a subject, justified a hope of greater returns. A young American who could give her nothing but pocket-money was a very moderate prize, and if she were prepared to marry for ambition (there was no such hardness in her face or tone, but then there never is), her mark would be at the least an English duke. I was received at Mrs. Pallant's lodgings with the announcement that she had left Homburg with her daughter half an hour before. The good woman who had entertained the pair professed to know nothing of their movements beyond the fact that they had gone to Frankfort, where however it was her belief that they did not intend to remain. They were evidently travelling beyond. Sudden? Oh yes, tremendously sudden. They must have spent the night in packing, they had so many things and such pretty ones; and their poor maid all the morning had scarcely had time to swallow her coffee. But they evidently were ladies accustomed to come and go. It did not matter: with such rooms as hers she never wanted; there was a new family coming in at three o'clock.

IV

This piece of strategy left me staring and I confess it made me rather angry. My only consolation was that Archie, when I told him, looked as blank as myself and that the trick touched him more nearly, for I was not in love with Louisa. We agreed that we required an explanation and we pretended to expect one the next day in the shape of a letter satisfactory even to the point of being apologetic. When I say 'we' pretended I mean that I did, for my suspicion that he knew (through an arrangement with Linda) what had become of our friends lasted only a moment. If his resentment was less than my own his surprise was equally great. I had been willing to bolt, but I felt rather slighted by the facility with which Mrs. Pallant had shown that she could part with us. Archie was not angry, because in the first place he was good-natured and in the second it was evidently not definite to him that he had been encouraged, having, I think, no very particular idea of what constituted encouragement. He was fresh from the wonderful country in which between the ingenuous young there may be so little question of 'intentions.' He was but dimly conscious of his own and would have had no opinion as to whether he had been provoked or jilted. I had no wish to exasperate him, but when at the end of three days more we were still without news of our late companions I remarked that it was very simple; it was plain they were just hiding from us; they thought us dangerous; they wished to avoid entanglements. They had found us too attentive and wished not to raise false hopes. He appeared to accept this explanation and even had the air (so at least I judged from his asking me no questions) of thinking that the matter might be delicate for myself. The poor youth was altogether much mystified, and I smiled at the image in his mind of Mrs. Pallant fleeing from his uncle's importunities.

We decided to leave Homburg, but if we did not pursue her it was not simply that we were ignorant of where she was. I could have found that out with a little trouble, but I was deterred by the reflection that this would be her own reasoning. She was dishonest and her departure was a provocation—I am afraid that it was in that stupid conviction that I made out a little independent itinerary with Archie. I even said to myself that we should learn where they were quite soon enough and that our patience—even my young man's—would be longer than theirs. Therefore I uttered a small private cry of triumph when three weeks later (we happened to be at Interlaken) he told me that he had received a note from Miss Pallant. His manner of telling me was to inquire whether there were any particular reasons why we should longer delay our projected visit to the Italian lakes; was not the fear of the hot weather, which was moreover in summer our native temperature, at an end, as it was already the middle of September? I answered that we would start on the morrow if he liked, and then, pleased apparently that I was so easy to deal with, he revealed his little secret. He showed me the letter, which was a graceful, natural document—it covered with a few flowing strokes but a single page of notepaper—not at all compromising to the young lady. If however it was almost the apology I had looked for (save that that should have come from the mother), it was not ostensibly in the least an invitation. It mentioned casually (the mention was mainly in the date) that they were on the Lago Maggiore, at Baveno; but it consisted mainly of the expression of a regret that they had to leave us at Homburg without giving notice. Linda did not say under what necessity they had found themselves; she only hoped we had not judged them too harshly and would accept 'these few hasty words' as a substitute for the omitted good-bye. She also hoped we were passing our time in an interesting manner and having the same lovely weather that prevailed south of the Alps; and she remained very sincerely, with the kindest remembrances to me.

The note contained no message from her mother and it was open to me to suppose, as I should judge, either that Mrs. Pallant had not known she was writing or that they wished to make us think she had not known. The letter might pass as a common civility of the girl's to a person with whom she had been on very familiar terms. It was however as something more than this that my nephew took it; at least so I was warranted in inferring from the very distinct nature of his determination to go to Baveno. I saw it was useless to drag him another way; he had money in his own pocket and was quite capable of giving me the slip. Yet—such are the sweet incongruities of youth—when I asked him if he had been thinking of Linda Pallant ever since they left us in the lurch he replied, 'Oh dear no; why should I?' This fib was accompanied by an exorbitant blush. Since he must obey the young lady's call I must also go and see where it would take him, and one splendid morning we started over the Simplon in a post-chaise.

I represented to him successfully that it would be in much better taste for us to alight at Stresa, which as every one knows is a resort of tourists, also on the shore of the major lake, at about a mile's distance from Baveno. If we stayed at the latter place we should have to inhabit the same hotel as our friends, and this would be indiscreet, considering our peculiar relations with them. Nothing would be easier than to go and come between the two points, especially by the water, which would give Archie a chance for unlimited paddling. His face lighted up at the vision of a pair of oars; he pretended to take my plea for discretion very seriously and I could see that he immediately began to calculate opportunities for being afloat with Linda. Our post-chaise (I had insisted on easy stages and we were three days on the way) deposited us at Stresa toward the middle of the afternoon, and it was within an amazingly short time that I found myself in a small boat with my nephew, who pulled us over to Baveno with vigorous strokes. I remember the sweetness of the whole impression (I had had it before, but to my companion it was new and he thought it as pretty as the opera); the enchanting beauty of the place and hour, the stillness of the air and water, with the romantic, fantastic Borromean Islands in the midst of them. We disembarked at the steps at the garden-foot of the hotel, and somehow it seemed a perfectly natural part of the lovely situation that I should immediately become conscious Mrs. Pallant and her daughter were sitting there—on the terrace—quietly watching us. They had all the air of expecting us and I think we looked for it in them. I had not even asked Archie if he had answered Linda's note; that was between themselves and in the way of supervision I had done enough in coming with him.

There is no doubt there was something very odd in our meeting with our friends—at least as between Louisa and me. I was too much taken up with that part of it to notice very much what was the manner of the encounter of the young people. I have sufficiently indicated that I could not get it out of my head that Mrs. Pallant was 'up to' something, and I am afraid she saw in my face that this suspicion had been the motive of my journey. I had come there to find her out. The knowledge of my purpose could not help her to make me very welcome, and that is why I say we met in strange conditions. However, on this occasion we observed all forms and the admirable scene gave us plenty to talk about. I made no reference before Linda to the retreat from Homburg. She looked even prettier than she had done on the eve of that manœuvre and gave no sign of an awkward consciousness. She struck me so, afresh, as a charming, clever girl that I was puzzled afresh to know why we should get—or should have got—into a tangle about her. People had to want to complicate a situation to do it on so simple a pretext as that Linda was admirable. So she was, and why should not the consequences be equally so? One of them, on the spot, was that at the end of a very short time Archie proposed to her to take a turn with him in his boat, which awaited us at the foot of the steps. She looked at her mother with a smiling 'May I, mamma?' and Mrs. Pallant answered, 'Certainly, darling, if you are not afraid.' At this—I scarcely knew why—I burst out laughing; it seemed so droll to me somehow that timidity should be imputed to this competent young lady. She gave me a quick, slightly sharp look as she turned away with my nephew; it appeared to challenge me a little—to say, 'Pray what is the matter with *you*?'

It was the first expression of the kind I had ever seen in her face. Mrs. Pallant's eyes, on the other hand, were not turned to mine; after we had been left there together she sat silent, not heeding me, looking at the lake and mountains—at the snowy crests which wore the flush of evening. She seemed not even to watch our young companions as they got into their boat and pushed off. For some minutes I respected her reverie; I walked slowly up and down the terrace and lighted a cigar, as she had always permitted me to do at Homburg. I noticed that she had an expression of weariness which I had never seen before; her delicate, agreeable face was pale; I made out that there were new lines of fatigue, almost of age, in it. At last I stopped in front of her and asked her, since she looked so sad, if she had any bad news.

'The only bad news was when I learned—through your nephew's note to Linda—that you were coming to us.'

'Ah, then he wrote?' I exclaimed.

'Certainly he wrote.'

'You take it all harder than I do,' I remarked, sitting down beside her. And then I added, smiling, 'Have you written to his mother?'

She slowly turned her face to me and rested her eyes on mine. 'Take care, take care, or you'll insult me,' she said, with an air of patience before the inevitable.

'Never, never! Unless you think I do so if I ask you if you knew when Linda wrote.'

She hesitated a moment. 'Yes; she showed me her letter. She wouldn't have done anything else. I let it go because I didn't know what it was best to do. I am afraid to oppose her, to her face.'

'Afraid, my dear friend, with that girl?'

'That girl? Much you know about her! It didn't follow that you would come—I didn't think it need follow.'

'I am like you,' I said—'I am afraid of my nephew. I don't venture to oppose him to his face. The only thing I could do under the circumstances was to come with him.'

'I see; I'm glad you have done it,' said Mrs. Pallant, thoughtfully.

'Oh, I was conscientious about that! But I have no authority; I can't order him nor forbid him—I can use no force.

Look at the way he is pulling that boat and see if you can fancy me.'

'You could tell him she's a bad, hard girl, who would poison any good man's life!' my companion suddenly broke out, with a kind of passion.

'Dear Mrs. Pallant, what do you mean?' I murmured, staring.

She bent her face into her hands, covering it over with them, and remained so for a minute; then she went on, in a different manner, as if she had not heard my question: 'I hoped you were too disgusted with us, after the way we left you planted.'

'It was disconcerting, assuredly, and it might have served if Linda hadn't written. That patched it up,' I said, laughing. But my laughter was hollow, for I had been exceedingly impressed with her little explosion of a moment before. 'Do you really mean she is bad?' I added.

Mrs. Pallant made no immediate answer to this; she only said that it did not matter after all whether the crisis should come a few weeks sooner or a few weeks later, since it was destined to come at the first opening. Linda had marked my young man—and when Linda had marked a thing!

'Bless my soul—how very grim! Do you mean she's in love with him?' I demanded, incredulous.

'It's enough if she makes him think she is—though even that isn't essential.'

'If she makes him think so? Dearest lady, what do you mean? I have observed her, I have watched her, and after all what has she done? She has been nice to him, but it would have been much more marked if she hadn't. She has really shown him nothing but the common friendliness of a bright, good-natured girl. Her note was nothing; he showed it to me.'

'I don't think you have heard every word that she has said to him,' Mrs. Pallant rejoined, with a persistence that struck me as unnatural.

'No more have you, I take it!' I exclaimed. She evidently meant more than she said, and this impression chilled me, made me really uncomfortable.

'No, but I know my own daughter. She's a very rare young woman.'

'You have a singular tone about her,' I responded—'such a tone as I think I have never heard on a mother's lips. I have observed it before, but never so accentuated.'

At this Mrs. Pallant got up; she stood there an instant, looking down at me. 'You make my reparation—my expiation—difficult!' And leaving me rather startled, she began to move along the terrace.

I overtook her presently and repeated her words. 'Your reparation—your expiation? What on earth do you mean by that?'

'You know perfectly what I mean—it is too magnanimous of you to pretend you don't.'

'Well, at any rate I don't see what good it does me or what it makes up to me for that you should abuse your daughter.'

'Oh, I don't care; I shall save him!' she exclaimed, as we went, with a kind of perverse cheerfulness. At the same moment two ladies, apparently English, came toward us (scattered groups had been sitting there and the inmates of the hotel were moving to and fro), and I observed the immediate charming transition (it seemed to me to show such years of social practice), by which, as they greeted us, she exchanged her excited, almost fevered expression for an air of recognition and pleasure. They stopped to speak to her and she asked with eagerness whether their mother were better. I strolled on and she presently rejoined me; after which she said impatiently, 'Come away from this—come down into the garden.' We descended into the garden, strolled through it and paused on the border of the lake.

V

The charm of the evening had deepened, the stillness was like a solemn expression on a beautiful face and the whole air of the place divine. In the fading light my nephew's boat was too far out to be perceived. I looked for it a little and then, as I gave it up, I remarked that from such an excursion as that, on such a lake, at such an hour, a young man and a young woman of ordinary sensibility could only come back doubly pledged to each other. To this observation Mrs. Pallant's answer was, superficially at least, irrelevant; she said after a pause:

'With you, my dear sir, one has certainly to dot one's "i's." Haven't you discovered, and didn't I tell you at Homburg, that we are miserably poor?'

'Isn't "miserably" rather too much, when you are living at an expensive hotel?'

'They take us *en pension*, for ever so little a day. I have been knocking about Europe long enough to learn there are certain ways of doing things. Besides, don't speak of hotels; we have spent half our life in them and Linda told me only last night that she hoped never to put her foot into one again. She thinks that when she comes to such a place as this it's the least that she should find a villa of her own.'

'Well, her companion there is perfectly competent to give her one. Don't think I have the least desire to push them into each other's arms; I only ask to wash my hands of them. But I should like to know why you want, as you said just now, to save him. When you speak as if your daughter were a monster I take it that you are not serious.'

She was facing me there in the twilight, and to let me know that she was more serious perhaps than she had ever been in her life she had only to look at me awhile without protestation. 'It's Linda's standard. God knows I myself could get on! She is ambitious, luxurious, determined to have what she wants, more than any one I have ever seen. Of course it's open to you to tell me that it's my fault, that I was so before her and have made her so. But does that make me like it any better?'

'Dear Mrs. Pallant, you are most extraordinary,' I stammered, infinitely surprised and not a little pained.

'Oh yes, you have made up your mind about me; you see me in a certain way and you don't like the trouble of changing. *Votre siège est fait.* But you will have to change—if you have any generosity!' Her eyes shone in the summer dusk and she looked remarkably handsome.

'Is this a part of the reparation, of the expiation?' I inquired. 'I don't see what you ever did to Archie.'

'It's enough that he belongs to you. But it isn't for you that I do it; it's for myself,' she went on.

'Doubtless you have your own reasons, which I can't penetrate. But can't you sacrifice something else?—must you sacrifice your child?'

'She's my punishment and she's my stigma!' cried Louisa Pallant, with veritable exaltation.

'It seems to me rather that you are hers.'

'Hers? What does *she* know of such things?—what can she ever feel? She's cased in steel; she has a heart of marble. It's true—it's true. She appals me!'

I laid my hand upon the poor lady's; I uttered, with the intention of checking and soothing her, the first incoherent words that came into my head and I drew her toward a bench which I perceived a few yards away. She dropped upon it; I placed myself near her and besought her to consider well what she was saying. She owed me nothing and I wished no one injured, no one denounced or exposed for my sake.

'For your sake? Oh, I am not thinking of you!' she answered; and indeed the next moment I thought my words rather fatuous. 'It's a satisfaction to my own conscience—for I have one, little as you think I have a right to speak of it. I have been punished by my sin itself. I have been hideously worldly, I have thought only of that, and I have taught her to be so—to do the same. That's the only instruction I have ever given her, and she has learned the lesson so well that now that I see it printed there in all her nature I am horrified at my work. For years we have lived that way; we have thought of nothing else. She has learned it so well that she has gone far beyond me. I say I am horrified, because she is horrible.'

'My poor extravagant friend,' I pleaded, 'isn't it still more so to hear a mother say such things?'

'Why so, if they are abominably true? Besides, I don't care what I say, if I save him.'

'Do you expect me to repeat to him——?'

'Not in the least,' she broke in; 'I will do it myself.' At this I uttered some strong inarticulate protest, and she went on with a sort of simplicity: 'I was very glad at first, but it would have been better if we hadn't met.'

'I don't agree to that, for you interest me immensely.'

'I don't care for that—if I can interest him.'

'You must remember then that your charges are strangely

vague, considering how violent they are. Never had a girl a more innocent appearance. You know how I have admired it.'

'You know nothing about her. *I* do, for she is the work of my hand!' Mrs. Pallant declared, with a bitter laugh. 'I have watched her for years and little by little, for the last two or three, it has come over me. There is not a tender spot in her whole composition. To arrive at a brilliant social position, if it were necessary, she would see me drown in this lake without lifting a finger, she would stand there and see it—she would push me in—and never feel a pang. That's my young lady! To climb up to the top and be splendid and envied there—to do it at any cost or by any meanness and cruelty, is the only thing she has a heart for. She would lie for it, she would steal for it, she would kill for it!' My companion brought out these words with a tremendous low distinctness and an air of sincerity that was really solemn. I watched her pale face and glowing eyes; she held me in a kind of stupor, but her strange, almost vindictive earnestness imposed itself. I found myself believing her, pitying her more than I pitied the girl. It was as if she had been bottled up for longer than she could bear, suffering more and more from the ferment of her knowledge. It relieved her to warn and denounce and expose. 'God has let me see it in time, in his mercy,' she continued; 'but his ways are strange, that he has let me see it in my daughter. It is myself that he has let me see, myself as I was for years. But she's worse—she is, I assure you; she's worse than I ever intended or dreamed.' Her hands were clasped tightly together in her lap; her low voice quavered and her breath came short; she looked up at the faint stars with religious perversity.

'Have you ever spoken to her as you speak to me?' I asked. 'Have you ever admonished her, reproached her?'

'Reproached her? How can I? when all she would have to say would be, "You—*you*—you base one—who made me!"'

'Then why do you want to play her a trick?'

'I'm not bound to tell you and you wouldn't understand if I did. I should play that boy a far worse trick if I were to hold my tongue.'

'If he loves her he won't believe a word you say.'

'Very possibly, but I shall have done my duty.'

'And shall you say to him simply what you have said to me?'

'Never mind what I shall say to him. It will be something that will perhaps affect him, if I lose no time.'

'If you are so bent on gaining time,' I said, 'why did you let her go out in the boat with him?'

'Let her? how could I prevent it?'

'But she asked your permission.'

'That's a part of all the comedy!'

We were silent a moment, after which I resumed: 'Then she doesn't know you hate her?'

'I don't know what she knows. She has depths and depths, and all of them bad. Besides, I don't hate her in the least; I pity her simply, for what I have made of her. But I pity still more the man who may find himself married to her.'

'There's not much danger of there being any such person, at the rate you go on.'

'Oh, perfectly; she'll marry some one. She'll marry a title as well as a fortune.'

'It's a pity my nephew hasn't a title,' I murmured, smiling.

She hesitated a moment. 'I see you think I want that and that I am acting a part. God forgive you! Your suspicion is perfectly natural: how can any one tell, with people like us?'

The way she uttered these last words brought tears to my eyes. I laid my hand on her arm, holding her awhile, and we looked at each other through the dusk. 'You couldn't do more if he were my son,' I said at last.

'Oh, if he had been your son he would have kept out of it! I like him for himself; he's simple and honest—he needs affection.'

'He would have an admirable, a devoted, mother-in-law,' I went on.

Mrs. Pallant gave a little impatient sigh and replied that she was not joking. We sat there some time longer, while I thought over what she had said to me and she apparently did the same. I confess that even close at her side, with the echo of her passionate, broken voice still in the air, some queer ideas came into my head. Was the comedy on *her* side and not on the girl's, and was she posturing as a magnanimous woman at poor Linda's expense? Was she determined, in spite of the young lady's preference, to keep her daughter for a grander personage than a young American whose dollars were

not numerous enough (numerous as they were) to make up
for his want of high relationships, and had she brought forth
these cruel imputations to help her to her end? If she was
prepared really to denounce the girl to Archie she would have
to go very far to overcome the suspicion he would be sure to
feel at so unnatural a proceeding. Was she prepared to go far
enough? The answer to these doubts was simply the way I had
been touched—it came back to me the next moment—when
she used the words, 'people like us.' The effect of them was
poignant. She made herself humble indeed and I felt in a manner ashamed, on my own side, that I saw her in the dust. She
said to me at last that I must wait no longer; I must go away
before the young people came back. They were staying very
long, too long; all the more reason that she should deal with
Archie that evening. I must drive back to Stresa or, if I liked,
I could go on foot: it was not far—for a man. She disposed
of me freely, she was so full of her purpose; and after we had
quitted the garden and returned to the terrace of the hotel
she seemed almost to push me to leave her—I felt her fine
hands, quivering a little, on my shoulders. I was ready to do
what she liked: she affected me painfully and I wanted to get
away from her. Before I went I asked her why Linda should
regard my young man as such a *parti*; it did not square after
all with her account of the girl's fierce ambitions. By that picture it would seem that a reigning prince was the least she
would look at.

'Oh, she has reflected well; she has regarded the question
in every light,' said Mrs. Pallant. 'If she has made up her mind
it is because she sees what she can do.'

'Do you mean that she has talked it over with you?'

'Lord! for what do you take us? We don't talk over things
to-day. We know each other's point of view and we only have
to act. We can take reasons, which are awkward things, for
granted.'

'But in this case she certainly doesn't know your point of
view, poor thing.'

'No—that's because I haven't played fair. Of course she
couldn't expect I would cheat. There ought to be honour
among thieves. But it was open to her to do the same.'

'How do you mean, to do the same?'

'She might have fallen in love with a poor man; then I should have been done.'

'A rich one is better; he can do more,' I replied, with conviction.

'So you would have reason to know if you had led the life that we have! Never to have had really enough—I mean to do just the few simple things we have wanted; never to have had the sinews of war, I suppose you would call them—the funds for a campaign; to have felt every day and every hour the hard, monotonous pinch and found the question of dollars and cents (and so horridly few of them) mixed up with every experience, with every impulse—that *does* make one mercenary, it does make money seem a good beyond all others, and it's quite natural it should. That is why Linda is of the opinion that a fortune is always a fortune. She knows all about that of your nephew, how it's invested, how it may be expected to increase, exactly on what sort of footing it would enable her to live. She has decided that it's enough, and enough is as good as a feast. She thinks she could lead him by the nose, and I daresay she could. She will make him live here: she has not the least intention of settling in America. I think she has views upon London, because in England he can hunt and shoot, and that will make him let her alone.'

'It strikes me that he would like that very much,' I interposed; 'that's not at all a bad programme, even from Archie's point of view.'

'It's no use of talking about princes,' Mrs. Pallant pursued, as if she had not heard me. 'Yes, they are most of them more in want of money even than we are. Therefore a title is out of the question, and we recognised that at an early stage. Your nephew is exactly the sort of young man we had constructed in advance—he was made on purpose. Dear Linda was her mother's own daughter when she recognised him on the spot! It's enough of a title to-day to be an American—with the way they have come up. It does as well as anything and it's a great simplification. If you don't believe me go to London and see.'

She had come with me out to the road. I had said I would walk back to Stresa and we stood there in the complete evening. As I took her hand, bidding her good-night, I exclaimed, 'Poor Linda—poor Linda!'

'Oh, she'll live to do better,' said Mrs. Pallant.

'How can she do better, since you have described this as perfection?'

She hesitated a moment. 'I mean better for Mr. Pringle.'

I still had her hand—I remained looking at her. 'How came it that you could throw me over—such a woman as you?'

'Ah, my friend, if I hadn't thrown you over I couldn't do this for you!' And disengaging herself she turned away quickly and went back to the hotel.

VI

I don't know whether she blushed as she made this avowal, which was a retraction of a former denial and the real truth, as I permitted myself to believe; but I did, while I took my way to Stresa—it is a walk of half an hour—in the darkness. The new and singular character in which she had appeared to me produced an effect of excitement which would have made it impossible for me to sit still in a carriage. This same agitation kept me up late after I had reached my hotel; as I knew that I should not sleep it was useless to go to bed. Long, however, as I deferred this ceremony Archie had not turned up when the lights in the hotel began to be put out. I felt even slightly nervous about him and wondered whether he had had an accident on the lake. I reflected that in this case—if he had not brought his companion back to Baveno—Mrs. Pallant would already have sent after me. It was foolish moreover to suppose that anything could have happened to him after putting off from Baveno by water to rejoin me, for the evening was absolutely windless and more than sufficiently clear and the lake as calm as glass. Besides I had unlimited confidence in his power to take care of himself in circumstances much more difficult. I went to my room at last; his own was at some distance, the people of the hotel not having been able—it was the height of the autumn season—to place us together. Before I went to bed I had occasion to ring for a servant, and then I learned by a chance inquiry that my nephew had returned an hour before and had gone straight to his own apartment. I had not supposed he could come in without my seeing him—I was wandering about the saloons

and terraces—and it had not occurred to me to knock at his
door. I had half a mind to do so then—I had such a curiosity
as to how I should find him; but I checked myself, for evidently he had not wished to see me. This did not diminish
my curiosity, and I slept even less than I had expected. His
dodging me that way (for if he had not perceived me downstairs he might have looked for me in my room) was a sign
that Mrs. Pallant's interview with him had really come off.
What had she said to him? What strong measures had she
taken? The impression of almost morbid eagerness of purpose
that she had given me suggested possibilities that I was afraid
to think of. She had spoken of these things as we parted there
as something she would do for me; but I had made the mental
comment, as I walked away from her, that she had not done
it yet. It would not really be done till Archie had backed out.
Perhaps it was done by this time; his avoiding me seemed
almost a proof. That was what I thought of most of the night.
I spent a considerable part of it at my window, looking out
at the sleeping mountains. *Had* he backed out?—was he making up his mind to back out? There was a strange contradiction in it; there were in fact more contradictions than ever. I
believed what Mrs. Pallant had told me about Linda, and yet
that other idea made me ashamed of my nephew. I was sorry
for the girl; I regretted her loss of a great chance, if loss it
was to be; and yet I hoped that the manner in which her
mother had betrayed her (there was no other word) to her
lover had been thoroughgoing. It would need very radical
measures on Mrs. Pallant's part to excuse Archie. For him too
I was sorry, if she had made an impression on him—the impression she desired. Once or twice I was on the point of
going in to condole with him, in my dressing-gown; I was
sure he too had jumped up from his bed and was looking out
of his window at the everlasting hills.

I am bound to say that he showed few symptoms when we
met in the morning and breakfasted together. Youth is
strange; it has resources that experience seems only to take
away from us. One of these is simply (in the given case) to
do nothing—to say nothing. As we grow older and cleverer
we think that is too simple, too crude; we dissimulate more
elaborately, but with an effect much less baffling. My young

man looked not in the least as if he had lain awake or had something on his mind; and when I asked him what he had done after my premature departure (I explained this by saying I had been tired of waiting for him—I was weary with my journey and wanted to go to bed), he replied: 'Oh, nothing in particular. I hung about the place; I like it better than this. We had an awfully jolly time on the water. *I* wasn't in the least tired.' I did not worry him with questions; it seemed to me indelicate to try to probe his secret. The only indication he gave was on my saying after breakfast that I should go over again to see our friends and my appearing to take for granted that he would be glad to accompany me. Then he remarked that he would stop at Stresa—he had paid them such a tremendous visit; also he had some letters to write. There was a freshness in his scruples about the length of his visits, and I knew something about his correspondence, which consisted entirely of twenty pages every week from his mother. But he satisfied my curiosity so little that it was really this sentiment that carried me back to Baveno. This time I ordered a conveyance, and as I got into it he stood watching me in the porch of the hotel with his hands in his pockets. Then it was for the first time that I saw in this young man's face the expression of a person slightly dazed, slightly foolish even, to whom something disagreeable has happened. Our eyes met as I observed him, and I was on the point of saying, 'You had really better come with me,' when he turned away. He went into the house as if he wished to escape from my call. I said to myself that Mrs. Pallant had warned him off but that it would not take much to bring him back.

The servant to whom I spoke at Baveno told me that my friends were in a certain summer-house in the garden, to which he led the way. The place had an empty air; most of the inmates of the hotel were dispersed on the lake, on the hills, in picnics, excursions, visits to the Borromean Islands. My guide was so far right as that Linda was in the summer-house, but she was there alone. On finding this to be the case I stopped short, rather awkwardly, for I had a sudden sense of being an unmasked hypocrite—a conspirator against her security and honour. But there was no awkwardness about Linda Pallant; she looked up with a little cry of pleasure from

the book she was reading and held out her hand with the
most engaging frankness. I felt as if I had no right to touch
her hand and I pretended not to see it. But this gave no chill
to her pretty manner; she moved a roll of tapestry off the
bench, so that I might sit down, and praised the place as a
delightful shady corner. She had never been fresher, fairer,
kinder; she made her mother's damning talk about her seem
a hideous dream. She told me Mrs. Pallant was coming to join
her; she had remained indoors to write a letter. One could
not write out there, though it was so nice in other respects:
the table was too rickety. They too then had pretexts between
them in the way of letters: I judged this to be a token that
the situation was tense. It was the only one however that
Linda gave: like Archie she was young enough to carry it off.
She had been used to seeing us always together and she made
no comment on my having come over without him. I waited
in vain for her to say something about it; this would only be
natural—it was almost unfriendly to omit it. At last I observed
that my nephew was very unsociable that morning; I had expected him to join me but he had left me to come alone.

'I am very glad,' she answered. 'You can tell him that if you
like.'

'If I tell him that he will come immediately.'

'Then don't tell him; I don't want him to come. He stayed
too long last night,' Linda went on, 'and kept me out on the
water till the most dreadful hours. That isn't done here, you
know, and every one was shocked when we came back—or
rather when we didn't come back. I begged him to bring me
in, but he wouldn't. When we did return—I almost had to
take the oars myself—I felt as if every one had been sitting up
to time us, to stare at us. It was very embarrassing.'

These words made an impression upon me; and as I have
treated the reader to most of the reflections—some of them
perhaps rather morbid—in which I indulged on the subject
of this young lady and her mother I may as well complete the
record and let him know that I now wondered whether
Linda—candid and accomplished maiden—had conceived the
fine idea of strengthening her hold of Archie by attempting
to prove that he had 'compromised' her. 'Ah, no doubt that
was the reason he had a bad conscience last evening!' I ex-

claimed. 'When he came back to Stresa he sneaked off to his room; he wouldn't look me in the face.'

'Mamma was so vexed that she took him apart and gave him a scolding,' the girl went on. 'And to punish *me* she sent me straight to bed. She has very old-fashioned ideas—haven't you, mamma?' she added, looking over my head at Mrs. Pallant, who had just come in behind me.

I forget what answer Mrs. Pallant made to Linda's appeal; she stood there with two letters, sealed and addressed, in her hand. She greeted me gaily and then asked her daughter if she had any postage-stamps. Linda consulted a somewhat shabby pocket-book and confessed that she was destitute; whereupon her mother gave her the letters, with the request that she would go into the hotel, buy the proper stamps at the office, carefully affix them and put the letters into the box. She was to pay for the stamps, not have them put on the bill— a preference for which Mrs. Pallant gave her reasons. I had bought some at Stresa that morning and I was on the point of offering them, when, apparently having guessed my intention, the elder lady silenced me with a look. Linda told her she had no money and she fumbled in her pocket for a franc. When she had found it and the girl had taken it Linda kissed her before going off with the letters.

'Darling mother, you haven't any too many of them, have you?' she murmured; and she gave me, sidelong, as she left us, the prettiest half comical, half pitiful smile.

'She's amazing—she's amazing,' said Mrs. Pallant, as we looked at each other.

'Does she know what you have done?'

'She knows I have done something and she is making up her mind what it is—or she will in the course of the next twenty-four hours, if your nephew doesn't come back. I think I can promise you he won't.'

'And won't she ask you?'

'Never!'

'Shall you not tell her? Can you sit down together in this summer-house, this divine day, with such a dreadful thing as that between you?'

'Don't you remember what I told you about our relations—that everything was implied between us and nothing expressed? The ideas we have had in common—our perpetual worldliness, our always looking out for chances—are not the sort of thing that can be uttered gracefully between persons who like to keep up forms, as we both do: so that if we understood each other it was enough. We shall understand each other now, as we have always done, and nothing will be changed, because there has always been something between us that couldn't be talked about.'

'Certainly, she is amazing—she is amazing,' I repeated; 'but so are you.' And then I asked her what she had said to my boy.

She seemed surprised. 'Hasn't he told you?'

'No, and he never will.'

'I am glad of that,' she said, simply.

'But I am not sure he won't come back. He didn't this morning, but he had already half a mind to.'

'That's your imagination,' said Mrs. Pallant, decisively. 'If you knew what I told him you would be sure.'

'And you won't let me know?'

'Never, my near friend.'

'And did he believe you?'

'Time will show; but I think so.'

'And how did you make it plausible to him that you should take so unnatural a course?'

For a moment she said nothing, only looking at me. Then at last—'I told him the truth.'

'The truth?' I repeated.

'Take him away—take him away!' she broke out. 'That's why I got rid of Linda, to tell you that you mustn't stay—you must leave Stresa to-morrow. This time it's you that must do it; I can't fly from you again—it costs too much!' And she smiled strangely.

'Don't be afraid; don't be afraid. We will leave to-morrow; I want to go myself.' I took her hand in farewell, and while I held it I said, 'The way you put it, about Linda, was very bad?'

'It was horrible.'

I turned away—I felt indeed that I wanted to leave the neighbourhood. She kept me from going to the hotel, as I might meet Linda coming back, which I was far from wishing to do, and showed me another way into the road. Then she turned round to meet her daughter and spend the rest of the morning in the summer-house with her, looking at the bright blue lake and the snowy crests of the Alps. When I reached Stresa again I found that Archie had gone off to Milan (to see the cathedral, the servant said), leaving a message for me to the effect that, as he should not be back for a day or two (though there were numerous trains), he had taken a small portmanteau with him. The next day I got a telegram from him notifying me that he had determined to go on to Venice and requesting me to forward the rest of his luggage. 'Please don't come after me,' this missive added; 'I want to be alone; I shall do no harm.' That sounded pathetic to me, in the light of what I knew, and I was glad to leave the poor boy to his own devices. He proceeded to Venice and I recrossed the Alps. For several weeks after this I expected to discover that he had rejoined Mrs. Pallant; but when we met in Paris, in November, I saw that he had nothing to hide from me, except indeed the secret of what that lady had told him. This he concealed from me then and has concealed ever since. He returned to America before Christmas and then I felt that the crisis had passed. I have never seen my old friend since. About a year after the time to which my story refers, Linda married, in London, a young Englishman, the possessor of a large fortune, a fortune acquired by his father in some useful industry. Mrs. Gimingham's photographs (such is her present name) may be obtained from the principal stationers. I am convinced her mother was sincere. My nephew has not changed his state yet, and now even my sister is beginning, for the first time, to desire it. I related to her as soon as I saw her the substance of the story I have written here, and (such is the inconsequence of women) nothing can exceed her reprobation of Louisa Pallant.

The Aspern Papers

I HAD TAKEN Mrs. Prest into my confidence; in truth without her I should have made but little advance, for the fruitful idea in the whole business dropped from her friendly lips. It was she who invented the short cut, who severed the Gordian knot. It is not supposed to be the nature of women to rise as a general thing to the largest and most liberal view—I mean of a practical scheme; but it has struck me that they sometimes throw off a bold conception—such as a man would not have risen to—with singular serenity. 'Simply ask them to take you in on the footing of a lodger'—I don't think that unaided I should have risen to that. I was beating about the bush, trying to be ingenious, wondering by what combination of arts I might become an acquaintance, when she offered this happy suggestion that the way to become an acquaintance was first to become an inmate. Her actual knowledge of the Misses Bordereau was scarcely larger than mine, and indeed I had brought with me from England some definite facts which were new to her. Their name had been mixed up ages before with one of the greatest names of the century, and they lived now in Venice in obscurity, on very small means, unvisited, unapproachable, in a dilapidated old palace on an out-of-the-way canal: this was the substance of my friend's impression of them. She herself had been established in Venice for fifteen years and had done a great deal of good there; but the circle of her benevolence did not include the two shy, mysterious and, as it was somehow supposed, scarcely respectable Americans (they were believed to have lost in their long exile all national quality, besides having had, as their name implied, some French strain in their origin), who asked no favours and desired no attention. In the early years of her residence she had made an attempt to see them, but this had been successful only as regards the little one, as Mrs. Prest called the niece; though in reality as I afterwards learned she was considerably the bigger of the two. She had heard Miss Bordereau was ill and had a suspicion that she was in want; and she had gone to the house to offer assistance, so that if

there were suffering (and American suffering), she should at
least not have it on her conscience. The 'little one' received her
in the great cold, tarnished Venetian *sala*, the central hall of the
house, paved with marble and roofed with dim cross-beams,
and did not even ask her to sit down. This was not encouraging
for me, who wished to sit so fast, and I remarked as much to
Mrs. Prest. She however replied with profundity, 'Ah, but
there's all the difference: I went to confer a favour and you will
go to ask one. If they are proud you will be on the right side.'
And she offered to show me their house to begin with—to row
me thither in her gondola. I let her know that I had already
been to look at it half a dozen times; but I accepted her invitation, for it charmed me to hover about the place. I had made
my way to it the day after my arrival in Venice (it had been
described to me in advance by the friend in England to whom
I owed definite information as to their possession of the papers), and I had besieged it with my eyes while I considered
my plan of campaign. Jeffrey Aspern had never been in it that
I knew of; but some note of his voice seemed to abide there
by a roundabout implication, a faint reverberation.

Mrs. Prest knew nothing about the papers, but she was interested in my curiosity, as she was always interested in the
joys and sorrows of her friends. As we went, however, in her
gondola, gliding there under the sociable hood with the
bright Venetian picture framed on either side by the movable
window, I could see that she was amused by my infatuation,
the way my interest in the papers had become a fixed idea.
'One would think you expected to find in them the answer to
the riddle of the universe,' she said; and I denied the impeachment only by replying that if I had to choose between that
precious solution and a bundle of Jeffrey Aspern's letters I
knew indeed which would appear to me the greater boon. She
pretended to make light of his genius and I took no pains to
defend him. One doesn't defend one's god: one's god is in
himself a defence. Besides, to-day, after his long comparative
obscuration, he hangs high in the heaven of our literature, for
all the world to see; he is a part of the light by which we walk.
The most I said was that he was no doubt not a woman's
poet: to which she rejoined aptly enough that he had been at
least Miss Bordereau's. The strange thing had been for me to

discover in England that she was still alive: it was as if I had been told Mrs. Siddons was, or Queen Caroline, or the famous Lady Hamilton, for it seemed to me that she belonged to a generation as extinct. 'Why, she must be tremendously old—at least a hundred,' I had said; but on coming to consider dates I saw that it was not strictly necessary that she should have exceeded by very much the common span. None the less she was very far advanced in life and her relations with Jeffrey Aspern had occurred in her early womanhood. 'That is her excuse,' said Mrs. Prest, half sententiously and yet also somewhat as if she were ashamed of making a speech so little in the real tone of Venice. As if a woman needed an excuse for having loved the divine poet! He had been not only one of the most brilliant minds of his day (and in those years, when the century was young, there were, as every one knows, many), but one of the most genial men and one of the handsomest.

The niece, according to Mrs. Prest, was not so old, and she risked the conjecture that she was only a grand-niece. This was possible; I had nothing but my share in the very limited knowledge of my English fellow-worshipper John Cumnor, who had never seen the couple. The world, as I say, had recognised Jeffrey Aspern, but Cumnor and I had recognised him most. The multitude, to-day, flocked to his temple, but of that temple he and I regarded ourselves as the ministers. We held, justly, as I think, that we had done more for his memory than any one else, and we had done it by opening lights into his life. He had nothing to fear from us because he had nothing to fear from the truth, which alone at such a distance of time we could be interested in establishing. His early death had been the only dark spot in his life, unless the papers in Miss Bordereau's hands should perversely bring out others. There had been an impression about 1825 that he had 'treated her badly,' just as there had been an impression that he had 'served,' as the London populace says, several other ladies in the same way. Each of these cases Cumnor and I had been able to investigate, and we had never failed to acquit him conscientiously of shabby behaviour. I judged him perhaps more indulgently than my friend; certainly, at any rate, it appeared to me that no man could have walked straighter in the given circumstances. These were almost always awkward. Half the women of his time, to speak liberally, had flung themselves at his head, and out of this pernicious fashion many complications, some of them grave, had not failed to arise. He was not a woman's poet, as I had said to Mrs. Prest, in the modern phase of his reputation; but the situation had been different when the man's own voice was mingled with his song. That voice, by every testimony, was one of the sweetest ever heard. 'Orpheus and the Mænads!' was the exclamation that rose to my lips when I first turned over his correspondence. Almost all the Mænads were unreasonable and many of them insupportable; it struck me in short that he was kinder, more considerate than, in his place (if I could imagine myself in such a place!) I should have been.

It was certainly strange beyond all strangeness, and I shall not take up space with attempting to explain it, that whereas in all these other lines of research we had to deal with phantoms and dust, the mere echoes of echoes, the one living source of information that had lingered on into our time had been unheeded by us. Every one of Aspern's contemporaries had, according to our belief, passed away; we had not been able to look into a single pair of eyes into which his had looked or to feel a transmitted contact in any aged hand that his had touched. Most dead of all did poor Miss Bordereau appear, and yet she alone had survived. We exhausted in the course of months our wonder that we had not found her out sooner, and the substance of our explanation was that she had kept so quiet. The poor lady on the whole had had reason for doing so. But it was a revelation to us that it was possible to keep so quiet as that in the latter half of the nineteenth century—the age of newspapers and telegrams and photographs and interviewers. And she had taken no great trouble about it either: she had not hidden herself away in an undiscoverable hole; she had boldly settled down in a city of exhibition. The only secret of her safety that we could perceive was that Venice contained so many curiosities that were greater than she. And then accident had somehow favoured her, as was shown for example in the fact that Mrs. Prest had never happened to mention her to me, though I had spent three weeks in Venice—under her nose, as it were—five years before. Mrs. Prest had not mentioned this much to any one; she appeared almost to have forgotten she was there. Of course she had not the responsibilities of an editor. It was no explanation of the old woman's having eluded us to say that she lived abroad, for our researches had again and again taken us (not only by correspondence but by personal inquiry) to France, to Germany, to Italy, in which countries, not counting his important stay in England, so many of the too few years of Aspern's career were spent. We were glad to think at least that in all our publishings (some people consider I believe that we have overdone them), we had only touched in passing and in the most discreet manner on Miss Bordereau's connection. Oddly enough, even if we had had the material (and we often wondered what had become of it), it would have been the most difficult episode to handle.

The gondola stopped, the old palace was there; it was a house of the class which in Venice carries even in extreme dilapidation the dignified name. 'How charming! It's gray and pink!' my companion exclaimed; and that is the most comprehensive description of it. It was not particularly old, only two or three centuries; and it had an air not so much of decay as of quiet discouragement, as if it had rather missed its career. But its wide front, with a stone balcony from end to end of the *piano nobile* or most important floor, was architectural enough, with the aid of various pilasters and arches; and the stucco with which in the intervals it had long ago been endued was rosy in the April afternoon. It overlooked a clean, melancholy, unfrequented canal, which had a narrow *riva* or convenient footway on either side. 'I don't know why—there are no brick gables,' said Mrs. Prest, 'but this corner has seemed to me before more Dutch than Italian, more like Amsterdam than like Venice. It's perversely clean, for reasons of its own; and though you can pass on foot scarcely any one ever thinks of doing so. It has the air of a Protestant Sunday. Perhaps the people are afraid of the Misses Bordereau. I daresay they have the reputation of witches.'

I forget what answer I made to this—I was given up to two other reflections. The first of these was that if the old lady lived in such a big, imposing house she could not be in any sort of misery and therefore would not be tempted by a chance to let a couple of rooms. I expressed this idea to Mrs.

Prest, who gave me a very logical reply. 'If she didn't live in a big house how could it be a question of her having rooms to spare? If she were not amply lodged herself you would lack ground to approach her. Besides, a big house here, and especially in this *quartier perdu*, proves nothing at all: it is perfectly compatible with a state of penury. Dilapidated old palazzi, if you will go out of the way for them, are to be had for five shillings a year. And as for the people who live in them—no, until you have explored Venice socially as much as I have you can form no idea of their domestic desolation. They live on nothing, for they have nothing to live on.' The other idea that had come into my head was connected with a high blank wall which appeared to confine an expanse of ground on one side of the house. Blank I call it, but it was figured over with the patches that please a painter, repaired breaches, crumblings of plaster, extrusions of brick that had turned pink with time; and a few thin trees, with the poles of certain rickety trellises, were visible over the top. The place was a garden and apparently it belonged to the house. It suddenly occurred to me that if it did belong to the house I had my pretext.

I sat looking out on all this with Mrs. Prest (it was covered with the golden glow of Venice) from the shade of our *felze*, and she asked me if I would go in then, while she waited for me, or come back another time. At first I could not decide—it was doubtless very weak of me. I wanted still to think I *might* get a footing, and I was afraid to meet failure, for it would leave me, as I remarked to my companion, without another arrow for my bow. 'Why not another?' she inquired, as I sat there hesitating and thinking it over; and she wished to know why even now and before taking the trouble of becoming an inmate (which might be wretchedly uncomfortable after all, even if it succeeded), I had not the resource of simply offering them a sum of money down. In that way I might obtain the documents without bad nights.

'Dearest lady,' I exclaimed, 'excuse the impatience of my tone when I suggest that you must have forgotten the very fact (surely I communicated it to you) which pushed me to throw myself upon your ingenuity. The old woman won't have the documents spoken of; they are personal, delicate, intimate, and she hasn't modern notions, God bless her! If I should sound that note first I should certainly spoil the game. I can arrive at the papers only by putting her off her guard, and I can put her off her guard only by ingratiating diplomatic practices. Hypocrisy, duplicity are my only chance. I am sorry for it, but for Jeffrey Aspern's sake I would do worse still. First I must take tea with her; then tackle the main job.' And I told over what had happened to John Cumnor when he wrote to her. No notice whatever had been taken of his first letter, and the second had been answered very sharply, in six lines, by the niece. 'Miss Bordereau requested her to say that she could not imagine what he meant by troubling them. They had none of Mr. Aspern's papers, and if they had should never think of showing them to any one on any account whatever. She didn't know what he was talking about and begged he would let her alone.' I certainly did not want to be met that way.

'Well,' said Mrs. Prest, after a moment, provokingly, 'perhaps after all they haven't any of his things. If they deny it flat how are you sure?'

'John Cumnor is sure, and it would take me long to tell you how his conviction, or his very strong presumption—strong enough to stand against the old lady's not unnatural fib—has built itself up. Besides, he makes much of the internal evidence of the niece's letter.'

'The internal evidence?'

'Her calling him "Mr. Aspern."'

'I don't see what that proves.'

'It proves familiarity, and familiarity implies the possession of mementoes, of relics. I can't tell you how that "Mr." touches me—how it bridges over the gulf of time and brings our hero near to me—nor what an edge it gives to my desire to see Juliana. You don't say "Mr." Shakespeare.'

'Would I, any more, if I had a box full of his letters?'

'Yes, if he had been your lover and some one wanted them!' And I added that John Cumnor was so convinced, and so all the more convinced by Miss Bordereau's tone, that he would have come himself to Venice on the business were it not that for him there was the obstacle that it would be difficult to disprove his identity with the person who had written to them, which the old ladies would be sure to suspect in spite of dissimulation and a change of name. If they were to ask him point-blank if he were not their correspondent it would be too awkward for him to lie; whereas I was fortunately not tied in that way. I was a fresh hand and could say no without lying.

'But you will have to change your name,' said Mrs. Prest. 'Juliana lives out of the world as much as it is possible to live, but none the less she has probably heard of Mr. Aspern's editors; she perhaps possesses what you have published.'

'I have thought of that,' I returned; and I drew out of my pocket-book a visiting-card, neatly engraved with a name that was not my own.

'You are very extravagant; you might have written it,' said my companion.

'This looks more genuine.'

'Certainly, you are prepared to go far! But it will be awkward about your letters; they won't come to you in that mask.'

'My banker will take them in and I will go every day to fetch them. It will give me a little walk.'

'Shall you only depend upon that?' asked Mrs. Prest. 'Aren't you coming to see me?'

'Oh, you will have left Venice, for the hot months, long before there are any results. I am prepared to roast all summer—as well as hereafter, perhaps you'll say! Meanwhile, John Cumnor will bombard me with letters addressed, in my feigned name, to the care of the *padrona*.'

'She will recognise his hand,' my companion suggested.

'On the envelope he can disguise it.'

'Well, you're a precious pair! Doesn't it occur to you that even if you are able to say you are not Mr. Cumnor in person they may still suspect you of being his emissary?'

'Certainly, and I see only one way to parry that.'

'And what may that be?'

I hesitated a moment. 'To make love to the niece.'

'Ah,' cried Mrs. Prest, 'wait till you see her!'

II

'I must work the garden—I must work the garden,' I said to myself, five minutes later, as I waited, upstairs, in the long, dusky sala, where the bare scagliola floor gleamed vaguely in a chink of the closed shutters. The place was impressive but it looked cold and cautious. Mrs. Prest had floated away, giving me a rendezvous at the end of half an hour by some neighbouring water-steps; and I had been let into the house, after pulling the rusty bell-wire, by a little red-headed, white-faced maid-servant, who was very young and not ugly and wore clicking pattens and a shawl in the fashion of a hood. She had not contented herself with opening the door from above by the usual arrangement of a creaking pulley, though she had looked down at me first from an upper window, dropping the inevitable challenge which in Italy precedes the hospitable act. As a general thing I was irritated by this survival of mediæval manners, though as I liked the old I suppose I ought to have liked it; but I was so determined to be genial that I took my false card out of my pocket and held it up to her, smiling as if it were a magic token. It had the effect of one indeed, for it brought her, as I say, all the way down. I begged her to hand it to her mistress, having first written on it in Italian the words, 'Could you very kindly see a gentleman, an American, for a moment?' The little maid was not hostile, and I reflected that even that was perhaps something gained. She coloured, she smiled and looked both frightened and pleased. I could see that my arrival was a great affair, that visits were rare in that house, and that she was a person who would have liked a sociable place. When she pushed forward the heavy door behind me I felt that I had a foot in the citadel. She pattered across the damp, stony lower hall and I followed her up the high staircase—stonier still, as it seemed—without an invitation. I think she had meant I should wait for her below, but such was not my idea, and I took up my station in the sala. She flitted, at the far end of it, into impenetrable regions, and I looked at the place with my heart beating as I had known it to do in the dentist's parlour. It was gloomy and stately, but it owed its character almost entirely to its noble shape and to the fine architectural doors—as high as the doors of houses—which, leading into the various rooms, repeated themselves on either side at intervals. They were surmounted with old faded painted escutcheons, and here and there, in the spaces between them, brown pictures, which I perceived to be bad, in battered frames, were suspended. With the exception of several straw-bottomed chairs with their backs to the wall, the grand obscure vista contained nothing else to minister to effect. It was evidently never used save as a passage, and little even as that. I may add that by the time the door opened again through which the maid-servant had escaped, my eyes had grown used to the want of light.

I had not meant by my private ejaculation that I must myself cultivate the soil of the tangled enclosure which lay beneath the windows, but the lady who came toward me from the distance over the hard, shining floor might have supposed as much from the way in which, as I went rapidly to meet her, I exclaimed, taking care to speak Italian: 'The garden, the garden—do me the pleasure to tell me if it's yours!'

She stopped short, looking at me with wonder; and then, 'Nothing here is mine,' she answered in English, coldly and sadly.

'Oh, you are English; how delightful!' I remarked, ingenuously. 'But surely the garden belongs to the house?'

'Yes, but the house doesn't belong to me.' She was a long, lean, pale person, habited apparently in a dull-coloured dressing-gown, and she spoke with a kind of mild literalness. She did not ask me to sit down, any more than years before (if she were the niece) she had asked Mrs. Prest, and we stood face to face in the empty pompous hall.

'Well then, would you kindly tell me to whom I must address myself? I'm afraid you'll think me odiously intrusive, but you know I *must* have a garden—upon my honour I must!'

Her face was not young, but it was simple; it was not fresh, but it was mild. She had large eyes which were not bright, and a great deal of hair which was not 'dressed,' and long fine hands which were—possibly—not clean. She clasped these members almost convulsively as, with a confused, alarmed look, she broke out, 'Oh, don't take it away from us; we like it ourselves!'

'You have the use of it then?'

'Oh yes. If it wasn't for that!' And she gave a shy, melancholy smile.

'Isn't it a luxury, precisely? That's why, intending to be in Venice some weeks, possibly all summer, and having some literary work, some reading and writing to do, so that I must be quiet, and yet if possible a great deal in the open air—that's why I have felt that a garden is really indispensable. I appeal to your own experience,' I went on, smiling. 'Now can't I look at yours?'

'I don't know, I don't understand,' the poor woman murmured, planted there and letting her embarrassed eyes wander all over my strangeness.

'I mean only from one of those windows—such grand ones as you have here—if you will let me open the shutters.' And I walked toward the back of the house. When I had advanced half-way I stopped and waited, as if I took it for granted she would accompany me. I had been of necessity very abrupt, but I strove at the same time to give her the impression of extreme courtesy. 'I have been looking at furnished rooms all over the place, and it seems impossible to find any with a garden attached. Naturally in a place like Venice gardens are rare. It's absurd if you like, for a man, but I can't live without flowers.'

'There are none to speak of down there.' She came nearer to me, as if, though she mistrusted me, I had drawn her by an invisible thread. I went on again, and she continued as she followed me: 'We have a few, but they are very common. It costs too much to cultivate them; one has to have a man.'

'Why shouldn't I be the man?' I asked. 'I'll work without wages; or rather I'll put in a gardener. You shall have the sweetest flowers in Venice.'

She protested at this, with a queer little sigh which might also have been a gush of rapture at the picture I presented. Then she observed, 'We don't know you—we don't know you.'

'You know me as much as I know you; that is much more, because you know my name. And if you are English I am almost a countryman.'

'We are not English,' said my companion, watching me helplessly while I threw open the shutters of one of the divisions of the wide high window.

'You speak the language so beautifully: might I ask what you are?' Seen from above the garden was certainly shabby; but I perceived at a glance that it had great capabilities. She made no rejoinder, she was so lost in staring at me, and I exclaimed, 'You don't mean to say you are also by chance American?'

'I don't know; we used to be.'

'Used to be? Surely you haven't changed?'

'It's so many years ago—we are nothing.'

'So many years that you have been living here? Well, I don't wonder at that; it's a grand old house. I suppose you all use the garden,' I went on, 'but I assure you I shouldn't be in your way. I would be very quiet and stay in one corner.'

'We all use it?' she repeated after me, vaguely, not coming close to the window but looking at my shoes. She appeared to think me capable of throwing her out.

'I mean all your family, as many as you are.'

'There is only one other; she is very old—she never goes down.'

'Only one other, in all this great house!' I feigned to be not only amazed but almost scandalised. 'Dear lady, you must have space then to spare!'

'To spare?' she repeated, in the same dazed way.

'Why, you surely don't live (two quiet women—I see *you* are quiet, at any rate) in fifty rooms!' Then with a burst of hope and cheer I demanded: 'Couldn't you let me two or three? That would set me up!'

I had now struck the note that translated my purpose and I need not reproduce the whole of the tune I played. I ended by making my interlocutress believe that I was an honourable person, though of course I did not even attempt to persuade her that I was not an eccentric one. I repeated that I had studies to pursue; that I wanted quiet; that I delighted in a garden and had vainly sought one up and down the city; that I would undertake that before another month was over the dear old house should be smothered in flowers. I think it was the flowers that won my suit, for I afterwards found that Miss Tita (for such the name of this high tremulous spinster proved somewhat incongruously to be) had an insatiable appetite for them. When I speak of my suit as won I mean that before I left her she had promised that she would refer the question to her aunt. I inquired who her aunt might be and she answered, 'Why, Miss Bordereau!' with an air of surprise, as if I might have been expected to know. There were contradictions like this in Tita Bordereau which, as I observed later, contributed to make her an odd and affecting person. It was the study of the two ladies to live so that the world should not touch them, and yet they had never altogether accepted the idea that it never heard of them. In Tita at any rate a grateful susceptibility to human contact had not died out, and contact of a limited order there would be if I should come to live in the house.

'We have never done anything of the sort; we have never had a lodger or any kind of inmate.' So much as this she made a point of saying to me. 'We are very poor, we live very badly. The rooms are very bare—that you might take; they have nothing in them. I don't know how you would sleep, how you would eat.'

'With your permission, I could easily put in a bed and a few tables and chairs. *C'est la moindre des choses* and the affair of an hour or two. I know a little man from whom I can hire what I should want for a few months, for a trifle, and my gondolier can bring the things round in his boat. Of course in this great house you must have a second kitchen, and my servant, who is a wonderfully handy fellow' (this personage was an evocation of the moment), 'can easily cook me a chop there. My tastes and habits are of the simplest; I live on flowers!' And then I ventured to add that if they were very poor it was all the more reason they should let their rooms. They were bad economists—I had never heard of such a waste of material.

I saw in a moment that the good lady had never before been spoken to in that way, with a kind of humorous firmness which did not exclude sympathy but was on the contrary founded on it. She might easily have told me that my sympathy was impertinent, but this by good fortune did not occur to her. I left her with the understanding that she would consider the matter with her aunt and that I might come back the next day for their decision.

'The aunt will refuse; she will think the whole proceeding very *louche*!' Mrs. Prest declared shortly after this, when I had resumed my place in her gondola. She had put the idea into my head and now (so little are women to be counted on) she appeared to take a despondent view of it. Her pessimism provoked me and I pretended to have the best hopes; I went so far as to say that I had a distinct presentiment that I should succeed. Upon this Mrs. Prest broke out, 'Oh, I see what's in your head! You fancy you have made such an impression in a quarter of an hour that she is dying for you to come and can be depended upon to bring the old one round. If you do get in you'll count it as a triumph.'

I did count it as a triumph, but only for the editor (in the last analysis), not for the man, who had not the tradition of personal conquest. When I went back on the morrow the little maid-servant conducted me straight through the long sala (it opened there as before in perfect perspective and was lighter now, which I thought a good omen) into the apartment from which the recipient of my former visit had emerged on that occasion. It was a large shabby parlour, with a fine old painted ceiling and a strange figure sitting alone at one of the windows. They come back to me now almost with the palpitation they caused, the successive feelings that accompanied my consciousness that as the door of the room closed behind me I was really face to face with the Juliana of some of Aspern's most exquisite and most renowned lyrics. I grew used to her afterwards, though never completely; but as she sat there before me my heart beat as fast as if the miracle of resurrection had taken place for my benefit. Her presence seemed somehow to contain his, and I felt nearer to him at that first moment of seeing her than I ever had been before or ever have been since. Yes, I remember my emotions in their order, even including a curious little tremor that took me when I saw that the niece was not there. With her, the day before, I had become sufficiently familiar, but it almost exceeded my courage (much as I had longed for the event) to be left alone with such a terrible relic as the aunt. She was too strange, too literally resurgent. Then came a check, with the perception that we were not really face to face, inasmuch as she had over her eyes a horrible green shade which, for her, served almost as a mask. I believed for the instant that she had put it on expressly, so that from underneath it she might scrutinise me without being scrutinised herself. At the same time it increased the presumption that there was a ghastly death's-head lurking behind it. The divine Juliana as a grinning skull—the vision hung there until it passed. Then it came to me that she *was* tremendously old—so old that death might take her at any moment, before I had time to get what I wanted from her. The next thought was a correction to that; it lighted up the situation. She would die next week, she would die to-morrow—then I could seize her papers. Meanwhile she sat there neither moving nor speaking. She was very small and shrunken, bent forward, with her hands in her lap. She was dressed in black and her head was wrapped in a piece of old black lace which showed no hair.

My emotion keeping me silent she spoke first, and the re-mark she made was exactly the most unexpected.

III

'Our house is very far from the centre, but the little canal is very *comme il faut.*'

'It's the sweetest corner of Venice and I can imagine noth-ing more charming,' I hastened to reply. The old lady's voice was very thin and weak, but it had an agreeable, cultivated murmur and there was wonder in the thought that that in-dividual note had been in Jeffrey Aspern's ear.

'Please to sit down there. I hear very well,' she said quietly, as if perhaps I had been shouting at her; and the chair she pointed to was at a certain distance. I took possession of it, telling her that I was perfectly aware that I had intruded, that I had not been properly introduced and could only throw myself upon her indulgence. Perhaps the other lady, the one I had had the honour of seeing the day before, would have explained to her about the garden. That was literally what had given me courage to take a step so unconventional. I had fallen in love at sight with the whole place (she herself prob-ably was so used to it that she did not know the impression it was capable of making on a stranger), and I had felt it was really a case to risk something. Was her own kindness in re-ceiving me a sign that I was not wholly out in my calculation? It would render me extremely happy to think so. I could give her my word of honour that I was a most respectable, inof-fensive person and that as an inmate they would be barely

conscious of my existence. I would conform to any regula-
tions, any restrictions if they would only let me enjoy the garden. Moreover I should be delighted to give her references,
guarantees; they would be of the very best, both in Venice
and in England as well as in America.

She listened to me in perfect stillness and I felt that she was
looking at me with great attention, though I could see only
the lower part of her bleached and shrivelled face. Independ-
ently of the refining process of old age it had a delicacy which
once must have been great. She had been very fair, she had
had a wonderful complexion. She was silent a little after I had
ceased speaking; then she inquired, 'If you are so fond of a
garden why don't you go to *terra firma*, where there are so
many far better than this?'

'Oh, it's the combination!' I answered, smiling; and then,
with rather a flight of fancy, 'It's the idea of a garden in the
middle of the sea.'

'It's not in the middle of the sea; you can't see the water.'

I stared a moment, wondering whether she wished to con-
vict me of fraud. 'Can't see the water? Why, dear madam, I
can come up to the very gate in my boat.'

She appeared inconsequent, for she said vaguely in reply to
this, 'Yes, if you have got a boat. I haven't any; it's many years
since I have been in one of the gondolas.' She uttered these
words as if the gondolas were a curious far-away craft which
she knew only by hearsay.

'Let me assure you of the pleasure with which I would put
mine at your service!' I exclaimed. I had scarcely said this
however before I became aware that the speech was in questionable taste and might also do me the injury of making me
appear too eager, too possessed of a hidden motive. But the
old woman remained impenetrable and her attitude bothered
me by suggesting that she had a fuller vision of me than I had
of her. She gave me no thanks for my somewhat extravagant
offer but remarked that the lady I had seen the day before
was her niece; she would presently come in. She had asked
her to stay away a little on purpose, because she herself wished
to see me at first alone. She relapsed into silence and I asked
myself why she had judged this necessary and what was coming yet; also whether I might venture on some judicious re-

mark in praise of her companion. I went so far as to say that
I should be delighted to see her again: she had been so very
courteous to me, considering how odd she must have thought
me—a declaration which drew from Miss Bordereau another
of her whimsical speeches.

'She has very good manners; I bred her up myself!' I was
on the point of saying that that accounted for the easy grace
of the niece, but I arrested myself in time, and the next moment the old woman went on: 'I don't care who you may
be—I don't want to know; it signifies very little to-day.' This
had all the air of being a formula of dismissal, as if her next
words would be that I might take myself off now that she had
had the amusement of looking on the face of such a monster
of indiscretion. Therefore I was all the more surprised when
she added, with her soft, venerable quaver, 'You may have as
many rooms as you like—if you will pay a good deal of
money.'

I hesitated but for a single instant, long enough to ask myself what she meant in particular by this condition. First it
struck me that she must have really a large sum in her mind;
then I reasoned quickly that her idea of a large sum would
probably not correspond to my own. My deliberation, I think,
was not so visible as to diminish the promptitude with which
I replied, 'I will pay with pleasure and of course in advance
whatever you may think it proper to ask me.'

'Well then, a thousand francs a month,' she rejoined instantly, while her baffling green shade continued to cover her
attitude.

The figure, as they say, was startling and my logic had been
at fault. The sum she had mentioned was, by the Venetian
measure of such matters, exceedingly large; there was many
an old palace in an out-of-the-way corner that I might on such
terms have enjoyed by the year. But so far as my small means
allowed I was prepared to spend money, and my decision was
quickly taken. I would pay her with a smiling face what she
asked, but in that case I would give myself the compensation
of extracting the papers from her for nothing. Moreover if she
had asked five times as much I should have risen to the occasion; so odious would it have appeared to me to stand chaf-
fering with Aspern's Juliana. It was queer enough to have a

question of money with her at all. I assured her that her views perfectly met my own and that on the morrow I should have the pleasure of putting three months' rent into her hand. She received this announcement with serenity and with no apparent sense that after all it would be becoming of her to say that I ought to see the rooms first. This did not occur to her and indeed her serenity was mainly what I wanted. Our little bargain was just concluded when the door opened and the younger lady appeared on the threshold. As soon as Miss Bordereau saw her niece she cried out almost gaily, 'He will give three thousand—three thousand to-morrow!'

Miss Tita stood still, with her patient eyes turning from one of us to the other; then she inquired, scarcely above her breath, 'Do you mean francs?'

'Did you mean francs or dollars?' the old woman asked of me at this.

'I think francs were what you said,' I answered, smiling.

'That is very good,' said Miss Tita, as if she had become conscious that her own question might have looked over-reaching.

'What do *you* know? You are ignorant,' Miss Bordereau remarked; not with acerbity but with a strange, soft coldness.

'Yes, of money—certainly of money!' Miss Tita hastened to exclaim.

'I am sure you have your own branches of knowledge,' I took the liberty of saying, genially. There was something painful to me, somehow, in the turn the conversation had taken, in the discussion of the rent.

'She had a very good education when she was young. I looked into that myself,' said Miss Bordereau. Then she added, 'But she has learned nothing since.'

'I have always been with you,' Miss Tita rejoined very mildly, and evidently with no intention of making an epigram.

'Yes, but for that!' her aunt declared, with more satirical force. She evidently meant that but for this her niece would never have got on at all; the point of the observation however being lost on Miss Tita, though she blushed at hearing her history revealed to a stranger. Miss Bordereau went on, addressing herself to me: 'And what time will you come to-morrow with the money?'

'The sooner the better. If it suits you I will come at noon.'

'I am always here but I have my hours,' said the old woman, as if her convenience were not to be taken for granted.

'You mean the times when you receive?'

'I never receive. But I will see you at noon, when you come with the money.'

'Very good, I shall be punctual;' and I added, 'May I shake hands with you, on our contract?' I thought there ought to be some little form, it would make me really feel easier, for I foresaw that there would be no other. Besides, though Miss Bordereau could not to-day be called personally attractive and there was something even in her wasted antiquity that bade one stand at one's distance, I felt an irresistible desire to hold in my own for a moment the hand that Jeffrey Aspern had pressed.

For a minute she made no answer and I saw that my proposal failed to meet with her approbation. She indulged in no movement of withdrawal, which I half expected; she only said coldly, 'I belong to a time when that was not the custom.'

I felt rather snubbed but I exclaimed good-humouredly to Miss Tita, 'Oh, you will do as well!' I shook hands with her while she replied, with a small flutter, 'Yes, yes, to show it's all arranged!'

'Shall you bring the money in gold?' Miss Bordereau demanded, as I was turning to the door.

I looked at her a moment. 'Aren't you a little afraid, after all, of keeping such a sum as that in the house?' It was not that I was annoyed at her avidity but I was really struck with the disparity between such a treasure and such scanty means of guarding it.

'Whom should I be afraid of if I am not afraid of you?' she asked with her shrunken grimness.

'Ah well,' said I, laughing, 'I shall be in point of fact a protector and I will bring gold if you prefer.'

'Thank you,' the old woman returned with dignity and with an inclination of her head which evidently signified that I might depart. I passed out of the room, reflecting that it would not be easy to circumvent her. As I stood in the sala again I saw that Miss Tita had followed me and I supposed that as her aunt had neglected to suggest that I should take a look at my quarters it was her purpose to repair the omission. But she made no such suggestion; she only stood there with a dim, though not a languid smile, and with an effect of irresponsible, incompetent youth which was almost comically at variance with the faded facts of her person. She was not infirm, like her aunt, but she struck me as still more helpless, because her inefficiency was spiritual, which was not the case with Miss Bordereau's. I waited to see if she would offer to show me the rest of the house, but I did not precipitate the question, inasmuch as my plan was from this moment to spend as much of my time as possible in her society. I only observed at the end of a minute:

'I have had better fortune than I hoped. It was very kind of her to see me. Perhaps you said a good word for me.'

'It was the idea of the money,' said Miss Tita.

'And did you suggest that?'

'I told her that you would perhaps give a good deal.'

'What made you think that?'

'I told her I thought you were rich.'

'And what put that idea into your head?'

'I don't know; the way you talked.'

'Dear me, I must talk differently now,' I declared. 'I'm sorry to say it's not the case.'

'Well,' said Miss Tita, 'I think that in Venice the *forestieri*, in general, often give a great deal for something that after all isn't much.' She appeared to make this remark with a comforting intention, to wish to remind me that if I had been extravagant I was not really foolishly singular. We walked together along the sala, and as I took its magnificent measure I said to her that I was afraid it would not form a part of my *quartiere*. Were my rooms by chance to be among those that opened into it? 'Not if you go above, on the second floor,' she answered with a little startled air, as if she had rather taken for granted I would know my proper place.

'And I infer that that's where your aunt would like me to be.'

'She said your apartments ought to be very distinct.'

'That certainly would be best.' And I listened with respect while she told me that up above I was free to take whatever I liked; that there was another staircase, but only from the floor on which we stood, and that to pass from it to the garden-story or to come up to my lodging I should have in effect to cross the great hall. This was an immense point gained; I foresaw that it would constitute my whole leverage in my relations with the two ladies. When I asked Miss Tita how I was to manage at present to find my way up she replied with an access of that sociable shyness which constantly marked her manner.

'Perhaps you can't. I don't see—unless I should go with you.' She evidently had not thought of this before.

We ascended to the upper floor and visited a long succession of empty rooms. The best of them looked over the garden; some of the others had a view of the blue lagoon, above the opposite rough-tiled housetops. They were all dusty and even a little disfigured with long neglect, but I saw that by spending a few hundred francs I should be able to convert three or four of them into a convenient habitation. My experiment was turning out costly, yet now that I had all but taken possession I ceased to allow this to trouble me. I mentioned to my companion a few of the things that I should put in, but she replied rather more precipitately than usual that I might do exactly what I liked; she seemed to wish to notify me that the Misses Bordereau would take no overt interest in my proceedings. I guessed that her aunt had instructed her to adopt this tone, and I may as well say now that I came afterwards to distinguish perfectly (as I believed) between the speeches she made on her own responsibility and those the old lady imposed upon her. She took no notice of the unswept condition of the rooms and indulged in no explanations nor apologies. I said to myself that this was a sign that Juliana and her niece (disenchanting idea!) were untidy persons, with a low Italian standard; but I afterwards recognised that a lodger who had forced an entrance had no *locus standi* as a critic. We looked out of a good many windows, for there was nothing within the rooms to look at, and still I wanted to linger. I asked her what several different objects in the prospect might be, but in no case did she appear to know. She was evidently not familiar with the view—it was as if she had not looked at it for years—and I presently saw that she was too preoccupied with something else to pretend to care for it. Suddenly she said—the remark was not suggested:

'I don't know whether it will make any difference to you, but the money is for me.'

'The money?'

'The money you are going to bring.'

'Why, you'll make me wish to stay here two or three years.' I spoke as benevolently as possible, though it had begun to act on my nerves that with these women so associated with Aspern the pecuniary question should constantly come back.

'That would be very good for me,' she replied, smiling.

'You put me on my honour!'

She looked as if she failed to understand this, but went on: 'She wants me to have more. She thinks she is going to die.'

'Ah, not soon, I hope!' I exclaimed, with genuine feeling. I had perfectly considered the possibility that she would destroy her papers on the day she should feel her end really approach. I believed that she would cling to them till then and I think I had an idea that she read Aspern's letters over every night or at least pressed them to her withered lips. I would have given a good deal to have a glimpse of the latter spectacle. I asked Miss Tita if the old lady were seriously ill and she replied that she was only very tired—she had lived so very, very long. That was what she said herself—she wanted to die for a change. Besides, all her friends were dead long ago; either they ought to have remained or she ought to have gone. That was another thing her aunt often said—she was not at all content.

'But people don't die when they like, do they?' Miss Tita inquired. I took the liberty of asking why, if there was actually enough money to maintain both of them, there would not be more than enough in case of her being left alone. She considered this difficult problem a moment and then she said, 'Oh, well, you know, she takes care of me. She thinks that when I'm alone I shall be a great fool, I shall not know how to manage.'

'I should have supposed rather that you took care of her. I'm afraid she is very proud.'

'Why, have you discovered that already?' Miss Tita cried, with the glimmer of an illumination in her face.

'I was shut up with her there for a considerable time, and she struck me, she interested me extremely. It didn't take me long to make my discovery. She won't have much to say to me while I'm here.'

'No, I don't think she will,' my companion averred.

'Do you suppose she has some suspicion of me?'

Miss Tita's honest eyes gave me no sign that I had touched a mark. 'I shouldn't think so—letting you in after all so easily.'

'Oh, so easily! she has covered her risk. But where is it that one could take an advantage of her?'

'I oughtn't to tell you if I knew, ought I?' And Miss Tita added, before I had time to reply to this, smiling dolefully, 'Do you think we have any weak points?'

'That's exactly what I'm asking. You would only have to mention them for me to respect them religiously.'

She looked at me, at this, with that air of timid but candid and even gratified curiosity with which she had confronted me from the first; and then she said, 'There is nothing to tell. We are terribly quiet. I don't know how the days pass. We have no life.'

'I wish I might think that I should bring you a little.'

'Oh, we know what we want,' she went on. 'It's all right.'

There were various things I desired to ask her: how in the world they did live; whether they had any friends or visitors, any relations in America or in other countries. But I judged such an inquiry would be premature; I must leave it to a later chance. 'Well, don't *you* be proud,' I contented myself with saying. 'Don't hide from me altogether.'

'Oh, I must stay with my aunt,' she returned, without looking at me. And at the same moment, abruptly, without any ceremony of parting, she quitted me and disappeared, leaving me to make my own way downstairs. I remained a while longer, wandering about the bright desert (the sun was pouring in) of the old house, thinking the situation over on the spot. Not even the pattering little *serva* came to look after me and I reflected that after all this treatment showed confidence.

IV

Perhaps it did, but all the same, six weeks later, towards the middle of June, the moment when Mrs. Prest undertook her annual migration, I had made no measureable advance. I was obliged to confess to her that I had no results to speak of. My first step had been unexpectedly rapid, but there was no appearance that it would be followed by a second. I was a thousand miles from taking tea with my hostesses—that privilege of which, as I reminded Mrs. Prest, we both had had a vision. She reproached me with wanting boldness and I answered that even to be bold you must have an opportunity: you may push on through a breach but you can't batter down a dead wall. She answered that the breach I had already made was big enough to admit an army and accused me of wasting precious hours in whimpering in her salon when I ought to have been carrying on the struggle in the field. It is true that I went to see her very often, on the theory that it would console me (I freely expressed my discouragement) for my want of success on my own premises. But I began to perceive that it did not console me to be perpetually chaffed for my scruples, especially when I was really so vigilant; and I was rather glad when my derisive friend closed her house for the summer. She had expected to gather amusement from the drama of my intercourse with the Misses Bordereau and she was disappointed that the intercourse, and consequently the drama, had not come off. 'They'll lead you on to your ruin,' she said before she left Venice. 'They'll get all your money without showing you a scrap.' I think I settled down to my business with more concentration after she had gone away.

It was a fact that up to that time I had not, save on a single brief occasion, had even a moment's contact with my queer hostesses. The exception had occurred when I carried them according to my promise the terrible three thousand francs. Then I found Miss Tita waiting for me in the hall, and she took the money from my hand so that I did not see her aunt. The old lady had promised to receive me, but she apparently thought nothing of breaking that vow. The money was contained in a bag of chamois leather, of respectable dimensions, which my banker had given me, and Miss Tita had to make a big fist to receive it. This she did with extreme solemnity, though I tried to treat the affair a little as a joke. It was in no jocular strain, yet it was with simplicity, that she inquired, weighing the money in her two palms: 'Don't you think it's too much?' To which I replied that that would depend upon the amount of pleasure I should get for it. Hereupon she turned away from me quickly, as she had done the day before, murmuring in a tone different from any she had used hitherto: 'Oh, pleasure, pleasure—there's no pleasure in this house!'

After this, for a long time, I never saw her, and I wondered that the common chances of the day should not have helped us to meet. It could only be evident that she was immensely on her guard against them; and in addition to this the house was so big that for each other we were lost in it. I used to look out for her hopefully as I crossed the sala in my comings and goings, but I was not rewarded with a glimpse of the tail of her dress. It was as if she never peeped out of her aunt's apartment. I used to wonder what she did there week after week and year after year. I had never encountered such a violent *parti pris* of seclusion; it was more than keeping quiet—it was like hunted creatures feigning death. The two ladies appeared to have no visitors whatever and no sort of contact with the world. I judged at least that people could not have come to the house and that Miss Tita could not have gone out without my having some observation of it. I did what I disliked myself for doing (reflecting that it was only once in a way): I questioned my servant about their habits and let him divine that I should be interested in any information he could pick up. But he picked up amazingly little for a knowing Venetian: it must be added that where there is a perpetual fast there are very few crumbs on the floor. His cleverness in other ways was sufficient, if it was not quite all that I had attributed to him on the occasion of my first interview with Miss Tita. He had helped my gondolier to bring me round a boat-load of furniture; and when these articles had been carried to the top of the palace and distributed according to our associated wisdom he organised my household with such promptitude as was consistent with the fact that it was composed exclusively of himself. He made me in short as comfortable as I could be with my indifferent prospects. I should have been glad if he had fallen in love with Miss Bordereau's maid or, failing this, had taken her in aversion; either event might have brought about some kind of catastrophe and a catastrophe might have led to some parley. It was my idea that she would have been sociable, and I myself on various occasions saw her flit to and fro on domestic errands, so that I was sure she was accessible. But I tasted of no gossip from that fountain, and I afterwards learned that Pasquale's affections were fixed upon an object that made him heedless of other women. This was a young lady with a powdered face, a yellow cotton gown and much leisure, who used often to come to see him. She practised, at her convenience, the art of a stringer of beads (these ornaments are made in Venice, in profusion; she had her pocket full of them and I used to find them on the floor of my apartment), and kept an eye on the maiden in the house. It was not for me of course to make the domestics tattle, and I never said a word to Miss Bordereau's cook.

It seemed to me a proof of the old lady's determination to have nothing to do with me that she should never have sent me a receipt for my three months' rent. For some days I looked out for it and then, when I had given it up, I wasted a good deal of time in wondering what her reason had been for neglecting so indispensable and familiar a form. At first I was tempted to send her a reminder, after which I relinquished the idea (against my judgment as to what was right in the particular case), on the general ground of wishing to keep quiet. If Miss Bordereau suspected me of ulterior aims she would suspect me less if I should be businesslike, and yet I consented not to be so. It was possible she intended her omission as an impertinence, a visible irony, to show how she could overreach people who attempted to overreach her. On that hypothesis it was well to let her see that one did not notice her little tricks. The real reading of the matter, I afterwards perceived, was simply the poor old woman's desire to emphasise the fact that I was in the enjoyment of a favour as rigidly limited as it had been liberally bestowed. She had given me part of her house and now she would not give me even a morsel of paper with her name on it. Let me say that even at first this did not make me too miserable, for the whole episode was essentially delightful to me. I foresaw that I should have a summer after my own literary heart, and the sense of holding my opportunity was much greater than the sense of losing it. There could be no Venetian business without patience, and since I adored the place I was much more in the spirit of it for having laid in a large provision. That spirit kept me perpetual company and seemed to look out at me from the revived immortal face—in which all his genius shone—of the great poet who was my prompter. I had invoked him and he had come; he hovered before me half the time; it was as if his bright ghost had returned to earth to tell me that he regarded the affair as his own no less than mine and that we should see it fraternally, cheerfully to a conclusion. It was as if he had said, 'Poor dear, be easy with her; she has some natural prejudices; only give her time. Strange as it may appear to you she was very attractive in 1820. Meanwhile are we not in Venice together, and what better place is there for the meeting of dear friends? See how it glows with the advancing summer; how the sky and the sea and the rosy air and the marble of the palaces all shimmer and melt together.' My eccentric private errand became a part of the general romance and the general glory—I felt even a mystic companionship, a moral fraternity with all those who in the past had been in the service of art. They had worked for beauty, for a devotion; and what else was I doing? That element was in everything that Jeffrey Aspern had written and I was only bringing it to the light.

I lingered in the sala when I went to and fro; I used to watch—as long as I thought decent—the door that led to Miss Bordereau's part of the house. A person observing me might have supposed I was trying to cast a spell upon it or attempting some odd experiment in hypnotism. But I was only praying it would open or thinking what treasure probably lurked behind it. I hold it singular, as I look back, that I should never have doubted for a moment that the sacred relics were there; never have failed to feel a certain joy at being under the same roof with them. After all they were under my hand—they had not escaped me yet; and they made my life continuous, in a fashion, with the illustrious life they had touched at the other end. I lost myself in this satisfaction to the point of assuming—in my quiet extravagance—that poor Miss Tita also went back, went back, as I used to phrase it. She did indeed, the gentle spinster, but not quite so far as Jeffrey Aspern, who was simple hearsay to her, quite as he was to me. Only she had lived for years with Juliana, she had seen and handled the papers and (even though she was stupid) some esoteric knowledge had rubbed off on her. That was what the old woman represented—esoteric knowledge; and this was the idea with which my editorial heart used to thrill. It literally beat faster often, of an evening, when I had been out, as I stopped with my candle in the re-echoing hall on my way up to bed. It was as if at such a moment as that, in the stillness, after the long contradiction of the day, Miss Bordereau's secrets were in the air, the wonder of her survival more palpable. These were the acute impressions. I had them in another form, with more of a certain sort of reciprocity, during the hours that I sat in the garden looking up over the top of my book at the closed windows of my hostess. In these windows no sign of life ever appeared; it was as if, for fear of my catching a glimpse of them, the two ladies passed their days in the dark. But this only proved to me that they had something to conceal; which was what I had wished to demonstrate. Their motionless shutters became as expressive as eyes consciously closed, and I took comfort in thinking that at all events though invisible themselves they saw me between the lashes.

I made a point of spending as much time as possible in the garden, to justify the picture I had originally given of my horticultural passion. And I not only spent time, but (hang it! as I said) I spent money. As soon as I had got my rooms arranged and could give the proper thought to the matter I surveyed the place with a clever expert and made terms for having it put in order. I was sorry to do this, for personally I liked it better as it was, with its weeds and its wild, rough tangle, its sweet, characteristic Venetian shabbiness. I had to be consistent, to keep my promise that I would smother the house in flowers. Moreover I formed this graceful project that by flowers I would make my way—I would succeed by big nosegays. I would batter the old women with lilies—I would bombard their citadel with roses. Their door would have to yield to the pressure when a mountain of carnations should be piled up against it. The place in truth had been brutally neglected. The Venetian capacity for dawdling is of the largest, and for a good many days unlimited litter was all my gardener had to show for his ministrations. There was a great digging of holes and carting about of earth, and after a while I grew so impatient that I had thoughts of sending for my bouquets to the nearest stand. But I reflected that the ladies would see through the chinks of their shutters that they must have been bought and might make up their minds from this that I was a humbug. So I composed myself and finally, though the delay was long, perceived some appearances of bloom. This encouraged me and I waited serenely enough till they multiplied. Meanwhile the real summer days arrived and began to pass, and as I look back upon them they seem to me almost the happiest of my life. I took more and more care to be in the garden whenever it was not too hot. I had an arbour arranged and a low table and an armchair put into it; and I carried out books and port-folios (I had always some business of writing in hand), and worked and waited and mused and hoped, while the golden hours elapsed and the plants drank in the light and the in-scrutable old palace turned pale and then, as the day waned, began to flush in it and my papers rustled in the wandering breeze of the Adriatic.

Considering how little satisfaction I got from it at first it is remarkable that I should not have grown more tired of won-dering what mystic rites of ennui the Misses Bordereau cele-brated in their darkened rooms; whether this had always been the tenor of their life and how in previous years they had escaped elbowing their neighbours. It was clear that they must have had other habits and other circumstances; that they must once have been young or at least middle-aged. There was no end to the questions it was possible to ask about them and no end to the answers it was not possible to frame. I had known many of my country-people in Europe and was familiar with the strange ways they were liable to take up there; but the Misses Bordereau formed altogether a new type of the American absentee. Indeed it was plain that the American name had ceased to have any application to them—I had seen this in the ten minutes I spent in the old woman's room. You could never have said whence they came, from the appearance of either of them; wherever it was they had long ago dropped the local accent and fashion. There was nothing in them that one recognised, and putting the question of speech aside they might have been Norwegians or Spaniards. Miss Bordereau, after all, had been in Europe nearly threequarters of a century; it appeared by some verses addressed to her by Aspern on the occasion of his own second absence from America—verses of which Cumnor and I had after infinite conjecture established solidly enough the date—that she was even then, as a girl of twenty, on the foreign side of the sea. There was an implication in the poem (I hope not just for the phrase) that he had come back for her sake. We had no real light upon her circumstances at that moment, any more than we had upon her origin, which we believed to be of the sort usually spoken of as modest. Cumnor had a theory that she had been a governess in some family in which the poet visited and that, in consequence of her position, there was from the first something unavowed, or rather something positively clandestine, in their relations. I on the other hand had hatched a little romance according to which she was the daughter of an artist, a painter or a sculptor, who had left the western world when the century was fresh, to study in the ancient schools. It was essential to my hypothesis that this amiable man should have lost his wife, should have been poor and unsuccessful and should have had a second daughter, of a disposition quite different from Juliana's. It was also indispensable that he should have been accompanied to Europe by these young ladies and should have established himself there for the remainder of a struggling, saddened life. There was a further implication that Miss Bordereau had had in her youth a perverse and adventurous, albeit a generous and fascinating character, and that she had passed through some singular vicissitudes. By what passions had she been ravaged, by what sufferings had she been blanched, what store of memories had she laid away for the monotonous future?

I asked myself these things as I sat spinning theories about her in my arbour and the bees droned in the flowers. It was incontestable that, whether for right or for wrong, most readers of certain of Aspern's poems (poems not as ambiguous as the sonnets—scarcely more divine, I think—of Shakespeare) had taken for granted that Juliana had not always adhered to the steep footway of renunciation. There hovered about her name a perfume of reckless passion, an intimation that she had not been exactly as the respectable young person in general. Was this a sign that her singer had betrayed her, had given her away, as we say nowadays, to posterity? Certain it is that it would have been difficult to put one's finger on the passage in which her fair fame suffered an imputation. Moreover was not any fame fair enough that was so sure of duration and was associated with works immortal through their beauty? It was a part of my idea that the young lady had had a foreign lover (and an unedifying tragical rupture) before her meeting with Jeffrey Aspern. She had lived with her father and sister in a queer old-fashioned, expatriated, artistic Bohemia, in the days when the æsthetic was only the academic and the painters who knew the best models for a *contadina* and *pifferaro* wore peaked hats and long hair. It was a society less furnished than the coteries of to-day (in its ignorance of the wonderful chances, the opportunities of the early bird, with which its path was strewn), with tatters of old stuff and fragments of old crockery; so that Miss Bordereau appeared not to have picked up or have inherited many objects of importance. There was no enviable *bric-à-brac*, with its provoking legend of cheapness, in the room in which I had seen her. Such a fact as that suggested bareness, but none the less it worked happily into the sentimental interest I had always taken in the early movements of my countrymen as visitors to Europe. When Americans went abroad in 1820 there was something romantic, almost heroic in it, as compared with the perpetual ferryings of the present hour, when photography and other conveniences have annihilated surprise. Miss Bordereau sailed with her family on a tossing brig, in the days of long voyages and sharp differences; she had her emotions on the top of yellow diligences, passed the night at inns where she dreamed of travellers' tales, and was struck, on reaching the eternal city, with the elegance of Roman pearls and scarfs. There was something touching to me in all that and my imagination frequently went back to the period. If Miss Bordereau carried it there of course Jeffrey Aspern at other times had done so a great deal more. It was a much more important fact, if one were looking at his genius critically, that he had lived in the days before the general transfusion. It had happened to me to regret that he had known Europe at all; I should have liked to see what he would have written without that experience, by which he had incontestably been enriched. But as his fate had ordered otherwise I went with him—I tried to judge how the old world would

have struck him. It was not only there, however, that I
watched him; the relations he had entertained with the new
had even a livelier interest. His own country after all had had
most of his life, and his muse, as they said at that time, was
essentially American. That was originally what I had loved him
for: that at a period when our native land was nude and crude
and provincial, when the famous 'atmosphere' it is supposed
to lack was not even missed, when literature was lonely there
and art and form almost impossible, he had found means to
live and write like one of the first; to be free and general and
not at all afraid; to feel, understand and express everything.

V

I was seldom at home in the evening, for when I attempted
to occupy myself in my apartments the lamplight brought in
a swarm of noxious insects, and it was too hot for closed windows. Accordingly I spent the late hours either on the water
(the moonlight of Venice is famous), or in the splendid square
which serves as a vast forecourt to the strange old basilica of
Saint Mark. I sat in front of Florian's *café*, eating ices, listening
to music, talking with acquaintances: the traveller will remember how the immense cluster of tables and little chairs
stretches like a promontory into the smooth lake of the Piazza. The whole place, of a summer's evening, under the stars
and with all the lamps, all the voices and light footsteps on
marble (the only sounds of the arcades that enclose it), is like
an open-air saloon dedicated to cooling drinks and to a still
finer degustation—that of the exquisite impressions received
during the day. When I did not prefer to keep mine to myself
there was always a stray tourist, disencumbered of his Bädeker,
to discuss them with, or some domesticated painter rejoicing
in the return of the season of strong effects. The wonderful
church, with its low domes and bristling embroideries, the
mystery of its mosaic and sculpture, looked ghostly in the
tempered gloom, and the sea-breeze passed between the twin
columns of the Piazzetta, the lintels of a door no longer
guarded, as gently as if a rich curtain were swaying there. I
used sometimes on these occasions to think of the Misses Bordereau and of the pity of their being shut up in apartments

which in the Venetian July even Venetian vastness did not prevent from being stuffy. Their life seemed miles away from the life of the Piazza, and no doubt it was really too late to make the austere Juliana change her habits. But poor Miss Tita would have enjoyed one of Florian's ices, I was sure; sometimes I even had thoughts of carrying one home to her. Fortunately my patience bore fruit and I was not obliged to do anything so ridiculous.

One evening about the middle of July I came in earlier than usual—I forget what chance had led to this—and instead of going up to my quarters made my way into the garden. The temperature was very high; it was such a night as one would gladly have spent in the open air and I was in no hurry to go to bed. I had floated home in my gondola, listening to the slow splash of the oar in the narrow dark canals, and now the only thought that solicited me was the vague reflection that it would be pleasant to recline at one's length in the fragrant darkness on a garden bench. The odour of the canal was doubtless at the bottom of that aspiration and the breath of the garden, as I entered it, gave consistency to my purpose. It was delicious—just such an air as must have trembled with Romeo's vows when he stood among the flowers and raised his arms to his mistress's balcony. I looked at the windows of the palace to see if by chance the example of Verona (Verona being not far off) had been followed; but everything was dim, as usual, and everything was still. Juliana, on summer nights in her youth, might have murmured down from open windows at Jeffrey Aspern, but Miss Tita was not a poet's mistress any more than I was a poet. This however did not prevent my gratification from being great as I became aware on reaching the end of the garden that Miss Tita was seated in my little bower. At first I only made out an indistinct figure, not in the least counting on such an overture from one of my hostesses; it even occurred to me that some sentimental maidservant had stolen in to keep a tryst with her sweetheart. I was going to turn away, not to frighten her, when the figure rose to its height and I recognised Miss Bordereau's niece. I must do myself the justice to say that I did not wish to frighten her either, and much as I had longed for some such accident I should have been capable of retreating. It was as if I had laid a trap for her by coming home earlier than usual and adding to that eccentricity by creeping into the garden. As she rose she spoke to me, and then I reflected that perhaps, secure in my almost inveterate absence, it was her nightly practice to take a lonely airing. There was no trap, in truth, because I had had no suspicion. At first I took for granted that the words she uttered expressed discomfiture at my arrival; but as she repeated them—I had not caught them clearly—I had the surprise of hearing her say, 'Oh, dear, I'm so very glad you've come!' She and her aunt had in common the property of unexpected speeches. She came out of the arbour almost as if she were going to throw herself into my arms.

I hasten to add that she did nothing of the kind; she did not even shake hands with me. It was a gratification to her to see me and presently she told me why—because she was nervous when she was out-of-doors at night alone. The plants and bushes looked so strange in the dark, and there were all sorts of queer sounds—she could not tell what they were—like the noises of animals. She stood close to me, looking about her with an air of greater security but without any demonstration of interest in me as an individual. Then I guessed that nocturnal prowlings were not in the least her habit, and I was also reminded (I had been struck with the circumstance in talking with her before I took possession) that it was impossible to overestimate her simplicity.

'You speak as if you were lost in the backwoods,' I said, laughing. 'How you manage to keep out of this charming place when you have only three steps to take to get into it, is more than I have yet been able to discover. You hide away mighty well so long as I am on the premises, I know; but I had a hope that you peeped out a little at other times. You and your poor aunt are worse off than Carmelite nuns in their cells. Should you mind telling me how you exist without air, without exercise, without any sort of human contact? I don't see how you carry on the common business of life.'

She looked at me as if I were talking some strange tongue and her answer was so little of an answer that I was considerably irritated. 'We go to bed very early—earlier than you would believe.' I was on the point of saying that this only deepened the mystery when she gave me some relief by adding, 'Before you came we were not so private. But I never have been out at night.'

'Never in these fragrant alleys, blooming here under your nose?'

'Ah,' said Miss Tita, 'they were never nice till now!' There was an unmistakable reference in this and a flattering comparison, so that it seemed to me I had gained a small advantage. As it would help me to follow it up to establish a sort of grievance I asked her why, since she thought my garden nice, she had never thanked me in any way for the flowers I had been sending up in such quantities for the previous three weeks. I had not been discouraged—there had been, as she would have observed, a daily armful; but I had been brought up in the common forms and a word of recognition now and then would have touched me in the right place.

'Why I didn't know they were for me!'

'They were for both of you. Why should I make a difference?'

Miss Tita reflected as if she might be thinking of a reason for that, but she failed to produce one. Instead of this she asked abruptly, 'Why in the world do you want to know us?'

'I ought after all to make a difference,' I replied. 'That question is your aunt's; it isn't yours. You wouldn't ask it if you hadn't been put up to it.'

'She didn't tell me to ask you,' Miss Tita replied, without confusion; she was the oddest mixture of the shrinking and the direct.

'Well, she has often wondered about it herself and expressed her wonder to you. She has insisted on it, so that she has put the idea into your head that I am unsufferably pushing. Upon my word I think I have been very discreet. And how completely your aunt must have lost every tradition of sociability, to see anything out of the way in the idea that respectable intelligent people, living as we do under the same roof, should occasionally exchange a remark! What could be more natural? We are of the same country and we have at least some of the same tastes, since, like you, I am intensely fond of Venice.'

My interlocutress appeared incapable of grasping more than one clause in any proposition, and she declared quickly, eagerly, as if she were answering my whole speech: 'I am not in the least fond of Venice. I should like to go far away!'

'Has she always kept you back so?' I went on, to show her that I could be as irrelevant as herself.

'She told me to come out to-night; she has told me very often,' said Miss Tita. 'It is I who wouldn't come. I don't like to leave her.'

'Is she too weak, is she failing?' I demanded, with more emotion, I think, than I intended to show. I judged this by the way her eyes rested upon me in the darkness. It embarrassed me a little, and to turn the matter off I continued genially: 'Do let us sit down together comfortably somewhere and you will tell me all about her.'

Miss Tita made no resistance to this. We found a bench less secluded, less confidential, as it were, than the one in the arbour; and we were still sitting there when I heard midnight ring out from those clear bells of Venice which vibrate with a solemnity of their own over the lagoon and hold the air so much more than the chimes of other places. We were together more than an hour and our interview gave, as it struck me, a great lift to my undertaking. Miss Tita accepted the situation without a protest; she had avoided me for three months, yet now she treated me almost as if these three months had made me an old friend. If I had chosen I might have inferred from this that though she had avoided me she had given a good deal of consideration to doing so. She paid no attention to the flight of time—never worried at my keeping her so long away from her aunt. She talked freely, answering questions and asking them and not even taking advantage of certain longish pauses with which they inevitably alternated to say she thought she had better go in. It was almost as if she were waiting for something—something I might say to her—and intended to give me my opportunity. I was the more struck by this as she told me that her aunt had been less well for a good many days and in a way that was rather new. She was weaker; at moments it seemed as if she had no strength at all; yet more than ever before she wished to be left alone. That was why she had told her to come out—not even to remain in her own room, which was alongside; she said her niece

irritated her, made her nervous. She sat still for hours together, as if she were asleep; she had always done that, musing
and dozing; but at such times formerly she gave at intervals
some small sign of life, of interest, liking her companion to
be near her with her work. Miss Tita confided to me that at
present her aunt was so motionless that she sometimes feared
she was dead; moreover she took hardly any food—one
couldn't see what she lived on. The great thing was that she
still on most days got up; the serious job was to dress her, to
wheel her out of her bedroom. She clung to as many of her
old habits as possible and she had always, little company as
they had received for years, made a point of sitting in the
parlour.

I scarcely knew what to think of all this—of Miss Tita's
sudden conversion to sociability and of the strange circumstance that the more the old lady appeared to decline toward
her end the less she should desire to be looked after. The story
did not hang together, and I even asked myself whether it
were not a trap laid for me, the result of a design to make me
show my hand. I could not have told why my companions (as
they could only by courtesy be called) should have this purpose—why they should try to trip up so lucrative a lodger. At
any rate I kept on my guard, so that Miss Tita should not
have occasion again to ask me if I had an *arrière-pensée*. Poor
woman, before we parted for the night my mind was at rest
as to *her* capacity for entertaining one.

She told me more about their affairs than I had hoped;
there was no need to be prying, for it evidently drew her out
simply to feel that I listened, that I cared. She ceased wondering why I cared, and at last, as she spoke of the brilliant
life they had led years before, she almost chattered. It was
Miss Tita who judged it brilliant; she said that when they first
came to live in Venice, years and years before (I saw that her
mind was essentially vague about dates and the order in which
events had occurred), there was scarcely a week that they had
not some visitor or did not make some delightful *passeggio* in
the city. They had seen all the curiosities; they had even been
to the Lido in a boat (she spoke as if I might think there was
a way on foot); they had had a collation there, brought in
three baskets and spread out on the grass. I asked her what

people they had known and she said, Oh! very nice ones—the Cavaliere Bombicci and the Contessa Altemura, with whom they had had a great friendship. Also English people—the Churtons and the Goldies and Mrs. Stock-Stock, whom they had loved dearly; she was dead and gone, poor dear. That was the case with most of their pleasant circle (this expression was Miss Tita's own), though a few were left, which was a wonder considering how they had neglected them. She mentioned the names of two or three Venetian old women; of a certain doctor, very clever, who was so kind—he came as a friend, he had really given up practice; of the *avvocato* Pochintesta, who wrote beautiful poems and had addressed one to her aunt. These people came to see them without fail every year, usually at the *capo d'anno*, and of old her aunt used to make them some little present—her aunt and she together: small things that she, Miss Tita, made herself, like paper lamp-shades or mats for the decanters of wine at dinner or those woollen things that in cold weather were worn on the wrists. The last few years there had not been many presents; she could not think what to make and her aunt had lost her interest and never suggested. But the people came all the same; if the Venetians liked you once they liked you for ever.

There was something affecting in the good faith of this sketch of former social glories; the picnic at the Lido had remained vivid through the ages and poor Miss Tita evidently was of the impression that she had had a brilliant youth. She had in fact had a glimpse of the Venetian world in its gossiping, home-keeping, parsimonious, professional walks; for I observed for the first time that she had acquired by contact something of the trick of the familiar, soft-sounding, almost infantile speech of the place. I judged that she had imbibed this invertebrate dialect, from the natural way the names of things and people—mostly purely local—rose to her lips. If she knew little of what they represented she knew still less of anything else. Her aunt had drawn in—her failing interest in the table-mats and lamp-shades was a sign of that—and she had not been able to mingle in society or to entertain it alone; so that the matter of her reminiscences struck one as an old world altogether. If she had not been so decent her references would have seemed to carry one back to the queer rococo

Venice of Casanova. I found myself falling into the error of
thinking of her too as one of Jeffrey Aspern's contemporaries;
this came from her having so little in common with my own.
It was possible, I said to myself, that she had not even heard
of him; it might very well be that Juliana had not cared to lift
even for her the veil that covered the temple of her youth. In
this case she perhaps would not know of the existence of the
papers, and I welcomed that presumption—it made me feel
more safe with her—until I remembered that we had believed
the letter of disavowal received by Cumnor to be in the hand-
writing of the niece. If it had been dictated to her she had of
course to know what it was about; yet after all the effect of it
was to repudiate the idea of any connection with the poet. I
held it probable at all events that Miss Tita had not read a
word of his poetry. Moreover if, with her companion, she had
always escaped the interviewer there was little occasion for her
having got it into her head that people were 'after' the letters.
People had not been after them, inasmuch as they had not
heard of them; and Cumnor's fruitless feeler would have been
a solitary accident.

When midnight sounded Miss Tita got up; but she stopped
at the door of the house only after she had wandered two or
three times with me round the garden. 'When shall I see you
again?' I asked, before she went in; to which she replied with
promptness that she should like to come out the next night.
She added however that she should not come—she was so far
from doing everything she liked.

'You might do a few things that I like,' I said with a sigh.

'Oh, you—I don't believe you!' she murmured, at this,
looking at me with her simple solemnity.

'Why don't you believe me?'

'Because I don't understand you.'

'That is just the sort of occasion to have faith.' I could not
say more, though I should have liked to, as I saw that I only
mystified her; for I had no wish to have it on my conscience
that I might pass for having made love to her. Nothing less
should I have seemed to do had I continued to beg a lady to
'believe in me' in an Italian garden on a mid-summer night.
There was some merit in my scruples, for Miss Tita lingered
and lingered: I perceived that she felt that she should not

really soon come down again and wished therefore to protract the present. She insisted too on making the talk between us personal to ourselves; and altogether her behaviour was such as would have been possible only to a completely innocent woman.

'I shall like the flowers better now that I know they are also meant for me.'

'How could you have doubted it? If you will tell me the kind you like best I will send a double lot of them.'

'Oh, I like them all best!' Then she went on, familiarly: 'Shall you study—shall you read and write—when you go up to your rooms?'

'I don't do that at night, at this season. The lamplight brings in the animals.'

'You might have known that when you came.'

'I did know it!'

'And in winter do you work at night?'

'I read a good deal, but I don't often write.' She listened as if these details had a rare interest, and suddenly a temptation quite at variance with the prudence I had been teaching myself associated itself with her plain, mild face. Ah yes, she was safe and I could make her safer! It seemed to me from one moment to another that I could not wait longer—that I really must take a sounding. So I went on: 'In general before I go to sleep—very often in bed (it's a bad habit, but I confess to it), I read some great poet. In nine cases out of ten it's a volume of Jeffrey Aspern.'

I watched her well as I pronounced that name but I saw nothing wonderful. Why should I indeed—was not Jeffrey Aspern the property of the human race?

'Oh, we read him—we *have* read him,' she quietly replied.

'He is my poet of poets—I know him almost by heart.'

For an instant Miss Tita hesitated; then her sociability was too much for her.

'Oh, by heart—that's nothing!' she murmured, smiling. 'My aunt used to know him—to know him'—she paused an instant and I wondered what she was going to say—'to know him as a visitor.'

'As a visitor?' I repeated, staring.

'He used to call on her and take her out.'

I continued to stare. 'My dear lady, he died a hundred years ago!'

'Well,' she said, mirthfully, 'my aunt is a hundred and fifty.'

'Mercy on us!' I exclaimed; 'why didn't you tell me before? I should like so to ask her about him.'

'She wouldn't care for that—she wouldn't tell you,' Miss Tita replied.

'I don't care what she cares for! She *must* tell me—it's not a chance to be lost.'

'Oh, you should have come twenty years ago: then she still talked about him.'

'And what did she say?' I asked, eagerly.

'I don't know—that he liked her immensely.'

'And she—didn't she like him?'

'She said he was a god.' Miss Tita gave me this information flatly, without expression; her tone might have made it a piece of trivial gossip. But it stirred me deeply as she dropped the words into the summer night; it seemed such a direct testimony.

'Fancy, fancy!' I murmured. And then, 'Tell me this, please —has she got a portrait of him? They are distressingly rare.'

'A portrait? I don't know,' said Miss Tita; and now there was discomfiture in her face. 'Well, good-night!' she added; and she turned into the house.

I accompanied her into the wide, dusky, stone-paved passage which on the ground floor corresponded with our grand sala. It opened at one end into the garden, at the other upon the canal, and was lighted now only by the small lamp that was always left for me to take up as I went to bed. An extinguished candle which Miss Tita apparently had brought down with her stood on the same table with it. 'Good-night, good-night!' I replied, keeping beside her as she went to get her light. 'Surely you would know, shouldn't you, if she had one?'

'If she had what?' the poor lady asked, looking at me queerly over the flame of her candle.

'A portrait of the god. I don't know what I wouldn't give to see it.'

'I don't know what she has got. She keeps her things locked up.' And Miss Tita went away, toward the staircase, with the sense evidently that she had said too much.

I let her go—I wished not to frighten her—and I contented myself with remarking that Miss Bordereau would not have locked up such a glorious possession as that—a thing a person would be proud of and hang up in a prominent place on the parlour-wall. Therefore of course she had not any portrait. Miss Tita made no direct answer to this and candle in hand, with her back to me, ascended two or three stairs. Then she stopped short and turned round, looking at me across the dusky space.

'Do you write—do you write?' There was a shake in her voice—she could scarcely bring out what she wanted to ask.

'Do I write? Oh, don't speak of my writing on the same day with Aspern's!'

'Do you write about *him*—do you pry into his life?'

'Ah, that's your aunt's question; it can't be yours!' I said, in a tone of slightly wounded sensibility.

'All the more reason then that you should answer it. Do you, please?'

I thought I had allowed for the falsehoods I should have to tell; but I found that in fact when it came to the point I had not. Besides, now that I had an opening there was a kind of relief in being frank. Lastly (it was perhaps fanciful, even fatuous), I guessed that Miss Tita personally would not in the last resort be less my friend. So after a moment's hesitation I answered, 'Yes, I have written about him and I am looking for more material. In heaven's name have you got any?'

'*Santo Dio!*' she exclaimed, without heeding my question; and she hurried upstairs and out of sight. I might count upon her in the last resort, but for the present she was visibly alarmed. The proof of it was that she began to hide again, so that for a fortnight I never beheld her. I found my patience ebbing and after four or five days of this I told the gardener to stop the flowers.

VI

One afternoon, as I came down from my quarters to go out, I found Miss Tita in the sala: it was our first encounter on that ground since I had come to the house. She put on no air of being there by accident; there was an ignorance of such arts in her angular, diffident directness. That I might be quite sure she was waiting for me she informed me of the fact and told me that Miss Bordereau wished to see me: she would take me into the room at that moment if I had time. If I had been late for a love-tryst I would have stayed for this, and I quickly signified that I should be delighted to wait upon the old lady. 'She wants to talk with you—to know you,' Miss Tita said, smiling as if she herself appreciated that idea; and she led me to the door of her aunt's apartment. I stopped her a moment before she had opened it, looking at her with some curiosity. I told her that this was a great satisfaction to me and a great honour; but all the same I should like to ask what had made Miss Bordereau change so suddenly. It was only the other day that she wouldn't suffer me near her. Miss Tita was not embarrassed by my question; she had as many little un-expected serenities as if she told fibs, but the odd part of them was that they had on the contrary their source in her truth-fulness. 'Oh, my aunt changes,' she answered; 'it's so terribly dull—I suppose she's tired.'

'But you told me that she wanted more and more to be alone.'

Poor Miss Tita coloured, as if she found me over-insistent. 'Well, if you don't believe she wants to see you—I haven't invented it! I think people often are capricious when they are very old.'

'That's perfectly true. I only wanted to be clear as to whether you have repeated to her what I told you the other night.'

'What you told me?'

'About Jeffrey Aspern—that I am looking for materials.'

'If I had told her do you think she would have sent for you?'

'That's exactly what I want to know. If she wants to keep him to herself she might have sent for me to tell me so.'

'She won't speak of him,' said Miss Tita. Then as she opened the door she added in a lower tone, 'I have told her nothing.'

The old woman was sitting in the same place in which I had seen her last, in the same position, with the same mysti-fying bandage over her eyes. Her welcome was to turn her almost invisible face to me and show me that while she sat silent she saw me clearly. I made no motion to shake hands with her; I felt too well on this occasion that that was out of place for ever. It had been sufficiently enjoined upon me that she was too sacred for that sort of reciprocity—too venerable to touch. There was something so grim in her aspect (it was partly the accident of her green shade), as I stood there to be measured, that I ceased on the spot to feel any doubt as to her knowing my secret, though I did not in the least suspect that Miss Tita had not just spoken the truth. She had not betrayed me, but the old woman's brooding instinct had served her; she had turned me over and over in the long, still hours and she had guessed. The worst of it was that she looked terribly like an old woman who at a pinch would burn her papers. Miss Tita pushed a chair forward, saying to me, 'This will be a good place for you to sit.' As I took possession of it I asked after Miss Bordereau's health; expressed the hope that in spite of the very hot weather it was satisfactory. She replied that it was good enough—good enough; that it was a great thing to be alive.

'Oh, as to that, it depends upon what you compare it with!' I exclaimed, laughing.

'I don't compare—I don't compare. If I did that I should have given everything up long ago.'

I liked to think that this was a subtle allusion to the rapture she had known in the society of Jeffrey Aspern—though it was true that such an allusion would have accorded ill with the wish I imputed to her to keep him buried in her soul. What it accorded with was my constant conviction that no human being had ever had a more delightful social gift than his, and what it seemed to convey was that nothing in the world was worth speaking of if one pretended to speak of that. But one did not! Miss Tita sat down beside her aunt, looking as if she had reason to believe some very remarkable conversation would come off between us.

'It's about the beautiful flowers,' said the old lady; 'you sent us so many—I ought to have thanked you for them before. But I don't write letters and I receive only at long intervals.'

She had not thanked me while the flowers continued to come, but she departed from her custom so far as to send for me as soon as she began to fear that they would not come any more. I noted this; I remembered what an acquisitive propensity she had shown when it was a question of extracting gold from me, and I privately rejoiced at the happy thought I had had in suspending my tribute. She had missed it and she was willing to make a concession to bring it back. At the first sign of this concession I could only go to meet her. 'I am afraid you have not had many, of late, but they shall begin again immediately—to-morrow, to-night.'

'Oh, do send us some to-night!' Miss Tita cried, as if it were an immense circumstance.

'What else should you do with them? It isn't a manly taste to make a bower of your room,' the old woman remarked.

'I don't make a bower of my room, but I am exceedingly fond of growing flowers, of watching their ways. There is nothing unmanly in that: it has been the amusement of philosophers, of statesmen in retirement; even I think of great captains.'

'I suppose you know you can sell them—those you don't use,' Miss Bordereau went on. 'I daresay they wouldn't give you much for them; still, you could make a bargain.'

'Oh, I have never made a bargain, as you ought to know. My gardener disposes of them and I ask no questions.'

'I would ask a few, I can promise you!' said Miss Bordereau; and it was the first time I had heard her laugh. I could not get used to the idea that this vision of pecuniary profit was what drew out the divine Juliana most.

'Come into the garden yourself and pick them; come as often as you like; come every day. They are all for you,' I pursued, addressing Miss Tita and carrying off this veracious statement by treating it as an innocent joke. 'I can't imagine why she doesn't come down,' I added, for Miss Bordereau's benefit.

'You must make her come; you must come up and fetch her,' said the old woman, to my stupefaction. 'That odd thing you have made in the corner would be a capital place for her to sit.'

The allusion to my arbour was irreverent; it confirmed the impression I had already received that there was a flicker of impertinence in Miss Bordereau's talk, a strange mocking lambency which must have been a part of her adventurous youth and which had outlived passions and faculties. None the less I asked, 'Wouldn't it be possible for you to come down there yourself? Wouldn't it do you good to sit there in the shade, in the sweet air?'

'Oh, sir, when I move out of this it won't be to sit in the air, and I'm afraid that any that may be stirring around me won't be particularly sweet! It will be a very dark shade indeed. But that won't be just yet,' Miss Bordereau continued, cannily, as if to correct any hopes that this courageous allusion to the last receptacle of her mortality might lead me to entertain. 'I have sat here many a day and I have had enough of arbours in my time. But I'm not afraid to wait till I'm called.'

Miss Tita had expected some interesting talk, but perhaps she found it less genial on her aunt's side (considering that I had been sent for with a civil intention) than she had hoped. As if to give the conversation a turn that would put our companion in a light more favourable she said to me, 'Didn't I tell you the other night that she had sent me out? You see that I can do what I like!'

'Do you pity her—do you teach her to pity herself?' Miss Bordereau demanded, before I had time to answer this appeal. 'She has a much easier life than I had when I was her age.'

'You must remember that it has been quite open to me to think you rather inhuman.'

'Inhuman? That's what the poets used to call the women a hundred years ago. Don't try that; you won't do as well as they!' Juliana declared. 'There is no more poetry in the world—that I know of at least. But I won't bandy words with you,' she pursued, and I well remember the old-fashioned, artificial sound she gave to the speech. 'You have made me talk, talk! It isn't good for me at all.' I got up at this and told her I would take no more of her time; but she detained me to ask, 'Do you remember, the day I saw you about the rooms, that you offered us the use of your gondola?' And when I assented, promptly, struck again with her disposition to make a 'good thing' of being there and wondering what she now had in her eye, she broke out, 'Why don't you take that girl out in it and show her the place?'

'Oh dear aunt, what do you want to do with me?' cried the 'girl,' with a piteous quaver. 'I know all about the place!'

'Well then, go with him as a cicerone!' said Miss Bordereau, with an effect of something like cruelty in her implacable power of retort—an incongruous suggestion that she was a sarcastic, profane, cynical old woman. 'Haven't we heard that there have been all sorts of changes in all these years? You ought to see them and at your age (I don't mean because you're so young), you ought to take the chances that come. You're old enough, my dear, and this gentleman won't hurt you. He will show you the famous sunsets, if they still go on— *do* they go on? The sun set for me so long ago. But that's not a reason. Besides, I shall never miss you; you think you are too important. Take her to the Piazza; it used to be very pretty,' Miss Bordereau continued, addressing herself to me. 'What have they done with the funny old church? I hope it hasn't tumbled down. Let her look at the shops; she may take some money, she may buy what she likes.'

Poor Miss Tita had got up, discountenanced and helpless, and as we stood there before her aunt it would certainly have seemed to a spectator of the scene that the old woman was amusing herself at our expense. Miss Tita protested, in a confusion of exclamations and murmurs; but I lost no time in saying that if she would do me the honour to accept the hospitality of my boat I would engage that she should not be bored. Or if she did not want so much of my company the boat itself, with the gondolier, was at her service; he was a capital oar and she might have every confidence. Miss Tita, without definitely answering this speech, looked away from me, out of the window, as if she were going to cry; and I remarked that once we had Miss Bordereau's approval we could easily come to an understanding. We would take an hour, whichever she liked, one of the very next days. As I made my obeisance to the old lady I asked her if she would kindly permit me to see her again.

For a moment she said nothing; then she inquired, 'Is it very necessary to your happiness?'

'It diverts me more than I can say.'

'You are wonderfully civil. Don't you know it almost kills *me*?'

'How can I believe that when I see you more animated, more brilliant than when I came in?'

'That is very true, aunt,' said Miss Tita. 'I think it does you good.'

'Isn't it touching, the solicitude we each have that the other shall enjoy herself?' sneered Miss Bordereau. 'If you think me brilliant to-day you don't know what you are talking about; you have never seen an agreeable woman. Don't try to pay me a compliment; I have been spoiled,' she went on. 'My door is shut, but you may sometimes knock.'

With this she dismissed me and I left the room. The latch closed behind me, but Miss Tita, contrary to my hope, had remained within. I passed slowly across the hall and before taking my way downstairs I waited a little. My hope was answered; after a minute Miss Tita followed me. 'That's a delightful idea about the Piazza,' I said. 'When will you go— to-night, to-morrow?'

She had been disconcerted, as I have mentioned, but I had already perceived and I was to observe again that when Miss Tita was embarrassed she did not (as most women would have done) turn away from you and try to escape, but came closer, as it were, with a deprecating, clinging appeal to be spared, to be protected. Her attitude was perpetually a sort of prayer for assistance, for explanation; and yet no woman in the world could have been less of a comedian. From the moment you were kind to her she depended on you absolutely; her self-consciousness dropped from her and she took the greatest intimacy, the innocent intimacy which was the only thing she could conceive, for granted. She told me she did not know what had got into her aunt; she had changed so quickly, she had got some idea. I replied that she must find out what the idea was and then let me know; we would go and have an ice together at Florian's and she should tell me while we listened to the band.

'Oh, it will take me a long time to find out!' she said, rather ruefully; and she could promise me this satisfaction neither for that night nor for the next. I was patient now, however, for I felt that I had only to wait; and in fact at the end of the week, one lovely evening after dinner, she stepped into my gondola, to which in honour of the occasion I had attached a second oar.

We swept in the course of five minutes into the Grand Canal; whereupon she uttered a murmur of ecstasy as fresh as if she had been a tourist just arrived. She had forgotten how splendid the great water-way looked on a clear, hot summer evening, and how the sense of floating between marble palaces and reflected lights disposed the mind to sympathetic talk. We floated long and far, and though Miss Tita gave no high-pitched voice to her satisfaction I felt that she surrendered herself. She was more than pleased, she was transported; the whole thing was an immense liberation. The gondola moved with slow strokes, to give her time to enjoy it, and she listened to the plash of the oars, which grew louder and more musically liquid as we passed into narrow canals, as if it were a revelation of Venice. When I asked her how long it was since she had been in a boat she answered, 'Oh, I don't know; a long time—not since my aunt began to be ill.' This was not the only example she gave me of her extreme vagueness about the previous years and the line which marked off the period when Miss Bordereau flourished. I was not at liberty to keep her out too long, but we took a considerable *giro* before going to the Piazza. I asked her no questions, keeping the conversation on purpose away from her domestic situation and the things I wanted to know; I poured treasures of information about Venice into her ears, described Florence and Rome, discoursed to her on the charms and advantages of travel. She reclined, receptive, on the deep leather cushions, turned her eyes conscientiously to everything I pointed out to her, and never mentioned to me till some time afterwards that she might be supposed to know Florence better than I, as she had lived there for years with Miss Bordereau. At last she asked, with the shy impatience of a child, 'Are we not really going to the Piazza? That's what I want to see!' I immediately gave the order that we should go straight; and then we sat silent with the expectation of arrival. As some time still passed, however, she said suddenly, of her own movement, 'I have found out what is the matter with my aunt: she is afraid you will go!'

'What has put that into her head?'

'She has had an idea you have not been happy. That is why she is different now.'

'You mean she wants to make me happier?'

'Well, she wants you not to go; she wants you to stay.'

'I suppose you mean on account of the rent,' I remarked candidly.

Miss Tita's candour showed itself a match for my own. 'Yes, you know; so that I shall have more.'

'How much does she want you to have?' I asked, laughing. 'She ought to fix the sum, so that I may stay till it's made up.'

'Oh, that wouldn't please me,' said Miss Tita. 'It would be unheard of, your taking that trouble.'

'But suppose I should have my own reasons for staying in Venice?'

'Then it would be better for you to stay in some other house.'

'And what would your aunt say to that?'

'She wouldn't like it at all. But I should think you would do well to give up your reasons and go away altogether.'

'Dear Miss Tita,' I said, 'it's not so easy to give them up!'

She made no immediate answer to this, but after a moment she broke out: 'I think I know what your reasons are!'

'I daresay, because the other night I almost told you how I wish you would help me to make them good.'

'I can't do that without being false to my aunt.'

'What do you mean, being false to her?'

'Why, she would never consent to what you want. She has been asked, she has been written to. It made her fearfully angry.'

'Then she *has* got papers of value?' I demanded, quickly.

'Oh, she has got everything!' sighed Miss Tita, with a curious weariness, a sudden lapse into gloom.

These words caused all my pulses to throb, for I regarded them as precious evidence. For some minutes I was too agitated to speak, and in the interval the gondola approached the Piazzetta. After we had disembarked I asked my companion whether she would rather walk round the square or go and sit at the door of the café; to which she replied that she would do whichever I liked best—I must only remember again how little time she had. I assured her there was plenty to do both, and we made the circuit of the long arcades. Her spirits revived at the sight of the bright shop-windows, and she

lingered and stopped, admiring or disapproving of their contents, asking me what I thought of things, theorising about
prices. My attention wandered from her; her words of a while
before, 'Oh, she has got everything!' echoed so in my consciousness. We sat down at last in the crowded circle at Florian's, finding an unoccupied table among those that were
ranged in the square. It was a splendid night and all the world
was out-of-doors; Miss Tita could not have wished the elements more auspicious for her return to society. I saw that
she enjoyed it even more than she told; she was agitated with
the multitude of her impressions. She had forgotten what an
attractive thing the world is, and it was coming over her that
somehow she had for the best years of her life been cheated
of it. This did not make her angry; but as she looked all over
the charming scene her face had, in spite of its smile of appreciation, the flush of a sort of wounded surprise. She became silent, as if she were thinking with a secret sadness of
opportunities, for ever lost, which ought to have been easy;
and this gave me a chance to say to her, 'Did you mean a
while ago that your aunt has a plan of keeping me on by
admitting me occasionally to her presence?'

'She thinks it will make a difference with you if you sometimes see her. She wants you so much to stay that she is willing
to make that concession.'

'And what good does she consider that I think it will do
me to see her?'

'I don't know; she thinks it's interesting,' said Miss Tita,
simply. 'You told her you found it so.'

'So I did; but every one doesn't think so.'

'No, of course not, or more people would try.'

'Well, if she is capable of making that reflection she is capable also of making this further one,' I went on: 'that I must
have a particular reason for not doing as others do, in spite
of the interest she offers—for not leaving her alone.' Miss Tita
looked as if she failed to grasp this rather complicated proposition; so I continued, 'If you have not told her what I said
to you the other night may she not at least have guessed it?'

'I don't know; she is very suspicious.'

'But she has not been made so by indiscreet curiosity, by
persecution?'

'No, no; it isn't that,' said Miss Tita, turning on me a somewhat troubled face. 'I don't know how to say it: it's on account of something—ages ago, before I was born—in her life.'

'Something? What sort of thing?' I asked, as if I myself could have no idea.

'Oh, she has never told me,' Miss Tita answered; and I was sure she was speaking the truth.

Her extreme limpidity was almost provoking, and I felt for the moment that she would have been more satisfactory if she had been less ingenuous. 'Do you suppose it's something to which Jeffrey Aspern's letters and papers—I mean the things in her possession—have reference?'

'I daresay it is!' my companion exclaimed, as if this were a very happy suggestion. 'I have never looked at any of those things.'

'None of them? Then how do you know what they are?'

'I don't,' said Miss Tita, placidly. 'I have never had them in my hands. But I have seen them when she has had them out.'

'Does she have them out often?'

'Not now, but she used to. She is very fond of them.'

'In spite of their being compromising?'

'Compromising?' Miss Tita repeated, as if she was ignorant of the meaning of the word. I felt almost as one who corrupts the innocence of youth.

'I mean their containing painful memories.'

'Oh, I don't think they are painful.'

'You mean you don't think they affect her reputation?'

At this a singular look came into the face of Miss Bordereau's niece—a kind of confession of helplessness, an appeal to me to deal fairly, generously with her. I had brought her to the Piazza, placed her among charming influences, paid her an attention she appreciated, and now I seemed to let her perceive that all this had been a bribe—a bribe to make her turn in some way against her aunt. She was of a yielding nature and capable of doing almost anything to please a person who was kind to her; but the greatest kindness of all would be not to presume too much on this. It was strange enough, as I afterwards thought, that she had not the least air of resenting my want of consideration for her aunt's character, which would have been in the worst possible taste if anything less vital (from my point of view) had been at stake. I don't think she really measured it. 'Do you mean that she did something bad?' she asked in a moment.

'Heaven forbid I should say so, and it's none of my business. Besides, if she did,' I added, laughing, 'it was in other ages, in another world. But why should she not destroy her papers?'

'Oh, she loves them too much.'

'Even now, when she may be near her end?'

'Perhaps when she's sure of that she will.'

'Well, Miss Tita,' I said, 'it's just what I should like you to prevent.'

'How can I prevent it?'

'Couldn't you get them away from her?'

'And give them to you?'

This put the case very crudely, though I am sure there was no irony in her intention. 'Oh, I mean that you might let me see them and look them over. It isn't for myself; there is no personal avidity in my desire. It is simply that they would be of such immense interest to the public, such immeasurable importance as a contribution to Jeffrey Aspern's history.'

She listened to me in her usual manner, as if my speech were full of reference to things she had never heard of, and I felt particularly like the reporter of a newspaper who forces his way into a house of mourning. This was especially the case when after a moment she said, 'There was a gentleman who some time ago wrote to her in very much those words. He also wanted her papers.'

'And did she answer him?' I asked, rather ashamed of myself for not having her rectitude.

'Only when he had written two or three times. He made her very angry.'

'And what did she say?'

'She said he was a devil,' Miss Tita replied, simply.

'She used that expression in her letter?'

'Oh no; she said it to me. She made me write to him.'

'And what did you say?'

'I told him there were no papers at all.'

'Ah, poor gentleman!' I exclaimed.

'I knew there were, but I wrote what she bade me.'

'Of course you had to do that. But I hope I shall not pass for a devil.'

'It will depend upon what you ask me to do for you,' said Miss Tita, smiling.

'Oh, if there is a chance of *your* thinking so my affair is in a bad way! I sha'n't ask you to steal for me, nor even to fib for you can't fib, unless on paper. But the principal thing is this—to prevent her from destroying the papers.'

'Why, I have no control of her,' said Miss Tita. 'It's she who controls me.'

'But she doesn't control her own arms and legs, does she? The way she would naturally destroy her letters would be to burn them. Now she can't burn them without fire, and she can't get fire unless you give it to her.'

'I have always done everything she has asked,' my companion rejoined. 'Besides, there's Olimpia.'

I was on the point of saying that Olimpia was probably corruptible, but I thought it best not to sound that note. So I simply inquired if that faithful domestic could not be managed.

'Every one can be managed by my aunt,' said Miss Tita. And then she observed that her holiday was over; she must go home.

I laid my hand on her arm, across the table, to stay her a moment. 'What I want of you is a general promise to help me.'

'Oh, how can I—how can I?' she asked, wondering and troubled. She was half surprised, half frightened at my wishing to make her play an active part.

'This is the main thing: to watch her carefully and warn me in time, before she commits that horrible sacrilege.'

'I can't watch her when she makes me go out.'

'That's very true.'

'And when you do too.'

'Mercy on us; do you think she will have done anything to-night?'

'I don't know; she is very cunning.'

'Are you trying to frighten me?' I asked.

I felt this inquiry sufficiently answered when my companion murmured in a musing, almost envious way, 'Oh, but she loves them—she loves them!'

This reflection, repeated with such emphasis, gave me great comfort; but to obtain more of that balm I said, 'If she shouldn't intend to destroy the objects we speak of before her death she will probably have made some disposition by will.'

'By will?'

'Hasn't she made a will for your benefit?'

'Why, she has so little to leave. That's why she likes money,' said Miss Tita.

'Might I ask, since we are really talking things over, what you and she live on?'

'On some money that comes from America, from a lawyer. He sends it every quarter. It isn't much!'

'And won't she have disposed of that?'

My companion hesitated—I saw she was blushing. 'I believe it's mine,' she said; and the look and tone which accompanied these words betrayed so the absence of the habit of thinking of herself that I almost thought her charming. The next instant she added, 'But she had a lawyer once, ever so long ago. And some people came and signed something.'

'They were probably witnesses. And you were not asked to sign? Well then,' I argued, rapidly and hopefully, 'it is because you are the legatee; she has left all her documents to you!'

'If she has it's with very strict conditions,' Miss Tita responded, rising quickly, while the movement gave the words a little character of decision. They seemed to imply that the bequest would be accompanied with a command that the articles bequeathed should remain concealed from every inquisitive eye and that I was very much mistaken if I thought she was the person to depart from an injunction so solemn.

'Oh, of course you will have to abide by the terms,' I said; and she uttered nothing to mitigate the severity of this conclusion. None the less, later, just before we disembarked at her own door, on our return, which had taken place almost in silence, she said to me abruptly, 'I will do what I can to help you.' I was grateful for this—it was very well so far as it went; but it did not keep me from remembering that night in a worried waking hour that I now had her word for it to reinforce my own impression that the old woman was very cunning.

VII

The fear of what this side of her character might have led her to do made me nervous for days afterwards. I waited for an intimation from Miss Tita; I almost figured to myself that it was her duty to keep me informed, to let me know definitely whether or no Miss Bordereau had sacrificed her treasures But as she gave no sign I lost patience and determined to judge so far as was possible with my own senses. I sent late one afternoon to ask if I might pay the ladies a visit, and my servant came back with surprising news. Miss Bordereau could be approached without the least difficulty; she had been moved out into the sala and was sitting by the window that overlooked the garden. I descended and found this picture correct; the old lady had been wheeled forth into the world and had a certain air, which came mainly perhaps from some brighter element in her dress, of being prepared again to have converse with it. It had not yet, however, begun to flock about her; she was perfectly alone and, though the door leading to her own quarters stood open, I had at first no glimpse of Miss Tita. The window at which she sat had the afternoon shade and, one of the shutters having been pushed back, she could see the pleasant garden, where the summer sun had by this time dried up too many of the plants—she could see the yellow light and the long shadows.

'Have you come to tell me that you will take the rooms for six months more?' she asked, as I approached her, startling me by something coarse in her cupidity almost as much as if she had not already given me a specimen of it. Juliana's desire to make our acquaintance lucrative had been, as I have sufficiently indicated, a false note in my image of the woman who had inspired a great poet with immortal lines; but I may say here definitely that I recognised after all that it behoved me to make a large allowance for her. It was I who had kindled the unholy flame; it was I who had put into her head that she had the means of making money. She appeared never to have thought of that; she had been living wastefully for years, in a house five times too big for her, on a footing that I could explain only by the presumption that, excessive as it was, the space she enjoyed cost her next to nothing and that small as were her revenues they left her, for Venice, an appreciable margin. I had descended on her one day and taught her to calculate, and my almost extravagant comedy on the subject of the garden had presented me irresistibly in the light of a victim. Like all persons who achieve the miracle of changing their point of view when they are old she had been intensely converted; she had seized my hint with a desperate, tremulous clutch.

I invited myself to go and get one of the chairs that stood, at a distance, against the wall (she had given herself no concern as to whether I should sit or stand); and while I placed it near her I began, gaily, 'Oh, dear madam, what an imagination you have, what an intellectual sweep! I am a poor devil of a man of letters who lives from day to day. How can I take palaces by the year? My existence is precarious. I don't know whether six months hence I shall have bread to put in my mouth. I have treated myself for once; it has been an immense luxury. But when it comes to going on——!'

'Are your rooms too dear? if they are you can have more for the same money,' Juliana responded. 'We can arrange, we can *combinare*, as they say here.'

'Well yes, since you ask me, they are too dear,' I said. 'Evidently you suppose me richer than I am.'

She looked at me in her barricaded way. 'If you write books don't you sell them?'

'Do you mean don't people buy them? A little—not so much as I could wish. Writing books, unless one be a great genius—and even then!—is the last road to fortune. I think there is no more money to be made by literature.'

'Perhaps you don't choose good subjects. What do you write about?' Miss Bordereau inquired.

'About the books of other people. I'm a critic, an historian, in a small way.' I wondered what she was coming to.

'And what other people, now?'

'Oh, better ones than myself: the great writers mainly—the great philosophers and poets of the past; those who are dead and gone and can't speak for themselves.'

'And what do you say about them?'

'I say they sometimes attached themselves to very clever women!' I answered, laughing. I spoke with great delibera-tion, but as my words fell upon the air they struck me as imprudent. However, I risked them and I was not sorry, for perhaps after all the old woman would be willing to treat. It seemed to be tolerably obvious that she knew my secret: why therefore drag the matter out? But she did not take what I had said as a confession; she only asked:

'Do you think it's right to rake up the past?'

'I don't know that I know what you mean by raking it up; but how can we get at it unless we dig a little? The present has such a rough way of treading it down.'

'Oh, I like the past, but I don't like critics,' the old woman declared, with her fine tranquillity.

'Neither do I, but I like their discoveries.'

'Aren't they mostly lies?'

'The lies are what they sometimes discover,' I said, smiling at the quiet impertinence of this. 'They often lay bare the truth.'

'The truth is God's, it isn't man's; we had better leave it alone. Who can judge of it—who can say?'

'We are terribly in the dark, I know,' I admitted; 'but if we give up trying what becomes of all the fine things? What be-comes of the work I just mentioned, that of the great philos-ophers and poets? It is all vain words if there is nothing to measure it by.'

'You talk as if you were a tailor,' said Miss Bordereau, whimsically; and then she added quickly, in a different man-ner, 'This house is very fine; the proportions are magnificent. To-day I wanted to look at this place again. I made them bring me out here. When your man came, just now, to learn if I would see you, I was on the point of sending for you, to ask if you didn't mean to go on. I wanted to judge what I'm letting you have. This sala is very grand,' she pursued, like an auctioneer, moving a little, as I guessed, her invisible eyes. 'I don't believe you often have lived in such a house, eh?'

'I can't often afford to!' I said.

'Well then, how much will you give for six months?'

I was on the point of exclaiming—and the air of excru-

ciation in my face would have denoted a moral fact—'Don't,
Juliana; for *his* sake, don't!' But I controlled myself and asked
less passionately: 'Why should I remain so long as that?'

'I thought you liked it,' said Miss Bordereau, with her shrivelled dignity.

'So I thought I should.'

For a moment she said nothing more, and I left my own
words to suggest to her what they might. I half expected her
to say, coldly enough, that if I had been disappointed we need
not continue the discussion, and this in spite of the fact that
I believed her now to have in her mind (however it had come
there), what would have told her that my disappointment was
natural. But to my extreme surprise she ended by observing:
'If you don't think we have treated you well enough perhaps
we can discover some way of treating you better.' This speech
was somehow so incongruous that it made me laugh again,
and I excused myself by saying that she talked as if I were a
sulky boy, pouting in the corner, to be 'brought round.' I had
not a grain of complaint to make; and could anything have
exceeded Miss Tita's graciousness in accompanying me a few
nights before to the Piazza? At this the old woman went on:
'Well, you brought it on yourself!' And then in a different
tone, 'She is a very nice girl.' I assented cordially to this proposition, and she expressed the hope that I did so not merely
to be obliging, but that I really liked her. Meanwhile I wondered still more what Miss Bordereau was coming to. 'Except
for me, to-day,' she said, 'she has not a relation in the world.'
Did she by describing her niece as amiable and unencumbered
wish to represent her as a *parti*?

It was perfectly true that I could not afford to go on with
my rooms at a fancy price and that I had already devoted to
my undertaking almost all the hard cash I had set apart for it.
My patience and my time were by no means exhausted, but I
should be able to draw upon them only on a more usual Venetian basis. I was willing to pay the venerable woman with
whom my pecuniary dealings were such a discord twice as
much as any other *padrona di casa* would have asked, but I
was not willing to pay her twenty times as much. I told her
so plainly, and my plainness appeared to have some success,

for she exclaimed, 'Very good; you have done what I asked —you have made an offer!'

'Yes, but not for half a year. Only by the month.'

'Oh, I must think of that then.' She seemed disappointed that I would not tie myself to a period, and I guessed that she wished both to secure me and to discourage me; to say, severely, 'Do you dream that you can get off with less than six months? Do you dream that even by the end of that time you will be appreciably nearer your victory?' What was more in my mind was that she had a fancy to play me the trick of making me engage myself when in fact she had annihilated the papers. There was a moment when my suspense on this point was so acute that I all but broke out with the question, and what kept it back was but a kind of instinctive recoil (lest it should be a mistake), from the last violence of self-exposure. She was such a subtle old witch that one could never tell where one stood with her. You may imagine whether it cleared up the puzzle when, just after she had said she would think of my proposal and without any formal transition, she drew out of her pocket with an embarrassed hand a small object wrapped in crumpled white paper. She held it there a moment and then she asked, 'Do you know much about curiosities?'

'About curiosities?'

'About antiquities, the old gimcracks that people pay so much for to-day. Do you know the kind of price they bring?'

I thought I saw what was coming, but I said ingenuously, 'Do you want to buy something?'

'No, I want to sell. What would an amateur give me for that?' She unfolded the white paper and made a motion for me to take from her a small oval portrait. I possessed myself of it with a hand of which I could only hope that she did not perceive the tremor, and she added, 'I would part with it only for a good price.'

At the first glance I recognised Jeffrey Aspern, and I was well aware that I flushed with the act. As she was watching me however I had the consistency to exclaim, 'What a striking face! Do tell me who it is.'

'It's an old friend of mine, a very distinguished man in his day. He gave it to me himself, but I'm afraid to mention his name, lest you never should have heard of him, critic and historian as you are. I know the world goes fast and one generation forgets another. He was all the fashion when I was young.'

She was perhaps amazed at my assurance, but I was surprised at hers; at her having the energy, in her state of health and at her time of life, to wish to sport with me that way simply for her private entertainment—the humour to test me and practise on me. This, at least, was the interpretation that I put upon her production of the portrait, for I could not believe that she really desired to sell it or cared for any information I might give her. What she wished was to dangle it before my eyes and put a prohibitive price on it. 'The face comes back to me, it torments me,' I said, turning the object this way and that and looking at it very critically. It was a careful but not a supreme work of art, larger than the ordinary miniature and representing a young man with a remarkably handsome face, in a high-collared green coat and a buff waistcoat. I judged the picture to have a valuable quality of resemblance and to have been painted when the model was about twenty-five years old. There are, as all the world knows, three other portraits of the poet in existence, but none of them is of so early a date as this elegant production. 'I have never seen the original but I have seen other likenesses,' I went on. 'You expressed doubt of this generation having heard of the gentleman, but he strikes me for all the world as a celebrity. Now who is he? I can't put my finger on him—I can't give him a label. Wasn't he a writer? Surely he's a poet.' I was determined that it should be she, not I, who should first pronounce Jeffrey Aspern's name.

My resolution was taken in ignorance of Miss Bordereau's extremely resolute character, and her lips never formed in my hearing the syllables that meant so much for her. She neglected to answer my question but raised her hand to take back the picture, with a gesture which though ineffectual was in a high degree peremptory. 'It's only a person who should know for himself that would give me my price,' she said with a certain dryness.

'Oh, then, you have a price?' I did not restore the precious thing; not from any vindictive purpose but because I instinc-

tively clung to it. We looked at each other hard while I retained it.

'I know the least I would take. What it occurred to me to
ask you about is the most I shall be able to get.'

She made a movement, drawing herself together as if, in a
spasm of dread at having lost her treasure, she were going to
attempt the immense effort of rising to snatch it from me. I
instantly placed it in her hand again, saying as I did so, 'I
should like to have it myself, but with your ideas I could never
afford it.'

She turned the small oval plate over in her lap, with its face
down, and I thought I saw her catch her breath a little, as if
she had had a strain or an escape. This however did not prevent her saying in a moment, 'You would buy a likeness of a
person you don't know, by an artist who has no reputation?'

'The artist may have no reputation, but that thing is wonderfully well painted,' I replied, to give myself a reason.

'It's lucky you thought of saying that, because the painter
was my father.'

'That makes the picture indeed precious!' I exclaimed,
laughing; and I may add that a part of my laughter came from
my satisfaction in finding that I had been right in my theory
of Miss Bordereau's origin. Aspern had of course met the
young lady when he went to her father's studio as a sitter. I
observed to Miss Bordereau that if she would entrust me with
her property for twenty-four hours I should be happy to take
advice upon it; but she made no answer to this save to slip it
in silence into her pocket. This convinced me still more that
she had no sincere intention of selling it during her lifetime,
though she may have desired to satisfy herself as to the sum
her niece, should she leave it to her, might expect eventually
to obtain for it. 'Well, at any rate I hope you will not offer it
without giving me notice,' I said, as she remained irresponsive. 'Remember that I am a possible purchaser.'

'I should want your money first!' she returned, with unexpected rudeness; and then, as if she bethought herself that
I had just cause to complain of such an insinuation and wished
to turn the matter off, asked abruptly what I talked about with
her niece when I went out with her that way in the evening.

'You speak as if we had set up the habit,' I replied. 'Certainly I should be very glad if it were to become a habit. But in that case I should feel a still greater scruple at betraying a lady's confidence.'

'Her confidence? Has she got confidence?'

'Here she is—she can tell you herself,' I said; for Miss Tita now appeared on the threshold of the old woman's parlour. 'Have you got confidence, Miss Tita? Your aunt wants very much to know.'

'Not in her, not in her!' the younger lady declared, shaking her head with a dolefulness that was neither jocular nor affected. 'I don't know what to do with her; she has fits of horrid imprudence. She is so easily tired—and yet she has begun to roam—to drag herself about the house.' And she stood looking down at her immemorial companion with a sort of helpless wonder, as if all their years of familiarity had not made her perversities, on occasion, any more easy to follow.

'I know what I'm about. I'm not losing my mind. I daresay you would like to think so,' said Miss Bordereau, with a cynical little sigh.

'I don't suppose you came out here yourself. Miss Tita must have had to lend you a hand,' I interposed, with a pacifying intention.

'Oh, she insisted that we should push her; and when she insists!' said Miss Tita, in the same tone of apprehension; as if there were no knowing what service that she disapproved of her aunt might force her next to render.

'I have always got most things done I wanted, thank God! The people I have lived with have humoured me,' the old woman continued, speaking out of the gray ashes of her vanity.

'I suppose you mean that they have obeyed you.'

'Well, whatever it is, when they like you.'

'It's just because I like you that I want to resist,' said Miss Tita, with a nervous laugh.

'Oh, I suspect you'll bring Miss Bordereau upstairs next, to pay me a visit,' I went on; to which the old lady replied:

'Oh no; I can keep an eye on you from here!'

'You are very tired; you will certainly be ill tonight!' cried Miss Tita.

'Nonsense, my dear; I feel better at this moment than I

have done for a month. To-morrow I shall come out again. I want to be where I can see this clever gentleman.'

'Shouldn't you perhaps see me better in your sitting-room?' I inquired.

'Don't you mean shouldn't you have a better chance at me?' she returned, fixing me a moment with her green shade.

'Ah, I haven't that anywhere! I look at you but I don't see you.'

'You excite her dreadfully—and that is not good,' said Miss Tita, giving me a reproachful, appealing look.

'I want to watch you—I want to watch you!' the old lady went on.

'Well then, let us spend as much of our time together as possible—I don't care where—and that will give you every facility.'

'Oh, I've seen you enough for to-day. I'm satisfied. Now I'll go home.' Miss Tita laid her hands on the back of her aunt's chair and began to push, but I begged her to let me take her place. 'Oh yes, you may move me this way—you sha'n't in any other!' Miss Bordereau exclaimed, as she felt herself propelled firmly and easily over the smooth, hard floor. Before we reached the door of her own apartment she commanded me to stop, and she took a long, last look up and down the noble sala. 'Oh, it's a magnificent house!' she murmured; after which I pushed her forward. When we had entered the parlour Miss Tita told me that she should now be able to manage, and at the same moment the little red-haired *donna* came to meet her mistress. Miss Tita's idea was evidently to get her aunt immediately back to bed. I confess that in spite of this urgency I was guilty of the indiscretion of lingering; it held me there to think that I was nearer the documents I coveted—that they were probably put away somewhere in the faded, unsociable room. The place had indeed a bareness which did not suggest hidden treasures; there were no dusky nooks nor curtained corners, no massive cabinets nor chests with iron bands. Moreover it was possible, it was perhaps even probable that the old lady had consigned her relics to her bedroom, to some battered box that was shoved under the bed, to the drawer of some lame dressing-table, where they would be in the range of vision by the dim

night-lamp. None the less I scrutinised every article of furniture, every conceivable cover for a hoard, and noticed that
there were half a dozen things with drawers, and in particular
a tall old secretary, with brass ornaments of the style of the
Empire—a receptacle somewhat rickety but still capable of
keeping a great many secrets. I don't know why this article
fascinated me so, inasmuch as I certainly had no definite purpose of breaking into it; but I stared at it so hard that Miss
Tita noticed me and changed colour. Her doing this made me
think I was right and that wherever they might have been
before the Aspern papers at that moment languished behind
the peevish little lock of the secretary. It was hard to remove
my eyes from the dull mahogany front when I reflected that
a simple panel divided me from the goal of my hopes; but I
remembered my prudence and with an effort took leave of
Miss Bordereau. To make the effort graceful I said to her that
I should certainly bring her an opinion about the little picture.

'The little picture?' Miss Tita asked, surprised.

'What do *you* know about it, my dear?' the old woman demanded. 'You needn't mind. I have fixed my price.'

'And what may that be?'

'A thousand pounds.'

'Oh Lord!' cried poor Miss Tita, irrepressibly.

'Is that what she talks to you about?' said Miss Bordereau.

'Imagine your aunt's wanting to know!' I had to separate
from Miss Tita with only those words, though I should have
liked immensely to add, 'For heaven's sake meet me to-night
in the garden!'

VIII

As it turned out the precaution had not been needed, for three
hours later, just as I had finished my dinner, Miss Bordereau's
niece appeared, unannounced, in the open doorway of the
room in which my simple repasts were served. I remember
well that I felt no surprise at seeing her; which is not a proof
that I did not believe in her timidity. It was immense, but in
a case in which there was a particular reason for boldness it
never would have prevented her from running up to my
rooms. I saw that she was now quite full of a particular reason;

it threw her forward—made her seize me, as I rose to meet her, by the arm.

'My aunt is very ill; I think she is dying!'

'Never in the world,' I answered, bitterly. 'Don't you be afraid!'

'Do go for a doctor—do, do! Olimpia is gone for the one we always have, but she doesn't come back; I don't know what has happened to her. I told her that if he was not at home she was to follow him where he had gone; but apparently she is following him all over Venice. I don't know what to do—she looks so as if she were sinking.'

'May I see her, may I judge?' I asked. 'Of course I shall be delighted to bring some one; but hadn't we better send my man instead, so that I may stay with you?'

Miss Tita assented to this and I despatched my servant for the best doctor in the neighbourhood. I hurried downstairs with her, and on the way she told me that an hour after I quitted them in the afternoon Miss Bordereau had had an attack of 'oppression,' a terrible difficulty in breathing. This had subsided but had left her so exhausted that she did not come up: she seemed all gone. I repeated that she was not gone, that she would not go yet; whereupon Miss Tita gave me a sharper sidelong glance than she had ever directed at me and said, 'Really, what do you mean? I suppose you don't accuse her of making-believe!' I forget what reply I made to this, but I grant that in my heart I thought the old woman capable of any weird manœuvre. Miss Tita wanted to know what I had done to her; her aunt had told her that I had made her so angry. I declared I had done nothing—I had been exceedingly careful; to which my companion rejoined that Miss Bordereau had assured her she had had a scene with me—a scene that had upset her. I answered with some resentment that it was a scene of her own making—that I couldn't think what she was angry with me for unless for not seeing my way to give a thousand pounds for the portrait of Jeffrey Aspern. 'And did she show you that? Oh gracious—oh deary me!' groaned Miss Tita, who appeared to feel that the situation was passing out of her control and that the elements of her fate were thickening around her. I said that I would give anything to possess it, yet that I had not a thousand pounds; but I stopped when we came to the door of Miss Bordereau's room. I had an immense curiosity to pass it, but I thought it my duty to represent to Miss Tita that if I made the invalid angry she ought perhaps to be spared the sight of me. 'The sight of you? Do you think she can *see*?' my companion demanded, almost with indignation. I did think so but forbore to say it, and I softly followed my conductress.

I remember that what I said to her as I stood for a moment beside the old woman's bed was, 'Does she never show you her eyes then? Have you never seen them?' Miss Bordereau had been divested of her green shade, but (it was not my fortune to behold Juliana in her nightcap) the upper half of her face was covered by the fall of a piece of dingy lacelike muslin, a sort of extemporised hood which, wound round her head, descended to the end of her nose, leaving nothing visible but her white withered cheeks and puckered mouth, closed tightly and, as it were, consciously. Miss Tita gave me a glance of surprise, evidently not seeing a reason for my impatience. 'You mean that she always wears something? She does it to preserve them.'

'Because they are so fine?'

'Oh, to-day, to-day!' And Miss Tita shook her head, speaking very low. 'But they used to be magnificent!'

'Yes indeed, we have Aspern's word for that.' And as I looked again at the old woman's wrappings I could imagine that she had not wished to allow people a reason to say that the great poet had overdone it. But I did not waste my time in considering Miss Bordereau, in whom the appearance of respiration was so slight as to suggest that no human attention could ever help her more. I turned my eyes all over the room, rummaging with them the closets, the chests of drawers, the tables. Miss Tita met them quickly and read, I think, what was in them; but she did not answer it, turning away restlessly, anxiously, so that I felt rebuked, with reason, for a preoccupation that was almost profane in the presence of our dying companion. All the same I took another look, endeavouring to pick out mentally the place to try first, for a person who should wish to put his hand on Miss Bordereau's papers directly after her death. The room was a dire confusion; it looked like the room of an old actress. There were clothes hanging over chairs, odd-looking, shabby bundles here and there, and various pasteboard boxes piled together, battered, bulging and discoloured, which might have been fifty years old. Miss Tita after a moment noticed the direction of my eyes again and, as if she guessed how I judged the air of the place (forgetting I had no business to judge it at all), said, perhaps to defend herself from the imputation of complicity in such untidiness:

'She likes it this way; we can't move things. There are old bandboxes she has had most of her life.' Then she added, half taking pity on my real thought, 'Those things were *there*.' And she pointed to a small, low trunk which stood under a sofa where there was just room for it. It appeared to be a queer, superannuated coffer, of painted wood, with elaborate handles and shrivelled straps and with the colour (it had last been endued with a coat of light green) much rubbed off. It evidently had travelled with Juliana in the olden time—in the days of her adventures, which it had shared. It would have made a strange figure arriving at a modern hotel.

'*Were* there—they aren't now?' I asked, startled by Miss Tita's implication.

She was going to answer, but at that moment the doctor came in—the doctor whom the little maid had been sent to fetch and whom she had at last overtaken. My servant, going on his own errand, had met her with her companion in tow, and in the sociable Venetian spirit, retracing his steps with them, had also come up to the threshold of Miss Bordereau's room, where I saw him peeping over the doctor's shoulder. I motioned him away the more instantly that the sight of his prying face reminded me that I myself had almost as little to do there—an admonition confirmed by the sharp way the little doctor looked at me, appearing to take me for a rival who had the field before him. He was a short, fat, brisk gentleman who wore the tall hat of his profession and seemed to look at everything but his patient. He looked particularly at me, as if it struck him that I should be better for a dose, so that I bowed to him and left him with the women, going down to smoke a cigar in the garden. I was nervous; I could not go further; I could not leave the place. I don't know exactly what I thought might happen, but it seemed to me important to be

there. I wandered about in the alleys—the warm night had
come on—smoking cigar after cigar and looking at the light
in Miss Bordereau's windows. They were open now, I could
see; the situation was different. Sometimes the light moved,
but not quickly; it did not suggest the hurry of a crisis. Was
the old woman dying or was she already dead? Had the doctor
said that there was nothing to be done at her tremendous age
but to let her quietly pass away; or had he simply announced
with a look a little more conventional that the end of the end
had come? Were the other two women moving about to perform the offices that follow in such a case? It made me uneasy
not to be nearer, as if I thought the doctor himself might
carry away the papers with him. I bit my cigar hard as it came
over me again that perhaps there were now no papers to carry!

I wandered about for an hour—for an hour and a half. I
looked out for Miss Tita at one of the windows, having a
vague idea that she might come there to give me some sign.
Would she not see the red tip of my cigar moving about in
the dark and feel that I wanted eminently to know what the
doctor had said? I am afraid it is a proof my anxieties had
made me gross that I should have taken in some degree for
granted that at such an hour, in the midst of the greatest
change that could take place in her life, they were uppermost
also in poor Miss Tita's mind. My servant came down and
spoke to me; he knew nothing save that the doctor had gone
after a visit of half an hour. If he had stayed half an hour then
Miss Bordereau was still alive: it could not have taken so much
time as that to enunciate the contrary. I sent the man out of
the house; there were moments when the sense of his curiosity
annoyed me and this was one of them. *He* had been watching
my cigar-tip from an upper window, if Miss Tita had not; he
could not know what I was after and I could not tell him,
though I was conscious he had fantastic private theories about
me which he thought fine and which I, had I known them,
should have thought offensive.

I went upstairs at last but I ascended no higher than the
sala. The door of Miss Bordereau's apartment was open,
showing from the parlour the dimness of a poor candle. I went
toward it with a light tread and at the same moment Miss Tita
appeared and stood looking at me as I approached. 'She's

better—she's better,' she said, even before I had asked. 'The doctor has given her something; she woke up, came back to life while he was there. He says there is no immediate danger.'

'No immediate danger? Surely he thinks her condition strange!'

'Yes, because she had been excited. That affects her dreadfully.'

'It will do so again then, because she excites herself. She did so this afternoon.'

'Yes; she mustn't come out any more,' said Miss Tita, with one of her lapses into a deeper placidity.

'What is the use of making such a remark as that if you begin to rattle her about again the first time she bids you?'

'I won't—I won't do it any more.'

'You must learn to resist her,' I went on.

'Oh yes, I shall; I shall do so better if you tell me it's right.'

'You mustn't do it for me; you must do it for yourself. It all comes back to you, if you are frightened.'

'Well, I am not frightened now,' said Miss Tita, cheerfully. 'She is very quiet.'

'Is she conscious again—does she speak?'

'No, she doesn't speak, but she takes my hand. She holds it fast.'

'Yes,' I rejoined, 'I can see what force she still has by the way she grabbed that picture this afternoon. But if she holds you fast how comes it that you are here?'

Miss Tita hesitated a moment; though her face was in deep shadow (she had her back to the light in the parlour and I had put down my own candle far off, near the door of the sala), I thought I saw her smile ingenuously. 'I came on purpose—I heard your step.'

'Why, I came on tiptoe, as inaudibly as possible.'

'Well, I heard you,' said Miss Tita.

'And is your aunt alone now?'

'Oh no; Olimpia is sitting there.'

On my side I hesitated. 'Shall we then step in there?' And I nodded at the parlour; I wanted more and more to be on the spot.

'We can't talk there—she will hear us.'

I was on the point of replying that in that case we would

sit silent, but I was too conscious that this would not do, as there was something I desired immensely to ask her. So I proposed that we should walk a little in the sala, keeping more at the other end, where we should not disturb the old lady. Miss Tita assented unconditionally; the doctor was coming again, she said, and she would be there to meet him at the door. We strolled through the fine superfluous hall, where on the marble floor—particularly as at first we said nothing—our footsteps were more audible than I had expected. When we reached the other end—the wide window, inveterately closed, connecting with the balcony that overhung the canal—I suggested that we should remain there, as she would see the doctor arrive still better. I opened the window and we passed out on the balcony. The air of the canal seemed even heavier, hotter than that of the sala. The place was hushed and void; the quiet neighbourhood had gone to sleep. A lamp, here and there, over the narrow black water, glimmered in double; the voice of a man going homeward singing, with his jacket on his shoulder and his hat on his ear, came to us from a distance. This did not prevent the scene from being very *comme il faut*, as Miss Bordereau had called it the first time I saw her. Presently a gondola passed along the canal with its slow rhythmical plash, and as we listened we watched it in silence. It did not stop, it did not carry the doctor; and after it had gone on I said to Miss Tita:

'And where are they now—the things that were in the trunk?'

'In the trunk?'

'That green box you pointed out to me in her room. You said her papers had been there; you seemed to imply that she had transferred them.'

'Oh yes; they are not in the trunk,' said Miss Tita.

'May I ask if you have looked?'

'Yes, I have looked—for you.'

'How for me, dear Miss Tita? Do you mean you would have given them to me if you had found them?' I asked, almost trembling.

She delayed to reply and I waited. Suddenly she broke out, 'I don't know what I would do—what I wouldn't!'

'Would you look again—somewhere else?'

She had spoken with a strange, unexpected emotion, and she went on in the same tone: 'I can't—I can't—while she lies there. It isn't decent.'

'No, it isn't decent,' I replied, gravely. 'Let the poor lady rest in peace.' And the words, on my lips, were not hypocritical, for I felt reprimanded and shamed.

Miss Tita added in a moment, as if she had guessed this and were sorry for me, but at the same time wished to explain that I did drive her on or at least did insist too much: 'I can't deceive her that way. I can't deceive her perhaps on her deathbed.'

'Heaven forbid I should ask you, though I have been guilty myself!'

'You have been guilty?'

'I have sailed under false colours.' I felt now as if I must tell her that I had given her an invented name, on account of my fear that her aunt would have heard of me and would refuse to take me in. I explained this and also that I had really been a party to the letter written to them by John Cumnor months before.

She listened with great attention, looking at me with parted lips, and when I had made my confession she said, 'Then your real name—what is it?' She repeated it over twice when I had told her, accompanying it with the exclamation 'Gracious, gracious!' Then she added, 'I like your own best.'

'So do I,' I said, laughing. 'Ouf! it's a relief to get rid of the other.'

'So it was a regular plot—a kind of conspiracy?'

'Oh, a conspiracy—we were only two,' I replied, leaving out Mrs. Prest of course.

She hesitated; I thought she was perhaps going to say that we had been very base. But she remarked after a moment, in a candid, wondering way, 'How much you must want them!'

'Oh, I do, passionately!' I conceded, smiling. And this chance made me go on, forgetting my compunction of a moment before. 'How can she possibly have changed their place herself? How can she walk? How can she arrive at that sort of muscular exertion? How can she lift and carry things?'

'Oh, when one wants and when one has so much will!' said Miss Tita, as if she had thought over my question already herself and had simply had no choice but that answer—the idea that in the dead of night, or at some moment when the coast was clear, the old woman had been capable of a miraculous effort.

'Have you questioned Olimpia? Hasn't she helped her—hasn't she done it for her?' I asked; to which Miss Tita replied promptly and positively that their servant had had nothing to do with the matter, though without admitting definitely that she had spoken to her. It was as if she were a little shy, a little ashamed now of letting me see how much she had entered into my uneasiness and had me on her mind. Suddenly she said to me, without any immediate relevance:

'I feel as if you were a new person, now that you have got a new name.'

'It isn't a new one; it is a very good old one, thank heaven!'

She looked at me a moment. 'I do like it better.'

'Oh, if you didn't I would almost go on with the other!'

'Would you really?'

I laughed again, but for all answer to this inquiry I said, 'Of course if she can rummage about that way she can perfectly have burnt them.'

'You must wait—you must wait,' Miss Tita moralised mournfully; and her tone ministered little to my patience, for it seemed after all to accept that wretched possibility. I would teach myself to wait, I declared nevertheless; because in the first place I could not do otherwise and in the second I had her promise, given me the other night, that she would help me.

'Of course if the papers are gone that's no use,' she said; not as if she wished to recede, but only to be conscientious.

'Naturally. But if you could only find out!' I groaned, quivering again.

'I thought you said you would wait.'

'Oh, you mean wait even for that?'

'For what then?'

'Oh, nothing,' I replied, rather foolishly, being ashamed to tell her what had been implied in my submission to delay—the idea that she would do more than merely find out. I know not whether she guessed this; at all events she appeared to become aware of the necessity for being a little more rigid.

'I didn't promise to deceive, did I? I don't think I did.'

'It doesn't much matter whether you did or not, for you couldn't!'

I don't think Miss Tita would have contested this even had she not been diverted by our seeing the doctor's gondola shoot into the little canal and approach the house. I noted that he came as fast as if he believed that Miss Bordereau was still in danger. We looked down at him while he disembarked and then went back into the sala to meet him. When he came up however I naturally left Miss Tita to go off with him alone, only asking her leave to come back later for news.

I went out of the house and took a long walk, as far as the Piazza, where my restlessness declined to quit me. I was unable to sit down (it was very late now but there were people still at the little tables in front of the cafés); I could only walk round and round, and I did so half a dozen times. I was uncomfortable, but it gave me a certain pleasure to have told Miss Tita who I really was. At last I took my way home again, slowly getting all but inextricably lost, as I did whenever I went out in Venice: so that it was considerably past midnight when I reached my door. The sala, upstairs, was as dark as usual and my lamp as I crossed it found nothing satisfactory to show me. I was disappointed, for I had notified Miss Tita that I would come back for a report, and I thought she might have left a light there as a sign. The door of the ladies' apartment was closed; which seemed an intimation that my faltering friend had gone to bed, tired of waiting for me. I stood in the middle of the place, considering, hoping she would hear me and perhaps peep out, saying to myself too that she would never go to bed with her aunt in a state so critical; she would sit up and watch—she would be in a chair, in her dressing-gown. I went nearer the door; I stopped there and listened. I heard nothing at all and at last I tapped gently. No answer came and after another minute I turned the handle. There was no light in the room; this ought to have prevented me from going in, but it had no such effect. If I have candidly narrated the importunities, the indelicacies, of which my desire to possess myself of Jeffrey Aspern's papers had rendered me capable I need not shrink from confessing this last indiscretion. I think it was the worst thing I did; yet there were extenuating circumstances. I was deeply though doubtless not disinterestedly anxious for more news of the old lady, and Miss Tita had accepted from me, as it were, a rendezvous which it might have been a point of honour with me to keep. It may be said that her leaving the place dark was a positive sign that she released me, and to this I can only reply that I desired not to be released.

The door of Miss Bordereau's room was open and I could see beyond it the faintness of a taper. There was no sound— my footstep caused no one to stir. I came further into the room; I lingered there with my lamp in my hand. I wanted to give Miss Tita a chance to come to me if she were with her aunt, as she must be. I made no noise to call her; I only waited to see if she would not notice my light. She did not, and I explained this (I found afterwards I was right) by the idea that she had fallen asleep. If she had fallen asleep her aunt was not on her mind, and my explanation ought to have led me to go out as I had come. I must repeat again that it did not, for I found myself at the same moment thinking of something else. I had no definite purpose, no bad intention, but I felt myself held to the spot by an acute, though absurd, sense of opportunity. For what I could not have said, inasmuch as it was not in my mind that I might commit a theft. Even if it had been I was confronted with the evident fact that Miss Bordereau did not leave her secretary, her cupboard and the drawers of her tables gaping. I had no keys, no tools and no ambition to smash her furniture. None the less it came to me that I was now, perhaps alone, unmolested, at the hour of temptation and secrecy, nearer to the tormenting treasure than I had ever been. I held up my lamp, let the light play on the different objects as if it could tell me something. Still there came no movement from the other room. If Miss Tita was sleeping she was sleeping sound. Was she doing so—generous creature— on purpose to leave me the field? Did she know I was there and was she just keeping quiet to see what I would do—what I *could* do? But what could I do, when it came to that? She herself knew even better than I how little.

I stopped in front of the secretary, looking at it very idiotically; for what had it to say to me after all? In the first place it was locked, and in the second it almost surely contained nothing in which I was interested. Ten to one the papers had been destroyed; and even if they had not been destroyed the old woman would not have put them in such a place as that after removing them from the green trunk—would not have transferred them, if she had the idea of their safety on her brain, from the better hiding-place to the worse. The secretary was more conspicuous, more accessible in a room in which she could no longer mount guard. It opened with a key, but there was a little brass handle, like a button, as well; I saw this as I played my lamp over it. I did something more than this at that moment: I caught a glimpse of the possibility that Miss Tita wished me really to understand. If she did not wish me to understand, if she wished me to keep away, why had she not locked the door of communication between the sitting-room and the sala? That would have been a definite sign that I was to leave them alone. If I did not leave them alone she meant me to come for a purpose—a purpose now indicated by the quick, fantastic idea that to oblige me she had unlocked the secretary. She had not left the key, but the lid would probably move if I touched the button. This theory fascinated me, and I bent over very close to judge. I did not propose to do anything, not even—not in the least—to let down the lid; I only wanted to test my theory, to see if the cover *would* move. I touched the button with my hand—a mere touch would tell me; and as I did so (it is embarrassing for me to relate it), I looked over my shoulder. It was a chance, an instinct, for I had not heard anything. I almost let my luminary drop and certainly I stepped back, straightening myself up at what I saw. Miss Bordereau stood there in her night-dress, in the doorway of her room, watching me; her hands were raised, she had lifted the everlasting curtain that covered half her face, and for the first, the last, the only time I beheld her extraordinary eyes. They glared at me, they made me horribly ashamed. I never shall forget her strange little bent white tottering figure, with its lifted head, her attitude, her expression; neither shall I forget the tone in which as I turned, looking at her, she hissed out passionately, furiously:

'Ah, you publishing scoundrel!'

I know not what I stammered, to excuse myself, to explain; but I went towards her, to tell her I meant no harm. She waved me off with her old hands, retreating before me in horror; and the next thing I knew she had fallen back with a quick spasm, as if death had descended on her, into Miss Tita's arms.

IX

I left Venice the next morning, as soon as I learnt that the old lady had not succumbed, as I feared at the moment, to the shock I had given her—the shock I may also say she had given me. How in the world could I have supposed her capable of getting out of bed by herself? I failed to see Miss Tita before going; I only saw the *donna*, whom I entrusted with a note for her younger mistress. In this note I mentioned that I should be absent but for a few days. I went to Treviso, to Bassano, to Castelfranco; I took walks and drives and looked at musty old churches with ill-lighted pictures and spent hours seated smoking at the doors of cafés, where there were flies and yellow curtains, on the shady side of sleepy little squares. In spite of these pastimes, which were mechanical and perfunctory, I scantily enjoyed my journey: there was too strong a taste of the disagreeable in my life. It had been devilish awkward, as the young men say, to be found by Miss Bordereau in the dead of night examining the attachment of her bureau; and it had not been less so to have to believe for a good many hours afterward that it was highly probable I had killed her. In writing to Miss Tita I attempted to minimise these irregularities; but as she gave me no word of answer I could not know what impression I made upon her. It rankled in my mind that I had been called a publishing scoundrel, for certainly I did publish and certainly I had not been very delicate. There was a moment when I stood convinced that the only way to make up for this latter fault was to take myself away altogether on the instant; to sacrifice my hopes and relieve the two poor women for ever of the oppression of my intercourse. Then I reflected that I had better try a short absence first, for I must already have had a sense (unexpressed and dim) that in disappearing completely it would not be merely my own hopes that I should condemn to extinction. It would perhaps be sufficient if I stayed away long enough to give the elder lady time to think she was rid of me. That she would wish to be rid of me after this (if I was not rid of her) was now not to be doubted: that nocturnal scene would have cured her of the disposition to put up with my company for the sake of my dollars. I said to myself that after all I could not abandon Miss Tita, and I continued to say this even while I observed that she quite failed to comply with my earnest request (I had given her two or three addresses, at little towns, *poste restante*) that she would let me know how she was getting on. I would have made my servant write to me but that he was unable to manage a pen. It struck me there was a kind of scorn in Miss Tita's silence (little disdainful as she had ever been), so that I was uncomfortable and sore. I had scruples about going back and yet I had others about not doing so, for I wanted to put myself on a better footing. The end of it was that I did return to Venice on the twelfth day; and as my gondola gently bumped against Miss Bordereau's steps a certain palpitation of suspense told me that I had done myself a violence in holding off so long.

I had faced about so abruptly that I had not telegraphed to my servant. He was therefore not at the station to meet me, but he poked out his head from an upper window when I reached the house. 'They have put her into the earth, *la vecchia*,' he said to me in the lower hall, while he shouldered my valise; and he grinned and almost winked, as if he knew I should be pleased at the news.

'She's dead!' I exclaimed, giving him a very different look.

'So it appears, since they have buried her.'

'It's all over? When was the funeral?'

'The other yesterday. But a funeral you could scarcely call it, signore; it was a dull little passeggio of two gondolas. Poveretta!' the man continued, referring apparently to Miss Tita. His conception of funerals was apparently that they were mainly to amuse the living.

I wanted to know about Miss Tita—how she was and where she was—but I asked him no more questions till we had got upstairs. Now that the fact had met me I took a bad view of it, especially of the idea that poor Miss Tita had had to manage by herself after the end. What did she know about arrangements, about the steps to take in such a case? Poveretta indeed! I could only hope that the doctor had given her assistance and that she had not been neglected by the old friends of whom she had told me, the little band of the faithful whose fidelity consisted in coming to the house once a year. I elicited from my servant that two old ladies and an old gentleman had in fact rallied round Miss Tita and had supported her (they had come for her in a gondola of their own) during the journey to the cemetery, the little red-walled island of tombs which lies to the north of the town, on the way to Murano. It appeared from these circumstances that the Misses Bordereau were Catholics, a discovery I had never made, as the old woman could not go to church and her niece, so far as I perceived, either did not or went only to early mass in the parish, before I was stirring. Certainly even the priests respected their seclusion; I had never caught the whisk of the curato's skirt. That evening, an hour later, I sent my servant down with five words written on a card, to ask Miss Tita if she would see me for a few moments. She was not in the house, where he had sought her, he told me when he came back, but in the garden walking about to refresh herself and gathering flowers. He had found her there and she would be very happy to see me.

I went down and passed half an hour with poor Miss Tita. She had always had a look of musty mourning (as if she were wearing out old robes of sorrow that would not come to an end), and in this respect there was no appreciable change in her appearance. But she evidently had been crying, crying a great deal—simply, satisfyingly, refreshingly, with a sort of primitive, retarded sense of loneliness and violence. But she had none of the formalism or the self-consciousness of grief, and I was almost surprised to see her standing there in the first dusk with her hands full of flowers, smiling at me with her reddened eyes. Her white face, in the frame of her mantilla, looked longer, leaner than usual. I had had an idea that she would be a good deal disgusted with me—would consider that I ought to have been on the spot to advise her, to help her; and, though I was sure there was no rancour in her composition and no great conviction of the importance of her affairs, I had prepared myself for a difference in her manner, for some little injured look, half familiar, half estranged, which should say to my conscience, 'Well, you are a nice person to have professed things!' But historic truth compels me to declare that Tita Bordereau's countenance expressed unqualified pleasure in seeing her late aunt's lodger. That touched him extremely and he thought it simplified his situation until he found it did not. I was as kind to her that evening as I knew how to be, and I walked about the garden with her for half an hour. There was no explanation of any sort between us; I did not ask her why she had not answered my letter. Still less did I repeat what I had said to her in that communication; if she chose to let me suppose that she had forgotten the position in which Miss Bordereau surprised me that night and the effect of the discovery on the old woman I was quite willing to take it that way: I was grateful to her for not treating me as if I had killed her aunt.

We strolled and strolled and really not much passed between us save the recognition of her bereavement, conveyed in my manner and in a visible air that she had of depending on me now, since I let her see that I took an interest in her. Miss Tita had none of the pride that makes a person wish to preserve the look of independence; she did not in the least pretend that she knew at present what would become of her. I forbore to touch particularly on that however, for I certainly was not prepared to say that I would take charge of her. I was cautious; not ignobly, I think, for I felt that her knowledge of life was so small that in her unsophisticated vision there would be no reason why—since I seemed to pity her—I should not look after her. She told me how her aunt had died, very peacefully at the last, and how everything had been done afterwards by the care of her good friends (fortunately, thanks to me, she said, smiling, there was money in the house; and she repeated that when once the Italians like you they are your friends for life); and when we had gone into this she asked me about my *giro*, my impressions, the places I had seen. I told her what I could, making it up partly, I am afraid, as in my depression I had not seen much; and after she had heard me she exclaimed, quite as if she had forgotten her aunt and her sorrow, 'Dear, dear, how much I should like to do such things—to take a little journey!' It came over me for the moment that I ought to propose some tour, say I would take her anywhere she liked; and I remarked at any rate that some excursion—to give her a change—might be managed: we would think of it, talk it over. I said never a word to her about the Aspern documents; asked no questions as to what she had ascertained or what had otherwise happened with regard to them before Miss Bordereau's death. It was not that I was not on pins and needles to know, but that I thought it more decent not to betray my anxiety so soon after the catastrophe. I hoped she herself would say something, but she never glanced that way, and I thought this natural at the time. Later however, that night, it occurred to me that her silence was somewhat strange; for if she had talked of my movements, of anything so detached as the Giorgione at Castelfranco, she might have alluded to what she could easily remember was in my mind. It was not to be supposed that the emotion produced by her aunt's death had blotted out the recollection that I was interested in that lady's relics, and I fidgeted afterwards as it came to me that her reticence might very possibly mean simply that nothing had been found. We separated in the garden (it was she who said she must go in); now that she was alone in the rooms I felt that (judged, at any rate, by Venetian ideas) I was on rather a different footing in regard to visiting her there. As I shook hands with her for good-night I asked her if she had any general plan—had thought over what she had better do. 'Oh yes, oh yes, but I haven't settled anything yet,' she replied, quite cheerfully. Was her cheerfulness explained by the impression that I would settle for her?

I was glad the next morning that we had neglected practical questions, for this gave me a pretext for seeing her again immediately. There was a very practical question to be touched upon. I owed it to her to let her know formally that of course I did not expect her to keep me on as a lodger, and also to show some interest in her own tenure, what she might have on her hands in the way of a lease. But I was not destined, as it happened, to converse with her for more than an instant on either of these points. I sent her no message; I simply went down to the sala and walked to and fro there. I knew she would come out; she would very soon discover I was there. Somehow I preferred not to be shut up with her; gardens and big halls seemed better places to talk. It was a splendid morning, with something in the air that told of the waning of the long Venetian summer; a freshness from the sea which stirred the flowers in the garden and made a pleasant draught in the house, less shuttered and darkened now than when the old woman was alive. It was the beginning of autumn, of the end of the golden months. With this it was the end of my experiment—or would be in the course of half an hour, when I should really have learned that the papers had been reduced to ashes. After that there would be nothing left for me but to go to the station; for seriously (and as it struck me in the morning light) I could not linger there to act as guardian to a piece of middle-aged female helplessness. If she had not saved the papers wherein should I be indebted to her? I think I winced a little as I asked myself how much, if she *had* saved them, I should have to recognise and, as it were, to reward such a courtesy. Might not that circumstance after all saddle me with a guardianship? If this idea did not make me more uncomfortable as I walked up and down it was because I was convinced I had nothing to look to. If the old woman had not destroyed everything before she pounced upon me in the parlour she had done so afterwards.

It took Miss Tita rather longer than I had expected to guess that I was there; but when at last she came out she looked at me without surprise. I said to her that I had been waiting for her and she asked why I had not let her know. I was glad the next day that I had checked myself before remarking that I had wished to see if a friendly intuition would not tell her: it became a satisfaction to me that I had not indulged in that rather tender joke. What I did say was virtually the truth—that I was too nervous, since I expected her now to settle my fate.

'Your fate?' said Miss Tita, giving me a queer look; and as she spoke I noticed a rare change in her. She was different from what she had been the evening before—less natural, less quiet. She had been crying the day before and she was not crying now, and yet she struck me as less confident. It was as if something had happened to her during the night, or at least as if she had thought of something that troubled her—something in particular that affected her relations with me, made them more embarrassing and complicated. Had she simply perceived that her aunt's not being there now altered my position?

'I mean about our papers. *Are* there any? You must know now.'

'Yes, there are a great many; more than I supposed.' I was struck with the way her voice trembled as she told me this.

'Do you mean that you have got them in there—and that I may see them?'

'I don't think you can see them,' said Miss Tita, with an extraordinary expression of entreaty in her eyes, as if the dearest hope she had in the world now was that I would not take them from her. But how could she expect me to make such a sacrifice as that after all that had passed between us? What had I come back to Venice for but to see them, to take them? My delight at learning they were still in existence was such that if the poor woman had gone down on her knees to beseech me never to mention them again I would have treated the proceeding as a bad joke. 'I have got them but I can't show them,' she added.

'Not even to me? Ah, Miss Tita!' I groaned, with a voice of infinite remonstrance and reproach.

She coloured and the tears came back to her eyes; I saw that it cost her a kind of anguish to take such a stand but that a dreadful sense of duty had descended upon her. It made me quite sick to find myself confronted with that particular obstacle; all the more that it appeared to me I had been extremely encouraged to leave it out of account. I almost considered that Miss Tita had assured me that if she had no greater hindrance than that——! 'You don't mean to say you made her a deathbed promise? It was precisely against your doing anything of that sort that I thought I was safe. Oh, I would rather she had burned the papers outright than that!'

'No, it isn't a promise,' said Miss Tita.

'Pray what is it then?'

She hesitated and then she said, 'She tried to burn them, but I prevented it. She had hid them in her bed.'

'In her bed?'

'Between the mattresses. That's where she put them when she took them out of the trunk. I can't understand how she did it, because Olimpia didn't help her. She tells me so and I believe her. My aunt only told her afterwards, so that she shouldn't touch the bed—anything but the sheets. So it was badly made,' added Miss Tita, simply.

'I should think so! And how did she try to burn them?'

'She didn't try much; she was too weak, those last days. But she told me—she charged me. Oh, it was terrible! She couldn't speak after that night; she could only make signs.'

'And what did you do?'

'I took them away. I locked them up.'

'In the secretary?'

'Yes, in the secretary,' said Miss Tita, reddening again.

'Did you tell her you would burn them?'

'No, I didn't—on purpose.'

'On purpose to gratify me?'

'Yes, only for that.'

'And what good will you have done me if after all you won't show them?'

'Oh, none; I know that—I know that.'

'And did she believe you had destroyed them?'

'I don't know what she believed at the last. I couldn't tell—she was too far gone.'

'Then if there was no promise and no assurance I can't see what ties you.'

'Oh, she hated it so—she hated it so! She was so jealous. But here's the portrait—you may have that,' Miss Tita announced, taking the little picture, wrapped up in the same manner in which her aunt had wrapped it, out of her pocket.

'I may have it—do you mean you give it to me?' I questioned, staring, as it passed into my hand.

'Oh yes.'

'But it's worth money—a large sum.'

'Well!' said Miss Tita, still with her strange look.

I did not know what to make of it, for it could scarcely mean that she wanted to bargain like her aunt. She spoke as if she wished to make me a present. 'I can't take it from you as a gift,' I said, 'and yet I can't afford to pay you for it according to the ideas Miss Bordereau had of its value. She rated it at a thousand pounds.'

'Couldn't we sell it?' asked Miss Tita.

'God forbid! I prefer the picture to the money.'

'Well then keep it.'

'You are very generous.'

'So are you.'

'I don't know why you should think so,' I replied, and this was a truthful speech, for the singular creature appeared to have some very fine reference in her mind, which I did not in the least seize.

'Well, you have made a great difference for me,' said Miss Tita.

I looked at Jeffrey Aspern's face in the little picture, partly in order not to look at that of my interlocutress, which had begun to trouble me, even to frighten me a little—it was so self-conscious, so unnatural. I made no answer to this last declaration; I only privately consulted Jeffrey Aspern's delightful eyes with my own (they were so young and brilliant, and yet so wise, so full of vision); I asked him what on earth was the matter with Miss Tita. He seemed to smile at me with friendly mockery, as if he were amused at my case. I had got into a pickle for him—as if he needed it! He was unsatisfactory, for the only moment since I had known him. Nevertheless, now that I held the little picture in my hand I felt that it would be a precious possession. 'Is this a bribe to make me give up the papers?' I demanded in a moment, perversely. 'Much as I value it, if I were to be obliged to choose, the papers are what I should prefer. Ah, but ever so much!'

'How can you choose—how can you choose?' Miss Tita asked, slowly, lamentably.

'I see! Of course there is nothing to be said, if you regard the interdiction that rests upon you as quite insurmountable. In this case it must seem to you that to part with them would be an impiety of the worst kind, a simple sacrilege!'

Miss Tita shook her head, full of her dolefulness. 'You would understand if you had known her. I'm afraid,' she quavered suddenly—'I'm afraid! She was terrible when she was angry.'

'Yes, I saw something of that, that night. She was terrible. Then I saw her eyes. Lord, they were fine!'

'I see them—they stare at me in the dark!' said Miss Tita.

'You are nervous, with all you have been through.'

'Oh yes, very—very!'

'You mustn't mind; that will pass away,' I said, kindly. Then

I added, resignedly, for it really seemed to me that I must accept the situation, 'Well, so it is, and it can't be helped. I must renounce.' Miss Tita, at this, looking at me, gave a low, soft moan, and I went on: 'I only wish to heaven she had destroyed them; then there would be nothing more to say. And I can't understand why, with her ideas, she didn't.'

'Oh, she lived on them!' said Miss Tita.

'You can imagine whether that makes me want less to see them,' I answered, smiling. 'But don't let me stand here as if I had it in my soul to tempt you to do anything base. Naturally you will understand I give up my rooms. I leave Venice immediately.' And I took up my hat, which I had placed on a chair. We were still there rather awkwardly, on our feet, in the middle of the sala. She had left the door of the apartments open behind her but she had not led me that way.

A kind of spasm came into her face as she saw me take my hat. 'Immediately—do you mean to-day?' The tone of the words was tragical—they were a cry of desolation.

'Oh no; not so long as I can be of the least service to you.'

'Well, just a day or two more—just two or three days,' she panted. Then controlling herself she added in another manner, 'She wanted to say something to me—the last day—something very particular, but she couldn't.'

'Something very particular?'

'Something more about the papers.'

'And did you guess—have you any idea?'

'No, I have thought—but I don't know. I have thought all kinds of things.'

'And for instance?'

'Well, that if you were a relation it would be different.'

'If I were a relation?'

'If you were not a stranger. Then it would be the same for you as for me. Anything that is mine—would be yours, and you could do what you like. I couldn't prevent you—and you would have no responsibility.'

She brought out this droll explanation with a little nervous rush, as if she were speaking words she had got by heart. They gave me an impression of subtlety and at first I failed to follow. But after a moment her face helped me to see further, and then a light came into my mind. It was embarrassing, and I bent my head over Jeffrey Aspern's portrait. What an odd expression was in his face! 'Get out of it as you can, my dear fellow!' I put the picture into the pocket of my coat and said to Miss Tita, 'Yes, I'll sell it for you. I sha'n't get a thousand pounds by any means, but I shall get something good.'

She looked at me with tears in her eyes, but she seemed to try to smile as she remarked, 'We can divide the money.'

'No, no, it shall be all yours.' Then I went on, 'I think I know what your poor aunt wanted to say. She wanted to give directions that her papers should be buried with her.'

Miss Tita appeared to consider this suggestion for a moment; after which she declared, with striking decision, 'Oh no, she wouldn't have thought that safe!'

'It seems to me nothing could be safer.'

'She had an idea that when people want to publish they are capable——' And she paused, blushing.

'Of violating a tomb? Mercy on us, what must she have thought of me!'

'She was not just, she was not generous!' Miss Tita cried with sudden passion.

The light that had come into my mind a moment before increased. 'Ah, don't say that, for we *are* a dreadful race.' Then I pursued, 'If she left a will, that may give you some idea.'

'I have found nothing of the sort—she destroyed it. She was very fond of me,' Miss Tita added, incongruously. 'She wanted me to be happy. And if any person should be kind to me—she wanted to speak of that.'

I was almost awestricken at the astuteness with which the good lady found herself inspired, transparent astuteness as it was and sewn, as the phrase is, with white thread. 'Depend upon it she didn't want to make any provision that would be agreeable to me.'

'No, not to you but to me. She knew I should like it if you could carry out your idea. Not because she cared for you but because she did think of me,' Miss Tita went on, with her unexpected, persuasive volubility. 'You could see them—you could use them.' She stopped, seeing that I perceived the sense of that conditional—stopped long enough for me to give some sign which I did not give. She must have been conscious however that though my face showed the greatest embarrassment that was ever painted on a human countenance it was not set as a stone, it was also full of compassion. It was a comfort to me a long time afterwards to consider that she could not have seen in me the smallest symptom of disrespect. 'I don't know what to do; I'm too tormented, I'm too ashamed!' she continued, with vehemence. Then turning away from me and burying her face in her hands she burst into a flood of tears. If she did not know what to do it may be imagined whether I did any better. I stood there dumb, watching her while her sobs resounded in the great empty hall. In a moment she was facing me again, with her streaming eyes. 'I would give you everything—and she would understand, where she is—she would forgive me!'

'Ah, Miss Tita—ah, Miss Tita,' I stammered, for all reply. I did not know what to do, as I say, but at a venture I made a wild, vague movement, in consequence of which I found myself at the door. I remember standing there and saying, 'It wouldn't do—it wouldn't do!' pensively, awkwardly, grotesquely, while I looked away to the opposite end of the sala as if there were a beautiful view there. The next thing I remember is that I was downstairs and out of the house. My gondola was there and my gondolier, reclining on the cushions, sprang up as soon as he saw me. I jumped in and to his usual *'Dove commanda?'* I replied, in a tone that made him stare, 'Anywhere, anywhere; out into the lagoon!'

He rowed me away and I sat there prostrate, groaning softly to myself, with my hat pulled over my face. What in the name of the preposterous did she mean if she did not mean to offer me her hand? That was the price—that was the price! And did she think I wanted it, poor deluded, infatuated, extravagant lady? My gondolier, behind me, must have seen my ears red as I wondered, sitting there under the fluttering *tenda*, with my hidden face, noticing nothing as we passed—wondered whether her delusion, her infatuation had been my own reckless work. Did she think I had made love to her, even to get the papers? I had not, I had not; I repeated that over to myself for an hour, for two hours, till I was wearied if not convinced. I don't know where my gondolier took me; we floated aimlessly about on the lagoon, with slow, rare strokes. At last I became conscious that we were near the Lido, far up, on the right hand, as you turn your back to Venice, and I made him put me ashore. I wanted to walk, to move, to shed some of my bewilderment. I crossed the narrow strip and got to the sea-beach—I took my way toward Malamocco. But presently I flung myself down again on the warm sand, in the breeze, on the coarse dry grass. It took it out of me to think I had been so much at fault, that I had unwittingly but none the less deplorably trifled. But I had not given her cause—distinctly I had not. I had said to Mrs. Prest that I would make love to her; but it had been a joke without consequences and I had never said it to Tita Bordereau. I had been as kind as possible, because I really liked her; but since when had that become a crime where a woman of such an age and such an appearance was concerned? I am far from remembering clearly the succession of events and feelings during this long day of confusion, which I spent entirely in wandering about, without going home, until late at night; it only comes back to me that there were moments when I pacified my conscience and others when I lashed it into pain. I did not laugh all day—that I do recollect; the case, however it might have struck others, seemed to me so little amusing. It would have been better perhaps for me to feel the comic side of it. At any rate, whether I had given cause or not it went without saying that I could not pay the price. I could not accept. I could not, for a bundle of tattered papers, marry a ridiculous, pathetic, provincial old woman. It was a proof that she did not think the idea would come to me, her having determined to suggest it herself in that practical, argumentative, heroic way, in which the timidity however had been so much more striking than the boldness that her reasons appeared to come first and her feelings afterward.

As the day went on I grew to wish that I had never heard of Aspern's relics, and I cursed the extravagant curiosity that had put John Cumnor on the scent of them. We had more than enough material without them and my predicament was the just punishment of that most fatal of human follies, our not having known when to stop. It was very well to say it was no predicament, that the way out was simple, that I had only to leave Venice by the first train in the morning, after writing

a note to Miss Tita, to be placed in her hand as soon as I got
clear of the house; for it was a strong sign that I was embarrassed that when I tried to make up the note in my mind in
advance (I would put it on paper as soon as I got home,
before going to bed), I could not think of anything but 'How
can I thank you for the rare confidence you have placed in
me?' That would never do; it sounded exactly as if an acceptance were to follow. Of course I might go away without writing a word, but that would be brutal and my idea was still to
exclude brutal solutions. As my confusion cooled I was lost
in wonder at the importance I had attached to Miss Bordereau's crumpled scraps; the thought of them became odious to
me and I was as vexed with the old witch for the superstition
that had prevented her from destroying them as I was with
myself for having already spent more money than I could afford in attempting to control their fate. I forget what I did,
where I went after leaving the Lido and at what hour or with
what recovery of composure I made my way back to my boat.
I only know that in the afternoon, when the air was aglow
with the sunset, I was standing before the church of Saints
John and Paul and looking up at the small square-jawed face
of Bartolommeo Colleoni, the terrible *condottiere* who sits so
sturdily astride of his huge bronze horse, on the high pedestal
on which Venetian gratitude maintains him. The statue is incomparable, the finest of all mounted figures, unless that of
Marcus Aurelius, who rides benignant before the Roman Cap-
itol, be finer: but I was not thinking of that; I only found
myself staring at the triumphant captain as if he had an oracle
on his lips. The western light shines into all his grimness at
that hour and makes it wonderfully personal. But he continued to look far over my head, at the red immersion of another
day—he had seen so many go down into the lagoon through
the centuries—and if he were thinking of battles and strata-
gems they were of a different quality from any I had to tell
him of. He could not direct me what to do, gaze up at him
as I might. Was it before this or after that I wandered about
for an hour in the small canals, to the continued stupefaction
of my gondolier, who had never seen me so restless and yet
so void of a purpose and could extract from me no order but
'Go anywhere—everywhere—all over the place'? He reminded

me that I had not lunched and expressed therefore respectfully
the hope that I would dine earlier. He had had long periods
of leisure during the day, when I had left the boat and rambled, so that I was not obliged to consider him, and I told
him that that day, for a change, I would touch no meat. It
was an effect of poor Miss Tita's proposal, not altogether auspicious, that I had quite lost my appetite. I don't know why
it happened that on this occasion I was more than ever struck
with that queer air of sociability, of cousinship and family life,
which makes up half the expression of Venice. Without streets
and vehicles, the uproar of wheels, the brutality of horses, and
with its little winding ways where people crowd together,
where voices sound as in the corridors of a house, where the
human step circulates as if it skirted the angles of furniture
and shoes never wear out, the place has the character of an
immense collective apartment, in which Piazza San Marco is
the most ornamented corner and palaces and churches, for
the rest, play the part of great divans of repose, tables of entertainment, expanses of decoration. And somehow the splendid common domicile, familiar, domestic and resonant, also
resembles a theatre, with actors clicking over bridges and, in
straggling processions, tripping along fondamentas. As you sit
in your gondola the footways that in certain parts edge the
canals assume to the eye the importance of a stage, meeting
it at the same angle, and the Venetian figures, moving to and
fro against the battered scenery of their little houses of comedy, strike you as members of an endless dramatic troupe.

I went to bed that night very tired, without being able to
compose a letter to Miss Tita. Was this failure the reason why
I became conscious the next morning as soon as I awoke of
a determination to see the poor lady again the first moment
she would receive me? That had something to do with it, but
what had still more was the fact that during my sleep a very
odd revulsion had taken place in my spirit. I found myself
aware of this almost as soon as I opened my eyes; it made me
jump out of my bed with the movement of a man who remembers that he has left the house-door ajar or a candle burning under a shelf. Was I still in time to save my goods? That
question was in my heart; for what had now come to pass was
that in the unconscious cerebration of sleep I had swung back

to a passionate appreciation of Miss Bordereau's papers. They were now more precious than ever and a kind of ferocity had come into my desire to possess them. The condition Miss Tita had attached to the possession of them no longer appeared an obstacle worth thinking of, and for an hour, that morning, my repentant imagination brushed it aside. It was absurd that I should be able to invent nothing; absurd to renounce so easily and turn away helpless from the idea that the only way to get hold of the papers was to unite myself to her for life. I would not unite myself and yet I would have them. I must add that by the time I sent down to ask if she would see me I had invented no alternative, though to do so I had had all the time that I was dressing. This failure was humiliating, yet what could the alternative be? Miss Tita sent back word that I might come; and as I descended the stairs and crossed the sala to her door—this time she received me in her aunt's forlorn parlour—I hoped she would not think my errand was to tell her I accepted her hand. She certainly would have made the day before the reflection that I declined it.

As soon as I came into the room I saw that she had drawn this inference, but I also saw something which had not been in my forecast. Poor Miss Tita's sense of her failure had produced an extraordinary alteration in her, but I had been too full of my literary concupiscence to think of that. Now I perceived it; I can scarcely tell how it startled me. She stood in the middle of the room with a face of mildness bent upon me, and her look of forgiveness, of absolution made her angelic. It beautified her; she was younger; she was not a ridiculous old woman. This optical trick gave her a sort of phantasmagoric brightness, and while I was still the victim of it I heard a whisper somewhere in the depths of my conscience: 'Why not, after all—why not?' It seemed to me I was ready to pay the price. Still more distinctly however than the whisper I heard Miss Tita's own voice. I was so struck with the different effect she made upon me that at first I was not clearly aware of what she was saying; then I perceived she had bade me good-bye—she said something about hoping I should be very happy.

'Good-bye—good-bye?' I repeated, with an inflection interrogative and probably foolish.

I saw she did not feel the interrogation, she only heard the words; she had strung herself up to accepting our separation and they fell upon her ear as a proof. 'Are you going to-day?' she asked. 'But it doesn't matter, for whenever you go I shall not see you again. I don't want to.' And she smiled strangely, with an infinite gentleness. She had never doubted that I had left her the day before in horror. How could she, since I had not come back before night to contradict, even as a simple form, such an idea? And now she had the force of soul—Miss Tita with force of soul was a new conception—to smile at me in her humiliation.

'What shall you do—where shall you go?' I asked.

'Oh, I don't know. I have done the great thing. I have destroyed the papers.'

'Destroyed them?' I faltered.

'Yes; what was I to keep them for? I burnt them last night, one by one, in the kitchen.'

'One by one?' I repeated, mechanically.

'It took a long time—there were so many.' The room seemed to go round me as she said this and a real darkness for a moment descended upon my eyes. When it passed Miss Tita was there still, but the transfiguration was over and she had changed back to a plain, dingy, elderly person. It was in this character she spoke as she said, 'I can't stay with you longer, I can't;' and it was in this character that she turned her back upon me, as I had turned mine upon her twenty-four hours before, and moved to the door of her room. Here she did what I had not done when I quitted her—she paused long enough to give me one look. I have never forgotten it and I sometimes still suffer from it, though it was not resentful. No, there was no resentment, nothing hard or vindictive in poor Miss Tita; for when, later, I sent her in exchange for the portrait of Jeffrey Aspern a larger sum of money than I had hoped to be able to gather for her, writing to her that I had sold the picture, she kept it with thanks; she never sent it back. I wrote to her that I had sold the picture, but I admitted to Mrs. Prest, at the time (I met her in London, in the autumn), that it hangs above my writing-table. When I look at it my chagrin at the loss of the letters becomes almost intolerable.

The Liar

T HE TRAIN was half an hour late and the drive from the
station longer than he had supposed, so that when he
reached the house its inmates had dispersed to dress for dinner
and he was conducted straight to his room. The curtains were
drawn in this asylum, the candles were lighted, the fire was
bright, and when the servant had quickly put out his clothes
the comfortable little place became suggestive—seemed to
promise a pleasant house, a various party, talks, acquaintances,
affinities, to say nothing of very good cheer. He was too occupied with his profession to pay many country visits, but he
had heard people who had more time for them speak of establishments where 'they do you very well.' He foresaw that
the proprietors of Stayes would do him very well. In his bedroom at a country house he always looked first at the books
on the shelf and the prints on the walls; he considered that
these things gave a sort of measure of the culture and even of
the character of his hosts. Though he had but little time to
devote to them on this occasion a cursory inspection assured
him that if the literature, as usual, was mainly American and
humorous the art consisted neither of the water-colour studies
of the children nor of 'goody' engravings. The walls were
adorned with old-fashioned lithographs, principally portraits
of country gentlemen with high collars and riding gloves: this
suggested—and it was encouraging—that the tradition of portraiture was held in esteem. There was the customary novel
of Mr. Le Fanu, for the bedside; the ideal reading in a country
house for the hours after midnight. Oliver Lyon could scarcely
forbear beginning it while he buttoned his shirt.

Perhaps that is why he not only found every one assembled
in the hall when he went down, but perceived from the way
the move to dinner was instantly made that they had been
waiting for him. There was no delay, to introduce him to a
lady, for he went out in a group of unmatched men, without
this appendage. The men, straggling behind, sidled and edged
as usual at the door of the dining-room, and the *dénouement*
of this little comedy was that he came to his place last of all.

This made him think that he was in a sufficiently distinguished company, for if he had been humiliated (which he was not), he could not have consoled himself with the reflection that such a fate was natural to an obscure, struggling young artist. He could no longer think of himself as very young, alas, and if his position was not so brilliant as it ought to be he could no longer justify it by calling it a struggle. He was something of a celebrity and he was apparently in a society of celebrities. This idea added to the curiosity with which he looked up and down the long table as he settled himself in his place.

It was a numerous party—five and twenty people; rather an odd occasion to have proposed to him, as he thought. He would not be surrounded by the quiet that ministers to good work; however, it had never interfered with his work to see the spectacle of human life before him in the intervals. And though he did not know it, it was never quiet at Stayes. When he was working well he found himself in that happy state— the happiest of all for an artist—in which things in general contribute to the particular idea and fall in with it, help it on and justify it, so that he feels for the hour as if nothing in the world can happen to him, even if it come in the guise of disaster or suffering, that will not be an enhancement of his subject. Moreover there was an exhilaration (he had felt it before) in the rapid change of scene—the jump, in the dusk of the afternoon, from foggy London and his familiar studio to a centre of festivity in the middle of Hertfordshire and a drama half acted, a drama of pretty women and noted men and wonderful orchids in silver jars. He observed as a not unimportant fact that one of the pretty women was beside him: a gentleman sat on his other hand. But he went into his neighbours little as yet: he was busy looking out for Sir David, whom he had never seen and about whom he naturally was curious.

Evidently, however, Sir David was not at dinner, a circum- stance sufficiently explained by the other circumstance which constituted our friend's principal knowledge of him—his being ninety years of age. Oliver Lyon had looked forward with great pleasure to the chance of painting a nonagenarian, and though the old man's absence from table was something of a disappointment (it was an opportunity the less to observe him before going to work), it seemed a sign that he was rather a sacred and perhaps therefore an impressive relic. Lyon looked at his son with the greater interest—wondered whether the glazed bloom of his cheek had been transmitted from Sir David. That would be jolly to paint, in the old man—the withered ruddiness of a winter apple, especially if the eye were still alive and the white hair carried out the frosty look. Arthur Ashmore's hair had a midsummer glow, but Lyon was glad his commission had been to delineate the father rather than the son, in spite of his never having seen the one and of the other being seated there before him now in the happy expansion of liberal hospitality.

Arthur Ashmore was a fresh-coloured, thick-necked English gentleman, but he was just not a subject; he might have been a farmer and he might have been a banker: you could scarcely paint him in characters. His wife did not make up the amount; she was a large, bright, negative woman, who had the same air as her husband of being somehow tremendously new; a sort of appearance of fresh varnish (Lyon could scarcely tell whether it came from her complexion or from her clothes), so that one felt she ought to sit in a gilt frame, suggesting reference to a catalogue or a price-list. It was as if she were already rather a bad though expensive portrait, knocked off by an eminent hand, and Lyon had no wish to copy that work. The pretty woman on his right was engaged with her neighbour and the gentleman on his other side looked shrinking and scared, so that he had time to lose himself in his favourite diversion of watching face after face. This amusement gave him the greatest pleasure he knew, and he often thought it a mercy that the human mask did interest him and that it was not less vivid than it was (sometimes it ran its success in this line very close), since he was to make his living by reproducing it. Even if Arthur Ashmore would not be inspiring to paint (a certain anxiety rose in him lest if he should make a hit with her father-in-law Mrs. Arthur should take it into her head that he had now proved himself worthy to *aborder* her husband); even if he had looked a little less like a page (fine as to print and margin) without punctuation, he would still be a refreshing, iridescent surface. But the gentleman four persons off—what was he? Would he be a subject, or was his face only the legible door-plate of his identity, burnished with punctual washing and shaving—the least thing that was decent that you would know him by?

This face arrested Oliver Lyon: it struck him at first as very handsome. The gentleman might still be called young, and his features were regular: he had a plentiful, fair moustache that curled up at the ends, a brilliant, gallant, almost adventurous air, and a big shining breastpin in the middle of his shirt. He appeared a fine satisfied soul, and Lyon perceived that wherever he rested his friendly eye there fell an influence as pleasant as the September sun—as if he could make grapes and pears or even human affection ripen by looking at them. What was odd in him was a certain mixture of the correct and the extravagant: as if he were an adventurer imitating a gentleman with rare perfection or a gentleman who had taken a fancy to go about with hidden arms. He might have been a dethroned prince or the war-correspondent of a newspaper: he represented both enterprise and tradition, good manners and bad taste. Lyon at length fell into conversation with the lady beside him—they dispensed, as he had had to dispense at dinner-parties before, with an introduction—by asking who this personage might be.

'Oh, he's Colonel Capadose, don't you know?' Lyon didn't know and he asked for further information. His neighbour had a sociable manner and evidently was accustomed to quick transitions; she turned from her other interlocutor with a methodical air, as a good cook lifts the cover of the next sauce-pan. 'He has been a great deal in India—isn't he rather celebrated?' she inquired. Lyon confessed he had never heard of him, and she went on, 'Well, perhaps he isn't; but he says he is, and if you think it, that's just the same, isn't it?'

'If *you* think it?'

'I mean if he thinks it—that's just as good, I suppose.'

'Do you mean that he says that which is not?'

'Oh dear, no—because I never know. He is exceedingly clever and amusing—quite the cleverest person in the house, unless indeed you are more so. But that I can't tell yet, can I? I only know about the people I know; I think that's celebrity enough!'

'Enough for them?'

'Oh, I see you're clever. Enough for me! But I have heard of you,' the lady went on. 'I know your pictures; I admire them. But I don't think you look like them.'

'They are mostly portraits,' Lyon said; 'and what I usually try for is not my own resemblance.'

'I see what you mean. But they have much more colour. And now you are going to do some one here?'

'I have been invited to do Sir David. I'm rather disappointed at not seeing him this evening.'

'Oh, he goes to bed at some unnatural hour—eight o'clock or something of that sort. You know he's rather an old mummy.'

'An old mummy?' Oliver Lyon repeated.

'I mean he wears half a dozen waistcoats, and that sort of thing. He's always cold.'

'I have never seen him and never seen any portrait or photograph of him,' Lyon said. 'I'm surprised at his never having had anything done—at their waiting all these years.'

'Ah, that's because he was afraid, you know; it was a kind of superstition. He was sure that if anything were done he would die directly afterwards. He has only consented to-day.'

'He's ready to die then?'

'Oh, now he's so old he doesn't care.'

'Well, I hope I shan't kill him,' said Lyon. 'It was rather unnatural in his son to send for me.'

'Oh, they have nothing to gain—everything is theirs already!' his companion rejoined, as if she took this speech quite literally. Her talkativeness was systematic—she fraternised as seriously as she might have played whist. 'They do as they like—they fill the house with people—they have *carte blanche*.'

'I see—but there's still the title.'

'Yes, but what is it?'

Our artist broke into laughter at this, whereat his companion stared. Before he had recovered himself she was scouring the plain with her other neighbour. The gentleman on his left at last risked an observation, and they had some fragmentary talk. This personage played his part with difficulty: he uttered a remark as a lady fires a pistol, looking the other way. To catch the ball Lyon had to bend his ear, and this movement led to his observing a handsome creature who was seated on the same side, beyond his interlocutor. Her profile was presented to him and at first he was only struck with its beauty; then it produced an impression still more agreeable—a sense of undimmed remembrance and intimate association. He had not recognised her on the instant only because he had so little expected to see her there; he had not seen her anywhere for so long, and no news of her ever came to him. She was often in his thoughts, but she had passed out of his life. He thought of her twice a week; that may be called often in relation to a person one has not seen for twelve years. The moment after he recognised her he felt how true it was that it was only she who could look like that: of the most charming head in the world (and this lady had it) there could never be a replica. She was leaning forward a little; she remained in profile, apparently listening to some one on the other side of her. She was listening, but she was also looking, and after a moment Lyon followed the direction of her eyes. They rested upon the gentleman who had been described to him as Colonel Capadose—rested, as it appeared to him, with a kind of habitual, visible complacency. This was not strange, for the Colonel was unmistakably formed to attract the sympathetic gaze of woman; but Lyon was slightly disappointed that she could let *him* look at her so long without giving him a glance. There was nothing between them to-day and he had no rights, but she must have known he was coming (it was of course not such a tremendous event, but she could not have been staying in the house without hearing of it), and it was not natural that that should absolutely fail to affect her.

She was looking at Colonel Capadose as if she were in love with him—a queer accident for the proudest, most reserved of women. But doubtless it was all right, if her husband liked it or didn't notice it: he had heard indefinitely, years before, that she was married, and he took for granted (as he had not heard that she had become a widow) the presence of the happy man on whom she had conferred what she had refused to *him*, the poor art-student at Munich. Colonel Capadose appeared to be aware of nothing, and this circumstance, incongruously enough, rather irritated Lyon than gratified him. Suddenly the lady turned her head, showing her full face to our hero. He was so prepared with a greeting that he instantly smiled, as a shaken jug overflows; but she gave him no response, turned away again and sank back in her chair. All that her face said in that instant was, 'You see I'm as handsome as ever.' To which he mentally subjoined, 'Yes, and as much good it does me!' He asked the young man beside him if he knew who that beautiful being was—the fifth person beyond him. The young man leaned forward, considered and then said, 'I think she's Mrs. Capadose.'

'Do you mean his wife—that fellow's?' And Lyon indicated the subject of the information given him by his other neighbour.

'Oh, is *he* Mr. Capadose?' said the young man, who appeared very vague. He admitted his vagueness and explained it by saying that there were so many people and he had come only the day before. What was definite to Lyon was that Mrs. Capadose was in love with her husband; so that he wished more than ever that he had married her.

'She's very faithful,' he found himself saying three minutes later to the lady on his right. He added that he meant Mrs. Capadose.

'Ah, you know her then?'

'I knew her once upon a time—when I was living abroad.'

'Why then were you asking me about her husband?'

'Precisely for that reason. She married after that—I didn't even know her present name.'

'How then do you know it now?'

'This gentleman has just told me—he appears to know.'

'I didn't know he knew anything,' said the lady, glancing forward.

'I don't think he knows anything but that.'

'Then you have found out for yourself that she is faithful. What do you mean by that?'

'Ah, you mustn't question me—I want to question you,' Lyon said. 'How do you all like her here?'

'You ask too much! I can only speak for myself. I think she's hard.'

'That's only because she's honest and straightforward.'

'Do you mean I like people in proportion as they deceive?'

'I think we all do, so long as we don't find them out,' Lyon

said. 'And then there's something in her face—a sort of Roman type, in spite of her having such an English eye. In fact
she's English down to the ground; but her complexion, her
low forehead and that beautiful close little wave in her dark
hair make her look like a glorified *contadina*.'

'Yes, and she always sticks pins and daggers into her head,
to increase that effect. I must say I like her husband better:
he is so clever.'

'Well, when I knew her there was no comparison that could
injure her. She was altogether the most delightful thing in
Munich.'

'In Munich?'

'Her people lived there; they were not rich—in pursuit of
economy in fact, and Munich was very cheap. Her father was
the younger son of some noble house; he had married a second time and had a lot of little mouths to feed. She was the
child of the first wife and she didn't like her stepmother, but
she was charming to her little brothers and sisters. I once
made a sketch of her as Werther's Charlotte, cutting bread
and butter while they clustered all round her. All the artists
in the place were in love with her but she wouldn't look at
"the likes" of us. She was too proud—I grant you that; but
she wasn't stuck up nor young ladyish; she was simple and
frank and kind about it. She used to remind me of Thackeray's
Ethel Newcome. She told me she must marry well: it was the
one thing she could do for her family. I suppose you would
say that she *has* married well.'

'She told *you*?' smiled Lyon's neighbour.

'Oh, of course I proposed to her too. But she evidently
thinks so herself!' he added.

When the ladies left the table the host as usual bade the
gentlemen draw together, so that Lyon found himself opposite to Colonel Capadose. The conversation was mainly about
the 'run,' for it had apparently been a great day in the hunt-
ing-field. Most of the gentlemen communicated their adventures and opinions, but Colonel Capadose's pleasant voice was
the most audible in the chorus. It was a bright and fresh but
masculine organ, just such a voice as, to Lyon's sense, such a
'fine man' ought to have had. It appeared from his remarks
that he was a very straight rider, which was also very much

what Lyon would have expected. Not that he swaggered, for his allusions were very quietly and casually made; but they were all to dangerous experiments and close shaves. Lyon perceived after a little that the attention paid by the company to the Colonel's remarks was not in direct relation to the interest they seemed to offer; the result of which was that the speaker, who noticed that *he* at least was listening, began to treat him as his particular auditor and to fix his eyes on him as he talked. Lyon had nothing to do but to look sympathetic and assent—Colonel Capadose appeared to take so much sympathy and assent for granted. A neighbouring squire had had an accident; he had come a cropper in an awkward place—just at the finish—with consequences that looked grave. He had struck his head; he remained insensible, up to the last accounts: there had evidently been concussion of the brain. There was some exchange of views as to his recovery—how soon it would take place or whether it would take place at all; which led the Colonel to confide to our artist across the table that *he* shouldn't despair of a fellow even if he didn't come round for weeks—for weeks and weeks and weeks—for months, almost for years. He leaned forward; Lyon leaned forward to listen, and Colonel Capadose mentioned that he knew from personal experience that there was really no limit to the time one might lie unconscious without being any the worse for it. It had happened to him in Ireland, years before; he had been pitched out of a dogcart, had turned a sheer somersault and landed on his head. They thought he was dead, but he wasn't; they carried him first to the nearest cabin, where he lay for some days with the pigs, and then to an inn in a neighbouring town—it was a near thing they didn't put him under ground. He had been completely insensible—without a ray of recognition of any human thing—for three whole months; had not a glimmer of consciousness of any blessed thing. It was touch and go to that degree that they couldn't come near him, they couldn't feed him, they could scarcely look at him. Then one day he had opened his eyes—as fit as a flea!

'I give you my honour it had done me good—it rested my brain.' He appeared to intimate that with an intelligence so active as his these periods of repose were providential. Lyon thought his story very striking, but he wanted to ask him whether he had not shammed a little—not in relating it, but in keeping so quiet. He hesitated however, in time, to imply a doubt—he was so impressed with the tone in which Colonel Capadose said that it was the turn of a hair that they hadn't buried him alive. That had happened to a friend of his in India—a fellow who was supposed to have died of jungle fever —they clapped him into a coffin. He was going on to recite the further fate of this unfortunate gentleman when Mr. Ashmore made a move and every one got up to adjourn to the drawing-room. Lyon noticed that by this time no one was heeding what his new friend said to him. They came round on either side of the table and met while the gentlemen dawdled before going out.

'And do you mean that your friend was literally buried alive?' asked Lyon, in some suspense.

Colonel Capadose looked at him a moment, as if he had already lost the thread of the conversation. Then his face brightened—and when it brightened it was doubly handsome. 'Upon my soul he was chucked into the ground!'

'And was he left there?'

'He was left there till I came and hauled him out.'

'*You* came?'

'I dreamed about him—it's the most extraordinary story: I heard him calling to me in the night. I took upon myself to dig him up. You know there are people in India—a kind of beastly race, the ghouls—who violate graves. I had a sort of presentiment that they would get at him first. I rode straight, I can tell you; and, by Jove, a couple of them had just broken ground! Crack—crack, from a couple of barrels, and they showed me their heels, as you may believe. Would you credit that I took him out myself? The air brought him to and he was none the worse. He has got his pension—he came home the other day; he would do anything for me.'

'He called to you in the night?' said Lyon, much startled.

'That's the interesting point. Now *what was it*? It wasn't his ghost, because he wasn't dead. It wasn't himself, because he couldn't. It was something or other! You see India's a strange country—there's an element of the mysterious: the air is full of things you can't explain.'

They passed out of the dining-room, and Colonel Capadose, who went among the first, was separated from Lyon; but a minute later, before they reached the drawing-room, he joined him again. 'Ashmore tells me who you are. Of course I have often heard of you—I'm very glad to make your acquaintance; my wife used to know you.'

'I'm glad she remembers me. I recognised her at dinner and I was afraid she didn't.'

'Ah, I daresay she was ashamed,' said the Colonel, with indulgent humour.

'Ashamed of me?' Lyon replied, in the same key.

'Wasn't there something about a picture? Yes; you painted her portrait.'

'Many times,' said the artist; 'and she may very well have been ashamed of what I made of her.'

'Well, I wasn't, my dear sir; it was the sight of that picture, which you were so good as to present to her, that made me first fall in love with her.'

'Do you mean that one with the children—cutting bread and butter?'

'Bread and butter? Bless me, no—vine leaves and a leopard skin—a kind of Bacchante.'

'Ah, yes,' said Lyon; 'I remember. It was the first decent portrait I painted. I should be curious to see it to-day.'

'Don't ask her to show it to you—she'll be mortified!' the Colonel exclaimed.

'Mortified?'

'We parted with it—in the most disinterested manner,' he laughed. 'An old friend of my wife's—her family had known him intimately when they lived in Germany—took the most extraordinary fancy to it: the Grand Duke of Silberstadt-Schreckenstein, don't you know? He came out to Bombay while we were there and he spotted your picture (you know he's one of the greatest collectors in Europe), and made such eyes at it that, upon my word—it happened to be his birthday—she told him he might have it, to get rid of him. He was perfectly enchanted—but we miss the picture.'

'It is very good of you,' Lyon said. 'If it's in a great collection—a work of my incompetent youth—I am infinitely honoured.'

'Oh, he has got it in one of his castles; I don't know which—you know he has so many. He sent us, before he left India—to return the compliment—a magnificent old vase.'

'That was more than the thing was worth,' Lyon remarked.

Colonel Capadose gave no heed to this observation; he seemed to be thinking of something. After a moment he said, 'If you'll come and see us in town she'll show you the vase.' And as they passed into the drawing-room he gave the artist a friendly propulsion. 'Go and speak to her; there she is—she'll be delighted.'

Oliver Lyon took but a few steps into the wide saloon; he stood there a moment looking at the bright composition of the lamplit group of fair women, the single figures, the great setting of white and gold, the panels of old damask, in the centre of each of which was a single celebrated picture. There was a subdued lustre in the scene and an air as of the shining trains of dresses tumbled over the carpet. At the furthest end of the room sat Mrs. Capadose, rather isolated; she was on a small sofa, with an empty place beside her. Lyon could not flatter himself she had been keeping it for him; her failure to respond to his recognition at table contradicted that, but he felt an extreme desire to go and occupy it. Moreover he had her husband's sanction; so he crossed the room, stepping over the tails of gowns, and stood before his old friend.

'I hope you don't mean to repudiate me,' he said.

She looked up at him with an expression of unalloyed pleasure. 'I am so glad to see you. I was delighted when I heard you were coming.'

'I tried to get a smile from you at dinner—but I couldn't.'

'I didn't see—I didn't understand. Besides, I hate smirking and telegraphing. Also I'm very shy—you won't have forgotten that. Now we can communicate comfortably.' And she made a better place for him on the little sofa. He sat down and they had a talk that he enjoyed, while the reason for which he used to like her so came back to him, as well as a good deal of the very same old liking. She was still the least spoiled beauty he had ever seen, with an absence of coquetry or any insinuating art that seemed almost like an omitted faculty; there were moments when she struck her interlocutor as some fine creature from an asylum—a surprising deaf-mute or one of the operative blind. Her noble pagan head gave her privileges that she neglected, and when people were admiring her brow she was wondering whether there were a good fire in her bedroom. She was simple, kind and good; inexpressive but not inhuman or stupid. Now and again she dropped something that had a sifted, selected air—the sound of an impression at first hand. She had no imagination, but she had added up her feelings, some of her reflections, about life. Lyon talked of the old days in Munich, reminded her of incidents, pleasures and pains, asked her about her father and the others; and she told him in return that she was so impressed with his own fame, his brilliant position in the world, that she had not felt very sure he would speak to her or that his little sign at table was meant for her. This was plainly a perfectly truthful speech—she was incapable of any other—and he was affected by such humility on the part of a woman whose grand line was unique. Her father was dead; one of her brothers was in the navy and the other on a ranch in America; two of her sisters were married and the youngest was just coming out and very pretty. She didn't mention her stepmother. She asked him about his own personal history and he said that the principal thing that had happened to him was that he had never married.

'Oh, you ought to,' she answered. 'It's the best thing.'

'I like that—from you!' he returned.

'Why not from me? I am very happy.'

'That's just why I can't be. It's cruel of you to praise your state. But I have had the pleasure of making the acquaintance of your husband. We had a good bit of talk in the other room.'

'You must know him better—you must know him really well,' said Mrs. Capadose.

'I am sure that the further you go the more you find. But he makes a fine show, too.'

She rested her good gray eyes on Lyon. 'Don't you think he's handsome?'

'Handsome and clever and entertaining. You see I'm generous.'

'Yes; you must know him well,' Mrs. Capadose repeated.

'He has seen a great deal of life,' said her companion.

'Yes, we have been in so many places. You must see my little girl. She is nine years old—she's too beautiful.'

'You must bring her to my studio some day—I should like to paint her.'

'Ah, don't speak of that,' said Mrs. Capadose. 'It reminds me of something so distressing.'

'I hope you don't mean when *you* used to sit to me—though that may well have bored you.'

'It's not what you did—it's what we have done. It's a confession I must make—it's a weight on my mind! I mean about that beautiful picture you gave me—it used to be so much admired. When you come to see me in London (I count on your doing that very soon) I shall see you looking all round. I can't tell you I keep it in my own room because I love it so, for the simple reason——' And she paused a moment.

'Because you can't tell wicked lies,' said Lyon.

'No, I can't. So before you ask for it——'

'Oh, I know you parted with it—the blow has already fallen,' Lyon interrupted.

'Ah then, you have heard? I was sure you would! But do you know what we got for it? Two hundred pounds.'

'You might have got much more,' said Lyon, smiling.

'That seemed a great deal at the time. We were in want of the money—it was a good while ago, when we first married. Our means were very small then, but fortunately that has changed rather for the better. We had the chance; it really seemed a big sum, and I am afraid we jumped at it. My husband had expectations which have partly come into effect, so that now we do well enough. But meanwhile the picture went.'

'Fortunately the original remained. But do you mean that two hundred was the value of the vase?' Lyon asked.

'Of the vase?'

'The beautiful old Indian vase—the Grand Duke's offering.'

'The Grand Duke?'

'What's his name?—Silberstadt-Schreckenstein. Your husband mentioned the transaction.'

'Oh, my husband,' said Mrs. Capadose; and Lyon saw that she coloured a little.

Not to add to her embarrassment, but to clear up the ambiguity, which he perceived the next moment he had better have left alone, he went on: 'He tells me it's now in his collection.'

'In the Grand Duke's? Ah, you know its reputation? I believe it contains treasures.' She was bewildered, but she recovered herself, and Lyon made the mental reflection that for some reason which would seem good when he knew it the husband and the wife had prepared different versions of the same incident. It was true that he did not exactly see Everina Brant preparing a version; that was not her line of old, and indeed it was not in her eyes to-day. At any rate they both had the matter too much on their conscience. He changed the subject, said Mrs. Capadose must really bring the little girl. He sat with her some time longer and thought—perhaps it was only a fancy—that she was rather absent, as if she were annoyed at their having been even for a moment at cross-purposes. This did not prevent him from saying to her at the last, just as the ladies began to gather themselves together to go to bed: 'You seem much impressed, from what you say, with my renown and my prosperity, and you are so good as greatly to exaggerate them. Would you have married me if you had known that I was destined to success?'

'I did know it.'

'Well, I didn't.'

'You were too modest.'

'You didn't think so when I proposed to you.'

'Well, if I had married you I couldn't have married *him*— and he's so nice,' Mrs. Capadose said. Lyon knew she thought it—he had learned that at dinner—but it vexed him a little to hear her say it. The gentleman designated by the pronoun came up, amid the prolonged handshaking for good-night, and Mrs. Capadose remarked to her husband as she turned away, 'He wants to paint Amy.'

'Ah, she's a charming child, a most interesting little creature,' the Colonel said to Lyon. 'She does the most remarkable things.'

Mrs. Capadose stopped, in the rustling procession that followed the hostess out of the room. 'Don't tell him, please don't,' she said.

'Don't tell him what?'

'Why, what she does. Let him find out for himself.' And she passed on.

'She thinks I swagger about the child—that I bore people,' said the Colonel. 'I hope you smoke.' He appeared ten minutes later in the smoking-room, in a brilliant equipment, a suit of crimson foulard covered with little white spots. He gratified Lyon's eye, made him feel that the modern age has its splendour too and its opportunities for costume. If his wife was an antique he was a fine specimen of the period of colour: he might have passed for a Venetian of the sixteenth century. They were a remarkable couple, Lyon thought, and as he looked at the Colonel standing in bright erectness before the chimney-piece while he emitted great smoke-puffs he did not wonder that Everina could not regret she had not married *him*. All the gentlemen collected at Stayes were not smokers and some of them had gone to bed. Colonel Capadose remarked that there probably would be a smallish muster, they had had such a hard day's work. That was the worst of a hunting-house—the men were so sleepy after dinner; it was devilish stupid for the ladies, even for those who hunted themselves—for women were so extraordinary, they never showed it. But most fellows revived under the stimulating influences of the smoking-room, and some of them, in this confidence, would turn up yet. Some of the grounds of their confidence—not all of them—might have been seen in a cluster of glasses and bottles on a table near the fire, which made the great salver and its contents twinkle sociably. The others lurked as yet in various improper corners of the minds of the most loquacious. Lyon was alone with Colonel Capadose for some moments before their companions, in varied eccentricities of uniform, straggled in, and he perceived that this wonderful man had but little loss of vital tissue to repair.

They talked about the house, Lyon having noticed an oddity of construction in the smoking-room; and the Colonel explained that it consisted of two distinct parts, one of which was of very great antiquity. They were two complete houses in short, the old one and the new, each of great extent and each very fine in its way. The two formed together an enormous structure—Lyon must make a point of going over it. The modern portion had been erected by the old man when he bought the property; oh yes, he had bought it, forty years before—it hadn't been in the family: there hadn't been any particular family for it to be in. He had had the good taste not to spoil the original house—he had not touched it beyond what was just necessary for joining it on. It was very curious indeed—a most irregular, rambling, mysterious pile, where they every now and then discovered a walled-up room or a secret staircase. To his mind it was essentially gloomy, however; even the modern additions, splendid as they were, failed to make it cheerful. There was some story about a skeleton having been found years before, during some repairs, under a stone slab of the floor of one of the passages; but the family were rather shy of its being talked about. The place they were in was of course in the old part, which contained after all some of the best rooms: he had an idea it had been the primitive kitchen, half modernised at some intermediate period.

'My room is in the old part too then—I'm very glad,' Lyon said. 'It's very comfortable and contains all the latest conveniences, but I observed the depth of the recess of the door and the evident antiquity of the corridor and staircase—the first short one—after I came out. That panelled corridor is admirable; it looks as if it stretched away, in its brown dimness (the lamps didn't seem to me to make much impression on it), for half a mile.'

'Oh, don't go to the end of it!' exclaimed the Colonel, smiling.

'Does it lead to the haunted room?' Lyon asked.

His companion looked at him a moment. 'Ah, you know about that?'

'No, I don't speak from knowledge, only from hope. I have never had any luck—I have never stayed in a dangerous house. The places I go to are always as safe as Charing Cross. I want to see—whatever there is, the regular thing. *Is* there a ghost here?'

'Of course there is—a rattling good one.'

'And have you seen him?'

'Oh, don't ask me what *I've* seen—I should tax your credulity. I don't like to talk of these things. But there are two or three as bad—that is, as good!—rooms as you'll find anywhere.'

'Do you mean in my corridor?' Lyon asked.

'I believe the worst is at the far end. But you would be ill-advised to sleep there.'

'Ill-advised?'

'Until you've finished your job. You'll get letters of importance the next morning, and you'll take the 10.20.'

'Do you mean I will invent a pretext for running away?'

'Unless you are braver than almost any one has ever been. They don't often put people to sleep there, but sometimes the house is so crowded that they have to. The same thing always happens—ill-concealed agitation at the breakfast-table and letters of the greatest importance. Of course it's a bachelor's room, and my wife and I are at the other end of the house. But we saw the comedy three days ago—the day after we got here. A young fellow had been put there—I forget his name—the house was so full; and the usual consequence followed. Letters at breakfast—an awfully queer face—an urgent call to town—so very sorry his visit was cut short. Ashmore and his wife looked at each other, and off the poor devil went.'

'Ah, that wouldn't suit me; I must paint my picture,' said Lyon. 'But do they mind your speaking of it? Some people who have a good ghost are very proud of it, you know.'

What answer Colonel Capadose was on the point of making to this inquiry our hero was not to learn, for at that moment their host had walked into the room accompanied by three or four gentlemen. Lyon was conscious that he was partly answered by the Colonel's not going on with the subject. This however on the other hand was rendered natural by the fact that one of the gentlemen appealed to him for an opinion on a point under discussion, something to do with the everlasting history of the day's run. To Lyon himself Mr. Ashmore began to talk, expressing his regret at having had so little direct conversation with him as yet. The topic that suggested itself was naturally that most closely connected with the motive of the artist's visit. Lyon remarked that it was a great disadvantage to him not to have had some preliminary acquaintance with Sir David—in most cases he found that so important. But the present sitter was so far advanced in life that there was doubtless no time to lose. 'Oh, I can tell you all about him,' said Mr. Ashmore; and for half an hour he told him a good deal.

It was very interesting as well as very eulogistic, and Lyon could see that he was a very nice old man, to have endeared himself so to a son who was evidently not a gusher. At last he got up—he said he must go to bed if he wished to be fresh for his work in the morning. To which his host replied, 'Then you must take your candle; the lights are out; I don't keep my servants up.'

In a moment Lyon had his glimmering taper in hand, and as he was leaving the room (he did not disturb the others with a good night; they were absorbed in the lemon-squeezer and the soda-water cork) he remembered other occasions on which he had made his way to bed alone through a darkened country-house; such occasions had not been rare, for he was almost always the first to leave the smoking-room. If he had not stayed in houses conspicuously haunted he had, none the less (having the artistic temperament), sometimes found the great black halls and staircases rather 'creepy': there had been often a sinister effect, to his imagination, in the sound of his tread in the long passages or the way the winter moon peeped into tall windows on landings. It occurred to him that if houses without supernatural pretensions could look so wicked at night, the old corridors of Stayes would certainly give him a sensation. He didn't know whether the proprietors were sensitive; very often, as he had said to Colonel Capadose, people enjoyed the impeachment. What determined him to speak, with a certain sense of the risk, was the impression that the Colonel told queer stories. As he had his hand on the door he said to Arthur Ashmore, 'I hope I shan't meet any ghosts.'

'Any ghosts?'

'You ought to have some—in this fine old part.'

'We do our best, but *que voulez-vous?*' said Mr. Ashmore. 'I don't think they like the hot-water pipes.'

'They remind them too much of their own climate? But haven't you a haunted room—at the end of my passage?'

'Oh, there are stories—we try to keep them up.'

'I should like very much to sleep there,' Lyon said.

'Well, you can move there to-morrow if you like.'

'Perhaps I had better wait till I have done my work.'

'Very good; but you won't work there, you know. My father will sit to you in his own apartments.'

'Oh, it isn't that; it's the fear of running away, like that gentleman three days ago.'

'Three days ago? What gentleman?' Mr. Ashmore asked.

'The one who got urgent letters at breakfast and fled by the 10.20. Did he stand more than one night?'

'I don't know what you are talking about. There was no such gentleman—three days ago.'

'Ah, so much the better,' said Lyon, nodding good-night and departing. He took his course, as he remembered it, with his wavering candle, and, though he encountered a great many gruesome objects, safely reached the passage out of which his room opened. In the complete darkness it seemed to stretch away still further, but he followed it, for the curiosity of the thing, to the end. He passed several doors with the name of the room painted upon them, but he found nothing else. He was tempted to try the last door—to look into the room of evil fame; but he reflected that this would be indiscreet, since Colonel Capadose handled the brush—as a *raconteur*—with such freedom. There might be a ghost and there might not; but the Colonel himself, he inclined to think, was the most mystifying figure in the house.

II

Lyon found Sir David Ashmore a capital subject and a very comfortable sitter into the bargain. Moreover he was a very agreeable old man, tremendously puckered but not in the least dim; and he wore exactly the furred dressing-gown that Lyon would have chosen. He was proud of his age but ashamed of his infirmities, which however he greatly exaggerated and which did not prevent him from sitting there as submissive as if portraiture in oils had been a branch of surgery. He demolished the legend of his having feared the operation would be fatal, giving an explanation which pleased our friend much better. He held that a gentleman should be painted but once in his life—that it was eager and fatuous to be hung up all over the place. That was good for women, who made a pretty wall-pattern; but the male face didn't lend itself to decorative repetition. The proper time for the likeness was at the last, when the whole man was there—you got the totality of his experience. Lyon could not reply that that period was not a real compendium—you had to allow so for leakage; for there had been no crack in Sir David's crystallisation. He spoke of his portrait as a plain map of the country, to be consulted by his children in a case of uncertainty. A proper map could be drawn up only when the country had been travelled. He gave Lyon his mornings, till luncheon, and they talked of many things, not neglecting, as a stimulus to gossip, the people in the house. Now that he did not 'go out,' as he said, he saw much less of the visitors at Stayes: people came and went whom he knew nothing about, and he liked to hear Lyon describe them. The artist sketched with a fine point and did not caricature, and it usually befell that when Sir David did not know the sons and daughters he had known the fathers and mothers. He was one of those terrible old gentlemen who are a repository of antecedents. But in the case of the Capadose family, at whom they arrived by an easy stage, his knowledge embraced two, or even three, generations. General Capadose was an old crony, and he remembered his father before him. The general was rather a smart soldier, but in private life of too speculative a turn—always sneaking into the City to put his money into some rotten thing. He married a girl who brought him something and they had half a dozen children. He scarcely knew what had become of the rest of them, except that one was in the Church and had found preferment—wasn't he Dean of Rockingham? Clement, the fellow who was at Stayes, had some military talent; he had served in the East, he had married a pretty girl. He had been at Eton with his son, and he used to come to Stayes in his holidays. Lately, coming back to England, he had turned up with his wife again; that was before he—the old man—had been put to grass. He was a taking dog, but he had a monstrous foible.

'A monstrous foible?' said Lyon.

'He's a thumping liar.'

Lyon's brush stopped short, while he repeated, for somehow the formula startled him, 'A thumping liar?'

'You are very lucky not to have found it out.'

'Well, I confess I have noticed a romantic tinge——'

'Oh, it isn't always romantic. He'll lie about the time of day, about the name of his hatter. It appears there are people like that.'

'Well, they are precious scoundrels,' Lyon declared, his voice trembling a little with the thought of what Everina Brant had done with herself.

'Oh, not always,' said the old man. 'This fellow isn't in the least a scoundrel. There is no harm in him and no bad intention; he doesn't steal nor cheat nor gamble nor drink; he's very kind—he sticks to his wife, is fond of his children. He simply can't give you a straight answer.'

'Then everything he told me last night, I suppose, was mendacious: he delivered himself of a series of the stiffest statements. They stuck, when I tried to swallow them, but I never thought of so simple an explanation.'

'No doubt he was in the vein,' Sir David went on. 'It's a natural peculiarity—as you might limp or stutter or be left-handed. I believe it comes and goes, like intermittent fever. My son tells me that his friends usually understand it and don't haul him up—for the sake of his wife.'

'Oh, his wife—his wife!' Lyon murmured, painting fast.

'I daresay she's used to it.'

'Never in the world, Sir David. How can she be used to it?'

'Why, my dear sir, when a woman's fond!—And don't they mostly handle the long bow themselves? They are connoisseurs—they have a sympathy for a fellow-performer.'

Lyon was silent a moment; he had no ground for denying that Mrs. Capadose was attached to her husband. But after a little he rejoined: 'Oh, not this one! I knew her years ago—before her marriage; knew her well and admired her. She was as clear as a bell.'

'I like her very much,' Sir David said, 'but I have seen her back him up.'

Lyon considered Sir David for a moment, not in the light of a model. 'Are you very sure?'

The old man hesitated; then he answered, smiling, 'You're in love with her.'

'Very likely. God knows I used to be!'

'She must help him out—she can't expose him.'

'She can hold her tongue,' Lyon remarked.

'Well, before you probably she will.'

'That's what I am curious to see.' And Lyon added, privately, 'Mercy on us, what he must have made of her!' He kept this reflection to himself, for he considered that he had sufficiently betrayed his state of mind with regard to Mrs. Capadose. None the less it occupied him now immensely, the question of how such a woman would arrange herself in such a predicament. He watched her with an interest deeply quickened when he mingled with the company; he had had his own troubles in life, but he had rarely been so anxious about anything as he was now to see what the loyalty of a wife and the infection of an example would have made of an absolutely truthful mind. Oh, he held it as immutably established that whatever other women might be prone to do she, of old, had been perfectly incapable of a deviation. Even if she had not been too simple to deceive she would have been too proud; and if she had not had too much conscience she would have had too little eagerness. It was the last thing she would have endured or condoned—the particular thing she would not have forgiven. Did she sit in torment while her husband turned his somersaults, or was she now too so perverse that she thought it a fine thing to be striking at the expense of one's honour? It would have taken a wondrous alchemy—working backwards, as it were—to produce this latter result. Besides these two alternatives (that she suffered tortures in silence and that she was so much in love that her husband's humiliating idiosyncrasy seemed to her only an added richness—a proof of life and talent), there was still the possibility that she had not found him out, that she took his false pieces at his own valuation. A little reflection rendered this hypothesis untenable; it was too evident that the account he gave of things must repeatedly have contradicted her own knowledge. Within an hour or two of his meeting them Lyon had seen her confronted with that perfectly gratuitous invention about the profit they had made off his early picture. Even then indeed she had not, so far as he could see, smarted, and—but for the present he could only contemplate the case.

Even if it had not been interfused, through his uneradicated tenderness for Mrs. Capadose, with an element of suspense, the question would still have presented itself to him as a very curious problem, for he had not painted portraits during so many years without becoming something of a psychologist. His inquiry was limited for the moment to the opportunity that the following three days might yield, as the Colonel and his wife were going on to another house. It fixed itself largely of course upon the Colonel too—this gentleman was such a rare anomaly. Moreover it had to go on very quickly. Lyon was too scrupulous to ask other people what they thought of the business—he was too afraid of exposing the woman he once had loved. It was probable also that light would come to him from the talk of the rest of the company: the Colonel's queer habit, both as it affected his own situation and as it affected his wife, would be a familiar theme in any house in which he was in the habit of staying. Lyon had not observed in the circles in which he visited any marked abstention from comment on the singularities of their members. It interfered with his progress that the Colonel hunted all day, while he plied his brushes and chatted with Sir David; but a Sunday intervened and that partly made it up. Mrs. Capadose fortunately did not hunt, and when his work was over she was not inaccessible. He took a couple of longish walks with her (she was fond of that), and beguiled her at tea into a friendly nook in the hall. Regard her as he might he could not make out to himself that she was consumed by a hidden shame; the sense of being married to a man whose word had no worth was not, in her spirit, so far as he could guess, the canker within the rose. Her mind appeared to have nothing on it but its own placid frankness, and when he looked into her eyes (deeply, as he occasionally permitted himself to do), they had no uncomfortable consciousness. He talked to her again and still again of the dear old days—reminded her of things that he had not (before this reunion) the least idea that he remembered. Then he spoke to her of her husband, praised his appearance, his talent for conversation, professed to have felt a quick friendship for him and asked (with an inward audacity at which he trembled a little) what manner of man he was. 'What manner?' said Mrs. Capadose. 'Dear me, how can one describe one's husband? I like him very much.'

'Ah, you have told me that already!' Lyon exclaimed, with exaggerated ruefulness.

'Then why do you ask me again?' She added in a moment, as if she were so happy that she could afford to take pity on him, 'He is everything that's good and kind. He's a soldier —and a gentleman—and a dear! He hasn't a fault. And he has great ability.'

'Yes; he strikes one as having great ability. But of course I can't think him a dear.'

'I don't care what you think him!' said Mrs. Capadose, looking, it seemed to him, as she smiled, handsomer than he had ever seen her. She was either deeply cynical or still more deeply impenetrable, and he had little prospect of winning from her the intimation that he longed for—some hint that it had come over her that after all she had better have married a man who was not a by-word for the most contemptible, the least heroic, of vices. Had she not seen—had she not felt— the smile go round when her husband executed some espe- cially characteristic conversational caper? How could a woman of her quality endure that day after day, year after year, except by her quality's altering? But he would believe in the alteration only when he should have heard *her* lie. He was fascinated by his problem and yet half exasperated, and he asked himself all kinds of questions. Did she not lie, after all, when she let his falsehoods pass without a protest? Was not her life a perpetual complicity, and did she not aid and abet him by the simple fact that she was not disgusted with him? Then again perhaps she *was* disgusted and it was the mere desperation of her pride that had given her an inscrutable mask. Perhaps she protested in private, passionately; perhaps every night, in their own apartments, after the day's hideous performance, she made him the most scorching scene. But if such scenes were of no avail and he took no more trouble to cure himself, how could she regard him, and after so many years of marriage too, with the perfectly artless complacency that Lyon had surprised in her in the course of the first day's dinner? If our friend had not been in love with her he could have taken the diverting view of the Colonel's delinquencies; but as it was they turned to the tragical in his mind, even while he had a sense that his solicitude might also have been laughed at.

The observation of these three days showed him that if Ca- padose was an abundant he was not a malignant liar and that his fine faculty exercised itself mainly on subjects of small direct importance. 'He is the liar platonic,' he said to himself; 'he is disinterested, he doesn't operate with a hope of gain or with a desire to injure. It is art for art and he is prompted by the love of beauty. He has an inner vision of what might have been, of what ought to be, and he helps on the good cause by the simple substitution of a *nuance*. He paints, as it were, and so do I!' His manifestations had a considerable variety, but a family likeness ran through them, which consisted mainly of their singular futility. It was this that made them offensive; they encumbered the field of conversation, took up valuable space, converted it into a sort of brilliant sun-shot fog. For a fib told under pressure a convenient place can usually be found, as for a person who presents himself with an author's order at the first night of a play. But the supererogatory lie is the gentleman without a voucher or a ticket who accommodates himself with a stool in the passage.

In one particular Lyon acquitted his successful rival; it had puzzled him that irrepressible as he was he had not got into a mess in the service. But he perceived that he respected the service—that august institution was sacred from his depredations. Moreover though there was a great deal of swagger in his talk it was, oddly enough, rarely swagger about his military exploits. He had a passion for the chase, he had followed it in far countries and some of his finest flowers were reminiscences of lonely danger and escape. The more solitary the scene the bigger of course the flower. A new acquaintance, with the Colonel, always received the tribute of a bouquet: that generalisation Lyon very promptly made. And this extraordinary man had inconsistencies and unexpected lapses— lapses into flat veracity. Lyon recognised what Sir David had told him, that his aberrations came in fits or periods—that he would sometimes keep the truce of God for a month at a time. The muse breathed upon him at her pleasure; she often left him alone. He would neglect the finest openings and then set sail in the teeth of the breeze. As a general thing he affirmed the false rather than denied the true; yet this proportion was sometimes strikingly reversed. Very often he joined in the laugh against himself—he admitted that he was trying it on and that a good many of his anecdotes had an experimental

character. Still he never completely retracted nor retreated—
he dived and came up in another place. Lyon divined that he
was capable at intervals of defending his position with violence, but only when it was a very bad one. Then he might
easily be dangerous—then he would hit out and become ca-
lumnious. Such occasions would test his wife's equanimity—
Lyon would have liked to see her there. In the smoking-room
and elsewhere the company, so far as it was composed of his
familiars, had an hilarious protest always at hand; but among
the men who had known him long his rich tone was an old
story, so old that they had ceased to talk about it, and Lyon
did not care, as I have said, to elicit the judgment of those
who might have shared his own surprise.

The oddest thing of all was that neither surprise nor familiarity prevented the Colonel's being liked; his largest drafts on
a sceptical attention passed for an overflow of life and gaiety—almost of good looks. He was fond of portraying his
bravery and used a very big brush, and yet he was unmistakably brave. He was a capital rider and shot, in spite of his fund
of anecdote illustrating these accomplishments: in short he
was very nearly as clever and his career had been very nearly
as wonderful as he pretended. His best quality however remained that indiscriminate sociability which took interest and
credulity for granted and about which he bragged least. It
made him cheap, it made him even in a manner vulgar; but
it was so contagious that his listener was more or less on his
side as against the probabilities. It was a private reflection of
Oliver Lyon's that he not only lied but made one feel one's
self a bit of a liar, even (or especially) if one contradicted him.
In the evening, at dinner and afterwards, our friend watched
his wife's face to see if some faint shade or spasm never passed
over it. But she showed nothing, and the wonder was that
when he spoke she almost always listened. That was her pride:
she wished not to be even suspected of not facing the music.
Lyon had none the less an importunate vision of a veiled figure coming the next day in the dusk to certain places to repair
the Colonel's ravages, as the relatives of kleptomaniacs punctually call at the shops that have suffered from their pilferings.
'I must apologise, of course it wasn't true, I hope no harm
is done, it is only his incorrigible——' Oh, to hear that

woman's voice in that deep abasement! Lyon had no nefarious plan, no conscious wish to practise upon her shame or her loyalty; but he did say to himself that he should like to bring her round to feel that there would have been more dignity in a union with a certain other person. He even dreamed of the hour when, with a burning face, she would ask *him* not to take it up. Then he should be almost consoled—he would be magnanimous.

Lyon finished his picture and took his departure, after having worked in a glow of interest which made him believe in his success, until he found he had pleased every one, especially Mr. and Mrs. Ashmore, when he began to be sceptical. The party at any rate changed: Colonel and Mrs. Capadose went their way. He was able to say to himself however that his separation from the lady was not so much an end as a beginning, and he called on her soon after his return to town. She had told him the hours she was at home—she seemed to like him. If she liked him why had she not married him or at any rate why was she not sorry she had not? If she was sorry she concealed it too well. Lyon's curiosity on this point may strike the reader as fatuous, but something must be allowed to a disappointed man. He did not ask much after all; not that she should love him to-day or that she should allow him to tell her that he loved her, but only that she should give him some sign she was sorry. Instead of this, for the present, she contented herself with exhibiting her little daughter to him. The child was beautiful and had the prettiest eyes of innocence he had ever seen: which did not prevent him from wondering whether she told horrid fibs. This idea gave him much entertainment—the picture of the anxiety with which her mother would watch as she grew older for the symptoms of heredity. That was a nice occupation for Everina Brant! Did she lie to the child herself, about her father—was that necessary, when she pressed her daughter to her bosom, to cover up his tracks? Did he control himself before the little girl—so that she might not hear him say things she knew to be other than he said? Lyon doubted this: his genius would be too strong for him, and the only safety for the child would be in her being too stupid to analyse. One couldn't judge yet—she was too young. If she should grow up clever she would be sure to tread in his steps—a delightful improvement in her mother's situation! Her little face was not shifty, but neither was her father's big one: so that proved nothing.

Lyon reminded his friends more than once of their promise that Amy should sit to him, and it was only a question of his leisure. The desire grew in him to paint the Colonel also—an operation from which he promised himself a rich private satisfaction. He would draw him out, he would set him up in that totality about which he had talked with Sir David, and none but the initiated would know. They, however, would rank the picture high, and it would be indeed six rows deep—a masterpiece of subtle characterisation, of legitimate treachery. He had dreamed for years of producing something which should bear the stamp of the psychologist as well as of the painter, and here at last was his subject. It was a pity it was not better, but that was not *his* fault. It was his impression that already no one drew the Colonel out more than he, and he did it not only by instinct but on a plan. There were moments when he was almost frightened at the success of his plan—the poor gentleman went so terribly far. He would pull up some day, look at Lyon between the eyes—guess he was being played upon—which would lead to his wife's guessing it also. Not that Lyon cared much for that however, so long as she failed to suppose (as she must) that *she* was a part of his joke. He formed such a habit now of going to see her of a Sunday afternoon that he was angry when she went out of town. This occurred often, as the couple were great visitors and the Colonel was always looking for sport, which he liked best when it could be had at other people's expense. Lyon would have supposed that this sort of life was particularly little to her taste, for he had an idea that it was in country-houses that her husband came out strongest. To let him go off without her, not to see him expose himself—that ought properly to have been a relief and a luxury to her. She told Lyon in fact that she preferred staying at home; but she neglected to say it was because in other people's houses she was on the rack: the reason she gave was that she liked so to be with the child. It was not perhaps criminal to draw such a bow, but it was vulgar: poor Lyon was delighted when he arrived at that formula. Certainly some day too he would cross the line—he would become a noxious animal. Yes, in the meantime he was vulgar, in spite of his talents, his fine person, his impunity. Twice, by exception, toward the end of the winter, when he left town for a few days' hunting, his wife remained at home. Lyon had not yet reached the point of asking himself whether the desire not to miss two of his visits had something to do with her immobility. That inquiry would perhaps have been more in place later, when he began to paint the child and she always came with her. But it was not in her to give the wrong name, to pretend, and Lyon could see that she had the maternal passion, in spite of the bad blood in the little girl's veins.

She came inveterately, though Lyon multiplied the sittings: Amy was never entrusted to the governess or the maid. He had knocked off poor old Sir David in ten days, but the portrait of the simple-faced child bade fair to stretch over into the following year. He asked for sitting after sitting, and it would have struck any one who might have witnessed the affair that he was wearing the little girl out. He knew better however and Mrs. Capadose also knew: they were present together at the long intermissions he gave her, when she left her pose and roamed about the great studio, amusing herself with its curiosities, playing with the old draperies and costumes, having unlimited leave to handle. Then her mother and Mr. Lyon sat and talked; he laid aside his brushes and leaned back in his chair; he always gave her tea. What Mrs. Capadose did not know was the way that during these weeks he neglected other orders: women have no faculty of imagination with regard to a man's work beyond a vague idea that it doesn't matter. In fact Lyon put off everything and made several celebrities wait. There were half-hours of silence, when he plied his brushes, during which he was mainly conscious that Everina was sitting there. She easily fell into that if he did not insist on talking, and she was not embarrassed nor bored by it. Sometimes she took up a book—there were plenty of them about; sometimes, a little way off, in her chair, she watched his progress (though without in the least advising or correcting), as if she cared for every stroke that represented her daughter. These strokes were occasionally a little wild; he was thinking so much more of his heart than of his hand. He was not more embarrassed than she was, but he was agitated: it was as if in the sittings (for the child, too, was beautifully quiet) something was growing between them or had already grown—a tacit confidence, an inexpressible secret. He felt it that way; but after all he could not be sure that she did. What he wanted her to do for him was very little; it was not even to confess that she was unhappy. He would be superabundantly gratified if she should simply let him know, even by a silent sign, that she recognised that with him her life would have been finer. Sometimes he guessed—his presumption went so far—that he might see this sign in her contentedly sitting there.

III

At last he broached the question of painting the Colonel: it was now very late in the season—there would be little time before the general dispersal. He said they must make the most of it; the great thing was to begin, then in the autumn, with the resumption of their London life, they could go forward. Mrs. Capadose objected to this that she really could not consent to accept another present of such value. Lyon had given her the portrait of herself of old, and he had seen what they had had the indelicacy to do with it. Now he had offered her this beautiful memorial of the child—beautiful it would evidently be when it was finished, if he could ever satisfy himself; a precious possession which they would cherish for ever. But his generosity must stop there—they couldn't be so tremendously 'beholden' to him. They couldn't order the picture—of course he would understand that, without her explaining: it was a luxury beyond their reach, for they knew the great prices he received. Besides, what had they ever done—what above all had *she* ever done, that he should overload them with benefits? No, he was too dreadfully good; it was really impossible that Clement should sit. Lyon listened to her without protest, without interruption, while he bent forward at his work, and at last he said: 'Well, if you won't take it why not let him sit for me for my own pleasure and profit? Let it be a favour, a service I ask of him. It will do me a lot of good to paint him and the picture will remain in my hands.'

'How will it do you a lot of good?' Mrs. Capadose asked.

'Why, he's such a rare model—such an interesting subject. He has such an expressive face. It will teach me no end of things.'

'Expressive of what?' said Mrs. Capadose.

'Why, of his nature.'

'And do you want to paint his nature?'

'Of course I do. That's what a great portrait gives you, and I shall make the Colonel's a great one. It will put me up high. So you see my request is eminently interested.'

'How can you be higher than you are?'

'Oh, I'm insatiable! Do consent,' said Lyon.

'Well, his nature is very noble,' Mrs. Capadose remarked.

'Ah, trust me, I shall bring it out!' Lyon exclaimed, feeling a little ashamed of himself.

Mrs. Capadose said before she went away that her husband would probably comply with his invitation, but she added, 'Nothing would induce me to let you pry into *me* that way!'

'Oh, you,' Lyon laughed—'I could do you in the dark!'

The Colonel shortly afterwards placed his leisure at the painter's disposal and by the end of July had paid him several visits. Lyon was disappointed neither in the quality of his sitter nor in the degree to which he himself rose to the occasion; he felt really confident that he should produce a fine thing. He was in the humour; he was charmed with his *motif* and deeply interested in his problem. The only point that troubled him was the idea that when he should send his picture to the Academy he should not be able to give the title, for the catalogue, simply as 'The Liar.' However, it little mattered, for he had now determined that this character should be perceptible even to the meanest intelligence—as overtopping as it had become to his own sense in the living man. As he saw nothing else in the Colonel to-day, so he gave himself up to the joy of painting nothing else. How he did it he could not have told you, but it seemed to him that the mystery of how to do it was revealed to him afresh every time he sat down to his work. It was in the eyes and it was in the mouth, it was in every line of the face and every fact of the attitude, in the indentation of the chin, in the way the hair was planted, the moustache was twisted, the smile came and went, the breath rose and fell. It was in the way he looked out at a bamboozled world in short—the way he would look out for ever. There were half a dozen portraits in Europe that Lyon rated as supreme; he regarded them as immortal, for they were as perfectly preserved as they were consummately painted. It was to this small exemplary group that he aspired to annex the canvas on which he was now engaged. One of the productions that helped to compose it was the magnificent Moroni of the National Gallery—the young tailor, in the white jacket, at his board with his shears. The Colonel was not a tailor, nor was Moroni's model, unlike many tailors, a liar; but as regards the masterly clearness with which the individual should be rendered his work would be on the same line as that. He had to a degree in which he had rarely had it before the satisfaction of feeling life grow and grow under his brush. The Colonel, as it turned out, liked to sit and he liked to talk while he was sitting: which was very fortunate, as his talk largely constituted Lyon's inspiration. Lyon put into practice that idea of drawing him out which he had been nursing for so many weeks: he could not possibly have been in a better relation to him for the purpose. He encouraged, beguiled, excited him, manifested an unfathomable credulity, and his only interruptions were when the Colonel did not respond to it. He had his intermissions, his hours of sterility, and then Lyon felt that the picture also languished. The higher his companion soared, the more gyrations he executed, in the blue, the better he painted; he couldn't make his flights long enough. He lashed him on when he flagged; his apprehension became great at moments that the Colonel would discover his game. But he never did, apparently; he basked and expanded in the fine steady light of the painter's attention. In this way the picture grew very fast; it was astonishing what a short business it was, compared with the little girl's. By the fifth of August it was pretty well finished: that was the date of the last sitting the Colonel was for the present able to give, as he was leaving town the next day with his wife. Lyon was amply content— he saw his way so clear: he should be able to do at his convenience what remained, with or without his friend's attendance. At any rate, as there was no hurry, he would let the thing stand over till his own return to London, in November, when he would come back to it with a fresh eye. On the Colonel's asking him if his wife might come and see it the next day, if she should find a minute—this was so greatly her desire—Lyon begged as a special favour that she would wait: he was so far from satisfied as yet. This was the repetition of a proposal Mrs. Capadose had made on the occasion of his last visit to her, and he had then asked for a delay—declared that he was by no means content. He was really delighted, and he was again a little ashamed of himself.

By the fifth of August the weather was very warm, and on that day, while the Colonel sat straight and gossiped, Lyon opened for the sake of ventilation a little subsidiary door which led directly from his studio into the garden and sometimes served as an entrance and an exit for models and for visitors of the humbler sort, and as a passage for canvases, frames, packing-boxes and other professional gear. The main entrance was through the house and his own apartments, and this approach had the charming effect of admitting you first to a high gallery, from which a crooked picturesque staircase enabled you to descend to the wide, decorated, encumbered room. The view of this room, beneath them, with all its artistic ingenuities and the objects of value that Lyon had collected, never failed to elicit exclamations of delight from persons stepping into the gallery. The way from the garden was plainer and at once more practicable and more private. Lyon's domain, in St. John's Wood, was not vast, but when the door stood open of a summer's day it offered a glimpse of flowers and trees, you smelt something sweet and you heard the birds. On this particular morning the side-door had been found convenient by an unannounced visitor, a youngish woman who stood in the room before the Colonel perceived her and whom he perceived before she was noticed by his friend. She was very quiet, and she looked from one of the men to the other. 'Oh, dear, here's another!' Lyon exclaimed, as soon as his eyes rested on her. She belonged, in fact, to a somewhat importunate class—the model in search of employment, and she explained that she had ventured to come straight in, that way, because very often when she went to call upon gentlemen the servants played her tricks, turned her off and wouldn't take in her name.

'But how did you get into the garden?' Lyon asked.

'The gate was open, sir—the servants' gate. The butcher's cart was there.'

'The butcher ought to have closed it,' said Lyon.

'Then you don't require me, sir?' the lady continued.

Lyon went on with his painting; he had given her a sharp look at first, but now his eyes lighted on her no more. The Colonel, however, examined her with interest. She was a person of whom you could scarcely say whether being young she looked old or old she looked young, she had at any rate evidently rounded several of the corners of life and had a face that was rosy but that somehow failed to suggest freshness. Nevertheless she was pretty and even looked as if at one time she might have sat for the complexion. She wore a hat with many feathers, a dress with many bugles, long black gloves, encircled with silver bracelets, and very bad shoes. There was something about her that was not exactly of the governess out of place nor completely of the actress seeking an engagement, but that savoured of an interrupted profession or even of a blighted career. She was rather soiled and tarnished, and after she had been in the room a few moments the air, or at any rate the nostril, became acquainted with a certain alcoholic waft. She was unpractised in the *h*, and when Lyon at last thanked her and said he didn't want her—he was doing nothing for which she could be useful—she replied with rather a wounded manner, 'Well, you know you *'ave* 'ad me!'

'I don't remember you,' Lyon answered.

'Well, I daresay the people that saw your pictures do! I haven't much time, but I thought I would look in.'

'I am much obliged to you.'

'If ever you should require me, if you just send me a post-card——'

'I never send postcards,' said Lyon.

'Oh well, I should value a private letter! Anything to Miss Geraldine, Mortimer Terrace Mews, Notting 'ill——'

'Very good; I'll remember,' said Lyon.

Miss Geraldine lingered. 'I thought I'd just stop, on the chance.'

'I'm afraid I can't hold out hopes, I'm so busy with portraits,' Lyon continued.

'Yes; I see you are. I wish I was in the gentleman's place.'

'I'm afraid in that case it wouldn't look like me,' said the Colonel, laughing.

'Oh, of course it couldn't compare—it wouldn't be so 'and-some! But I do hate them portraits!' Miss Geraldine declared. 'It's so much bread out of our mouths.'

'Well, there are many who can't paint them,' Lyon suggested, comfortingly.

'Oh, I've sat to the very first—and only to the first! There's many that couldn't do anything without me.'

'I'm glad you're in such demand.' Lyon was beginning to be bored and he added that he wouldn't detain her—he would send for her in case of need.

'Very well; remember it's the Mews—more's the pity! You don't sit so well as *us*!' Miss Geraldine pursued, looking at the Colonel. 'If *you* should require me, sir——'

'You put him out; you embarrass him,' said Lyon.

'Embarrass him, oh gracious!' the visitor cried, with a laugh which diffused a fragrance. 'Perhaps *you* send postcards, eh?' she went on to the Colonel; and then she retreated with a wavering step. She passed out into the garden as she had come.

'How very dreadful—she's drunk!' said Lyon. He was painting hard, but he looked up, checking himself: Miss Geraldine, in the open doorway, had thrust back her head.

'Yes, I do hate it—that sort of thing!' she cried with an explosion of mirth which confirmed Lyon's declaration. And then she disappeared.

'What sort of thing—what does she mean?' the Colonel asked.

'Oh, my painting you, when I might be painting her.'

'And have you ever painted her?'

'Never in the world; I have never seen her. She is quite mistaken.'

The Colonel was silent a moment; then he remarked, 'She was very pretty—ten years ago.'

'I daresay, but she's quite ruined. For me the least drop too much spoils them; I shouldn't care for her at all.'

'My dear fellow, she's not a model,' said the Colonel, laughing.

'To-day, no doubt, she's not worthy of the name; but she has been one.'

'*Jamais de la vie!* That's all a pretext.'

'A pretext?' Lyon pricked up his ears—he began to wonder what was coming now.

'She didn't want you—she wanted me.'

'I noticed she paid you some attention. What does she want of you?'

'Oh, to do me an ill turn. She hates me—lots of women do. She's watching me—she follows me.'

Lyon leaned back in his chair—he didn't believe a word of this. He was all the more delighted with it and with the Colonel's bright, candid manner. The story had bloomed, fragrant, on the spot. 'My dear Colonel!' he murmured, with friendly interest and commiseration.

'I was annoyed when she came in—but I wasn't startled,' his sitter continued.

'You concealed it very well, if you were.'

'Ah, when one has been through what I have! To-day however I confess I was half prepared. I have seen her hanging about—she knows my movements. She was near my house this morning—she must have followed me.'

'But who is she then—with such a *toupet*?'

'Yes, she has that,' said the Colonel; 'but as you observe she was primed. Still, there was a cheek, as they say, in her coming in. Oh, she's a bad one! She isn't a model and she never was; no doubt she has known some of those women and picked up their form. She had hold of a friend of mine ten years ago—a stupid young gander who might have been left to be plucked but whom I was obliged to take an interest in for family reasons. It's a long story—I had really forgotten all about it. She's thirty-seven if she's a day. I cut in and made him get rid of her—I sent her about her business. She knew it was me she had to thank. She has never forgiven me—I think she's off her head. Her name isn't Geraldine at all and I doubt very much if that's her address.'

'Ah, what is her name?' Lyon asked, most attentive. The details always began to multiply, to abound, when once his companion was well launched—they flowed forth in battalions.

'It's Pearson—Harriet Pearson; but she used to call her-self Grenadine—wasn't that a rum appellation? Grenadine—Geraldine—the jump was easy.' Lyon was charmed with the promptitude of this response, and his interlocutor went on: 'I hadn't thought of her for years—I had quite lost sight of her. I don't know what her idea is, but practically she's harmless. As I came in I thought I saw her a little way up the road. She must have found out I come here and have arrived before me. I daresay—or rather I'm sure—she is waiting for me there now.'

'Hadn't you better have protection?' Lyon asked, laughing.

'The best protection is five shillings—I'm willing to go that length. Unless indeed she has a bottle of vitriol. But they only throw vitriol on the men who have deceived them, and I never deceived her—I told her the first time I saw her that it wouldn't do. Oh, if she's there we'll walk a little way together and talk it over and, as I say, I'll go as far as five shillings.'

'Well,' said Lyon, 'I'll contribute another five.' He felt that this was little to pay for his entertainment.

That entertainment was interrupted however for the time by the Colonel's departure. Lyon hoped for a letter recounting the fictive sequel; but apparently his brilliant sitter did not operate with the pen. At any rate he left town without writing; they had taken a rendezvous for three months later. Oliver Lyon always passed the holidays in the same way; during the first weeks he paid a visit to his elder brother, the happy possessor, in the south of England, of a rambling old house with formal gardens, in which he delighted, and then he went abroad—usually to Italy or Spain. This year he carried out his custom after taking a last look at his all but finished work and feeling as nearly pleased with it as he ever felt with the translation of the idea by the hand—always, as it seemed to him, a pitiful compromise. One yellow afternoon, in the country, as he was smoking his pipe on one of the old terraces he was seized with the desire to see it again and do two or three things more to it: he had thought of it so often while he lounged there. The impulse was too strong to be dismissed, and though he expected to return to town in the course of another week he was unable to face the delay. To look at the picture for five minutes would be enough—it would clear up certain questions which hummed in his brain; so that the next morning, to give himself this luxury, he took the train for London. He sent no word in advance; he would lunch at his club and probably return into Sussex by the 5.45.

In St. John's Wood the tide of human life flows at no time very fast, and in the first days of September Lyon found unmitigated emptiness in the straight sunny roads where the little plastered garden-walls, with their incommunicative doors, looked slightly Oriental. There was definite stillness in his own house, to which he admitted himself by his pass-key, having a theory that it was well sometimes to take servants unprepared. The good woman who was mainly in charge and who cumulated the functions of cook and housekeeper was, however, quickly summoned by his step, and (he cultivated frankness of intercourse with his domestics) received him without the confusion of surprise. He told her that she needn't mind the place being not quite straight, he had only come up for a few hours—he should be busy in the studio. To this she replied that he was just in time to see a lady and a gentleman who were there at the moment—they had arrived five minutes before. She had told them he was away from home but they said it was all right; they only wanted to look at a picture and would be very careful of everything. 'I hope it is all right, sir,' the housekeeper concluded. 'The gentleman says he's a sitter and he gave me his name—rather an odd name; I think it's military. The lady's a very fine lady, sir; at any rate there they are.'

'Oh, it's all right,' Lyon said, the identity of his visitors being clear. The good woman couldn't know, for she usually had little to do with the comings and goings; his man, who showed people in and out, had accompanied him to the country. He was a good deal surprised at Mrs. Capadose's having come to see her husband's portrait when she knew that the artist himself wished her to forbear; but it was a familiar truth to him that she was a woman of a high spirit. Besides, perhaps the lady was not Mrs. Capadose; the Colonel might have brought some inquisitive friend, a person who wanted a portrait of *her* husband. What were they doing in town, at any rate, at that moment? Lyon made his way to the studio with a certain curiosity; he wondered vaguely what his friends were 'up to.' He pushed aside the curtain that hung in the door of communication—the door opening upon the gallery which it had been found convenient to construct at the time the studio was added to the house. When I say he pushed it aside I should amend my phrase; he laid his hand upon it, but at that moment he was arrested by a very singular sound. It came from the floor of the room beneath him and it startled him extremely, consisting apparently as it did of a passionate wail—a sort of smothered shriek—accompanied by a violent burst of tears. Oliver Lyon listened intently a moment, and then he passed out upon the balcony, which was covered with an old thick Moorish rug. His step was noiseless, though he had not endeavoured to make it so, and after that first instant he found himself profiting irresistibly by the accident of his not having attracted the attention of the two persons in the studio, who were some twenty feet below him. In truth they were so deeply and so strangely engaged that their unconsciousness of observation was explained. The scene that took place before Lyon's eyes was one of the most extraordinary they had ever rested upon. Delicacy and the failure to comprehend kept him at first from interrupting it—for what he saw was a woman who had thrown herself in a flood of tears on her companion's bosom—and these influences were succeeded after a minute (the minutes were very few and very short) by a definite motive which presently had the force to make him step back behind the curtain. I may add that it also had the force to make him avail himself for further contemplation of a crevice formed by his gathering together the two halves of the *portière*. He was perfectly aware of what he was about—he was for the moment an eavesdropper, a spy; but he was also aware that a very odd business, in which his confidence had been trifled with, was going forward, and that if in a measure it didn't concern him, in a measure it very definitely did. His observation, his reflections, accomplished themselves in a flash.

His visitors were in the middle of the room; Mrs. Capadose clung to her husband, weeping, sobbing as if her heart would break. Her distress was horrible to Oliver Lyon but his astonishment was greater than his horror when he heard the Colonel respond to it by the words, vehemently uttered, 'Damn him, damn him, damn him!' What in the world had happened? why was she sobbing and whom was he damning? What had happened, Lyon saw the next instant, was that the Colonel had finally rummaged out his unfinished portrait (he knew the corner where the artist usually placed it, out of the way, with its face to the wall) and had set it up before his wife on an empty easel. She had looked at it a few moments and then—apparently—what she saw in it had produced an explosion of dismay and resentment. She was too busy sobbing and the Colonel was too busy holding her and reiterating his objurgation, to look round or look up. The scene was so unexpected to Lyon that he could not take it, on the spot, as a proof of the triumph of his hand—of a tremendous hit: he could only wonder what on earth was the matter. The idea of the triumph came a little later. Yet he could see the portrait from where he stood; he was startled with its look of life—he had not thought it so masterly. Mrs. Capadose flung herself away from her husband—she dropped into the nearest chair, buried her face in her arms, leaning on a table. Her weeping suddenly ceased to be audible, but she shuddered there as if she were overwhelmed with anguish and shame. Her husband remained a moment staring at the picture; then he went to her, bent over her, took hold of her again, soothed her. 'What is it, darling, what the devil is it?' he demanded.

Lyon heard her answer. 'It's cruel—oh, it's too cruel!'

'Damn him—damn him—damn him!' the Colonel repeated.

'It's all there—it's all there!' Mrs. Capadose went on.

'Hang it, what's all there?'

'Everything there oughtn't to be—everything he has seen—it's too dreadful!'

'Everything he has seen? Why, ain't I a good-looking fellow? He has made me rather handsome.'

Mrs. Capadose had sprung up again; she had darted another glance at the painted betrayal. 'Handsome? Hideous, hideous! Not that—never, never!'

'Not *what*, in heaven's name?' the Colonel almost shouted. Lyon could see his flushed, bewildered face.

'What he has made of you—what you know! *He* knows—
he has seen. Every one will know—every one will see. Fancy
that thing in the Academy!'

'You're going wild, darling; but if you hate it so it needn't
go.'

'Oh, he'll send it—it's so good! Come away—come away!'
Mrs. Capadose wailed, seizing her husband.

'It's so good?' the poor man cried.

'Come away—come away,' she only repeated; and she
turned toward the staircase that ascended to the gallery.

'Not that way—not through the house, in the state you're
in,' Lyon heard the Colonel object. 'This way—we can pass,'
he added; and he drew his wife to the small door that opened
into the garden. It was bolted, but he pushed the bolt and
opened the door. She passed out quickly, but he stood there
looking back into the room. 'Wait for me a moment!' he cried
out to her; and with an excited stride he re-entered the studio.
He came up to the picture again, and again he stood looking
at it. 'Damn him—damn him—damn him!' he broke out once
more. It was not clear to Lyon whether this malediction had
for its object the original or the painter of the portrait. The
Colonel turned away and moved rapidly about the room, as
if he were looking for something; Lyon was unable for the
instant to guess his intention. Then the artist said to himself,
below his breath, 'He's going to do it a harm!' His first
impulse was to rush down and stop him; but he paused,
with the sound of Everina Brant's sobs still in his ears. The
Colonel found what he was looking for—found it among
some odds and ends on a small table and rushed back with it
to the easel. At one and the same moment Lyon perceived
that the object he had seized was a small Eastern dagger
and that he had plunged it into the canvas. He seemed animated by a sudden fury, for with extreme vigour of hand he
dragged the instrument down (Lyon knew it to have no very
fine edge) making a long, abominable gash. Then he plucked
it out and dashed it again several times into the face of the
likeness, exactly as if he were stabbing a human victim: it had
the oddest effect—that of a sort of figurative suicide. In a few
seconds more the Colonel had tossed the dagger away—he
looked at it as he did so, as if he expected it to reek with

blood—and hurried out of the place, closing the door after him.

The strangest part of all was—as will doubtless appear—that Oliver Lyon made no movement to save his picture. But he did not feel as if he were losing it or cared not if he were, so much more did he feel that he was gaining a certitude. His old friend *was* ashamed of her husband, and he had made her so, and he had scored a great success, even though the picture had been reduced to rags. The revelation excited him so—as indeed the whole scene did—that when he came down the steps after the Colonel had gone he trembled with his happy agitation; he was dizzy and had to sit down a moment. The portrait had a dozen jagged wounds—the Colonel literally had hacked it to death. Lyon left it where it was, never touched it, scarcely looked at it; he only walked up and down his studio, still excited, for an hour. At the end of this time his good woman came to recommend that he should have some luncheon; there was a passage under the staircase from the offices.

'Ah, the lady and gentleman have gone, sir? I didn't hear them.'

'Yes; they went by the garden.'

But she had stopped, staring at the picture on the easel. 'Gracious, how you 'ave served it, sir!'

Lyon imitated the Colonel. 'Yes, I cut it up—in a fit of disgust.'

'Mercy, after all your trouble! Because they weren't pleased, sir?'

'Yes; they weren't pleased.'

'Well, they must be very grand! Blessed if I would!'

'Have it chopped up; it will do to light fires,' Lyon said.

He returned to the country by the 3.30 and a few days later passed over to France. During the two months that he was absent from England he expected something—he could hardly have said what; a manifestation of some sort on the Colonel's part. Wouldn't he write, wouldn't he explain, wouldn't he take for granted Lyon had discovered the way he had, as the cook said, served him and deem it only decent to take pity in some fashion or other on his mystification? Would he plead guilty or would he repudiate suspicion? The latter course would be difficult and make a considerable draft upon

his genius, in view of the certain testimony of Lyon's housekeeper, who had admitted the visitors and would establish the
connection between their presence and the violence wrought.
Would the Colonel proffer some apology or some amends, or
would any word from him be only a further expression of that
destructive petulance which our friend had seen his wife so
suddenly and so potently communicate to him? He would
have either to declare that he had not touched the picture or
to admit that he had, and in either case he would have to tell
a fine story. Lyon was impatient for the story and, as no letter
came, disappointed that it was not produced. His impatience
however was much greater in respect to Mrs. Capadose's version, if version there was to be; for certainly that would be
the real test, would show how far she would go for her husband, on the one side, or for him, Oliver Lyon, on the other.
He could scarcely wait to see what line she would take;
whether she would simply adopt the Colonel's, whatever it
might be. He wanted to draw her out without waiting, to get
an idea in advance. He wrote to her, to this end, from Venice,
in the tone of their established friendship, asking for news,
narrating his wanderings, hoping they should soon meet in
town and not saying a word about the picture. Day followed
day, after the time, and he received no answer; upon which
he reflected that she couldn't trust herself to write—was still
too much under the influence of the emotion produced by
his 'betrayal.' Her husband had espoused that emotion and
she had espoused the action he had taken in consequence of
it, and it was a complete rupture and everything was at an
end. Lyon considered this prospect rather ruefully, at the same
time that he thought it deplorable that such charming people
should have put themselves so grossly in the wrong. He was
at last cheered, though little further enlightened, by the arrival
of a letter, brief but breathing good-humour and hinting neither at a grievance nor at a bad conscience. The most interesting part of it to Lyon was the postscript, which consisted
of these words: 'I have a confession to make to you. We were
in town for a couple of days, the 1st of September, and I took
the occasion to defy your authority—it was very bad of me
but I couldn't help it. I made Clement take me to your studio—I wanted so dreadfully to see what you had done with

him, your wishes to the contrary notwithstanding. We made your servants let us in and I took a good look at the picture. It is really wonderful!' 'Wonderful' was non-committal, but at least with this letter there was no rupture.

The third day after Lyon's return to London was a Sunday, so that he could go and ask Mrs. Capadose for luncheon. She had given him in the spring a general invitation to do so and he had availed himself of it several times. These had been the occasions (before he sat to him) when he saw the Colonel most familiarly. Directly after the meal his host disappeared (he went out, as he said, to call on *his* women) and the second half-hour was the best, even when there were other people. Now, in the first days of December, Lyon had the luck to find the pair alone, without even Amy, who appeared but little in public. They were in the drawing-room, waiting for the repast to be announced, and as soon as he came in the Colonel broke out, 'My dear fellow, I'm delighted to see you! I'm so keen to begin again.'

'Oh, do go on, it's so beautiful,' Mrs. Capadose said, as she gave him her hand.

Lyon looked from one to the other; he didn't know what he had expected, but he had not expected this. 'Ah, then, you think I've got something?'

'You've got everything,' said Mrs. Capadose, smiling from her golden-brown eyes.

'She wrote you of our little crime?' her husband asked. 'She dragged me there—I had to go.' Lyon wondered for a moment whether he meant by their little crime the assault on the canvas; but the Colonel's next words didn't confirm this interpretation. 'You know I like to sit—it gives such a chance to my *bavardise*. And just now I have time.'

'You must remember I had almost finished,' Lyon remarked.

'So you had. More's the pity. I should like you to begin again.'

'My dear fellow, I shall have to begin again!' said Oliver Lyon with a laugh, looking at Mrs. Capadose. She did not meet his eyes—she had got up to ring for luncheon. 'The picture has been smashed,' Lyon continued.

'Smashed? Ah, what did you do that for?' Mrs. Capadose

asked, standing there before him in all her clear, rich beauty. Now that she looked at him she was impenetrable.

'I didn't—I found it so—with a dozen holes punched in it!'

'I say!' cried the Colonel.

Lyon turned his eyes to him, smiling. 'I hope *you* didn't do it?'

'Is it ruined?' the Colonel inquired. He was as brightly true as his wife and he looked simply as if Lyon's question could not be serious. 'For the love of sitting to you? My dear fellow, if I had thought of it I would!'

'Nor you either?' the painter demanded of Mrs. Capadose.

Before she had time to reply her husband had seized her arm, as if a highly suggestive idea had come to him. 'I say, my dear, that woman—that woman!'

'That woman?' Mrs. Capadose repeated; and Lyon too wondered what woman he meant.

'Don't you remember when we came out, she was at the door—or a little way from it? I spoke to you of her—I told you about her. Geraldine—Grenadine—the one who burst in that day,' he explained to Lyon. 'We saw her hanging about—I called Everina's attention to her.'

'Do you mean she got at my picture?'

'Ah yes, I remember,' said Mrs. Capadose, with a sigh.

'She burst in again—she had learned the way—she was waiting for her chance,' the Colonel continued. 'Ah, the little brute!'

Lyon looked down; he felt himself colouring. This was what he had been waiting for—the day the Colonel should wantonly sacrifice some innocent person. And could his wife be a party to that final atrocity? Lyon had reminded himself repeatedly during the previous weeks that when the Colonel perpetrated his misdeed she had already quitted the room; but he had argued none the less—it was a virtual certainty—that he had on rejoining her immediately made his achievement plain to her. He was in the flush of performance; and even if he had not mentioned what he had done she would have guessed it. He did not for an instant believe that poor Miss Geraldine had been hovering about his door, nor had the account given by the Colonel the summer before of his relations with this lady deceived him in the slightest degree. Lyon had never seen her before the day she planted herself in his studio; but he knew her and classified her as if he had made her. He was acquainted with the London female model in all her varieties—in every phase of her development and every step of her decay. When he entered his house that September morning just after the arrival of his two friends there had been no symptoms whatever, up and down the road, of Miss Geraldine's reappearance. That fact had been fixed in his mind by his recollecting the vacancy of the prospect when his cook told him that a lady and a gentleman were in his studio: he had wondered there was not a carriage nor a cab at his door. Then he had reflected that they would have come by the underground railway; he was close to the Marlborough Road station and he knew the Colonel, coming to his sittings, more than once had availed himself of that convenience. 'How in the world did she get in?' He addressed the question to his companions indifferently.

'Let us go down to luncheon,' said Mrs. Capadose, passing out of the room.

'We went by the garden—without troubling your servant—I wanted to show my wife.' Lyon followed his hostess with her husband and the Colonel stopped him at the top of the stairs. 'My dear fellow, I *can't* have been guilty of the folly of not fastening the door?'

'I am sure I don't know, Colonel,' Lyon said as they went down. 'It was a very determined hand—a perfect wild-cat.'

'Well, she *is* a wild-cat—confound her! That's why I wanted to get him away from her.'

'But I don't understand her motive.'

'She's off her head—and she hates me; that was her motive.'

'But she doesn't hate me, my dear fellow!' Lyon said, laughing.

'She hated the picture—don't you remember she said so? The more portraits there are the less employment for such as her.'

'Yes; but if she is not really the model she pretends to be, how can that hurt her?' Lyon asked.

The inquiry baffled the Colonel an instant—but only an

instant. 'Ah, she was in a vicious muddle! As I say, she's off her head.'

They went into the dining-room, where Mrs. Capadose was taking her place. 'It's too bad, it's too horrid!' she said. 'You see the fates are against you. Providence won't let you be so disinterested—painting masterpieces for nothing.'

'Did *you* see the woman?' Lyon demanded, with something like a sternness that he could not mitigate.

Mrs. Capadose appeared not to perceive it or not to heed it if she did. 'There was a person, not far from your door, whom Clement called my attention to. He told me something about her but we were going the other way.'

'And do you think she did it?'

'How can I tell? If she did she was mad, poor wretch.'

'I should like very much to get hold of her,' said Lyon. This was a false statement, for he had no desire for any further conversation with Miss Geraldine. He had exposed his friends to himself, but he had no desire to expose them to any one else, least of all to themselves.

'Oh, depend upon it she will never show again. You're safe!' the Colonel exclaimed.

'But I remember her address—Mortimer Terrace Mews, Notting Hill.'

'Oh, that's pure humbug; there isn't any such place.'

'Lord, what a deceiver!' said Lyon.

'Is there any one else you suspect?' the Colonel went on.

'Not a creature.'

'And what do your servants say?'

'They say it wasn't *them*, and I reply that I never said it was. That's about the substance of our conferences.'

'And when did they discover the havoc?'

'They never discovered it at all. I noticed it first—when I came back.'

'Well, she could easily have stepped in,' said the Colonel. 'Don't you remember how she turned up that day, like the clown in the ring?'

'Yes, yes; she could have done the job in three seconds, except that the picture wasn't out.'

'My dear fellow, don't curse me!—but of course I dragged it out.'

'You didn't put it back?' Lyon asked tragically.

'Ah, Clement, Clement, didn't I tell you to?' Mrs. Capadose exclaimed in a tone of exquisite reproach.

The Colonel groaned, dramatically; he covered his face with his hands. His wife's words were for Lyon the finishing touch; they made his whole vision crumble—his theory that she had secretly kept herself true. Even to her old lover she wouldn't be so! He was sick; he couldn't eat; he knew that he looked very strange. He murmured something about it being useless to cry over spilled milk—he tried to turn the conversation to other things. But it was a horrid effort and he wondered whether they felt it as much as he. He wondered all sorts of things: whether they guessed he disbelieved them (that he had seen them of course they would never guess); whether they had arranged their story in advance or it was only an inspiration of the moment; whether she had resisted, protested, when the Colonel proposed it to her, and then had been borne down by him; whether in short she didn't loathe herself as she sat there. The cruelty, the cowardice of fastening their unholy act upon the wretched woman struck him as monstrous—no less monstrous indeed than the levity that could make them run the risk of her giving them, in her righteous indignation, the lie. Of course that risk could only exculpate her and not inculpate them—the probabilities protected them so perfectly; and what the Colonel counted on (what he would have counted upon the day he delivered himself, after first seeing her, at the studio, if he had thought about the matter then at all and not spoken from the pure spontaneity of his genius) was simply that Miss Geraldine had really vanished for ever into her native unknown. Lyon wanted so much to quit the subject that when after a little Mrs. Capadose said to him, 'But can nothing be done, can't the picture be repaired? You know they do such wonders in that way now,' he only replied, 'I don't know, I don't care, it's all over, *n'en parlons plus!*' Her hypocrisy revolted him. And yet, by way of plucking off the last veil of her shame, he broke out to her again, shortly afterward, 'And you *did* like it, really?' To which she returned, looking him straight in his face, without a blush, a pallor, an evasion, 'Oh, I loved it!' Truly her husband had trained her well. After that Lyon said no more and his com-

panions forbore temporarily to insist, like people of tact and
sympathy aware that the odious accident had made him sore.

When they quitted the table the Colonel went away without
coming upstairs; but Lyon returned to the drawing-room with
his hostess, remarking to her however on the way that he
could remain but a moment. He spent that moment—it prolonged itself a little—standing with her before the chimney-
piece. She neither sat down nor asked him to; her manner
denoted that she intended to go out. Yes, her husband had
trained her well; yet Lyon dreamed for a moment that now
he was alone with her she would perhaps break down, retract,
apologise, confide, say to him, 'My dear old friend, forgive
this hideous comedy—you understand!' And then how he
would have loved her and pitied her, guarded her, helped her
always! If she were not ready to do something of that sort
why had she treated him as if he were a dear old friend; why
had she let him for months suppose certain things—or almost;
why had she come to his studio day after day to sit near him
on the pretext of her child's portrait, as if she liked to think
what might have been? Why had she come so near a tacit
confession, in a word, if she was not willing to go an inch
further? And she was not willing—she was not; he could see
that as he lingered there. She moved about the room a little,
rearranging two or three objects on the tables, but she did
nothing more. Suddenly he said to her: 'Which way was she
going, when you came out?'

'She—the woman we saw?'

'Yes, your husband's strange friend. It's a clew worth following.' He had no desire to frighten her; he only wanted to
communicate the impulse which would make her say, 'Ah,
spare me—and spare *him*! There was no such person.'

Instead of this Mrs. Capadose replied, 'She was going away
from us—she crossed the road. We were coming towards the
station.'

'And did she appear to recognise the Colonel—did she look
round?'

'Yes; she looked round, but I didn't notice much. A hansom
came along and we got into it. It was not till then that
Clement told me who she was: I remember he said that she was
there for no good. I suppose we ought to have gone back.'

'Yes; you would have saved the picture.'

For a moment she said nothing; then she smiled. 'For you, I am very sorry. But you must remember that I possess the original!'

At this Lyon turned away. 'Well, I must go,' he said; and he left her without any other farewell and made his way out of the house. As he went slowly up the street the sense came back to him of that first glimpse of her he had had at Stayes—the way he had seen her gaze across the table at her husband. Lyon stopped at the corner, looking vaguely up and down. He would never go back—he couldn't. She was still in love with the Colonel—he had trained her too well.

The Modern Warning

WHEN he reached the hotel Macarthy Grice was apprised, to his great disappointment, of the fact that his mother and sister were absent for the day, and he reproached himself with not having been more definite in announcing his arrival to them in advance. It was a little his nature to expect people to know things about himself that he had not told them and to be vexed when he found they were ignorant of them. I will not go so far as to say that he was inordinately conceited, but he had a general sense that he himself knew most things without having them pumped into him. He had been uncertain about his arrival and, since he disembarked at Liverpool, had communicated his movements to the two ladies who after spending the winter in Rome were awaiting him at Caden-abbia only by notes as brief as telegrams and on several occasions by telegrams simply. It struck his mother that he spent a great deal of money on these latter missives—which were mainly negative, mainly to say that he could not yet say when he *should* be able to start for the Continent. He had had business in London and had apparently been a good deal vexed by the discovery that, most of the people it was necessary for him to see being out of town, the middle of August was a bad time for transacting it. Mrs. Grice gathered that he had had annoyances and disappointments, but she hoped that by the time he should join them his serenity would have been restored. She had not seen him for a year and her heart hungered for her boy. Family feeling was strong among these three though Macarthy's manner of showing it was sometimes peculiar, and her affection for her son was jealous and passionate; but she and Agatha made no secret between themselves of the fact that the privilege of being his mother and his sister was mainly sensible when things were going well with him. They were a little afraid they were not going well just now and they asked each other why he could not leave his affairs alone for a few weeks anyway and treat his journey to Europe as a complete holiday—a course which would do him infinitely more good. He took life too hard and was overworked and overstrained. It was only to each other however that the anxious and affectionate women made these reflections, for they knew it was of no use to say such things to Macarthy. It was not that he answered them angrily; on the contrary he never noticed them at all. The answer was in the very essence of his nature: he was indomitably ambitious.

They had gone on the steamboat to the other end of the lake and could not possibly be back for several hours. There was a *festa* going on at one of the villages—in the hills, a little way from the lake—and several ladies and gentlemen had gone from the hotel to be present at it. They would find carriages at the landing and they would drive to the village, after which the same vehicles would bring them back to the boat. This information was given to Macarthy Grice by the secretary of the hotel, a young man with a very low shirt collar, whose nationality puzzled and even defied him by its indefiniteness (he liked to know whom he was talking to even when he could not have the satisfaction of feeling that it was an American), and who suggested to him that he might follow and overtake his friends in the next steamer. As however there appeared to be some danger that in this case he should cross them on their way back he determined simply to lounge about the lake-side and the grounds of the hotel. The place was lovely, the view magnificent, and there was a coming and going of little boats, of travellers of every nationality, of itinerant vendors of small superfluities. Macarthy observed these things as patiently as his native restlessness allowed—and indeed that quality was reinforced to-day by an inexplicable tendency to fidget. He changed his place twenty times; he lighted a cigar and threw it away; he ordered some luncheon and when it came had no appetite for it. He felt nervous and he wondered what he was nervous about; whether he were afraid that during their excursion an accident had befallen his mother or Agatha. He was not usually a prey to small timidities, and indeed it cost him a certain effort to admit that a little Italian lake could be deep enough to drown a pair of independent Americans or that Italian horses could have the high spirit to run away with them. He talked with no one, for the Americans seemed to him all taken up with each other and the English all taken up with themselves. He had a few elementary principles for use in travelling (he had travelled little, but he had an abundant supply of theory on the subject), and one of them was that with Englishmen an American should never open the conversation. It was his belief that in doing so an American was exposed to be snubbed, or even insulted, and this belief was unshaken by the fact that Englishmen very often spoke to him, Macarthy, first.

The afternoon passed, little by little, and at last, as he stood there with his hands in his pockets and his hat pulled over his nose to keep the western sun out of his eyes, he saw the boat that he was waiting for round a distant point. At this stage the little annoyance he had felt at the trick his relations had unwittingly played him passed completely away and there was nothing in his mind but the eagerness of affection, the joy of reunion—of the prospective embrace. This feeling was in his face, in the fixed smile with which he watched the boat grow larger and larger. If we watch the young man himself as he does so we shall perceive him to be a tallish, lean personage, with an excessive slope of the shoulders, a very thin neck, a short light beard and a bright, sharp, expressive eye. He almost always wore his hat too much behind or too much in front; in the former case it showed a very fine high forehead. He looked like a man of intellect whose body was not much to him and its senses and appetites not importunate. His feet were small and he always wore a double-breasted frockcoat, which he never buttoned. His mother and sister thought him very handsome. He had this appearance especially of course when, making them out on the deck of the steamer, he began to wave his hat and his hand to them. They responded in the most demonstrative manner and when they got near enough his mother called out to him over the water that she could not forgive herself for having lost so much of his visit. This was a bold proceeding for Mrs. Grice, who usually held back. Only she had been uncertain—she had not expected him that day in particular. 'It's my fault!—it's my fault!' exclaimed a gentleman beside her, whom our young man had not yet noticed, raising his hat slightly as he spoke. Agatha, on the other side, said nothing—she only smiled at her brother. He had not seen her for so many months that he had almost forgotten how pretty she was. She looked lovely, under the shadow of her hat and of the awning of the steamer, as she stood there with happiness in her face and a big bunch of familiar flowers in her hand. Macarthy was proud of many things, but on this occasion he was proudest of having such a charming sister. Before they all disembarked he had time to observe the gentleman who had spoken to him—an extraordinarily fair, clean-looking man, with a white waistcoat, a white hat, a glass in one eye and a flower in his button-hole. Macarthy wondered who he was, but only vaguely, as it explained him sufficiently to suppose that he was a gentleman staying at the hotel who had made acquaintance with his mother and sister and taken part in the excursion. The only thing Grice had against him was that he had the air of an American who tried to look like an Englishman—a definite and conspicuous class to the young man's sense and one in regard to which he entertained a peculiar abhorrence. He was sorry his relatives should associate themselves with persons of that stamp; he would almost have preferred that they should become acquainted with the genuine English. He happened to perceive that the individual in question looked a good deal at him; but he disappeared instantly and discreetly when the boat drew up at the landing and the three Grices—I had almost written the three Graces—pressed each other in their arms.

Half an hour later Macarthy sat between the two ladies at the table d'hôte, where he had a hundred questions to answer and to ask. He was still more struck with Agatha's improvement; she was older, handsomer, brighter: she had turned completely into a young lady and into a very accomplished one. It seemed to him that there had been a change for the better in his mother as well, the only change of that sort of which the good lady was susceptible, an amelioration of health, a fresher colour and a less frequent cough. Mrs. Grice was a gentle, sallow, serious little woman, the main principle of whose being was the habit of insisting that nothing that concerned herself was of the least consequence. She thought it indelicate to be ill and obtrusive even to be better, and discouraged all conversation of which she was in any degree the subject. Fortunately she had not been able to prevent her children from discussing her condition sufficiently to agree—it

took but few words, for they agreed easily, that is Agatha always agreed with her brother—that she must have a change
of climate and spend a winter or two in the south of Europe.
Mrs. Grice kept her son's birthday all the year and knew an
extraordinary number of stitches in knitting. Her friends constantly received from her, by post, offerings of little mats for
the table, done up in an envelope, usually without any writing.
She could make little mats in forty or fifty different ways. Toward the end of the dinner Macarthy, who up to this moment
had been wholly occupied with his companions, began to look
around him and to ask questions about the people opposite.
Then he leaned forward a little and turned his eye up and
down the row of their fellow-tourists on the same side. It was
in this way that he perceived the gentleman who had said from
the steamer that it was *his* fault that Mrs. Grice and her daughter had gone away for so many hours and who now was seated
at some distance below the younger lady. At the moment
Macarthy leaned forward this personage happened to be looking toward him, so that he caught his eye. The stranger smiled
at him and nodded, as if an acquaintance might be considered
to have been established between them, rather to Macarthy's
surprise. He drew back and asked his sister who he was—the
fellow who had been with them on the boat.

'He's an Englishman—Sir Rufus Chasemore,' said the girl.
Then she added, 'Such a nice man.'

'Oh, I thought he was an American making a fool of himself!' Macarthy rejoined.

'There's nothing of the fool about him,' Agatha declared,
laughing; and in a moment she added that Sir Rufus's usual
place was beside hers, on her left hand. On this occasion he
had moved away.

'What do you mean by this occasion?' her brother inquired.

'Oh, because you are here.'

'And is he afraid of me?'

'Yes, I think he is.'

'He doesn't behave so, anyway.'

'Oh, he has very good manners,' said the girl.

'Well, I suppose he's bound to do that. Isn't he a kind of
nobleman?' Macarthy asked.

'Well no, not exactly a nobleman.'

'Well, some kind of a panjandarum. Hasn't he got one of their titles?'

'Yes, but not a very high one,' Agatha explained. 'He's only a K.C.B. And also an M.P.'

'A K.C.B. and an M.P.? What the deuce is all that?' And when Agatha had elucidated these mystic signs, as to which the young man's ignorance was partly simulated, he remarked that the Post-office ought to charge her friend double for his letters—for requiring that amount of stuff in his address. He also said that he owed him one for leading them astray at a time when they were bound to be on hand to receive one who was so dear to them. To this Agatha replied:

'Ah, you see, Englishmen are like that. They expect women to be so much honoured by their wanting them to do anything. And it must always be what *they* like, of course.'

'What the men like? Well, that's all right, only they mustn't be Englishmen,' said Macarthy Grice.

'Oh, if one is going to be a slave I don't know that the nationality of one's master matters!' his sister exclaimed. After which his mother began to ask him if he had seen anything during the previous months of their Philadelphia cousins— some cousins who wrote their name Gryce and for whom Macarthy had but a small affection.

After dinner the three sat out on the terrace of the hotel, in the delicious warmth of the September night. There were boats on the water, decked with coloured lanterns; music and song proceeded from several of them and every influence was harmonious. Nevertheless by the time Macarthy had finished a cigar it was judged best that the old lady should withdraw herself from the evening air. She went into the salon of the hotel, and her children accompanied her, against her protest, so that she might not be alone. Macarthy liked better to sit with his mother in a drawing-room which the lamps made hot than without her under the stars. At the end of a quarter of an hour he became aware that his sister had disappeared, and as some time elapsed without her returning he asked his mother what had become of her.

'I guess she has gone to walk with Sir Rufus,' said the old lady, candidly.

'Why, you seem to do everything Sir Rufus wants, down

here!' her son exclaimed. 'How did he get such a grip on you?'

'Well, he has been most kind, Macarthy,' Mrs. Grice returned, not appearing to deny that the Englishman's influence was considerable.

'I have heard it stated that it's not the custom, down here, for young girls to walk round—at night—with foreign lords.'

'Oh, he's not foreign and he's most reliable,' said the old lady, very earnestly. It was not in her nature to treat such a question, or indeed any question, as unimportant.

'Well, that's all right,' her son remarked, in a tone which implied that he was in good-humour and wished not to have his equanimity ruffled. Such accidents with Macarthy Grice were not light things. All the same at the end of five minutes more, as Agatha did not reappear, he expressed the hope that nothing of any kind had sprung up between her and the K.C.B.

'Oh, I guess they are just conversing by the lake. I'll go and find them if you like,' said Mrs. Grice.

'Well, haven't they been conversing by the lake—and on the lake—all day?' asked the young man, without taking up her proposal.

'Yes, of course we had a great deal of bright talk while we were out. It was quite enough for me to listen to it. But he is most kind—and he knows everything, Macarthy.'

'Well, that's all right!' exclaimed the young man again. But a few moments later he returned to the charge and asked his mother if the Englishman were paying any serious attention—she knew what he meant—to Agatha. 'Italian lakes and summer evenings and glittering titles and all that sort of thing—of course you know what they may lead to.'

Mrs. Grice looked anxious and veracious, as she always did, and appeared to consider a little. 'Well, Macarthy, the truth is just this. Your sister is so attractive and so admired that it seems as if wherever she went there was a great interest taken in her. Sir Rufus certainly does like to converse with her, but so have many others—and so would any one in their place. And Agatha is full of conscience. For me that's her highest attraction.'

'I'm very much pleased with her—she's a lovely creature,' Macarthy remarked.

'Well, there's no one whose appreciation could gratify her more than yours. She has praised you up to Sir Rufus,' added the old lady, simply.

'Dear mother, what has *he* got to do with it?' her son demanded, staring. 'I don't care what Sir Rufus thinks of me.'

Fortunately the good lady was left only for a moment confronted with this inquiry, for Agatha now re-entered the room, passing in from the terrace by one of the long windows and accompanied precisely by the gentleman whom her relatives had been discussing. She came toward them smiling and perhaps even blushing a little, but with an air of considerable resolution, and she said to Macarthy, 'Brother, I want to make you acquainted with a good friend of ours, Sir Rufus Chasemore.'

'Oh, I asked Miss Grice to be so good.' The Englishman laughed, looking easy and genial.

Macarthy got up and extended his hand, with a 'Very happy to know you, sir,' and the two men stood a moment looking at each other while Agatha, beside them, bent her regard upon both. I shall not attempt to translate the reflections which rose in the young lady's mind as she did so, for they were complicated and subtle and it is quite difficult enough to reproduce our own more casual impression of the contrast between her companions. This contrast was extreme and complete, and it was not weakened by the fact that both the men had the signs of character and ability. The American was thin, dry, fine, with something in his face which seemed to say that there was more in him of the spirit than of the letter. He looked unfinished and yet somehow he looked mature, though he was not advanced in life. The Englishman had more detail about him, something stippled and retouched, an air of having been more artfully fashioned, in conformity with traditions and models. He wore old clothes which looked new, while his transatlantic brother wore new clothes which looked old. He thought he had never heard the American tone so marked as on the lips of Mr. Macarthy Grice, who on his side found in the accent of his sister's friend a strange, exaggerated, even affected variation of the tongue in which he supposed himself to have been brought up. In general he was much irritated by the tricks which the English played with the English language, deprecating especially their use of familiar slang.

'Miss Grice tells me that you have just crossed the ditch, but I'm afraid you are not going to stay with us long,' Sir Rufus remarked, with much pleasantness.

'Well, no, I shall return as soon as I have transacted my business,' Macarthy replied. 'That's all I came for.'

'You don't do us justice; you ought to follow the example of your mother and sister and take a look round,' Sir Rufus went on, with another laugh. He was evidently of a mirthful nature.

'Oh, I have been here before; I've seen the principal curiosities.'

'He has seen everything thoroughly,' Mrs. Grice murmured over her crotchet.

'Ah, I daresay you have seen much more than we poor natives. And your own country is so interesting. I have an immense desire to see that.'

'Well, it certainly repays observation,' said Macarthy Grice.

'You wouldn't like it at all; you would find it awful,' his sister remarked, sportively, to Sir Rufus.

'Gracious, daughter!' the old lady exclaimed, trying to catch Agatha's eye.

'That's what she's always telling me, as if she were trying to keep me from going. I don't know what she has been doing over there that she wants to prevent me from finding out.' Sir Rufus's eyes, while he made this observation, rested on the young lady in the most respectful yet at the same time the most complacent manner.

She smiled back at him and said with a laugh still clearer than his own, 'I know the kind of people who will like America and the kind of people who won't.'

'Do you know the kind who will like *you* and the kind who won't?' Sir Rufus Chasemore inquired.

'I don't know that in some cases it particularly matters what people like,' Macarthy interposed, with a certain severity.

'Well, I must say I like people to like my country,' said Agatha.

'You certainly take the best way to make them, Miss Grice!' Sir Rufus exclaimed.

'Do you mean by dissuading them from visiting it, sir?' Macarthy asked.

'Oh dear no; by being so charming a representative of it. But I shall most positively go on the first opportunity.'

'I hope it won't be while we are on this side,' said Mrs. Grice, very civilly.

'You will need us over there to explain everything,' her daughter added.

The Englishman looked at her a moment with his glass in his eye. 'I shall certainly pretend to be very stupid.' Then he went on, addressing himself to Macarthy: 'I have an idea that you have some rocks ahead, but that doesn't diminish—in fact it increases—my curiosity to see the country.'

'Oh, I suspect we'll scratch along all right,' Macarthy replied, with rather a grim smile, in a tone which conveyed that the success of American institutions might not altogether depend on Sir Rufus's judgment of them. He was on the point of expressing his belief, further, that there were European countries which would be glad enough to exchange their 'rocks' for those of the United States; but he kept back this reflection, as it might appear too pointed and he wished not to be rude to a man who seemed on such sociable terms with his mother and sister. In the course of a quarter of an hour the ladies took their departure for the upper regions and Macarthy Grice went off with them. The Englishman looked for him again however, as something had been said about their smoking a cigar together before they went to bed; but he never turned up, so that Sir Rufus puffed his own weed in solitude, strolling up and down the terrace without mingling with the groups that remained and looking much at the starlit lake and mountains.

II

The next morning after breakfast Mrs. Grice had a conversation with her son in her own room. Agatha had not yet appeared, and she explained that the girl was sleeping late, having been much fatigued by her excursion the day before as well as by the excitement of her brother's arrival. Macarthy thought it a little singular that she should bear her fatigue so much less well than her mother, but he understood everything in a moment, as soon as the old lady drew him toward her with her little conscious, cautious face, taking his hand in hers. She had had a long and important talk with Agatha the previous evening, after they went upstairs, and she had extracted from the girl some information which she had within a day or two begun very much to desire.

'It's about Sir Rufus Chasemore. I couldn't but think you would wonder—just as I was wondering myself,' said Mrs. Grice. 'I felt as if I couldn't be satisfied till I had asked. I don't know how you will feel about it. I am afraid it will upset you a little; but anything that you may think—well, yes, it *is* the case.'

'Do you mean she is engaged to be married to your Englishman?' Macarthy demanded, with a face that suddenly flushed.

'No, she's not engaged. I presume she wouldn't take that step without finding out how you'd feel. In fact that's what she said last night.'

'I feel like thunder, I feel like hell!' Macarthy exclaimed; 'and I hope you'll tell her so.'

Mrs. Grice looked frightened and pained. 'Well, my son, I'm glad you've come, if there is going to be any trouble.'

'Trouble—what trouble should there be? He can't marry her if she won't have him.'

'Well, she didn't say she wouldn't have him; she said the question hadn't come up. But she thinks it would come up if she were to give him any sort of opening. That's what I thought and that's what I wanted to make sure of.'

Macarthy looked at his mother for some moments in extreme seriousness; then he took out his watch and looked at that. 'What time is the first boat?' he asked.

'I don't know—there are a good many.'

'Well, we'll take the first—we'll quit this.' And the young man put back his watch and got up with decision.

His mother sat looking at him rather ruefully. 'Would you feel so badly if she were to do it?'

'She may do it without my consent; she shall never do it with,' said Macarthy Grice.

'Well, I could see last evening, by the way you acted—' his mother murmured, as if she thought it her duty to try and enter into his opposition.

'How did I act, ma'am?'

'Well, you acted as if you didn't think much of the English.'

'Well, I don't,' said the young man.

'Agatha noticed it and she thought Sir Rufus noticed it too.'

'They have such thick hides in general that they don't notice anything. But if he is more sensitive than the others perhaps it will keep him away.'

'Would you like to wound him, Macarthy?' his mother inquired, with an accent of timid reproach.

'Wound him? I should like to kill him! Please to let Agatha know that we'll move on,' the young man added.

Mrs. Grice got up as if she were about to comply with this injunction, but she stopped in the middle of the room and asked of her son, with a quaint effort at conscientious impartiality which would have made him smile if he had been capable of smiling in such a connection, 'Don't you think that in some respects the English are a fine nation?'

'Well, yes; I like them for pale ale and note-paper and umbrellas; and I got a firstrate trunk there the other day. But I want my sister to marry one of her own people.'

'Yes, I presume it would be better,' Mrs. Grice remarked. 'But Sir Rufus has occupied very high positions in his own country.'

'I know the kind of positions he has occupied; I can tell what they were by looking at him. The more he has done of that the more intensely he represents what I don't like.'

'Of course he would stand up for England,' Mrs. Grice felt herself compelled to admit.

'Then why the mischief doesn't he do so instead of running round after Americans?' Macarthy demanded.

'He doesn't run round after us; but we knew his sister, Lady Bolitho, in Rome. She is a most sweet woman and we saw a great deal of her; she took a great fancy to Agatha. I surmise that she mentioned us to him pretty often when she went back to England, and when he came abroad for his autumn holiday, as he calls it—he met us first in the Engadine, three or four weeks ago, and came down here with us—it seemed as if we already knew him and he knew us. He is very talented and he is quite well off.'

'Mother,' said Macarthy Grice, going close to the old lady and speaking very gravely, 'why do you know so much about him? Why have you gone into it so?'

'I haven't gone into it; I only know what he has told us.'

'But why have you given him the right to tell you? How does it concern you whether he is well off?'

The poor woman began to look flurried and scared. 'My son, I have given him no right; I don't know what you mean. Besides, it wasn't he who told us he is well off; it was his sister.'

'It would have been better if you hadn't known his sister,' said the young man, gloomily.

'Gracious, Macarthy, we must know some one!' Mrs. Grice rejoined, with a flicker of spirit.

'I don't see the necessity of your knowing the English.'

'Why Macarthy, can't we even *know* them?' pleaded his mother.

'You see the sort of thing it gets you into.'

'It hasn't got us into anything. Nothing has been done.'

'So much the better, mother darling,' said the young man. 'In that case we will go on to Venice. Where is he going?'

'I don't know, but I suppose he won't come on to Venice if we don't ask him.'

'I don't believe any delicacy would prevent him,' Macarthy rejoined. 'But he loathes me; that's an advantage.'

'He *loathes* you—when he wanted so to know you?'

'Oh yes, I understand. Well, now he knows me! He knows he hates everything I like and I hate everything he likes.'

'He doesn't imagine you hate your sister, I suppose!' said the old lady, with a little vague laugh.

'Mother,' said Macarthy, still in front of her with his hands in his pockets, 'I verily believe I should hate her if she were to marry him.'

'Oh, gracious, my son, don't, don't!' cried Mrs. Grice, throwing herself into his arms with a shudder of horror and burying her face on his shoulder.

Her son held her close and as he bent over her he went on: 'Dearest mother, don't you see that we must remain together, that at any rate we mustn't be separated by different ideas, different associations and institutions? I don't believe any family has ever had more of the feeling that holds people closely together than we have had: therefore for heaven's sake let us keep it, let us find our happiness in it as we always have done. Of course Agatha will marry some day; but why need she marry in such a way as to make a gulf? You and she are all I have, and—I may be selfish—I should like very much to keep you.'

'Of course I will let her know the way you feel,' said the old lady, a moment later, rearranging her cap and her shawl and putting away her pocket-handkerchief.

'It's a matter she certainly ought to understand. She would wish to, unless she is very much changed,' Macarthy added, as if he saw all this with high lucidity.

'Oh, she isn't changed—she'll never change!' his mother exclaimed, with rebounding optimism. She thought it wicked not to take cheerful views.

'She wouldn't if she were to marry an Englishman,' he declared, as Mrs. Grice left him to go to her daughter.

She told him an hour later that Agatha would be quite ready to start for Venice on the morrow and that she said he need have no fear that Sir Rufus Chasemore would follow them. He was naturally anxious to know from her what words she had had with Agatha, but the only very definite information he extracted was to the effect that the girl had declared with infinite feeling that she would never marry an enemy of her country. When he saw her later in the day he thought she had been crying; but there was nothing in her manner to show that she resented any pressure her mother might have represented to her that he had put upon her or that she was making a reluctant sacrifice. Agatha Grice was very fond of her brother, whom she knew to be upright, distinguished and exceedingly mindful of the protection and support that he owed her mother and herself. He was perverse and obstinate, but she was aware that in essentials he was supremely tender, and he had always been very much the most eminent figure in her horizon.

No allusion was made between them to Sir Rufus Chasemore, though the silence on either side was rather a conscious one, and they talked of the prospective pleasures of Venice and of the arrangements Macarthy would be able to make in regard to his mother's spending another winter in Rome. He was to accompany them to Venice and spend a fortnight with them there, after which he was to return to London to terminate his business and then take his way back to New York. There was a plan of his coming to see them again later in the winter, in Rome, if he should succeed in getting six weeks off. As a man of energy and decision, though indeed of a somewhat irritable stomach, he made light of the Atlantic voyage: it was a rest and a relief, alternating with his close attention to business. That the disunion produced by the state of Mrs. Grice's health was a source of constant regret and even of much depression to him was well known to his mother and sister, who would not have broken up his home by coming to live in Europe if he had not insisted upon it. Macarthy was in the highest degree conscientious; he was capable of suffering the extremity of discomfort in a cause which he held to be right. But his mother and sister *were* his home, all the same, and in their absence he was perceptibly desolate. Fortunately it had been hoped that a couple of southern winters would quite set Mrs. Grice up again and that then everything in America would be as it had been before. Agatha's affection for her brother was very nearly as great as his affection for herself; but it took the form of wishing that his loneliness might be the cause of his marrying some thoroughly nice girl, inasmuch as after all her mother and she might not always be there. Fraternal tenderness in Macarthy's bosom followed a different logic. He was so fond of his sister that he had a secret hope that she would never marry at all. He had spoken otherwise to his mother, because that was the only way not to seem offensively selfish; but the essence of his thought was that on the day Agatha should marry she would throw him over. On the day she should marry an Englishman she would not throw him over—she would betray him. That is she would betray her country, and it came to the same thing. Macarthy's patriotism was of so intense a hue that to his own sense the national life and his own life flowed in an indistinguishable current.

The particular Englishman he had his eye upon now was not, as a general thing, visible before luncheon. He had told Agatha, who mentioned it to her brother, that in the morning

he was immersed in work—in letter-writing. Macarthy wondered what his work might be, but did not condescend to
inquire. He was enlightened however by happening by an odd
chance to observe an allusion to Sir Rufus in a copy of the
London *Times* which he took up in the reading-room of the
hotel. This occurred in a letter to the editor of the newspaper,
the writer of which accused Agatha's friend of having withheld
from the public some information to which the public was
entitled. The information had respect to 'the situation in
South Africa,' and Sir Rufus was plainly an agent of the British
government, the head of some kind of department or sub-
department. This did not make Macarthy like him any better.
He was displeased with the idea of England's possessing col-
onies at all and considered that she had acquired them by
force and fraud and held them by a frail and unnatural tenure.
It appeared to him that any man who occupied a place in this
unrighteous system must have false, detestable views.

Sir Rufus Chasemore turned up on the terrace in the afternoon and bore himself with the serenity of a man unconscious
of the damaging inferences that had been formed about him.
Macarthy neither avoided him nor sought him out—he even
relented a little toward him mentally when he thought of the
loss he was about to inflict on him; but when the Englishman
approached him and appeared to wish to renew their conversation of the evening before it struck him that he was wanting
in delicacy. There was nothing strange in that however, for
delicacy and tact were not the strong point of one's transatlantic cousins, with whom one had always to dot one's i's. It
seemed to Macarthy that Sir Rufus Chasemore ought to have
guessed that he cared little to keep up an acquaintance with
him, though indeed the young American would have been at
a loss to say how he was to guess it, inasmuch as he would
have resented the imputation that he himself had been rude
enough to make such a fact patent. The American ladies were
in their apartments, occupied in some manner connected with
their intended retreat, and there was nothing for Macarthy
but to stroll up and down for nearly half an hour with the
personage who was so provokingly the cause of it. It had come
over him now that he should have liked extremely to spend
several days on the lake of Como. The place struck him as

much more delicious than it had done while he chafed the day before at the absence of his relations. He was angry with the Englishman for forcing him to leave it and still more angry with him for showing so little responsibility or even perception in regard to the matter. It occurred to him while he was in this humour that it might be a good plan to make himself so disagreeable that Sir Rufus would take to his heels and never reappear, fleeing before the portent of such an insufferable brother-in-law. But this plan demanded powers of execution which Macarthy did not flatter himself that he possessed: he felt that it was impossible to him to divest himself of his character of a polished American gentleman.

If he found himself dissenting from most of the judgments and opinions which Sir Rufus Chasemore happened to express in the course of their conversation there was nothing perverse in that: it was a simple fact apparently that the Englishman had nothing in common with him and was predestined to enunciate propositions to which it was impossible for him to assent. Moreover how could he assent to propositions enunciated in that short, offhand, clipping tone, with the words running into each other and the voice rushing up and down the scale? Macarthy, who spoke very slowly, with great distinctness and in general with great correctness, was annoyed not only by his companion's intonation but by the odd and, as it seemed to him, licentious application that he made of certain words. He struck him as wanting in reverence for the language, which Macarthy had an idea, not altogether unjust, that he himself deeply cherished. He would have admitted that these things were small and not great, but in the usual relations of life the small things count more than the great, and they sufficed at any rate to remind him of the essential antipathy and incompatibility which he had always believed to exist between an Englishman and an American. They were, in the very nature of things, disagreeable to each other—both mentally and physically irreconcilable. In cases where this want of correspondence had been bridged over it was because the American had made weak concessions, had been shamefully accommodating. That was a kind of thing the Englishman, to do him justice, never did; he had at least the courage of his prejudices. It was not unknown to Macarthy that the repug-

nance in question appeared to be confined to the American
male, as was shown by a thousand international marriages,
which had transplanted as many of his countrywomen to unnatural British homes. That variation had to be allowed for,
and the young man felt that he was allowing for it when he
reflected that probably his own sister liked the way Sir Rufus
Chasemore spoke. In fact he was intimately convinced she
liked it, which was a reason the more for their quitting
Cadenabbia the next morning.

Sir Rufus took the opposite point of view quite as much as
himself, only he took it gaily and familiarly and laughed about
it, as if he were amused at the preferences his companion betrayed and especially amused that he should hold them so
gravely, so almost gloomily. This sociable jocosity, as if they
had known each other three months was what appeared to
Macarthy so indelicate. They talked no politics and Sir Rufus
said nothing more about America; but it stuck out of the Englishman at every pore that he was a resolute and consistent
conservative, a prosperous, accomplished, professional, official
Tory. It gave Macarthy a kind of palpitation to think that his
sister had been in danger of associating herself with such ar-
rogant doctrines. Not that a woman's political creed mattered;
but that of her husband did. He had an impression that he
himself was a passionate democrat, an unshrinking radical. It
was a proof of how far Sir Rufus's manner was from being
satisfactory to his companion that the latter was unable to
guess whether he already knew of the sudden determination
of his American friends to leave Cadenabbia or whether their
intention was first revealed to him in Macarthy's casual mention of it, which apparently put him out not at all, eliciting
nothing more than a frank, cheerful expression of regret.
Macarthy somehow mistrusted a man who could conceal his
emotions like that. How could he have known they were going unless Agatha had told him, and how could Agatha have
told him, since she could not as yet have seen him? It did not
even occur to the young man to suspect that she might have
conveyed the unwelcome news to him by a letter. And if he
had not known it why was he not more startled and discom-
fited when Macarthy dealt the blow? The young American
made up his mind at last that the reason why Sir Rufus was

not startled was that he had thought in advance it would be
no more than natural that the newly-arrived brother should
wish to spoil his game. But in that case why was he not angry
with him for such a disposition? Why did he come after him
and insist on talking with him? There seemed to Macarthy
something impudent in this incongruity—as if to the mind of
an English statesman the animosity of a Yankee lawyer were
really of too little account.

III

It may be intimated to the reader that Agatha Grice had written no note to her English friend, and she held no communication with him of any sort, till after she had left the table
d'hôte with her mother and brother in the evening. Sir Rufus
had seated himself at dinner in the same place as the night
before; he was already occupying it and he simply bowed to
her with a smile, from a distance, when she came into the
room. As she passed out to the terrace later with her companions he overtook her and said to her in a lower tone of
voice than usual that he had been exceedingly sorry to hear
that she was leaving Cadenabbia so soon. Was it really true?
could not they put it off a little? should not they find the
weather too hot in Venice and the mosquitoes too numerous?
Agatha saw that Sir Rufus asked these questions with the intention of drawing her away, engaging her in a walk, in some
talk to which they should have no listeners; and she resisted
him at first a little, keeping near the others because she had
made up her mind that morning in deep and solitary meditation that she would force him to understand that further
acquaintance could lead to nothing profitable for either party.
It presently came over her, however, that it would take some
little time to explain this truth and that the time might be
obtained by their walking a certain distance along the charming shore of the lake together. The windows of the hotel and
of the little water-side houses and villas projected over the
place long shafts of lamplight which shimmered on the water,
broken by the slow-moving barges laden with musicians, and
gave the whole region the air of an illuminated garden surrounding a magnificent pond. Agatha made the further re-

flection that it would be only common kindness to give Sir Rufus an opportunity to say anything he wished to say; that is within the limits she was prepared to allow: they had been too good friends to separate without some of the forms of regret, without a backward look at least, since they might not enjoy a forward one. In short she had taken in the morning a resolution so virtuous, founded on so high and large a view of the whole situation, that she felt herself entitled to some reward, some present liberty of action. She turned away from her relatives with Sir Rufus—she observed that they paid no attention to her—and in a few moments she was strolling by his side at a certain distance from the hotel.

'I will tell you what I should like to do,' he said, as they went; 'I should like to turn up in Venice—about a week hence.'

'I don't recommend you to do that,' the girl replied, promptly enough; though as soon as she had spoken she bethought herself that she could give him no definite reason why he should not follow her; she could give him no reason at all that would not be singularly wanting in delicacy. She had a moment of vexation with her brother for having put her in a false position; it was the first, for in the morning when her mother repeated to her what Macarthy had said and she perceived all that it implied she had not been in the least angry with him—she sometimes indeed wondered why she was not—and she did not propose to become so for Sir Rufus Chasemore. What she had been was sad—touched too with a sense of horror—horror at the idea that she might be in danger of denying, under the influence of an insinuating alien, the pieties and sanctities in which she had been brought up. Sir Rufus *was* a tremendous conservative, though perhaps that did not matter so much, and he had let her know at an early stage of their acquaintance that he had never liked Americans in the least as a people. As it was apparent that he liked her—all American and very American as she was—she had regarded this shortcoming only in its minor bearings, and it had even gratified her to form a private project of converting him to a friendlier view. If she had not found him a charming man she would not have cared what he thought about her country-people; but, as it happened, she did find him a charming man, and it grieved her to see a mind that was really worthy of the finest initiations (as regarded the American question) wasting itself on poor prejudices. Somehow, by showing him how nice she was herself she could make him like the people better with whom she had so much in common, and as he admitted that his observation of them had after all been very restricted she would also make him know them better. This prospect drew her on till suddenly her brother sounded the note of warning. When it came she understood it perfectly; she could not pretend that she did not. If she were not careful she would give her country away: in the privacy of her own room she had coloured up to her hair at the thought. She had a lurid vision in which the chance seemed to be greater that Sir Rufus Chasemore would bring her over to his side than that she should make him like anything he had begun by disliking; so that she resisted, with the conviction that the complications which might arise from allowing a prejudiced Englishman to possess himself, as he evidently desired to do, of her affections, would be much greater than a sensitive girl with other loyalties to observe might be able to manage. A moment after she had said to her companion that she did not recommend him to come to Venice she added that of course he was free to do as he liked: only why should he come if he was sure the place was so uncomfortable? To this Sir Rufus replied that it signified little how uncomfortable it was if she should be there and that there was nothing he would not put up with for the sake of a few days more of her society.

'Oh, if it's for that you are coming,' the girl replied, laughing and feeling nervous—feeling that something was in the air which she had wished precisely to keep out of it—'Oh, if it's for that you are coming you had very much better not take the trouble. You would have very little of my society. While my brother is with us all my time will be given up to him.'

'Confound your brother!' Sir Rufus exclaimed. Then he went on: 'You told me yourself he wouldn't be with you long. After he's gone you will be free again and you will still be in Venice, shan't you? I do want to float in a gondola with you.'

'It's very possible my brother may be with us for weeks.'

Sir Rufus hesitated a moment. 'I see what you mean—that he won't leave you so long as I am about the place. In that case if you are so fond of him you ought to take it as a kindness of me to hover about.' Before the girl had time to make a rejoinder to this ingenious proposition he added, 'Why in the world has he taken such a dislike to me?'

'I know nothing of any dislike,' Agatha said, not very honestly. 'He has expressed none to me.'

'He has to me then. He quite loathes me.'

She was silent a little; then she inquired, 'And do you like him very much?'

'I think he's immense fun! He's very clever, like most of the Americans I have seen, including yourself. I should like to show him I like him, and I have salaamed and kowtowed to him whenever I had a chance; but he won't let me get near him. Hang it, it's cruel!'

'It's not directed to you in particular, any dislike he may have. I have told you before that he doesn't like the English,' Agatha remarked.

'Bless me—no more do I! But my best friends have been among them.'

'I don't say I agree with my brother and I don't say I disagree with him,' Sir Rufus's companion went on. 'I have told you before that we are of Irish descent, on my mother's side. Her mother was a Macarthy. We have kept up the name and we have kept up the feeling.'

'I see—so that even if the Yankee were to let me off the Paddy would come down! That's a most unholy combination. But you remember, I hope, what I have also told you—that I am quite as Irish as you can ever be. I had an Irish grandmother—a beauty of beauties, a certain Lady Laura Fitzgibbon, *qui vaut bien la vôtre*. A charming old woman she was.'

'Oh, well, she wasn't of our kind!' the girl exclaimed, laughing.

'You mean that yours wasn't charming? In the presence of her granddaughter permit me to doubt it.'

'Well, I suppose that those hostilities of race—transmitted and hereditary, as it were—are the greatest of all.' Agatha

Grice uttered this sage reflection by no means in the tone of
successful controversy and with the faintest possible tremor in
her voice.

'Good God! do you mean to say that an hostility of race, a
legendary feud, is to prevent you and me from meeting again?'
The Englishman stopped short as he made this inquiry, but
Agatha continued to walk, as if that might help her to elude
it. She had come out with a perfectly sincere determination
to prevent Sir Rufus from saying what she believed he wanted
to say, and if her voice had trembled just now it was because
it began to come over her that her preventive measures would
fail. The only tolerably efficacious one would be to turn
straight round and go home. But there would be a rudeness
in this course and even a want of dignity; and besides she did
not wish to go home. She compromised by not answering her
companion's question, and though she could not see him she
was aware that he was looking after her with an expression in
his face of high impatience momentarily baffled. She knew
that expression and thought it handsome; she knew all his
expressions and thought them all handsome. He overtook her
in a few moments and then she was surprised that he should
be laughing as he exclaimed: 'It's too absurd!—it's too absurd!' It was not long however before she understood the
nature of his laughter, as she understood everything else. If
she was nervous he was scarcely less so; his whole manner now
expressed the temper of a man wishing to ascertain rapidly
whether he may enjoy or must miss great happiness. Before
she knew it he had spoken the words which she had flattered
herself he should not speak; he had said that since there appeared to be a doubt whether they should soon meet again it
was important he should seize the present occasion. He was
very glad after all, because for several days he had been wanting to speak. He loved her as he had never loved any woman
and he besought her earnestly to believe it. What was this
crude stuff about disliking the English and disliking the Americans? what had questions of nationality to do with it any more
than questions of ornithology? It was a question simply of
being his wife, and that was rather between themselves, was
it not? He besought her to consider it, as *he* had been turning
it over from almost the first hour he met her. It was not in

Agatha's power to go her way now, because he had laid his hand upon her in a manner that kept her motionless, and while he talked to her in low, kind tones, touching her face with the breath of supplication, she stood there in the warm darkness, very pale, looking as if she were listening to a threat of injury rather than to a declaration of love. 'Of course I ought to speak to your mother,' he said; 'I ought to have spoken to her first. But your leaving at an hour's notice and apparently wishing to shake me off has given me no time. For God's sake give me your permission and I will do it to night.'

'Don't—don't speak to my mother,' said Agatha, mournfully.

'Don't tell me to-morrow then that she won't hear of it!'

'She likes you, Sir Rufus,' the girl rejoined, in the same singular, hopeless tone.

'I hope you don't mean to imply by that that you don't!'

'No; I like you of course; otherwise I should never have allowed myself to be in this position, because I hate it!' The girl uttered these last words with a sudden burst of emotion and an equally sudden failure of sequence, and turning round quickly began to walk in the direction from which they had come. Her companion, however, was again beside her, close to her, and he found means to prevent her from going as fast as she wished. History has lost the record of what at that moment he said to her; it was something that made her exclaim in a voice which seemed on the point of breaking into tears: 'Please don't say that or anything like it again, Sir Rufus, or I shall have to take leave of you for ever this instant, on the spot.' He strove to be obedient and they walked on a little in silence; after which she resumed, with a slightly different manner: 'I am very sorry you have said this to-night. You have troubled and distressed me; it isn't a good time.'

'I wonder if you would favour me with your idea of what might be a good time?'

'I don't know. Perhaps never. I am greatly obliged to you for the honour you have done me. I beg you to believe me when I say this. But I don't think I shall ever marry. I have other duties. I can't do what I like with my life.'

At this Sir Rufus made her stop again, to tell him what she meant by such an extraordinary speech. What overwhelming duties had she, pray, and what restrictions upon her life that made her so different from other women? He could not, for his part, imagine a woman more free. She explained that she had her mother, who was terribly delicate and who must be her first thought and her first care. Nothing would induce her to leave her mother. She was all her mother had except Macarthy, and he was absorbed in his profession.

'What possible question need there be of your leaving her?' the Englishman demanded. 'What could be more delightful than that she should live with us and that we should take care of her together? You say she is so good as to like me, and I assure you I like *her*—most uncommonly.'

'It would be impossible that we should take her away from my brother,' said the girl, after an hesitation.

'Take her away?' And Sir Rufus Chasemore stood staring. 'Well, if he won't look after her himself—you say he is so taken up with his work—he has no earthly right to prevent other people from doing so.'

'It's not a man's business—it's mine—it's her daughter's.'

'That's exactly what I think, and what in the world do I wish but to help you? If she requires a mild climate we will find some lovely place in the south of England and be as happy there as the day is long.'

'So that Macarthy would have to come *there* to see his mother? Fancy Macarthy in the south of England—especially as happy as the day is long! He would find the day very long,' Agatha Grice continued, with the strange little laugh which expressed—or rather which disguised—the mixture of her feelings. 'He would never consent.'

'Never consent to what? Is what you mean to say that he would never consent to your marriage? I certainly never dreamed that you would have to ask him. Haven't you defended to me again and again the freedom, the independence with which American girls marry? Where is the independence when it comes to your own case?' Sir Rufus Chasemore paused a moment and then he went on with bitterness: 'Why don't you say outright that you are afraid of your brother? Miss Grice, I never dreamed that that would be your answer to an offer of everything that a man—and a man of some distinction, I may say, for it would be affectation in me to pretend that I consider myself a nonentity—can lay at the feet of a woman.'

The girl did not reply immediately; she appeared to think over intently what he had said to her, and while she did so she turned her white face and her charming serious eyes upon him. When at last she spoke it was in a very gentle, considerate tone. 'You are wrong in supposing that I am afraid of my brother. How can I be afraid of a person of whom I am so exceedingly fond?'

'Oh, the two things are quite consistent,' said Sir Rufus Chasemore, impatiently. 'And is it impossible that I should ever inspire you with a sentiment which you would consent to place in the balance with this intense fraternal affection?' He had no sooner spoken those somewhat sarcastic words than he broke out in a different tone: 'Oh Agatha, for pity's sake don't make difficulties where there are no difficulties!'

'I don't make them; I assure you they exist. It is difficult to explain them, but I can see them, I can feel them. Therefore we mustn't talk this way any more. Please, please don't,' the girl pursued, imploringly. 'Nothing is possible to-day. Some day or other very likely there will be changes. Then we shall meet; then we shall talk again.'

'I like the way you ask me to wait ten years. What do you mean by "changes"? Before heaven, I shall never change,' Sir Rufus declared.

Agatha Grice hesitated. 'Well, perhaps you will like us better.'

'Us? Whom do you mean by "us"? Are you coming back to that beastly question of one's feelings—real or supposed it doesn't matter—about your great and glorious country? Good God, it's too monstrous! One tells a girl one adores her and she replies that she doesn't care so long as one doesn't adore her compatriots. What do you want me to do to them? What do you want me to say? I will say anything in the English language, or in the American, that you like. I'll say that they're the greatest of the great and have every charm and virtue under heaven. I'll go down on my stomach before them and remain there for ever. I can't do more than that!'

Whether this extravagant profession had the effect of making Agatha Grice ashamed of having struck that note in regard

to her companion's international attitude, or whether her
nerves were simply upset by his vehemence, his insistence, is
more than I can say: what is certain is that her rejoinder to
this last speech was a sudden burst of tears. They fell for a
moment rapidly, soundlessly, but she was quicker still in
brushing them away. 'You may laugh at me or you may despise
me,' she said when she could speak, 'and I daresay my state
of mind is deplorably narrow. But I couldn't be happy with
you if you hated my country.'

'You would hate mine back and we should pass the liveliest,
jolliest days!' returned the Englishman, gratified, softened, enchanted by her tears. 'My dear girl, what is a woman's country? It's her house and her garden, her children and her social
world. You exaggerate immensely the difference which that
part of the business makes. I assure you that if you were to
marry me it would be the last thing you would find yourself
thinking of. However, to prove how little I hate your country
I am perfectly willing to go there and live with you.'

'Oh, Sir Rufus Chasemore!' murmured Agatha Grice, protestingly.

'You don't believe me?'

She believed him not a bit and yet to hear him make such
an offer was sweet to her, for it gave her a sense of the reality
of his passion. 'I shouldn't ask that—I shouldn't even like it,'
she said; and then he wished to know what she would like. 'I
should like you to let me go—not to press me, not to distress
me any more now. I shall think of everything—of course you
know that. But it will take me a long time. That's all I can
tell you now, but I think you ought to be content.' He was
obliged to say that he was content, and they resumed their
walk in the direction of the hotel. Shortly before they reached
it Agatha exclaimed with a certain irrelevance, 'You ought to
go there first; then you would know.'

'Then I should know what?'

'Whether you would like it.'

'Like your great country? Good Lord, what difference does
it make whether I like it or not?'

'No—that's just it—you don't care,' said Agatha; 'yet you
said to my brother that you wanted immensely to go.'

'So I do; I am ashamed not to have been; that's an immense

drawback to-day, in England, to a man in public life. Something has always stopped me off, tiresomely, from year to year.
Of course I shall go the very first moment I can take the time.'

'It's a pity you didn't go this year instead of coming down
here,' the girl observed, rather sententiously.

'I thank my stars I didn't!' he responded, in a very different
tone.

'Well, I should try to make you like it,' she went on. 'I
think it very probable I should succeed.'

'I think it very probable you could do with me exactly whatever you might attempt.'

'Oh, you hypocrite!' the girl exclaimed; and it was on this
that she separated from him and went into the house. It
soothed him to see her do so instead of rejoining her mother
and brother, whom he distinguished at a distance sitting on
the terrace. She had perceived them there as well, but she
would go straight to her room; she preferred the company of
her thoughts. It suited Sir Rufus Chasemore to believe that
those thoughts would plead for him and eventually win his
suit. He gave a melancholy, loverlike sigh, however, as he
walked toward Mrs. Grice and her son. He could not keep
away from them, though he was so interested in being and
appearing discreet. The girl had told him that her mother
liked him, and he desired both to stimulate and to reward that
inclination. Whatever he desired he desired with extreme def-
initeness and energy. He would go and sit down beside the
little old lady (with whom hitherto he had no very direct conversation), and talk to her and be kind to her and amuse her.
It must be added that he rather despaired of the success of
these arts as he saw Macarthy Grice, on becoming aware of
his approach, get up and walk away.

IV

'It sometimes seems to me as if he didn't marry on purpose
to make me feel badly.' That was the only fashion, as yet, in
which Lady Chasemore had given away her brother to her
husband. The words fell from her lips some five years after
Macarthy's visit to the lake of Como—two years after her
mother's death—a twelvemonth after her marriage. The same

idea came into her mind—a trifle whimsically perhaps, only
this time she forbore to express it—as she stood by her husband's side, on the deck of the steamer, half an hour before
they reached the wharf at New York. Six years had elapsed
between the scenes at Cadenabbia and their disembarkation
in that city. Agatha knew that Macarthy would be on the
wharf to meet them, and that he should be there alone was
natural enough. But she had a prevision of their return with
him—she also knew he expected that—to the house, so narrow but fortunately rather deep, in Thirty-seventh street, in
which such a happy trio had lived in the old days before this
unexpressed but none the less perceptible estrangement. As
her marriage had taken place in Europe (Sir Rufus coming to
her at Bologna, in the very midst of the Parliamentary session,
the moment he heard, by his sister, of her mother's death: this
was really the sign of devotion that had won her); as the ceremony of her nuptials, I say—a very simple one—had been
performed in Paris, so that her absence from her native land
had had no intermission, she had not seen the house since she
left it with her mother for that remedial pilgrimage in the
course of which poor Mrs. Grice, travelling up from Rome in
the spring, after her third winter there (two had been so far
from sufficing), was to succumb, from one day to the other,
to inflammation of the lungs. She saw it over again now, even
before she left the ship, and felt in advance all that it would
imply to find Macarthy living there as a bachelor, struggling
with New York servants, unaided and unrelieved by the sister
whose natural place might by many people have been thought
to be the care of his establishment, as her natural reward
would have been the honours of such a position. Lady Chasemore was prepared to feel pang upon pang when she should
perceive how much less comfortably he lived than he would
have lived if she had not quitted him. She knew that their
second cousins in Boston, whose sense of duty was so terrible
(even her poor mother, who never had a thought for herself,
used to try as much as possible to conceal her life from them),
considered that she had in a manner almost immoral deserted
him for the sake of an English title. When they went ashore
and drove home with Macarthy Agatha received exactly the
impression she had expected: her brother's life struck her as

bare, ungarnished, helpless, socially and domestically speaking. He had not the art of keeping house, naturally, and in New York, unless one were a good deal richer than he, it was very difficult to do that sort of thing by deputy. But Lady Chasemore made no further allusion to the idea that he remained single out of perversity. The situation was too serious for that or for any other flippant speech.

It was a delicate matter for the brothers-in-law to spend two or three weeks together; not however because when the moment for her own real decision came Macarthy had protested in vivid words against her marriage. By the time he arrived from America after his mother's death the Englishman was in possession of the field and it was too late to save her. He had had the opportunity to show her kindness for which her situation made her extremely grateful—he had indeed rendered her services which Macarthy himself, though he knew they were the result of an interested purpose, could not but appreciate. When her brother met her in Paris he saw that she was already lost to him: she had ceased to struggle, she had accepted the fate of a Briton's bride. It appeared that she was much in love with her Briton—that was necessarily the end of it. Macarthy offered no opposition, and she would have liked it better if he had, as it would have given her a chance to put him in the wrong a little more than, formally at least, she had been able to do. He knew that she knew what he thought and how he felt, and there was no need of saying any more about it. No doubt he would not have accepted a sacrifice from her even if she had been capable of making it (there were moments when it seemed to her that even at the last, if he had appealed to her directly and with tenderness, she would have renounced); but it was none the less clear to her that he was deeply disappointed at her having found it in her heart to separate herself so utterly. And there was something in his whole attitude which seemed to say that it was not only from him that she separated herself, but from all her fellow-countrymen besides and from everything that was best and finest in American life. He regarded her marriage as an abjuration, an apostasy, a kind of moral treachery. It was of no use to say to him that she was doing nothing original or extraordinary, to ask him if he did not know that in England, at the point things had come to, American wives were as thick as blackberries, so that if she were doing wrong she was doing wrong with—well, almost the majority: for he had an answer to such cheap arguments, an answer according to which it appeared that the American girls who had done what she was about to do were notoriously poor specimens, the most frivolous and feather-headed young persons in the country. They had no conception of the great meaning of American institutions, no appreciation of their birthright, and they were doubtless very worthy recruits to a debauched and stultified aristocracy. The pity of Agatha's desertion was that *she* had been meant for better things, she had appreciated her birthright, or if she had not it had not been the fault of a brother who had taken so much pains to form her mind and character. The sentiment of her nationality had been cultivated in her; it was not a mere brute instinct or customary prejudice—it was a responsibility, a faith, a religion. She was not a poor specimen but a remarkably fine one; she was intelligent, she was clever, she was sensitive, she could understand difficult things and feel great ones.

Of course in those days of trouble in Paris, when it was arranged that she should be married immediately (as if there had really been an engagement to Sir Rufus from the night before their flight from Cadenabbia), of course she had had a certain amount of talk with Macarthy about the matter, and at such moments she had almost wished to drive him to protest articulately, so that she might as explicitly reassure him, endeavour to bring him round. But he had never said to her personally what he had said to her mother at Cadenabbia— what her mother, frightened and distressed, had immediately repeated to her. The most he said was that he hoped she was conscious of all the perfectly different and opposed things she and her husband would represent when they should find themselves face to face. He hoped she had measured in advance the strain that might arise from the fact that in so many ways her good would be his evil, her white his black and *vice versâ*—the fact in a word that by birth, tradition, convictions, she was the product of a democratic society, while the very breath of Sir Rufus's nostrils was the denial of human equality. She had replied, 'Oh yes, I have thought of everything;' but in reality she had not thought that she was in any very aggressive manner a democrat or even that she had a representative function. She had not thought that Macarthy in his innermost soul was a democrat either; and she had even wondered what would happen if in regard to some of those levelling theories he had suddenly been taken at his word. She knew however that nothing would have made him more angry than to hint that anything could happen which would find him unprepared, and she was ashamed to repudiate the opinions, the general character her brother attributed to her, to fall below the high standard he had set up for her. She had moreover no wish to do so. She was well aware that there were many things in English life that she should not like, and she was never a more passionate American than the day she married Sir Rufus Chasemore.

To what extent she remained one an observer of the deportment of this young lady would at first have had considerable difficulty in judging. The question of the respective merits of the institutions of the two countries came up very little in her life. Her husband had other things to think of than the great republic beyond the sea, and her horizon, social and political, had practically the same large but fixed line as his. Sir Rufus was immersed in politics and in administrative questions; but these things belonged wholly to the domestic field; they were embodied in big blue-books with terrible dry titles (Agatha had tried conscientiously to acquaint herself with the contents of some of them), which piled themselves up on the table of his library. The conservatives had come into power just after his marriage, and he had held honourable though not supereminent office. His duties had nothing to do with foreign relations; they were altogether of an economical and statistical kind. He performed them in a manner which showed perhaps that he was conscious of some justice in the reproach usually addressed to the Tories—the taunt that they always came to grief in the department of industry and finance. His wife was sufficiently in his confidence to know how much he had it at heart to prove that a conservative administration could be strong in ciphering. He never spoke to her of her own country—they had so many other things to talk about—but if there was nothing in his behaviour to betray the assumption that she had given it up, so on the other hand there was nothing to show that he doubted of her having done so. What he had said about a woman's country being her husband and children, her house and garden and visiting list, was very considerably verified; for it was certain that her ladyship's new career gave her, though she had no children, plenty of occupation. Even if it had not however she would have found a good deal of work to her hand in loving her husband, which she continued to do with the most com-mendable zeal. He seemed to her a very magnificent person, bullying her not half so much as she expected. There were times when it even occurred to her that he really did not bully her enough, for she had always had an idea that it would be agreeable to be subjected to this probation by some one she should be very fond of.

After they had been married a year he became a permanent official, in succession to a gentleman who was made a peer on his retirement from the post to which Sir Rufus was ap-pointed. This gave Lady Chasemore an opportunity to reflect that she might some day be a peeress, it being reasonable to suppose that the same reward would be meted out to her husband on the day on which, in the fulness of time and of credit, he also should retire. She was obliged to admit to her-self that the reflection was unattended with any sense of hor-ror; it exhilarated her indeed to the point of making her smile at the contingency of Macarthy's finding himself the brother of a member of the aristocracy. As a permanent official her husband was supposed to have no active political opinions; but she could not flatter herself that she perceived any dimi-nution of his conservative zeal. Even if she had done so it would have made little difference, for it had not taken her long to discover that she had married into a tremendous Tory 'set'—a set in which people took for granted she had feelings that she was not prepared to publish on the housetops. It was scarcely worth while however to explain at length that she had not been brought up in that way, partly because the people would not have understood and partly because really after all they did not care. How little it was possible in general to care her career in England helped her in due time to discover. The people who cared least appeared to be those who were most convinced that everything in the national life was going to the dogs. Lady Chasemore was not struck with this tendency herself; but if she had been the belief would have worried her more than it seemed to worry her friends. She liked most of them extremely and thought them very kind, very easy to live with; but she liked London much better than the country, rejoiced much when her husband's new post added to the number of months he would have annually to spend there (they ended by being there as much as any one), and had grave doubts as to whether she would have been able to 'stand' it if her lot had been cast among those members of her new circle who lived mainly on their acres.

All the same, though what she had to bear she bore very easily, she indulged in a good deal of private meditation on some of the things that failed to catch her sympathy. She did not always mention them to her husband, but she always intended to mention them. She desired he should not think that she swallowed his country whole, that she was stupidly undiscriminating. Of course he knew that she was not stupid and of course also he knew that she could not fail to be painfully impressed by the misery and brutality of the British populace. She had never anywhere else seen anything like that. Of course, furthermore, she knew that Sir Rufus had given and would give in the future a great deal of thought to legislative measures directed to elevating gradually the condition of the lower orders. It came over Lady Chasemore at times that it would be well if some of these measures might arrive at maturity with as little delay as possible.

The night before she quitted England with her husband they slept at an hotel at Liverpool, in order to embark early on the morrow. Sir Rufus went out to attend to some business and, the evening being very close, she sat at the window of their sitting-room and looked out on a kind of square which stretched in front of the hotel. The night was muggy, the window was open and she was held there by a horrible fascination. Dusky forms of vice and wretchedness moved about in the stuffy darkness, visions of grimy, half-naked, whining beggary hovered before her, curses and the sound of blows came to her ears; there were young girls, frousy and violent, who evidently were drunk, as every one seemed to be, more or less, which was little wonder, as four public-houses flared into the impure night, visible from where Lady Chasemore sat, and they appeared to be gorged with customers, half of whom were women. The impression came back to her that the horrible place had made upon her and upon her mother when they landed in England years before, and as she turned from the window she liked to think that she was going to a country where, at any rate, there would be less of that sort of thing. When her husband came in he said it was of course a beastly place but much better than it used to be—which she was glad to hear. She made some allusion to the confidence they might have that they should be treated to no such scenes as that in *her* country: whereupon he remonstrated, jocosely expressing a hope that they should not be deprived of a glimpse of the celebrated American drinks and bar-room fights.

It must be added that in New York he made of his brother-in-law no inquiry about these phenomena—a reserve, a magnanimity keenly appreciated by his wife. She appreciated altogether the manner in which he conducted himself during their visit to the United States and felt that if she had not already known that she had married a perfect gentleman the fact would now have been revealed to her. For she had to make up her mind to this, that after all (it was vain to shut one's eyes to it) Sir Rufus personally did not like the United States: he did not like them yet he made an immense effort to behave as if he did. She was grateful to him for that; it assuaged her nervousness (she was afraid there might be 'scenes' if he should break out with some of his displeasures); so grateful that she almost forgot to be disappointed at the failure of her own original intent, to be distressed at seeing or rather at guessing (for he was reserved about it even to her), that a nearer view of American institutions had not had the effect which she once promised herself a nearer view should have. She had married him partly to bring him over to an admiration of her country (she had never told any one this, for she was too proud to make the confidence to an English person and if she had made it to an American the answer would have been so prompt, 'What on earth does it

signify what he thinks of it?' no one, of course, being obliged
to understand that it might signify to *her*); she had united
herself to Sir Rufus in this missionary spirit and now not only
did her proselyte prove unamenable but the vanity of her enterprise became a fact of secondary importance. She wondered
a little that she did not suffer more from it, and this is partly
why she rejoiced that her husband kept most of his observations to himself: it gave her a pretext for not being ashamed.
She had flattered herself before that in general he had the
manners of a diplomatist (she did not suspect that this was
not the opinion of all his contemporaries), and his behaviour
during the first few weeks at least of their stay in the western
world struck her as a triumph of diplomacy. She had really
passed from caring whether he disliked American manners to
caring primarily whether he showed he disliked them—a transition which on her own side she was very sensible it was
important to conceal from Macarthy. To love a man who
could feel no tenderness for the order of things which had
encompassed her early years and had been intimately mixed
with her growth, which was a part of the conscience, the piety
of many who had been most dear to her and whose memory
would be dear to her always—that was an irregularity which
was after all shut up in her own breast, where she could trust
her dignity to get some way or other the upper hand of it.
But to be pointed at as having such a problem as that on one's
back was quite another affair; it was a kind of exposure of
one's sanctities, a surrender of private judgment. Lady Chasemore had by this time known her husband long enough to
enter into the logic of his preferences; if he disliked or disapproved what he saw in America his reasons for doing so had
ceased to be a mystery. They were the very elements of his
character, the joints and vertebration of his general creed. All
the while she was absent from England with him (it was not
very long, their whole tour, including the two voyages, being
included in ten weeks), she knew more or less the impression
that things would have made upon him; she knew that both
in the generals and in the particulars American life would have
gone against his grain, contradicted his traditions, violated his
taste.

V

All the same he was determined to see it thoroughly, and this is doubtless one of the reasons why after the first few days she cherished the hope that they should be able to get off at the end without any collision with Macarthy. Of course it was to be taken into account that Macarthy's own demeanour was much more that of a man of the world than she had ventured to hope. He appeared for the time almost to have smothered his national consciousness, which had always been so acute, and to have accepted his sister's perfidious alliance. She could see that he was delighted that she should be near him again—so delighted that he neglected to look for the signs of corruption in her or to manifest any suspicion that in fact, now that she was immersed in them again, she regarded her old associations with changed eyes. So, also, if she had not already been aware of how much Macarthy was a gentleman she would have seen it from the way he rose to the occasion. Accordingly they were all superior people and all was for the best in Lady Chasemore's simple creed. Her brother asked her no questions whatever about her life in England, but his letters had already enlightened her as to his determination to avoid that topic. They had hitherto not contained a single inquiry on the subject of her occupations and pursuits, and if she had been domiciled in the moon he could not have indulged in less reference to public or private events in the British islands. It was a tacit form of disapprobation of her being connected with that impertinent corner of the globe; but it had never prevented her from giving him the fullest information on everything he never asked about. He never took up her allusions, and when she poured forth information to him now in regard to matters concerning her life in her new home (on these points she was wilfully copious and appealing), he listened with a sort of exaggerated dumb deference, as if she were reciting a lesson and he must sit quiet till she should come to the end. Usually when she stopped he simply sighed, then directed the conversation to something as different as possible. It evidently pleased him however to see that she enjoyed her native air and her temporary reunion with some of her old familiars. This was a graceful inconsistency on his part: it showed that he had not completely given her up. Perhaps he thought Sir Rufus would die and that in this case she would come back and live in New York. She was careful not to tell him that such a calculation was baseless, that with or without Sir Rufus she should never be able to settle in her native city as Lady Chasemore. He was scrupulously polite to Sir Rufus, and this personage asked Agatha why he never by any chance addressed him save by his title. She could see what her husband meant, but even in the privacy of the conjugal chamber she was loyal enough to Macarthy not to reply, 'Oh, it's a mercy he doesn't say simply "Sir!"'

The English visitor was prodigiously active; he desired to leave nothing unexplored, unattempted; his purpose was to inspect institutions, to collect statistics, to talk with the principal people, to see the workings of the political machine, and Macarthy acquitted himself scrupulously, even zealously, in the way of giving him introductions and facilities. Lady Chasemore reflected with pleasure that it was in her brother's power to do the honours of his native land very completely. She suspected indeed that as he did not like her husband (he *couldn't* like him, in spite of Sir Rufus's now comporting himself so sweetly), it was a relief to him to pass him on to others—to work him off, as it were, into penitentiaries and chambers of commerce. Sir Rufus's frequent expeditions to these establishments and long interviews with local worthies of every kind kept him constantly out of the house and removed him from contact with his host, so that as Macarthy was extremely busy with his own profession (Sir Rufus was greatly struck with the way he worked; he had never seen a gentleman work so hard, without any shooting or hunting or fishing), it may be said, though it sounds odd, that the two men met very little directly—met scarcely more than in the evening or in other words always in company. During the twenty days the Chasemores spent together in New York they either dined out or were members of a party given at home by Macarthy, and on these occasions Sir Rufus found plenty to talk about with his new acquaintance. His wife flattered herself he was liked, he was so hilarious and so easy. He had a very appreciative manner, but she really wished sometimes that he might have subdued his hilarity a little; there were moments when perhaps it looked as if he took everything in the United States as if it were more than all else amusing. She knew exactly how it must privately affect Macarthy, this implication that it was merely a comical country; but after all it was not very easy to say how Macarthy would have preferred that a stranger, or that Sir Rufus in particular, should take the great republic. A cheerful view, yet untinged by the sense of drollery—that would have been the right thing if it could have been arrived at. At all events (and this was something gained), if Sir Rufus was in his heart a pessimist in regard to things he did not like he was not superficially sardonic. And then he asked questions by the million; and what was curiosity but an homage?

It will be inferred, and most correctly, that Macarthy Grice was not personally in any degree for his brother-in-law the showman of the exhibition. He caused him to be conducted, but he did not conduct him. He listened to his reports of what he had seen (it was at breakfast mainly that these fresh intimations dropped from Sir Rufus's lips), with very much the same cold patience (as if he were civilly forcing his attention) with which he listened to Agatha's persistent anecdotes of things that had happened to her in England. Of course with Sir Rufus there could be no question of persistence; he cared too little whether Macarthy cared or not and he did not stick to this everlasting subject of American institutions either to entertain him or to entertain himself—all he wanted was to lead on to further researches and discoveries. Macarthy always met him with the same response, 'Oh, So-and-So is the man to tell you all about that. If you wish I will give you a letter to him.' Sir Rufus always wished and certainly Macarthy wrote a prodigious number of letters. The inquiries and conclusions of his visitor (so far as Sir Rufus indulged in the latter) all bore on special points; he was careful to commit himself to no crude generalisations. He had to remember that he had still the rest of the country to see, and after a little discussion (which was confined to Lady Chasemore and her husband) it was decided that he should see it without his wife, who would await his return among her friends in New York. This arrangement was much to her taste, but it gives again the measure of the degree to which she had renounced her early dream of interpreting the western world to Sir Rufus. If she was not to be at his side at the moment, on the spot, of course she could not interpret—he would get a tremendous start of her. In short by staying quietly with Macarthy during his absence she almost gave up the great advantage she had hitherto had of knowing more about America than her husband could. She liked however to feel that she was making a sacrifice—making one indeed both to Sir Rufus and to her brother. The idea of giving up something for Macarthy (she only wished it had been something more) did her great good—sweetened the period of her husband's absence.

The whole season had been splendid, but at this moment the golden days of the Indian summer descended upon the shining city and steeped it in a kind of fragrant haze. For two or three weeks New York seemed to Lady Chasemore poetical; the marble buildings looked yellow in the sleeping sunshine and her native land exhibited for the occasion an atmosphere. Vague memories came back to her of her younger years, of things that had to do somehow with the blurred brightness of the late autumn in the country. She walked about, she walked irresponsibly for hours; she did not care, as she had to care in London. She met friends in the streets and turned and walked with them; and pleasures as simple as this acquired an exaggerated charm for her. She liked walking and as an American girl had indulged the taste freely; but in London she had no time but to drive—besides which there were other tiresome considerations. Macarthy came home from his office earlier and she went to meet him in Washington Square and walked up the Fifth Avenue with him in the rich afternoon. It was many years since she had been in New York and she found herself taking a kind of relapsing interest in changes and improvements. There were houses she used to know, where friends had lived in the old days and where they lived no more (no one in New York seemed to her to live where they used to live), which reminded her of incidents she had long ago forgotten, incidents that it pleased and touched her now to recall. Macarthy became very easy and sociable; he even asked her a few questions about her arrangements and habits in England and struck her (though she had never been particularly aware of it before) as having a great deal of the

American humour. On one occasion he stayed away from work altogether and took her up the Hudson, on the steamer, to West Point—an excursion in which she found a peculiar charm. Every day she lunched intimately with a dozen ladies, at the house of one or other of them.

In due time Sir Rufus returned from Canada, the Mississippi, the Rocky Mountains and California; he had achieved marvels in the way of traversing distances and seeing manners and men with rapidity and facility. Everything had been settled in regard to their sailing for England almost directly after his return; there were only to be two more days in New York, then a rush to Boston, followed by another rush to Philadelphia and Washington. Macarthy made no inquiry whatever of his brother-in-law touching his impression of the great West; he neglected even to ask him if he had been favourably impressed with Canada. There would not have been much opportunity however, for Sir Rufus on his side was extremely occupied with the last things he had to do. He had not even time as yet to impart his impressions to his wife, and she forbore to interrogate him, feeling that the voyage close at hand would afford abundant leisure for the history of his adventures. For the moment almost the only light that he threw upon them was by saying to Agatha (not before Macarthy) that it was a pleasure to him to see a handsome woman again, as he had not had that satisfaction in the course of his travels. Lady Chasemore wondered, exclaimed, protested, eliciting from him the declaration that to his sense, and in the interior at least, the beauty of the women was, like a great many other things, a gigantic American fraud. Sir Rufus had looked for it in vain—he went so far as to say that he had, in the course of extensive wanderings about the world, seen no female type on the whole less to his taste than that of the ladies in whose society, in hundreds (there was no paucity of specimens), in the long, hot, heaving trains, he had traversed a large part of the American continent. His wife inquired whether by chance he preferred the young persons they had (or at least she had) observed at Liverpool the night before their departure; to which he replied that they were no doubt sad creatures, but that the looks of a woman mattered only so long as one lived with her, and he did not live, and never should live, with the daughters of that grimy seaport. With the women in the American cars he had been living—oh, tremendously! and they were deucedly plain. Thereupon Lady Chasemore wished to know whether he did not think Mrs. Eugene had beauty, and Mrs. Ripley, and her sister Mrs. Redwood, and Mrs. Long, and several other ornaments of the society in which they had mingled during their stay in New York. 'Mrs. Eugene is Mrs. Eugene and Mrs. Redwood is Mrs. Redwood,' Sir Rufus retorted; 'but the women in the cars weren't either, and all the women I saw were like the women in the cars.'—'Well, there may be something in the cars,' said Lady Chasemore, pensively; and she mentioned that it was very odd that during her husband's absence, as she roamed about New York, she should have made precisely the opposite reflection and been struck with the number of pretty faces. 'Oh, pretty faces, pretty faces, I daresay!' But Sir Rufus had no time to develop this vague rejoinder.

When they came back from Washington to sail Agatha told her brother that he was going to write a book about America: it was for this he had made so many inquiries and taken so many notes. She had not known it before; it was only while they were in Washington that he told her he had made up his mind to it. Something he saw or heard in Washington appeared to have brought this resolution to a point. Lady Chasemore privately thought it rather a formidable fact; her husband had startled her a good deal in announcing his intention. She had said, 'Of course it will be friendly—you'll say nice things?' And he had replied, 'My poor child, they will abuse me like a pickpocket.' This had scarcely been reassuring, so that she had had it at heart to probe the question further, in the train, after they left Washington. But as it happened, in the train, all the way, Sir Rufus was engaged in conversation with a Democratic Congressman whom he had picked up she did not know how—very certainly he had not met him at any respectable house in Washington. They sat in front of her in the car, with their heads almost touching, and although she was a better American than her husband she should not have liked hers to be so close to that of the Democratic Congressman. Now of course she knew that Sir Rufus was taking in material for his book. This idea made her uncomfortable and she would have liked immensely to separate him from his companion—she scarcely knew why, after all, except that she could not believe the Representative represented anything very nice. She promised herself to ascertain thoroughly, after they should be comfortably settled in the ship, the animus with which the book was to be written. She was a very good sailor and she liked to talk at sea; there her husband would not be able to escape from her, and she foresaw the manner in which she should catechise him. It exercised her greatly in advance and she was more agitated than she could easily have expressed by the whole question of the book. Meanwhile, however, she was careful not to show her agitation to Macarthy. She referred to her husband's project as casually as possible, and the reason she referred to it was that this seemed more loyal—more loyal to Macarthy. If the book, when written, should attract attention by the severity of its criticism (and that by many qualities it would attract attention of the widest character Lady Chasemore could not doubt), she should feel more easy not to have had the air of concealing from her brother that such a work was in preparation, which would also be the air of having a bad conscience about it. It was to prove, both to herself and Macarthy, that she had a good conscience that she told him of Sir Rufus's design. The habit of detachment from matters connected with his brother-in-law's activity was strong in him; nevertheless he was not able to repress some sign of emotion—he flushed very perceptibly. Quickly, however, he recovered his appearance of considering that the circumstance was one in which he could not hope to interest himself much; though the next moment he observed, with a certain inconsequence, 'I am rather sorry to hear it.'

'Why are you sorry?' asked Agatha. She was surprised and indeed gratified that he should commit himself even so far as to express regret. What she had supposed he would say, if he should say anything, was that he was obliged to her for the information, but that if it was given him with any expectation that he might be induced to read the book he must really let her know that such an expectation was extremely vain. He could have no more affinity with Sir Rufus's printed ideas than with his spoken ones.

'Well, it will be rather disagreeable for you,' he said, in answer to her question. 'Unless indeed you don't care what he says.'

'But I do care. The book will be sure to be very able. Do you mean if it should be severe—that would be disagreeable for me? Very certainly it would; it would put me in a false, in a ridiculous position, and I don't see how I should bear it,' Lady Chasemore went on, feeling that her candour was generous and wishing it to be. 'But I shan't allow it to be severe. To prevent that, if it's necessary, I will write every word of it myself.'

She laughed as she took this vow, but there was nothing in Macarthy's face to show that *he* could lend himself to a mirthful treatment of the question. 'I think an Englishman had better look at home,' he said, 'and if he does so I don't easily see how the occupation should leave him any leisure or any assurance for reading lectures to other nations. The self-complacency of your husband's countrymen is colossal, imperturbable. Therefore, with the tight place they find themselves in to-day and with the judgment of the rest of the world upon them being what it is, it's grotesque to see them still sitting in their old judgment-seat and pronouncing upon the shortcomings of people who are full of the life that has so long since left *them*.' Macarthy Grice spoke slowly, mildly, with a certain dryness, as if he were delivering himself once for all and would not return to the subject. The quietness of his manner made the words solemn for his sister, and she stared at him a moment, wondering, as if they pointed to strange things which she had hitherto but imperfectly apprehended.

'The judgment of the rest of the world—what is that?'

'Why, that they are simply finished; that they don't count.'

'Oh, a nation must count which produces such men as my husband,' Agatha rejoined, with another laugh. Macarthy was on the point of retorting that it counted as the laughing-stock of the world (that of course was something), but he checked himself and she moreover checked him by going on: 'Why Macarthy, you ought to come out with a book yourself about the English. You would steal my husband's thunder.'

'Nothing would induce me to do anything of the sort; I pity them too much.'

'You pity them?' Lady Chasemore exclaimed. 'It would amuse my husband to hear that.'

'Very likely, and it would be exactly a proof of what is so pitiable—the contrast between their gross pretensions and the real facts of their condition. They have pressing upon them at once every problem, every source of weakness, every danger that can threaten the life of a people, and they have nothing to meet the situation with but their classic stupidity.'

'Well, that has been useful to them before,' said Lady Chasemore, smiling. Her smile was a little forced and she coloured as her brother had done when she first spoke to him. She found it impossible not to be impressed by what he said and yet she was vexed that she was, because this was far from her desire.

He looked at her as if he saw some warning in her face and continued: 'Excuse my going so far. In this last month that we have spent together so happily for me I had almost forgotten that you are one of them.'

Lady Chasemore said nothing—she did not deny that she was one of them. If her husband's country was denounced —after all he had not written his book yet—she felt as if such a denial would be a repudiation of one of the responsibilities she had taken in marrying him.

VI

The postman was at the door in Grosvenor Crescent when she came back from her drive; the servant took the letters from his hand as she passed into the house. In the hall she stopped to see which of the letters were for her; the butler gave her two and retained those that were for Sir Rufus. She asked him what orders Sir Rufus had given about his letters and he replied that they were to be forwarded up to the following night. This applied only to letters, not to parcels, pamphlets and books. 'But would he wish this to go, my lady?' the man asked, holding up a small packet; he added that it appeared to be a kind of document. She took it from him: her eye had caught a name printed on the wrapper and though she made no great profession of literature she recognised the name as that of a distinguished publisher and the packet as a roll of proof-sheets. She turned it up and down while the servant waited; it had quite a different look from the bundles of printed official papers which the postman was perpetually leaving and which, when she scanned the array on the hall-table in her own interest, she identified even at a distance. They were certainly the sheets, at least the first, of her husband's book—those of which he had said to her on the steamer, on the way back from New York a year before, 'My dear child, when I tell you that you shall see them—every page of them—that you shall have complete control of them!' Since she was to have complete control of them she began with telling the butler not to forward them—to lay them on the hall-table. She went upstairs to dress—she was dining out in her husband's absence—and when she came down to re-enter her carriage she saw the packet lying where it had been placed. So many months had passed that she had ended by forgetting that the book was on the stocks; nothing had happened to remind her of it. She had believed indeed that it was not on the stocks and even that the project would die a natural death. Sir Rufus would have no time to carry it out—he had returned from America to find himself more than ever immersed in official work—and if he did not put his hand to it within two or three years at the very most he would never do so at all, for he would have lost the freshness of his impressions, on which the success of the whole thing would depend. He had his notes of course, but none the less a delay would be fatal to the production of the volume (it was to be only a volume and not a big one), inasmuch as by the time it should be published it would have to encounter the objection that everything changed in America in two or three years and no one wanted to know anything about a dead past.

Such had been the reflections with which Lady Chasemore consoled herself for the results of those inquiries she had promised herself, in New York, to make when once she should be ensconced in a sea-chair by her husband's side and which she had in fact made to her no small discomposure. Meanwhile apparently he had stolen a march upon her, he had put his hand to *The Modern Warning* (that was to be the title, as she had learned on the ship), he had worked at it in his odd hours, he had sent it to the printers and here were the first-fruits of it. Had he had a bad conscience about it—was that the reason he had been so quiet? She did not believe much in his bad conscience, for he had been tremendously, formidably explicit when they talked the matter over; had let her know as fully as possible what he intended to do. Then it was that he relieved himself, that in the long, unoccupied hours of their fine voyage (he was in wonderful 'form' at sea) he took her into the confidence of his real impressions—made her understand how things had struck him in the United States. They had not struck him well; oh no, they had not struck him well at all! But at least he had prepared her and therefore since then he had nothing to hide. It was doubtless an accident that he appeared to have kept his work away from her, for sometimes, in other cases, he had paid her intelligence the compliment (was it not for that in part he had married her?) of supposing that she could enter into it. It was probable that in this case he had wanted first to see for himself how his chapters would look in print. Very likely even he had not written the whole book, nor even half of it; he had only written the opening pages and had them 'set up': she remembered to have heard him speak of this as a very convenient system. It would be very convenient for her as well and she should also be much interested in seeing how they looked. On the table, in their neat little packet, they seemed half to solicit her, half to warn her off.

They were still there of course when she came back from her dinner, and this time she took possession of them. She carried them upstairs and in her dressing-room, when she had been left alone in her wrapper, she sat down with them under the lamp. The packet lay in her lap a long time, however, before she decided to detach the envelope. Her hesitation came not from her feeling in any degree that this roll of printed sheets had the sanctity of a letter, a seal that she might not discreetly break, but from an insurmountable nervousness as to what she might find within. She sat there for an hour, with her head resting on the back of her chair and her eyes closed; but she had not fallen asleep—Lady Chasemore was very wide-awake indeed. She was living for the moment in a kind of concentration of memory, thinking over everything that had fallen from her husband's lips after he began, as I

have said, to relieve himself. It turned out that the opinion he
had formed of the order of society in the United States was
even less favourable than she had had reason to fear. There
were not many things it would have occurred to him to commend, and the few exceptions related to the matters that were
not most characteristic of the country—not idiosyncrasies of
American life. The idiosyncrasies he had held to be one and
all detestable. The whole spectacle was a vivid warning, a con-
summate illustration of the horrors of democracy. The only
thing that had saved the misbegotten republic as yet was its
margin, its geographical vastness; but that was now dis-
counted and exhausted. For the rest every democratic vice was
in the ascendant and could be studied there *sur le vif*; he could
not be too thankful that he had not delayed longer to go over
and master the subject. He had come back with a head full of
lessons and a heart fired with the resolve to enforce them
upon his own people, who, as Agatha knew, had begun to
move in the same lamentable direction. As she listened to him
she perceived the mistake she had made in not going to the
West with him, for it was from that part of the country that
he had drawn his most formidable anecdotes and examples.
Of these he produced a terrific array; he spoke by book, he
overflowed with facts and figures, and his wife felt herself sub-
merged by the deep, bitter waters. She even felt what a pity
it was that she had not dragged him away from that vulgar
little legislator whom he had stuck to so in the train, coming
from Washington; yet it did not matter—a little more or a
little less—the whole affair had rubbed him so the wrong way,
exasperated his taste, confounded his traditions. He proved to
have disliked quite unspeakably things that she supposed he
liked, to have suffered acutely on occasions when she thought
he was really pleased. It would appear that there had been no
occasion, except once sitting at dinner between Mrs. Redwood and Mrs. Eugene, when he was really pleased. Even his
long chat with the Pennsylvania representative had made him
almost ill at the time. His wife could be none the less struck
with the ability which had enabled him to absorb so much
knowledge in so short a time; he had not only gobbled up
facts, he had arranged them in a magnificent order, and she
was proud of his being so clever even when he made her bleed

by the way he talked. He had had no intention whatever of this, and he was as much surprised as touched when she broke out into a passionate appeal to him not to publish such horrible misrepresentations. She defended her country with exaltation, and so far as was possible in the face of his own flood of statistics, of anecdotes of 'lobbying,' of the corruption of public life, for which she was unprepared, endeavouring to gainsay him in the particulars as well as in the generals, she maintained that he had seen everything wrong, seen it through the distortion of prejudice, of a hostile temperament, in the light—or rather in the darkness—of wishing to find weapons to worry the opposite party in England. Of course America had its faults, but on the whole it was a much finer country than any other, finer even than his clumsy, congested old England, where there was plenty to do to sweep the house clean, if he would give a little more of his time to that. Scandals for scandals she had heard more since she came to England than all the years she had lived at home. She forbore to quote Macarthy to him (she had reasons for not doing so), but something of the spirit of Macarthy flamed up in her as she spoke.

Sir Rufus smiled at her vehemence; he took it in perfectly good part, though it evidently left him not a little astonished. He had forgotten that America was hers—that she had any allegiance but the allegiance of her marriage. He had made her his own and, being the intense Englishman that he was, it had never occurred to him to doubt that she now partook of his quality in the same degree as himself. He had assimilated her, as it were, completely, and he had assumed that she had also assimilated him and his country with him—a process which would have for its consequence that the other country, the ugly, vulgar, importunate one, would be, as he mentally phrased it to himself, 'shunted.' That it had not been was the proof of rather a morbid sensibility, which tenderness and time would still assuage. Sir Rufus was tender, he reassured his wife on the spot, in the first place by telling her that she knew nothing whatever about the United States (it was astonishing how little many of the people in the country itself knew about them), and in the second by promising her that he would not print a word to which her approval should not be expressly given. She should countersign every page before it went to press, and none should leave the house without her *visé*. She wished to know if he possibly could have forgotten—so strange would it be—that she had told him long ago, at Cadenabbia, how horrible it would be to her to find herself married to a man harbouring evil thoughts of her fatherland. He remembered this declaration perfectly and others that had followed it, but was prepared to ask if she on her side recollected giving him notice that she should convert him into an admirer of transatlantic peculiarities. She had had an excellent opportunity, but she had not carried out her plan. He had been passive in her hands, she could have done what she liked with him (had not he offered, that night by the lake of Como, to throw up his career and go and live with her in some beastly American town? and he had really meant it—upon his honour he had!), so that if the conversion had not come off whose fault was it but hers? She had not gone to work with any sort of earnestness. At all events now it was too late; he had seen for himself—the impression was made. Two points were vivid beyond the others in Lady Chasemore's evocation of the scene on the ship; one was her husband's insistence on the fact that he had not the smallest animosity to the American people, but had only his own English brothers in view, wished only to protect and save them, to point a certain moral as it never had been pointed before; the other was his pledge that nothing should be made public without her assent.

As at last she broke the envelope of the packet in her lap she wondered how much she should find to assent to. More perhaps than a third person judging the case would have expected; for after what had passed between them Sir Rufus must have taken great pains to tone down his opinions—or at least the expression of them.

VII

He came back to Grosvenor Place the next evening very late and on asking for his wife was told that she was in her apartments. He was furthermore informed that she was to have dined out but had given it up, countermanding the carriage at the last moment and despatching a note instead. On Sir

Rufus's asking if she were ill it was added that she had seemed
not quite right and had not left the house since the day before.
A minute later he found her in her own sitting-room, where
she appeared to have been walking up and down. She stopped
when he entered and stood there looking at him; she was in
her dressing-gown, very pale, and she received him without a
smile. He went up to her, kissed her, saw something strange
in her eyes and asked with eagerness if she had been suffering.
'Yes, yes,' she said, 'but I have not been ill,' and the next
moment flung herself upon his neck and buried her face there,
sobbing yet at the same time stifling her sobs. Inarticulate
words were mingled with them and it was not till after a moment he understood that she was saying, 'How could you?
ah, how *could* you?' He failed to understand her allusion, and
while he was still in the dark she recovered herself and broke
away from him. She went quickly to a drawer and possessed
herself of a parcel of papers which she held out to him, this
time without meeting his eyes. 'Please take them away—take
them away for ever. It's your book—the things from the
printers. I saw them on the table—I guessed what they were—
I opened them to see. I read them—I read them. Please take
them away.'

He had by this time become aware that even though she
had flung herself upon his breast his wife was animated by a
spirit of the deepest reproach, an exquisite sense of injury.
When he first saw the papers he failed to recognise his book:
it had not been in his mind. He took them from her with an
exclamation of wonder, accompanied by a laugh which was
meant in kindness, and turned them over, glancing at page
after page. Disconcerted as he was at the condition in which
Agatha presented herself he was still accessible to that agreeable titillation which a man feels on seeing his prose 'set up.'
Sir Rufus had been quoted and reported by the newspapers
and had put into circulation several little pamphlets, but this
was his first contribution to the regular literature of his country, and his publishers had given him a very handsome page.
Its striking beauty held him a moment; then his eyes passed
back to his wife, who with her grand, cold, wounded air was
also very handsome. 'My dear girl, do you think me an awful
brute? have I made you ill?' he asked. He declared that he

had no idea he had gone so far as to shock her—he had left out such a lot; he had tried to keep the sting out of everything; he had made it all butter and honey. But he begged her not to get into a state; he would go over the whole thing with her if she liked—make any changes she should require. It would spoil the book, but he would rather do that than spoil her perfect temper. It was in a highly jocular manner that he made this allusion to her temper, and it was impressed upon her that he was not too much discomposed by her discomposure to be able to joke. She took notice of two things: the first of which was that he had a perfectly good conscience and that no accusing eye that might have been turned upon him would have made him change colour. He had no sense that he had broken faith with her, and he really thought his horrible book was very mild. He spoke the simple truth in saying that for her sake he had endeavoured to qualify his strictures, and strange as it might appear he honestly believed he had succeeded. Later, at other times, Agatha wondered what he would have written if he had felt himself free. What she observed in the second place was that though he saw she was much upset he did not in the least sound the depth of her distress or, as she herself would have said, of her shame. He never would—he never would; he could not enter into her feelings, because he could not believe in them: they could only strike him as exaggerated and factitious. He had given her a country, a magnificent one, and why in the name of common sense was she making him a scene about another? It was morbid—it was mad.

When he accused her of this extravagance it was very simple for her to meet his surprise with a greater astonishment— astonishment at his being able to allow so little for her just susceptibility. He could not take it seriously that she had American feelings; he could not believe that it would make a terrible difference in her happiness to go about the world as the wife, the cynical, consenting wife of the author of a blow dealt with that brutality at a breast to which she owed filial honour. She did not say to him that she should never hold her head up before Macarthy again (her strength had been that hitherto, as against Macarthy, she was perfectly straight), but it was in a great degree the prefigurement of her brother's

cold, lifelong scorn that had kindled in her, while she awaited
her husband's return, the passion with which she now protested. He would never read *The Modern Warning* but he
would hear all about it; he would meet it in the newspapers,
in every one's talk; the very voices of the air would distil the
worst pages into his ear and make the scandal of her participation even greater than—as heaven knew—it would deserve
to be. She thought of the month of renewed association, of
happy, pure impressions that she had spent a year before in
the midst of American kindness, in the midst of memories
more innocent than her visions of to-day; and the effect of
this retrospect was galling in the face of her possible shame.
Shame—shame: she repeated that word to Sir Rufus in a tone
which made him stare, as if it dawned upon him that her
reason was perhaps deserting her. That shame should attach
itself to his wife in consequence of any behaviour of *his* was
an idea that he had to make a very considerable effort to
embrace; and while his candour betrayed it his wife was
touched even through her resentment by seeing that she had
not made him angry. He thought she was strangely unreasonable, but he was determined not to fall into that vice on his
own side. She was silent about Macarthy because Sir Rufus
had accused her before her marriage of being afraid of him,
and she had then resolved never again to incur such a taunt;
but before things had gone much further between them she
reminded her husband that she had Irish blood, the blood of
the people, in her veins and that he must take that into account in measuring the provocation he might think it safe to
heap upon her. She was far from being a fanatic on this subject, as he knew; but when America was made out to be an
object of holy horror to virtuous England she could not but
remember that millions of her Celtic cousins had found refuge
there from the blessed English dispensation and be struck with
his recklessness in challenging comparisons which were better
left to sleep.

When his wife began to represent herself as Irish Sir Rufus
evidently thought her 'off her head' indeed: it was the first he
had heard of it since she communicated the mystic fact to him
on the lake of Como. Nevertheless he argued with her for half
an hour as if she were sane, and before they separated he made

her a liberal concession, such as only a perfectly lucid mind would be able to appreciate. This was a simple indulgence, at the end of their midnight discussion; it was not dictated by any recognition of his having been unjust; for though his wife reiterated this charge with a sacred fire in her eyes which made them more beautiful than he had ever known them he took his stand, in his own stubborn opinion, too firmly upon piles of evidence, revelations of political fraud and corruption, and the 'whole tone of the newspapers'—to speak only of that. He remarked to her that clearly he must simply give way to her opposition. If she were going to suffer so inordinately it settled the question. The book should not be published and they would say no more about it. He would put it away, he would burn it up and *The Modern Warning* should be as if it had never been. Amen! amen! Lady Chasemore accepted this sacrifice with eagerness, although her husband (it must be added) did not fail to place before her the exceeding greatness of it. He did not lose his temper, he was not petulant nor spiteful, he did not throw up his project and his vision of literary distinction in a huff; but he called her attention very vividly and solemnly to the fact that in deferring to the feelings she so uncompromisingly expressed he renounced the dream of rendering a signal service to his country. There was a certain bitterness in his smile as he told her that *her* wish was the only thing in the world that could have made him throw away such a golden opportunity. The rest of his life would never offer him such another; but patriotism might go to the dogs if only it were settled that she should not have a grudge. He did not care what became of poor old England if once that precious result were obtained; poor old England might pursue impure delusions and rattle down hill as fast as she chose for want of the word his voice would have spoken—really inspired as he held it to be by the justice of his cause.

Lady Chasemore flattered herself that they did not drop the subject that night in acrimony; there was nothing of this in the long kiss which she took from her husband's lips, with wet eyes, with a grateful, comprehensive murmur. It seemed to her that nothing could be fairer or finer than their mutual confidence; her husband's concession was gallant in the extreme; but even more than this was it impressed upon her that her own affection was perfect, since it could accept such a renunciation without a fear of the aftertaste. She had been in love with Sir Rufus from the day he sought her hand at Cadenabbia, but she was never so much in love with him as during the weeks that immediately followed his withdrawal of his book. It was agreed between them that neither of them would speak of the circumstance again, but she at least, in private, devoted an immense deal of meditation to it. It gave her a tremendous reprieve, lifted a nightmare off her breast, and that in turn gave her freedom to reflect that probably few men would have made such a graceful surrender. She wanted him to understand, or at any rate she wanted to understand herself, that in all its particulars too she thoroughly appreciated it; if he really was unable to conceive how she could feel as she did, it was all the more generous of him to comply blindly, to take her at her word, little as he could make of it. It did not become less obvious to Lady Chasemore, but quite the contrary, as the weeks went on, that *The Modern Warning* would have been a masterpiece of its class. In her room, that evening, her husband had told her that the best of him intellectually had gone into it, that he believed he had uttered certain truths there as they never would be uttered again—contributed his grain of gold to the limited sum of human wisdom. He had done something to help his country, and then—to please her—he had undone it. Above all it was delightful to her that he had not been sullen or rancorous about it, that he never made her pay for his magnanimity. He neither sighed nor scowled nor took on the air of a domestic martyr; he came and went with his usual step and his usual smile, remaining to all appearance the same fresh-coloured, decided, accomplished high official.

Therefore it is that I find it difficult to explain how it was that Lady Chasemore began to feel at the end of a few months that their difficulties had after all not become the mere reminiscence of a flurry, making present security more deep. What if the flurry continued impalpably, insidiously, under the surface? She thought there had been no change, but now she suspected that there was at least a difference. She had read Tennyson and she knew the famous phrase about the little rift within the lute. It came back to her with a larger meaning, it haunted her at last, and she asked herself whether when she accepted her husband's relinquishment it had been her happiness and his that she staked and threw away. In the light of this fear she struck herself as having lived in a fool's paradise—a misfortune from which she had ever prayed to be delivered. She wanted in every situation to know the worst, and in this case she had not known it; at least she knew it only now, in the shape of the formidable fact that Sir Rufus's outward good manners misrepresented his real reaction. At present she began anxiously, broodingly to take this reaction for granted and to see signs of it in the very things which she had regarded at first as signs of resignation. She secretly watched his face; she privately counted his words. When she began to do this it was no very long time before she made up her mind that the latter had become much fewer—that Sir Rufus talked to her very much less than he had done of old. He took no revenge, but he was cold, and in his coldness there was something horribly inevitable. He looked at her less and less, whereas formerly his eyes had had no more agreeable occupation. She tried to teach herself that her suspicions were woven of air and were an offence to a just man's character; she remembered that Sir Rufus had told her she was morbid, and if the charge had not been true at the time it might very well be true now. But the effect of this reflection was only to suggest to her that Sir Rufus himself was morbid and that her behaviour had made him so. It was the last thing that would be in his nature, but she had subjected that nature to an injurious strain. He was feeling it now; he was feeling that he had failed in the duty of a good citizen: a good citizen being what he had ever most earnestly proposed to himself to be. Lady Chasemore pictured to herself that his cheek burned for this when it was turned away from her—that he ground his teeth with shame in the watches of the night. Then it came over her with unspeakable bitterness that there had been no real solution of their difficulty; that it was too great to be settled by so simple an arrangement as that—an arrangement too primitive for a complicated world. Nothing was less simple than to bury one's gold and live without the interest.

It is a singular circumstance, and suggesting perhaps a perversion of the imagination under the influence of distress, but

Lady Chasemore at this time found herself thinking with a kind of baffled pride of the merits of *The Modern Warning* as a literary composition, a political essay. It would have been dreadful for her, but at least it would have been superb, and that was what was naturally enough present to the defeated author as he tossed through the sleepless hours. She determined at last to question him, to confess her fears, to make him tell her whether his weakness—if he considered it a weakness—really did rankle; though when he made the sacrifice months before (nearly a year had come round) he had let her know that he wished the subject buried between them for evermore. She approached it with some trepidation, and the manner in which he looked at her as she stammered out her inquiry was not such as to make the effort easier. He waited in silence till she had expressed herself as she best could, without helping her, without showing that he guessed her trouble, her need to be assured that he did not feel her to have been cruel. Did he?—*did* he? that was what she wanted to be certain of. Sir Rufus's answer was in itself a question; he demanded what she meant by imputing to him such hypocrisy, such bad faith. What did she take him for and what right had he given her to make a new scene, when he flattered himself the last pretext had been removed? If he had been dissatisfied she might be very sure he would have told her so; and as he had not told her she might pay him the compliment to believe he was honest. He expressed the hope—and for the first time in his life he was stern with her—that this would be the last endeavour on her part to revive an odious topic. His sternness was of no avail; it neither wounded her nor comforted her; it only had the effect of making her perfectly sure that he suffered and that he regarded himself as a kind of traitor. He was one more in the long list of those whom a woman had ruined, who had sold themselves, sold their honour and the commonwealth, for a fair face, a quiet life, a show of tears, a bribe of caresses. The vision of this smothered pain, which he tried to carry off as a gentleman should, only ministered to the love she had ever borne him—the love that had had the power originally to throw her into his arms in the face of an opposing force. As month followed month all her nature centred itself in this feeling; she loved him more than ever and yet she had been the cause of the most tormenting thing that had ever happened to him. This was a tragic contradiction, impossible to bear, and she sat staring at it with tears of rage.

One day she had occasion to tell him that she had received a letter from Macarthy, who announced that he should soon sail for Europe, even intimated that he should spend two or three weeks in London. He had been overworked, it was years since he had had a proper holiday, and the doctor threatened him with nervous prostration unless he very soon broke off everything. His sister had a vision of his reason for offering to let her see him in England; it was a piece of appreciation on Macarthy's part, a reward for their having behaved—that is, for Sir Rufus's having behaved, apparently under her influence—better than might have been expected. He had the good taste not to bring out his insolent book, and Macarthy gave this little sign, the most mollified thing he had done as yet, that he noticed. If Lady Chasemore had not at this moment been thinking of something else it might have occurred to her that nervous prostration, in her brother's organism, had already set in. The prospect of his visit held Sir Rufus's attention very briefly, and in a few minutes Agatha herself ceased to dwell upon it. Suddenly, illogically, fantastically, she could not have told why, at that moment and in that place, for she had had no such intention when she came into the room, she broke out: 'My own darling, do you know what has come over me? I have changed entirely—I see it differently; I want you to publish that grand thing.' And she stood there smiling at him, expressing the transformation of her feeling so well that he might have been forgiven for not doubting it.

Nevertheless he did doubt it, especially at first. But she repeated, she pressed, she insisted; once she had spoken in this sense she abounded and overflowed. It went on for several days (he had begun by refusing to listen to her, for even in touching the question she had violated his express command), and by the end of a week she persuaded him that she had really come round. She was extremely ingenious and plausible in tracing the process by which she had done so, and she drew from him the confession (they kissed a great deal after it was made) that the manuscript of *The Modern Warning* had not been destroyed at all, but was safely locked up in a cabinet, together with the interrupted proofs. She doubtless placed her tergiversation in a more natural light than her biographer has been able to do: he however will spare the reader the exertion of following the impalpable clue which leads to the heart of the labyrinth. A month was still to elapse before Macarthy would show himself, and during this time she had the leisure and freedom of mind to consider the sort of face with which she should meet him, her husband having virtually promised that he would send the book back to the printers. Now, of course, she renounced all pretension of censorship; she had nothing to do with it; it might be whatever he liked; she gave him formal notice that she should not even look at it after it was printed. It was his affair altogether now—it had ceased to be hers. A hard crust had formed itself in the course of a year over a sensibility that was once so tender; this she admitted was very strange, but it would be stranger still if (with the value that he had originally set upon his opportunity) he should fail to feel that he might hammer away at it. In this case would not the morbidness be quite on *his* side? Several times, during the period that preceded Macarthy's arrival, Lady Chasemore saw on the table in the hall little packets which reminded her of the roll of proofs she had opened that evening in her room. Her courage never failed her, and an observer of her present relations with her husband might easily have been excused for believing that the solution which at one time appeared so illusory was now valid for earthly purposes. Sir Rufus was immensely taken up with the resumption of his task; the revision of his original pages went forward the more rapidly that in fact, though his wife was unaware of it, they had repeatedly been in his hands since he put them away. He had retouched and amended them, by the midnight lamp, disinterestedly, platonically, hypothetically; and the alterations and improvements which suggest themselves when valuable ideas are laid by to ripen, like a row of pears on a shelf, started into life and liberty. Sir Rufus was as happy as a man who after having been obliged for a long time to entertain a passion in secret finds it recognised and legitimated, finds that the obstacles are removed and he may conduct his beloved to the altar.

Nevertheless when Macarthy Grice alighted at the door of

his sister's house—he had assented at the last to her urgent request that he would make it his habitation during his stay in London—he stepped into an atmosphere of sudden alarm and dismay. It was late in the afternoon, a couple of hours before dinner, and it so happened that Sir Rufus drove up at the moment the American traveller issued from the carriage that had been sent for him. The two men exchanged greetings on the steps of the house, but in the next breath Macarthy's host asked what had become of Agatha, whether she had not gone to the station to meet him, as she had announced at noon, when Sir Rufus saw her last, that she intended.

It appeared that she had not accompanied the carriage; Macarthy had been met only by one of the servants, who had been with the Chasemores to America and was therefore in a position to recognise him. This functionary said to Sir Rufus that her ladyship had sent him down word an hour before the carriage started that she had altered her intention and he was to go on without her. By this time the door of the house had been thrown open; the butler and the other footman had come to the front. They had not, however, their usual perpendicular demeanour, and the master's eye immediately saw that there was something wrong in the house. This apprehension was confirmed by the butler on the instant, before he had time to ask a question. 'We are afraid her ladyship is ill, sir; rather seriously, sir; we have but this moment discovered it, sir; her maid is with her, sir, and the other women.'

Sir Rufus started; he paused but a single instant, looking from one of the men to the other. Their faces were very white; they had a strange, scared expression. 'What do you mean by rather seriously?—what the devil has happened?' But he had sprung to the stairs—he was half-way up before they could answer.

'You had better go up, sir, really,' said the butler to Macarthy, who was planted there and had turned as white as himself. 'We are afraid she has taken something.'

'Taken something?'

'By mistake, sir, you know, sir,' quavered the footman, looking at his companion. There were tears in the footman's eyes. Macarthy felt sick.

'And there's no doctor? You don't send? You stand gaping?'

'We are going, sir—we have already gone!' cried both the men together. 'He'll come from the hospital, round the corner; he'll be here by the time you're upstairs. It was but this very moment, sir, just before you rang the bell,' one of them went on. The footman who had come with Macarthy from Euston dashed out of the house and he himself followed the direction his brother-in-law had taken. The butler was with him, saying he didn't know what—that it was only while they were waiting—that it would be a stroke for Sir Rufus. He got before him, on the upper landing; he led the way to Lady Chasemore's room, the door of which was open, revealing a horrible hush and, beyond the interior, a flurried, gasping flight of female domestics. Sir Rufus was there, he was at the bed still; he had cleared the room; two of the women had remained, they had hold of Lady Chasemore, who lay there passive, with a lifeless arm that caught Macarthy's eye—calling her, chafing her, pushing each other, saying that she would come to in a minute. Sir Rufus had apparently been staring at his wife in stupefaction and horror, but as Macarthy came to the bed he caught her up in his arms, pressing her to his bosom, and the American visitor met his face glaring at him over her shoulder, convulsed and transformed. 'She has taken something, but only by mistake:' he was conscious that the butler was saying that again, behind him, in his ear.

'By God, you have killed her! it's *your* infernal work!' cried Sir Rufus, in a voice that matched his terrible face.

'*I* have killed her?' answered Macarthy, bewildered and appalled.

'Your damned fantastic opposition—the fear of meeting you,' Sir Rufus went on. But his words lost themselves, as he bent over her, in violent kisses and imprecations, in demands whether nothing could be done, why the doctor was not there; in clumsy passionate attempts to arouse, to revive.

'Oh, I am sure she wanted you to come. She was very well this morning, sir,' the waiting-maid broke out, to Macarthy, contradicting Sir Rufus in her fright and protesting again that it was nothing, that it was a faint, for the very pleasure, that her ladyship would come round. The other woman had picked up a little phial. She thrust it at Macarthy with the boldness of their common distress, and as he took it from her mechanically he perceived that it was empty and had a strange odour. He sniffed it—then with a shout of horror flung it away. He rushed at his sister and for a moment almost had a struggle with her husband for the possession of her body, in which, as soon as he touched it, he felt the absence of life. Then she was on the bed again, beautiful, irresponsive, inanimate, and they were both beside her for an instant, after which Sir Rufus broke away and staggered out of the room. It seemed an eternity to Macarthy while he waited, though it had already come over him that he was waiting only for something still worse. The women talked, tried to tell him things; one of them said something about the pity of his coming all the way from America on purpose. Agatha was beautiful; there was no disfigurement. The butler had gone out with Sir Rufus and he came back with him, reappearing first, and with the doctor. Macarthy did not even heed what the doctor said. By this time he knew it all for himself. He flung himself into a chair, overwhelmed, covering his face with the cape of his ulster. The odour of the little phial was in his nostrils. He let the doctor lead him out without resistance, scarcely with consciousness, after some minutes.

Lady Chasemore had taken something—the doctor gave it a name—but it was not by mistake. In the hall, downstairs, he stood looking at Macarthy, kindly, soothingly, tentatively, with his hand on his shoulder. 'Had she—a—had she some domestic grief?' Macarthy heard him ask. He could not stay in the house—not with Chasemore. The servant who had brought him from the station took him to an hotel, with his luggage, in the carriage, which was still at the door—a horrible hotel where, in a dismal, dingy back room, with chimney-pots outside, he spent a night of unsurpassable anguish. He could not understand, and he howled to himself, 'Why, *why*, just now?' Sir Rufus, in the other house, had exactly such another vigil: it was plain enough that this was the case when, the next morning, he came to the hotel. He held out his hand to Macarthy—he appeared to take back his monstrous words of the evening before. He made him return to Grosvenor Crescent; he made him spend three days there, three days during which the two men scarcely exchanged a word. But the rest of the holiday that Macarthy had undertaken for the benefit of his health was passed upon the Continent, with little present evidence that he should find what he had sought. *The Modern Warning* has not yet been published, but it may still appear. This doubtless will depend upon whether, this time, the sheets have really been destroyed—buried in Lady Chasemore's grave or only put back into the cabinet.

A London Life

IT WAS RAINING, apparently, but she didn't mind—she would put on stout shoes and walk over to Plash. She was restless and so fidgety that it was a pain; there were strange voices that frightened her—they threw out the ugliest intimations—in the empty rooms at home. She would see old Mrs. Berrington, whom she liked because she was so simple, and old Lady Davenant, who was staying with her and who was interesting for reasons with which simplicity had nothing to do. Then she would come back to the children's tea—she liked even better the last half-hour in the schoolroom, with the bread and butter, the candles and the red fire, the little spasms of confidence of Miss Steet the nursery-governess, and the society of Scratch and Parson (their nicknames would have made you think they were dogs) her small, magnificent nephews, whose flesh was so firm yet so soft and their eyes so charming when they listened to stories. Plash was the dower-house and about a mile and a half, through the park, from Mellows. It was not raining after all, though it had been; there was only a grayness in the air, covering all the strong, rich green, and a pleasant damp, earthy smell, and the walks were smooth and hard, so that the expedition was not arduous.

The girl had been in England more than a year, but there were some satisfactions she had not got used to yet nor ceased to enjoy, and one of these was the accessibility, the convenience of the country. Within the lodge-gates or without them it seemed all alike a park—it was all so intensely 'property.' The very name of Plash, which was quaint and old, had not lost its effect upon her, nor had it become indifferent to her that the place was a dower-house—the little red-walled, ivied asylum to which old Mrs. Berrington had retired when, on his father's death, her son came into the estates. Laura Wing thought very ill of the custom of the expropriation of the widow in the evening of her days, when honour and abundance should attend her more than ever; but her condemnation of this wrong forgot itself when so many of the consequences looked right—barring a little dampness: which

435

was the fate sooner or later of most of her unfavourable judgments of English institutions. Iniquities in such a country somehow always made pictures; and there had been dowerhouses in the novels, mainly of fashionable life, on which her later childhood was fed. The iniquity did not as a general thing prevent these retreats from being occupied by old ladies with wonderful reminiscences and rare voices, whose reverses had not deprived them of a great deal of becoming hereditary lace. In the park, half-way, suddenly, Laura stopped, with a pain—a moral pang—that almost took away her breath; she looked at the misty glades and the dear old beeches (so familiar they were now and loved as much as if she owned them); they seemed in their unlighted December bareness conscious of all the trouble, and they made her conscious of all the change. A year ago she knew nothing, and now she knew almost everything; and the worst of her knowledge (or at least the worst of the fears she had raised upon it) had come to her in that beautiful place, where everything was so full of peace and purity, of the air of happy submission to immemorial law. The place was the same but her eyes were different: they had seen such sad, bad things in so short a time. Yes, the time was short and everything was strange. Laura Wing was too uneasy even to sigh, and as she walked on she lightened her tread almost as if she were going on tiptoe.

At Plash the house seemed to shine in the wet air—the tone of the mottled red walls and the limited but perfect lawn to be the work of an artist's brush. Lady Davenant was in the drawing-room, in a low chair by one of the windows, reading the second volume of a novel. There was the same look of crisp chintz, of fresh flowers wherever flowers could be put, of a wall-paper that was in the bad taste of years before, but had been kept so that no more money should be spent, and was almost covered over with amateurish drawings and superior engravings, framed in narrow gilt with large margins. The room had its bright, durable, sociable air, the air that Laura Wing liked in so many English things—that of being meant for daily life, for long periods, for uses of high decency. But more than ever to-day was it incongruous that such an habitation, with its chintzes and its British poets, its well-worn carpets and domestic art—the whole aspect so unmeretricious and sincere—should have to do with lives that were not right. Of course however it had to do only indirectly, and the wrong life was not old Mrs. Berrington's nor yet Lady Davenant's. If Selina and Selina's doings were not an implication of such an interior any more than it was for them an explication, this was because she had come from so far off, was a foreign element altogether. Yet it was there she had found her occasion, all the influences that had altered her so (her sister had a theory that she was metamorphosed, that when she was young she seemed born for innocence) if not at Plash at least at Mellows, for the two places after all had ever so much in common, and there were rooms at the great house that looked remarkably like Mrs. Berrington's parlour.

Lady Davenant always had a head-dress of a peculiar style, original and appropriate—a sort of white veil or cape which came in a point to the place on her forehead where her smooth hair began to show and then covered her shoulders. It was always exquisitely fresh and was partly the reason why she struck the girl rather as a fine portrait than as a living person. And yet she was full of life, old as she was, and had been made finer, sharper and more delicate, by nearly eighty years of it. It was the hand of a master that Laura seemed to see in her face, the witty expression of which shone like a lamp through the ground-glass of her good breeding; nature was always an artist, but not so much of an artist as that. Infinite knowledge the girl attributed to her, and that was why she liked her a little fearfully. Lady Davenant was not as a general thing fond of the young or of invalids; but she made an exception as regards youth for the little girl from America, the sister of the daughter-in-law of her dearest friend. She took an interest in Laura partly perhaps to make up for the tepidity with which she regarded Selina. At all events she had assumed the general responsibility of providing her with a husband. She pretended to care equally little for persons suffering from other forms of misfortune, but she was capable of finding excuses for them when they had been sufficiently to blame. She expected a great deal of attention, always wore gloves in the house and never had anything in her hand but a book. She neither embroidered nor wrote—only read and talked. She had no special conversation for girls but generally addressed

them in the same manner that she found effective with her
contemporaries. Laura Wing regarded this as an honour, but
very often she didn't know what the old lady meant and was
ashamed to ask her. Once in a while Lady Davenant was
ashamed to tell. Mrs. Berrington had gone to a cottage to see
an old woman who was ill—an old woman who had been in
her service for years, in the old days. Unlike her friend she
was fond of young people and invalids, but she was less interesting to Laura, except that it was a sort of fascination to
wonder how she could have such abysses of placidity. She had
long cheeks and kind eyes and was devoted to birds; somehow
she always made Laura think secretly of a tablet of fine white
soap—nothing else was so smooth and clean.

'And what's going on *chez vous*—who is there and what are
they doing?' Lady Davenant asked, after the first greetings.

'There isn't any one but me—and the children—and the
governess.'

'What, no party—no private theatricals? How do you live?'

'Oh, it doesn't take so much to keep me going,' said Laura.
'I believe there were some people coming on Saturday, but
they have been put off, or they can't come. Selina has gone
to London.'

'And what has she gone to London for?'

'Oh, I don't know—she has so many things to do.'

'And where is Mr. Berrington?'

'He has been away somewhere; but I believe he is coming
back to-morrow—or next day.'

'Or the day after?' said Lady Davenant. 'And do they never
go away together?' she continued after a pause.

'Yes, sometimes—but they don't come back together.'

'Do you mean they quarrel on the way?'

'I don't know what they do, Lady Davenant—I don't understand,' Laura Wing replied, with an unguarded tremor in
her voice. 'I don't think they are very happy.'

'Then they ought to be ashamed of themselves. They have
got everything so comfortable—what more do they want?'

'Yes, and the children are such dears!'

'Certainly—charming. And is she a good person, the present governess? Does she look after them properly?'

'Yes—she seems very good—it's a blessing. But I think she's unhappy too.'

'Bless us, what a house! Does she want some one to make love to her?'

'No, but she wants Selina to see—to appreciate,' said the young girl.

'And doesn't she appreciate—when she leaves them that way quite to the young woman?'

'Miss Steet thinks she doesn't notice how they come on—she is never there.'

'And has she wept and told you so? You know they are always crying, governesses—whatever line you take. You shouldn't draw them out too much—they are always looking for a chance. She ought to be thankful to be let alone. You mustn't be too sympathetic—it's mostly wasted,' the old lady went on.

'Oh, I'm not—I assure you I'm not,' said Laura Wing. 'On the contrary, I see so much about me that I don't sympathise with.'

'Well, you mustn't be an impertinent little American either!' her interlocutress exclaimed. Laura sat with her for half an hour and the conversation took a turn through the affairs of Plash and through Lady Davenant's own, which were visits in prospect and ideas suggested more or less directly by them as well as by the books she had been reading, a heterogeneous pile on a table near her, all of them new and clean, from a circulating library in London. The old woman had ideas and Laura liked them, though they often struck her as very sharp and hard, because at Mellows she had no diet of that sort. There had never been an idea in the house, since she came at least, and there was wonderfully little reading. Lady Davenant still went from country-house to country-house all winter, as she had done all her life, and when Laura asked her she told her the places and the people she probably should find at each of them. Such an enumeration was much less interesting to the girl than it would have been a year before: she herself had now seen a great many places and people and the freshness of her curiosity was gone. But she still cared for Lady Davenant's descriptions and judgments, because they were the thing in her life which (when she met the old woman from time to time) most represented talk—the rare sort of talk that was not mere chaff. That was what she had dreamed of before she came to England, but in Selina's set the dream had not come true. In Selina's set people only harried each other from morning till night with extravagant accusations—it was all a kind of horse-play of false charges. When Lady Davenant was accusatory it was within the limits of perfect verisimilitude.

Laura waited for Mrs. Berrington to come in but she failed to appear, so that the girl gathered her waterproof together with an intention of departure. But she was secretly reluctant, because she had walked over to Plash with a vague hope that some soothing hand would be laid upon her pain. If there was no comfort at the dower-house she knew not where to look for it, for there was certainly none at home—not even with Miss Steet and the children. It was not Lady Davenant's leading characteristic that she was comforting, and Laura had not aspired to be coaxed or coddled into forgetfulness: she wanted rather to be taught a certain fortitude—how to live and hold up one's head even while knowing that things were very bad. A brazen indifference—it was not exactly that that she wished to acquire; but were there not some sorts of indifference that were philosophic and noble? Could Lady Davenant not teach them, if she should take the trouble? The girl remembered to have heard that there had been years before some disagreeable occurrences in *her* family; it was not a race in which the ladies inveterately turned out well. Yet who to-day had the stamp of honour and credit—of a past which was either no one's business or was part and parcel of a fair public record—and carried it so much as a matter of course? She herself had been a good woman and that was the only thing that told in the long run. It was Laura's own idea to be a good woman and that this would make it an advantage for Lady Davenant to show her how not to feel too much. As regards feeling enough, that was a branch in which she had no need to take lessons.

The old woman liked cutting new books, a task she never remitted to her maid, and while her young visitor sat there she went through the greater part of a volume with the paper-knife. She didn't proceed very fast—there was a kind of patient, awkward fumbling of her aged hands; but as she passed her knife into the last leaf she said abruptly—'And how is your sister going on? She's very light!' Lady Davenant added before Laura had time to reply.

'Oh, Lady Davenant!' the girl exclaimed, vaguely, slowly, vexed with herself as soon as she had spoken for having uttered the words as a protest, whereas she wished to draw her companion out. To correct this impression she threw back her waterproof.

'Have you ever spoken to her?' the old woman asked.

'Spoken to her?'

'About her behaviour. I daresay you haven't—you Americans have such a lot of false delicacy. I daresay Selina wouldn't speak to you if you were in her place (excuse the supposition!) and yet she is capable——' But Lady Davenant paused, preferring not to say of what young Mrs. Berrington was capable. 'It's a bad house for a girl.'

'It only gives me a horror,' said Laura, pausing in turn.

'A horror of your sister? That's not what one should aim at. You ought to get married—and the sooner the better. My dear child, I have neglected you dreadfully.'

'I am much obliged to you, but if you think marriage looks to me happy!' the girl exclaimed, laughing without hilarity.

'Make it happy for some one else and you will be happy enough yourself. You ought to get out of your situation.'

Laura Wing was silent a moment, though this was not a new reflection to her. 'Do you mean that I should leave Selina altogether? I feel as if I should abandon her—as if I should be a coward.'

'Oh, my dear, it isn't the business of little girls to serve as parachutes to fly-away wives! That's why if you haven't spoken to her you needn't take the trouble at this time of day. Let her go—let her go!'

'Let her go?' Laura repeated, staring.

Her companion gave her a sharper glance. 'Let her stay, then! Only get out of the house. You can come to me, you know, whenever you like. I don't know another girl I would say that to.'

'Oh, Lady Davenant,' Laura began again, but she only got as far as this; in a moment she had covered her face with her hands—she had burst into tears.

'Ah my dear, don't cry or I shall take back my invitation! It would never do if you were to *larmoyer*. If I have offended you by the way I have spoken of Selina I think you are too sensitive. We shouldn't feel more for people than they feel for themselves. She has no tears, I'm sure.'

'Oh, she has, she has!' cried the girl, sobbing with an odd effect as she put forth this pretension for her sister.

'Then she's worse than I thought. I don't mind them so much when they are merry but I hate them when they are sentimental.'

'She's so changed—so changed!' Laura Wing went on.

'Never, never, my dear: *c'est de naissance*.'

'You never knew my mother,' returned the girl; 'when I think of mother——' The words failed her while she sobbed.

'I daresay she was very nice,' said Lady Davenant gently. 'It would take that to account for you: such women as Selina are always easily enough accounted for. I didn't mean it was inherited—for that sort of thing skips about. I daresay there was some improper ancestress—except that you Americans don't seem to have ancestresses.'

Laura gave no sign of having heard these observations; she was occupied in brushing away her tears. 'Everything is so changed—you don't know,' she remarked in a moment. 'Nothing could have been happier—nothing could have been sweeter. And now to be so dependent—so helpless—so poor!'

'Have you nothing at all?' asked Lady Davenant, with simplicity.

'Only enough to pay for my clothes.'

'That's a good deal, for a girl. You are uncommonly dressy, you know.'

'I'm sorry I seem so. That's just the way I don't want to look.'

'You Americans can't help it; you "wear" your very features and your eyes look as if they had just been sent home. But I confess you are not so smart as Selina.'

'Yes, isn't she splendid?' Laura exclaimed, with proud inconsequence. 'And the worse she is the better she looks.'

'Oh my child, if the bad women looked as bad as they are——! It's only the good ones who can afford that,' the old lady murmured.

'It was the last thing I ever thought of—that I should be ashamed,' said Laura.

'Oh, keep your shame till you have more to do with it. It's like lending your umbrella—when you have only one.'

'If anything were to happen—publicly—I should die, I should die!' the girl exclaimed passionately and with a motion that carried her to her feet. This time she settled herself for departure. Lady Davenant's admonition rather frightened than sustained her.

The old woman leaned back in her chair, looking up at her. 'It would be very bad, I daresay. But it wouldn't prevent me from taking you in.'

Laura Wing returned her look, with eyes slightly distended, musing. 'Think of having to come to that!'

Lady Davenant burst out laughing. 'Yes, yes, you must come; you are so original!'

'I don't mean that I don't feel your kindness,' the girl broke out, blushing. 'But to be only protected—always protected: is that a life?'

'Most women are only too thankful and I am bound to say I think you are *difficile*.' Lady Davenant used a good many French words, in the old-fashioned manner and with a pronunciation not perfectly pure: when she did so she reminded Laura Wing of Mrs. Gore's novels. 'But you shall be better protected than even by me. *Nous verrons cela*. Only you must stop crying—this isn't a crying country.'

'No, one must have courage here. It takes courage to marry for such a reason.'

'Any reason is good enough that keeps a woman from being an old maid. Besides, you will like him.'

'He must like me first,' said the girl, with a sad smile.

'There's the American again! It isn't necessary. You are too proud—you expect too much.'

'I'm proud for what I am—that's very certain. But I don't expect anything,' Laura Wing declared. 'That's the only form my pride takes. Please give my love to Mrs. Berrington. I am so sorry—so sorry,' she went on, to change the talk from the subject of her marrying. She wanted to marry but she wanted also not to want it and, above all, not to appear to. She lingered in the room, moving about a little; the place was always so pleasant to her that to go away—to return to her own barren home—had the effect of forfeiting a sort of privilege of sanctuary. The afternoon had faded but the lamps had been brought in, the smell of flowers was in the air and the old house of Plash seemed to recognise the hour that suited it best. The quiet old lady in the firelight, encompassed with the symbolic security of chintz and water-colour, gave her a sudden vision of how blessed it would be to jump all the middle dangers of life and have arrived at the end, safely, sensibly, with a cap and gloves and consideration and memories. 'And, Lady Davenant, what does *she* think?' she asked abruptly, stopping short and referring to Mrs. Berrington.

'Think? Bless your soul, she doesn't do that! If she did, the things she says would be unpardonable.'

'The things she says?'

'That's what makes them so beautiful—that they are not spoiled by preparation. You could never think of them *for* her.' The girl smiled at this description of the dearest friend of her interlocutress, but she wondered a little what Lady Davenant would say to visitors about *her* if she should accept a refuge under her roof. Her speech was after all a flattering proof of confidence. 'She wishes it had been you—I happen to know that,' said the old woman.

'It had been me?'

'That Lionel had taken a fancy to.'

'I wouldn't have married him,' Laura rejoined, after a moment.

'Don't say that or you will make me think it won't be easy to help you. I shall depend upon you not to refuse anything so good.'

'I don't call him good. If he were good his wife would be better.'

'Very likely; and if you had married him *he* would be better, and that's more to the purpose. Lionel is as idiotic as a comic song, but you have cleverness for two.'

'And you have it for fifty, dear Lady Davenant. Never, never —I shall never marry a man I can't respect!' Laura Wing exclaimed.

She had come a little nearer her old friend and taken her

hand; her companion held her a moment and with the other hand pushed aside one of the flaps of the waterproof. 'And what is it your clothing costs you?' asked Lady Davenant, looking at the dress underneath and not giving any heed to this declaration.

'I don't exactly know: it takes almost everything that is sent me from America. But that is dreadfully little—only a few pounds. I am a wonderful manager. Besides,' the girl added, 'Selina wants one to be dressed.'

'And doesn't she pay any of your bills?'

'Why, she gives me everything—food, shelter, carriages.'

'Does she never give you money?'

'I wouldn't take it,' said the girl. 'They need everything they have—their life is tremendously expensive.'

'That I'll warrant!' cried the old woman. 'It was a most beautiful property, but I don't know what has become of it now. *Ce n'est pas pour vous blesser*, but the hole you Americans *can* make——'

Laura interrupted immediately, holding up her head; Lady Davenant had dropped her hand and she had receded a step. 'Selina brought Lionel a very considerable fortune and every penny of it was paid.'

'Yes, I know it was; Mrs. Berrington told me it was most satisfactory. That's not always the case with the fortunes you young ladies are supposed to bring!' the old lady added, smiling.

The girl looked over her head a moment. 'Why do your men marry for money?'

'Why indeed, my dear? And before your troubles what used your father to give you for your personal expenses?'

'He gave us everything we asked—we had no particular allowance.'

'And I daresay you asked for everything?' said Lady Davenant.

'No doubt we were very dressy, as you say.'

'No wonder he went bankrupt—for he did, didn't he?'

'He had dreadful reverses but he only sacrificed himself— he protected others.'

'Well, I know nothing about these things and I only ask *pour me renseigner*,' Mrs. Berrington's guest went on. 'And after their reverses your father and mother lived I think only a short time?'

Laura Wing had covered herself again with her mantle; her eyes were now bent upon the ground and, standing there before her companion with her umbrella and her air of momentary submission and self-control, she might very well have been a young person in reduced circumstances applying for a place. 'It was short enough but it seemed—some parts of it—terribly long and painful. My poor father—my dear father,' the girl went on. But her voice trembled and she checked herself.

'I feel as if I were cross-questioning you, which God forbid!' said Lady Davenant. 'But there is one thing I should really like to know. Did Lionel and his wife, when you were poor, come freely to your assistance?'

'They sent us money repeatedly—it was *her* money of course. It was almost all we had.'

'And if you have been poor and know what poverty is tell me this: has it made you afraid to marry a poor man?'

It seemed to Lady Davenant that in answer to this her young friend looked at her strangely; and then the old woman heard her say something that had not quite the heroic ring she expected. 'I am afraid of so many things to-day that I don't know where my fears end.'

'I have no patience with the highstrung way you take things. But I have to know, you know.'

'Oh, don't try to know any more shames—any more horrors!' the girl wailed with sudden passion, turning away.

Her companion got up, drew her round again and kissed her. 'I think you would fidget me,' she remarked as she released her. Then, as if this were too cheerless a leave-taking, she added in a gayer tone, as Laura had her hand on the door: 'Mind what I tell you, my dear; let her go!' It was to this that the girl's lesson in philosophy reduced itself, she reflected, as she walked back to Mellows in the rain, which had now come on, through the darkening park.

II

The children were still at tea and poor Miss Steet sat between them, consoling herself with strong cups, crunching melancholy morsels of toast and dropping an absent gaze on her little companions as they exchanged small, loud remarks. She always sighed when Laura came in—it was her way of expressing appreciation of the visit—and she was the one person whom the girl frequently saw who seemed to her more unhappy than herself. But Laura envied her—she thought her position had more dignity than that of her employer's dependent sister. Miss Steet had related her life to the children's pretty young aunt and this personage knew that though it had had painful elements nothing so disagreeable had ever befallen her or was likely to befall her as the odious possibility of her sister's making a scandal. She had two sisters (Laura knew all about them) and one of them was married to a clergyman in Staffordshire (a very ugly part) and had seven children and four hundred a year; while the other, the eldest, was enormously stout and filled (it was a good deal of a squeeze) a position as matron in an orphanage at Liverpool. Neither of them seemed destined to go into the English divorce-court, and such a circumstance on the part of one's near relations struck Laura as in itself almost sufficient to constitute happiness. Miss Steet never lived in a state of nervous anxiety—everything about her was respectable. She made the girl almost angry sometimes, by her drooping, martyr-like air: Laura was near breaking out at her with, 'Dear me, what have *you* got to complain of? Don't you earn your living like an honest girl and are you obliged to see things going on about you that you hate?'

But she could not say things like that to her, because she had promised Selina, who made a great point of this, that she would never be too familiar with her. Selina was not without her ideas of decorum—very far from it indeed; only she erected them in such queer places. She was not familiar with her children's governess; she was not even familiar with the children themselves. That was why after all it was impossible to address much of a remonstrance to Miss Steet when she sat as if she were tied to the stake and the fagots were being lighted. If martyrs in this situation had tea and cold meat served them they would strikingly have resembled the provoking young woman in the schoolroom at Mellows. Laura could not have denied that it was natural she should have liked it better if Mrs. Berrington would *sometimes* just look in and give a sign that she was pleased with her system; but poor Miss Steet only knew by the servants or by Laura whether Mrs. Berrington were at home or not: she was for the most part not, and the governess had a way of silently intimating (it was the manner she put her head on one side when she looked at Scratch and Parson—of course *she* called them Geordie and Ferdy) that she was immensely handicapped and even that they were. Perhaps they were, though they certainly showed it little in their appearance and manner, and Laura was at least sure that if Selina had been perpetually dropping in Miss Steet would have taken that discomfort even more tragically. The sight of this young woman's either real or fancied wrongs did not diminish her conviction that she herself would have found courage to become a governess. She would have had to teach very young children, for she believed she was too ignorant for higher flights. But Selina would never have consented to that—she would have considered it a disgrace or even worse—a *pose*. Laura had proposed to her six months before that she should dispense with a paid governess and suffer *her* to take charge of the little boys: in that way she should not feel so completely dependent—she should be doing something in return. 'And pray what would happen when you came to dinner? Who would look after them then?' Mrs. Berrington had demanded, with a very shocked air. Laura had replied that perhaps it was not absolutely necessary that she should come to dinner—she could dine early, with the children; and that if her presence in the drawing-room should be required the children had their nurse—and what did they have their nurse for? Selina looked at her as if she was deplorably superficial and told her that they had their nurse to dress them and look after their clothes—did she wish the poor little ducks to go in rags? She had her own ideas of thoroughness and when Laura hinted that after all at that hour the children were in bed she declared that even when they were asleep she desired the governess to be at hand—that was the way a mother felt who really took an interest. Selina was wonderfully thorough; she said something about the evening hours in the quiet schoolroom being the proper time for the governess to 'get up' the children's lessons for the next day. Laura Wing was conscious of her own ignorance; nevertheless she presumed to believe that she could have taught Geordie and Ferdy the alphabet without anticipatory nocturnal researches. She wondered what her sister supposed Miss Steet taught them—whether she had a cheap theory that they were in Latin and algebra.

The governess's evening hours in the quiet schoolroom would have suited Laura well—so at least she believed; by touches of her own she would make the place even prettier than it was already, and in the winter nights, near the bright fire, she would get through a delightful course of reading. There was the question of a new piano (the old one was pretty bad—Miss Steet had a finger!) and perhaps she should have to ask Selina for that—but it would be all. The schoolroom at Mellows was not a charmless place and the girl often wished that she might have spent her own early years in so dear a scene. It was a sort of panelled parlour, in a wing, and looked out on the great cushiony lawns and a part of the terrace where the peacocks used most to spread their tails. There were quaint old maps on the wall, and 'collections'—birds and shells—under glass cases, and there was a wonderful pictured screen which old Mrs. Berrington had made when Lionel was young out of primitive woodcuts illustrative of nursery-tales. The place was a setting for rosy childhood, and Laura believed her sister never knew how delightful Scratch and Parson looked there. Old Mrs. Berrington had known in the case of Lionel—it had all been arranged for him. That was the story told by ever so many other things in the house, which betrayed the full perception of a comfortable, liberal, deeply domestic effect, addressed to eternities of possession, characteristic thirty years before of the unquestioned and unquestioning old lady whose sofas and 'corners' (she had perhaps been the first person in England to have corners) demonstrated the most of her cleverness.

Laura Wing envied English children, the boys at least, and even her own chubby nephews, in spite of the cloud that hung over them; but she had already noted the incongruity that appeared to-day between Lionel Berrington at thirty-five and the influences that had surrounded his younger years. She did not dislike her brother-in-law, though she admired him scantily, and she pitied him; but she marvelled at the waste involved in some human institutions (the English country gentry for instance) when she perceived that it had taken so much to produce so little. The sweet old wainscoted parlour, the view of the garden that reminded her of scenes in Shakespeare's comedies, all that was exquisite in the home of his fore-fathers—what visible reference was there to these fine things in poor Lionel's stable-stamped composition? When she came in this evening and saw his small sons making competitive noises in their mugs (Miss Steet checked this impropriety on her entrance) she asked herself what *they* would have to show twenty years later for the frame that made them just then a picture. Would they be wonderfully ripe and noble, the perfection of human culture? The contrast was before her again, the sense of the same curious duplicity (in the literal meaning of the word) that she had felt at Plash—the way the genius of such an old house was all peace and decorum and the spirit that prevailed there, outside of the schoolroom, was contentious and impure. She had often been struck with it be-fore—with that perfection of machinery which can still at certain times make English life go on of itself with a stately rhythm long after there is corruption within it.

She had half a purpose of asking Miss Steet to dine with her that evening downstairs, so absurd did it seem to her that two young women who had so much in common (enough at least for that) should sit feeding alone at opposite ends of the big empty house, melancholy on such a night. She would not have cared just now whether Selina did think such a course familiar: she indulged sometimes in a kind of angry humility, placing herself near to those who were laborious and sordid. But when she observed how much cold meat the governess had already consumed she felt that it would be a vain form to propose to her another repast. She sat down with her and presently, in the firelight, the two children had placed themselves in position for a story. They were dressed like the mariners of England and they smelt of the ablutions to which they had been condemned before tea and the odour of which was but partly overlaid by that of bread and butter. Scratch wanted an old story and Parson a new, and they exchanged from side to side a good many powerful arguments. While they were so engaged Miss Steet narrated at her visitor's invitation the walk she had taken with them and revealed that she had been thinking for a long time of asking Mrs. Berrington—if she only had an opportunity—whether she should approve of her giving them a few elementary notions of botany. But the opportunity had not come—she had had the idea for a long time past. She was rather fond of the study herself; she had gone into it a little—she seemed to intimate that there had been times when she extracted a needed comfort from it. Laura suggested that botany might be a little dry for such young children in winter, from text-books—that the better way would be perhaps to wait till the spring and show them out of doors, in the garden, some of the peculiarities of plants. To this Miss Steet rejoined that her idea had been to teach some of the general facts slowly—it would take a long time—and then they would be all ready for the spring. She spoke of the spring as if it would not arrive for a terribly long time. She had hoped to lay the question before Mrs. Berrington that week—but was it not already Thursday? Laura said, 'Oh yes, you had better do anything with the children that will keep them profitably occupied;' she came very near saying anything that would occupy the governess herself.

She had rather a dread of new stories—it took the little boys so long to get initiated and the first steps were so terribly bestrewn with questions. Receptive silence, broken only by an occasional rectification on the part of the listener, never descended until after the tale had been told a dozen times. The matter was settled for 'Riquet with the Tuft,' but on this occasion the girl's heart was not much in the entertainment. The children stood on either side of her, leaning against her, and she had an arm round each; their little bodies were thick and strong and their voices had the quality of silver bells. Their mother had certainly gone too far; but there was nevertheless a limit to the tenderness one could feel for the neglected, compromised bairns. It was difficult to take a sentimental view of them—they would never take such a view of themselves. Geordie would grow up to be a master-hand at polo and care more for that pastime than for anything in life, and Ferdy perhaps would develop into 'the best shot in England.' Laura felt these possibilities stirring within them; they were in the things they said to her, in the things they said to each other. At any rate they would never reflect upon anything in the world. They contradicted each other on a question of ancestral history to which their attention apparently had been drawn by their nurse, whose people had been tenants for generations. Their grandfather had had the hounds for fifteen years—Ferdy maintained that he had always had them. Geordie ridiculed this idea, like a man of the world; he had had them till he went into volunteering—then he had got up a magnificent regiment, he had spent thousands of pounds on it. Ferdy was of the opinion that this was wasted money—he himself intended to have a real regiment, to be a colonel in the Guards. Geordie looked as if he thought that a superficial ambition and could see beyond it; his own most definite view was that he would have back the hounds. He didn't see why papa didn't have them—unless it was because he wouldn't take the trouble.

'I know—it's because mamma is an American!' Ferdy announced, with confidence.

'And what has that to do with it?' asked Laura.

'Mamma spends so much money—there isn't any more for anything!'

This startling speech elicited an alarmed protest from Miss Steet; she blushed and assured Laura that she couldn't imagine where the child could have picked up such an extraordinary idea. 'I'll look into it—you may be sure I'll look into it,' she said; while Laura told Ferdy that he must never, never, never, under any circumstances, either utter or listen to a word that should be wanting in respect to his mother.

'If any one should say anything against any of my people I would give him a good one!' Geordie shouted, with his hands in his little blue pockets.

'I'd hit him in the eye!' cried Ferdy, with cheerful inconsequence.

'Perhaps you don't care to come to dinner at half-past seven,' the girl said to Miss Steet; 'but I should be very glad—I'm all alone.'

'Thank you so much. All alone, really?' murmured the governess.

'Why don't you get married? then you wouldn't be alone,' Geordie interposed, with ingenuity.

'Children, you are really too dreadful this evening!' Miss Steet exclaimed.

'I shan't get married—I want to have the hounds,' proclaimed Geordie, who had apparently been much struck with his brother's explanation.

'I will come down afterwards, about half-past eight, if you will allow me,' said Miss Steet, looking conscious and responsible.

'Very well—perhaps we can have some music; we will try something together.'

'Oh, music—*we* don't go in for music!' said Geordie, with clear superiority; and while he spoke Laura saw Miss Steet get up suddenly, looking even less alleviated than usual. The door of the room had been pushed open and Lionel Berrington stood there. He had his hat on and a cigar in his mouth and his face was red, which was its common condition. He took off his hat as he came into the room, but he did not stop smoking and he turned a little redder than before. There were several ways in which his sister-in-law often wished he had been very different, but she had never disliked him for a certain boyish shyness that was in him, which came out in his dealings with almost all women. The governess of his children made him uncomfortable and Laura had already noticed that he had the same effect upon Miss Steet. He was fond of his children, but he saw them hardly more frequently than their mother and they never knew whether he were at home or away. Indeed his goings and comings were so frequent that Laura herself scarcely knew: it was an accident that on this occasion his absence had been marked for her. Selina had had her reasons for wishing not to go up to town while her husband was still at Mellows, and she cherished the irritating belief that he stayed at home on purpose to watch her—to keep her from going away. It was her theory that she herself was perpetually at home—that few women were more domestic, more glued to the fireside and absorbed in the duties belonging to it; and unreasonable as she was she recognised the fact that for her to establish this theory she must make her husband sometimes see her at Mellows. It was not enough for her to maintain that he would see her if he were sometimes there himself. Therefore she disliked to be caught in the crude fact of absence—to go away under his nose; what she preferred was to take the next train after his own and return an hour or two before him. She managed this often with great ability, in spite of her not being able to be sure when he *would* return. Of late however she had ceased to take so much trouble, and Laura, by no desire of the girl's own, was enough in the confidence of her impatiences and perversities to know that for her to have wished (four days before the moment I write of) to put him on a wrong scent—or to keep him at least off the right one—she must have had something more dreadful than usual in her head. This was why the girl had been so nervous and why the sense of an impending catastrophe, which had lately gathered strength in her mind, was at present almost intolerably pressing: she knew how little Selina could afford to be more dreadful than usual.

Lionel startled her by turning up in that unexpected way, though she could not have told herself when it would have been natural to expect him. This attitude, at Mellows, was left to the servants, most of them inscrutable and incommunicative and erect in a wisdom that was founded upon telegrams—you couldn't speak to the butler but he pulled one out of his pocket. It was a house of telegrams; they crossed each other a dozen times an hour, coming and going, and Selina in particular lived in a cloud of them. Laura had but vague ideas as to what they were all about; once in a while, when they fell under her eyes, she either failed to understand them or judged them to be about horses. There were an immense number of horses, in one way and another, in Mrs. Berrington's life. Then she had so many friends, who were always rushing about like herself and making appointments and putting them off and wanting to know if she were going to certain places or whether she would go if they did or whether she would come up to town and dine and 'do a theatre.' There were also a good many theatres in the existence of this busy lady. Laura remembered how fond their poor father had been of telegraphing, but it was never about the theatre: at all events she tried to give her sister the benefit or the excuse of heredity. Selina had her own opinions, which were superior to this: she once remarked to Laura that it was idiotic for a woman to write—to telegraph was the only way not to get into trouble. If doing so sufficed to keep a lady out of it Mrs. Berrington's life should have flowed like the rivers of Eden.

III

Laura, as soon as her brother-in-law had been in the room a moment, had a particular fear; she had seen him twice noticeably under the influence of liquor; she had not liked it at all and now there were some of the same signs. She was afraid the children would discover them, or at any rate Miss Steet, and she felt the importance of not letting him stay in the room. She thought it almost a sign that he should have come there at all—he was so rare an apparition. He looked at her very hard, smiling as if to say, 'No, no, I'm not—not if you think it!' She perceived with relief in a moment that he was not very bad, and liquor disposed him apparently to tenderness, for he indulged in an interminable kissing of Geordie and Ferdy, during which Miss Steet turned away delicately, looking out of the window. The little boys asked him no questions to celebrate his return—they only announced that they were going to learn botany, to which he replied: 'Are you, really? Why, I never did,' and looked askance at the governess, blushing as if to express the hope that she would let him off from carrying that subject further. To Laura and to Miss Steet he was amiably explanatory, though his explanations were not quite coherent. He had come back an hour before—he was going to spend the night—he had driven over from Churton—he was thinking of taking the last train up to town. Was Laura dining at home? Was any one coming? He should enjoy a quiet dinner awfully.

'Certainly I'm alone,' said the girl. 'I suppose you know Selina is away.'

'Oh yes—I know where Selina is!' And Lionel Berrington looked round, smiling at every one present, including Scratch and Parson. He stopped while he continued to smile and Laura wondered what he was so much pleased at. She preferred not to ask—she was sure it was something that wouldn't give *her* pleasure; but after waiting a moment her brother-in-law went on: 'Selina's in Paris, my dear; that's where Selina is!'

'In Paris?' Laura repeated.

'Yes, in Paris, my dear—God bless her! Where else do you suppose? Geordie my boy, where should *you* think your mummy would naturally be?'

'Oh, I don't know,' said Geordie, who had no reply ready that would express affectingly the desolation of the nursery. 'If I were mummy I'd travel.'

'Well now that's your mummy's idea—she has gone to travel,' returned the father. 'Were you ever in Paris, Miss Steet?'

Miss Steet gave a nervous laugh and said No, but she had been to Boulogne; while to her added confusion Ferdy announced that he knew where Paris was—it was in America. 'No, it ain't—it's in Scotland!' cried Geordie; and Laura asked Lionel how he knew—whether his wife had written to him.

'Written to me? when did she ever write to me? No, I saw a fellow in town this morning who saw her there—at breakfast yesterday. He came over last night. That's how I know my wife's in Paris. You can't have better proof than that!'

'I suppose it's a very pleasant season there,' the governess murmured, as if from a sense of duty, in a distant, discomfortable tone.

'I daresay it's very pleasant indeed—I daresay it's awfully amusing!' laughed Mr. Berrington. 'Shouldn't you like to run over with me for a few days, Laura—just to have a go at the theatres? I don't see why we should always be moping at home. We'll take Miss Steet and the children and give mummy a pleasant surprise. Now who do you suppose she was with, in Paris—who do you suppose she was seen with?'

Laura had turned pale, she looked at him hard, imploringly, in the eyes: there was a name she was terribly afraid he would mention. 'Oh sir, in that case we had better go and get ready!' Miss Steet quavered, betwixt a laugh and a groan, in a spasm of discretion; and before Laura knew it she had gathered Geordie and Ferdy together and swept them out of the room.

The door closed behind her with a very quick softness and Lionel remained a moment staring at it.

'I say, what does she mean?—ain't that damned impertinent?' he stammered. 'What did she think I was going to say? Does she suppose I would say any harm before—before *her*? Dash it, does she suppose I would give away my wife to the servants?' Then he added, 'And I wouldn't say any harm before you, Laura. You are too good and too nice and I like you too much!'

'Won't you come downstairs? won't you have some tea?' the girl asked, uneasily.

'No, no, I want to stay here—I like this place,' he replied, very gently and reasoningly. 'It's a deuced nice place—it's an awfully jolly room. It used to be this way—always—when I was a little chap. I was a rough one, my dear; I wasn't a pretty little lamb like that pair. I think it's because you look after them—that's what makes 'em so sweet. The one in my time—what was her name? I think it was Bald or Bold—I rather think she found me a handful. I used to kick her shins—I was decidedly vicious. And do *you* see it's kept so well, Laura?' he went on, looking round him. ''Pon my soul, it's the prettiest room in the house. What does she want to go to Paris for when she has got such a charming house? Now can you answer me that, Laura?'

'I suppose she has gone to get some clothes: her dressmaker lives in Paris, you know.'

'Dressmaker? Clothes? Why, she has got whole rooms full of them. Hasn't she got whole rooms full of them?'

'Speaking of clothes I must go and change mine,' said Laura. 'I have been out in the rain—I have been to Plash—I'm decidedly damp.'

'Oh, you have been to Plash? You have seen my mother? I hope she's in very good health.' But before the girl could reply to this he went on: 'Now, I want you to guess who she's in Paris with. Motcomb saw them together—at that place, what's his name? close to the Madeleine.' And as Laura was silent, not wishing at all to guess, he continued—'It's the ruin of any woman, you know; I can't think what she has got in her head.' Still Laura said nothing, and as he had hold of her arm, she having turned away, she led him this time out of the room. She had a horror of the name, the name that was in her mind and that was apparently on his lips, though his tone was so singular, so contemplative. 'My dear girl, she's with Lady Ringrose—what do you say to that?' he exclaimed, as they passed along the corridor to the staircase.

'With Lady Ringrose?'

'They went over on Tuesday—they are knocking about there alone.'

'I don't know Lady Ringrose,' Laura said, infinitely relieved that the name was not the one she had feared. Lionel leaned on her arm as they went downstairs.

'I rather hope not—I promise you she has never put her foot in this house! If Selina expects to bring her here I should like half an hour's notice; yes, half an hour would do. She might as well be seen with——' And Lionel Berrington checked himself. 'She has had at least fifty——' And again he stopped short. 'You must pull me up, you know, if I say anything you don't like!'

'I don't understand you—let me alone, please!' the girl broke out, disengaging herself with an effort from his arm. She hurried down the rest of the steps and left him there looking after her, and as she went she heard him give an irrelevant laugh.

IV

She determined not to go to dinner—she wished for that day not to meet him again. He would drink more—he would be worse—she didn't know what he might say. Besides she was too angry—not with him but with Selina—and in addition to being angry she was sick. She knew who Lady Ringrose was; she knew so many things to-day that when she was younger—and only a little—she had not expected ever to know. Her eyes had been opened very wide in England and certainly they had been opened to Lady Ringrose. She had heard what she had done and perhaps a good deal more, and it was not very different from what she had heard of other women. She knew Selina had been to her house; she had an impression that her ladyship had been to Selina's, in London, though she herself had not seen her there. But she had not known they were so intimate as that—that Selina would rush over to Paris with her. What they had gone to Paris for was not necessarily criminal; there were a hundred reasons, familiar to ladies who were fond of change, of movement, of the theatres and of new bonnets; but nevertheless it was the fact of this little excursion quite as much as the companion that excited Laura's disgust.

She was not ready to say that the companion was any worse, though Lionel appeared to think so, than twenty other women who were her sister's intimates and whom she herself had seen in London, in Grosvenor Place, and even under the motherly old beeches at Mellows. But she thought it unpleasant and base in Selina to go abroad that way, like a commercial traveller, capriciously, clandestinely, without giving notice, when she had left her to understand that she was simply spending three or four days in town. It was bad taste and bad form, it was *cabotin* and had the mark of Selina's complete, irremediable frivolity—the worst accusation (Laura tried to cling to that opinion) that she laid herself open to. Of course frivolity that was never ashamed of itself was like a neglected cold—you could die of it morally as well as of anything else. Laura knew this and it was why she was inexpressibly vexed with her sister. She hoped she should get a letter from Selina the next morning (Mrs. Berrington would show at least that remnant of propriety) which would give her a chance to despatch her an answer that was already writing itself in her brain. It scarcely diminished Laura's eagerness for such an opportunity that she had a vision of Selina's showing her letter, laughing, across the table, at the place near the Madeleine, to Lady Ringrose (who would be painted—Selina herself, to do her justice, was not yet) while the French waiters, in white aprons, contemplated *ces dames*. It was new work for our young lady to judge of these shades—the gradations, the probabilities of license, and of the side of the line on which, or rather how far on the wrong side, Lady Ringrose was situated.

A quarter of an hour before dinner Lionel sent word to her room that she was to sit down without him—he had a headache and wouldn't appear. This was an unexpected grace and it simplified the position for Laura; so that, smoothing her

ruffles, she betook herself to the table. Before doing this however she went back to the schoolroom and told Miss Steet she
must contribute her company. She took the governess (the
little boys were in bed) downstairs with her and made her sit
opposite, thinking she would be a safeguard if Lionel were to
change his mind. Miss Steet was more frightened than herself—she was a very shrinking bulwark. The dinner was dull
and the conversation rare; the governess ate three olives and
looked at the figures on the spoons. Laura had more than
ever her sense of impending calamity; a draught of misfortune
seemed to blow through the house; it chilled her feet under
her chair. The letter she had in her head went out like a flame
in the wind and her only thought now was to telegraph to
Selina the first thing in the morning, in quite different words.
She scarcely spoke to Miss Steet and there was very little the
governess could say to her: she had already related her history
so often. After dinner she carried her companion into the
drawing-room, by the arm, and they sat down to the piano
together. They played duets for an hour, mechanically, violently; Laura had no idea what the music was—she only knew
that their playing was execrable. In spite of this—'That's a
very nice thing, that last,' she heard a vague voice say, behind
her, at the end; and she became aware that her brother-in-law
had joined them again.

Miss Steet was pusillanimous—she retreated on the spot,
though Lionel had already forgotten that he was angry at the
scandalous way she had carried off the children from the
schoolroom. Laura would have gone too if Lionel had not
told her that he had something very particular to say to her.
That made her want to go more, but she had to listen to him
when he expressed the hope that she hadn't taken offence at
anything he had said before. He didn't strike her as tipsy now;
he had slept it off or got rid of it and she saw no traces of his
headache. He was still conspicuously cheerful, as if he had got
some good news and were very much encouraged. She knew
the news he had got and she might have thought, in view of
his manner, that it could not really have seemed to him so
bad as he had pretended to think it. It was not the first time
however that she had seen him pleased that he had a case
against his wife, and she was to learn on this occasion how

extreme a satisfaction he could take in his wrongs. She would not sit down again; she only lingered by the fire, pretending to warm her feet, and he walked to and fro in the long room, where the lamplight to-night was limited, stepping on certain figures of the carpet as if his triumph were alloyed with hesitation.

'I never know how to talk to you—you are so beastly clever,' he said. 'I can't treat you like a little girl in a pinafore—and yet of course you are only a young lady. You're so deuced good—that makes it worse,' he went on, stopping in front of her with his hands in his pockets and the air he himself had of being a good-natured but dissipated boy; with his small stature, his smooth, fat, suffused face, his round, watery, light-coloured eyes and his hair growing in curious infantile rings. He had lost one of his front teeth and always wore a stiff white scarf, with a pin representing some symbol of the turf or the chase. 'I don't see why *she* couldn't have been a little more like you. If I could have had a shot at you first!'

'I don't care for any compliments at my sister's expense,' Laura said, with some majesty.

'Oh I say, Laura, don't put on so many frills, as Selina says. You know what your sister is as well as I do!' They stood looking at each other a moment and he appeared to see something in her face which led him to add—'You know, at any rate, how little we hit it off.'

'I know you don't love each other—it's too dreadful.'

'Love each other? she hates me as she'd hate a hump on her back. She'd do me any devilish turn she could. There isn't a feeling of loathing that she doesn't have for me! She'd like to stamp on me and hear me crack, like a black beetle, and she never opens her mouth but she insults me.' Lionel Berrington delivered himself of these assertions without violence, without passion or the sting of a new discovery; there was a familiar gaiety in his trivial little tone and he had the air of being so sure of what he said that he did not need to exaggerate in order to prove enough.

'Oh, Lionel!' the girl murmured, turning pale. 'Is that the particular thing you wished to say to me?'

'And you can't say it's my fault—you won't pretend to do that, will you?' he went on. 'Ain't I quiet, ain't I kind, don't

I go steady? Haven't I given her every blessed thing she has ever asked for?'

'You haven't given her an example!' Laura replied, with spirit. 'You don't care for anything in the wide world but to amuse yourself, from the beginning of the year to the end. No more does she—and perhaps it's even worse in a woman. You are both as selfish as you can live, with nothing in your head or your heart but your vulgar pleasure, incapable of a concession, incapable of a sacrifice!' She at least spoke with passion; something that had been pent up in her soul broke out and it gave her relief, almost a momentary joy.

It made Lionel Berrington stare; he coloured, but after a moment he threw back his head with laughter. 'Don't you call me kind when I stand here and take all that? If I'm so keen for my pleasure what pleasure do *you* give me? Look at the way I take it, Laura. You ought to do me justice. Haven't I sacrificed my home? and what more can a man do?'

'I don't think you care any more for your home than Selina does. And it's so sacred and so beautiful, God forgive you! You are all blind and senseless and heartless and I don't know what poison is in your veins. There is a curse on you and there will be a judgment!' the girl went on, glowing like a young prophetess.

'What do you want me to do? Do you want me to stay at home and read the Bible?' her companion demanded with an effect of profanity, confronted with her deep seriousness.

'It wouldn't do you any harm, once in a while.'

'There will be a judgment on *her*—that's very sure, and I know where it will be delivered,' said Lionel Berrington, indulging in a visible approach to a wink. 'Have I done the half to her she has done to me? I won't say the half but the hundredth part? Answer me truly, my dear!'

'I don't know what she has done to you,' said Laura, impatiently.

'That's exactly what I want to tell you. But it's difficult. I'll bet you five pounds she's doing it now!'

'You are too unable to make yourself respected,' the girl remarked, not shrinking now from the enjoyment of an advantage—that of feeling herself superior and taking her opportunity.

Her brother-in-law seemed to feel for the moment the prick of this observation. 'What has such a piece of nasty boldness as that to do with respect? She's the first that ever defied me!' exclaimed the young man, whose aspect somehow scarcely confirmed this pretension. 'You know all about her—don't make believe you don't,' he continued in another tone. 'You see everything—you're one of the sharp ones. There's no use beating about the bush, Laura—you've lived in this precious house and you're not so green as that comes to. Besides, you're so good yourself that you needn't give a shriek if one is obliged to say what one means. Why didn't you grow up a little sooner? Then, over there in New York, it would certainly have been you I would have made up to. *You* would have respected me—eh? now don't say you wouldn't.' He rambled on, turning about the room again, partly like a person whose sequences were naturally slow but also a little as if, though he knew what he had in mind, there were still a scruple attached to it that he was trying to rub off.

'I take it that isn't what I must sit up to listen to, Lionel, is it?' Laura said, wearily.

'Why, you don't want to go to bed at nine o'clock, do you? That's all rot, of course. But I want you to help me.'

'To help you—how?'

'I'll tell you—but you must give me my head. I don't know what I said to you before dinner—I had had too many brandy and sodas. Perhaps I was too free; if I was I beg your pardon. I made the governess bolt—very proper in the superintendent of one's children. Do you suppose they saw anything? I shouldn't care for that. I did take half a dozen or so; I was thirsty and I was awfully gratified.'

'You have little enough to gratify you.'

'Now that's just where you are wrong. I don't know when I've fancied anything so much as what I told you.'

'What you told me?'

'About her being in Paris. I hope she'll stay a month!'

'I don't understand you,' Laura said.

'Are you very sure, Laura? My dear, it suits my book! Now you know yourself he's not the first.'

Laura was silent; his round eyes were fixed on her face and she saw something she had not seen before—a little shining point which on Lionel's part might represent an idea, but which made his expression conscious as well as eager. 'He?' she presently asked. 'Whom are you speaking of?'

'Why, of Charley Crispin, G——' And Lionel Berrington accompanied this name with a startling imprecation.

'What has he to do——?'

'He has everything to do. Isn't he with her there?'

'How should I know? You said Lady Ringrose.'

'Lady Ringrose is a mere blind—and a devilish poor one at that. I'm sorry to have to say it to you, but he's her lover. I mean Selina's. And he ain't the first.'

There was another short silence while they stood opposed, and then Laura asked—and the question was unexpected—'Why do you call him Charley?'

'Doesn't he call me Lion, like all the rest?' said her brother-in-law, staring.

'You're the most extraordinary people. I suppose you have a certain amount of proof before you say such things to me?'

'Proof, I've oceans of proof! And not only about Crispin, but about Deepmere.'

'And pray who is Deepmere?'

'Did you never hear of Lord Deepmere? He has gone to India. That was before you came. I don't say all this for my pleasure, Laura,' Mr. Berrington added.

'Don't you, indeed?' asked the girl with a singular laugh. 'I thought you were so glad.'

'I'm glad to know it but I'm not glad to tell it. When I say I'm glad to know it I mean I'm glad to be fixed at last. Oh, I've got the tip! It's all open country now and I know just how to go. I've gone into it most extensively; there's nothing you can't find out to-day—if you go to the right place. I've—I've——' He hesitated a moment, then went on: 'Well, it's no matter what I've done. I know where I am and it's a great comfort. She's up a tree, if ever a woman was. Now we'll see who's a beetle and who's a toad!' Lionel Berrington concluded, gaily, with some incongruity of metaphor.

'It's not true—it's not true—it's not true,' Laura said, slowly.

'That's just what she'll say—though that's not the way she'll say it. Oh, if she could get off by your saying it for her!—for you, my dear, would be believed.'

'Get off—what do you mean?' the girl demanded, with a coldness she failed to feel, for she was tingling all over with shame and rage.

'Why, what do you suppose I'm talking about? I'm going to haul her up and to have it out.'

'You're going to make a scandal?'

'*Make* it? Bless my soul, it isn't me! And I should think it was made enough. I'm going to appeal to the laws of my country—that's what I'm going to do. She pretends I'm stopped, whatever she does. But that's all gammon—I ain't!'

'I understand—but you won't do anything so horrible,' said Laura, very gently.

'Horrible as you please, but less so than going on in this way; I haven't told you the fiftieth part—you will easily understand that I can't. They are not nice things to say to a girl like you—especially about Deepmere, if you didn't know it. But when they happen you've got to look at them, haven't you? That's the way I look at it.'

'It's not true—it's not true—it's not true,' Laura Wing repeated, in the same way, slowly shaking her head.

'Of course you stand up for your sister—but that's just what I wanted to say to you, that you ought to have some pity for *me* and some sense of justice. Haven't I always been nice to you? Have you ever had so much as a nasty word from me?'

This appeal touched the girl; she had eaten her brother-in-law's bread for months, she had had the use of all the luxuries with which he was surrounded, and to herself personally she had never known him anything but good-natured. She made no direct response however; she only said—'Be quiet, be quiet and leave her to me. I will answer for her.'

'Answer for her—what do you mean?'

'She shall be better—she shall be reasonable—there shall be no more talk of these horrors. Leave her to me—let me go away with her somewhere.'

'Go away with her? I wouldn't let you come within a mile of her, if you were *my* sister!'

'Oh, shame, shame!' cried Laura Wing, turning away from him.

She hurried to the door of the room, but he stopped her before she reached it. He got his back to it, he barred her way and she had to stand there and hear him. 'I haven't said what I wanted—for I told you that I wanted you to help me. I ain't cruel—I ain't insulting—you can't make out that against me; I'm sure you know in your heart that I've swallowed what would sicken most men. Therefore I will say that you ought to be fair. You're too clever not to be; *you* can't pretend to swallow——' He paused a moment and went on, and she saw it was his idea—an idea very simple and bold. He wanted her to side with him—to watch for him—to help him to get his divorce. He forbore to say that she owed him as much for the hospitality and protection she had in her poverty enjoyed, but she was sure that was in his heart. 'Of course she's your sister, but when one's sister's a perfect bad 'un there's no law to force one to jump into the mud to save her. It *is* mud, my dear, and mud up to your neck. You had much better think of her children—you had much better stop in *my* boat.'

'Do you ask me to help you with evidence against her?' the girl murmured. She had stood there passive, waiting while he talked, covering her face with her hands, which she parted a little, looking at him.

He hesitated a moment. 'I ask you not to deny what you have seen—what you feel to be true.'

'Then of the abominations of which you say you have proof, you haven't proof'

'Why haven't I proof?'

'If you want *me* to come forward!'

'I shall go into court with a strong case. You may do what you like. But I give you notice and I expect you not to forget that I have given it. Don't forget—because you'll be asked —that I have told you to-night where she is and with whom she is and what measures I intend to take.'

'Be asked—be asked?' the girl repeated.

'Why, of course you'll be cross-examined.'

'Oh, mother, mother!' cried Laura Wing. Her hands were over her face again and as Lionel Berrington, opening the door, let her pass, she burst into tears. He looked after her, distressed, compunctious, half-ashamed, and he exclaimed to

himself—'The bloody brute, the bloody brute!' But the words
had reference to his wife.

V

'And are you telling me the perfect truth when you say that
Captain Crispin was not there?'

'The perfect truth?' Mrs. Berrington straightened herself to
her height, threw back her head and measured her interlocutress up and down; it is to be surmised that this was one of
the many ways in which she knew she looked very handsome
indeed. Her interlocutress was her sister, and even in a discussion with a person long since initiated she was not incapable of feeling that her beauty was a new advantage. On this
occasion she had at first the air of depending upon it mainly
to produce an effect upon Laura; then, after an instant's reflection, she determined to arrive at her result in another way.
She exchanged her expression of scorn (of resentment at her
veracity's being impugned) for a look of gentle amusement;
she smiled patiently, as if she remembered that of course Laura
couldn't understand of what an impertinence she had been
guilty. There was a quickness of perception and lightness of
hand which, to her sense, her American sister had never acquired: the girl's earnest, almost barbarous probity blinded
her to the importance of certain pleasant little forms. 'My
poor child, the things you do say! One doesn't put a question
about the perfect truth in a manner that implies that a person
is telling a perfect lie. However, as it's only you, I don't mind
satisfying your clumsy curiosity. I haven't the least idea whether
Captain Crispin was there or not. I know nothing of his movements and he doesn't keep me informed—why should he, poor
man?—of his whereabouts. He was not there for me—isn't that
all that need interest you? As far as I was concerned he might
have been at the North Pole. I neither saw him nor heard of
him. I didn't see the end of his nose!' Selina continued, still
with her wiser, tolerant brightness, looking straight into her sister's eyes. Her own were clear and lovely and she was but little
less handsome than if she had been proud and freezing. Laura
wondered at her more and more; stupefied suspense was now
almost the girl's constant state of mind.

Mrs. Berrington had come back from Paris the day before but had not proceeded to Mellows the same night, though there was more than one train she might have taken. Neither had she gone to the house in Grosvenor Place but had spent the night at an hotel. Her husband was absent again; he was supposed to be in Grosvenor Place, so that they had not yet met. Little as she was a woman to admit that she had been in the wrong she was known to have granted later that at this moment she had made a mistake in not going straight to her own house. It had given Lionel a degree of advantage, made it appear perhaps a little that she had a bad conscience and was afraid to face him. But she had had her reasons for putting up at an hotel, and she thought it unnecessary to express them very definitely. She came home by a morning train, the second day, and arrived before luncheon, of which meal she partook in the company of her sister and in that of Miss Steet and the children, sent for in honour of the occasion. After luncheon she let the governess go but kept Scratch and Parson—kept them on ever so long in the morning-room where she remained; longer than she had ever kept them before. Laura was conscious that she ought to have been pleased at this, but there was a perversity even in Selina's manner of doing right; for she wished immensely now to see her alone—she had something so serious to say to her. Selina hugged her children repeatedly, encouraging their sallies; she laughed extravagantly at the artlessness of their remarks, so that at table Miss Steet was quite abashed by her unusual high spirits. Laura was unable to question her about Captain Crispin and Lady Ringrose while Geordie and Ferdy were there: they would not understand, of course, but names were always reflected in their limpid little minds and they gave forth the image later—often in the most extraordinary connections. It was as if Selina knew what she was waiting for and were determined to make her wait. The girl wished her to go to her room, that she might follow her there. But Selina showed no disposition to retire, and one could never entertain the idea for her, on any occasion, that it would be suitable that she should change her dress. The dress she wore—whatever it was—was too becoming to her, and to the moment, for that. Laura noticed how the very folds of her garment told that she had been to Paris;

she had spent only a week there but the mark of her *couturière* was all over her: it was simply to confer with this great artist that, from her own account, she had crossed the Channel. The signs of the conference were so conspicuous that it was as if she had said, 'Don't you see the proof that it was for nothing but *chiffons*?' She walked up and down the room with Geordie in her arms, in an access of maternal tenderness; he was much too big to nestle gracefully in her bosom, but that only made her seem younger, more flexible, fairer in her tall, strong slimness. Her distinguished figure bent itself hither and thither, but always in perfect freedom, as she romped with her children; and there was another moment, when she came slowly down the room, holding one of them in each hand and singing to them while they looked up at her beauty, charmed and listening and a little surprised at such new ways—a moment when she might have passed for some grave, antique statue of a young matron, or even for a picture of Saint Cecilia. This morning, more than ever, Laura was struck with her air of youth, the inextinguishable freshness that would have made any one exclaim at her being the mother of such bouncing little boys. Laura had always admired her, thought her the prettiest woman in London, the beauty with the finest points; and now these points were so vivid (especially her finished slenderness and the grace, the natural elegance of every turn—the fall of her shoulders had never looked so perfect) that the girl almost detested them: they appeared to her a kind of advertisement of danger and even of shame.

Miss Steet at last came back for the children, and as soon as she had taken them away Selina observed that she would go over to Plash—just as she was: she rang for her hat and jacket and for the carriage. Laura could see that she would not give her just yet the advantage of a retreat to her room. The hat and jacket were quickly brought, but after they were put on Selina kept her maid in the drawing-room, talking to her a long time, telling her elaborately what she wished done with the things she had brought from Paris. Before the maid departed the carriage was announced, and the servant, leaving the door of the room open, hovered within earshot. Laura then, losing patience, turned out the maid and closed the door; she stood before her sister, who was prepared for her

drive. Then she asked her abruptly, fiercely, but colouring with
her question, whether Captain Crispin had been in Paris. We
have heard Mrs. Berrington's answer, with which her strenuous sister was imperfectly satisfied; a fact the perception of
which it doubtless was that led Selina to break out, with a
greater show of indignation: 'I never heard of such extraordinary ideas for a girl to have, and such extraordinary things
for a girl to talk about! My dear, you have acquired a freedom—you have emancipated yourself from conventionality
—and I suppose I must congratulate you.' Laura only stood
there, with her eyes fixed, without answering the sally, and
Selina went on, with another change of tone: 'And pray if he
was there, what is there so monstrous? Hasn't it happened
that he is in London when I am there? Why is it then so awful
that he should be in Paris?'

'Awful, awful, too awful,' murmured Laura, with intense
gravity, still looking at her—looking all the more fixedly that
she knew how little Selina liked it.

'My dear, you do indulge in a style of innuendo, for a respectable young woman!' Mrs. Berrington exclaimed, with an
angry laugh. 'You have ideas that when I was a girl——' She
paused, and her sister saw that she had not the assurance to
finish her sentence on that particular note.

'Don't talk about my innuendoes and my ideas—you might
remember those in which I have heard you indulge! Ideas?
what ideas did I ever have before I came here?' Laura Wing
asked, with a trembling voice. 'Don't pretend to be shocked,
Selina; that's too cheap a defence. You have said things to
me—if you choose to talk of freedom! What is the talk of your
house and what does one hear if one lives with you? I don't
care what I hear now (it's all odious and there's little choice
and my sweet sensibility has gone God knows where!) and
I'm very glad if you understand that I don't care what I say.
If one talks about your affairs, my dear, one mustn't be too
particular!' the girl continued, with a flash of passion.

Mrs. Berrington buried her face in her hands. 'Merciful
powers, to be insulted, to be covered with outrage, by one's
wretched little sister!' she moaned.

'I think you should be thankful there is one human being
—however wretched—who cares enough for you to care

about the truth in what concerns you,' Laura said. 'Selina, Selina—are you hideously deceiving us?'

'Us?' Selina repeated, with a singular laugh. 'Whom do you mean by us?'

Laura Wing hesitated; she had asked herself whether it would be best she should let her sister know the dreadful scene she had had with Lionel; but she had not, in her mind, settled that point. However, it was settled now in an instant. 'I don't mean your friends—those of them that I have seen. I don't think *they* care a straw—I have never seen such people. But last week Lionel spoke to me—he told me he *knew* it, as a certainty.'

'Lionel spoke to you?' said Mrs. Berrington, holding up her head with a stare. 'And what is it that he knows?'

'That Captain Crispin was in Paris and that you were with him. He believes you went there to meet him.'

'He said this to *you?*'

'Yes, and much more—I don't know why I should make a secret of it.'

'The disgusting beast!' Selina exclaimed slowly, solemnly. 'He enjoys the right—the legal right—to pour forth his vileness upon *me*; but when he is so lost to every feeling as to begin to talk to you in such a way——!' And Mrs. Berrington paused, in the extremity of her reprobation.

'Oh, it was not his talk that shocked me—it was his believing it,' the girl replied. 'That, I confess, made an impression on me.'

'Did it indeed? I'm infinitely obliged to you! You are a tender, loving little sister.'

'Yes, I am, if it's tender to have cried about you—all these days—till I'm blind and sick!' Laura replied. 'I hope you are prepared to meet him. His mind is quite made up to apply for a divorce.'

Laura's voice almost failed her as she said this—it was the first time that in talking with Selina she had uttered that horrible word. She had heard it however, often enough on the lips of others; it had been bandied lightly enough in her presence under those somewhat austere ceilings of Mellows, of which the admired decorations and mouldings, in the taste of the middle of the last century, all in delicate plaster and

reminding her of Wedgewood pottery, consisted of slim festoons, urns and trophies and knotted ribbons, so many sym-
bols of domestic affection and irrevocable union. Selina herself
had flashed it at her with light superiority, as if it were some
precious jewel kept in reserve, which she could convert at any
moment into specie, so that it would constitute a happy provision for her future. The idea—associated with her own point
of view—was apparently too familiar to Mrs. Berrington to be
the cause of her changing colour; it struck her indeed, as presented by Laura, in a ludicrous light, for her pretty eyes expanded a moment and she smiled pityingly. 'Well, you are a
poor dear innocent, after all. Lionel would be about as able
to divorce me—even if I were the most abandoned of my
sex—as he would be to write a leader in the *Times*.'

'I know nothing about that,' said Laura.

'So I perceive—as I also perceive that you must have shut
your eyes very tight. Should you like to know a few of the
reasons—heaven forbid I should attempt to go over them all;
there are millions!—why his hands are tied?'

'Not in the least.'

'Should you like to know that his own life is too base for
words and that his impudence in talking about me would be
sickening if it weren't grotesque?' Selina went on, with increasing emotion. 'Should you like me to tell you to what he
has stooped—to the very gutter—and the charming history
of his relations with——'

'No, I don't want you to tell me anything of the sort,'
Laura interrupted. 'Especially as you were just now so pained
by the license of my own allusions.'

'You listen to him then—but it suits your purpose not to
listen to me!'

'Oh, Selina, Selina!' the girl almost shrieked, turning away.

'Where have your eyes been, or your senses, or your powers
of observation? You can be clever enough when it suits you!'
Mrs. Berrington continued, throwing off another ripple of derision. 'And now perhaps, as the carriage is waiting, you will
let me go about my duties.'

Laura turned again and stopped her, holding her arm as she
passed toward the door. 'Will you swear—will you swear by
everything that is most sacred?'

'Will I swear what?' And now she thought Selina visibly blanched.

'That you didn't lay eyes on Captain Crispin in Paris.'

Mrs. Berrington hesitated, but only for an instant. 'You are really too odious, but as you are pinching me to death I will swear, to get away from you. I never laid eyes on him.'

The organs of vision which Mrs. Berrington was ready solemnly to declare that she had not misapplied were, as her sister looked into them, an abyss of indefinite prettiness. The girl had sounded them before without discovering a conscience at the bottom of them, and they had never helped any one to find out anything about their possessor except that she was one of the beauties of London. Even while Selina spoke Laura had a cold, horrible sense of not believing her, and at the same time a desire, colder still, to extract a reiteration of the pledge. Was it the asseveration of her innocence that she wished her to repeat, or only the attestation of her falsity? One way or the other it seemed to her that this would settle something, and she went on inexorably—'By our dear mother's memory—by our poor father's?'

'By my mother's, by my father's,' said Mrs. Berrington, 'and by that of any other member of the family you like!' Laura let her go; she had not been pinching her, as Selina described the pressure, but had clung to her with insistent hands. As she opened the door Selina said, in a changed voice: 'I suppose it's no use to ask you if you care to drive to Plash.'

'No, thank you, I don't care—I shall take a walk.'

'I suppose, from that, that your friend Lady Davenant has gone.'

'No, I think she is still there.'

'That's a bore!' Selina exclaimed, as she went off.

VI

Laura Wing hastened to her room to prepare herself for her walk; but when she reached it she simply fell on her knees, shuddering, beside her bed. She buried her face in the soft counterpane of wadded silk; she remained there a long time, with a kind of aversion to lifting it again to the day. It burned with horror and there was coolness in the smooth glaze of the silk. It seemed to her that she had been concerned in a hideous transaction, and her uppermost feeling was, strangely enough, that she was ashamed—not of her sister but of herself. She did not believe her—that was at the bottom of everything, and she had made her lie, she had brought out her perjury, she had associated it with the sacred images of the dead. She took no walk, she remained in her room, and quite late, towards six o'clock, she heard on the gravel, outside of her windows, the wheels of the carriage bringing back Mrs. Berrington. She had evidently been elsewhere as well as to Plash; no doubt she had been to the vicarage—she was capable even of that. She could pay 'duty-visits,' like that (she called at the vicarage about three times a year), and she could go and be nice to her mother-in-law with her fresh lips still fresher for the lie she had just told. For it was as definite as an aching nerve to Laura that she did not believe her, and if she did not believe her the words she had spoken were a lie. It was the lie, the lie to *her* and which she had dragged out of her that seemed to the girl the ugliest thing. If she had admitted her folly, if she had explained, attenuated, sophisticated, there would have been a difference in her favour; but now she was bad because she was hard. She had a surface of polished metal. And she could make plans and calculate, she could act and do things for a particular effect. She could go straight to old Mrs. Berrington and to the parson's wife and his many daughters (just as she had kept the children after luncheon, on purpose, so long) because that looked innocent and domestic and denoted a mind without a feather's weight upon it.

A servant came to the young lady's door to tell her that tea was ready; and on her asking who else was below (for she had heard the wheels of a second vehicle just after Selina's return), she learned that Lionel had come back. At this news she requested that some tea should be brought to her room—she determined not to go to dinner. When the dinner-hour came she sent down word that she had a headache, that she was going to bed. She wondered whether Selina would come to her (she could forget disagreeable scenes amazingly); but her fervent hope that she would stay away was gratified. Indeed she would have another call upon her attention if her meeting with her husband was half as much of a concussion as was to have been expected. Laura had found herself listening hard, after knowing that her brother-in-law was in the house: she half expected to hear indications of violence—loud cries or the sound of a scuffle. It was a matter of course to her that some dreadful scene had not been slow to take place, something that discretion should keep her out of even if she had not been too sick. She did not go to bed—partly because she didn't know what might happen in the house. But she was restless also for herself: things had reached a point when it seemed to her that she must make up her mind. She left her candles unlighted—she sat up till the small hours, in the glow of the fire. What had been settled by her scene with Selina was that worse things were to come (looking into her fire, as the night went on, she had a rare prevision of the catastrophe that hung over the house), and she considered, or tried to consider, what it would be best for her, in anticipation, to do. The first thing was to take flight.

It may be related without delay that Laura Wing did not take flight and that though the circumstance detracts from the interest that should be felt in her character she did not even make up her mind. That was not so easy when action had to ensue. At the same time she had not the excuse of a conviction that by not acting—that is by not withdrawing from her brother-in-law's roof—she should be able to hold Selina up to her duty, to drag her back into the straight path. The hopes connected with that project were now a phase that she had left behind her; she had not to-day an illusion about her sister large enough to cover a sixpence. She had passed through the period of superstition, which had lasted the longest—the time when it seemed to her, as at first, a kind of profanity to doubt of Selina and judge her, the elder sister whose beauty and success she had ever been proud of and who carried herself, though with the most good-natured fraternisings, as one native to an upper air. She had called herself in moments of early penitence for irrepressible suspicion a little presumptuous prig: so strange did it seem to her at first, the impulse of criticism in regard to her bright protectress. But the revolution was over and she had a desolate, lonely freedom which struck her as not the most cynical thing in the world only because Selina's behaviour was more so. She supposed she should learn, though she was afraid of the knowledge, what had passed between that lady and her husband while her vigil ached itself away. But it appeared to her the next day, to her surprise, that nothing was changed in the situation save that Selina knew at present how much more she was suspected. As this had not a chastening effect upon Mrs. Berrington nothing had been gained by Laura's appeal to her. Whatever Lionel had said to his wife he said nothing to Laura: he left her at perfect liberty to forget the subject he had opened up to her so luminously. This was very characteristic of his good-nature; it had come over him that after all she wouldn't like it, and if the free use of the gray ponies could make up to her for the shock she might order them every day in the week and banish the unpleasant episode from her mind.

Laura ordered the gray ponies very often: she drove herself all over the country. She visited not only the neighbouring but the distant poor, and she never went out without stopping for one of the vicar's fresh daughters. Mellows was now half the time full of visitors and when it was not its master and mistress were staying with their friends either together or singly. Sometimes (almost always when she was asked) Laura Wing accompanied her sister and on two or three occasions she paid an independent visit. Selina had often told her that she wished her to have her own friends, so that the girl now felt a great desire to show her that she had them. She had arrived at no decision whatever; she had embraced in intention no particular course. She drifted on, shutting her eyes, averting her head and, as it seemed to herself, hardening her heart. This admission will doubtless suggest to the reader that she was a weak, inconsequent, spasmodic young person, with a standard not really, or at any rate not continuously, high; and I have no desire that she shall appear anything but what she was. It must even be related of her that since she could not escape and live in lodgings and paint fans (there were reasons why this combination was impossible) she determined to try and be happy in the given circumstances—to float in shallow, turbid water. She gave up the attempt to understand the cynical *modus vivendi* at which her companions seemed to have arrived; she knew it was not final but it served them sufficiently for the time; and if it served them why should it not serve her, the dependent, impecunious, tolerated little sister, representative of the class whom it behoved above all to mind their own business? The time was coming round when they would all move up to town, and there, in the crowd, with the added movement, the strain would be less and indifference easier.

Whatever Lionel had said to his wife that evening she had found something to say to him: that Laura could see, though not so much from any change in the simple expression of his little red face and in the vain bustle of his existence as from the grand manner in which Selina now carried herself. She was 'smarter' than ever and her waist was smaller and her back straighter and the fall of her shoulders finer; her long eyes were more oddly charming and the extreme detachment of her elbows from her sides conduced still more to the exhibition of her beautiful arms. So she floated, with a serenity not disturbed by a general tardiness, through the interminable succession of her engagements. Her photographs were not to be purchased in the Burlington Arcade—she had kept out of that; but she looked more than ever as they would have represented her if they had been obtainable there. There were times when Laura thought her brother-in-law's formless desistence too frivolous for nature: it even gave her a sense of deeper dangers. It was as if he had been digging away in the dark and they would all tumble into the hole. It happened to her to ask herself whether the things he had said to her the afternoon he fell upon her in the schoolroom had not all been a clumsy practical joke, a crude desire to scare, that of a schoolboy playing with a sheet in the dark; or else brandy and soda, which came to the same thing. However this might be she was obliged to recognise that the impression of brandy and soda had not again been given her. More striking still however was Selina's capacity to recover from shocks and condone imputations; she kissed again—kissed Laura—without tears, and proposed problems connected with the rearrangement of trimmings and of the flowers at dinner, as candidly—as earnestly—as if there had never been an intenser question between them. Captain Crispin was not mentioned; much less of course, so far as Laura was concerned, was he seen. But Lady Ringrose appeared; she came down for two days, during an absence of Lionel's. Laura, to her surprise, found her no such Jezebel but a clever little woman with a single eye-glass and short hair who had read Lecky and could give her useful hints about water-colours: a reconciliation that encouraged the girl, for this was the direction in which it now seemed to her best that she herself should grow.

VII

In Grosvenor Place, on Sunday afternoon, during the first weeks of the season, Mrs. Berrington was usually at home: this indeed was the only time when a visitor who had not made an appointment could hope to be admitted to her presence. Very few hours in the twenty-four did she spend in her own house. Gentlemen calling on these occasions rarely found her sister: Mrs. Berrington had the field to herself. It was understood between the pair that Laura should take this time for going to see her old women: it was in that manner that Selina qualified the girl's independent social resources. The old women however were not a dozen in number; they consisted mainly of Lady Davenant and the elder Mrs. Berrington, who had a house in Portman Street. Lady Davenant lived at Queen's Gate and also was usually at home of a Sunday afternoon: her visitors were not all men, like Selina Berrington's, and Laura's maidenly bonnet was not a false note in her drawing-room. Selina liked her sister, naturally enough, to make herself useful, but of late, somehow, they had grown rarer, the occasions that depended in any degree upon her aid, and she had never been much appealed to—though it would have seemed natural she should be—on behalf of the weekly chorus of gentlemen. It came to be recognised on Selina's part that nature had dedicated her more to the relief of old women than to that of young men. Laura had a distinct sense of interfering with the free interchange of anecdote and pleasantry that went on at her sister's fireside: the anecdotes were mostly such an immense secret that they could not be told fairly if she were there, and she had their privacy on her conscience. There was an exception however; when Selina expected Americans she naturally asked her to stay at home: not apparently so much because their conversation would be good for her as because hers would be good for them.

One Sunday, about the middle of May, Laura Wing prepared herself to go and see Lady Davenant, who had made a long absence from town at Easter but would now have returned. The weather was charming, she had from the first established her right to tread the London streets alone (if she was a poor girl she could have the detachment as well as the helplessness of it) and she promised herself the pleasure of a walk along the park, where the new grass was bright. A moment before she quitted the house her sister sent for her to the drawing-room; the servant gave her a note scrawled in pencil: 'That man from New York is here—Mr. Wendover, who brought me the introduction the other day from the Schoolings. He's rather a dose—you must positively come down and talk to him. Take him out with you if you can.' The description was not alluring, but Selina had never made a request of her to which the girl had not instantly responded: it seemed to her she was there for that. She joined the circle in the drawing-room and found that it consisted of five persons, one of whom was Lady Ringrose. Lady Ringrose was at all times and in all places a fitful apparition; she had described herself to Laura during her visit at Mellows as 'a bird on the branch.' She had no fixed habit of receiving on Sunday, she was in and out as she liked, and she was one of the few specimens of her sex who, in Grosvenor Place, ever turned up, as she said, on the occasions to which I allude. Of the three gentlemen two were known to Laura; she could have told you at least that the big one with the red hair was in the Guards and the other in the Rifles; the latter looked like a rosy child and as if he ought to be sent up to play with Geordie and Ferdy: his social nickname indeed was the Baby. Selina's admirers were of all ages—they ranged from infants to octogenarians.

She introduced the third gentleman to her sister; a tall, fair, slender young man who suggested that he had made a mistake in the shade of his tight, perpendicular coat, ordering it of too heavenly a blue. This added however to the candour of his appearance, and if he was a dose, as Selina had described him, he could only operate beneficently. There were moments when Laura's heart rather yearned towards her countrymen, and now, though she was preoccupied and a little disappointed at having been detained, she tried to like Mr. Wendover, whom her sister had compared invidiously, as it seemed to her, with her other companions. It struck her that his surface at least was as glossy as theirs. The Baby, whom she remembered to have heard spoken of as a dangerous flirt, was in conversation with Lady Ringrose and the guardsman with Mrs. Berrington; so she did her best to entertain the American visitor, as to whom any one could easily see (she thought) that he had brought a letter of introduction—he wished so to maintain the credit of those who had given it to him. Laura scarcely knew these people, American friends of her sister who had spent a period of festivity in London and gone back across the sea before her own advent; but Mr. Wendover gave her all possible information about them. He lingered upon them, returned to them, corrected statements he had made at first, discoursed upon them earnestly and exhaustively. He seemed to fear to leave them, lest he should find nothing again so good, and he indulged in a parallel that was almost elaborate between Miss Fanny and Miss Katie. Selina told her sister afterwards that she had overheard him—that he talked of them as if he had been a nursemaid; upon which Laura defended the young man even to extravagance. She reminded her sister that people in London were always saying Lady Mary and Lady Susan: why then shouldn't Americans use the Christian name, with the humbler prefix with which they had to content themselves? There had been a time when Mrs. Berrington had been happy enough to be Miss Lina, even though she was the elder sister; and the girl liked to think there were still old friends—friends of the family, at home, for whom, even should she live to sixty years of spinsterhood, she would never be anything but Miss Laura. This was as good as Donna Anna or Donna Elvira: English people could never call people as other people did, for fear of resembling the servants.

Mr. Wendover was very attentive, as well as communicative; however his letter might be regarded in Grosvenor Place he evidently took it very seriously himself; but his eyes wandered considerably, none the less, to the other side of the room, and Laura felt that though he had often seen persons like her before (not that he betrayed this too crudely) he had never seen any one like Lady Ringrose. His glance rested also on Mrs. Berrington, who, to do her justice, abstained from showing, by the way she returned it, that she wished her sister to get him out of the room. Her smile was particularly pretty on Sunday afternoons and he was welcome to enjoy it as a part of the decoration of the place. Whether or no the young man should prove interesting he was at any rate interested; indeed she afterwards learned that what Selina deprecated in him was the fact that he would eventually display a fatiguing intensity of observation. He would be one of the sort who noticed all kinds of little things—things she never saw or heard of—in the newspapers or in society, and would call upon her (a dreadful prospect) to explain or even to defend them. She had not come there to explain England to the Americans; the more particularly as her life had been a burden to her during the first years of her marriage through her having to explain America to the English. As for defending England to her countrymen she had much rather defend it *from* them: there were too many—too many for those who were already there. This was the class she wished to spare—she didn't care about the English. They could obtain an eye for an eye and a cutlet for a cutlet by going over there; which she had no desire to do—not for all the cutlets in Christendom!

When Mr. Wendover and Laura had at last cut loose from the Schoolings he let her know confidentially that he had come over really to see London: he had time, that year; he didn't know when he should have it again (if ever, as he said) and he had made up his mind that this was about the best use he could make of four months and a half. He had heard so much of it; it was talked of so much today; a man felt as if he ought to know something about it. Laura wished the others could hear this—that England was coming up, was making her way at last to a place among the topics of societies more universal. She thought Mr. Wendover after all remarkably like an Englishman, in spite of his saying that he believed she had resided in London quite a time. He talked a great deal about things being characteristic, and wanted to know, lowering his voice to make the inquiry, whether Lady Ringrose were not particularly so. He had heard of her very often, he said; and he observed that it was very interesting to see her: he could not have used a different tone if he had been speaking of the prime minister or the laureate. Laura was ignorant of what he had heard of Lady Ringrose; she doubted whether it could be the same as what she had heard from her brother-in-law: if this had been the case he never would have mentioned it. She foresaw that his friends in London would have a good deal to do in the way of telling him whether this or that were characteristic or not; he would go about in much the same way that English travellers did in America, fixing his attention mainly on society (he let Laura know that this was especially what he wished to go into) and neglecting the antiquities and sights, quite as if he failed to believe in their importance. He would ask questions it was impossible to answer; as to whether for instance society were very different in the two countries. If you said yes you gave a wrong impression and if you said no you didn't give a right one: that was the kind of thing that Selina had suffered from. Laura found her new acquaintance, on the present occasion and later, more philosophically analytic of his impressions than those of her countrymen she had hitherto encountered in her new home: the latter, in regard to such impressions, usually exhibited either a profane levity or a tendency to mawkish idealism.

Mrs. Berrington called out at last to Laura that she must not stay if she had prepared herself to go out: whereupon the girl, having nodded and smiled good-bye at the other members of the circle, took a more formal leave of Mr. Wendover—expressed the hope, as an American girl does in such a case, that they should see him again. Selina asked him to come and dine three days later; which was as much as to say that relations might be suspended till then. Mr. Wendover took it so, and having accepted the invitation he departed at the same time as Laura. He passed out of the house with her and in the street she asked him which way he was going. He was too tender, but she liked him; he appeared not to deal in chaff and that was a change that relieved her—she had so often had to pay out that coin when she felt wretchedly poor. She hoped he would ask her leave to go with her the way she was going—and this not on particular but on general grounds. It would be American, it would remind her of old times; she

should like him to be as American as that. There was no reason for her taking so quick an interest in his nature, inasmuch
as she had not fallen under his spell; but there were moments
when she felt a whimsical desire to be reminded of the way
people felt and acted at home. Mr. Wendover did not disappoint her, and the bright chocolate-coloured vista of the Fifth
Avenue seemed to surge before her as he said, 'May I have
the pleasure of making my direction the same as yours?' and
moved round, systematically, to take his place between her and
the curbstone. She had never walked much with young men
in America (she had been brought up in the new school, the
school of attendant maids and the avoidance of certain streets)
and she had very often done so in England, in the country;
yet, as at the top of Grosvenor Place she crossed over to the
park, proposing they should take that way, the breath of her
native land was in her nostrils. It was certainly only an American who could have the tension of Mr. Wendover; his solemnity almost made her laugh, just as her eyes grew dull when
people 'slanged' each other hilariously in her sister's house;
but at the same time he gave her a feeling of high respectability. It would be respectable still if she were to go on with
him indefinitely—if she never were to come home at all. He
asked her after a while, as they went, whether he had violated
the custom of the English in offering her his company;
whether in that country a gentleman might walk with a young
lady—the first time he saw her—not because their roads lay
together but for the sake of the walk.

'Why should it matter to me whether it is the custom of
the English? I am not English,' said Laura Wing. Then her
companion explained that he only wanted a general guidance—that with her (she was so kind) he had not the sense
of having taken a liberty. The point was simply—and rather
comprehensively and strenuously he began to set forth the
point. Laura interrupted him; she said she didn't care about
it and he almost irritated her by telling her she was kind. She
was, but she was not pleased at its being recognised so soon;
and he was still too importunate when he asked her whether
she continued to go by American usage, didn't find that if
one lived there one had to conform in a great many ways to
the English. She was weary of the perpetual comparison, for

she not only heard it from others—she heard it a great deal from herself. She held that there were certain differences you felt, if you belonged to one or the other nation, and that was the end of it: there was no use trying to express them. Those you *could* express were not real or not important ones and were not worth talking about. Mr. Wendover asked her if she liked English society and if it were superior to American; also if the tone were very high in London. She thought his questions 'academic'—the term she used to see applied in the *Times* to certain speeches in Parliament. Bending his long leanness over her (she had never seen a man whose material presence was so insubstantial, so unoppressive) and walking almost sidewise, to give her a proper attention, he struck her as innocent, as incapable of guessing that she had had a certain observation of life. They were talking about totally different things: English society, as he asked her judgment upon it and she had happened to see it, was an affair that he didn't suspect. If she were to give him that judgment it would be more than he doubtless bargained for; but she would do it not to make him open his eyes—only to relieve herself. She had thought of that before in regard to two or three persons she had met—of the satisfaction of breaking out with some of her feelings. It would make little difference whether the person understood her or not; the one who should do so best would be far from understanding everything. 'I want to get out of it, please—out of the set I live in, the one I have tumbled into through my sister, the people you saw just now. There are thousands of people in London who are different from that and ever so much nicer; but I don't see them, I don't know how to get at them; and after all, poor dear man, what power have you to help me?' That was in the last analysis the gist of what she had to say.

Mr. Wendover asked her about Selina in the tone of a person who thought Mrs. Berrington a very important phenomenon, and that by itself was irritating to Laura Wing. Important—gracious goodness, no! She might have to live with her, to hold her tongue about her; but at least she was not bound to exaggerate her significance. The young man forbore decorously to make use of the expression, but she could see that he supposed Selina to be a professional beauty

and she guessed that as this product had not yet been domesticated in the western world the desire to behold it, after
having read so much about it, had been one of the motives
of Mr. Wendover's pilgrimage. Mrs. Schooling, who must
have been a goose, had told him that Mrs. Berrington, though
transplanted, was the finest flower of a rich, ripe society and
as clever and virtuous as she was beautiful. Meanwhile Laura
knew what Selina thought of Fanny Schooling and her incurable provinciality. 'Now was that a good example of London
talk—what I heard (I only heard a little of it, but the conversation was more general before you came in) in your sister's
drawing-room? I don't mean literary, intellectual talk—I
suppose there are special places to hear that; I mean—I
mean——' Mr. Wendover went on with a deliberation which
gave his companion an opportunity to interrupt him. They
had arrived at Lady Davenant's door and she cut his meaning
short. A fancy had taken her, on the spot, and the fact that it
was whimsical seemed only to recommend it.

'If you want to hear London talk there will be some very
good going on in here,' she said. 'If you would like to come
in with me——?'

'Oh, you are very kind—I should be delighted,' replied Mr.
Wendover, endeavouring to emulate her own more rapid
processes. They stepped into the porch and the young man,
anticipating his companion, lifted the knocker and gave a
postman's rap. She laughed at him for this and he looked
bewildered; the idea of taking him in with her had become
agreeably exhilarating. Their acquaintance, in that moment,
took a long jump. She explained to him who Lady Davenant
was and that if he was in search of the characteristic it would
be a pity he shouldn't know her; and then she added, before
he could put the question:

'And what I am doing is *not* in the least usual. No, it is not
the custom for young ladies here to take strange gentlemen
off to call on their friends the first time they see them.'

'So that Lady Davenant will think it rather extraordinary?'
Mr. Wendover eagerly inquired; not as if that idea frightened
him, but so that his observation on this point should also be
well founded. He had entered into Laura's proposal with
complete serenity.

'Oh, most extraordinary!' said Laura, as they went in. The old lady however concealed such surprise as she may have felt, and greeted Mr. Wendover as if he were any one of fifty familiars. She took him altogether for granted and asked him no questions about his arrival, his departure, his hotel or his business in England. He noticed, as he afterwards confided to Laura, her omission of these forms; but he was not wounded by it—he only made a mark against it as an illustration of the difference between English and American manners: in New York people always asked the arriving stranger the first thing about the steamer and the hotel. Mr. Wendover appeared greatly impressed with Lady Davenant's antiquity, though he confessed to his companion on a subsequent occasion that he thought her a little flippant, a little frivolous even for her years. 'Oh yes,' said the girl, on that occasion, 'I have no doubt that you considered she talked too much, for one so old. In America old ladies sit silent and listen to the young.' Mr. Wendover stared a little and replied to this that with her—with Laura Wing—it was impossible to tell which side she was on, the American or the English: sometimes she seemed to take one, sometimes the other. At any rate, he added, smiling, with regard to the other great division it was easy to see—she was on the side of the old. 'Of course I am,' she said; 'when one *is* old!' And then he inquired, according to his wont, if she were thought so in England; to which she answered that it was England that had made her so.

Lady Davenant's bright drawing-room was filled with mementoes and especially with a collection of portraits of distinguished people, mainly fine old prints with signatures, an array of precious autographs. 'Oh, it's a cemetery,' she said, when the young man asked her some question about one of the pictures; 'they are my contemporaries, they are all dead and those things are the tombstones, with the inscriptions. I'm the grave-digger, I look after the place and try to keep it a little tidy. I have dug my own little hole,' she went on, to Laura, 'and when you are sent for you must come and put me in.' This evocation of mortality led Mr. Wendover to ask her if she had known Charles Lamb; at which she stared for an instant, replying: 'Dear me, no—one didn't meet him.'

'Oh, I meant to say Lord Byron,' said Mr. Wendover.

'Bless me, yes; I was in love with him. But he didn't notice me, fortunately—we were so many. He was very nice-looking but he was very vulgar.' Lady Davenant talked to Laura as if Mr. Wendover had not been there; or rather as if his interests and knowledge were identical with hers. Before they went away the young man asked her if she had known Garrick and she replied: 'Oh, dear, no, we didn't have them in our houses, in those days.'

'He must have been dead long before you were born!' Laura exclaimed.

'I daresay; but one used to hear of him.'

'I think I meant Edmund Kean,' said Mr. Wendover.

'You make little mistakes of a century or two,' Laura Wing remarked, laughing. She felt now as if she had known Mr. Wendover a long time.

'Oh, he was very clever,' said Lady Davenant.

'Very magnetic, I suppose,' Mr. Wendover went on.

'What's that? I believe he used to get tipsy.'

'Perhaps you don't use that expression in England?' Laura's companion inquired.

'Oh, I daresay we do, if it's American; we talk American now. You seem very good-natured people, but such a jargon as you *do* speak!'

'I like *your* way, Lady Davenant,' said Mr. Wendover, benevolently, smiling.

'You might do worse,' cried the old woman; and then she added: 'Please go out!' They were taking leave of her but she kept Laura's hand and, for the young man, nodded with decision at the open door. 'Now, wouldn't *he* do?' she asked, after Mr. Wendover had passed into the hall.

'Do for what?'

'For a husband, of course.'

'For a husband—for whom?'

'Why—for me,' said Lady Davenant.

'I don't know—I think he might tire you.'

'Oh—if he's tiresome!' the old lady continued, smiling at the girl.

'I think he is very good,' said Laura.

'Well then, he'll do.'

'Ah, perhaps *you* won't!' Laura exclaimed, smiling back at her and turning away.

VIII

She was of a serious turn by nature and unlike many serious people she made no particular study of the art of being gay. Had her circumstances been different she might have done so, but she lived in a merry house (heaven save the mark! as she used to say) and therefore was not driven to amuse herself for conscience sake. The diversions she sought were of a serious cast and she liked those best which showed most the note of difference from Selina's interests and Lionel's. She felt that she was most divergent when she attempted to cultivate her mind, and it was a branch of such cultivation to visit the curiosities, the antiquities, the monuments of London. She was fond of the Abbey and the British Museum—she had extended her researches as far as the Tower. She read the works of Mr. John Timbs and made notes of the old corners of history that had not yet been abolished—the houses in which great men had lived and died. She planned a general tour of inspection of the ancient churches of the City and a pilgrimage to the queer places commemorated by Dickens. It must be added that though her intentions were great her adventures had as yet been small. She had wanted for opportunity and independence; people had other things to do than to go with her, so that it was not till she had been some time in the country and till a good while after she had begun to go out alone that she entered upon the privilege of visiting public institutions by herself. There were some aspects of London that frightened her, but there were certain spots, such as the Poets' Corner in the Abbey or the room of the Elgin marbles, where she liked better to be alone than not to have the right companion. At the time Mr. Wendover presented himself in Grosvenor Place she had begun to put in, as they said, a museum or something of that sort whenever she had a chance. Besides her idea that such places were sources of knowledge (it is to be feared that the poor girl's notions of knowledge were at once conventional and crude) they were also occasions for detachment, an escape from worrying thoughts. She forgot Selina and she 'qualified' herself a little—though for what she hardly knew.

The day Mr. Wendover dined in Grosvenor Place they talked about St. Paul's, which he expressed a desire to see, wishing to get some idea of the great past, as he said, in England as well as of the present. Laura mentioned that she had spent half an hour the summer before in the big black temple on Ludgate Hill; whereupon he asked her if he might entertain the hope that—if it were not disagreeable to her to go again—she would serve as his guide there. She had taken him to see Lady Davenant, who was so remarkable and worth a long journey, and now he should like to pay her back—to show *her* something. The difficulty would be that there was probably nothing she had not seen; but if she could think of anything he was completely at her service. They sat together at dinner and she told him she would think of something before the repast was over. A little while later she let him know that a charming place had occurred to her—a place to which she was afraid to go alone and where she should be grateful for a protector: she would tell him more about it afterwards. It was then settled between them that on a certain afternoon of the same week they would go to St. Paul's together, extending their ramble as much further as they had time. Laura lowered her voice for this discussion, as if the range of allusion had had a kind of impropriety. She was now still more of the mind that Mr. Wendover was a good young man—he had such worthy eyes. His principal defect was that he treated all subjects as if they were equally important; but that was perhaps better than treating them with equal levity. If one took an interest in him one might not despair of teaching him to discriminate.

Laura said nothing at first to her sister about her appointment with him: the feelings with which she regarded Selina were not such as to make it easy for her to talk over matters of conduct, as it were, with this votary of pleasure at any price, or at any rate to report her arrangements to her as one would do to a person of fine judgment. All the same, as she had a horror of positively hiding anything (Selina herself did that enough for two) it was her purpose to mention at luncheon

on the day of the event that she had agreed to accompany
Mr. Wendover to St. Paul's. It so happened however that Mrs.
Berrington was not at home at this repast; Laura partook of
it in the company of Miss Steet and her young charges. It very
often happened now that the sisters failed to meet in the
morning, for Selina remained very late in her room and there
had been a considerable intermission of the girl's earlier custom of visiting her there. It was Selina's habit to send forth
from this fragrant sanctuary little hieroglyphic notes in which
she expressed her wishes or gave her directions for the day.
On the morning I speak of her maid put into Laura's hand
one of these communications, which contained the words:
'Please be sure and replace me with the children at lunch—I
meant to give them that hour to-day. But I have a frantic
appeal from Lady Watermouth; she is worse and beseeches me
to come to her, so I rush for the 12.30 train.' These lines
required no answer and Laura had no questions to ask about
Lady Watermouth. She knew she was tiresomely ill, in exile,
condemned to forego the diversions of the season and calling
out to her friends, in a house she had taken for three months
at Weybridge (for a certain particular air) where Selina had
already been to see her. Selina's devotion to her appeared
commendable—she had her so much on her mind. Laura had
observed in her sister in relation to other persons and objects
these sudden intensities of charity, and she had said to herself,
watching them—'Is it because she is bad?—does she want to
make up for it somehow and to buy herself off from the
penalties?'

Mr. Wendover called for his *cicerone* and they agreed to go
in a romantic, Bohemian manner (the young man was very
docile and appreciative about this), walking the short distance
to the Victoria station and taking the mysterious underground
railway. In the carriage she anticipated the inquiry that she
figured to herself he presently would make and said, laughing:
'No, no, this is very exceptional; if we were both English—
and both what we are, otherwise—we wouldn't do this.'

'And if only one of us were English?'

'It would depend upon which one.'

'Well, say me.'

'Oh, in that case I certainly—on so short an acquaintance—would not go sight-seeing with you.'

'Well, I am glad I'm American,' said Mr. Wendover, sitting opposite to her.

'Yes, you may thank your fate. It's much simpler,' Laura added.

'Oh, you spoil it!' the young man exclaimed—a speech of which she took no notice but which made her think him brighter, as they used to say at home. He was brighter still after they had descended from the train at the Temple station (they had meant to go on to Blackfriars, but they jumped out on seeing the sign of the Temple, fired with the thought of visiting that institution too) and got admission to the old garden of the Benchers, which lies beside the foggy, crowded river, and looked at the tombs of the crusaders in the low Romanesque church, with the cross-legged figures sleeping so close to the eternal uproar, and lingered in the flagged, homely courts of brick, with their much-lettered door-posts, their dull old windows and atmosphere of consultation—lingered to talk of Johnson and Goldsmith and to remark how London opened one's eyes to Dickens; and he was brightest of all when they stood in the high, bare cathedral, which suggested a dirty whiteness, saying it was fine but wondering why it was not finer and letting a glance as cold as the dusty, colourless glass fall upon epitaphs that seemed to make most of the defunct bores even in death. Mr. Wendover was decorous but he was increasingly gay, and these qualities appeared in him in spite of the fact that St. Paul's was rather a disappointment. Then they felt the advantage of having the other place—the one Laura had had in mind at dinner—to fall back upon: that perhaps would prove a compensation. They entered a hansom now (they had to come to that, though they had walked also from the Temple to St. Paul's) and drove to Lincoln's Inn Fields, Laura making the reflection as they went that it was really a charm to roam about London under valid protection—such a mixture of freedom and safety—and that perhaps she had been unjust, ungenerous to her sister. A good-natured, positively charitable doubt came into her mind—a doubt that Selina might have the benefit of. What she liked in her present undertaking was the element of the *imprévu* that it contained, and perhaps it was simply the same happy sense of getting the laws of London—once in a way—off her back that had led Selina to go over to Paris to ramble about with Captain Crispin. Possibly they had done nothing worse than go together to the Invalides and Notre Dame; and if any one were to meet *her* driving that way, so far from home, with Mr. Wendover—Laura, mentally, did not finish her sentence, overtaken as she was by the reflection that she had fallen again into her old assumption (she had been in and out of it a hundred times), that Mrs. Berrington *had* met Captain Crispin—the idea she so passionately repudiated. She at least would never deny that she had spent the afternoon with Mr. Wendover: she would simply say that he was an American and had brought a letter of introduction.

The cab stopped at the Soane Museum, which Laura Wing had always wanted to see, a compatriot having once told her that it was one of the most curious things in London and one of the least known. While Mr. Wendover was discharging the vehicle she looked over the important old-fashioned square (which led her to say to herself that London was endlessly big and one would never know all the places that made it up) and saw a great bank of cloud hanging above it—a definite portent of a summer storm. 'We are going to have thunder; you had better keep the cab,' she said; upon which her companion told the man to wait, so that they should not afterwards, in the wet, have to walk for another conveyance. The heterogeneous objects collected by the late Sir John Soane are arranged in a fine old dwelling-house, and the place gives one the impression of a sort of Saturday afternoon of one's youth—a long, rummaging visit, under indulgent care, to some eccentric and rather alarming old travelled person. Our young friends wandered from room to room and thought everything queer and some few objects interesting; Mr. Wendover said it would be a very good place to find a thing you couldn't find anywhere else—it illustrated the prudent virtue of keeping. They took note of the sarcophagi and pagodas, the artless old maps and medals. They admired the fine Hogarths; there were uncanny, unexpected objects that Laura edged away from, that she would have preferred not to be in the room with. They had been there half an hour—it had grown much darker—when they heard a tremendous peal of thunder and became aware that the storm had broken. They watched it a while from the upper windows—a violent June shower, with quick sheets of lightning and a rainfall that danced on the pavements. They took it sociably, they lingered at the window, inhaling the odour of the fresh wet that splashed over the sultry town. They would have to wait till it had passed, and they resigned themselves serenely to this idea, repeating very often that it would pass very soon. One of the keepers told them that there were other rooms to see—that there were very interesting things in the basement. They made their way down—it grew much darker and they heard a great deal of thunder—and entered a part of the house which presented itself to Laura as a series of dim, irregular vaults—passages and little narrow avenues—encumbered with strange vague things, obscured for the time but some of which had a wicked, startling look, so that she wondered how the keepers could stay there. 'It's very fearful—it looks like a cave of idols!' she said to her companion; and then she added—'Just look there—is that a person or a thing?' As she spoke they drew nearer to the object of her reference—a figure in the middle of a small vista of curiosities, a figure which answered her question by uttering a short shriek as they approached. The immediate cause of this cry was apparently a vivid flash of lightning, which penetrated into the room and illuminated both Laura's face and that of the mysterious person. Our young lady recognised her sister, as Mrs. Berrington had evidently recognised her. 'Why, Selina!' broke from her lips before she had time to check the words. At the same moment the figure turned quickly away, and then Laura saw that it was accompanied by another, that of a tall gentleman with a light beard which shone in the dusk. The two persons retreated together—dodged out of sight, as it were, disappearing in the gloom or in the labyrinth of the objects exhibited. The whole encounter was but the business of an instant.

'Was it Mrs. Berrington?' Mr. Wendover asked with interest while Laura stood staring.

'Oh no, I only thought it was at first,' she managed to reply, very quickly. She had recognised the gentleman—he had the

fine fair beard of Captain Crispin—and her heart seemed to
her to jump up and down. She was glad her companion could
not see her face, and yet she wanted to get out, to rush up
the stairs, where he would see it again, to escape from the
place. She wished not to be there with *them*—she was overwhelmed with a sudden horror. 'She has lied—she has lied
again—she has lied!'—that was the rhythm to which her
thought began to dance. She took a few steps one way and
then another: she was afraid of running against the dreadful
pair again. She remarked to her companion that it was time
they should go off, and then when he showed her the way
back to the staircase she pleaded that she had not half seen
the things. She pretended suddenly to a deep interest in them,
and lingered there roaming and prying about. She was flurried
still more by the thought that he would have seen her flurry,
and she wondered whether he believed the woman who had
shrieked and rushed away was *not* Selina. If she was not Selina
why had she shrieked? and if she was Selina what would Mr.
Wendover think of her behaviour, and of her own, and of the
strange accident of their meeting? What must she herself think
of that? so astonishing it was that in the immensity of London
so infinitesimally small a chance should have got itself enacted.
What a queer place to come to—for people like them! They
would get away as soon as possible, of that she could be sure;
and she would wait a little to give them time.

Mr. Wendover made no further remark—that was a relief;
though his silence itself seemed to show that he was mystified.
They went upstairs again and on reaching the door found to
their surprise that their cab had disappeared—a circumstance
the more singular as the man had not been paid. The rain was
still coming down, though with less violence, and the square
had been cleared of vehicles by the sudden storm. The doorkeeper, perceiving the dismay of our friends, explained that
the cab had been taken up by another lady and another gentleman who had gone out a few minutes before; and when
they inquired how he had been induced to depart without the
money they owed him the reply was that there evidently had
been a discussion (he hadn't heard it, but the lady seemed in
a fearful hurry) and the gentleman had told him that they
would make it all up to him and give him a lot more into the

bargain. The doorkeeper hazarded the candid surmise that the cabby would make ten shillings by the job. But there were plenty more cabs; there would be one up in a minute and the rain moreover was going to stop. 'Well, that *is* sharp practice!' said Mr. Wendover. He made no further allusion to the identity of the lady.

IX

The rain did stop while they stood there, and a brace of hansoms was not slow to appear. Laura told her companion that he must put her into one—she could go home alone: she had taken up enough of his time. He deprecated this course very respectfully; urged that he had it on his conscience to deliver her at her own door; but she sprang into the cab and closed the apron with a movement that was a sharp prohibition. She wanted to get away from him—it would be too awkward, the long, pottering drive back. Her hansom started off while Mr. Wendover, smiling sadly, lifted his hat. It was not very comfortable, even without him; especially as before she had gone a quarter of a mile she felt that her action had been too marked—she wished she had let him come. His puzzled, innocent air of wondering what was the matter annoyed her; and she was in the absurd situation of being angry at a desistence which she would have been still angrier if he had been guiltless of. It would have comforted her (because it would seem to share her burden) and yet it would have covered her with shame if he had guessed that what she saw was wrong. It would not occur to him that there was a scandal so near her, because he thought with no great promptitude of such things; and yet, since there was—but since there was after all Laura scarcely knew what attitude would sit upon him most gracefully. As to what he might be prepared to suspect by having heard what Selina's reputation was in London, of that Laura was unable to judge, not knowing what was said, because of course it was not said to *her*. Lionel would undertake to give her the benefit of this any moment she would allow him, but how in the world could *he* know either, for how could things be said to him? Then, in the rattle of the hansom, passing through streets for which the girl had no eyes, 'She has lied, she has lied, she has lied!' kept repeating itself. Why had she written and signed that wanton falsehood about her going down to Lady Watermouth? How could she have gone to Lady Watermouth's when she was making so very different and so extraordinary a use of the hours she had announced her intention of spending there? What had been the need of that misrepresentation and why did she lie before she was driven to it?

It was because she was false altogether and deception came out of her with her breath; she was so depraved that it was easier to her to fabricate than to let it alone. Laura would not have asked her to give an account of her day, but she would ask her now. She shuddered at one moment, as she found herself saying—even in silence—such things of her sister, and the next she sat staring out of the front of the cab at the stiff problem presented by Selina's turning up with the partner of her guilt at the Soane Museum, of all places in the world. The girl shifted this fact about in various ways, to account for it—not unconscious as she did so that it was a pretty exercise of ingenuity for a nice girl. Plainly, it was a rare accident: if it had been their plan to spend the day together the Soane Museum had not been in the original programme. They had been near it, they had been on foot and they had rushed in to take refuge from the rain. But how did they come to be near it and above all to be on foot? How could Selina do anything so reckless from her own point of view as to walk about the town—even an out-of-the-way part of it—with her suspected lover? Laura Wing felt the want of proper knowledge to explain such anomalies. It was too little clear to her where ladies went and how they proceeded when they consorted with gentlemen in regard to their meetings with whom they had to lie. She knew nothing of where Captain Crispin lived; very possibly—for she vaguely remembered having heard Selina say of him that he was very poor—he had chambers in that part of the town, and they were either going to them or coming from them. If Selina had neglected to take her way in a four-wheeler with the glasses up it was through some chance that would not seem natural till it was explained, like that of their having darted into a public institution. Then no doubt it would hang together with the rest only too well. The explanation most exact would probably be that the pair had snatched a walk together (in the course of a day of many edifying episodes) for the 'lark' of it, and for the sake of the walk had taken the risk, which in that part of London, so detached from all gentility, had appeared to them small. The last thing Selina could have expected was to meet her sister in such a strange corner —her sister with a young man of her own!

She was dining out that night with both Selina and Lionel —a conjunction that was rather rare. She was by no means always invited with them, and Selina constantly went without her husband. Appearances, however, sometimes got a sop thrown them; three or four times a month Lionel and she entered the brougham together like people who still had forms, who still said 'my dear.' This was to be one of those occasions, and Mrs. Berrington's young unmarried sister was included in the invitation. When Laura reached home she learned, on inquiry, that Selina had not yet come in, and she went straight to her own room. If her sister had been there she would have gone to hers instead— she would have cried out to her as soon as she had closed the door: 'Oh, stop, stop—in God's name, stop before you go any further, before exposure and ruin and shame come down and bury us!' That was what was in the air—the vulgarest disgrace, and the girl, harder now than ever about her sister, was conscious of a more passionate desire to save herself. But Selina's absence made the difference that during the next hour a certain chill fell upon this impulse from other feelings: she found suddenly that she was late and she began to dress. They were to go together after dinner to a couple of balls; a diversion which struck her as ghastly for people who carried such horrors in their breasts. Ghastly was the idea of the drive of husband, wife and sister in pursuit of pleasure, with falsity and detection and hate between them. Selina's maid came to her door to tell her that she was in the carriage—an extraordinary piece of punctuality, which made her wonder, as Selina was always dreadfully late for everything. Laura went down as quickly as she could, passed through the open door, where the servants were grouped in the foolish majesty of their superfluous attendance, and through the file of dingy gazers who had paused at the sight of the carpet across the pavement and the waiting carriage, in which Selina sat in pure white splendour. Mrs. Berrington had a tiara on her head and a proud patience in her face, as if her sister were really a sore trial. As soon as the girl had taken her place she said to the footman: 'Is Mr. Berrington there?'—to which the man replied: 'No ma'am, not yet.' It was not new to Laura that if there was any one later as a general thing than Selina it was Selina's husband. 'Then he must take a hansom. Go on.' The footman mounted and they rolled away.

There were several different things that had been present to Laura's mind during the last couple of hours as destined to mark—one or the other—this present encounter with her sister; but the words Selina spoke the moment the brougham began to move were of course exactly those she had not foreseen. She had considered that she might take this tone or that tone or even no tone at all; she was quite prepared for her presenting a face of blankness to any form of interrogation and saying, 'What on earth are you talking about?' It was in short conceivable to her that Selina would deny absolutely that she had been in the museum, that they had stood face to face and that she had fled in confusion. She was capable of explaining the incident by an idiotic error on Laura's part, by her having seized on another person, by her seeing Captain Crispin in every bush; though doubtless she would be taxed (of course she would say *that* was the woman's own affair) to supply a reason for the embarrassment of the other lady. But she was not prepared for Selina's breaking out with: 'Will you be so good as to inform me if you are engaged to be married to Mr. Wendover?'

'Engaged to him? I have seen him but three times.'

'And is that what you usually do with gentlemen you have seen three times?'

'Are you talking about my having gone with him to see some sights? I see nothing wrong in that. To begin with you see what he is. One might go with him anywhere. Then he brought us an introduction—we have to do something for him. Moreover you threw him upon me the moment he came—you asked me to take charge of him.'

'I didn't ask you to be indecent! If Lionel were to know it he wouldn't tolerate it, so long as you live with us.'

great many 'My loves' and 'Not for the worlds.' Lionel Berrington disappeared after dinner, without holding any communication with his wife, and Laura expected to find that he had taken the carriage, to repay her in kind for her having driven off from Grosvenor Place without him. But it was not new to the girl that he really spared his wife more than she spared him; not so much perhaps because he wouldn't do the 'nastiest' thing as because he couldn't. Selina could always be nastier. There was ever a whimsicality in her actions: if two or three hours before it had been her fancy to keep a third person out of the carriage she had now her reasons for bringing such a person in. Laura knew that she would not only pretend, but would really believe, that her vindication of her conduct on their way to dinner had been powerful and that she had won a brilliant victory. What need, therefore, to thresh out further a subject that she had chopped into atoms? Laura Wing, however, had needs of her own, and her remaining in the carriage when the footman next opened the door was intimately connected with them.

'I don't care to go in,' she said to her sister. 'If you will allow me to be driven home and send back the carriage for you, that's what I shall like best.'

Selina stared and Laura knew what she would have said if she could have spoken her thought. 'Oh, you are furious that I haven't given you a chance to fly at me again, and you must take it out in sulks!' These were the ideas—ideas of 'fury' and sulks—into which Selina could translate feelings that sprang from the pure depths of one's conscience. Mrs. Collingwood protested—she said it was a shame that Laura shouldn't go in and enjoy herself when she looked so lovely. 'Doesn't she look lovely?' She appealed to Mrs. Berrington. 'Bless us, what's the use of being pretty? Now, if she had *my* face!'

'I think she looks rather cross,' said Selina, getting out with her friend and leaving her sister to her own inventions. Laura had a vision, as the carriage drove away again, of what her situation would have been, or her peace of mind, if Selina and Lionel had been good, attached people like the Collingwoods, and at the same time of the singularity of a good woman's being ready to accept favours from a person as to whose behaviour she had the lights that must have come to the lady in question in regard to Selina. She accepted favours herself and she only wanted to be good: that was oppressively true; but if she had not been Selina's sister she would never drive in her carriage. That conviction was strong in the girl as this vehicle conveyed her to Grosvenor Place; but it was not in its nature consoling. The prevision of disgrace was now so vivid to her that it seemed to her that if it had not already overtaken them she had only to thank the loose, mysterious, rather ignoble tolerance of people like Mrs. Collingwood. There were plenty of that species, even among the good; perhaps indeed expo-sure and dishonour would begin only when the bad had got hold of the facts. Would the bad be most horrified and do most to spread the scandal? There were, in any event, plenty of them too.

Laura sat up for her sister that night, with that nice question to help her to torment herself—whether if she was hard and merciless in judging Selina it would be with the bad too that she would associate herself. Was she all wrong after all—was she cruel by being too rigid? Was Mrs. Collingwood's attitude the right one and ought she only to propose to herself to 'allow' more and more, and to allow ever, and to smooth things down by gentleness, by sympathy, by not looking at them too hard? It was not the first time that the just measure of things seemed to slip from her hands as she became con-scious of possible, or rather of very actual, differences of stan-dard and usage. On this occasion Geordie and Ferdy asserted themselves, by the mere force of lying asleep upstairs in their little cribs, as on the whole the proper measure. Laura went into the nursery to look at them when she came home—it was her habit almost any night—and yearned over them as moth-ers and maids do alike over the pillow of rosy childhood. They were an antidote to all casuistry; for Selina to forget *them*— that was the beginning and the end of shame. She came back to the library, where she should best hear the sound of her sister's return; the hours passed as she sat there, without bringing round this event. Carriages came and went all night; the soft shock of swift hoofs was on the wooden roadway long after the summer dawn grew fair—till it was merged in the rumble of the awakening day. Lionel had not come in when she returned, and he continued absent, to Laura's satisfaction;

for if she wanted not to miss Selina she had no desire at present to have to tell her brother-in-law why she was sitting up. She prayed Selina might arrive first: then she would have more time to think of something that harassed her particularly—the question of whether she ought to tell Lionel that she had seen her in a far-away corner of the town with Captain Crispin. Almost impossible as she found it now to feel any tenderness for her, she yet detested the idea of bearing witness against her: notwithstanding which it appeared to her that she could make up her mind to do this if there were a chance of its preventing the last scandal—a catastrophe to which she saw her sister rushing straight. That Selina was capable at a given moment of going off with her lover, and capable of it precisely because it was the greatest ineptitude as well as the greatest wickedness—there was a voice of prophecy, of warning, to this effect in the silent, empty house. If repeating to Lionel what she had seen would contribute to prevent anything, or to stave off the danger, was it not her duty to denounce his wife, flesh and blood of her own as she was, to his further reprobation? This point was not intolerably difficult to determine, as she sat there waiting, only because even what was righteous in that reprobation could not present itself to her as fruitful or efficient. What could Lionel frustrate, after all, and what intelligent or authoritative step was he capable of taking? Mixed with all that now haunted her was her consciousness of what his own absence at such an hour represented in the way of the unedifying. He might be at some sporting club or he might be anywhere else; at any rate he was not where he ought to be at three o'clock in the morning. Such the husband such the wife, she said to herself; and she felt that Selina would have a kind of advantage, which she grudged her, if she should come in and say: 'And where is *he*, please—where is he, the exalted being on whose behalf you have undertaken to preach so much better than he himself practises?'

But still Selina failed to come in—even to take that advantage; yet in proportion as her waiting was useless did the girl find it impossible to go to bed. A new fear had seized her, the fear that she would never come back at all—that they were already in the presence of the dreaded catastrophe. This made her so nervous that she paced about the lower rooms, listening to every sound, roaming till she was tired. She knew it was absurd, the image of Selina taking flight in a ball-dress; but she said to herself that she might very well have sent other clothes away, in advance, somewhere (Laura had her own ripe views about the maid); and at any rate, for herself, that was the fate she had to expect, if not that night then some other one soon, and it was all the same: to sit counting the hours till a hope was given up and a hideous certainty remained. She had fallen into such a state of apprehension that when at last she heard a carriage stop at the door she was almost happy, in spite of her prevision of how disgusted her sister would be to find her. They met in the hall—Laura went out as she heard the opening of the door. Selina stopped short, seeing her, but said nothing—on account apparently of the presence of the sleepy footman. Then she moved straight to the stairs, where she paused again, asking the footman if Mr. Berrington had come in.

'Not yet, ma'am,' the footman answered.

'Ah!' said Mrs. Berrington, dramatically, and ascended the stairs.

'I have sat up on purpose—I want particularly to speak to you,' Laura remarked, following her.

'Ah!' Selina repeated, more superior still. She went fast, almost as if she wished to get to her room before her sister could overtake her. But the girl was close behind her, she passed into the room with her. Laura closed the door; then she told her that she had found it impossible to go to bed without asking her what she intended to do.

'Your behaviour is too monstrous!' Selina flashed out. 'What on earth do you wish to make the servants suppose?'

'Oh, the servants—in *this* house; as if one could put any idea into their heads that is not there already!' Laura thought. But she said nothing of this—she only repeated her question: aware that she was exasperating to her sister but also aware that she could not be anything else. Mrs. Berrington, whose maid, having outlived surprises, had gone to rest, began to divest herself of some of her ornaments, and it was not till after a moment, during which she stood before the glass, that she made that answer about doing as she had always done. To this Laura rejoined that she ought to put herself in her place enough to feel how important it was to *her* to know what was likely to happen, so that she might take time by the forelock and think of her own situation. If anything should happen she would infinitely rather be out of it—be as far away as possible. Therefore she must take her measures.

It was in the mirror that they looked at each other—in the strange, candle-lighted duplication of the scene that their eyes met. Selina drew the diamonds out of her hair, and in this occupation, for a minute, she was silent. Presently she asked: 'What are you talking about—what do you allude to as happening?'

'Why, it seems to me that there is nothing left for you but to go away with him. If there is a prospect of that insanity——' But here Laura stopped; something so unexpected was taking place in Selina's countenance—the movement that precedes a sudden gush of tears. Mrs. Berrington dashed down the glittering pins she had detached from her tresses, and the next moment she had flung herself into an armchair and was weeping profusely, extravagantly. Laura forbore to go to her; she made no motion to soothe or reassure her; she only stood and watched her tears and wondered what they signified. Somehow even the slight refreshment she felt at having affected her in that particular and, as it had lately come to seem, improbable way did not suggest to her that they were precious symptoms. Since she had come to disbelieve her word so completely there was nothing precious about Selina any more. But she continued for some moments to cry passionately, and while this lasted Laura remained silent. At last from the midst of her sobs Selina broke out, 'Go away, go away—leave me alone!'

'Of course I infuriate you,' said the girl; 'but how can I see you rush to your ruin—to that of all of us—without holding on to you and dragging you back?'

'Oh, you don't understand anything about anything!' Selina wailed, with her beautiful hair tumbling all over her.

'I certainly don't understand how you can give such a tremendous handle to Lionel.'

At the mention of her husband's name Selina always gave a bound, and she sprang up now, shaking back her dense braids. 'I give him no handle and you don't know what you are talking about! I know what I am doing and what becomes me, and I don't care if I do. He is welcome to all the handles in the world, for all that he can do with them!'

'In the name of common pity think of your children!' said Laura.

'Have I ever thought of anything else? Have you sat up all night to have the pleasure of accusing me of cruelty? Are there sweeter or more delightful children in the world, and isn't that a little *my* merit, pray?' Selina went on, sweeping away her tears. 'Who has made them what they are, pray?—is it their lovely father? Perhaps you'll say it's you! Certainly you have been nice to them, but you must remember that you only came here the other day. Isn't it only for them that I am trying to keep myself alive?'

This formula struck Laura Wing as grotesque, so that she replied with a laugh which betrayed too much her impression, 'Die for them—that would be better!'

Her sister, at this, looked at her with an extraordinary cold gravity. 'Don't interfere between me and my children. And for God's sake cease to harry me!'

Laura turned away: she said to herself that, given that intensity of silliness, of course the worst would come. She felt sick and helpless, and, practically, she had got the certitude she both wanted and dreaded. 'I don't know what has become of your mind,' she murmured; and she went to the door. But before she reached it Selina had flung herself upon her in one of her strange but, as she felt, really not encouraging revulsions. Her arms were about her, she clung to her, she covered Laura with the tears that had again begun to flow. She besought her to save her, to stay with her, to help her against herself, against *him*, against Lionel, against everything—to forgive her also all the horrid things she had said to her. Mrs. Berrington melted, liquefied, and the room was deluged with her repentance, her desolation, her confession, her promises and the articles of apparel which were detached from her by the high tide of her agitation. Laura remained with her for an hour, and before they separated the culpable woman had taken a tremendous vow—kneeling before her sister with her head in her lap—never again, as long as she lived, to consent

to see Captain Crispin or to address a word to him, spoken
or written. The girl went terribly tired to bed.

A month afterwards she lunched with Lady Davenant,
whom she had not seen since the day she took Mr. Wendover
to call upon her. The old woman had found herself obliged
to entertain a small company, and as she disliked set parties
she sent Laura a request for sympathy and assistance. She had
disencumbered herself, at the end of so many years, of the
burden of hospitality; but every now and then she invited people, in order to prove that she was not too old. Laura suspected her of choosing stupid ones on purpose to prove it
better—to show that she could submit not only to the
extraordinary but, what was much more difficult, to the usual.
But when they had been properly fed she encouraged them
to disperse; on this occasion as the party broke up Laura was
the only person she asked to stay. She wished to know in the
first place why she had not been to see her for so long, and
in the second how that young man had behaved—the one she
had brought that Sunday. Lady Davenant didn't remember
his name, though he had been so good-natured, as she said,
since then, as to leave a card. If he had behaved well that was
a very good reason for the girl's neglect and Laura need give
no other. Laura herself would not have behaved well if at such
a time she had been running after old women. There was
nothing, in general, that the girl liked less than being spoken
of, off-hand, as a marriageable article—being planned and arranged for in this particular. It made too light of her independence, and though in general such inventions passed for
benevolence they had always seemed to her to contain at bottom an impertinence—as if people could be moved about like
a game of chequers. There was a liberty in the way Lady Davenant's imagination disposed of her (with such an *insouciance*
of her own preferences), but she forgave that, because after
all this old friend was not obliged to think of her at all.

'I knew that you were almost always out of town now, on
Sundays—and so have we been,' Laura said. 'And then I have
been a great deal with my sister—more than before.'

'More than before what?'

'Well, a kind of estrangement we had, about a certain
matter.'

'And now you have made it all up?'

'Well, we have been able to talk of it (we couldn't before—without painful scenes), and that has cleared the air. We have gone about together a good deal,' Laura went on. 'She has wanted me constantly with her.'

'That's very nice. And where has she taken you?' asked the old lady.

'Oh, it's I who have taken her, rather.' And Laura hesitated.

'Where do you mean?—to say her prayers?'

'Well, to some concerts—and to the National Gallery.'

Lady Davenant laughed, disrespectfully, at this, and the girl watched her with a mournful face. 'My dear child, you are too delightful! You are trying to reform her? by Beethoven and Bach, by Rubens and Titian?'

'She is very intelligent, about music and pictures—she has excellent ideas,' said Laura.

'And you have been trying to draw them out? that is very commendable.'

'I think you are laughing at me, but I don't care,' the girl declared, smiling faintly.

'Because you have a consciousness of success?—in what do they call it?—the attempt to raise her tone? You have been trying to wind her up, and you *have* raised her tone?'

'Oh, Lady Davenant, I don't know and I don't understand!' Laura broke out. 'I don't understand anything any more—I have given up trying.'

'That's what I recommended you to do last winter. Don't you remember that day at Plash?'

'You told me to let her go,' said Laura.

'And evidently you haven't taken my advice.'

'How can I—how can I?'

'Of course, how can you? And meanwhile if she doesn't go it's so much gained. But even if she should, won't that nice young man remain?' Lady Davenant inquired. 'I hope very much Selina hasn't taken you altogether away from him.'

Laura was silent a moment; then she returned: 'What nice young man would ever look at me, if anything bad should happen?'

'I would never look at *him* if he should let that prevent

him!' the old woman cried. 'It isn't for your sister he loves you, I suppose; is it?'

'He doesn't love me at all.'

'Ah, then he does?' Lady Davenant demanded, with some eagerness, laying her hand on the girl's arm. Laura sat near her on her sofa and looked at her, for all answer to this, with an expression of which the sadness appeared to strike the old woman freshly. 'Doesn't he come to the house—doesn't he say anything?' she continued, with a voice of kindness.

'He comes to the house—very often.'

'And don't you like him?'

'Yes, very much—more than I did at first.'

'Well, as you liked him at first well enough to bring him straight to see me, I suppose that means that now you are immensely pleased with him.'

'He's a gentleman,' said Laura.

'So he seems to me. But why then doesn't he speak out?'

'Perhaps that's the very reason! Seriously,' the girl added, 'I don't know what he comes to the house for.'

'Is he in love with your sister?'

'I sometimes think so.'

'And does she encourage him?'

'She detests him.'

'Oh, then, I like him! I shall immediately write to him to come and see me: I shall appoint an hour and give him a piece of my mind.'

'If I believed that, I should kill myself,' said Laura.

'You may believe what you like; but I wish you didn't show your feelings so in your eyes. They might be those of a poor widow with fifteen children. When I was young I managed to be happy, whatever occurred; and I am sure I looked so.'

'Oh yes, Lady Davenant—for you it was different. You were safe, in so many ways,' Laura said. 'And you were surrounded with consideration.'

'I don't know; some of us were very wild, and exceedingly ill thought of, and I didn't cry about it. However, there are natures and natures. If you will come and stay with me to-morrow I will take you in.'

'You know how kind I think you, but I have promised Selina not to leave her.'

'Well, then, if she keeps you she must at least go straight!' cried the old woman, with some asperity. Laura made no answer to this and Lady Davenant asked, after a moment: 'And what is Lionel doing?'

'I don't know—he is very quiet.'

'Doesn't it please him—his wife's improvement?' The girl got up; apparently she was made uncomfortable by the ironical effect, if not by the ironical intention, of this question. Her old friend was kind but she was penetrating; her very next words pierced further. 'Of course if you are really protecting her I can't count upon you': a remark not adapted to enliven Laura, who would have liked immensely to transfer herself to Queen's Gate and had her very private ideas as to the efficacy of her protection. Lady Davenant kissed her and then suddenly said—'Oh, by the way, his address; you must tell me that.'

'His address?'

'The young man's whom you brought here. But it's no matter,' the old woman added; 'the butler will have entered it—from his card.'

'Lady Davenant, you won't do anything so loathsome!' the girl cried, seizing her hand.

'Why is it loathsome, if he comes so often? It's rubbish, his caring for Selina—a married woman—when you are there.'

'Why is it rubbish—when so many other people do?'

'Oh, well, he is different—I could see that; or if he isn't he ought to be!'

'He likes to observe—he came here to take notes,' said the girl. 'And he thinks Selina a very interesting London specimen.'

'In spite of her dislike of him?'

'Oh, he doesn't know that!' Laura exclaimed.

'Why not? he isn't a fool.'

'Oh, I have made it seem——' But here Laura stopped; her colour had risen.

Lady Davenant stared an instant. 'Made it seem that she inclines to him? Mercy, to do that how fond of him you must be!' An observation which had the effect of driving the girl straight out of the house.

XI

On one of the last days of June Mrs. Berrington showed her sister a note she had received from 'your dear friend,' as she called him, Mr. Wendover. This was the manner in which she usually designated him, but she had naturally, in the present phase of her relations with Laura, never indulged in any renewal of the eminently perverse insinuations by means of which she had attempted, after the incident at the Soane Museum, to throw dust in her eyes. Mr. Wendover proposed to Mrs. Berrington that she and her sister should honour with their presence a box he had obtained for the opera three nights later—an occasion of high curiosity, the first appearance of a young American singer of whom considerable things were expected. Laura left it to Selina to decide whether they should accept this invitation, and Selina proved to be of two or three differing minds. First she said it wouldn't be convenient to her to go, and she wrote to the young man to this effect. Then, on second thoughts, she considered she might very well go, and telegraphed an acceptance. Later she saw reason to regret her acceptance and communicated this circumstance to her sister, who remarked that it was still not too late to change. Selina left her in ignorance till the next day as to whether she had retracted; then she told her that she had let the matter stand—they would go. To this Laura replied that she was glad—for Mr. Wendover. 'And for yourself,' Selina said, leaving the girl to wonder why every one (this universality was represented by Mrs. Lionel Berrington and Lady Davenant) had taken up the idea that she entertained a passion for her compatriot. She was clearly conscious that this was not the case; though she was glad her esteem for him had not yet suffered the disturbance of her seeing reason to believe that Lady Davenant had already meddled, according to her terrible threat. Laura was surprised to learn afterwards that Selina had, in London parlance, 'thrown over' a dinner in order to make the evening at the opera fit in. The dinner would have made her too late, and she didn't care about it: she wanted to hear the whole opera.

The sisters dined together alone, without any question of Lionel, and on alighting at Covent Garden found Mr. Wendover awaiting them in the portico. His box proved commodious and comfortable, and Selina was gracious to him: she thanked him for his consideration in not stuffing it full of people. He assured her that he expected but one other inmate—a gentleman of a shrinking disposition, who would take up no room. The gentleman came in after the first act; he was introduced to the ladies as Mr. Booker, of Baltimore. He knew a great deal about the young lady they had come to listen to, and he was not so shrinking but that he attempted to impart a portion of his knowledge even while she was singing. Before the second act was over Laura perceived Lady Ringrose in a box on the other side of the house, accompanied by a lady unknown to her. There was apparently another person in the box, behind the two ladies, whom they turned round from time to time to talk with. Laura made no observation about Lady Ringrose to her sister, and she noticed that Selina never resorted to the glass to look at her. That Mrs. Berrington had not failed to see her, however, was proved by the fact that at the end of the second act (the opera was Meyerbeer's *Huguenots*) she suddenly said, turning to Mr. Wendover: 'I hope you won't mind very much if I go for a short time to sit with a friend on the other side of the house.' She smiled with all her sweetness as she announced this intention, and had the benefit of the fact that an apologetic expression is highly becoming to a pretty woman. But she abstained from looking at her sister, and the latter, after a wondering glance at her, looked at Mr. Wendover. She saw that he was disappointed—even slightly wounded: he had taken some trouble to get his box and it had been no small pleasure to him to see it graced by the presence of a celebrated beauty. Now his situation collapsed if the celebrated beauty were going to transfer her light to another quarter. Laura was unable to imagine what had come into her sister's head—to make her so inconsiderate, so rude. Selina tried to perform her act of defection in a soothing, conciliating way, so far as appealing eyebeams went; but she gave no particular reason for her escapade, withheld the name of the friends in question and betrayed no consciousness that it was not usual for ladies to roam about the lobbies. Laura asked her no question, but she said to her, after an hesitation: 'You won't be long, surely.

You know you oughtn't to leave me here.' Selina took no notice of this—excused herself in no way to the girl. Mr. Wendover only exclaimed, smiling in reference to Laura's last remark: 'Oh, so far as leaving you here goes——!' In spite of his great defect (and it was his only one, that she could see) of having only an ascending scale of seriousness, she judged him interestedly enough to feel a real pleasure in noticing that though he was annoyed at Selina's going away and not saying that she would come back soon, he conducted himself as a gentleman should, submitted respectfully, gallantly, to her wish. He suggested that her friends might perhaps, instead, be induced to come to his box, but when she had objected, 'Oh, you see, there are too many,' he put her shawl on her shoulders, opened the box, offered her his arm. While this was going on Laura saw Lady Ringrose studying them with her glass. Selina refused Mr. Wendover's arm; she said, 'Oh no, you stay with *her*—I daresay *he'll* take me:' and she gazed inspiringly at Mr. Booker. Selina never mentioned a name when the pronoun would do. Mr. Booker of course sprang to the service required and led her away, with an injunction from his friend to bring her back promptly. As they went off Laura heard Selina say to her companion—and she knew Mr. Wendover could also hear it—'Nothing would have induced me to leave her alone with *you!*' She thought this a very extraordinary speech—she thought it even vulgar; especially considering that she had never seen the young man till half an hour before and since then had not exchanged twenty words with him. It came to their ears so distinctly that Laura was moved to notice it by exclaiming, with a laugh: 'Poor Mr. Booker, what does she suppose I would do to him?'

'Oh, it's for you she's afraid,' said Mr. Wendover.

Laura went on, after a moment: 'She oughtn't to have left me alone with you, either.'

'Oh yes, she ought—after all!' the young man returned.

The girl had uttered these words from no desire to say something flirtatious, but because they simply expressed a part of the judgment she passed, mentally, on Selina's behaviour. She had a sense of wrong—of being made light of; for Mrs. Berrington certainly knew that honourable women didn't (for the appearance of the thing) arrange to leave their unmarried sister sitting alone, publicly, at the playhouse, with a couple of young men—the couple that there would be as soon as Mr. Booker should come back. It displeased her that the people in the opposite box, the people Selina had joined, should see her exhibited in this light. She drew the curtain of the box a little, she moved a little more behind it, and she heard her companion utter a vague appealing, protecting sigh, which seemed to express his sense (her own corresponded with it) that the glory of the occasion had somehow suddenly departed. At the end of some minutes she perceived among Lady Ringrose and her companions a movement which appeared to denote that Selina had come in. The two ladies in front turned round—something went on at the back of the box. 'She's there,' Laura said, indicating the place; but Mrs. Berrington did not show herself—she remained masked by the others. Neither was Mr. Booker visible; he had not, seemingly, been persuaded to remain, and indeed Laura could see that there would not have been room for him. Mr. Wendover observed, ruefully, that as Mrs. Berrington evidently could see nothing at all from where she had gone she had exchanged a very good place for a very bad one. 'I can't imagine—I can't imagine——' said the girl; but she paused, losing herself in reflections and wonderments, in conjectures that soon became anxieties. Suspicion of Selina was now so rooted in her heart that it could make her unhappy even when it pointed nowhere, and by the end of half an hour she felt how little her fears had really been lulled since that scene of dishevelment and contrition in the early dawn.

The opera resumed its course, but Mr. Booker did not come back. The American singer trilled and warbled, executed remarkable flights, and there was much applause, every symptom of success; but Laura became more and more unaware of the music—she had no eyes but for Lady Ringrose and her friend. She watched them earnestly—she tried to sound with her glass the curtained dimness behind them. Their attention was all for the stage and they gave no present sign of having any fellow-listeners. These others had either gone away or were leaving them very much to themselves. Laura was unable to guess any particular motive on her sister's part, but the conviction grew within her that she had not put such an affront on Mr. Wendover simply in order to have a little chat with Lady Ringrose. There was something else, there was some one else, in the affair; and when once the girl's idea had become as definite as that it took but little longer to associate itself with the image of Captain Crispin. This image made her draw back further behind her curtain, because it brought the blood to her face; and if she coloured for shame she coloured also for anger. Captain Crispin was there, in the opposite box; those horrible women concealed him (she forgot how harmless and well-read Lady Ringrose had appeared to her that time at Mellows); they had lent themselves to this abominable proceeding. Selina was nestling there in safety with him, by their favour, and she had had the baseness to lay an honest girl, the most loyal, the most unselfish of sisters, under contribution to the same end. Laura crimsoned with the sense that she had been, unsuspectingly, part of a scheme, that she was being used as the two women opposite were used, but that she had been outraged into the bargain, inasmuch as she was not, like them, a conscious accomplice and not a person to be given away in that manner before hundreds of people. It came back to her how bad Selina had been the day of the business in Lincoln's Inn Fields, and how in spite of intervening comedies the woman who had then found such words of injury would be sure to break out in a new spot with a new weapon. Accordingly, while the pure music filled the place and the rich picture of the stage glowed beneath it, Laura found herself face to face with the strange inference that the evil of Selina's nature made her wish—since she had given herself to it—to bring her sister to her own colour by putting an appearance of 'fastness' upon her. The girl said to herself that she would have succeeded, in the cynical view of London; and to her troubled spirit the immense theatre had a myriad eyes, eyes that she knew, eyes that would know her, that would see her sitting there with a strange young man. She had recognised many faces already and her imagination quickly multiplied them. However, after she had burned a while with this particular revolt she ceased to think of herself and of what, as regarded herself, Selina had intended: all her thought went to the mere calculation of Mrs. Berrington's return. As she did not return, and still did not, Laura felt a sharp constriction of the heart. She knew not what she feared—she knew not what she supposed. She was so nervous (as she had been the night she waited, till morning, for her sister to re-enter the house in Grosvenor Place) that when Mr. Wendover occasionally made a remark to her she failed to understand him, was unable to answer him. Fortunately he made very few; he was preoccupied—either wondering also what Selina was 'up to' or, more probably, simply absorbed in the music. What she *had* comprehended, however, was that when at three different moments she had said, restlessly, 'Why doesn't Mr. Booker come back?' he replied, 'Oh, there's plenty of time—we are very comfortable.' These words she was conscious of; she particularly noted them and they interwove themselves with her restlessness. She also noted, in her tension, that after her third inquiry Mr. Wendover said something about looking up his friend, if she didn't mind being left alone a moment. He quitted the box and during this interval Laura tried more than ever to see with her glass what had become of her sister. But it was as if the ladies opposite had arranged themselves, had arranged their curtains, on purpose to frustrate such an attempt: it was impossible to her even to assure herself of what she had begun to suspect, that Selina was now not with them. If she was not with them where in the world had she gone? As the moments elapsed, before Mr. Wendover's return, she went to the door of the box and stood watching the lobby, for the chance that he would bring back the absentee. Presently she saw him coming alone, and something in the expression of his face made her step out into the lobby to meet him. He was smiling, but he looked embarrassed and strange, especially when he saw her standing there as if she wished to leave the place.

'I hope you don't want to go,' he said, holding the door for her to pass back into the box.

'Where are they—where are they?' she demanded, remaining in the corridor.

'I saw our friend—he has found a place in the stalls, near the door by which you go into them—just here under us.'

'And does he like that better?'

Mr. Wendover's smile became perfunctory as he looked

down at her. 'Mrs. Berrington has made such an amusing request of him.'

'An amusing request?'

'She made him promise not to come back.'

'Made him promise——?' Laura stared.

'She asked him—as a particular favour to her—not to join us again. And he said he wouldn't.'

'Ah, the monster!' Laura exclaimed, blushing crimson.

'Do you mean poor Mr. Booker?' Mr. Wendover asked. 'Of course he had to assure her that the wish of so lovely a lady was law. But he doesn't understand!' laughed the young man.

'No more do I. And where is the lovely lady?' said Laura, trying to recover herself.

'He hasn't the least idea.'

'Isn't she with Lady Ringrose?'

'If you like I will go and see.'

Laura hesitated, looking down the curved lobby, where there was nothing to see but the little numbered doors of the boxes. They were alone in the lamplit bareness; the *finale* of the act was ringing and booming behind them. In a moment she said: 'I'm afraid I must trouble you to put me into a cab.'

'Ah, you won't see the rest? *Do* stay—what difference does it make?' And her companion still held open the door of the box. Her eyes met his, in which it seemed to her that as well as in his voice there was conscious sympathy, entreaty, vindication, tenderness. Then she gazed into the vulgar corridor again; something said to her that if she should return she would be taking the most important step of her life. She considered this, and while she did so a great burst of applause filled the place as the curtain fell. 'See what we are losing! And the last act is so fine,' said Mr. Wendover. She returned to her seat and he closed the door of the box behind them.

Then, in this little upholstered receptacle which was so public and yet so private, Laura Wing passed through the strangest moments she had known. An indication of their strangeness is that when she presently perceived that while she was in the lobby Lady Ringrose and her companion had quite disappeared, she observed the circumstance without an exclamation, holding herself silent. Their box was empty, but Laura

looked at it without in the least feeling this to be a sign that
Selina would now come round. She would never come round
again, nor would she have gone home from the opera. That
was by this time absolutely definite to the girl, who had first
been hot and now was cold with the sense of what Selina's
injunction to poor Mr. Booker exactly meant. It was worthy
of her, for it was simply a vicious little kick as she took her
flight. Grosvenor Place would not shelter her that night and
would never shelter her more: that was the reason she tried
to spatter her sister with the mud into which she herself had
jumped. She would not have dared to treat her in such a fashion if they had had a prospect of meeting again. The strangest
part of this remarkable juncture was that what ministered
most to our young lady's suppressed emotion was not the
tremendous reflection that this time Selina had really 'bolted'
and that on the morrow all London would know it: all that
had taken the glare of certainty (and a very hideous hue it
was), whereas the chill that had fallen upon the girl now was
that of a mystery which waited to be cleared up. Her heart
was full of suspense—suspense of which she returned the pressure, trying to twist it into expectation. There was a certain
chance in life that sat there beside her, but it would go for
ever if it should not move nearer that night; and she listened,
she watched, for it to move. I need not inform the reader that
this chance presented itself in the person of Mr. Wendover,
who more than any one she knew had it in his hand to trans-
mute her detestable position. To-morrow he would know, and
would think sufficiently little of a young person of *that* breed:
therefore it could only be a question of his speaking on the
spot. That was what she had come back into the box for—to
give him his opportunity. It was open to her to think he had
asked for it—adding everything together.

The poor girl added, added, deep in her heart, while she
said nothing. The music was not there now, to keep them
silent; yet he remained quiet, even as she did, and that for
some minutes was a part of her addition. She felt as if she
were running a race with failure and shame; she would get in
first if she should get in before the degradation of the morrow.
But this was not very far off, and every minute brought it
nearer. It would be there in fact, virtually, that night, if Mr.

Wendover should begin to realise the brutality of Selina's not turning up at all. The comfort had been, hitherto, that he didn't realise brutalities. There were certain violins that emitted tentative sounds in the orchestra; they shortened the time and made her uneasier—fixed her idea that he could lift her out of her mire if he would. It didn't appear to prove that he would, his also observing Lady Ringrose's empty box without making an encouraging comment upon it. Laura waited for him to remark that her sister obviously would turn up now; but no such words fell from his lips. He must either like Selina's being away or judge it damningly, and in either case why didn't he speak? If he had nothing to say, why *had* he said, why had he done, what did he mean——? But the girl's inward challenge to him lost itself in a mist of faintness; she was screwing herself up to a purpose of her own, and it hurt almost to anguish, and the whole place, around her, was a blur and swim, through which she heard the tuning of fiddles. Before she knew it she had said to him, 'Why have you come so often?'

'So often? To see you, do you mean?'

'To see *me*—it was for that? Why have you come?' she went on. He was evidently surprised, and his surprise gave her a point of anger, a desire almost that her words should hurt him, lash him. She spoke low, but she heard herself, and she thought that if what she said sounded to *him* in the same way——! 'You have come very often—too often, too often!'

He coloured, he looked frightened, he was, clearly, extremely startled. 'Why, you have been so kind, so delightful,' he stammered.

'Yes, of course, and so have you! Did you come for Selina? She is married, you know, and devoted to her husband.' A single minute had sufficed to show the girl that her companion was quite unprepared for her question, that he was distinctly not in love with her and was face to face with a situation entirely new. The effect of this perception was to make her say wilder things.

'Why, what is more natural, when one likes people, than to come often? Perhaps I have bored you—with our American way,' said Mr. Wendover.

'And is it because you like me that you have kept me here?'

Laura asked. She got up, leaning against the side of the box; she had pulled the curtain far forward and was out of sight of the house.

He rose, but more slowly; he had got over his first confusion. He smiled at her, but his smile was dreadful. 'Can you have any doubt as to what I have come for? It's a pleasure to me that you have liked me well enough to ask.'

For an instant she thought he was coming nearer to her, but he didn't: he stood there twirling his gloves. Then an unspeakable shame and horror—horror of herself, of him, of everything—came over her, and she sank into a chair at the back of the box, with averted eyes, trying to get further into her corner. 'Leave me, leave me, go away!' she said, in the lowest tone that he could hear. The whole house seemed to her to be listening to her, pressing into the box.

'Leave you alone—in this place—when I love you? I can't do that—indeed I can't.'

'You don't love me—and you torture me by staying!' Laura went on, in a convulsed voice. 'For God's sake go away and don't speak to me, don't let me see you or hear of you again!'

Mr. Wendover still stood there, exceedingly agitated, as well he might be, by this inconceivable scene. Unaccustomed feelings possessed him and they moved him in different directions. Her command that he should take himself off was passionate, yet he attempted to resist, to speak. How would she get home—would she see him to-morrow—would she let him wait for her outside? To this Laura only replied: 'Oh dear, oh dear, if you would only go!' and at the same instant she sprang up, gathering her cloak around her as if to escape from him, to rush away herself. He checked this movement, however, clapping on his hat and holding the door. One moment more he looked at her—her own eyes were closed; then he exclaimed, pitifully, 'Oh Miss Wing, oh Miss Wing!' and stepped out of the box.

When he had gone she collapsed into one of the chairs again and sat there with her face buried in a fold of her mantle. For many minutes she was perfectly still—she was ashamed even to move. The one thing that could have justified her, blown away the dishonour of her monstrous overture, would have been, on his side, the quick response of unmistakable passion. It had not come, and she had nothing left but to loathe herself. She did so, violently, for a long time, in the dark corner of the box, and she felt that he loathed her too. 'I love you!'—how pitifully the poor little make-believe words had quavered out and how much disgust they must have represented! 'Poor man—poor man!' Laura Wing suddenly found herself murmuring: compassion filled her mind at the sense of the way she had used him. At the same moment a flare of music broke out: the last act of the opera had begun and she had sprung up and quitted the box.

The passages were empty and she made her way without trouble. She descended to the vestibule; there was no one to stare at her and her only fear was that Mr. Wendover would be there. But he was not, apparently, and she saw that she should be able to go away quickly. Selina would have taken the carriage—she could be sure of that; or if she hadn't it wouldn't have come back yet; besides, she couldn't possibly wait there so long as while it was called. She was in the act of asking one of the attendants, in the portico, to get her a cab, when some one hurried up to her from behind, overtaking her—a gentleman in whom, turning round, she recognised Mr. Booker. He looked almost as bewildered as Mr. Wendover, and his appearance disconcerted her almost as much as that of his friend would have done. 'Oh, are you going away, alone? What must you think of me?' this young man exclaimed; and he began to tell her something about her sister and to ask her at the same time if he might not go with her—help her in some way. He made no inquiry about Mr. Wendover, and she afterwards judged that that distracted gentleman had sought him out and sent him to her assistance; also that he himself was at that moment watching them from behind some column. He would have been hateful if he had shown himself; yet (in this later meditation) there was a voice in her heart which commended his delicacy. He effaced himself to look after her—he provided for her departure by proxy.

'A cab, a cab—that's all I want!' she said to Mr. Booker; and she almost pushed him out of the place with the wave of the hand with which she indicated her need. He rushed off to call one, and a minute afterwards the messenger whom she had already despatched rattled up in a hansom. She quickly got into it, and as she rolled away she saw Mr. Booker returning in all haste with another. She gave a passionate moan—this common confusion seemed to add a grotesqueness to her predicament.

XII

The next day, at five o'clock, she drove to Queen's Gate, turning to Lady Davenant in her distress in order to turn somewhere. Her old friend was at home and by extreme good fortune alone; looking up from her book, in her place by the window, she gave the girl as she came in a sharp glance over her glasses. This glance was acquisitive; she said nothing, but laying down her book stretched out her two gloved hands. Laura took them and she drew her down toward her, so that the girl sunk on her knees and in a moment hid her face, sobbing, in the old woman's lap. There was nothing said for some time: Lady Davenant only pressed her tenderly—stroked her with her hands. 'Is it very bad?' she asked at last. Then Laura got up, saying as she took a seat, 'Have you heard of it and do people know it?'

'I haven't heard anything. Is it very bad?' Lady Davenant repeated.

'We don't know where Selina is—and her maid's gone.'

Lady Davenant looked at her visitor a moment. 'Lord, what an ass!' she then ejaculated, putting the paper-knife into her book to keep her place. 'And whom has she persuaded to take her—Charles Crispin?' she added.

'We suppose—we suppose——' said Laura.

'And he's another,' interrupted the old woman. And who supposes—Geordie and Ferdy?'

'I don't know; it's all black darkness!'

'My dear, it's a blessing, and now you can live in peace.'

'In peace!' cried Laura; 'with my wretched sister leading such a life?'

'Oh, my dear, I daresay it will be very comfortable; I am sorry to say anything in favour of such doings, but it very often is. Don't worry; you take her too hard. Has she gone abroad?' the old lady continued. 'I daresay she has gone to some pretty, amusing place.'

'I don't know anything about it. I only know she is gone. I was with her last evening and she left me without a word.'

'Well, that was better. I hate 'em when they make parting scenes: it's too mawkish!'

'Lionel has people watching them,' said the girl; 'agents, detectives, I don't know what. He has had them for a long time; I didn't know it.'

'Do you mean you would have told her if you had? What is the use of detectives now? Isn't he rid of her?'

'Oh, I don't know, he's as bad as she; he talks too horribly—he wants every one to know it,' Laura groaned.

'And has he told his mother?'

'I suppose so: he rushed off to see her at noon. She'll be overwhelmed.'

'Overwhelmed? Not a bit of it!' cried Lady Davenant, almost gaily. 'When did anything in the world overwhelm her and what do you take her for? She'll only make some delightful odd speech. As for people knowing it,' she added, 'they'll know it whether he wants them or not. My poor child, how long do you expect to make believe?'

'Lionel expects some news to-night,' Laura said. 'As soon as I know where she is I shall start.'

'Start for where?'

'To go to her—to do something.'

'Something preposterous, my dear. Do you expect to bring her back?'

'He won't take her in,' said Laura, with her dried, dismal eyes. 'He wants his divorce—it's too hideous!'

'Well, as she wants hers what is simpler?'

'Yes, she wants hers. Lionel swears by all the gods she can't get it.'

'Bless me, won't one do?' Lady Davenant asked. 'We shall have some pretty reading.'

'It's awful, awful, awful!' murmured Laura.

'Yes, they oughtn't to be allowed to publish them. I wonder if we couldn't stop that. At any rate he had better be quiet: tell him to come and see me.'

'You won't influence him; he's dreadful against her. Such a house as it is to-day!'

'Well, my dear, naturally.'

'Yes, but it's terrible for me: it's all more sickening than I can bear.'

'My dear child, come and stay with me,' said the old woman, gently.

'Oh, I can't desert her; I can't abandon her!'

'Desert—abandon? What a way to put it! Hasn't she abandoned you?'

'She has no heart—she's too base!' said the girl. Her face was white and the tears now began to rise to her eyes again.

Lady Davenant got up and came and sat on the sofa beside her: she put her arms round her and the two women embraced. 'Your room is all ready,' the old lady remarked. And then she said, 'When did she leave you? When did you see her last?'

'Oh, in the strangest, maddest, cruelest way, the way most insulting to me. We went to the opera together and she left me there with a gentleman. We know nothing about her since.'

'With a gentleman?'

'With Mr. Wendover—that American, and something too dreadful happened.'

'Dear me, did he kiss you?' asked Lady Davenant.

Laura got up quickly, turning away. 'Good-bye, I'm going, I'm going!' And in reply to an irritated, protesting exclamation from her companion she went on, 'Anywhere—anywhere to get away!'

'To get away from your American?'

'I asked him to marry me!' The girl turned round with her tragic face.

'He oughtn't to have left that to you.'

'I knew this horror was coming and it took possession of me, there in the box, from one moment to the other—the idea of making sure of some other life, some protection, some respectability. First I thought he liked me, he had behaved as if he did. And I like him, he is a very good man. So I asked him, I couldn't help it, it was too hideous—I offered myself!' Laura spoke as if she were telling that she had stabbed him, standing there with dilated eyes.

Lady Davenant got up again and went to her; drawing off

her glove she felt her cheek with the back of her hand. 'You are ill, you are in a fever. I'm sure that whatever you said it was very charming.'

'Yes, I am ill,' said Laura.

'Upon my honour you shan't go home, you shall go straight to bed. And what did he say to you?'

'Oh, it was too miserable!' cried the girl, pressing her face again into her companion's kerchief. 'I was all, all mistaken; he had never thought!'

'Why the deuce then did he run about that way after you? He was a brute to say it!'

'He didn't say it and he never ran about. He behaved like a perfect gentleman.'

'I've no patience—I wish I had seen him that time!' Lady Davenant declared.

'Yes, that would have been nice! You'll never see him; if he *is* a gentleman he'll rush away.'

'Bless me, what a rushing away!' murmured the old woman. Then passing her arm round Laura she added, 'You'll please to come upstairs with me.'

Half an hour later she had some conversation with her butler which led to his consulting a little register into which it was his law to transcribe with great neatness, from their cards, the addresses of new visitors. This volume, kept in the drawer of the hall table, revealed the fact that Mr. Wendover was staying in George Street, Hanover Square. 'Get into a cab immediately and tell him to come and see me this evening,' Lady Davenant said. 'Make him understand that it interests him very nearly, so that no matter what his engagements may be he must give them up. Go quickly and you'll just find him: he'll be sure to be at home to dress for dinner.' She had calculated justly, for a few minutes before ten o'clock the door of her drawing-room was thrown open and Mr. Wendover was announced.

'Sit there,' said the old lady; 'no, not that one, nearer to me. We must talk low. My dear sir, I won't bite you!'

'Oh, this is very comfortable,' Mr. Wendover replied vaguely, smiling through his visible anxiety. It was no more than natural that he should wonder what Laura Wing's peremptory friend wanted of him at that hour of the night; but nothing could exceed the gallantry of his attempt to conceal the symptoms of alarm.

'You ought to have come before, you know,' Lady Davenant went on. 'I have wanted to see you more than once.'

'I have been dining out—I hurried away. This was the first possible moment, I assure you.'

'I too was dining out and I stopped at home on purpose to see you. But I didn't mean to-night, for you have done very well. I was quite intending to send for you—the other day. But something put it out of my head. Besides, I knew she wouldn't like it.'

'Why, Lady Davenant, I made a point of calling, ever so long ago—after that day!' the young man exclaimed, not reassured, or at any rate not enlightened.

'I daresay you did—but you mustn't justify yourself; that's just what I don't want; it isn't what I sent for you for. I have something very particular to say to you, but it's very difficult. Voyons un peu!'

The old woman reflected a little, with her eyes on his face, which had grown more grave as she went on; its expression intimated that he failed as yet to understand her and that he at least was not exactly trifling. Lady Davenant's musings apparently helped her little, if she was looking for an artful approach; for they ended in her saying abruptly, 'I wonder if you know what a capital girl she is.'

'Do you mean—do you mean——?' stammered Mr. Wendover, pausing as if he had given her no right not to allow him to conceive alternatives.

'Yes, I do mean. She's upstairs, in bed.'

'Upstairs in bed!' The young man stared.

'Don't be afraid—I'm not going to send for her!' laughed his hostess; 'her being here, after all, has nothing to do with it, except that she *did* come—yes, certainly, she did come. But my keeping her—that was my doing. My maid has gone to Grosvenor Place to get her things and let them know that she will stay here for the present. Now am I clear?'

'Not in the least,' said Mr. Wendover, almost sternly.

Lady Davenant, however, was not of a composition to suspect him of sternness or to care very much if she did, and she went on, with her quick discursiveness: 'Well, we must be patient; we shall work it out together. I was afraid you would go away, that's why I lost no time. Above all I want you to understand that she has not the least idea that I have sent for you, and you must promise me never, never, never to let her know. She would be monstrous angry. It is quite my own idea—I have taken the responsibility. I know very little about you of course, but she has spoken to me well of you. Besides, I am very clever about people, and I liked you that day, though you seemed to think I was a hundred and eighty.'

'You do me great honour,' Mr. Wendover rejoined.

'I'm glad you're pleased! You must be if I tell you that I like you now even better. I see what you are, except for the question of fortune. It doesn't perhaps matter much, but have you any money? I mean have you a fine income?'

'No, indeed I haven't!' And the young man laughed in his bewilderment. 'I have very little money indeed.'

'Well, I daresay you have as much as I. Besides, that would be a proof she is not mercenary.'

'You haven't in the least made it plain whom you are talking about,' said Mr. Wendover. 'I have no right to assume any-thing.'

'Are you afraid of betraying her? I am more devoted to her even than I want you to be. She has told me what happened between you last night—what she said to you at the opera. That's what I want to talk to you about.'

'She was very strange,' the young man remarked.

'I am not so sure that she was strange. However, you are welcome to think it, for goodness knows she says so herself. She is overwhelmed with horror at her own words; she is absolutely distracted and prostrate.'

Mr. Wendover was silent a moment. 'I assured her that I admire her—beyond every one. I was most kind to her.'

'Did you say it in that tone? You should have thrown your-self at her feet! From the moment you didn't—surely you understand women well enough to know.'

'You must remember where we were—in a public place, with very little room for throwing!' Mr. Wendover exclaimed.

'Ah, so far from blaming you she says your behaviour was perfect. It's only I who want to have it out with you,' Lady

Davenant pursued. 'She's so clever, so charming, so good and so unhappy.'

'When I said just now she was strange, I meant only in the way she turned against me.'

'She turned against you?'

'She told me she hoped she should never see me again.'

'And you, should you like to see her?'

'Not now—not now!' Mr. Wendover exclaimed, eagerly.

'I don't mean now, I'm not such a fool as that. I mean some day or other, when she has stopped accusing herself, if she ever does.'

'Ah, Lady Davenant, you must leave that to me,' the young man returned, after a moment's hesitation.

'Don't be afraid to tell me I'm meddling with what doesn't concern me,' said his hostess. 'Of course I know I'm meddling; I sent for you here to meddle. Who wouldn't, for that creature? She makes one melt.'

'I'm exceedingly sorry for her. I don't know what she thinks she said.'

'Well, that she asked you why you came so often to Grosvenor Place. I don't see anything so awful in that, if you did go.'

'Yes, I went very often. I liked to go.'

'Now, that's exactly where I wish to prevent a misconception,' said Lady Davenant. 'If you liked to go you had a reason for liking, and Laura Wing was the reason, wasn't she?'

'I thought her charming, and I think her so now more than ever.'

'Then you are a dear good man. Vous faisiez votre cour, in short.'

Mr. Wendover made no immediate response: the two sat looking at each other. 'It isn't easy for me to talk of these things,' he said at last; 'but if you mean that I wished to ask her to be my wife I am bound to tell you that I had no such intention.'

'Ah, then I'm at sea. You thought her charming and you went to see her every day. What then did you wish?'

'I didn't go every day. Moreover I think you have a very different idea in this country of what constitutes—well, what constitutes making love. A man commits himself much sooner.'

'Oh, I don't know what *your* odd ways may be!' Lady Davenant exclaimed, with a shade of irritation.

'Yes, but I was justified in supposing that those ladies did: they at least are American.'

' "They," my dear sir! For heaven's sake don't mix up that nasty Selina with it!'

'Why not, if I admired her too? I do extremely, and I thought the house most interesting.'

'Mercy on us, if that's your idea of a nice house! But I don't know—I have always kept out of it,' Lady Davenant added, checking herself. Then she went on, 'If you are so fond of Mrs. Berrington I am sorry to inform you that she is absolutely good-for-nothing.'

'Good-for-nothing?'

'Nothing to speak of! I have been thinking whether I would tell you, and I have decided to do so because I take it that your learning it for yourself would be a matter of but a very short time. Selina has bolted, as they say.'

'Bolted?' Mr. Wendover repeated.

'I don't know what you call it in America.'

'In America we don't do it.'

'Ah, well, if they stay, as they do usually abroad, that's better. I suppose you didn't think her capable of behaving herself, did you?'

'Do you mean she has left her husband—with some one else?'

'Neither more nor less; with a fellow named Crispin. It appears it all came off last evening, and she had her own reasons for doing it in the most offensive way—publicly, clumsily, with the vulgarest bravado. Laura has told me what took place, and you must permit me to express my surprise at your not having divined the miserable business.'

'I saw something was wrong, but I didn't understand. I'm afraid I'm not very quick at these things.'

'Your state is the more gracious; but certainly you are not quick if you could call there so often and not see through Selina.'

'Mr. Crispin, whoever he is, was never there,' said the young man.

'Oh, she was a clever hussy!' his companion rejoined.

'I knew she was fond of amusement, but that's what I liked to see. I wanted to see a house of that sort.'

'Fond of amusement is a very pretty phrase!' said Lady Davenant, laughing at the simplicity with which her visitor accounted for his assiduity. 'And did Laura Wing seem to you in her place in a house of that sort?'

'Why, it was natural she should be with her sister, and she always struck me as very gay.'

'That was your enlivening effect! And did she strike you as very gay last night, with this scandal hanging over her?'

'She didn't talk much,' said Mr. Wendover.

'She knew it was coming—she felt it, she saw it, and that's what makes her sick now, that at *such* a time she should have challenged you, when she felt herself about to be associated (in people's minds, of course) with such a vile business. In people's minds and in yours—when you should know what had happened.'

'Ah, Miss Wing isn't associated——' said Mr. Wendover. He spoke slowly, but he rose to his feet with a nervous movement that was not lost upon his companion: she noted it indeed with a certain inward sense of triumph. She was very deep, but she had never been so deep as when she made up her mind to mention the scandal of the house of Berrington to her visitor and intimated to him that Laura Wing regarded herself as near enough to it to receive from it a personal stain. 'I'm extremely sorry to hear of Mrs. Berrington's misconduct,' he continued gravely, standing before her. 'And I am no less obliged to you for your interest.'

'Don't mention it,' she said, getting up too and smiling. 'I mean my interest. As for the other matter, it will all come out. Lionel will haul her up.'

'Dear me, how dreadful!'

'Yes, dreadful enough. But don't betray me.'

'Betray you?' he repeated, as if his thoughts had gone astray a moment.

'I mean to the girl. Think of her shame!'

'Her shame?' Mr. Wendover said, in the same way.

'It seemed to her, with what was becoming so clear to her, that an honest man might save her from it, might give her his name and his faith and help her to traverse the bad place. She exaggerates the badness of it, the stigma of her relationship. Good heavens, at that rate where would some of us be? But those are her ideas, they are absolutely sincere, and they had possession of her at the opera. She had a sense of being lost and was in a real agony to be rescued. She saw before her a kind gentleman who had seemed—who had certainly seemed——' And Lady Davenant, with her fine old face lighted by her bright sagacity and her eyes on Mr. Wendover's, paused, lingering on this word. 'Of course she must have been in a state of nerves.'

'I am very sorry for her,' said Mr. Wendover, with his gravity that committed him to nothing.

'So am I! And of course if you were not in love with her you weren't, were you?'

'I must bid you good-bye, I am leaving London.' That was the only answer Lady Davenant got to her inquiry.

'Good-bye then. She is the nicest girl I know. But once more, mind you don't let her suspect!'

'How can I let her suspect anything when I shall never see her again?'

'Oh, don't say that,' said Lady Davenant, very gently.

'She drove me away from her with a kind of ferocity.'

'Oh, gammon!' cried the old woman.

'I'm going home,' he said, looking at her with his hand on the door.

'Well, it's the best place for you. And for her too!' she added as he went out. She was not sure that the last words reached him.

XIII

Laura Wing was sharply ill for three days, but on the fourth she made up her mind she was better, though this was not the opinion of Lady Davenant, who would not hear of her getting up. The remedy she urged was lying still and yet lying still; but this specific the girl found well-nigh intolerable—it was a form of relief that only ministered to fever. She assured her friend that it killed her to do nothing: to which her friend replied by asking her what she had a fancy to do. Laura had her idea and held it tight, but there was no use in producing it before Lady Davenant, who would have knocked it to pieces. On the afternoon of the first day Lionel Berrington came, and though his intention was honest he brought no healing. Hearing she was ill he wanted to look after her—he wanted to take her back to Grosvenor Place and make her comfortable: he spoke as if he had every convenience for producing that condition, though he confessed there was a little bar to it in his own case. This impediment was the 'cheeky' aspect of Miss Steet, who went sniffing about as if she knew a lot, if she should only condescend to tell it. He saw more of the children now; 'I'm going to have 'em in every day, poor little devils,' he said; and he spoke as if the discipline of suffering had already begun for him and a kind of holy change had taken place in his life. Nothing had been said yet in the house, of course, as Laura knew, about Selina's disappearance, in the way of treating it as irregular; but the servants pretended so hard not to be aware of anything in particular that they were like pickpockets looking with unnatural interest the other way after they have cribbed a fellow's watch. To a certainty, in a day or two, the governess would give him warning: she would come and tell him she couldn't stay in such a place, and he would tell her, in return, that she was a little donkey for not knowing that the place was much more respectable now than it had ever been.

This information Selina's husband imparted to Lady Davenant, to whom he discoursed with infinite candour and humour, taking a highly philosophical view of his position and declaring that it suited him down to the ground. His wife couldn't have pleased him better if she had done it on purpose; he knew where she had been every hour since she quitted Laura at the opera—he knew where she was at that moment and he was expecting to find another telegram on his return to Grosvenor Place. So if it suited *her* it was all right, wasn't it? and the whole thing would go as straight as a shot. Lady Davenant took him up to see Laura, though she viewed their meeting with extreme disfavour, the girl being in no state for talking. In general Laura had little enough mind for it, but she insisted on seeing Lionel: she declared that if this were not allowed her she would go after him, ill as she was—she would dress herself and drive to his house. She dressed herself now, after a fashion; she got upon a sofa to receive him. Lady Davenant left him alone with her for twenty minutes, at the end of which she returned to take him away. This interview was not fortifying to the girl, whose idea—the idea of which I have said that she was tenacious—was to go after her sister, to take possession of her, cling to her and bring her back. Lionel, of course, wouldn't hear of taking her back, nor would Selina presumably hear of coming; but this made no difference in Laura's heroic plan. She would work it, she would compass it, she would go down on her knees, she would find the eloquence of angels, she would achieve miracles. At any rate it made her frantic not to try, especially as even in fruitless action she should escape from herself—an object of which her horror was not yet extinguished.

As she lay there through inexorably conscious hours the picture of that hideous moment in the box alternated with the vision of her sister's guilty flight. She wanted to fly, herself—to go off and keep going for ever. Lionel was fussily kind to her and he didn't abuse Selina—he didn't tell her again how that lady's behaviour suited his book. He simply resisted, with a little exasperating, dogged grin, her pitiful appeal for knowledge of her sister's whereabouts. He knew what she wanted it for and he wouldn't help her in any such game. If she would promise, solemnly, to be quiet, he would tell her when she got better, but he wouldn't lend her a hand to make a fool of herself. Her work was cut out for her—she was to stay and mind the children: if she was so keen to do her duty she needn't go further than that for it. He talked a great deal about the children and figured himself as pressing the little deserted darlings to his bosom. He was not a comedian, and she could see that he really believed he was going to be better and purer now. Laura said she was sure Selina would make an attempt to get them—or at least one of them; and he replied, grimly, 'Yes, my dear, she had better try!' The girl was so angry with him, in her hot, tossing weakness, for refusing to tell her even whether the desperate pair had crossed the Channel, that she was guilty of the immorality of regretting that the difference in badness between husband and wife was so distinct (for it was distinct, she could see that) as he made his dry little remark about Selina's trying. He told her he had already seen his solicitor, the clever Mr. Smallshaw, and she said she didn't care.

On the fourth day of her absence from Grosvenor Place she got up, at an hour when she was alone (in the afternoon, rather late), and prepared herself to go out. Lady Davenant had admitted in the morning that she was better, and fortunately she had not the complication of being subject to a medical opinion, having absolutely refused to see a doctor. Her old friend had been obliged to go out—she had scarcely quitted her before—and Laura had requested the hovering, rustling lady's-maid to leave her alone: she assured her she was doing beautifully. Laura had no plan except to leave London that night; she had a moral certainty that Selina had gone to the Continent. She had always done so whenever she had a chance, and what chance had ever been larger than the present? The Continent was fearfully vague, but she would deal sharply with Lionel—she would show him she had a right to knowledge. He would certainly be in town; he would be in a complacent bustle with his lawyers. She had told him that she didn't believe he had yet gone to them, but in her heart she believed it perfectly. If he didn't satisfy her she would go to Lady Ringrose, odious as it would be to her to ask a favour of this depraved creature: unless indeed Lady Ringrose had joined the little party to France, as on the occasion of Selina's last journey thither. On her way downstairs she met one of the footmen, of whom she made the request that he would call her a cab as quickly as possible—she was obliged to go out for half an hour. He expressed the respectful hope that she was better and she replied that she was perfectly well—he would please tell her ladyship when she came in. To this the footman rejoined that her ladyship *had* come in—she had returned five minutes before and had gone to her room. 'Miss Frothingham told her you were asleep, Miss,' said the man, 'and her ladyship said it was a blessing and you were not to be disturbed.'

'Very good, I will see her,' Laura remarked, with dissimulation: 'only please let me have my cab.'

The footman went downstairs and she stood there listening; presently she heard the house-door close—he had gone out on his errand. Then she descended very softly—she prayed he might not be long. The door of the drawing-room stood open as she passed it, and she paused before it, thinking she heard sounds in the lower hall. They appeared to subside and then she found herself faint—she was terribly impatient for her cab. Partly to sit down till it came (there was a seat on the landing, but another servant might come up or down and see her), and partly to look, at the front window, whether it were not coming, she went for a moment into the drawing-room. She stood at the window, but the footman was slow; then she sank upon a chair—she felt very weak. Just after she had done so she became aware of steps on the stairs and she got up quickly, supposing that her messenger had returned, though she had not heard wheels. What she saw was not the footman she had sent out, but the expansive person of the butler, followed apparently by a visitor. This functionary ushered the visitor in with the remark that he would call her ladyship, and before she knew it she was face to face with Mr. Wendover. At the same moment she heard a cab drive up, while Mr. Wendover instantly closed the door.

'Don't turn me away; do see me—do see me!' he said. 'I asked for Lady Davenant—they told me she was at home. But it was you I wanted, and I wanted her to help me. I was going away—but I couldn't. You look very ill—do listen to me! You don't understand—I will explain everything. Ah, how ill you look!' the young man cried, as the climax of this sudden, soft, distressed appeal. Laura, for all answer, tried to push past him, but the result of this movement was that she found herself enclosed in his arms. He stopped her, but she disengaged herself, she got her hand upon the door. He was leaning against it, so she couldn't open it, and as she stood there panting she shut her eyes, so as not to see him. 'If you would let me tell you what I think—I would do anything in the world for you!' he went on.

'Let me go—you persecute me!' the girl cried, pulling at the handle.

'You don't do me justice—you are too cruel!' Mr. Wendover persisted.

'Let me go—let me go!' she only repeated, with her high, quavering, distracted note; and as he moved a little she got the door open. But he followed her out: would she see him that night? Where was she going? might he not go with her? would she see him to-morrow?

'Never, never, never!' she flung at him as she hurried away. The butler was on the stairs, descending from above; so he checked himself, letting her go. Laura passed out of the house and flew into her cab with extraordinary speed, for Mr. Wendover heard the wheels bear her away while the servant was saying to him in measured accents that her ladyship would come down immediately.

Lionel was at home, in Grosvenor Place: she burst into the library and found him playing papa. Geordie and Ferdy were sporting around him, the presence of Miss Steet had been dispensed with, and he was holding his younger son by the stomach, horizontally, between his legs, while the child made little sprawling movements which were apparently intended to represent the act of swimming. Geordie stood impatient on the brink of the imaginary stream, protesting that it was his turn now, and as soon as he saw his aunt he rushed at her with the request that she would take him up in the same fashion. She was struck with the superficiality of their childhood; they appeared to have no sense that she had been away and no care that she had been ill. But Lionel made up for this; he greeted her with affectionate jollity, said it was a good job she had come back, and remarked to the children that they would have great larks now that auntie was home again. Ferdy asked if she had been with mummy, but didn't wait for an answer, and she observed that they put no question about their mother and made no further allusion to her while they remained in the room. She wondered whether their father had enjoined upon them not to mention her, and reflected that even if he had such a command would not have been efficacious. It added to the ugliness of Selina's flight that even her children didn't miss her, and to the dreariness, somehow, to Laura's sense, of the whole situation that one could neither spend tears on the mother and wife, because she was not worth it, nor sentimentalise about the little boys, because they didn't inspire it. 'Well, you do look seedy—I'm bound to say that!' Lionel exclaimed; and he recommended strongly a glass of port, while Ferdy, not seizing this reference, suggested that daddy should take her by the waistband and teach her to 'strike out.' He represented himself in the act of drowning, but Laura interrupted this entertainment, when the servant answered the bell (Lionel having rung for the port), by requesting that the children should be conveyed to Miss Steet. 'Tell her she must never go away again,' Lionel said to Geordie, as the butler took him by the hand; but the only touching consequence of this injunction was that the child piped back to his father, over his shoulder, 'Well, you mustn't either, you know!'

'You must tell me or I'll kill myself—I give you my word!' Laura said to her brother-in-law, with unnecessary violence, as soon as they had left the room.

'I say, I say,' he rejoined, 'you *are* a wilful one! What do you want to threaten me for? Don't you know me well enough to know that ain't the way? That's the tone Selina used to take. Surely you don't want to begin and imitate her!' She only sat there, looking at him, while he leaned against the chimney-piece smoking a short cigar. There was a silence, during which she felt the heat of a certain irrational anger at the thought that a little ignorant, red-faced jockey should have the luck to be in the right as against her flesh and blood. She considered him helplessly, with something in her eyes that had never been there before—something that, apparently, after a moment, made an impression on him. Afterwards, however, she saw very well that it was not her threat that had moved him, and even at the moment she had a sense, from the way he looked back at her, that this was in no manner the first time a baffled woman had told him that she would kill herself. He had always accepted his kinship with her, but even in her trouble it was part of her consciousness that he now lumped her with a mixed group of female figures, a little wavering and dim, who were associated in his memory with 'scenes,' with importunities and bothers. It is apt to be the disadvantage of women, on occasions of measuring their strength with men, that they may perceive that the man has a larger experience and that they themselves are a part of it. It is doubtless as a provision against such emergencies that nature has opened to them operations of the mind that are independent of experience. Laura felt the dishonour of her race the more that her brother-in-law seemed so gay and bright about it: he had an air of positive prosperity, as if his misfortune had turned into that. It came to her that he really liked the idea of the public *éclaircissement*—the fresh occupation, the bustle and importance and celebrity of it. That was sufficiently incredible, but as she was on the wrong side it was also humiliating. Besides, higher spirits always suggest finer wisdom, and such an attribute on Lionel's part was most humiliating of all. 'I haven't the least objection at present to telling you what you want to know. I shall have made my little arrangements very soon and you will be subpœnaed.'

'Subpœnaed?' the girl repeated, mechanically.

'You will be called as a witness on my side.'

'On your side.'

'Of course you're on my side, ain't you?'

'Can they force me to come?' asked Laura, in answer to this.

'No, they can't force you, if you leave the country.'

'That's exactly what I want to do.'

'That will be idiotic,' said Lionel, 'and very bad for your sister. If you don't help me you ought at least to help her.'

She sat a moment with her eyes on the ground. 'Where is she—where is she?' she then asked.

'They are at Brussels, at the Hôtel de Flandres. They appear to like it very much.'

'Are you telling me the truth?'

'Lord, my dear child, *I* don't lie!' Lionel exclaimed. 'You'll make a jolly mistake if you go to her,' he added. 'If you have seen her with him how can you speak for her?'

'I won't see her with him.'

'That's all very well, but he'll take care of that. Of course if you're ready for perjury——!' Lionel exclaimed.

'I'm ready for anything.'

'Well, I've been kind to you, my dear,' he continued, smoking, with his chin in the air.

'Certainly you have been kind to me.'

'If you want to defend her you had better keep away from

her,' said Lionel. 'Besides for yourself, it won't be the best thing in the world—to be known to have been in it.'

'I don't care about myself,' the girl returned, musingly.

'Don't you care about the children, that you are so ready to throw them over? For you would, my dear, you know. If you go to Brussels you never come back here—you never cross this threshold—you never touch them again!'

Laura appeared to listen to this last declaration, but she made no reply to it; she only exclaimed after a moment, with a certain impatience, 'Oh, the children will do anyway!' Then she added passionately, 'You *won't*, Lionel; in mercy's name tell me that you won't!'

'I won't what?'

'Do the awful thing you say.'

'Divorce her? The devil I won't!'

'Then why do you speak of the children—if you have no pity for them?'

Lionel stared an instant. 'I thought you said yourself that they would do anyway!'

Laura bent her head, resting it on the back of her hand, on the leathern arm of the sofa. So she remained, while Lionel stood smoking; but at last, to leave the room, she got up with an effort that was a physical pain. He came to her, to detain her, with a little good intention that had no felicity for her, trying to take her hand persuasively. 'Dear old girl, don't try and behave just as *she* did! If you'll stay quietly here I won't call you, I give you my honour I won't; there! You want to see the doctor—that's the fellow you want to see. And what good will it do you, even if you bring her home in pink paper? Do you candidly suppose I'll ever look at her—except across the court-room?'

'I must, I must, I must!' Laura cried, jerking herself away from him and reaching the door.

'Well then, good-bye,' he said, in the sternest tone she had ever heard him use.

She made no answer, she only escaped. She locked herself in her room; she remained there an hour. At the end of this time she came out and went to the door of the schoolroom, where she asked Miss Steet to be so good as to come and speak to her. The governess followed her to her apartment and there Laura took her partly into her confidence. There were things she wanted to do before going, and she was too weak to act without assistance. She didn't want it from the servants, if only Miss Steet would learn from them whether Mr. Berrington were dining at home. Laura told her that her sister was ill and she was hurrying to join her abroad. It had to be mentioned, that way, that Mrs. Berrington had left the country, though of course there was no spoken recognition between the two women of the reasons for which she had done so. There was only a tacit hypocritical assumption that she was on a visit to friends and that there had been nothing queer about her departure. Laura knew that Miss Steet knew the truth, and the governess knew that she knew it. This young woman lent a hand, very confusedly, to the girl's prep-arations; she ventured not to be sympathetic, as that would point too much to badness, but she succeeded perfectly in being dismal. She suggested that Laura was ill herself, but Laura replied that this was no matter when her sister was so much worse. She elicited the fact that Mr. Berrington was dining out—the butler believed with his mother—but she was of no use when it came to finding in the 'Bradshaw' which she brought up from the hall the hour of the night-boat to Ostend. Laura found it herself; it was conveniently late, and it was a gain to her that she was very near the Victoria station, where she would take the train for Dover. The governess wanted to go to the station with her, but the girl would not listen to this—she would only allow her to see that she had a cab. Laura let her help her still further; she sent her down to talk to Lady Davenant's maid when that personage arrived in Grosvenor Place to inquire, from her mistress, what in the world had become of poor Miss Wing. The maid intimated, Miss Steet said on her return, that her ladyship would have come herself, only she was too angry. She was very bad in-deed. It was an indication of this that she had sent back her young friend's dressing-case and her clothes. Laura also bor-rowed money from the governess—she had too little in her pocket. The latter brightened up as the preparations ad-vanced; she had never before been concerned in a flurried night-episode, with an unavowed clandestine side; the very imprudence of it (for a sick girl alone) was romantic, and before Laura had gone down to the cab she began to say that foreign life must be fascinating and to make wistful reflections. She saw that the coast was clear, in the nursery—that the children were asleep, for their aunt to come in. She kissed Ferdy while her companion pressed her lips upon Geordie, and Geordie while Laura hung for a moment over Ferdy. At the door of the cab she tried to make her take more money, and our heroine had an odd sense that if the vehicle had not rolled away she would have thrust into her hand a keepsake for Captain Crispin.

A quarter of an hour later Laura sat in the corner of a railway-carriage, muffled in her cloak (the July evening was fresh, as it so often is in London—fresh enough to add to her sombre thoughts the suggestion of the wind in the Channel), waiting in a vain torment of nervousness for the train to set itself in motion. Her nervousness itself had led her to come too early to the station, and it seemed to her that she had already waited long. A lady and a gentleman had taken their place in the carriage (it was not yet the moment for the outward crowd of tourists) and had left their appurtenances there while they strolled up and down the platform. The long English twilight was still in the air, but there was dusk under the grimy arch of the station and Laura flattered herself that the off-corner of the carriage she had chosen was in shadow. This, however, apparently did not prevent her from being recognised by a gentleman who stopped at the door, looking in, with the movement of a person who was going from carriage to carriage. As soon as he saw her he stepped quickly in, and the next moment Mr. Wendover was seated on the edge of the place beside her, leaning toward her, speaking to her low, with clasped hands. She fell back in her seat, closing her eyes again. He barred the way out of the compartment.

'I have followed you here—I saw Miss Steet—I want to implore you not to go! Don't, don't! I know what you're doing. Don't go, I beseech you. I saw Lady Davenant, I wanted to ask her to help me, I could bear it no longer. I have thought of you, night and day, these four days. Lady Davenant has told me things, and I entreat you not to go!'

Laura opened her eyes (there was something in his voice,

in his pressing nearness), and looked at him a moment: it was the first time she had done so since the first of those detestable moments in the box at Covent Garden. She had never spoken to him of Selina in any but an honourable sense. Now she said, 'I'm going to my sister.'

'I know it, and I wish unspeakably you would give it up—it isn't good—it's a great mistake. Stay here and let me talk to you.'

The girl raised herself, she stood up in the carriage. Mr. Wendover did the same; Laura saw that the lady and gentleman outside were now standing near the door. 'What have you to say? It's my own business!' she returned, between her teeth. 'Go out, go out, go out!'

'Do you suppose I would speak if I didn't care—do you suppose I would care if I didn't love you?' the young man murmured, close to her face.

'What is there to care about? Because people will know it and talk? If it's bad it's the right thing for me! If I don't go to her where else shall I go?'

'Come to me, dearest, dearest!' Mr. Wendover went on. 'You are ill, you are mad! I love you—I assure you I do!'

She pushed him away with her hands. 'If you follow me I will jump off the boat!'

'Take your places, take your places!' cried the guard, on the platform. Mr. Wendover had to slip out, the lady and gentleman were coming in. Laura huddled herself into her corner again and presently the train drew away.

Mr. Wendover did not get into another compartment; he went back that evening to Queen's Gate. He knew how interested his old friend there, as he now considered her, would be to hear what Laura had undertaken (though, as he learned, on entering her drawing-room again, she had already heard of it from her maid), and he felt the necessity to tell her once more how her words of four days before had fructified in his heart, what a strange, ineffaceable impression she had made upon him: to tell her in short and to repeat it over and over, that he had taken the most extraordinary fancy——! Lady Davenant was tremendously vexed at the girl's perversity, but she counselled him patience, a long, persistent patience. A week later she heard from Laura Wing, from Antwerp, that she was sailing to America from that port—a letter containing no mention whatever of Selina or of the reception she had found at Brussels. To America Mr. Wendover followed his young compatriot (that at least she had no right to forbid), and there, for the moment, he has had a chance to practise the humble virtue recommended by Lady Davenant. He knows she has no money and that she is staying with some distant relatives in Virginia; a situation that he—perhaps too superficially—figures as unspeakably dreary. He knows further that Lady Davenant has sent her fifty pounds, and he himself has ideas of transmitting funds, not directly to Virginia but by the roundabout road of Queen's Gate. Now, however, that Lionel Berrington's deplorable suit is coming on he reflects with some satisfaction that the Court of Probate and Divorce is far from the banks of the Rappahannock. 'Berrington *versus* Berrington and Others' is coming on—but these are matters of the present hour.

The Lesson of the Master

H E HAD been informed that the ladies were at church, but that was corrected by what he saw from the top of the steps (they descended from a great height in two arms, with a circular sweep of the most charming effect) at the threshold of the door which, from the long, bright gallery, overlooked the immense lawn. Three gentlemen, on the grass, at a distance, sat under the great trees; but the fourth figure was not a gentleman, the one in the crimson dress which made so vivid a spot, told so as a "bit of colour" amid the fresh, rich green. The servant had come so far with Paul Overt to show him the way and had asked him if he wished first to go to his room. The young man declined this privilege, having no disorder to repair after so short and easy a journey and liking to take a general perceptive possession of the new scene immediately, as he always did. He stood there a little with his eyes on the group and on the admirable picture—the wide grounds of an old country-house near London (that only made it better,) on a splendid Sunday in June. "But that lady, who is she?" he said to the servant before the man went away.

"I think it's Mrs. St. George, sir."

"Mrs. St. George, the wife of the distinguished——" Then Paul Overt checked himself, doubting whether the footman would know.

"Yes, sir—probably, sir," said the servant, who appeared to wish to intimate that a person staying at Summersoft would naturally be, if only by alliance, distinguished. His manner, however, made poor Overt feel for the moment as if he himself were but little so.

"And the gentlemen?" he inquired.

"Well, sir, one of them is General Fancourt."

"Ah yes, I know; thank you." General Fancourt was distinguished, there was no doubt of that, for something he had done, or perhaps even had not done (the young man could not remember which) some years before in India. The servant went away, leaving the glass doors open into the gallery, and Paul Overt remained at the head of the wide double staircase, saying to himself that the place was sweet and promised a pleasant visit, while he leaned on the balustrade of fine old ironwork which, like all the other details, was of the same period as the house. It all went together and spoke in one voice—a rich English voice of the early part of the eighteenth century. It might have been church-time on a summer's day in the reign of Queen Anne; the stillness was too perfect to be modern, the nearness counted so as distance and there was something so fresh and sound in the originality of the large smooth house, the expanse of whose beautiful brickwork, which had been kept clear of messy creepers (as a woman with a rare complexion disdains a veil,) was pink rather than red. When Paul Overt perceived that the people under the trees were noticing him he turned back through the open doors into the great gallery which was the pride of the place. It traversed the mansion from end to end and seemed—with its bright colours, its high panelled windows, its faded, flowered chintzes, its quickly-recognised portraits and pictures, the blue and white china of its cabinets and the attenuated festoons and rosettes of its ceiling—a cheerful upholstered avenue into the other century.

The young man was slightly nervous; that belonged in general to his disposition as a student of fine prose, with his dose of the artist's restlessness; and there was a particular excitement in the idea that Henry St. George might be a member of the party. For the younger writer he had remained a high literary figure, in spite of the lower range of production to which he had fallen after his three first great successes, the comparative absence of quality in his later work. There had been moments when Paul Overt almost shed tears upon this; but now that he was near him (he had never met him,) he was conscious only of the fine original source and of his own immense debt. After he had taken a turn or two up and down the gallery he came out again and descended the steps. He was but slenderly supplied with a certain social boldness (it was really a weakness in him,) so that, conscious of a want of acquaintance with the four persons in the distance, he indulged in a movement as to which he had a certain safety in feeling that it did not necessarily appear to commit him to an attempt to join them. There was a fine English awkwardness in it—he felt this too as he sauntered vaguely and obliquely across the lawn, as if to take an independent line. Fortunately there was an equally fine English directness in the way one of the gentlemen presently rose and made as if to approach him, with an air of conciliation and reassurance. To this demonstration Paul Overt instantly responded, though he knew the gentleman was not his host. He was tall, straight and elderly, and had a pink, smiling face and a white moustache. Our young man met him half way while he laughed and said: "A——Lady Watermouth told us you were coming; she asked me just to look after you." Paul Overt thanked him (he liked him without delay,) and turned round with him, walking toward the others. "They've all gone to church—all except us," the stranger continued as they went; "we're just sitting here—it's so jolly." Overt rejoined that it was jolly indeed— it was such a lovely place; he mentioned that he had not seen it before—it was a charming impression.

"Ah, you've not been here before?" said his companion. "It's a nice little place—not much to *do*, you know." Overt wondered what he wanted to "do"—he felt as if he himself were doing a good deal. By the time they came to where the others sat he had guessed his initiator was a military man, and (such was the turn of Overt's imagination,) this made him still more sympathetic. He would naturally have a passion for activity—for deeds at variance with the pacific, pastoral scene. He was evidently so good-natured, however, that he accepted the inglorious hour for what it was worth. Paul Overt shared it with him and with his companions for the next twenty minutes; the latter looked at him and he looked at them without knowing much who they were, while the talk went on without enlightening him much as to what it was about. It was indeed about nothing in particular, and wandered, with casual, pointless pauses and short terrestrial flights, amid the names of persons and places—names which, for him, had no great power of evocation. It was all sociable and slow, as was right and natural on a warm Sunday morning.

Overt's first attention was given to the question, privately considered, of whether one of the two younger men would be Henry St. George. He knew many of his distinguished contemporaries by their photographs, but he had never, as it happened, seen a portrait of the great misguided novelist. One of the gentlemen was out of the question—he was too young; and the other scarcely looked clever enough, with such mild, undiscriminating eyes. If those eyes were St. George's the problem presented by the ill-matched parts of his genius was still more difficult of solution. Besides, the deportment of the personage possessing them was not, as regards the lady in the red dress, such as could be natural, towards his wife, even to a writer accused by several critics of sacrificing too much to manner. Lastly, Paul Overt had an indefinite feeling that if the gentleman with the sightless eyes bore the name that had set his heart beating faster (he also had contradictory, conventional whiskers—the young admirer of the celebrity had never in a mental vision seen *his* face in so vulgar a frame), he would have given him a sign of recognition or of friendliness—would have heard of him a little, would know something about *Ginistrella*, would have gathered at least that that recent work of fiction had made an impression on the discerning. Paul Overt had a dread of being grossly proud, but it seemed to him that his self-consciousness took no undue license in thinking that the authorship of *Ginistrella* constituted a degree of identity. His soldierly friend became clear enough; he was "Fancourt," but he was also the General; and he mentioned to our young man in the course of a few moments that he had but lately returned from twenty years' service abroad.

"And do you mean to remain in England?" Overt asked.

"Oh yes, I have bought a little house in London."

"And I hope you like it," said Overt, looking at Mrs. St. George.

"Well, a little house in Manchester Square—there's a limit to the enthusiasm that that inspires."

"Oh, I meant being at home again—being in London."

"My daughter likes it—that's the main thing. She's very fond of art and music and literature and all that kind of thing. She missed it in India and she finds it in London, or she hopes she will find it. Mr. St. George has promised to help her—he has been awfully kind to her. She has gone to church—she's fond of that too—but they'll all be back in a quarter of an hour. You must let me introduce you to her—she will be so glad to know you. I dare say she has read every word you have written."

"I shall be delighted—I haven't written very many," said Overt, who felt without resentment that the General at least was very vague about that. But he wondered a little why, since he expressed this friendly disposition, it did not occur to him to pronounce the word which would put him in relation with Mrs. St. George. If it was a question of introductions Miss Fancourt (apparently she was unmarried,) was far away and the wife of his illustrious *confrère* was almost between them. This lady struck Paul Overt as a very pretty woman, with a surprising air of youth and a high smartness of aspect which seemed to him (he could scarcely have said why,) a sort of mystification. St. George certainly had every right to a charming wife, but he himself would never have taken the important little woman in the aggressively Parisian dress for the domestic partner of a man of letters. That partner in general, he knew, was far from presenting herself in a single type: his observation had instructed him that she was not inveterately, not necessarily dreary. But he had never before seen her look so much as if her prosperity had deeper foundations than an ink-spotted study-table littered with proof-sheets. Mrs. St. George might have been the wife of a gentleman who "kept" books rather than wrote them, who carried on great affairs in the City and made better bargains than those that poets make with publishers. With this she hinted at a success more personal, as if she had been the most characteristic product of an age in which society, the world of conversation, is a great drawing-room with the City for its antechamber. Overt judged her at first to be about thirty years of age; then, after a while, he perceived that she was much nearer fifty. But she juggled away the twenty years somehow—you only saw them in a rare glimpse, like the rabbit in the conjurer's sleeve. She was extraordinarily white, and everything about her was pretty—her eyes, her ears, her hair, her voice, her hands, her feet (to which her relaxed attitude in her wicker chair gave a great publicity,) and the numerous ribbons and trinkets with which she was bedecked. She looked as if she had put on her best clothes to go to church and then had decided that they were too good for that and had stayed at home. She told a story of some length about the shabby way Lady Jane had treated the Duchess, as well as an anecdote in relation to a purchase she had made in Paris (on her way back from Cannes,) for Lady Egbert, who had never refunded the money. Paul Overt suspected her of a tendency to figure great people as larger than life, until he noticed the manner in which she handled Lady Egbert, which was so subversive that it reassured him. He felt that he should have understood her better if he might have met her eye; but she scarcely looked at him. "Ah, here they come—all the good ones!" she said at last; and Paul Overt saw in the distance the return of the churchgoers—several persons, in couples and threes, advancing in a flicker of sun and shade at the end of a large green vista formed by the level grass and the overarching boughs.

"If you mean to imply that we are bad, I protest," said one of the gentlemen—"after making oneself agreeable all the morning!"

"Ah, if they've found you agreeable!" Mrs. St. George exclaimed, smiling. "But if we are good the others are better."

"They must be angels then," observed the General.

"Your husband was an angel, the way he went off at your bidding," the gentleman who had first spoken said to Mrs. St. George.

"At my bidding?"

"Didn't you make him go to church?"

"I never made him do anything in my life but once, when I made him burn up a bad book. That's all!" At her "That's all!" Paul broke into an irrepressible laugh; it lasted only a second, but it drew her eyes to him. His own met them, but not long enough to help him to understand her; unless it were a step towards this that he felt sure on the instant that the burnt book (the way she alluded to it!) was one of her husband's finest things.

"A bad book?" her interlocutor repeated.

"I didn't like it. He went to church because your daughter went," she continued, to General Fancourt. "I think it my duty to call your attention to his demeanour to your daughter."

"Well, if you don't mind it, I don't," the General laughed.
"Il s'attache à ses pas. But I don't wonder—she's so
charming."

"I hope she won't make him burn any books!" Paul Overt
ventured to exclaim.

"If she would make him write a few it would be more to
the purpose," said Mrs. St. George. "He has been of an in-
dolence this year!"

Our young man stared—he was so struck with the lady's
phraseology. Her "Write a few" seemed to him almost as
good as her "That's all." Didn't she, as the wife of a rare
artist, know what it was to produce *one* perfect work of art?
How in the world did she think they were turned off? His
private conviction was that admirably as Henry St. George
wrote, he had written for the last ten years, and especially for
the last five, only too much, and there was an instant during
which he felt the temptation to make this public. But before
he had spoken a diversion was effected by the return of the
absent guests. They strolled up dispersedly—there were eight
or ten of them—and the circle under the trees rearranged itself
as they took their place in it. They made it much larger; so
that Paul Overt could feel (he was always feeling that sort of
thing, as he said to himself,) that if the company had already
been interesting to watch it would now become a great deal
more so. He shook hands with his hostess, who welcomed
him without many words, in the manner of a woman able to
trust him to understand—conscious that, in every way, so
pleasant an occasion would speak for itself. She offered him
no particular facility for sitting by her, and when they had all
subsided again he found himself still next General Fancourt,
with an unknown lady on his other flank.

"That's my daughter—that one opposite," the General said
to him without loss of time. Overt saw a tall girl, with magnificent red hair, in a dress of a pretty grey-green tint and of
a limp silken texture, in which every modern effect had been
avoided. It had therefore somehow the stamp of the latest
thing, so that Overt quickly perceived she was eminently a
contemporary young lady.

"She's very handsome—very handsome," he repeated,

looking at her. There was something noble in her head, and she appeared fresh and strong.

Her father surveyed her with complacency; then he said: "She looks too hot—that's her walk. But she'll be all right presently. Then I'll make her come over and speak to you."

"I should be sorry to give you that trouble; if you were to take me over there—" the young man murmured.

"My dear sir, do you suppose I put myself out that way? I don't mean for you, but for Marian," the General added.

"*I* would put myself out for her, soon enough," Overt replied; after which he went on: "Will you be so good as to tell me which of those gentlemen is Henry St. George?"

"The fellow talking to my girl. By Jove, he *is* making up to her—they're going off for another walk."

"Ah, is that he, really?" The young man felt a certain surprise, for the personage before him contradicted a preconception which had been vague only till it was confronted with the reality. As soon as this happened the mental image, retiring with a sigh, became substantial enough to suffer a slight wrong. Overt, who had spent a considerable part of his short life in foreign lands, made now, but not for the first time, the reflection that whereas in those countries he had almost always recognised the artist and the man of letters by his personal "type," the mould of his face, the character of his head, the expression of his figure and even the indications of his dress, in England this identification was as little as possible a matter of course, thanks to the greater conformity, the habit of sinking the profession instead of advertising it, the general diffusion of the air of the gentleman—the gentleman committed to no particular set of ideas. More than once, on returning to his own country, he had said to himself in regard to the people whom he met in society: "One sees them about and one even talks with them; but to find out what they *do* one would really have to be a detective." In respect to several individuals whose work he was unable to like (perhaps he was wrong) he found himself adding, "No wonder they conceal it—it's so bad!" He observed that oftener than in France and in Germany his artist looked like a gentleman (that is, like an English one,) while he perceived that outside of a few exceptions his

gentleman didn't look like an artist. St. George was not one
of the exceptions; that circumstance he definitely apprehended
before the great man had turned his back to walk off with
Miss Fancourt. He certainly looked better behind than any
foreign man of letters, and beautifully correct in his tall black
hat and his superior frock coat. Somehow, all the same, these
very garments (he wouldn't have minded them so much on a
weekday,) were disconcerting to Paul Overt, who forgot for
the moment that the head of the profession was not a bit
better dressed than himself. He had caught a glimpse of a
regular face, with a fresh colour, a brown moustache and a
pair of eyes surely never visited by a fine frenzy, and he promised himself to study it on the first occasion. His temporary
opinion was that St. George looked like a lucky stock-
broker—a gentleman driving eastward every morning from a
sanitary suburb in a smart dog-cart. That carried out the
impression already derived from his wife. Paul Overt's glance,
after a moment, travelled back to this lady, and he saw that
her own had followed her husband as he moved off with Miss
Fancourt. Overt permitted himself to wonder a little whether
she were jealous when another woman took him away. Then
he seemed to perceive that Mrs. St. George was not glaring
at the indifferent maiden—her eyes rested only on her husband, and with unmistakable serenity. That was the way she
wanted him to be—she liked his conventional uniform. Overt
had a great desire to hear more about the book she had induced him to destroy.

II.

As they all came out from luncheon General Fancourt took
hold of Paul Overt and exclaimed, "I say, I want you to know
my girl!" as if the idea had just occurred to him and he had
not spoken of it before. With the other hand he possessed
himself of the young lady and said: "You know all about him.
I've seen you with his books. She reads everything—everything!" he added to the young man. The girl smiled at him
and then laughed at her father. The General turned away and
his daughter said:
    "Isn't papa delightful?"

"He is indeed, Miss Fancourt."

"As if I read you because I read 'everything'!"

"Oh, I don't mean for saying that," said Paul Overt. "I liked him from the moment he spoke to me. Then he promised me this privilege."

"It isn't for you he means it, it's for me. If you flatter yourself that he thinks of anything in life but me you'll find you are mistaken. He introduces every one to me. He thinks me insatiable."

"You speak like him," said Paul Overt, laughing.

"Ah, but sometimes I want to," the girl replied, colouring. "I don't read everything—I read very little. But I *have* read you."

"Suppose we go into the gallery," said Paul Overt. She pleased him greatly, not so much because of this last remark (though that of course was not disagreeable to him,) as because, seated opposite to him at luncheon, she had given him for half an hour the impression of her beautiful face. Something else had come with it—a sense of generosity, of an enthusiasm which, unlike many enthusiasms, was not all manner. That was not spoiled for him by the circumstance that the repast had placed her again in familiar contact with Henry St. George. Sitting next to her he was also opposite to our young man, who had been able to observe that he multiplied the attentions which his wife had brought to the General's notice. Paul Overt had been able to observe further that this lady was not in the least discomposed by these demonstrations and that she gave every sign of an unclouded spirit. She had Lord Masham on one side of her and on the other the accomplished Mr. Mulliner, editor of the new high-class, lively evening paper which was expected to meet a want felt in circles increasingly conscious that Conservatism must be made amusing, and unconvinced when assured by those of another political colour that it was already amusing enough. At the end of an hour spent in her company Paul Overt thought her still prettier than she had appeared to him at first, and if her profane allusions to her husband's work had not still rung in his ears he should have liked her—so far as it could be a question of that in connection with a woman to whom he had not yet spoken and to whom probably he should never speak if it were

left to her. Pretty women evidently were necessary to Henry
St. George, and for the moment it was Miss Fancourt who
was most indispensable. If Overt had promised himself to take
a better look at him the opportunity now was of the best, and
it brought consequences which the young man felt to be important. He saw more in his face, and he liked it the better
for its not telling its whole story in the first three minutes.
That story came out as one read, in little instalments (it was
excusable that Overt's mental comparisons should be somewhat professional,) and the text was a style considerably involved—a language not easy to translate at sight. There were
shades of meaning in it and a vague perspective of history
which receded as you advanced. Of two facts Paul Overt had
taken especial notice. The first of these was that he liked the
countenance of the illustrious novelist much better when it
was in repose than when it smiled; the smile displeased him
(as much as anything from that source could,) whereas the
quiet face had a charm which increased in proportion as it
became completely quiet. The change to the expression of
gaiety excited on Overt's part a private protest which resembled that of a person sitting in the twilight and enjoying it,
when the lamp is brought in too soon. His second reflection
was that, though generally he disliked the sight of a man of
that age using arts to make himself agreeable to a pretty girl,
he was not struck in this case by the ugliness of the thing,
which seemed to prove that St. George had a light hand or
the air of being younger than he was, or else that Miss Fancourt showed that *she* was not conscious of an anomaly.

Overt walked with her into the gallery, and they strolled to
the end of it, looking at the pictures, the cabinets, the charming vista, which harmonised with the prospect of the summer
afternoon, resembling it in its long brightness, with great divans and old chairs like hours of rest. Such a place as that had
the added merit of giving persons who came into it plenty to
talk about. Miss Fancourt sat down with Paul Overt on a
flowered sofa, the cushions of which, very numerous, were
tight, ancient cubes, of many sizes, and presently she said:
"I'm so glad to have a chance to thank you."

"To thank me?"

"I liked your book so much. I think it's splendid."

She sat there smiling at him, and he never asked himself which book she meant; for after all he had written three or four. That seemed a vulgar detail, and he was not even gratified by the idea of the pleasure she told him—her bright, handsome face told him—he had given her. The feeling she appealed to, or at any rate the feeling she excited, was something larger—something that had little to do with any quickened pulsation of his own vanity. It was responsive admiration of the life she embodied, the young purity and richness of which appeared to imply that real success was to resemble *that*, to live, to bloom, to present the perfection of a fine type, not to have hammered out headachy fancies with a bent back at an ink-stained table. While her grey eyes rested on him (there was a wideish space between them, and the division of her rich-coloured hair, which was so thick that it ventured to be smooth, made a free arch above them,) he was almost ashamed of that exercise of the pen which it was her present inclination to eulogise. He was conscious that he should have liked better to please her in some other way. The lines of her face were those of a woman grown, but there was something childish in her complexion and the sweetness of her mouth. Above all she was natural—that was indubitable now—more natural than he had supposed at first, perhaps on account of her æsthetic drapery, which was conventionally unconventional, suggesting a tortuous spontaneity. He had feared that sort of thing in other cases, and his fears had been justified; though he was an artist to the essence, the modern reactionary nymph, with the brambles of the woodland caught in her folds and a look as if the satyrs had toyed with her hair, was apt to make him uncomfortable. Miss Fancourt was really more candid than her costume, and the best proof of it was her supposing that such garments suited her liberal character. She was robed like a pessimist, but Overt was sure she liked the taste of life. He thanked her for her appreciation—aware at the same time that he didn't appear to thank her enough and that she might think him ungracious. He was afraid she would ask him to explain something that he had written, and he always shrank from that (perhaps too timidly,) for to his own ear the explanation of a work of art sounded fatuous. But he liked her so much as to feel a confidence that in the long run he should be able to show her that he was not rudely evasive. Moreover it was very certain that she was not quick to take offence; she was not irritable, she could be trusted to wait. So when he said to her, "Ah! don't talk of anything I have done, *here*; there is another man in the house who is the actuality!" when he uttered this short, sincere protest, it was with the sense that she would see in the words neither mock humility nor the ungraciousness of a successful man bored with praise.

"You mean Mr. St. George—isn't he delightful?"

Paul Overt looked at her a moment; there was a species of morning-light in her eyes.

"Alas, I don't know him. I only admire him at a distance."

"Oh, you must know him—he wants so to talk to you," rejoined Miss Fancourt, who evidently had the habit of saying the things that, by her quick calculation, would give people pleasure. Overt divined that she would always calculate on everything's being simple between others.

"I shouldn't have supposed he knew anything about me," Paul said, smiling.

"He does then—everything. And if he didn't, I should be able to tell him."

"To tell him everything?"

"You talk just like the people in your book!" the girl exclaimed.

"Then they must all talk alike."

"Well, it must be so difficult. Mr. St. George tells me it is, terribly. I've tried too and I find it so. I've tried to write a novel."

"Mr. St. George oughtn't to discourage you," said Paul Overt.

"You do much more—when you wear that expression."

"Well, after all, why try to be an artist?" the young man went on. "It's so poor—so poor!"

"I don't know what you mean," said Marian Fancourt, looking grave.

"I mean as compared with being a person of action—as living your works."

"But what is art but a life—if it be real?" asked the girl. "I think it's the only one—everything else is so clumsy!" Paul

Overt laughed, and she continued: "It's so interesting, meeting so many celebrated people."

"So I should think; but surely it isn't new to you."

"Why, I have never seen any one—any one: living always in Asia."

"But doesn't Asia swarm with personages? Haven't you administered provinces in India and had captive rajahs and tributary princes chained to your car?"

"I was with my father, after I left school to go out there. It was delightful being with him—we are alone together in the world, he and I—but there was none of the society I like best. One never heard of a picture—never of a book, except bad ones."

"Never of a picture? Why, wasn't all life a picture?"

Miss Fancourt looked over the delightful place where they sat. "Nothing to compare with this. I adore England!" she exclaimed.

"Ah, of course I don't deny that we must do something with it yet."

"It hasn't been touched, really," said the girl.

"Did Henry St. George say that?"

There was a small and, as he felt it, venial intention of irony in his question; which, however, the girl took very simply, not noticing the insinuation. "Yes, he says it has not been touched—not touched comparatively," she answered, eagerly. "He's so interesting about it. To listen to him makes one want so to do something."

"It would make me want to," said Paul Overt, feeling strongly, on the instant, the suggestion of what she said and of the emotion with which she said it, and what an incentive, on St. George's lips, such a speech might be.

"Oh, you—as if you hadn't! I should like so to hear you talk together," the girl added, ardently.

"That's very genial of you; but he would have it all his own way. I'm prostrate before him."

Marian Fancourt looked earnest for a moment. "Do you think then he's so perfect?"

"Far from it. Some of his later books seem to me awfully queer."

"Yes, yes—he knows that."

Paul Overt stared. "That they seem to me awfully queer?"

"Well yes, or at any rate that they are not what they should be. He told me he didn't esteem them. He has told me such wonderful things—he's so interesting."

There was a certain shock for Paul Overt in the knowledge that the fine genius they were talking of had been reduced to so explicit a confession and had made it, in his misery, to the first comer; for though Miss Fancourt was charming, what was she after all but an immature girl encountered at a country-house? Yet precisely this was a part of the sentiment that he himself had just expressed; he would make way completely for the poor peccable great man, not because he didn't read him clear, but altogether because he did. His consideration was half composed of tenderness for superficialities which he was sure St. George judged privately with supreme sternness and which denoted some tragic intellectual secret. He would have his reasons for his psychology *à fleur de peau*, and these reasons could only be cruel ones, such as would make him dearer to those who already were fond of him. "You excite my envy. I judge him, I discriminate—but I love him," Overt said in a moment. "And seeing him for the first time this way is a great event for me."

"How momentous—how magnificent!" cried the girl. "How delicious to bring you together!"

"*Your* doing it—that makes it perfect," Overt responded.

"He's as eager as you," Miss Fancourt went on. "But it's so odd you shouldn't have met."

"It's not so odd as it seems. I've been out of England so much—repeated absences during all these last years."

"And yet you write of it as well as if you were always here."

"It's just the being away perhaps. At any rate the best bits, I suspect, are those that were done in dreary places abroad."

"And why were they dreary?"

"Because they were health-resorts—where my poor mother was dying."

"Your poor mother?" the girl murmured, kindly.

"We went from place to place to help her to get better. But she never did. To the deadly Riviera (I hate it!) to the high

Alps, to Algiers, and far away—a hideous journey—to Colorado."

"And she isn't better?" Miss Fancourt went on.

"She died a year ago."

"Really?—like mine! Only that is far away. Some day you must tell me about your mother," she added.

Overt looked at her a moment. "What right things you say! If you say them to St. George I don't wonder he's in bondage."

"I don't know what you mean. He doesn't make speeches and professions at all—he isn't ridiculous."

"I'm afraid you consider that I am."

"No, I don't," the girl replied, rather shortly. "He understands everything."

Overt was on the point of saying jocosely: "And I don't—is that it?" But these words, before he had spoken, changed themselves into others slightly less trivial: "Do you suppose he understands his wife?"

Miss Fancourt made no direct answer to his question; but after a moment's hesitation she exclaimed: "Isn't she charming?"

"Not in the least!"

"Here he comes. Now you must know him," the girl went on. A small group of visitors had gathered at the other end of the gallery and they had been joined for a moment by Henry St. George, who strolled in from a neighbouring room. He stood near them a moment, not, apparently, falling into the conversation, but taking up an old miniature from a table and vaguely examining it. At the end of a minute he seemed to perceive Miss Fancourt and her companion in the distance; whereupon, laying down his miniature, he approached them with the same procrastinating air, with his hands in his pockets, looking to right and left at the pictures. The gallery was so long that this transit took some little time, especially as there was a moment when he stopped to admire the fine Gainsborough. "He says she has been the making of him," Miss Fancourt continued, in a voice slightly lowered.

"Ah, he's often obscure!" laughed Paul Overt.

"Obscure?" she repeated, interrogatively. Her eyes rested

upon her other friend, and it was not lost upon Paul that they appeared to send out great shafts of softness. "He is going to speak to us!" she exclaimed, almost breathlessly. There was a sort of rapture in her voice; Paul Overt was startled. "Bless my soul, is she so fond of him as that—is she in love with him?" he mentally inquired. "Didn't I tell you he was eager?" she added, to her companion.

"It's eagerness dissimulated," the young man rejoined, as the subject of their observation lingered before his Gainsborough. "He edges toward us shyly. Does he mean that she saved him by burning that book?"

"That book? what book did she burn?" The girl turned her face quickly upon him.

"Hasn't he told you, then?"

"Not a word."

"Then he doesn't tell you everything!" Paul Overt had guessed that Miss Fancourt pretty much supposed he did. The great man had now resumed his course and come nearer; nevertheless Overt risked the profane observation: "St. George and the dragon, the anecdote suggests!"

Miss Fancourt, however, did not hear it; she was smiling at her approaching friend. "He *is* eager—he is!" she repeated.

"Eager for you—yes."

The girl called out frankly, joyously: "I know you want to know Mr. Overt. You'll be great friends, and it will always be delightful to me to think that I was here when you first met and that I had something to do with it."

There was a freshness of intention in this speech which carried it off; nevertheless our young man was sorry for Henry St. George, as he was sorry at any time for any one who was publicly invited to be responsive and delightful. He would have been so contented to believe that a man he deeply admired attached an importance to him that he was determined not to play with such a presumption if it possibly were vain. In a single glance of the eye of the pardonable master he discovered (having the sort of divination that belonged to his talent,) that this personage was full of general good-will, but had not read a word he had written. There was even a relief, a simplification, in that: liking him so much already for what he had done, how could he like him more for having been struck with a certain promise? He got up, trying to show his compassion, but at the same instant he found himself encompassed by St. George's happy personal art—a manner of which it was the essence to conjure away false positions. It all took place in a moment. He was conscious that he knew him now, conscious of his handshake and of the very quality of his hand; of his face, seen nearer and consequently seen better, of a general fraternising assurance, and in particular of the circumstance that St. George didn't dislike him (as yet at least,) for being imposed by a charming but too gushing girl, valuable enough without such danglers. At any rate no irritation was reflected in the voice with which he questioned Miss Fancourt in respect to some project of a walk—a general walk of the company round the park. He had said something to Overt about a talk—"We must have a tremendous lot of talk; there are so many things, aren't there?"—but Paul perceived that this idea would not in the present case take very immediate effect. All the same he was extremely happy, even after the matter of the walk had been settled (the three presently passed back to the other part of the gallery, where it was discussed with several members of the party,) even when, after they had all gone out together, he found himself for half an hour in contact with Mrs. St. George. Her husband had taken the advance with Miss Fancourt, and this pair were quite out of sight. It was the prettiest of rambles for a summer afternoon—a grassy circuit, of immense extent, skirting the limit of the park within. The park was completely surrounded by its old mottled but perfect red wall, which, all the way on their left, made a picturesque accompaniment. Mrs. St. George mentioned to him the surprising number of acres that were thus enclosed, together with numerous other facts relating to the property and the family, and its other properties: she could not too strongly urge upon him the importance of seeing their other houses. She ran over the names of these and rang the changes on them with the facility of practice, making them appear an almost endless list. She had received Paul Overt very amiably when he broke ground with her by telling her that he had just had the joy of making her husband's acquaintance, and struck him as so alert and so accommodating a little woman that he was rather ashamed of his *mot* about her to Miss Fancourt; though he reflected that a hundred other people, on a hundred occasions, would have been sure to make it. He got on with Mrs. St. George, in short, better than he expected; but this did not prevent her from suddenly becoming aware that she was faint with fatigue and must take her way back to the house by the shortest cut. She hadn't the strength of a kitten, she said—she was awfully seedy; a state of things that Overt had been too preoccupied to perceive— preoccupied with a private effort to ascertain in what sense she could be held to have been the making of her husband. He had arrived at a glimmering of the answer when she announced that she must leave him, though this perception was of course provisional. While he was in the very act of placing himself at her disposal for the return the situation underwent a change; Lord Masham suddenly turned up, coming back to them, overtaking them, emerging from the shrubbery—Overt could scarcely have said how he appeared, and Mrs. St. George had protested that she wanted to be left alone and not to break up the party. A moment later she was walking off with Lord Masham. Paul Overt fell back and joined Lady Watermouth, to whom he presently mentioned that Mrs. St. George had been obliged to renounce the attempt to go further.

"She oughtn't to have come out at all," her ladyship remarked, rather grumpily.

"Is she so very much of an invalid?"

"Very bad indeed." And his hostess added, with still greater austerity: "She oughtn't to come to stay with one!" He wondered what was implied by this, and presently gathered that it was not a reflection on the lady's conduct or her moral nature: it only represented that her strength was not equal to her aspirations.

III.

The smoking-room at Summersoft was on the scale of the rest of the place; that is it was high and light and commodious, and decorated with such refined old carvings and mouldings that it seemed rather a bower for ladies who should sit at work at fading crewels than a parliament of gentlemen smoking strong cigars. The gentlemen mustered there in considerable force on the Sunday evening, collecting mainly at one end, in front of one of the cool fair fireplaces of white marble, the entablature of which was adorned with a delicate little Italian "subject." There was another in the wall that faced it, and, thanks to the mild summer night, there was no fire in either; but a nucleus for aggregation was furnished on one side by a table in the chimney-corner laden with bottles, decanters and tall tumblers. Paul Overt was an insincere smoker; he puffed cigarettes occasionally for reasons with which tobacco had nothing to do. This was particularly the case on the occasion of which I speak; his motive was the vision of a little direct talk with Henry St. George. The "tremendous" communion of which the great man had held out hopes to him earlier in the day had not yet come off, and this saddened him considerably, for the party was to go its several ways immediately after breakfast on the morrow. He had, however, the disappointment of finding that apparently the author of *Shadow mere* was not disposed to prolong his vigil. He was not among the gentlemen assembled in the smoking-room when Overt entered it, nor was he one of those who turned up, in bright habiliments, during the next ten minutes. The young man waited a little, wondering whether he had only gone to put on something extraordinary; this would account for his delay as well as contribute further to Overt's observation of his tendency to do the approved superficial thing. But he didn't arrive—he must have been putting on something more extraordinary than was probable. Paul gave him up, feeling a little injured, a little wounded at his not having managed to say twenty words to him. He was not angry, but he puffed his cigarette sighingly, with the sense of having lost a precious chance. He wandered away with his regret, moved slowly round the room, looking at the old prints on the walls. In this attitude he presently felt a hand laid on his shoulder and a friendly voice in his ear. "This is good. I hoped I should find you. I came down on purpose." St. George was there, without a change of dress and with a kind face—his graver one—to which Overt eagerly responded. He explained that it was only for the Master—the idea of a little talk—that he had sat up and that, not finding him, he had been on the point of going to bed.

"Well, you know, I don't smoke—my wife doesn't let me," said St. George, looking for a place to sit down. "It's very good for me—very good for me. Let us take that sofa."

"Do you mean smoking is good for you?"

"No, no, her not letting me. It's a great thing to have a wife who proves to one all the things one can do without. One might never find them out for oneself. She doesn't allow me to touch a cigarette."

They took possession of the sofa, which was at a distance from the group of smokers, and St. George went on: "Have you got one yourself?"

"Do you mean a cigarette?"

"Dear no! a wife."

"No; and yet I would give up my cigarette for one."

"You would give up a good deal more than that," said St. George. "However, you would get a great deal in return. There is a great deal to be said for wives," he added, folding his arms and crossing his outstretched legs. He declined tobacco altogether and sat there without returning fire. Paul Overt stopped smoking, touched by his courtesy; and after all they were out of the fumes, their sofa was in a far-away corner. It would have been a mistake, St. George went on, a great mistake for them to have separated without a little chat; "for I know all about you," he said, "I know you're very remarkable. You've written a very distinguished book."

"And how do you know it?" Overt asked.

"Why, my dear fellow, it's in the air, it's in the papers, it's everywhere," St. George replied, with the immediate familiarity of a *confrère*—a tone that seemed to his companion the very rustle of the laurel. "You're on all men's lips and, what's better, you're on all women's. And I've just been reading your book."

"Just? You hadn't read it this afternoon," said Overt.

"How do you know that?"

"You know how I know it," the young man answered, laughing.

"I suppose Miss Fancourt told you."

"No, indeed; she led me rather to suppose that you had."

"Yes; that's much more what she would do. Doesn't she shed a rosy glow over life? But you didn't believe her?" asked St. George.

"No, not when you came to us there."

"Did I pretend? did I pretend badly?" But without waiting for an answer to this St. George went on: "You ought always to believe such a girl as that—always, always. Some women are meant to be taken with allowances and reserves; but you must take *her* just as she is."

"I like her very much," said Paul Overt.

Something in his tone appeared to excite on his companion's part a momentary sense of the absurd; perhaps it was the air of deliberation attending this judgment. St. George broke into a laugh and returned: "It's the best thing you can do with her. She's a rare young lady! In point of fact, however, I confess I hadn't read you this afternoon."

"Then you see how right I was in this particular case not to believe Miss Fancourt."

"How right? how can I agree to that, when I lost credit by it?"

"Do you wish to pass for exactly what she represents you? Certainly you needn't be afraid," Paul said.

"Ah, my dear young man, don't talk about passing—for the likes of me! I'm passing away—nothing else than that. She has a better use for her young imagination (isn't it fine?) than in 'representing' in any way such a weary, wasted, used-up animal!" St. George spoke with a sudden sadness which produced a protest on Paul's part; but before the protest could be uttered he went on, reverting to the latter's successful novel: "I had no idea you were so good—one hears of so many things. But you're surprisingly good."

"I'm going to be surprisingly better," said Overt.

"I see that and it's what fetches me. I don't see so much else—as one looks about—that's going to be surprisingly better. They're going to be consistently worse—most of the things. It's so much easier to be worse—heaven knows I've found it so. I'm not in a great glow, you know, about what's being attempted, what's being done. But you *must* be better —you must keep it up. I haven't, of course. It's very difficult

—that's the devil of the whole thing; but I see you can. It will be a great disgrace if you don't."

"It's very interesting to hear you speak of yourself; but I don't know what you mean by your allusions to your having fallen off," Paul Overt remarked, with pardonable hypocrisy. He liked his companion so much now that it had ceased for the moment to be vivid to him that there had been any decline.

"Don't say that—don't say that," St. George replied gravely, with his head resting on the top of the back of the sofa and his eyes on the ceiling. "You know perfectly what I mean. I haven't read twenty pages of your book without seeing that you can't help it."

"You make me very miserable," Paul murmured.

"I'm glad of that, for it may serve as a kind of warning. Shocking enough it must be, especially to a young, fresh mind, full of faith,—the spectacle of a man meant for better things sunk at my age in such dishonour." St. George, in the same contemplative attitude, spoke softly but deliberately, and without perceptible emotion. His tone indeed suggested an impersonal lucidity which was cruel—cruel to himself—and which made Paul lay an argumentative hand on his arm. But he went on, while his eyes seemed to follow the ingenuities of the beautiful Adams ceiling: "Look at me well and take my lesson to heart, for it *is* a lesson. Let that good come of it at least that you shudder with your pitiful impression and that this may help to keep you straight in the future. Don't become in your old age what I am in mine—the depressing, the deplorable illustration of the worship of false gods!"

"What do you mean by your old age?" Paul Overt asked.

"It has made me old. But I like your youth."

Overt answered nothing—they sat for a minute in silence. They heard the others talking about the governmental majority. Then, "What do you mean by false gods?" Paul inquired.

"The idols of the market—money and luxury and 'the world,' placing one's children and dressing one's wife—everything that drives one to the short and easy way. Ah, the vile things they make one do!"

"But surely one is right to want to place one's children."

"One has no business to have any children," St. George declared, placidly. "I mean of course if one wants to do something good."

"But aren't they an inspiration—an incentive?"

"An incentive to damnation, artistically speaking."

"You touch on very deep things—things I should like to discuss with you," Paul Overt said. "I should like you to tell me volumes about yourself. This is a festival for *me*!"

"Of course it is, cruel youth. But to show you that I'm still not incapable, degraded as I am, of an act of faith, I'll tie my vanity to the stake for you and burn it to ashes. You must come and see me—you must come and see us. Mrs. St. George is charming; I don't know whether you have had any opportunity to talk with her. She will be delighted to see you; she likes great celebrities, whether incipient or predominant. You must come and dine—my wife will write to you. Where are you to be found?"

"This is my little address"—and Overt drew out his pocketbook and extracted a visiting-card. On second thoughts, however, he kept it back, remarking that he would not trouble his friend to take charge of it but would come and see him straightway in London and leave it at his door if he should fail to obtain admittance.

"Ah! you probably will fail; my wife's always out, or when she isn't out she's knocked up from having been out. You must come and dine—though that won't do much good either, for my wife insists on big dinners. You must come down and see us in the country, that's the best way; we have plenty of room, and it isn't bad."

"You have a house in the country?" Paul asked, enviously.

"Ah, not like this! But we have a sort of place we go to—an hour from Euston. That's one of the reasons."

"One of the reasons?"

"Why my books are so bad."

"You must tell me all the others!" Paul exclaimed, laughing.

St. George made no direct rejoinder to this; he only inquired rather abruptly: "Why have I never seen you before?"

The tone of the question was singularly flattering to his new comrade; it seemed to imply that he perceived now that for years he had missed something. "Partly, I suppose, because there has been no particular reason why you should see me. I haven't lived in the world—in your world. I have spent many years out of England, in different places abroad."

"Well, please don't do it any more. You must do England—there's such a lot of it."

"Do you mean I must write about it?" Paul asked, in a voice which had the note of the listening candour of a child.

"Of course you must. And tremendously well, do you mind? That takes off a little of my esteem for this thing of yours—that it goes on abroad. Hang abroad! Stay at home and do things here—do subjects we can measure."

"I'll do whatever you tell me," said Paul Overt, deeply attentive. "But excuse me if I say I don't understand how you have been reading my book," he subjoined. "I've had you before me all the afternoon, first in that long walk, then at tea on the lawn, till we went to dress for dinner, and all the evening at dinner and in this place."

St. George turned his face round with a smile. "I only read for a quarter of an hour."

"A quarter of an hour is liberal, but I don't understand where you put it in. In the drawing-room, after dinner, you were not reading, you were talking to Miss Fancourt."

"It comes to the same thing, because we talked about *Ginistrella*. She described it to me—she lent it to me."

"Lent it to you?"

"She travels with it."

"It's incredible," Paul Overt murmured, blushing.

"It's glorious for you; but it also turned out very well for me. When the ladies went off to bed she kindly offered to send the book down to me. Her maid brought it to me in the hall and I went to my room with it. I hadn't thought of coming here, I do that so little. But I don't sleep early, I always have to read for an hour or two. I sat down to your novel on the spot, without undressing, without taking off anything but my coat. I think that's a sign that my curiosity had been strongly roused about it. I read a quarter of an hour, as I tell you, and even in a quarter of an hour I was greatly struck."

"Ah, the beginning isn't very good—it's the whole thing!"

said Overt, who had listened to this recital with extreme interest. "And you laid down the book and came after me?" he asked.

"That's the way it moved me. I said to myself, 'I see it's off his own bat, and he's there, by the way, and the day's over and I haven't said twenty words to him.' It occurred to me that you would probably be in the smoking-room and that it wouldn't be too late to repair my omission. I wanted to do something civil to you, so I put on my coat and came down. I shall read your book again when I go up."

Paul Overt turned round in his place—he was exceedingly touched by the picture of such a demonstration in his favour. "You're really the kindest of men. *Cela s'est passé comme ça?* and I have been sitting here with you all this time and never apprehended it and never thanked you!"

"Thank Miss Fancourt—it was she who wound me up. She has made me feel as if I had read your novel."

"She's an angel from heaven!" Paul Overt exclaimed.

"She is indeed. I have never seen anyone like her. Her interest in literature is touching—something quite peculiar to herself; she takes it all so seriously. She feels the arts and she wants to feel them more. To those who practise them it's almost humiliating—her curiosity, her sympathy, her good faith. How can anything be as fine as she supposes it?"

"She's a rare organisation," Paul Overt sighed.

"The richest I have ever seen—an artistic intelligence really of the first order. And lodged in such a form!" St. George exclaimed.

"One would like to paint such a girl as that," Overt continued.

"Ah, there it is—there's nothing like life! When you're finished, squeezed dry and used up and you think the sack's empty, you're still spoken to, you still get touches and thrills, the idea springs up—out of the lap of the actual—and shows you there's always something to be done. But I shan't do it—she's not for me!"

"How do you mean, not for you?"

"Oh, it's all over—she's for you, if you like."

"Ah, much less!" said Paul Overt. "She's not for a dingy

little man of letters; she's for the world, the bright rich world of bribes and rewards. And the world will take hold of her—it will carry her away."

"It will try; but it's just a case in which there may be a fight. It would be worth fighting, for a man who had it in him, with youth and talent on his side."

These words rang not a little in Paul Overt's consciousness—they held him silent a moment. "It's a wonder she has remained as she is—giving herself away so, with so much to give away."

"Do you mean so ingenuous—so natural? Oh, she doesn't care a straw—she gives away because she overflows. She has her own feelings, her own standards; she doesn't keep remembering that she must be proud. And then she hasn't been here long enough to be spoiled; she has picked up a fashion or two, but only the amusing ones. She's a provincial—a provincial of genius; her very blunders are charming, her mistakes are interesting. She has come back from Asia with all sorts of excited curiosities and unappeased appetites. She's first-rate herself and she expends herself on the second-rate. She's life herself and she takes a rare interest in imitations. She mixes all things up, but there are none in regard to which she hasn't perceptions. She sees things in a perspective—as if from the top of the Himalayas—and she enlarges everything she touches. Above all she exaggerates—to herself, I mean. She exaggerates you and me!"

There was nothing in this description to allay the excitement produced in the mind of our younger friend by such a sketch of a fine subject. It seemed to him to show the art of St. George's admired hand, and he lost himself in it, gazing at the vision (it hovered there before him,) of a woman's figure which should be part of the perfection of a novel. At the end of a moment he became aware that it had turned into smoke, and out of the smoke—the last puff of a big cigar—proceeded the voice of General Fancourt, who had left the others and come and planted himself before the gentlemen on the sofa. "I suppose that when you fellows get talking you sit up half the night."

"Half the night?—*jamais de la vie!* I follow a hygiene," St. George replied, rising to his feet.

"I see, you're hothouse plants," laughed the General. "That's the way you produce your flowers."

"I produce mine between ten and one every morning; I bloom with a regularity!" St. George went on.

"And with a splendour!" added the polite General, while Paul Overt noted how little the author of *Shadowmere* minded, as he phrased it to himself, when he was addressed as a celebrated story-teller. The young man had an idea that *he* should never get used to that—it would always make him uncomfortable (from the suspicion that people would think they had to,) and he would want to prevent it. Evidently his more illustrious congener had toughened and hardened—had made himself a surface. The group of men had finished their cigars and taken up their bedroom candlesticks; but before they all passed out Lord Watermouth invited St. George and Paul Overt to drink something. It happened that they both declined, upon which General Fancourt said: "Is that the hygiene? You don't sprinkle the flowers?"

"Oh, I should drown them!" St. George replied; but leaving the room beside Overt he added whimsically, for the latter's benefit, in a lower tone: "My wife doesn't let me."

"Well, I'm glad I'm not one of you fellows!" the General exclaimed.

The nearness of Summersoft to London had this consequence, chilling to a person who had had a vision of sociability in a railway-carriage, that most of the company, after breakfast, drove back to town, entering their own vehicles, which had come out to fetch them, while their servants returned by train with their luggage. Three or four young men, among whom was Paul Overt, also availed themselves of the common convenience; but they stood in the portico of the house and saw the others roll away. Miss Fancourt got into a victoria with her father, after she had shaken hands with Paul Overt and said, smiling in the frankest way in the world—"I *must* see you more. Mrs. St. George is so nice: she has promised to ask us both to dinner together." This lady and her husband took their places in a perfectly-appointed brougham (she required a closed carriage,) and as our young man waved his hat to them in response to their nods and flourishes he reflected that, taken together, they were an honourable image of success, of the material rewards and the social credit of literature. Such things were not the full measure, but all the same he felt a little proud for literature.

IV.

Before a week had elapsed Paul Overt met Miss Fancourt in Bond Street, at a private view of the works of a young artist in "black and white" who had been so good as to invite him to the stuffy scene. The drawings were admirable, but the crowd in the one little room was so dense that he felt as if he were up to his neck in a big sack of wool. A fringe of people at the outer edge endeavoured by curving forward their backs and presenting, below them, a still more convex surface of resistance to the pressure of the mass, to preserve an interval between their noses and the glazed mounts of the pictures; while the central body, in the comparative gloom projected by a wide horizontal screen, hung under the skylight and allowing only a margin for the day, remained upright, dense and vague, lost in the contemplation of its own ingredients. This contemplation sat especially in the sad eyes of certain female heads, surmounted with hats of strange convolution and plumage, which rose on long necks above the others. One of the heads, Paul Overt perceived, was much the most beautiful of the collection, and his next discovery was that it belonged to Miss Fancourt. Its beauty was enhanced by the glad smile that she sent him across surrounding obstructions, a smile which drew him to her as fast as he could make his way. He had divined at Summersoft that the last thing her nature contained was an affectation of indifference; yet even with this circumspection he had a freshness of pleasure in seeing that she did not pretend to await his arrival with composure. She smiled as radiantly as if she wished to make him hurry, and as soon as he came within earshot she said to him, in her voice of joy: "He's here—he's here—he's coming back in a moment!"

"Ah, your father?" Paul responded, as she offered him her hand.

"Oh dear no, this isn't in my poor father's line. I mean Mr.

St. George. He has just left me to speak to some one—he's coming back. It's he who brought me—wasn't it charming?"

"Ah, that gives him a pull over me—I couldn't have 'brought' you, could I?"

"If you had been so kind as to propose it—why not you as well as he?" the girl asked, with a face which expressed no cheap coquetry, but simply affirmed a happy fact.

"Why, he's a *père de famille*. They have privileges," Paul Overt explained. And then, quickly: "Will you go to see places with *me*?" he broke out.

"Anything you like!" she smiled. "I know what you mean, that girls have to have a lot of people——" She interrupted herself to say: "I don't know; I'm free. I have always been like that," she went on; "I can go anywhere with any one. I'm so glad to meet you," she added, with a sweet distinctness that made the people near her turn round.

"Let me at least repay that speech by taking you out of this squash," said Paul Overt. "Surely people are not happy here!"

"No, they are *mornes*, aren't they? But I am very happy indeed, and I promised Mr. St. George to remain in this spot till he comes back. He's going to take me away. They send him invitations for things of this sort—more than he wants. It was so kind of him to think of me."

"They also send me invitations of this kind—more than I want. And if thinking of *you* will do it——!" Paul went on.

"Oh, I delight in them—everything that's life—everything that's London!"

"They don't have private views in Asia, I suppose. But what a pity that for this year, in this fertile city, they are pretty well over."

"Well, next year will do, for I hope you believe we are going to be friends always. Here he comes!" Miss Fancourt continued, before Paul had time to respond.

He made out St. George in the gaps of the crowd, and this perhaps led to his hurrying a little to say: "I hope that doesn't mean that I'm to wait till next year to see you."

"No, no; are we not to meet at dinner on the 25th?" she answered, with an eagerness greater even than his own.

"That's almost next year. Is there no means of seeing you before?"

She stared, with all her brightness. "Do you mean that you would *come?*"

"Like a shot, if you'll be so good as to ask me!"

"On Sunday, then—this next Sunday?"

"What have I done that you should doubt it?" the young man demanded, smiling.

Miss Fancourt turned instantly to St. George, who had now joined them, and announced triumphantly: "He's coming on Sunday—this next Sunday!"

"Ah, my day—my day too!" said the famous novelist, laughing at Paul Overt.

"Yes, but not yours only. You shall meet in Manchester Square; you shall talk—you shall be wonderful!"

"We don't meet often enough," St. George remarked, shaking hands with his disciple. "Too many things—ah, too many things! But we must make it up in the country in September. You won't forget that you've promised me that?"

"Why, he's coming on the 25th; you'll see him then," said Marian Fancourt.

"On the 25th?" St. George asked, vaguely.

"We dine with you; I hope you haven't forgotten. He's dining out," she added gaily to Paul Overt.

"Oh, bless me, yes; that's charming! And you're coming? My wife didn't tell me," St. George said to Paul. "Too many things—too many things!" he repeated.

"Too many people—too many people!" Paul exclaimed, giving ground before the penetration of an elbow.

"You oughtn't to say that; they all read you."

"Me? I should like to see them! Only two or three at most," the young man rejoined.

"Did you ever hear anything like that? he knows how good he is!" St. George exclaimed, laughing, to Miss Fancourt. "They read *me*, but that doesn't make me like them any better. Come away from them, come away!" And he led the way out of the exhibition.

"He's going to take me to the Park," the girl said, with elation, to Paul Overt, as they passed along the corridor which led to the street.

"Ah, does he go there?" Paul asked, wondering at the idea as a somewhat unexpected illustration of St. George's *moeurs*.

"It's a beautiful day; there will be a great crowd. We're going to look at the people, to look at types," the girl went on. "We shall sit under the trees; we shall walk by the Row."

"I go once a year, on business," said St. George, who had overheard Paul's question.

"Or with a country cousin, didn't you tell me? I'm the country cousin!" she went on, over her shoulder, to Paul, as her companion drew her toward a hansom to which he had signalled. The young man watched them get in; he returned, as he stood there, the friendly wave of the hand with which, ensconced in the vehicle beside Miss Fancourt, St. George took leave of him. He even lingered to see the vehicle start away and lose itself in the confusion of Bond Street. He followed it with his eyes; it was embarrassingly suggestive. "She's not for me!" the great novelist had said emphatically at Summersoft; but his manner of conducting himself toward her appeared not exactly in harmony with such a conviction. How could he have behaved differently if she *had* been for him? An indefinite envy rose in Paul Overt's heart as he took his way on foot alone, and the singular part of it was that it was directed to each of the occupants of the hansom. How much he should like to rattle about London with such a girl! How much he should like to go and look at "types" with St. George!

The next Sunday, at four o'clock, he called in Manchester Square, where his secret wish was gratified by his finding Miss Fancourt alone. She was in a large, bright, friendly, occupied room, which was painted red all over, draped with the quaint, cheap, florid stuffs that are represented as coming from southern and eastern countries, where they are fabled to serve as the counterpanes of the peasantry, and bedecked with pottery of vivid hues, ranged on casual shelves, and with many watercolour drawings from the hand (as the visitor learned,) of the young lady, commemorating, with courage and skill, the sunsets, the mountains, the temples and palaces of India. Overt sat there an hour—more than an hour, two hours—and all the while no one came in. Miss Fancourt was so good as to remark, with her liberal humanity, that it was delightful they were not interrupted; it was so rare in London, especially at that season, that people got a good talk. But fortunately

now, of a fine Sunday, half the world went out of town, and
that made it better for those who didn't go, when they were
in sympathy. It was the defect of London (one of two or three,
the very short list of those she recognised in the teeming
world-city that she adored,) that there were too few good
chances for talk; one never had time to carry anything far.

"Too many things—too many things!" Paul Overt said,
quoting St. George's exclamation of a few days before.

"Ah yes, for him there are too many; his life is too complicated."

"Have you seen it *near*? That's what I should like to do; it
might explain some mysteries," Paul Overt went on. The girl
asked him what mysteries he meant, and he said: "Oh, peculiarities of his work, inequalities, superficialities. For one
who looks at it from the artistic point of view it contains a
bottomless ambiguity."

"Oh, do describe that more—it's so interesting. There are
no such suggestive questions. I'm so fond of them. He thinks
he's a failure—fancy!" Miss Fancourt added.

"That depends upon what his ideal may have been. Ah,
with his gifts it ought to have been high. But till one knows
what he really proposed to himself—Do *you* know, by
chance?" the young man asked, breaking off.

"Oh, he doesn't talk to me about himself. I can't make him.
It's too provoking."

Paul Overt was on the point of asking what then he did
talk about; but discretion checked this inquiry, and he said
instead: "Do you think he's unhappy at home?"

"At home?"

"I mean in his relations with his wife. He has a mystifying
little way of alluding to her."

"Not to me," said Marian Fancourt, with her clear eyes.
"That wouldn't be right, would it?" she asked, seriously.

"Not particularly; so I am glad he doesn't mention her to
you. To praise her might bore you, and he has no business to
do anything else. Yet he knows you better than me."

"Ah, but he respects *you*!" the girl exclaimed, enviously.

Her visitor stared a moment; then he broke into a laugh.
"Doesn't he respect you?"

"Of course, but not in the same way. He respects what you've done—he told me so, the other day."

"When you went to look at types?"

"Ah, we found so many—he has such an observation of them! He talked a great deal about your book. He says it's really important."

"Important! Ah! the grand creature," Paul murmured, hilarious.

"He was wonderfully amusing, he was inexpressibly droll, while we walked about. He sees everything; he has so many comparisons, and they are always exactly right. *C'est d'un trouvé!* as they say."

"Yes, with his gifts, such things as he ought to have done!" Paul Overt remarked.

"And don't you think he *has* done them?"

He hesitated a moment. "A part of them—and of course even that part is immense. But he might have been one of the greatest! However, let us not make this an hour of qualifications. Even as they stand, his writings are a mine of gold."

To this proposition Marian Fancourt ardently responded, and for half an hour the pair talked over the master's principal productions. She knew them well—she knew them even better than her visitor, who was struck with her critical intelligence and with something large and bold in the movement in her mind. She said things that startled him and that evidently had come to her directly; they were not picked-up phrases, she placed them too well. St. George had been right about her being first-rate, about her not being afraid to gush, not remembering that she must be proud. Suddenly something reminded her, and she said: "I recollect that he did speak of Mrs. St. George to me once. He said, *à propos* of something or other, that she didn't care for perfection."

"That's a great crime, for an artist's wife," said Paul Overt.

"Yes, poor thing!" and the young lady sighed, with a suggestion of many reflections, some of them mitigating. But she added in a moment, "Ah, perfection, perfection—how one ought to go in for it! I wish I could."

"Every one can, in his way," said Paul Overt.

"In *his* way, yes; but not in hers. Women are so ham-

pered—so condemned! But it's a kind of dishonour if you
don't, when you want to *do* something, isn't it?" Miss Fancourt pursued, dropping one train in her quickness to take up
another, an accident that was common with her. So these two
young persons sat discussing high themes in their eclectic
drawing-room, in their London season—discussing, with extreme seriousness, the high theme of perfection. And it must
be said, in extenuation of this eccentricity, that they were interested in the business; their tone was genuine, their emotion
real; they were not posturing for each other or for some one
else.

The subject was so wide that they found it necessary to
contract it; the perfection to which for the moment they
agreed to confine their speculations was that of which the
valid work of art is susceptible. Miss Fancourt's imagination,
it appeared, had wandered far in that direction, and her visitor
had the rare delight of feeling that their conversation was a
full interchange. This episode will have lived for years in his
memory and even in his wonder; it had the quality that fortune distils in a single drop at a time—the quality that lubri-
cates ensuing weeks and months. He has still a vision of the
room, whenever he likes—the bright, red, sociable, talkative
room, with the curtains that, by a stroke of successful audacity,
had the note of vivid blue. He remembers where certain
things stood, the book that was open on the table and the
particular odour of the flowers that were placed on the left,
somewhere behind him. These facts were the fringe, as it
were, of a particular consciousness which had its birth in those
two hours and of which perhaps the most general description
would be to mention that it led him to say over and over
again to himself: "I had no idea there was any one like this—I
had no idea there was any one like this!" Her freedom amazed
him and charmed him—it seemed so to simplify the practical
question. She was on the footing of an independent personage—a motherless girl who had passed out of her teens and
had a position, responsibilities, and was not held down to the
limitations of a little miss. She came and went without the
clumsiness of a chaperon; she received people alone and,
though she was totally without hardness, the question of protection or patronage had no relevancy in regard to her. She

gave such an impression of purity combined with naturalness
that, in spite of her eminently modern situation, she suggested
no sort of sisterhood with the "fast" girl. Modern she was,
indeed, and made Paul Overt, who loved old colour, the
golden glaze of time, think with some alarm of the muddled
palette of the future. He couldn't get used to her interest in
the arts he cared for; it seemed too good to be real—it was
so unlikely an adventure to tumble into such a well of sympathy. One might stray into the desert easily—that was on the
cards and that was the law of life; but it was too rare an accident to stumble on a crystal well. Yet if her aspirations
seemed at one moment too extravagant to be real, they struck
him at the next as too intelligent to be false. They were both
noble and crude, and whims for whims, he liked them better
than any he had met. It was probable enough she would leave
them behind—exchange them for politics, or "smartness," or
mere prolific maternity, as was the custom of scribbling, daub-
ing, educated, flattered girls, in an age of luxury and a society
of leisure. He noted that the water-colours on the walls of the
room she sat in had mainly the quality of being *naïves*, and
reflected that *naïveté* in art is like a cipher in a number: its
importance depends upon the figure it is united with. But
meanwhile he had fallen in love with her.

Before he went away he said to Miss Fancourt: "I thought
St. George was coming to see you to-day—but he doesn't
turn up."

For a moment he supposed she was going to reply, "*Comment donc?* Did you come here only to meet him?" But the
next he became aware of how little such a speech would have
fallen in with any flirtatious element he had as yet perceived
in her. She only replied: "Ah yes, but I don't think he'll come.
He recommended me not to expect him." Then she added,
laughing: "He said it wasn't fair to you. But I think I could
manage two."

"So could I," Paul Overt rejoined, stretching the point a
little to be humorous. In reality his appreciation of the occasion was so completely an appreciation of the woman before
him that another figure in the scene, even so esteemed a one
as St. George, might for the hour have appealed to him vainly.
As he went away he wondered what the great man had meant

by its not being fair to him; and, still more than that, whether he had actually stayed away out of the delicacy of such an idea. As he took his course, swinging his stick, through the Sunday solitude of Manchester Square, with a good deal of emotion fermenting in his soul, it appeared to him that he was living in a world really magnanimous. Miss Fancourt had told him that there was an uncertainty about her being, and her father's being, in town on the following Sunday, but that she had the hope of a visit from him if they should not go away. She promised to let him know if they stayed at home, then he could act accordingly. After he had passed into one of the streets that lead out of the square, he stopped, without definite intentions, looking sceptically for a cab. In a moment he saw a hansom roll through the square from the other side and come a part of the way toward him. He was on the point of hailing the driver when he perceived that he carried a fare; then he waited, seeing him prepare to deposit his passenger by pulling up at one of the houses. The house was apparently the one he himself had just quitted; at least he drew that inference as he saw that the person who stepped out of the hansom was Henry St. George. Paul Overt turned away quickly, as if he had been caught in the act of spying. He gave up his cab—he preferred to walk; he would go nowhere else. He was glad St. George had not given up his visit altogether—that would have been too absurd. Yes, the world was magnanimous, and Overt felt so too as, on looking at his watch, he found it was only six o'clock, so that he could mentally congratulate his successor on having an hour still to sit in Miss Fancourt's drawing-room. He himself might use that hour for another visit, but by the time he reached the Marble Arch the idea of another visit had become incongruous to him. He passed beneath that architectural effort and walked into the Park till he got upon the grass. Here he continued to walk; he took his way across the elastic turf and came out by the Serpentine. He watched with a friendly eye the diversions of the London people, and bent a glance almost encouraging upon the young ladies paddling their sweethearts on the lake, and the guardsmen tickling tenderly with their bearskins the artificial flowers in the Sunday hats of their partners. He prolonged his meditative walk; he went into Kensington Gardens—he sat upon the penny chairs—he looked at the little sail-boats launched upon the round pond—he was glad he had no engagement to dine. He repaired for this purpose, very late, to his club, where he found himself unable to order a repast and told the waiter to bring whatever he would. He did not even observe what he was served with, and he spent the evening in the library of the establishment, pretending to read an article in an American magazine. He failed to discover what it was about; it appeared in a dim way to be about Marian Fancourt.

Quite late in the week she wrote to him that she was not to go into the country—it had only just been settled. Her father, she added, would never settle anything—he put it all on her. She felt her responsibility—she had to—and since she was forced that was the way she had decided. She mentioned no reasons, which gave Paul Overt all the clearer field for bold conjecture about them. In Manchester Square, on this second Sunday, he esteemed his fortune less good, for she had three or four other visitors. But there were three or four compensations; the greatest, perhaps, of which was that, learning from her that her father had, after all, at the last hour, gone out of town alone, the bold conjecture I just now spoke of found itself becoming a shade more bold. And then her presence was her presence, and the personal red room was there and was full of it, whatever phantoms passed and vanished, emitting incomprehensible sounds. Lastly, he had the resource of staying till every one had come and gone and of supposing that this pleased her, though she gave no particular sign. When they were alone together he said to her: "But St. George did come—last Sunday. I saw him as I looked back."

"Yes; but it was the last time."

"The last time?"

"He said he would never come again."

Paul Overt stared. "Does he mean that he wishes to cease to see you?"

"I don't know what he means," the girl replied, smiling. "He won't, at any rate, see me here."

"And, pray, why not?"

"I don't know," said Marian Fancourt; and her visitor thought he had not yet seen her more beautiful than in uttering these unsatisfactory words.

v.

"Oh, I say, I want you to remain," Henry St. George said to him at eleven o'clock, the night he dined with the head of the profession. The company had been numerous and they were taking their leave; our young man, after bidding good-night to his hostess, had put out his hand in farewell to the master of the house. Besides eliciting from St. George the protest I have quoted this movement provoked a further observation about such a chance to have a talk, their going into his room, his having still everything to say. Paul Overt was delighted to be asked to stay; nevertheless he mentioned jocularly the literal fact that he had promised to go to another place, at a distance.

"Well then, you'll break your promise, that's all. You humbug!" St. George exclaimed, in a tone that added to Overt's contentment.

"Certainly, I'll break it; but it was a real promise."

"Do you mean to Miss Fancourt? You're following her?" St. George asked.

Paul Overt answered by a question. "Oh, is *she* going?"

"Base impostor!" his ironic host went on; "I've treated you handsomely on the article of that young lady: I won't make another concession. Wait three minutes—I'll be with you." He gave himself to his departing guests, went with the long-trained ladies to the door. It was a hot night, the windows were open, the sound of the quick carriages and of the linkmen's call came into the house. The company had been brilliant; a sense of festal things was in the heavy air: not only the influence of that particular entertainment, but the suggestion of the wide hurry of pleasure which, in London, on summer nights, fills so many of the happier quarters of the complicated town. Gradually Mrs. St. George's drawing-room emptied itself; Paul Overt was left alone with his hostess, to whom he explained the motive of his waiting. "Ah yes, some intellectual, some *professional*, talk," she smiled; "at this season doesn't one miss it? Poor dear Henry, I'm so glad!" The young man looked out of the window a moment, at the called hansoms that lurched up, at the smooth broughams that rolled away. When he turned round Mrs. St. George had disappeared; her husband's voice came up to him from below—he was laughing and talking, in the portico, with some lady who awaited her carriage. Paul had solitary possession, for some minutes, of the warm, deserted rooms, where the covered, tinted lamplight was soft, the seats had been pushed about and the odour of flowers lingered. They were large, they were pretty, they contained objects of value; everything in the picture told of a "good house." At the end of five minutes a servant came in with a request from Mr. St. George that he would join him downstairs; upon which, descending, he followed his conductor through a long passage to an apartment thrown out, in the rear of the habitation, for the special requirements, as he guessed, of a busy man of letters.

St. George was in his shirt-sleeves in the middle of a large, high room—a room without windows, but with a wide skylight at the top, like a place of exhibition. It was furnished as a library, and the serried bookshelves rose to the ceiling, a surface of incomparable tone, produced by dimly-gilt "backs," which was interrupted here and there by the suspension of old prints and drawings. At the end furthest from the door of admission was a tall desk, of great extent, at which the person using it could only write standing, like a clerk in a counting-house; and stretching from the door to this structure was a large plain band of crimson cloth, as straight as a garden-path and almost as long, where, in his mind's eye, Paul Overt immediately saw his host pace to and fro during his hours of composition. The servant gave him a coat, an old jacket with an air of experience, from a cupboard in the wall, retiring afterwards with the garment he had taken off. Paul Overt welcomed the coat; it was a coat for talk and promised confidences—it must have received so many—and had pathetic literary elbows. "Ah, we're practical—we're practical!" St. George said, as he saw his visitor looking the place over. "Isn't it a good big cage, to go round and round? My wife invented it and she locks me up here every morning."

"You don't miss a window—a place to look out?"

"I did at first, awfully; but her calculation was just. It saves time, it has saved me many months in these ten years. Here I stand, under the eye of day—in London of course, very often, it's rather a bleared old eye—walled in to my trade. I can't get away, and the room is a fine lesson in concentration. I've learned the lesson, I think; look at that big bundle of proof and admit that I have." He pointed to a fat roll of papers, on one of the tables, which had not been undone.

"Are you bringing out another——?" Paul Overt asked, in a tone of whose deficiencies he was not conscious till his companion burst out laughing, and indeed not even then.

"You humbug—you humbug! Don't I know what you think of them?" St. George inquired, standing before him with his hands in his pockets and with a new kind of smile. It was as if he were going to let his young votary know him well now.

"Upon my word, in that case you know more than I do!" Paul ventured to respond, revealing a part of the torment of being able neither clearly to esteem him nor distinctly to renounce him.

"My dear fellow," said his companion, "don't imagine I talk about my books, specifically; it isn't a decent subject—*il ne manquerait plus que ça*—I'm not so bad as you may apprehend! About myself, a little, if you like; though it wasn't for that I brought you down here. I want to ask you something—very much indeed—I value this chance. Therefore sit down. We are practical, but there *is* a sofa, you see, for she does humour me a little, after all. Like all really great administrators she knows when to." Paul Overt sank into the corner of a deep leathern couch, but his interlocutor remained standing and said: "If you don't mind, in this room this is my habit. From the door to the desk and from the desk to the door. That shakes up my imagination, gently; and don't you see what a good thing it is that there's no window for her to fly out of? The eternal standing as I write (I stop at that bureau and put it down, when anything comes, and so we go on,) was rather wearisome at first, but we adopted it with an eye to the long run; you're in better order (if your legs don't break down!) and you can keep it up for more years. Oh, we're practical—we're practical!" St. George repeated, going to the table and taking up, mechanically, the bundle of proofs. He pulled off the wrapper, he turned the papers over with a sudden change of attention which only made him more interesting to Paul Overt. He lost himself a moment, examining the sheets of his new book, while the younger man's eyes wandered over the room again.

"Lord, what good things I should do if I had such a charming place as this to do them in!" Paul reflected. The outer world, the world of accident and ugliness was so successfully excluded, and within the rich, protecting square, beneath the patronising sky, the figures projected for an artistic purpose could hold their particular revel. It was a prevision of Paul Overt's rather than an observation on actual data, for which the occasions had been too few, that his new friend would have the quality, the charming quality, of surprising him by flashing out in personal intercourse, at moments of suspended, or perhaps even of diminished expectation. A happy relation with him would be a thing proceeding by jumps, not by traceable stages.

"Do you read them—really?" he asked, laying down the proofs on Paul's inquiring of him how soon the work would be published. And when the young man answered, "Oh yes, always," he was moved to mirth again by something he caught in his manner of saying that. "You go to see your grandmother on her birthday—and very proper it is, especially as she won't last for ever. She has lost every faculty and every sense; she neither sees, nor hears, nor speaks; but all customary pieties and kindly habits are respectable. But you're strong if you *do* read 'em! *I* couldn't, my dear fellow. You *are* strong, I know; and that's just a part of what I wanted to say to you. You're very strong indeed. I've been going into your other things—they've interested me exceedingly. Some one ought to have told me about them before—some one I could believe. But whom can one believe? You're wonderfully in the good direction—it's extremely curious work. Now do you mean to keep it up?—that's what I want to ask you."

"Do I mean to do others?" Paul Overt asked, looking up from his sofa at his erect inquisitor and feeling partly like a happy little boy when the schoolmaster is gay and partly like some pilgrim of old who might have consulted the oracle. St.

George's own performance had been infirm, but as an adviser he would be infallible.

"Others—others? Ah, the number won't matter; one other would do, if it were really a further step—a throb of the same effort. What I mean is, have you it in your mind to go in for some sort of little perfection?"

"Ah, perfection!" Overt sighed, "I talked of that the other Sunday with Miss Fancourt."

"Oh yes, they'll talk of it, as much as you like! But they do mighty little to help one to it. There's no obligation, of course; only you strike me as capable," St. George went on. "You must have thought it all over. I can't believe you're without a plan. That's the sensation you give me, and it's so rare that it really stirs up one; it makes you remarkable. If you haven't a plan and you don't mean to keep it up, of course it's all right, it's no one's business, no one can force you, and not more than two or three people will notice that you don't go straight. The others—*all* the rest, every blessed soul in England, will think you do—will think you *are* keeping it up: upon my honour they will! I shall be one of the two or three who know better. Now the question is whether you can do it for two or three. Is that the stuff you're made of?"

"I could do it for one, if you were the one."

"Don't say that—I don't deserve it; it scorches me," St. George exclaimed, with eyes suddenly grave and glowing. "The 'one' is of course oneself—one's conscience, one's idea, the singleness of one's aim. I think of that pure spirit as a man thinks of a woman whom, in some detested hour of his youth, he has loved and forsaken. She haunts him with reproachful eyes, she lives for ever before him. As an artist, you know, I've married for money." Paul stared and even blushed a little, confounded by this avowal; whereupon his host, observing the expression of his face, dropped a quick laugh and went on: "You don't follow my figure. I'm not speaking of my dear wife, who had a small fortune, which, however, was not my bribe. I fell in love with her, as many other people have done. I refer to the mercenary muse whom I led to the altar of literature. Don't do that, my boy. She'll lead you a life!"

"Haven't you been happy!"

"Happy? It's a kind of hell."

"There are things I should like to ask you," Paul Overt said, hesitating.

"Ask me anything in all the world. I'd turn myself inside out to save you."

"To save me?" Paul repeated.

"To make you stick to it—to make you see it through. As I said to you the other night at Summersoft, let my example be vivid to you."

"Why, your books are not so bad as that," said Paul, laughing and feeling that he breathed the air of art.

"So bad as what?"

"Your talent is so great that it is in everything you do, in what's less good as well as in what's best. You've some forty volumes to show for it—forty volumes of life, of observation, of magnificent ability."

"I'm very clever, of course I know that," St. George replied, quietly. "Lord, what rot they'd all be if I hadn't been! I'm a successful charlatan—I've been able to pass off my system. But do you know what it is? It's *carton-pierre.*"

"*Carton-pierre?*"

"Lincrusta-Walton!"

"Ah, don't say such things—you make me bleed!" the younger man protested. "I see you in a beautiful, fortunate home, living in comfort and honour."

"Do you call it honour?" St. George interrupted, with an intonation that often comes back to his companion. "That's what I want *you* to go in for. I mean the real thing. This is brummagaem."

"Brummagaem?" Paul ejaculated, while his eyes wandered, by a movement natural at the moment, over the luxurious room.

"Ah, they make it so well to-day; it's wonderfully deceptive!"

"Is it deceptive that I find you living with every appearance of domestic felicity—blessed with a devoted, accomplished wife, with children whose acquaintance I haven't yet had the pleasure of making, but who *must* be delightful young people, from what I know of their parents?"

"It's all excellent, my dear fellow—heaven forbid I should deny it. I've made a great deal of money; my wife has known how to take care of it, to use it without wasting it, to put a good bit of it by, to make it fructify. I've got a loaf on the shelf; I've got everything, in fact, but the great thing——"

"The great thing?"

"The sense of having done the best—the sense, which is the real life of the artist and the absence of which is his death, of having drawn from his intellectual instrument the finest music that nature had hidden in it, of having played it as it should be played. He either does that or he doesn't—and if he doesn't he isn't worth speaking of. And precisely those who really know don't speak of him. He may still hear a great chatter, but what he hears most is the incorruptible silence of Fame. I have squared her, you may say, for my little hour— but what is my little hour? Don't imagine for a moment I'm such a cad as to have brought you down here to abuse or to complain of my wife to you. She is a woman of very distinguished qualities, to whom my obligations are immense; so that, if you please, we will say nothing about her. My boys—my children are all boys—are straight and strong, thank God! and have no poverty of growth about them, no penury of needs. I receive, periodically, the most satisfactory attestation from Harrow, from Oxford, from Sandhurst (oh, we have done the best for them!) of their being living, thriving, consuming organisms."

"It must be delightful to feel that the son of one's loins is at Sandhurst," Paul remarked enthusiastically.

"It is—it's charming. Oh, I'm a patriot!"

"Then what did you mean—the other night at Summersoft—by saying that children are a curse?"

"My dear fellow, on what basis are we talking?" St. George asked, dropping upon the sofa, at a short distance from his visitor. Sitting a little sideways he leaned back against the opposite arm with his hands raised and interlocked behind his head. "On the supposition that a certain perfection is possible and even desirable—isn't it so? Well, all I say is that one's children interfere with perfection. One's wife interferes. Marriage interferes."

"You think then the artist shouldn't marry?"

"He does so at his peril—he does so at his cost."

"Not even when his wife is in sympathy with his work?"

"She never is—she can't be! Women don't know what work is."

"Surely, they work themselves," Paul Overt objected.

"Yes, very badly. Oh, of course, often, they think they understand, they think they sympathise. Then it is that they are most dangerous. Their idea is that you shall do a great lot and get a great lot of money. Their great nobleness and virtue, their exemplary conscientiousness as British females, is in keeping you up to that. My wife makes all my bargains with my publishers for me, and she has done so for twenty years. She does it consummately well; that's why I'm really pretty well off. Are you not the father of their innocent babes, and will you withhold from them their natural sustenance? You asked me the other night if they were not an immense incentive. Of course they are—there's no doubt of that!"

"For myself, I have an idea I need incentives," Paul Overt dropped.

"Ah well, then, *n'en parlons plus*!" said his companion, smiling.

"You are an incentive, I maintain," the young man went on. "You don't affect me in the way you apparently would like to. Your great success is what I see—the pomp of Ennismore Gardens!"

"Success?—do you call it success to be spoken of as you would speak of me if you were sitting here with another artist—a young man intelligent and sincere like yourself? Do you call it success to make you blush—as you would blush—if some foreign critic (some fellow, of course, I mean, who should know what he was talking about and should have shown you he did, as foreign critics like to show it!) were to say to you: 'He's the one, in this country, whom they consider the most perfect, isn't he?' Is it success to be the occasion of a young Englishman's having to stammer as you would have to stammer at such a moment for old England? No, no; success is to have made people tremble after another fashion. Do try it!"

"Try it?"

"Try to do some really good work."

"Oh, I want to, heaven knows!"

"Well, you can't do it without sacrifices; don't believe that for a moment," said Henry St. George. "I've made none. I've had everything. In other words, I've missed everything."

"You've had the full, rich, masculine, human, general life, with all the responsibilities and duties and burdens and sorrows and joys—all the domestic and social initiations and complications. They must be immensely suggestive, immensely amusing."

"Amusing?"

"For a strong man—yes."

"They've given me subjects without number, if that's what you mean; but they've taken away at the same time the power to use them. I've touched a thousand things, but which one of them have I turned into gold? The artist has to do only with that—he knows nothing of any baser metal. I've led the life of the world, with my wife and my progeny; the clumsy, expensive, materialised, brutalised, Philistine, snobbish life of London. We've got everything handsome, even a carriage—we are prosperous, hospitable, eminent people. But, my dear fellow, don't try to stultify yourself and pretend you don't know what we *haven't* got. It's bigger than all the rest. Between artists—come! You know as well as you sit there that you would put a pistol-ball into your brain if you had written my books!"

It appeared to Paul Overt that the tremendous talk promised by the master at Summersoft had indeed come off, and with a promptitude, a fulness, with which his young imagination had scarcely reckoned. His companion made an immense impression on him and he throbbed with the excitement of such deep soundings and such strange confidences. He throbbed indeed with the conflict of his feelings—bewilderment and recognition and alarm, enjoyment and protest and assent, all commingled with tenderness (and a kind of shame in the participation,) for the sores and bruises exhibited by so fine a creature, and with a sense of the tragic secret that he nursed under his trappings. The idea of *his* being made the occasion of such an act of humility made him flush and pant, at the same time that his perception, in certain directions, had been too much awakened to conceal from him anything that St. George really meant. It had been his odd fortune to blow upon the deep waters, to make them surge and break in waves of strange eloquence. He launched himself into a passionate contradiction of his host's last declaration; tried to enumerate to him the parts of his work he loved, the splendid things he had found in it, beyond the compass of any other writer of the day. St. George listened awhile, courteously; then he said, laying his hand on Paul Overt's:

"That's all very well; and if your idea is to do nothing better there is no reason why you shouldn't have as many good things as I—as many human and material appendages, as many sons or daughters, a wife with as many gowns, a house with as many servants, a stable with as many horses, a heart with as many aches." He got up when he had spoken thus, and then stood a moment near the sofa, looking down on his agitated pupil. "Are you possessed of any money?" it occurred to him to ask.

"None to speak of."

"Oh, well, there's no reason why you shouldn't make a goodish income—if you set about it the right way. Study *me* for that—study me well. You may really have a carriage."

Paul Overt sat there for some moments without speaking. He looked straight before him—he turned over many things. His friend had wandered away from him, taking up a parcel of letters that were on the table where the roll of proofs had lain. "What was the book Mrs. St. George made you burn—the one she didn't like?" he abruptly inquired.

"The book she made me burn—how did you know that?" St. George looked up from his letters.

"I heard her speak of it at Summersoft."

"Ah, yes; she's proud of it. I don't know—it was rather good."

"What was it about?"

"Let me see." And St. George appeared to make an effort to remember. "Oh, yes, it was about myself." Paul Overt gave an irrepressible groan for the disappearance of such a production, and the elder man went on: "Oh, but *you* should write it—*you* should do me. There's a subject, my boy: no end of stuff in it!"

Again Paul was silent, but after a little he spoke. "Are there no women that really understand—that can take part in a sacrifice?"

"How can they take part? They themselves are the sacrifice. They're the idol and the altar and the flame."

"Isn't there even *one* who sees further?" Paul continued.

For a moment St. George made no answer to this; then, having torn up his letters, he stood before his disciple again, ironic. "Of course I know the one you mean. But not even Miss Fancourt."

"I thought you admired her so much."

"It's impossible to admire her more. Are you in love with her?" St. George asked.

"Yes," said Paul Overt.

"Well, then, give it up."

Paul stared. "Give up my love?"

"Bless me, no; your idea."

"My idea?"

"The one you talked with her about. The idea of perfection."

"She would help it—she would help it!" cried the young man.

"For about a year—the first year, yes. After that she would be as a millstone round its neck."

"Why, she has a passion for completeness, for good work—for everything you and I care for most."

" 'You and I' is charming, my dear fellow! She has it indeed, but she would have a still greater passion for her children; and very proper too. She would insist upon everything's being made comfortable, advantageous, propitious for them. That isn't the artist's business."

"The artist—the artist! Isn't he a man all the same?"

St. George hesitated. "Sometimes I really think not. You know as well as I what he has to do: the concentration, the finish, the independence that he must strive for, from the moment that he begins to respect his work. Ah, my young friend, his relation to women, especially in matrimony, is at the mercy of this damning fact—that whereas he can in the nature of things have but one standard, they have about fifty. That's what makes them so superior," St. George added, laughing. "Fancy an artist with a plurality of standards," he went on. "To *do* it—to do it and make it divine is the only thing he has to think about. 'Is it done or not?' is his only question.

Not 'Is it done as well as a proper solicitude for my dear little family will allow?' He has nothing to do with the relative, nothing to do with a dear little family!"

"Then you don't allow him the common passions and affections of men?"

"Hasn't he a passion, an affection, which includes all the rest? Besides, let him have all the passions he likes—if he only keeps his independence. He must afford to be poor."

Paul Overt slowly got up. "Why did you advise me to make up to her, then?"

St. George laid his hand on his shoulder. "Because she would make an adorable wife! And I hadn't read you then."

"I wish you had left me alone!" murmured the young man.

"I didn't know that that wasn't good enough for you," St. George continued.

"What a false position, what a condemnation of the artist, that he's a mere disfranchised monk and can produce his effect only by giving up personal happiness. What an arraignment of art!" Paul Overt pursued, with a trembling voice.

"Ah, you don't imagine, by chance, that I'm defending art? Arraignment, I should think so! Happy the societies in which it hasn't made its appearance; for from the moment it comes they have a consuming ache, they have an incurable corruption in their bosom. Assuredly, the artist is in a false position. But I thought we were taking him for granted. Pardon me," St. George continued; "*Ginistrella* made me!"

Paul Overt stood looking at the floor—one o'clock struck, in the stillness, from a neighbouring church-tower. "Do you think she would ever look at me?" he asked at last.

"Miss Fancourt—as a suitor? Why shouldn't I think it? That's why I've tried to favour you—I have had a little chance or two of bettering your opportunity."

"Excuse my asking you, but do you mean by keeping away yourself?" Paul said, blushing.

"I'm an old idiot—my place isn't there," St. George replied, gravely.

"I'm nothing, yet; I've no fortune; and there must be so many others."

"You're a gentleman and a man of genius. I think you might do something."

"But if I must give that up—the genius?"

"Lots of people, you know, think I've kept mine."

"You have a genius for torment!" Paul Overt exclaimed; but taking his companion's hand in farewell as a mitigation of this judgment.

"Poor child, I do bother you. Try, try, then! I think your chances are good, and you'll win a great prize."

Paul held the other's hand a minute; he looked into his face. "No, I *am* an artist—I can't help it!"

"Ah, show it then!" St. George broke out—"let me see before I die the thing I most want, the thing I yearn for—a life in which the passion is really intense. If you can be rare, don't fail of it! Think what it is—how it counts—how it lives!" They had moved to the door and St. George had closed both his own hands over that of his companion. Here they paused again and Paul Overt ejaculated—"I want to live!"

"In what sense?"

"In the greatest sense."

"Well then, stick to it—see it through."

"With your sympathy—your help?"

"Count on that—you'll be a great figure to me. Count on my highest appreciation, my devotion. You'll give me satisfaction!—if that has any weight with you." And as Paul appeared still to waver, St. George added: "Do you remember what you said to me at Summersoft?"

"Something infatuated, no doubt!"

"'I'll do anything in the world you tell me.' You said that."

"And you hold me to it?"

"Ah, what am I?" sighed the master, shaking his head.

"Lord, what things I shall have to do!" Paul almost moaned as he turned away.

VI.

"It goes on too much abroad—hang abroad!" These, or something like them, had been St. George's remarkable words in relation to the action of *Ginistrella*; and yet, though they had made a sharp impression on Paul Overt, like almost all the master's spoken words, the young man, a week after the conversation I have narrated, left England for a long absence and full of projects of work. It is not a perversion of the truth to say that that conversation was the direct cause of his departure. If the oral utterance of the eminent writer had the privilege of moving him deeply it was especially on his turning it over at leisure, hours and days afterward, that it appeared to yield its full meaning and exhibit its extreme importance. He spent the summer in Switzerland, and having, in September, begun a new task, he determined not to cross the Alps till he should have made a good start. To this end he returned to a quiet corner that he knew well, on the edge of the Lake of Geneva, within sight of the towers of Chillon: a region and a view for which he had an affection springing from old associations, capable of mysterious little revivals and refreshments. Here he lingered late, till the snow was on the nearer hills, almost down to the limit to which he could climb when his stint was done, on the shortening afternoons. The autumn was fine, the lake was blue, and his book took form and direction. These circumstances, for the time, embroidered his life, and he suffered it to cover him with its mantle. At the end of six weeks he appeared to himself to have learned St. George's lesson by heart—to have tested and proved its doctrine. Nevertheless he did a very inconsistent thing: before crossing the Alps he wrote to Marian Fancourt. He was aware of the perversity of this act, and it was only as a luxury, an amusement, the reward of a strenuous autumn, that he justified it. She had not asked any such favour of him when he went to see her three days before he left London—three days after their dinner in Ennismore Gardens. It is true that she had no reason to, for he had not mentioned that he was on the eve of such an excursion. He hadn't mentioned it because he didn't know it; it was that particular visit that made the matter clear. He had paid the visit to see how much he really cared for her, and quick departure, without so much as a farewell, was the sequel to this inquiry, the answer to which had been a distinct superlative. When he wrote to her from Clarens he noted that he owed her an explanation (more than three months after!) for the omission of such a form.

She answered him briefly but very promptly, and gave him a striking piece of news: the death, a week before, of Mrs. St. George. This exemplary woman had succumbed, in the country, to a violent attack of inflammation of the lungs—he would remember that for a long time she had been delicate. Miss Fancourt added that she heard her husband was overwhelmed with the blow; he would miss her unspeakably—she had been everything to him. Paul Overt immediately wrote to St. George. He had wished to remain in communication with him, but had hitherto lacked the right excuse for troubling so busy a man. Their long nocturnal talk came back to him in every detail, but this did not prevent his expressing a cordial sympathy with the head of the profession, for had not that very talk made it clear that the accomplished lady was the influence that ruled his life? What catastrophe could be more cruel than the extinction of such an influence? This was exactly the tone that St. George took in answering his young friend, upwards of a month later. He made no allusion, of course, to their important discussion. He spoke of his wife as frankly and generously as if he had quite forgotten that occasion, and the feeling of deep bereavement was visible in his words. "She took every thing off my hands—off my mind. She carried on our life with the greatest art, the rarest devotion, and I was free, as few men can have been, to drive my pen, to shut myself up with my trade. This was a rare service—the highest she could have rendered me. Would I could have acknowledged it more fitly!"

A certain bewilderment, for Paul Overt, disengaged itself from these remarks: they struck him as a contradiction, a retractation. He had certainly not expected his correspondent to rejoice in the death of his wife, and it was perfectly in order that the rupture of a tie of more than twenty years should have left him sore. But if she was such a benefactress as that, what in the name of consistency had St. George meant by turning *him* upside down that night—by dosing him to that degree, at the most sensitive hour of his life, with the doctrine of renunciation? If Mrs. St. George was an irreparable loss, then her husband's inspired advice had been a bad joke and renunciation was a mistake. Overt was on the point of rushing back to London to show that, for his part, he was perfectly willing to consider it so, and he went so far as to take the manuscript of the first chapters of his new book out of his table-drawer, to insert it into a pocket of his portmanteau.

This led to his catching a glimpse of some pages he had not looked at for months, and that accident, in turn, to his being struck with the high promise they contained—a rare result of such retrospections, which it was his habit to avoid as much as possible. They usually made him feel that the glow of composition might be a purely subjective and a very barren emotion. On this occasion a certain belief in himself disengaged itself whimsically from the serried erasures of his first draft, making him think it best after all to carry out his present experiment to the end. If he could write as well as that under the influence of renunciation, it would be a pity to change the conditions before the termination of the work. He would go back to London of course, but he would go back only when he should have finished his book. This was the vow he privately made, restoring his manuscript to the table-drawer. It may be added that it took him a long time to finish his book, for the subject was as difficult as it was fine and he was literally embarrassed by the fulness of his notes. Something within him told him that he must make it supremely good —otherwise he should lack, as regards his private behaviour, a handsome excuse. He had a horror of this deficiency and found himself as firm as need be on the question of the lamp and the file. He crossed the Alps at last and spent the winter, the spring, the ensuing summer, in Italy, where still, at the end of a twelve-month, his task was unachieved. "Stick to it—see it through:" this general injunction of St. George's was good also for the particular case. He applied it to the utmost, with the result that when in its slow order, the summer had come round again he felt that he had given all that was in him. This time he put his papers into his portmanteau, with the address of his publisher attached, and took his way northward.

He had been absent from London for two years—two years which were a long period and had made such a difference in his own life (through the production of a novel far stronger, he believed, than *Ginistrella*) that he turned out into Piccadilly, the morning after his arrival, with an indefinite expectation of changes, of finding that things had happened. But there were few transformations in Piccadilly (only three or four big red houses where there had been low black ones), and the brightness of the end of June peeped through the rusty railings of the Green Park and glittered in the varnish of the rolling carriages as he had seen it in other, more cursory Junes. It was a greeting that he appreciated; it seemed friendly and pointed, added to the exhilaration of his finished book, of his having his own country and the huge, oppressive, amusing city that suggested everything, that contained everything, under his hand again. "Stay at home and do things here—do subjects we can measure," St. George had said; and now it appeared to him that he should ask nothing better than to stay at home for ever. Late in the afternoon he took his way to Manchester Square, looking out for a number he had not forgotten. Miss Fancourt, however, was not within, so that he turned, rather dejectedly, from the door. This movement brought him face to face with a gentleman who was approaching it and whom he promptly perceived to be Miss Fancourt's father. Paul saluted this personage, and the General returned his greeting with his customary good manner—a manner so good, however, that you could never tell whether it meant that he placed you. Paul Overt felt the impulse to speak to him; then, hesitating, became conscious both that he had nothing particular to say and that though the old soldier remembered him he remembered him wrong. He therefore passed on, without calculating on the irresistible effect that his own evident recognition would have upon the General, who never neglected a chance to gossip. Our young man's face was expressive, and observation seldom let it pass. He had not taken ten steps before he heard himself called after with a friendly, semi-articulate "A—I beg your pardon!" He turned round and the General, smiling at him from the steps, said: "Won't you come in? I won't leave you the advantage of me!" Paul declined to come in, and then was sorry he had done so, for Miss Fancourt, so late in the afternoon, might return at any moment. But her father gave him no second chance; he appeared mainly to wish not to have struck him as inhospitable. A further look at the visitor told him more about him, enough at least to enable him to say—"You've come back, you've come back?" Paul was on the point of replying that he had come back the night before, but he bethought himself to suppress this strong light on the immediacy of his visit, and, giving merely a general assent, remarked that he was extremely sorry not to have found Miss Fancourt. He had come late, in the hope that she would be in. "I'll tell her— I'll tell her," said the old man; and then he added quickly, gallantly, "You'll be giving us something new? It's a long time, isn't it?" Now he remembered him right.

"Rather long. I'm very slow," said Paul. "I met you at Summersoft a long time ago."

"Oh, yes, with Henry St George. I remember very well. Before his poor wife——" General Fancourt paused a moment, smiling a little less. "I daresay you know."

"About Mrs. St. George's death? Oh yes, I heard at the time."

"Oh no; I mean—I mean he's to be married."

"Ah! I've not heard that." Just as Paul was about to add, "To whom?" the General crossed his intention with a question.

"When did you come back? I know you've been away— from my daughter. She was very sorry. You ought to give her something new."

"I came back last night," said our young man, to whom something had occurred which made his speech, for the moment, a little thick.

"Ah, most kind of you to come so soon. Couldn't you turn up at dinner?"

"At dinner?" Paul Overt repeated, not liking to ask whom St. George was going to marry, but thinking only of that.

"There are several people, I believe. Certainly St. George. Or afterwards, if you like better. I believe my daughter expects——." He appeared to notice something in Overt's upward face (on his steps he stood higher) which led him to interrupt himself, and the interruption gave him a momentary sense of awkwardness, from which he sought a quick issue. "Perhaps then you haven't heard she's to be married."

"To be married?" Paul stared.

"To Mr. St. George—it has just been settled. Odd marriage, isn't it?" Paul uttered no opinion on this point: he only continued to stare. "But I daresay it will do—she's so awfully literary!" said the General.

Paul had turned very red. "Oh, it's a surprise—very in-

teresting, very charming! I'm afraid I can't dine—so many
thanks!"

"Well, you must come to the wedding!" cried the General.
"Oh, I remember that day at Summersoft. He's a very good
fellow."

"Charming—charming!" Paul stammered, retreating. He
shook hands with the General and got off. His face was red
and he had the sense of its growing more and more crimson.
All the evening at home—he went straight to his rooms and
remained there dinnerless—his cheek burned at intervals as if
it had been smitten. He didn't understand what had happened
to him, what trick had been played him, what treachery practised. "None, none," he said to himself. "I've nothing to do
with it. I'm out of it—it's none of my business." But that
bewildered murmur was followed again and again by the incongruous ejaculation—"Was it a plan—was it a plan?" Sometimes he cried to himself, breathless, "Am I a dupe—am I a
dupe?" If he was, he was an absurd, and abject one. It seemed
to him he had never lost her till now. He had renounced her,
yes; but that was another affair—that was a closed but not a
locked door. Now he felt as if the door had been slammed in
his face. Did he expect her to wait—was she to give him his
time like that: two years at a stretch? He didn't know what
he had expected—he only knew what he hadn't. It wasn't
this—it wasn't this. Mystification, bitterness and wrath rose
and boiled in him when he thought of the deference, the
devotion, the credulity with which he had listened to St.
George. The evening wore on and the light was long; but
even when it had darkened he remained without a lamp. He
had flung himself on the sofa, and he lay there through the
hours with his eyes either closed or gazing into the gloom, in
the attitude of a man teaching himself to bear something, to
bear having been made a fool of. He had made it too
easy—that idea passed over him like a hot wave. Suddenly, as
he heard eleven o'clock strike, he jumped up, remembering
what General Fancourt had said about his coming after dinner. He would go—he would see her at least; perhaps he
should see what it meant. He felt as if some of the elements
of a hard sum had been given him and the others were

wanting: he couldn't do his sum till he was in possession of them all.

He dressed quickly, so that by half-past eleven he was at Manchester Square. There were a good many carriages at the door—a party was going on; a circumstance which at the last gave him a slight relief, for now he would rather see her in a crowd. People passed him on the staircase; they were going away, going "on," with the hunted, herdlike movement of London society at night. But sundry groups remained in the drawing-room, and it was some minutes, as she didn't hear him announced, before he discovered her and spoke to her. In this short interval he had perceived that St. George was there, talking to a lady before the fireplace; but he looked away from him, for the moment, and therefore failed to see whether the author of *Shadowmere* noticed him. At all events he didn't come to him. Miss Fancourt did, as soon as she saw him; she almost rushed at him, smiling, rustling, radiant, beautiful. He had forgotten what her head, what her face offered to the sight; she was in white, there were gold figures on her dress, and her hair was like a casque of gold. In a single moment he saw she was happy, happy with a kind of aggressiveness, of splendour. But she would not speak to him of that, she would speak only of himself.

"I'm so delighted; my father told me. How kind of you to come!" She struck him as so fresh and brave, while his eyes moved over her, that he said to himself, irresistibly: "Why to *him*, why not to youth, to strength, to ambition, to a future? Why, in her rich young capacity, to failure, to abdication, to superannuation?" In his thought, at that sharp moment, he blasphemed even against all that had been left of his faith in the peccable master. "I'm so sorry I missed you," she went on. "My father told me. How charming of you to have come so soon!"

"Does that surprise you?" Paul Overt asked.

"The first day? No, from you—nothing that's nice." She was interrupted by a lady who bade her good-night, and he seemed to read that it cost her nothing to speak to one in that tone; it was her old bounteous, demonstrative way, with a certain added amplitude that time had brought; and if it began to operate on the spot, at such a juncture in her history, perhaps in the other days too it had meant just as little or as much—a sort of mechanical charity, with the difference now that she was satisfied, ready to give but asking nothing. Oh, she was satisfied—and why shouldn't she be? Why shouldn't she have been surprised at his coming the first day—for all the good she had ever got from him? As the lady continued to hold her attention Paul Overt turned from her with a strange irritation in his complicated artistic soul and a kind of disinterested disappointment. She was so happy that it was almost stupid—it seemed to deny the extraordinary intelligence he had formerly found in her. Didn't she know how bad St. George could be, hadn't she perceived the deplorable thinness——? If she didn't she was nothing, and if she did why such an insolence of serenity? This question expired as our young man's eyes settled at last upon the genius who had advised him in a great crisis. St. George was still before the chimney-piece, but now he was alone (fixed, waiting, as if he meant to remain after every one), and he met the clouded gaze of the young friend who was tormented with uncertainty as to whether he had the right (which his resentment would have enjoyed,) to regard himself as his victim. Somehow, the fantastic inquiry I have just noted was answered by St. George's aspect. It was as fine in its way as Marian Fancourt's —it denoted the happy human being; but somehow it represented to Paul Overt that the author of *Shadowmere* had now definitively ceased to count—ceased to count as a writer. As he smiled a welcome across the room he was almost *banal*, he was almost smug. Paul had the impression that for a moment he hesitated to make a movement forward, as if he had a bad conscience; but the next they had met in the middle of the room and had shaken hands, expressively, cordially on St. George's part. Then they had passed together to where the elder man had been standing, while St. George said: "I hope you are never going away again. I have been dining here; the General told me." He was handsome, he was young, he looked as if he had still a great fund of life. He bent the friendliest, most unconfessing eyes upon Paul Overt; asked him about everything, his health, his plans, his late occupations, the new book. "When will it be out—soon, soon, I hope? Splendid, eh? That's right; you're a comfort! I've read you all over again, the last six months." Paul waited to see if he would tell him what the General had told him in the afternoon, and what Miss Fancourt, verbally at least, of course had not. But as it didn't come out he asked at last: "Is it true, the great news I hear, that you're to be married?"

"Ah, you *have* heard it then?"

"Didn't the General tell you?" Paul Overt went on.

"Tell me what?"

"That he mentioned it to me this afternoon?"

"My dear fellow, I don't remember. We've been in the midst of people. I'm sorry, in that case, that I lose the pleasure, myself, of announcing to you a fact that touches me so nearly. It *is* a fact, strange as it may appear. It has only just become one. Isn't it ridiculous?" St. George made this speech without confusion, but on the other hand, so far as Paul could see, without latent impudence. It appeared to his interlocutor that, to talk so comfortably and coolly, he must simply have forgotten what had passed between them. His next words, however, showed that he had not, and they had, as an appeal to Paul's own memory, an effect which would have been ludicrous if it had not been cruel. "Do you recollect the talk we had at my house that night, into which Miss Fancourt's name entered? I've often thought of it since."

"Yes—no wonder you said what you did," said Paul, looking at him.

"In the light of the present occasion? Ah! but there was no light then. How could I have foreseen this hour?"

"Didn't you think it probable?"

"Upon my honour, no," said Henry St. George. "Certainly, I owe you that assurance. Think how my situation has changed."

"I see—I see," Paul murmured.

His companion went on, as if, now that the subject had been broached, he was, as a man of imagination and tact, perfectly ready to give every satisfaction—being able to enter fully into everything another might feel. "But it's not only that—for honestly, at my age, I never dreamed——a widower, with big boys and with so little else! It has turned out differently from any possible calculation, and I am fortunate beyond all measure. She has been so free, and yet she consents. Better than any one else perhaps—for I remember how you liked her, before you went away, and how she liked you—you can intelligently congratulate me."

"She has been so free!" Those words made a great impression on Paul Overt, and he almost writhed under that irony in them as to which it little mattered whether it was intentional or casual. Of course she had been free and, appreciably perhaps, by his own act; for was not St. George's allusion to her having liked him a part of the irony too? "I thought that by your theory you disapproved of a writer's marrying."

"Surely—surely. But you don't call me a writer?"

"You ought to be ashamed," said Paul.

"Ashamed of marrying again?"

"I won't say that—but ashamed of your reasons."

"You must let me judge of them, my friend."

"Yes; why not? For you judged wonderfully of mine."

The tone of these words appeared suddenly, for Henry St. George, to suggest the unsuspected. He stared as if he read a bitterness in them. "Don't you think I have acted fair?"

"You might have told me at the time, perhaps."

"My dear fellow, when I say I couldn't pierce futurity!"

"I mean afterwards."

St. George hesitated. "After my wife's death?"

"When this idea came to you."

"Ah, never, never! I wanted to save you, rare and precious as you are."

"Are you marrying Miss Fancourt to save me?"

"Not absolutely, but it adds to the pleasure. I shall be the making of you," said St. George, smiling. "I was greatly struck, after our talk, with the resolute way you quitted the country and still more, perhaps, with your force of character in remaining abroad. You're very strong—you're wonderfully strong."

Paul Overt tried to sound his pleasant eyes; the strange thing was that he appeared sincere—not a mocking fiend. He turned away, and as he did so he heard St. George say something about his giving them the proof, being the joy of his old age. He faced him again, taking another look. "Do you mean to say you've stopped writing?"

"My dear fellow, of course I have. It's too late. Didn't I tell you?"

"I can't believe it!"

"Of course you can't—with your own talent! No, no; for the rest of my life I shall only read you."

"Does she know that—Miss Fancourt?"

"She will—she will." Our young man wondered whether St. George meant this as a covert intimation that the assistance he should derive from that young lady's fortune, moderate as it was, would make the difference of putting it in his power to cease to work, ungratefully, an exhausted vein. Somehow, standing there in the ripeness of his successful manhood, he did not suggest that any of his veins were exhausted. "Don't you remember the moral I offered myself to you—that night—as pointing?" St. George continued. "Consider, at any rate, the warning I am at present."

This was too much—he *was* the mocking fiend. Paul separated from him with a mere nod for good-night; the sense that he might come back to him some time in the far future but could not fraternise with him now. It was necessary to his sore spirit to believe for the hour that he had a grievance—all the more cruel for not being a legal one. It was doubtless in the attitude of hugging this wrong that he descended the stairs without taking leave of Miss Fancourt, who had not been in view at the moment he quitted the room. He was glad to get out into the honest, dusky, unsophisticating night, to move fast, to take his way home on foot. He walked a long time, missing his way, not thinking of it. He was thinking of too many other things. His steps recovered their direction, however, and at the end of an hour he found himself before his door, in the small, inexpensive, empty street. He lingered, questioning himself still, before going in, with nothing around and above him but moonless blackness, a bad lamp or two and a few faraway dim stars. To these last faint features he raised his eyes; he had been saying to himself that there would have been mockery indeed if now, on his new foundation, at the end of a year, St. George should put forth something with his early quality—something of the type of *Shadowmere* and finer than his finest. Greatly as he admired his talent Paul literally hoped such an incident would not occur; it seemed to him just then that he scarcely should be able to endure it. St. George's words were still in his ears, "You're very strong—wonderfully strong." Was he really? Certainly, he would have to be; and it would be a sort of revenge. *Is* he? the reader may ask in turn, if his interest has followed the perplexed young man so far. The best answer to that perhaps is that he is doing his best but that it is too soon to say. When the new book came out in the autumn Mr. and Mrs. St. George found it really magnificent. The former still has published nothing, but Paul Overt does not even yet feel safe. I may say for him, however, that if this event were to befall he would really be the very first to appreciate it: which is perhaps a proof that St. George was essentially right and that Nature dedicated him to intellectual, not to personal passion.

The Patagonia

THE HOUSES were dark in the August night and the perspective of Beacon Street, with its double chain of lamps,
was a foreshortened desert. The club on the hill alone, from
its semi-cylindrical front, projected a glow upon the dusky
vagueness of the Common, and as I passed it I heard in the
hot stillness the click of a pair of billiard balls. As 'every one'
was out of town perhaps the servants, in the extravagance of
their leisure, were profaning the tables. The heat was insufferable and I thought with joy of the morrow, of the deck of
the steamer, the freshening breeze, the sense of getting out
to sea. I was even glad of what I had learned in the afternoon
at the office of the company—that at the eleventh hour an
old ship with a lower standard of speed had been put on in
place of the vessel in which I had taken my passage. America
was roasting, England might very well be stuffy, and a slow
passage (which at that season of the year would probably
also be a fine one) was a guarantee of ten or twelve days of
fresh air.

I strolled down the hill without meeting a creature, though
I could see through the palings of the Common that that
recreative expanse was peopled with dim forms. I remembered
Mrs. Nettlepoint's house—she lived in those days (they are
not so distant, but there have been changes) on the water-
side, a little way beyond the spot at which the Public Garden
terminates; and I reflected that like myself she would be
spending the night in Boston if it were true that, as had been
mentioned to me a few days before at Mount Desert, she was
to embark on the morrow for Liverpool. I presently saw this
appearance confirmed by a light above her door and in two
or three of her windows, and I determined to ask for her,
having nothing to do till bedtime. I had come out simply to
pass an hour, leaving my hotel to the blaze of its gas and the
perspiration of its porters; but it occurred to me that my old
friend might very well not know of the substitution of the
Patagonia for the *Scandinavia*, so that it would be an act of
consideration to prepare her mind. Besides, I could offer to

help her, to look after her in the morning: lone women are grateful for support in taking ship for far countries.

As I stood on her doorstep I remembered that as she had a son she might not after all be so lone; yet at the same time it was present to me that Jasper Nettlepoint was not quite a young man to lean upon, having (as I at least supposed) a life of his own and tastes and habits which had long since drawn him away from the maternal side. If he did happen just now to be at home my solicitude would of course seem officious; for in his many wanderings—I believed he had roamed all over the globe—he would certainly have learned how to manage. None the less I was very glad to show Mrs. Nettlepoint I thought of her. With my long absence I had lost sight of her; but I had liked her of old; she had been a close friend of my sisters; and I had in regard to her that sense which is pleasant to those who, in general, have grown strange or detached— the feeling that she at least knew all about me. I could trust her at any time to tell people what a respectable person I was. Perhaps I was conscious of how little I deserved this indulgence when it came over me that for years I had not communicated with her. The measure of this neglect was given by my vagueness of mind about her son. However, I really belonged nowadays to a different generation: I was more the old lady's contemporary than Jasper's.

Mrs. Nettlepoint was at home: I found her in her back drawing-room, where the wide windows opened upon the water. The room was dusky—it was too hot for lamps—and she sat slowly moving her fan and looking out on the little arm of the sea which is so pretty at night, reflecting the lights of Cambridgeport and Charlestown. I supposed she was musing upon the loved ones she was to leave behind, her married daughters, her grandchildren; but she struck a note more specifically Bostonian as she said to me, pointing with her fan to the Back Bay—'I shall see nothing more charming than that over there, you know!' She made me very welcome, but her son had told her about the *Patagonia*, for which she was sorry, as this would mean a longer voyage. She was a poor creature on shipboard and mainly confined to her cabin, even in weather extravagantly termed fine—as if any weather could be fine at sea.

'Ah, then your son's going with you?' I asked.

'Here he comes, he will tell you for himself much better than I am able to do.'

Jasper Nettlepoint came into the room at that moment, dressed in white flannel and carrying a large fan.

'Well, my dear, have you decided?' his mother continued, with some irony in her tone. 'He hasn't yet made up his mind, and we sail at ten o'clock!'

'What does it matter, when my things are put up?' said the young man. 'There is no crowd at this moment, there will be cabins to spare. I'm waiting for a telegram—that will settle it. I just walked up to the club to see if it was come—they'll send it there because they think the house is closed. Not yet, but I shall go back in twenty minutes.'

'Mercy, how you rush about in this temperature!' his mother exclaimed, while I reflected that it was perhaps *his* billiard-balls I had heard ten minutes before. I was sure he was fond of billiards.

'Rush? not in the least. I take it uncommonly easy.'

'Ah, I'm bound to say you do,' Mrs. Nettlepoint exclaimed, inconsequently. I divined that there was a certain tension between the pair and a want of consideration on the young man's part, arising perhaps from selfishness. His mother was nervous, in suspense, wanting to be at rest as to whether she should have his company on the voyage or be obliged to make it alone. But as he stood there smiling and slowly moving his fan he struck me somehow as a person on whom this fact would not sit very heavily. He was of the type of those whom other people worry about, not of those who worry about other people. Tall and strong, he had a handsome face, with a round head and close-curling hair; the whites of his eyes and the enamel of his teeth, under his brown moustache, gleamed vaguely in the lights of the Back Bay. I made out that he was sunburnt, as if he lived much in the open air, and that he looked intelligent but also slightly brutal, though not in a morose way. His brutality, if he had any, was bright and finished. I had to tell him who I was, but even then I saw that he failed to place me and that my explanations gave me in his mind no great identity or at any rate no great importance. I foresaw that he would in intercourse make me feel sometimes very young and sometimes very old. He mentioned, as if to show his mother that he might safely be left to his own devices, that he had once started from London to Bombay at three-quarters of an hour's notice.

'Yes, and it must have been pleasant for the people you were with!'

'Oh, the people I was with——!' he rejoined; and his tone appeared to signify that such people would always have to come off as they could. He asked if there were no cold drinks in the house, no lemonade, no iced syrups; in such weather something of that sort ought always to be kept going. When his mother remarked that surely at the club they *were* going he went on, 'Oh, yes, I had various things there; but you know I have walked down the hill since. One should have something at either end. May I ring and see?' He rang while Mrs. Nettlepoint observed that with the people they had in the house—an establishment reduced naturally at such a moment to its simplest expression (they were burning-up candle-ends and there were no luxuries) she would not answer for the service. The matter ended in the old lady's going out of the room in quest of syrup with the female domestic who had appeared in response to the bell and in whom Jasper's appeal aroused no visible intelligence.

She remained away some time and I talked with her son, who was sociable but desultory and kept moving about the room, always with his fan, as if he were impatient. Sometimes he seated himself for an instant on the window-sill, and then I saw that he was in fact very good-looking; a fine brown, clean young athlete. He never told me on what special contingency his decision depended; he only alluded familiarly to an expected telegram, and I perceived that he was probably not addicted to copious explanations. His mother's absence was an indication that when it was a question of gratifying him she had grown used to spare no pains, and I fancied her rummaging in some close storeroom, among old preserve-pots, while the dull maid-servant held the candle awry. I know not whether this same vision was in his own eyes; at all events it did not prevent him from saying suddenly, as he looked at his watch, that I must excuse him, as he had to go back to the club. He would return in half an hour—or in less. He walked away and I sat there alone, conscious, in the dark, dismantled, simplified room, in the deep silence that rests on American towns during the hot season (there was now and then a far cry or a plash in the water, and at intervals the tinkle of the bells of the horse-cars on the long bridge, slow in the suffocating night), of the strange influence, half sweet, half sad, that abides in houses uninhabited or about to become so—in places muffled and bereaved, where the unheeded sofas and patient belittered tables seem to know (like the disconcerted dogs) that it is the eve of a journey.

After a while I heard the sound of voices, of steps, the rustle of dresses, and I looked round, supposing these things to be the sign of the return of Mrs. Nettlepoint and her handmaiden, bearing the refreshment prepared for her son. What I saw however was two other female forms, visitors just admitted apparently, who were ushered into the room. They were not announced—the servant turned her back on them and rambled off to our hostess. They came forward in a wavering, tentative, unintroduced way—partly, I could see, because the place was dark and partly because their visit was in its nature experimental, a stretch of confidence. One of the ladies was stout and the other was slim, and I perceived in a moment that one was talkative and the other silent. I made out further that one was elderly and the other young and that the fact that they were so unlike did not prevent their being mother and daughter. Mrs. Nettlepoint reappeared in a very few minutes, but the interval had sufficed to establish a communication (really copious for the occasion) between the strangers and the unknown gentleman whom they found in possession, hat and stick in hand. This was not my doing (for what had I to go upon?) and still less was it the doing of the person whom I supposed and whom I indeed quickly and definitely learned to be the daughter. She spoke but once— when her companion informed me that she was going out to Europe the next day to be married. Then she said, 'Oh, mother!' protestingly, in a tone which struck me in the darkness as doubly strange, exciting my curiosity to see her face.

It had taken her mother but a moment to come to that and

to other things besides, after I had explained that I myself was waiting for Mrs. Nettlepoint, who would doubtless soon come back.

'Well, she won't know me—I guess she hasn't ever heard much about me,' the good lady said; 'but I have come from Mrs. Allen and I guess that will make it all right. I presume you know Mrs. Allen?'

I was unacquainted with this influential personage, but I assented vaguely to the proposition. Mrs. Allen's emissary was good-humoured and familiar, but rather appealing than insistent (she remarked that if her friend *had* found time to come in the afternoon—she had so much to do, being just up for the day, that she couldn't be sure—it would be all right); and somehow even before she mentioned Merrimac Avenue (they had come all the way from there) my imagination had associated her with that indefinite social limbo known to the properly-constituted Boston mind as the South End—a nebulous region which condenses here and there into a pretty face, in which the daughters are an 'improvement' on the mothers and are sometimes acquainted with gentlemen resident in more distinguished districts of the New England capital—gentlemen whose wives and sisters in turn are not acquainted with them.

When at last Mrs. Nettlepoint came in, accompanied by candles and by a tray laden with glasses of coloured fluid which emitted a cool tinkling, I was in a position to officiate as master of the ceremonies, to introduce Mrs. Mavis and Miss Grace Mavis, to represent that Mrs. Allen had recommended them—nay, had urged them—to come that way, informally, and had been prevented only by the pressure of occupations so characteristic of her (especially when she was up from Mattapoisett just for a few hours' shopping) from herself calling in the course of the day to explain who they were and what was the favour they had to ask of Mrs. Nettlepoint. Good-natured women understand each other even when divided by the line of topographical fashion, and our hostess had quickly mastered the main facts: Mrs. Allen's visit in the morning in Merrimac Avenue to talk of Mrs. Amber's great idea, the classes at the public schools in vacation (she was interested with an equal charity to that of Mrs. Mavis—even in such

weather!—in those of the South End) for games and exercises
and music, to keep the poor unoccupied children out of the
streets; then the revelation that it had suddenly been settled
almost from one hour to the other that Grace should sail for
Liverpool, Mr. Porterfield at last being ready. He was taking
a little holiday; his mother was with him, they had come over
from Paris to see some of the celebrated old buildings in England, and he had telegraphed to say that if Grace would start
right off they would just finish it up and be married. It often
happened that when things had dragged on that way for years
they were all huddled up at the end. Of course in such a case
she, Mrs. Mavis, had had to fly round. Her daughter's passage
was taken, but it seemed too dreadful that she should make
her journey all alone, the first time she had ever been at sea,
without any companion or escort. *She* couldn't go—Mr. Mavis
was too sick: she hadn't even been able to get him off to the
seaside.

'Well, Mrs. Nettlepoint is going in that ship,' Mrs. Allen
had said; and she had represented that nothing was simpler
than to put the girl in her charge. When Mrs. Mavis had replied that that was all very well but that she didn't know the
lady, Mrs. Allen had declared that that didn't make a speck of
difference, for Mrs. Nettlepoint was kind enough for anything. It was easy enough to know her, if that was all the
trouble. All Mrs. Mavis would have to do would be to go up
to her the next morning when she took her daughter to the
ship (she would see her there on the deck with her party) and
tell her what she wanted. Mrs. Nettlepoint had daughters herself and she would easily understand. Very likely she would
even look after Grace a little on the other side, in such a queer
situation, going out alone to the gentleman she was engaged
to; she would just help her to turn round before she was married. Mr. Porterfield seemed to think they wouldn't wait long,
once she was there: they would have it right over at the American consul's. Mrs. Allen had said it would perhaps be better
still to go and see Mrs. Nettlepoint beforehand, that day, to
tell her what they wanted: then they wouldn't seem to spring
it on her just as she was leaving. She herself (Mrs. Allen)
would call and say a word for them if she could save ten
minutes before catching her train. If she hadn't come it was

because she hadn't saved her ten minutes; but she had made them feel that they must come all the same. Mrs. Mavis liked that better, because on the ship in the morning there would be such a confusion. She didn't think her daughter would be any trouble—conscientiously she didn't. It was just to have some one to speak to her and not sally forth like a servant-girl going to a situation.

'I see, I am to act as a sort of bridesmaid and to give her away,' said Mrs. Nettlepoint. She was in fact kind enough for anything and she showed on this occasion that it was easy enough to know her. There is nothing more tiresome than complications at sea, but she accepted without a protest the burden of the young lady's dependence and allowed her, as Mrs. Mavis said, to hook herself on. She evidently had the habit of patience, and her reception of her visitors' story reminded me afresh (I was reminded of it whenever I returned to my native land) that my dear compatriots are the people in the world who most freely take mutual accommodation for granted. They have always had to help themselves, and by a magnanimous extension they confound helping each other with that. In no country are there fewer forms and more reciprocities.

It was doubtless not singular that the ladies from Merrimac Avenue should not feel that they were importunate: what was striking was that Mrs. Nettlepoint did not appear to suspect it. However, she would in any case have thought it inhuman to show that—though I could see that under the surface she was amused at everything the lady from the South End took for granted. I know not whether the attitude of the younger visitor added or not to the merit of her good-nature. Mr. Porterfield's intended took no part in her mother's appeal, scarcely spoke, sat looking at the Back Bay and the lights on the long bridge. She declined the lemonade and the other mixtures which, at Mrs. Nettlepoint's request, I offered her, while her mother partook freely of everything and I reflected (for I as freely consumed the reviving liquid) that Mr. Jasper had better hurry back if he wished to profit by the refreshment prepared for him.

Was the effect of the young woman's reserve ungracious, or was it only natural that in her particular situation she

should not have a flow of compliment at her command? I
noticed that Mrs. Nettlepoint looked at her often, and certainly though she was undemonstrative Miss Mavis was interesting. The candle-light enabled me to see that if she was not
in the very first flower of her youth she was still a handsome
girl. Her eyes and hair were dark, her face was pale and she
held up her head as if, with its thick braids, it were an appurtenance she was not ashamed of. If her mother was excellent
and common she was not common (not flagrantly so) and
perhaps not excellent. At all events she would not be, in appearance at least, a dreary appendage, and (in the case of a
person 'hooking on') that was always something gained. Is it
because something of a romantic or pathetic interest usually
attaches to a good creature who has been the victim of a 'long
engagement' that this young lady made an impression on me
from the first—favoured as I had been so quickly with this
glimpse of her history? Certainly she made no positive appeal;
she only held her tongue and smiled, and her smile corrected
whatever suggestion might have forced itself upon me that
the spirit was dead—the spirit of that promise of which she
found herself doomed to carry out the letter.

What corrected it less, I must add, was an odd recollection
which gathered vividness as I listened to it—a mental association which the name of Mr. Porterfield had evoked. Surely I
had a personal impression, over-smeared and confused, of the
gentleman who was waiting at Liverpool, or who would be,
for Mrs. Nettlepoint's *protégée*. I had met him, known him,
some time, somewhere, somehow, in Europe. Was he not
studying something—very hard—somewhere, probably in
Paris, ten years before, and did he not make extraordinarily
neat drawings, linear and architectural? Didn't he go to a *table
d'hôte*, at two francs twenty-five, in the Rue Bonaparte, which
I then frequented, and didn't he wear spectacles and a Scotch
plaid arranged in a manner which seemed to say, 'I have trust-
worthy information that that is the way they do it in the High-
lands'? Was he not exemplary and very poor, so that I
supposed he had no overcoat and his tartan was what he slept
under at night? Was he not working very hard still, and
wouldn't he be in the natural course, not yet satisfied that he
knew enough to launch out? He would be a man of long

preparations—Miss Mavis's white face seemed to speak to one
of that. It appeared to me that if I had been in love with her
I should not have needed to lay such a train to marry her.
Architecture was his line and he was a pupil of the Ecole des
Beaux Arts. This reminiscence grew so much more vivid with
me that at the end of ten minutes I had a curious sense of
knowing—by implication—a good deal about the young lady.

Even after it was settled that Mrs. Nettlepoint would do
everything for her that she could her mother sat a little, sip-
ping her syrup and telling how 'low' Mr. Mavis had been. At
this period the girl's silence struck me as still more conscious,
partly perhaps because she deprecated her mother's loquacity
(she was enough of an 'improvement' to measure that) and
partly because she was too full of pain at the idea of leaving
her infirm, her perhaps dying father. I divined that they were
poor and that she would take out a very small purse for her
trousseau. Moreover for Mr. Porterfield to make up the sum
his own case would have had to change. If he had enriched
himself by the successful practice of his profession I had not
encountered the buildings he had reared—his reputation had
not come to my ears.

Mrs. Nettlepoint notified her new friends that she was a
very inactive person at sea: she was prepared to suffer to the
full with Miss Mavis, but she was not prepared to walk with
her, to struggle with her, to accompany her to the table. To
this the girl replied that she would trouble her little, she was
sure: she had a belief that she should prove a wretched sailor
and spend the voyage on her back. Her mother scoffed at this
picture, prophesying perfect weather and a lovely time, and I
said that if I might be trusted, as a tame old bachelor fairly
sea-seasoned, I should be delighted to give the new member
of our party an arm or any other countenance whenever she
should require it. Both the ladies thanked me for this (taking
my description only too literally), and the elder one declared
that we were evidently going to be such a sociable group that
it was too bad to have to stay at home. She inquired of Mrs.
Nettlepoint if there were any one else—if she were to be accompanied by some of her family; and when our hostess mentioned her son—there was a chance of his embarking but
(wasn't it absurd?) he had not decided yet, she rejoined with

extraordinary candour—'Oh dear, I do hope he'll go: that would be so pleasant for Grace.'

Somehow the words made me think of poor Mr. Porterfield's tartan, especially as Jasper Nettlepoint strolled in again at that moment. His mother instantly challenged him: it was ten o'clock; had he by chance made up his great mind? Apparently he failed to hear her, being in the first place surprised at the strange ladies and then struck with the fact that one of them was not strange. The young man, after a slight hesitation, greeted Miss Mavis with a handshake and an 'Oh, good evening, how do you do?' He did not utter her name, and I could see that he had forgotten it; but she immediately pronounced his, availing herself of an American girl's discretion to introduce him to her mother.

'Well, you might have told me you knew him all this time!' Mrs. Mavis exclaimed. Then smiling at Mrs. Nettlepoint she added, 'It would have saved me a worry, an acquaintance already begun.'

'Ah, my son's acquaintances——!' Mrs. Nettlepoint murmured.

'Yes, and my daughter's too!' cried Mrs. Mavis, jovially. 'Mrs. Allen didn't tell us *you* were going,' she continued, to the young man.

'She would have been clever if she had been able to!' Mrs. Nettlepoint ejaculated.

'Dear mother, I have my telegram,' Jasper remarked, looking at Grace Mavis.

'I know you very little,' the girl said, returning his observation.

'I've danced with you at some ball—for some sufferers by something or other.'

'I think it was an inundation,' she replied, smiling. 'But it was a long time ago—and I haven't seen you since.'

'I have been in far countries—to my loss. I should have said it was for a big fire.'

'It was at the Horticultural Hall. I didn't remember your name,' said Grace Mavis.

'That is very unkind of you, when I recall vividly that you had a pink dress.'

'Oh, I remember that dress—you looked lovely in it!' Mrs.

Mavis broke out. 'You must get another just like it—on the other side.'

'Yes, your daughter looked charming in it,' said Jasper Nettlepoint. Then he added, to the girl—'Yet you mentioned my name to your mother.'

'It came back to me—seeing you here. I had no idea this was your home.'

'Well, I confess it isn't, much. Oh, there are some drinks!' Jasper went on, approaching the tray and its glasses.

'Indeed there are and quite delicious,' Mrs. Mavis declared.

'Won't you have another then?—a pink one, like your daughter's gown.'

'With pleasure, sir. Oh, do see them over,' Mrs. Mavis continued, accepting from the young man's hand a third tumbler.

'My mother and that gentleman? Surely they can take care of themselves,' said Jasper Nettlepoint.

'But my daughter—she has a claim as an old friend.'

'Jasper, what does your telegram say?' his mother interposed.

He gave no heed to her question: he stood there with his glass in his hand, looking from Mrs. Mavis to Miss Grace.

'Ah, leave her to me, madam; I'm quite competent,' I said to Mrs. Mavis.

Then the young man looked at me. The next minute he asked of the young lady—'Do you mean you are going to Europe?'

'Yes, to-morrow; in the same ship as your mother.'

'That's what we've come here for, to see all about it,' said Mrs. Mavis.

'My son, take pity on me and tell me what light your telegram throws,' Mrs. Nettlepoint went on.

'I will, dearest, when I've quenched my thirst.' And Jasper slowly drained his glass.

'Well, you're worse than Gracie,' Mrs. Mavis commented. 'She was first one thing and then the other—but only about up to three o'clock yesterday.'

'Excuse me—won't you take something?' Jasper inquired of Gracie; who however declined, as if to make up for her mother's copious *consommation*. I made privately the reflection that the two ladies ought to take leave, the question of

Mrs. Nettlepoint's goodwill being so satisfactorily settled and the meeting of the morrow at the ship so near at hand; and I went so far as to judge that their protracted stay, with their hostess visibly in a fidget, was a sign of a want of breeding. Miss Grace after all then was not such an improvement on her mother, for she easily might have taken the initiative of departure, in spite of Mrs. Mavis's imbibing her glass of syrup in little interspaced sips, as if to make it last as long as possible. I watched the girl with an increasing curiosity; I could not help asking myself a question or two about her and even perceiving already (in a dim and general way) that there were some complications in her position. Was it not a complication that she should have wished to remain long enough to assuage a certain suspense, to learn whether or no Jasper were going to sail? Had not something particular passed between them on the occasion or at the period to which they had covertly alluded, and did she really not know that her mother was bringing her to *his* mother's, though she apparently had thought it well not to mention the circumstance? Such things were complications on the part of a young lady betrothed to that curious cross-barred phantom of a Mr. Porterfield. But I am bound to add that she gave me no further warrant for suspecting them than by the simple fact of her encouraging her mother, by her immobility, to linger. Somehow I had a sense that *she* knew better. I got up myself to go, but Mrs. Nettlepoint detained me after seeing that my movement would not be taken as a hint, and I perceived she wished me not to leave my fellow-visitors on her hands. Jasper complained of the closeness of the room, said that it was not a night to sit in a room—one ought to be out in the air, under the sky. He denounced the windows that overlooked the water for not opening upon a balcony or a terrace, until his mother, whom he had not yet satisfied about his telegram, reminded him that there was a beautiful balcony in front, with room for a dozen people. She assured him we would go and sit there if it would please him.

'It will be nice and cool to-morrow, when we steam into the great ocean,' said Miss Mavis, expressing with more vivacity than she had yet thrown into any of her utterances my own thought of half an hour before. Mrs. Nettlepoint replied that it would probably be freezing cold, and her son murmured that he would go and try the drawing-room balcony and report upon it. Just as he was turning away he said, smiling, to Miss Mavis—'Won't you come with me and see if it's pleasant?'

'Oh, well, we had better not stay all night!' her mother exclaimed, but without moving. The girl moved, after a moment's hesitation; she rose and accompanied Jasper into the other room. I observed that her slim tallness showed to advantage as she walked and that she looked well as she passed, with her head thrown back, into the darkness of the other part of the house. There was something rather marked, rather surprising (I scarcely knew why, for the act was simple enough) in her doing so, and perhaps it was our sense of this that held the rest of us somewhat stiffly silent as she remained away. I was waiting for Mrs. Mavis to go, so that I myself might go; and Mrs. Nettlepoint was waiting for her to go so that I might not. This doubtless made the young lady's absence appear to us longer than it really was—it was probably very brief. Her mother moreover, I think, had a vague consciousness of embarrassment. Jasper Nettlepoint presently returned to the back drawing-room to get a glass of syrup for his companion, and he took occasion to remark that it was lovely on the balcony: one really got some air, the breeze was from that quarter. I remembered, as he went away with his tinkling tumbler, that from *my* hand, a few minutes before, Miss Mavis had not been willing to accept this innocent offering. A little later Mrs. Nettlepoint said—'Well, if it's so pleasant there we had better go ourselves.' So we passed to the front and in the other room met the two young people coming in from the balcony. I wondered in the light of subsequent events exactly how long they had been sitting there together. (There were three or four cane chairs which had been placed there for the summer.) If it had been but five minutes, that only made subsequent events more curious. 'We must go, mother,' Miss Mavis immediately said; and a moment later, with a little renewal of chatter as to our general meeting on the ship, the visitors had taken leave. Jasper went down with them to the door and as soon as they had gone out Mrs. Nettlepoint exclaimed—'Ah, but she'll be a bore—she'll be a bore!'

'Not through talking too much—surely.'

'An affectation of silence is as bad. I hate that particular *pose*; it's coming up very much now; an imitation of the English, like everything else. A girl who tries to be statuesque at sea—that will act on one's nerves!'

'I don't know what she tries to be, but she succeeds in being very handsome.'

'So much the better for you. I'll leave her to you, for I shall be shut up. I like her being placed under my "care." '

'She will be under Jasper's,' I remarked.

'Ah, he won't go—I want it too much.'

'I have an idea he will go.'

'Why didn't he tell me so then—when he came in?'

'He was diverted by Miss Mavis—a beautiful unexpected girl sitting there.'

'Diverted from his mother—trembling for his decision?'

'She's an old friend; it was a meeting after a long separation.'

'Yes, such a lot of them as he knows!' said Mrs. Nettlepoint.

'Such a lot of them?'

'He has so many female friends—in the most varied circles.'

'Well, we can close round her then—for I on my side knew, or used to know, her young man.'

'Her young man?'

'The *fiancé*, the intended, the one she is going out to. He can't by the way be very young now.'

'How odd it sounds!' said Mrs. Nettlepoint.

I was going to reply that it was not odd if you knew Mr. Porterfield, but I reflected that that perhaps only made it odder. I told my companion briefly who he was—that I had met him in the old days in Paris, when I believed for a fleeting hour that I could learn to paint, when I lived with the *jeunesse des écoles*, and her comment on this was simply—'Well, he had better have come out for her!'

'Perhaps so. She looked to me as she sat there as if she might change her mind at the last moment.'

'About her marriage?'

'About sailing. But she won't change now.'

Jasper came back, and his mother instantly challenged him. 'Well, *are* you going?'

'Yes, I shall go,' he said, smiling. 'I have got my telegram.'

'Oh, your telegram!' I ventured to exclaim. 'That charming girl is your telegram.'

He gave me a look, but in the dusk I could not make out very well what it conveyed. Then he bent over his mother, kissing her. 'My news isn't particularly satisfactory. I am going for *you*.'

'Oh, you humbug!' she rejoined. But of course she was delighted.

II

People usually spend the first hours of a voyage in squeezing themselves into their cabins, taking their little precautions, either so excessive or so inadequate, wondering how they can pass so many days in such a hole and asking idiotic questions of the stewards, who appear in comparison such men of the world. My own initiations were rapid, as became an old sailor, and so it seemed were Miss Mavis's, for when I mounted to the deck at the end of half an hour I found her there alone, in the stern of the ship, looking back at the dwindling continent. It dwindled very fast for so big a place. I accosted her, having had no conversation with her amid the crowd of leave-takers and the muddle of farewells before we put off; we talked a little about the boat, our fellow-passengers and our prospects, and then I said—'I think you mentioned last night a name I know—that of Mr. Porterfield.'

'Oh no, I never uttered it,' she replied, smiling at me through her closely-drawn veil.

'Then it was your mother.'

'Very likely it was my mother.' And she continued to smile, as if I ought to have known the difference.

'I venture to allude to him because I have an idea I used to know him,' I went on.

'Oh, I see.' Beyond this remark she manifested no interest in my having known him.

'That is if it's the same one.' It seemed to me it would be

silly to say nothing more; so I added 'My Mr. Porterfield was called David.'

'Well, so is ours.' 'Ours' struck me as clever.

'I suppose I shall see him again if he is to meet you at Liverpool,' I continued.

'Well, it will be bad if he doesn't.'

It was too soon for me to have the idea that it would be bad if he did: that only came later. So I remarked that I had not seen him for so many years that it was very possible I should not know him.

'Well, I have not seen him for a great many years, but I expect I shall know him all the same.'

'Oh, with you it's different,' I rejoined, smiling at her. 'Hasn't he been back since those days?'

'I don't know what days you mean.'

'When I knew him in Paris—ages ago. He was a pupil of the Ecole des Beaux Arts. He was studying architecture.'

'Well, he is studying it still,' said Grace Mavis.

'Hasn't he learned it yet?'

'I don't know what he has learned. I shall see.' Then she added: 'Architecture is very difficult and he is tremendously thorough.'

'Oh, yes, I remember that. He was an admirable worker. But he must have become quite a foreigner, if it's so many years since he has been at home.'

'Oh, he is not changeable. If he were changeable——' But here my interlocutress paused. I suspect she had been going to say that if he were changeable he would have given her up long ago. After an instant she went on: 'He wouldn't have stuck so to his profession. You can't make much by it.'

'You can't make much?'

'It doesn't make you rich.'

'Oh, of course you have got to practise it—and to practise it long.'

'Yes—so Mr. Porterfield says.'

Something in the way she uttered these words made me laugh—they were so serene an implication that the gentleman in question did not live up to his principles. But I checked myself, asking my companion if she expected to remain in Europe long—to live there.

'Well, it will be a good while if it takes me as long to come back as it has taken me to go out.'

'And I think your mother said last night that it was your first visit.'

Miss Mavis looked at me a moment. 'Didn't mother talk!'

'It was all very interesting.'

She continued to look at me. 'You don't think that.'

'What have I to gain by saying it if I don't?'

'Oh, men have always something to gain.'

'You make me feel a terrible failure, then! I hope at any rate that it gives you pleasure—the idea of seeing foreign lands.'

'Mercy—I should think so.'

'It's a pity our ship is not one of the fast ones, if you are impatient.'

She was silent a moment; then she exclaimed, 'Oh, I guess it will be fast enough!'

That evening I went in to see Mrs. Nettlepoint and sat on her sea-trunk, which was pulled out from under the berth to accommodate me. It was nine o'clock but not quite dark, as our northward course had already taken us into the latitude of the longer days. She had made her nest admirably and lay upon her sofa in a becoming dressing-gown and cap, resting from her labours. It was her regular practice to spend the voyage in her cabin, which smelt good (such was the refinement of her art), and she had a secret peculiar to herself for keeping her port open without shipping seas. She hated what she called the mess of the ship and the idea, if she should go above, of meeting stewards with plates of supererogatory food. She professed to be content with her situation (we promised to lend each other books and I assured her familiarly that I should be in and out of her room a dozen times a day), and pitied me for having to mingle in society. She judged this to be a limited privilege, for on the deck before we left the wharf she had taken a view of our fellow-passengers.

'Oh, I'm an inveterate, almost a professional observer,' I replied, 'and with that vice I am as well occupied as an old woman in the sun with her knitting. It puts it in my power, in any situation, to *see* things. I shall see them even here and I shall come down very often and tell you about them. You are not interested to-day, but you will be to-morrow, for a ship is a great school of gossip. You won't believe the number of researches and problems you will be engaged in by the middle of the voyage.'

'I? Never in the world—lying here with my nose in a book and never seeing anything.'

'You will participate at second hand. You will see through my eyes, hang upon my lips, take sides, feel passions, all sorts of sympathies and indignations. I have an idea that your young lady is the person on board who will interest me most.'

'Mine, indeed! She has not been near me since we left the dock.'

'Well, she is very curious.'

'You have such cold-blooded terms,' Mrs. Nettlepoint murmured. '*Elle ne sait pas se conduire*; she ought to have come to ask about me.'

'Yes, since you are under her care,' I said, smiling. 'As for her not knowing how to behave—well, that's exactly what we shall see.'

'You will, but not I! I wash my hands of her.'

'Don't say that—don't say that.'

Mrs. Nettlepoint looked at me a moment. 'Why do you speak so solemnly?'

In return I considered her. 'I will tell you before we land. And have you seen much of your son?'

'Oh yes, he has come in several times. He seems very much pleased. He has got a cabin to himself.'

'That's great luck,' I said, 'but I have an idea he is always in luck. I was sure I should have to offer him the second berth in my room.'

'And you wouldn't have enjoyed that, because you don't like him,' Mrs. Nettlepoint took upon herself to say.

'What put that into your head?'

'It isn't in my head—it's in my heart, my *cœur de mère*. We guess those things. You think he's selfish—I could see it last night.'

'Dear lady,' I said, 'I have no general ideas about him at all. He is just one of the phenomena I am going to observe. He seems to me a very fine young man. However,' I added, 'since you have mentioned last night I will admit that I thought he rather tantalised you. He played with your suspense.'

'Why, he came at the last just to please me,' said Mrs. Nettlepoint.

I was silent a moment. 'Are you sure it was for your sake?'

'Ah, perhaps it was for yours!'

'When he went out on the balcony with that girl perhaps she asked him to come,' I continued.

'Perhaps she did. But why should he do everything she asks him?'

'I don't know yet, but perhaps I shall know later. Not that he will tell me—for he will never tell me anything: he is not one of those who tell.'

'If she didn't ask him, what you say is a great wrong to her,' said Mrs. Nettlepoint.

'Yes, if she didn't. But you say that to protect Jasper, not to protect her,' I continued, smiling.

'You *are* cold-blooded—it's uncanny!' my companion exclaimed.

'Ah, this is nothing yet! Wait a while—you'll see. At sea in general I'm awful—I pass the limits. If I have outraged her in thought I will jump overboard. There are ways of asking (a man doesn't need to tell a woman that) without the crude words.'

'I don't know what you suppose between them,' said Mrs. Nettlepoint.

'Nothing but what was visible on the surface. It transpired, as the newspapers say, that they were old friends.'

'He met her at some promiscuous party—I asked him about it afterwards. She is not a person he could ever think of seriously.'

'That's exactly what I believe.'

'You don't observe—you imagine,' Mrs. Nettlepoint pursued. 'How do you reconcile her laying a trap for Jasper with her going out to Liverpool on an errand of love?'

'I don't for an instant suppose she laid a trap; I believe she acted on the impulse of the moment. She is going out to Liverpool on an errand of marriage; that is not necessarily the same thing as an errand of love, especially for one who happens to have had a personal impression of the gentleman she is engaged to.'

'Well, there are certain decencies which in such a situation the most abandoned of her sex would still observe. You apparently judge her capable—on no evidence—of violating them.'

'Ah, you don't understand the shades of things,' I rejoined. 'Decencies and violations—there is no need for such heavy artillery! I can perfectly imagine that without the least immodesty she should have said to Jasper on the balcony, in fact if not in words—"I'm in dreadful spirits, but if you come I shall feel better, and that will be pleasant for you too."'

'And why is she in dreadful spirits?'

'She isn't!' I replied, laughing.

'What is she doing?'

'She is walking with your son.'

Mrs. Nettlepoint said nothing for a moment; then she broke out, inconsequently—'Ah, she's horrid!'

'No, she's charming!' I protested.

'You mean she's "curious"?'

'Well, for me it's the same thing!'

This led my friend of course to declare once more that I was cold-blooded. On the afternoon of the morrow we had another talk, and she told me that in the morning Miss Mavis had paid her a long visit. She knew nothing about anything, but her intentions were good and she was evidently in her own eyes conscientious and decorous. And Mrs. Nettlepoint concluded these remarks with the exclamation 'Poor young thing!'

'You think she is a good deal to be pitied, then?'

'Well, her story sounds dreary—she told me a great deal of it. She fell to talking little by little and went from one thing to another. She's in that situation when a girl *must* open herself—to some woman.'

'Hasn't she got Jasper?' I inquired.

'He isn't a woman. You strike me as jealous of him,' my companion added.

'I daresay *he* thinks so—or will before the end. Ah no—ah no!' And I asked Mrs. Nettlepoint if our young lady struck her as a flirt. She gave me no answer, but went on to remark that it was odd and interesting to her to see the way a girl like Grace Mavis resembled the girls of the kind she herself knew better, the girls of 'society,' at the same time that she differed from them; and the way the differences and resemblances were mixed up, so that on certain questions you couldn't tell where you would find her. You would think she would feel as you did because you had found her feeling so, and then suddenly, in regard to some other matter (which was yet quite the same) she would be terribly wanting. Mrs. Nettlepoint proceeded to observe (to such idle speculations does the vanity of a sea-voyage give encouragement) that she wondered whether it were better to be an ordinary girl very well brought up or an extraordinary girl not brought up at all.

'Oh, I go in for the extraordinary girl under all circumstances.'

'It is true that if you are *very* well brought up you are not ordinary,' said Mrs. Nettlepoint, smelling her strong salts. 'You are a lady, at any rate. *C'est toujours ça.*'

'And Miss Mavis isn't one—is that what you mean?'

'Well—you have seen her mother.'

'Yes, but I think your contention would be that among such people the mother doesn't count.'

'Precisely; and that's bad.'

'I see what you mean. But isn't it rather hard? If your mother doesn't know anything it is better you should be independent of her, and yet if you are that constitutes a bad note.' I added that Mrs. Mavis had appeared to count sufficiently two nights before. She had said and done everything she wanted, while the girl sat silent and respectful. Grace's attitude (so far as her mother was concerned) had been eminently decent.

'Yes, but she couldn't bear it,' said Mrs. Nettlepoint.

'Ah, if you know it I may confess that she has told me as much.'

Mrs. Nettlepoint stared. 'Told you? There's one of the things they do!'

'Well, it was only a word. Won't you let me know whether you think she's a flirt?'

'Find out for yourself, since you pretend to study folks.'

'Oh, your judgment would probably not at all determine mine. It's in regard to yourself that I ask it.'

'In regard to myself?'

'To see the length of maternal immorality.'

Mrs. Nettlepoint continued to repeat my words. 'Maternal immorality?'

'You desire your son to have every possible distraction on his voyage, and if you can make up your mind in the sense I refer to that will make it all right. He will have no responsibility.'

'Heavens, how you analyse! I haven't in the least your passion for making up my mind.'

'Then if you chance it you'll be more immoral still.'

'Your reasoning is strange,' said the poor lady; 'when it was you who tried to put it into my head yesterday that she had asked him to come.'

'Yes, but in good faith.'

'How do you mean in good faith?'

'Why, as girls of that sort do. Their allowance and measure in such matters is much larger than that of young ladies who have been, as you say, *very* well brought up; and yet I am not sure that on the whole I don't think them the more innocent. Miss Mavis is engaged, and she's to be married next week, but it's an old, old story, and there's no more romance in it than if she were going to be photographed. So her usual life goes on, and her usual life consists (and that of ces demoiselles in general) in having plenty of gentlemen's society. Having it I mean without having any harm from it.'

'Well, if there is no harm from it what are you talking about and why am I immoral?'

I hesitated, laughing. 'I retract—you are sane and clear. I am sure she thinks there won't be any harm,' I added. 'That's the great point.'

'The great point?'

'I mean, to be settled.'

'Mercy, we are not trying them! How can *we* settle it?'

'I mean of course in our minds. There will be nothing more interesting for the next ten days for our minds to exercise themselves upon.'

'They will get very tired of it,' said Mrs. Nettlepoint.

'No, no, because the interest will increase and the plot will thicken. It can't help it.' She looked at me as if she thought me slightly Mephistophelean, and I went on—'So she told you everything in her life was dreary?'

'Not everything but most things. And she didn't tell me so much as I guessed it. She'll tell me more the next time. She will behave properly now about coming in to see me; I told her she ought to.'

'I am glad of that,' I said. 'Keep her with you as much as possible.'

'I don't follow you much,' Mrs. Nettlepoint replied, 'but so far as I do I don't think your remarks are in very good taste.'

'I'm too excited, I lose my head, cold-blooded as you think me. Doesn't she like Mr. Porterfield?'

'Yes, that's the worst of it.'

'The worst of it?'

'He's so good—there's no fault to be found with him. Otherwise she would have thrown it all up. It has dragged on since she was eighteen: she became engaged to him before he went abroad to study. It was one of those childish muddles which parents in America might prevent so much more than they do. The thing is to insist on one's daughter's waiting, on the engagement's being long; and then after you have got that started to take it on every occasion as little seriously as possible—to make it die out. You can easily tire it out. However, Mr. Porterfield has taken it seriously for some years. He has done his part to keep it alive. She says he adores her.'

'His part? Surely his part would have been to marry her by this time.'

'He has absolutely no money.'

'He ought to have got some, in seven years.'

'So I think she thinks. There are some sorts of poverty that are contemptible. But he has a little more now. That's why he won't wait any longer. His mother has come out, she has something—a little—and she is able to help him. She will live with them and bear some of the expenses, and after her death the son will have what there is.'

'How old is she?' I asked, cynically.

'I haven't the least idea. But it doesn't sound very inspiring. He has not been to America since he first went out.'

'That's an odd way of adoring her.'

'I made that objection mentally, but I didn't express it to her. She met it indeed a little by telling me that he had had other chances to marry.'

'That surprises me,' I remarked. 'And did she say that *she* had had?'

'No, and that's one of the things I thought nice in her; for she must have had. She didn't try to make out that he had spoiled her life. She has three other sisters and there is very little money at home. She has tried to make money; she has written little things and painted little things, but her talent is apparently not in that direction. Her father has had a long illness and has lost his place—he was in receipt of a salary in connection with some waterworks—and one of her sisters has lately become a widow, with children and without means. And so as in fact she never has married any one else, whatever opportunities she may have encountered, she appears to have just made up her mind to go out to Mr. Porterfield as the least of her evils. But it isn't very amusing.'

'That only makes it the more honourable. She will go through with it, whatever it costs, rather than disappoint him after he has waited so long. It is true,' I continued, 'that when a woman acts from a sense of honour——'

'Well, when she does?' said Mrs. Nettlepoint, for I hesitated perceptibly.

'It is so extravagant a course that some one has to pay for it.'

'You are very impertinent. We all have to pay for each other, all the while; and for each other's virtues as well as vices.'

'That's precisely why I shall be sorry for Mr. Porterfield when she steps off the ship with her little bill. I mean with her teeth clenched.'

'Her teeth are not in the least clenched. She is in perfect good-humour.'

'Well, we must try and keep her so,' I said. 'You must take care that Jasper neglects nothing.'

I know not what reflection this innocent pleasantry of mine provoked on the good lady's part; the upshot of them at all events was to make her say—'Well, I never asked her to come; I'm very glad of that. It is all their own doing.'

'Their own—you mean Jasper's and hers?'

'No indeed. I mean her mother's and Mrs. Allen's; the girl's too of course. They put themselves upon us.'

'Oh yes, I can testify to that. Therefore I'm glad too. We should have missed it, I think.'

'How seriously you take it!' Mrs. Nettlepoint exclaimed.

'Ah, wait a few days!' I replied, getting up to leave her.

III

The *Patagonia* was slow, but she was spacious and comfortable, and there was a kind of motherly decency in her long, nursing rock and her rustling, old-fashioned gait. It was as if she wished not to present herself in port with the splashed eagerness of a young creature. We were not numerous enough to squeeze each other and yet we were not too few to entertain—with that familiarity and relief which figures and objects acquire on the great bare field of the ocean, beneath the great bright glass of the sky. I had never liked the sea so much before, indeed I had never liked it at all; but now I had a revelation of how, in a midsummer mood, it could please. It was darkly and magnificently blue and imperturbably quiet —save for the great regular swell of its heart-beats, the pulse of its life, and there grew to be something so agreeable in the sense of floating there in infinite isolation and leisure that it was a positive satisfaction the *Patagonia* was not a racer. One had never thought of the sea as the great place of safety, but now it came over one that there is no place so safe from the land. When it does not give you trouble it takes it away— takes away letters and telegrams and newspapers and visits and duties and efforts, all the complications, all the superfluities and superstitions that we have stuffed into our terrene life. The simple absence of the post, when the particular conditions enable you to enjoy the great fact by which it is produced, becomes in itself a kind of bliss, and the clean stage of the deck shows you a play that amuses, the personal drama of the voyage, the movement and interaction, in the strong sea-light, of figures that end by representing something—something moreover of which the interest is never, even in its keenness, too great to suffer you to go to sleep. I, at any rate, dozed a great deal, lying on my rug with a French novel, and when I opened my eyes I generally saw Jasper Nettlepoint passing with his mother's *protégée* on his arm. Somehow at these moments, between sleeping and waking, I had an inconsequent sense that they were a part of the French novel. Perhaps this was because I had fallen into the trick, at the start, of regarding Grace Mavis almost as a married woman, which, as every one knows, is the necessary status of the heroine of such a work. Every revolution of our engine at any rate would contribute to the effect of making her one.

In the saloon, at meals, my neighbour on the right was a certain little Mrs. Peck, a very short and very round person whose head was enveloped in a 'cloud' (a cloud of dirty white wool) and who promptly let me know that she was going to Europe for the education of her children. I had already perceived (an hour after we left the dock) that some energetic step was required in their interest, but as we were not in Europe yet the business could not be said to have begun. The four little Pecks, in the enjoyment of untrammelled leisure, swarmed about the ship as if they had been pirates boarding her, and their mother was as powerless to check their license as if she had been gagged and stowed away in the hold. They were especially to be trusted to run between the legs of the stewards when these attendants arrived with bowls of soup for the languid ladies. Their mother was too busy recounting to her fellow-passengers how many years Miss Mavis had been engaged. In the blank of a marine existence things that are nobody's business very soon become everybody's, and this was just one of those facts that are propagated with a mysterious and ridiculous rapidity. The whisper that carries them is very small, in the great scale of things, of air and space and progress, but it is also very safe, for there is no compression, no sounding-board, to make speakers responsible. And then repetition at sea is somehow not repetition; monotony is in the air, the mind is flat and everything recurs—the bells, the meals, the stewards' faces, the romp of children, the walk, the clothes, the very shoes and buttons of passengers taking their exercise. These things grow at last so insipid that, in comparison, revelations as to the personal history of one's companions have a taste, even when one cares little about the people.

Jasper Nettlepoint sat on my left hand when he was not upstairs seeing that Miss Mavis had her repast comfortably on deck. His mother's place would have been next mine had she shown herself, and then that of the young lady under her care. The two ladies, in other words, would have been between us, Jasper marking the limit of the party on that side. Miss Mavis was present at luncheon the first day, but dinner passed without her coming in, and when it was half over Jasper remarked that he would go up and look after her.

'Isn't that young lady coming—the one who was here to lunch?' Mrs. Peck asked of me as he left the saloon.

'Apparently not. My friend tells me she doesn't like the saloon.'

'You don't mean to say she's sick, do you?'

'Oh no, not in this weather. But she likes to be above.'

'And is that gentleman gone up to her?'

'Yes, she's under his mother's care.'

'And is his mother up there, too?' asked Mrs. Peck, whose processes were homely and direct.

'No, she remains in her cabin. People have different tastes. Perhaps that's one reason why Miss Mavis doesn't come to table,' I added—'her chaperon not being able to accompany her.'

'Her chaperon?'

'Mrs. Nettlepoint—the lady under whose protection she is.'

'Protection?' Mrs. Peck stared at me a moment, moving some valued morsel in her mouth; then she exclaimed, familiarly, 'Pshaw!' I was struck with this and I was on the point of asking her what she meant by it when she continued: 'Are we not going to see Mrs. Nettlepoint?'

'I am afraid not. She vows that she won't stir from her sofa.'

'Pshaw!' said Mrs. Peck again. 'That's quite a disappointment.'

'Do you know her then?'

'No, but I know all about her.' Then my companion added—'You don't meant to say she's any relation?'

'Do you mean to me?'

'No, to Grace Mavis.'

'None at all. They are very new friends, as I happen to know. Then you are acquainted with our young lady?' I had not noticed that any recognition passed between them at luncheon.

'Is she yours too?' asked Mrs. Peck, smiling at me.

'Ah, when people are in the same boat—literally—they belong a little to each other.'

'That's so,' said Mrs. Peck. 'I don't know Miss Mavis but I know all about her—I live opposite to her on Merrimac Avenue. I don't know whether you know that part.'

'Oh yes—it's very beautiful.'

The consequence of this remark was another 'Pshaw!' But Mrs. Peck went on—'When you've lived opposite to people like that for a long time you feel as if you were acquainted. But she didn't take it up to-day; she didn't speak to me. She knows who I am as well as she knows her own mother.'

'You had better speak to her first—she's shy,' I remarked.

'Shy? Why she's nearly thirty years old. I suppose you know where she's going.'

'Oh yes—we all take an interest in that.'

'That young man, I suppose, particularly.'

'That young man?'

'The handsome one, who sits there. Didn't you tell me he is Mrs. Nettlepoint's son?'

'Oh yes; he acts as her deputy. No doubt he does all he can to carry out her function.'

Mrs. Peck was silent a moment. I had spoken jocosely, but she received my pleasantry with a serious face. 'Well, she might let him eat his dinner in peace!' she presently exclaimed.

'Oh, he'll come back!' I said, glancing at his place. The repast continued and when it was finished I screwed my chair round to leave the table. Mrs. Peck performed the same movement and we quitted the saloon together. Outside of it was a kind of vestibule, with several seats, from which you could descend to the lower cabins or mount to the promenade-deck. Mrs. Peck appeared to hesitate as to her course and then solved the problem by going neither way. She dropped upon one of the benches and looked up at me.

'I thought you said he would come back.'

'Young Nettlepoint? I see he didn't. Miss Mavis then has given him half of her dinner.'

'It's very kind of her! She has been engaged for ages.'

'Yes, but that will soon be over.'

'So I suppose—as quick as we land. Every one knows it on Merrimac Avenue. Every one there takes a great interest in it.'

'Ah, of course, a girl like that: she has many friends.'

'I mean even people who don't know her.'

'I see,' I went on: 'she is so handsome that she attracts attention, people enter into her affairs.'

'She *used* to be pretty, but I can't say I think she's anything remarkable to-day. Anyhow, if she attracts attention she ought to be all the more careful what she does. You had better tell her that.'

'Oh, it's none of my business!' I replied, leaving Mrs. Peck and going above. The exclamation, I confess, was not perfectly in accordance with my feeling, or rather my feeling was not perfectly in harmony with the exclamation. The very first thing I did on reaching the deck was to notice that Miss Mavis was pacing it on Jasper Nettlepoint's arm and that whatever beauty she might have lost, according to Mrs. Peck's insinuation, she still kept enough to make one's eyes follow her. She had put on a sort of crimson hood, which was very becoming to her and which she wore for the rest of the voyage. She walked very well, with long steps, and I remember that at this moment the ocean had a gentle evening swell which made the great ship dip slowly, rhythmically, giving a movement that was graceful to graceful pedestrians and a more awkward one to the awkward. It was the loveliest hour of a fine day, the clear early evening, with the glow of the sunset in the air and a purple colour in the sea. I always thought that the waters ploughed by the Homeric heroes must have looked like that. I perceived on that particular occasion moreover that Grace Mavis would for the rest of the voyage be the most visible thing on the ship; the figure that would count most in the composition of groups. She couldn't help it, poor girl; nature had made her conspicuous—important, as the painters say. She paid for it by the exposure it brought with it—the danger that people would, as I had said to Mrs. Peck, enter into her affairs.

Jasper Nettlepoint went down at certain times to see his mother, and I watched for one of these occasions (on the third day out) and took advantage of it to go and sit by Miss Mavis. She wore a blue veil drawn tightly over her face, so that if the smile with which she greeted me was dim I could account for it partly by that.

'Well, we are getting on—we are getting on,' I said, cheerfully, looking at the friendly, twinkling sea.

'Are we going very fast?'

'Not fast, but steadily. *Ohne Hast, ohne Rast*—do you know German?'

'Well, I've studied it—some.'

'It will be useful to you over there when you travel.'

'Well yes, if we do. But I don't suppose we shall much. Mr. Nettlepoint says we ought,' my interlocutress added in a moment.

'Ah, of course *he* thinks so. He has been all over the world.'

'Yes, he has described some of the places. That's what I should like. I didn't know I should like it so much.'

'Like what so much?'

'Going on this way. I could go on for ever, for ever and ever.'

'Ah, you know it's not always like this,' I rejoined.

'Well, it's better than Boston.'

'It isn't so good as Paris,' I said, smiling.

'Oh, I know all about Paris. There is no freshness in that. I feel as if I had been there.'

'You mean you have heard so much about it?'

'Oh yes, nothing else for ten years.'

I had come to talk with Miss Mavis because she was attractive, but I had been rather conscious of the absence of a good topic, not feeling at liberty to revert to Mr. Porterfield. She had not encouraged me, when I spoke to her as we were leaving Boston, to go on with the history of my acquaintance with this gentleman; and yet now, unexpectedly, she appeared to imply (it was doubtless one of the disparities mentioned by Mrs. Nettlepoint) that he might be glanced at without indelicacy.

'I see, you mean by letters,' I remarked.

'I shan't live in a good part. I know enough to know that,' she went on.

'Dear young lady, there are no bad parts,' I answered, reassuringly.

'Why, Mr. Nettlepoint says it's horrid.'

'It's horrid?'

'Up there in the Batignolles. It's worse than Merrimac Avenue.'

'Worse—in what way?'

'Why, even less where the nice people live.'

'He oughtn't to say that,' I returned. 'Don't you call Mr. Porterfield a nice person?' I ventured to subjoin.

'Oh, it doesn't make any difference.' She rested her eyes on me a moment through her veil, the texture of which gave them a suffused prettiness. 'Do you know him very well?' she asked.

'Mr. Porterfield?'

'No, Mr. Nettlepoint.'

'Ah, very little. He's a good deal younger than I.'

She was silent a moment; after which she said: 'He's younger than me, too.' I know not what drollery there was in this but it was unexpected and it made me laugh. Neither do I know whether Miss Mavis took offence at my laughter, though I remember thinking at the moment with compunction that it had brought a certain colour to her cheek. At all events she got up, gathering her shawl and her books into her arm. 'I'm going down—I'm tired.'

'Tired of me, I'm afraid.'

'No, not yet.'

'I'm like you,' I pursued. 'I should like it to go on and on.'

She had begun to walk along the deck to the companion-way and I went with her. 'Oh, no, I shouldn't, after all!'

I had taken her shawl from her to carry it, but at the top of the steps that led down to the cabins I had to give it back. 'Your mother would be glad if she could know,' I observed as we parted.

'If she could know?'

'How well you are getting on. And that good Mrs. Allen.'

'Oh, mother, mother! She made me come, she pushed me off.' And almost as if not to say more she went quickly below.

I paid Mrs. Nettlepoint a morning visit after luncheon and another in the evening, before she 'turned in.' That same day, in the evening, she said to me suddenly, 'Do you know what I have done? I have asked Jasper.'

'Asked him what?'

'Why, if *she* asked him, you know.'

'I don't understand.'

'You do perfectly. If that girl really asked him—on the balcony—to sail with us.'

'My dear friend, do you suppose that if she did he would tell you?'

'That's just what he says. But he says she didn't.'

'And do you consider the statement valuable?' I asked, laughing out. 'You had better ask Miss Gracie herself.'

Mrs. Nettlepoint stared. 'I couldn't do that.'

'Incomparable friend, I am only joking. What does it signify now?'

'I thought you thought everything signified. You were so full of signification!'

'Yes, but we are farther out now, and somehow in mid-ocean everything becomes absolute.'

'What else *can* he do with decency?' Mrs. Nettlepoint went on. 'If, as my son, he were never to speak to her it would be very rude and you would think that stranger still. Then *you* would do what he does, and where would be the difference?'

'How do you know what he does? I haven't mentioned him for twenty-four hours.'

'Why, she told me herself: she came in this afternoon.'

'What an odd thing to tell you!' I exclaimed.

'Not as she says it. She says he's full of attention, perfectly devoted—looks after her all the while. She seems to want me to know it, so that I may commend him for it.'

'That's charming; it shows her good conscience.'

'Yes, or her great cleverness.'

Something in the tone in which Mrs. Nettlepoint said this caused me to exclaim in real surprise, 'Why, what do you suppose she has in her mind?'

'To get hold of him, to make him go so far that he can't retreat, to marry him, perhaps.'

'To marry him? And what will she do with Mr. Porterfield?'

'She'll ask me just to explain to him—or perhaps you.'

'Yes, as an old friend!' I replied, laughing. But I asked more seriously, 'Do you see Jasper caught like that?'

'Well, he's only a boy—he's younger at least than she.'

'Precisely; she regards him as a child.'

'As a child?'

'She remarked to me herself to-day that he is so much younger.'

Mrs. Nettlepoint stared. 'Does she talk of it with you? That shows she has a plan, that she has thought it over!'

I have sufficiently betrayed that I deemed Grace Mavis a singular girl, but I was far from judging her capable of laying a trap for our young companion. Moreover my reading of Jasper was not in the least that he was catchable—could be made to do a thing if he didn't want to do it. Of course it was not impossible that he might be inclined, that he might take it (or already have taken it) into his head to marry Miss Mavis; but to believe this I should require still more proof than his always being with her. He wanted at most to marry her for the voyage. 'If you have questioned him perhaps you have tried to make him feel responsible,' I said to his mother.

'A little, but it's very difficult. Interference makes him perverse. One has to go gently. Besides, it's too absurd—think of her age. If she can't take care of herself!' cried Mrs. Nettlepoint.

'Yes, let us keep thinking of her age, though it's not so prodigious. And if things get very bad you have one resource left,' I added.

'What is that?'

'You can go upstairs.'

'Ah, never, never! If it takes that to save her she must be lost. Besides, what good would it do? If I were to go up she could come down here.'

'Yes, but you could keep Jasper with you.'

'Could I?' Mrs. Nettlepoint demanded, in the manner of a woman who knew her son.

In the saloon the next day, after dinner, over the red cloth of the tables, beneath the swinging lamps and the racks of tumblers, decanters and wine-glasses, we sat down to whist, Mrs. Peck, among others, taking a hand in the game. She played very badly and talked too much, and when the rubber was over assuaged her discomfiture (though not mine—we had been partners) with a Welsh rabbit and a tumbler of something hot. We had done with the cards, but while she waited for this refreshment she sat with her elbows on the table shuffling a pack.

'She hasn't spoken to me yet—she won't do it,' she remarked in a moment.

'Is it possible there is any one on the ship who hasn't spoken to you?'

'Not that girl—she knows too well!' Mrs. Peck looked round our little circle with a smile of intelligence—she had familiar, communicative eyes. Several of our company had assembled, according to the wont, the last thing in the evening, of those who are cheerful at sea, for the consumption of grilled sardines and devilled bones.

'What then does she know?'

'Oh, she knows that I know.'

'Well, we know what Mrs. Peck knows,' one of the ladies of the group observed to me, with an air of privilege.

'Well, you wouldn't know if I hadn't told you—from the way she acts,' said Mrs. Peck, with a small laugh.

'She is going out to a gentleman who lives over there—he's waiting there to marry her,' the other lady went on, in the tone of authentic information. I remember that her name was Mrs. Gotch and that her mouth looked always as if she were whistling.

'Oh, he knows—I've told him,' said Mrs. Peck.

'Well, I presume every one knows,' Mrs. Gotch reflected.

'Dear madam, is it every one's business?' I asked.

'Why, don't you think it's a peculiar way to act?' Mrs. Gotch was evidently surprised at my little protest.

'Why, it's right there—straight in front of you, like a play at the theatre—as if you had paid to see it,' said Mrs. Peck. 'If you don't call it public——!'

'Aren't you mixing things up? What do you call public?'

'Why, the way they go on. They are up there now.'

'They cuddle up there half the night,' said Mrs. Gotch. 'I don't know when they come down. Any hour you like—when all the lights are out they are up there still.'

'Oh, you can't tire them out. They don't want relief—like the watch!' laughed one of the gentlemen.

'Well, if they enjoy each other's society what's the harm?' another asked. 'They'd do just the same on land.'

'They wouldn't do it on the public streets, I suppose,' said Mrs. Peck. 'And they wouldn't do it if Mr. Porterfield was round!'

'Isn't that just where your confusion comes in?' I inquired. 'It's public enough that Miss Mavis and Mr. Nettlepoint are always together, but it isn't in the least public that she is going to be married.'

'Why, how can you say—when the very sailors know it! The captain knows it and all the officers know it; they see them there—especially at night, when they're sailing the ship.'

'I thought there was some rule——' said Mrs. Gotch.

'Well, there is—that you've got to behave yourself,' Mrs. Peck rejoined. 'So the captain told me—he said they have some rule. He said they have to have, when people are too demonstrative.'

'Too demonstrative?'

'When they attract so much attention.'

'Ah, it's we who attract the attention—by talking about what doesn't concern us and about what we really don't know,' I ventured to declare.

'She said the captain said he would tell on her as soon as we arrive,' Mrs. Gotch interposed.

'*She* said——?' I repeated, bewildered.

'Well, he did say so, that he would think it his duty to inform Mr. Porterfield, when he comes on to meet her—if they keep it up in the same way,' said Mrs. Peck.

'Oh, they'll keep it up, don't you fear!' one of the gentlemen exclaimed.

'Dear madam, the captain is laughing at you.'

'No, he ain't—he's right down scandalised. He says he regards us all as a real family and wants the family to be properly behaved.' I could see Mrs. Peck was irritated by my controversial tone: she challenged me with considerable spirit. 'How can you say I don't know it when all the street knows it and has known it for years—for years and years?' She spoke as if the girl had been engaged at least for twenty. 'What is she going out for, if not to marry him?'

'Perhaps she is going to see how he looks,' suggested one of the gentlemen.

'He'd look queer—if he knew.'

'Well, I guess he'll know,' said Mrs. Gotch.

'She'd tell him herself—she wouldn't be afraid,' the gentleman went on.

'Well, she might as well kill him. He'll jump overboard.'

'Jump overboard?' cried Mrs. Gotch, as if she hoped then that Mr. Porterfield would be told.

'He has just been waiting for this—for years,' said Mrs. Peck.

'Do you happen to know him?' I inquired.

Mrs. Peck hesitated a moment. 'No, but I know a lady who does. Are you going up?'

I had risen from my place—I had not ordered supper. 'I'm going to take a turn before going to bed.'

'Well then, you'll see!'

Outside the saloon I hesitated, for Mrs. Peck's admonition made me feel for a moment that if I ascended to the deck I should have entered in a manner into her little conspiracy. But the night was so warm and splendid that I had been intending to smoke a cigar in the air before going below, and I did not see why I should deprive myself of this pleasure in order to seem not to mind Mrs. Peck. I went up and saw a few figures sitting or moving about in the darkness. The ocean looked black and small, as it is apt to do at night, and the long mass of the ship, with its vague dim wings, seemed to take up a great part of it. There were more stars than one saw on land and the heavens struck one more than ever as larger than the earth. Grace Mavis and her companion were not, so far as I perceived at first, among the few passengers who were lingering late, and I was glad, because I hated to hear her talked about in the manner of the gossips I had left at supper. I wished there had been some way to prevent it, but I could think of no way but to recommend her privately to change her habits. That would be a very delicate business, and perhaps it would be better to begin with Jasper, though that would be delicate too. At any rate one might let him know, in a friendly spirit, to how much remark he exposed the young lady—leaving this revelation to work its way upon him. Unfortunately I could not altogether believe that the pair were unconscious of the observation and the opinion of the passengers. They were not a boy and a girl; they had a certain social perspective in their eye. I was not very clear as to the details of that behaviour which had made them (according to the version of my good friends in the saloon) a scandal to the ship, for though I looked at them a good deal I evidently had not looked at them so continuously and so hungrily as Mrs. Peck. Nevertheless the probability was that they knew what was thought of them—what naturally would be—and simply didn't care. That made Miss Mavis out rather cynical and even a little immodest; and yet, somehow, if she had such qualities I did not dislike her for them. I don't know what strange, secret excuses I found for her. I presently indeed encountered a need for them on the spot, for just as I was on the point of going below again, after several restless turns and (within the limit where smoking was allowed) as many puffs at a cigar as I cared for, I became aware that a couple of figures were seated behind one of the lifeboats that rested on the deck. They were so placed as to be visible only to a person going close to the rail and peering a little sidewise. I don't think I peered, but as I stood a moment beside the rail my eye was attracted by a dusky object which protruded beyond the boat and which, as I saw at a second glance, was the tail of a lady's dress. I bent forward an instant, but even then I saw very little more; that scarcely mattered, however, for I took for granted on the spot that the persons concealed in so snug a corner were Jasper Nettlepoint and Mr. Porterfield's intended. Concealed was the word, and I thought it a real pity; there was bad taste in it. I immediately turned away and the next moment I found myself face to face with the captain of the ship. I had already had some conversation with him (he had been so good as to invite me, as he had invited Mrs. Nettlepoint and her son and the young lady travelling with them, and also Mrs. Peck, to sit at his table) and had observed with pleasure that he had the art, not universal on the Atlantic liners, of mingling urbanity with seamanship.

'They don't waste much time—your friends in there,' he said, nodding in the direction in which he had seen me looking.

'Ah well, they haven't much to lose.'

'That's what I mean. I'm told *she* hasn't.'

I wanted to say something exculpatory but I scarcely knew what note to strike. I could only look vaguely about me at the starry darkness and the sea that seemed to sleep. 'Well, with these splendid nights, this perfection of weather, people are beguiled into late hours.'

'Yes. We want a nice little blow,' the captain said.

'A nice little blow?'

'That would clear the decks!'

The captain was rather dry and he went about his business. He had made me uneasy and instead of going below I walked a few steps more. The other walkers dropped off pair by pair (they were all men) till at last I was alone. Then, after a little, I quitted the field. Jasper and his companion were still behind their lifeboat. Personally I greatly preferred good weather, but as I went down I found myself vaguely wishing, in the interest of I scarcely knew what, unless of decorum, that we might have half a gale.

Miss Mavis turned out, in sea-phrase, early; for the next morning I saw her come up only a little while after I had finished my breakfast, a ceremony over which I contrived not to dawdle. She was alone and Jasper Nettlepoint, by a rare accident, was not on deck to help her. I went to meet her (she was encumbered as usual with her shawl, her sun-umbrella and a book) and laid my hands on her chair, placing it near the stern of the ship, where she liked best to be. But I proposed to her to walk a little before she sat down and she took my arm after I had put her accessories into the chair. The deck was clear at that hour and the morning light was gay; one got a sort of exhilarated impression of fair conditions and an absence of hindrance. I forget what we spoke of first, but it was because I felt these things pleasantly, and not to torment my companion nor to test her, that I could not help exclaiming cheerfully, after a moment, as I have mentioned having done the first day, 'Well, we are getting on, we are getting on!'

'Oh yes, I count every hour.'

'The last days always go quicker,' I said, 'and the last hours——'

'Well, the last hours?' she asked; for I had instinctively checked myself.

'Oh, one is so glad then that it is almost the same as if one had arrived. But we ought to be grateful when the elements have been so kind to us,' I added. 'I hope you will have enjoyed the voyage.'

She hesitated a moment, then she said, 'Yes, much more than I expected.'

'Did you think it would be very bad?'

'Horrible, horrible!'

The tone of these words was strange but I had not much time to reflect upon it, for turning round at that moment I saw Jasper Nettlepoint come towards us. He was separated from us by the expanse of the white deck and I could not help looking at him from head to foot as he drew nearer. I know not what rendered me on this occasion particularly sensitive to the impression, but it seemed to me that I saw him as I had never seen him before—saw him inside and out, in the intense sea-light, in his personal, his moral totality. It was a quick, vivid revelation; if it only lasted a moment it had a simplifying, certifying effect. He was intrinsically a pleasing apparition, with his handsome young face and a certain absence of compromise in his personal arrangements which, more than any one I have ever seen, he managed to exhibit on shipboard. He had none of the appearance of wearing out old clothes that usually prevails there, but dressed straight, as I heard some one say. This gave him a practical, successful air, as of a young man who would come best out of any predicament. I expected to feel my companion's hand loosen itself on my arm, as indication that now she must go to him, and was almost surprised she did not drop me. We stopped as we met and Jasper bade us a friendly good-morning. Of course the remark was not slow to be made that we had another lovely day, which led him to exclaim, in the manner of one to whom criticism came easily, 'Yes, but with this sort of thing consider what one of the others would do!'

'One of the other ships?'

'We should be there now, or at any rate to-morrow.'

'Well then, I'm glad it isn't one of the others,' I said, smiling at the young lady on my arm. My remark offered her a chance to say something appreciative and gave him one even more; but neither Jasper nor Grace Mavis took advantage of the opportunity. What they did do, I perceived, was to look at each other for an instant; after which Miss Mavis turned her eyes silently to the sea. She made no movement and uttered no word, contriving to give me the sense that she had all at once become perfectly passive, that she somehow declined responsibility. We remained standing there with Jasper in front of us, and if the touch of her arm did not suggest that I should give her up, neither did it intimate that we had better pass on. I had no idea of giving her up, albeit one of the things that I seemed to discover just then in Jasper's physiognomy was an imperturbable implication that she was his property. His eye met mine for a moment, and it was exactly as if he had said to me, 'I know what you think, but I don't care a rap.' What I really thought was that he was selfish beyond the limits: that was the substance of my little revelation. Youth is almost always selfish, just as it is almost always conceited, and, after all, when it is combined with health and good parts, good looks and good spirits, it has a right to be, and I easily forgive it if it be really youth. Still it is a question of degree, and what stuck out of Jasper Nettlepoint (if one felt that sort of thing) was that his egotism had a hardness, his love of his own way an avidity. These elements were jaunty and prosperous, they were accustomed to triumph. He was fond, very fond, of women; they were necessary to him and that was in his type; but he was not in the least in love with Grace Mavis. Among the reflections I quickly made this was the one that was most to the point. There was a degree of awkwardness, after a minute, in the way we were planted there, though the apprehension of it was doubtless not in the least with him.

'How is your mother this morning?' I asked.

'You had better go down and see.'

'Not till Miss Mavis is tired of me.'

She said nothing to this and I made her walk again. For some minutes she remained silent; then, rather unexpectedly, she began: 'I've seen you talking to that lady who sits at our table—the one who has so many children.'

'Mrs. Peck? Oh yes, I have talked with her.'

'Do you know her very well?'

'Only as one knows people at sea. An acquaintance makes itself. It doesn't mean very much.'

'She doesn't speak to me—she might if she wanted.'

'That's just what she says of you—that you might speak to her.'

'Oh, if she's waiting for that——!' said my companion, with a laugh. Then she added—'She lives in our street, nearly opposite.'

'Precisely. That's the reason why she thinks you might speak; she has seen you so often and seems to know so much about you.'

'What does she know about me?'

'Ah, you must ask her—I can't tell you!'

'I don't care what she knows,' said my young lady. After a moment she went on—'She must have seen that I'm not very sociable.' And then—'What are you laughing at?'

My laughter was for an instant irrepressible—there was something so droll in the way she had said that.

'Well, you are not sociable and yet you are. Mrs. Peck is, at any rate, and thought that ought to make it easy for you to enter into conversation with her.'

'Oh, I don't care for her conversation—I know what it amounts to.' I made no rejoinder—I scarcely knew what rejoinder to make—and the girl went on, 'I know what she thinks and I know what she says.' Still I was silent, but the next moment I saw that my delicacy had been wasted, for Miss Mavis asked, 'Does she make out that she knows Mr. Porterfield?'

'No, she only says that she knows a lady who knows him.'

'Yes, I know—Mrs. Jeremie. Mrs. Jeremie's an idiot!' I was not in a position to controvert this, and presently my young lady said she would sit down. I left her in her chair—I saw that she preferred it—and wandered to a distance. A few minutes later I met Jasper again, and he stopped of his own accord and said to me—

'We shall be in about six in the evening, on the eleventh day—they promise it.'

'If nothing happens, of course.'

'Well, what's going to happen?'

'That's just what I'm wondering!' And I turned away and went below with the foolish but innocent satisfaction of thinking that I had mystified him.

IV

'I don't know what to do, and you must help me,' Mrs. Nettlepoint said to me that evening, as soon as I went in to see her.

'I'll do what I can—but what's the matter?'

'She has been crying here and going on—she has quite upset me.'

'Crying? She doesn't look like that.'

'Exactly, and that's what startled me. She came in to see me this afternoon, as she has done before, and we talked about the weather and the run of the ship and the manners of the stewardess and little commonplaces like that, and then suddenly, in the midst of it, as she sat there, *à propos* of nothing, she burst into tears. I asked her what ailed her and tried to comfort her, but she didn't explain; she only said it was nothing, the effect of the sea, of leaving home. I asked her if it had anything to do with her prospects, with her marriage; whether she found as that drew near that her heart was not in it; I told her that she mustn't be nervous, that I could enter into that—in short I said what I could. All that she replied was that she *was* nervous, very nervous, but that it was already over; and then she jumped up and kissed me and went away. Does she look as if she had been crying?' Mrs. Nettlepoint asked.

'How can I tell, when she never quits that horrid veil? It's as if she were ashamed to show her face.'

'She's keeping it for Liverpool. But I don't like such incidents,' said Mrs. Nettlepoint. 'I shall go upstairs.'

'And is that where you want me to help you?'

'Oh, your arm and that sort of thing, yes. But something more. I feel as if something were going to happen.'

'That's exactly what I said to Jasper this morning.'

'And what did he say?'

'He only looked innocent, as if he thought I meant a fog or a storm.'

'Heaven forbid—it isn't that! I shall never be good-natured again,' Mrs. Nettlepoint went on; 'never have a girl put upon me that way. You always pay for it, there are always tiresome complications. What I am afraid of is after we get there. She'll throw up her engagement; there will be dreadful scenes; I shall be mixed up with them and have to look after her and keep her with me. I shall have to stay there with her till she can be sent back, or even take her up to London. *Voyez-vous ça?*'

I listened respectfully to this and then I said: 'You are afraid of your son.'

'Afraid of him?'

'There are things you might say to him—and with your manner; because you have one when you choose.'

'Very likely, but what is my manner to his? Besides, I have said everything to him. That is I have said the great thing, that he is making her immensely talked about.'

'And of course in answer to that he has asked you how you know, and you have told him I have told you.'

'I had to; and he says it's none of your business.'

'I wish he would say that to my face.'

'He'll do so perfectly, if you give him a chance. That's where you can help me. Quarrel with him—he's rather good at a quarrel, and that will divert him and draw him off.'

'Then I'm ready to discuss the matter with him for the rest of the voyage.'

'Very well; I count on you. But he'll ask you, as he asks me, what the deuce you want him to do.'

'To go to bed,' I replied, laughing.

'Oh, it isn't a joke.'

'That's exactly what I told you at first.'

'Yes, but don't exult; I hate people who exult. Jasper wants to know why he should mind her being talked about if she doesn't mind it herself.'

'I'll tell him why,' I replied; and Mrs. Nettlepoint said she should be exceedingly obliged to me and repeated that she would come upstairs.

I looked for Jasper above that same evening, but circumstances did not favour my quest. I found him—that is I discovered that he was again ensconced behind the lifeboat with Miss Mavis; but there was a needless violence in breaking into their communion, and I put off our interview till the next day. Then I took the first opportunity, at breakfast, to make sure of it. He was in the saloon when I went in and was preparing to leave the table; but I stopped him and asked if he would give me a quarter of an hour on deck a little later—there was something particular I wanted to say to him. He said, 'Oh yes, if you like,' with just a visible surprise, but no look of an uncomfortable consciousness. When I had finished my breakfast I found him smoking on the forward-deck and I immediately began: 'I am going to say something that you won't at all like; to ask you a question that you will think impertinent.'

'Impertinent? that's bad.'

'I am a good deal older than you and I am a friend—of many years—of your mother. There's nothing I like less than to be meddlesome, but I think these things give me a certain right—a sort of privilege. For the rest, my inquiry will speak for itself.'

'Why so many preliminaries?' the young man asked, smiling.

We looked into each other's eyes a moment. What indeed was his mother's manner—her best manner—compared with his? 'Are you prepared to be responsible?'

'To you?'

'Dear no—to the young lady herself. I am speaking of course of Miss Mavis.'

'Ah yes, my mother tells me you have her greatly on your mind.'

'So has your mother herself—now.'

'She is so good as to say so—to oblige you.'

'She would oblige me a great deal more by reassuring me. I am aware that you know I have told her that Miss Mavis is greatly talked about.'

'Yes, but what on earth does it matter?'

'It matters as a sign.'

'A sign of what?'

'That she is in a false position.'

Jasper puffed his cigar, with his eyes on the horizon. 'I don't know whether it's *your* business, what you are attempting to discuss; but it really appears to me it is none of mine. What have I to do with the tattle with which a pack of old women console themselves for not being sea-sick?'

'Do you call it tattle that Miss Mavis is in love with you?'

'Drivelling.'

'Then you are very ungrateful. The tattle of a pack of old women has this importance, that she suspects or knows that it exists, and that nice girls are for the most part very sensitive to that sort of thing. To be prepared not to heed it in this case she must have a reason, and the reason must be the one I have taken the liberty to call your attention to.'

'In love with me in six days, just like that?' said Jasper, smoking.

'There is no accounting for tastes, and six days at sea are equivalent to sixty on land. I don't want to make you too proud. Of course if you recognise your responsibility it's all right and I have nothing to say.'

'I don't see what you mean,' Jasper went on.

'Surely you ought to have thought of that by this time. She's engaged to be married and the gentleman she is engaged to is to meet her at Liverpool. The whole ship knows it (I didn't tell them!) and the whole ship is watching her. It's impertinent if you like, just as I am, but we make a little world here together and we can't blink its conditions. What I ask you is whether you are prepared to allow her to give up the gentleman I have just mentioned for your sake.'

'For my sake?'

'To marry her if she breaks with him.'

Jasper turned his eyes from the horizon to my own, and I found a strange expression in them. 'Has Miss Mavis commissioned you to make this inquiry?'

'Never in the world.'

'Well then, I don't understand it.'

'It isn't from another I make it. Let it come from your-self—*to* yourself.'

'Lord, you must think I lead myself a life! That's a question the young lady may put to me any moment that it pleases her.'

'Let me then express the hope that she will. But what will you answer?'

'My dear sir, it seems to me that in spite of all the titles you have enumerated you have no reason to expect I will tell you.' He turned away and I exclaimed, sincerely, 'Poor girl!' At this he faced me again and, looking at me from head to foot, demanded: 'What is it you want me to do?'

'I told your mother that you ought to go to bed.'

'You had better do that yourself!'

This time he walked off, and I reflected rather dolefully that the only clear result of my experiment would probably have been to make it vivid to him that she was in love with him. Mrs. Nettlepoint came up as she had announced, but the day was half over: it was nearly three o'clock. She was accompanied by her son, who established her on deck, arranged her chair and her shawls, saw that she was protected from sun and wind, and for an hour was very properly attentive. While this went on Grace Mavis was not visible, nor did she reappear during the whole afternoon. I had not observed that she had as yet been absent from the deck for so long a period. Jasper went away, but he came back at intervals to see how his mother got on, and when she asked him where Miss Mavis was he said he had not the least idea. I sat with Mrs. Nettlepoint at her particular request: she told me she knew that if I left her Mrs. Peck and Mrs. Gotch would come to speak to her. She was flurried and fatigued at having to make an effort, and I think that Grace Mavis's choosing this occasion for retirement suggested to her a little that she had been made a fool of. She remarked that the girl's not being there showed her complete want of breeding and that she was really very good to have put herself out for her so; she was a common creature and that was the end of it. I could see that Mrs. Nettlepoint's advent quickened the speculative activity of the other ladies; they watched her from the opposite side of the deck, keeping their eyes fixed on her very much as the man at the wheel kept his on the course of the ship. Mrs. Peck plainly meditated an approach, and it was from this danger that Mrs. Nettlepoint averted her face.

'It's just as we said,' she remarked to me as we sat there. 'It is like the bucket in the well. When I come up that girl goes down.'

'Yes, but you've succeeded, since Jasper remains here.'

'Remains? I don't see him.'

'He comes and goes—it's the same thing.'

'He goes more than he comes. But *n'en parlons plus*; I haven't gained anything. I don't admire the sea at all—what is it but a magnified water-tank? I shan't come up again.'

'I have an idea she'll stay in her cabin now,' I said. 'She tells me she has one to herself.' Mrs. Nettlepoint replied that she might do as she liked, and I repeated to her the little conversation I had had with Jasper.

She listened with interest, but 'Marry her? mercy!' she exclaimed. 'I like the manner in which you give my son away.'

'You wouldn't accept that.'

'Never in the world.'

'Then I don't understand your position.'

'Good heavens, I have none! It isn't a position to be bored to death.'

'You wouldn't accept it even in the case I put to him—that of her believing she had been encouraged to throw over poor Porterfield?'

'Not even—not even. Who knows what she believes?'

'Then you do exactly what I said you would—you show me a fine example of maternal immorality.'

'Maternal fiddlesticks! It was she began it.'

'Then why did you come up to-day?'

'To keep you quiet.'

Mrs. Nettlepoint's dinner was served on deck, but I went into the saloon. Jasper was there but not Grace Mavis, as I had half expected. I asked him what had become of her, if she were ill (he must have thought I had an ignoble pertinacity), and he replied that he knew nothing whatever about her. Mrs. Peck talked to me about Mrs. Nettlepoint and said it had been a great interest to her to see her; only it was a pity she didn't seem more sociable. To this I replied that she had to beg to be excused—she was not well.

'You don't mean to say she's sick, on this pond?'

'No, she's unwell in another way.'

'I guess I know the way!' Mrs. Peck laughed. And then she added, 'I suppose she came up to look after her charge.'

'Her charge?'

'Why, Miss Mavis. We've talked enough about that.'

'Quite enough. I don't know what that had to do with it. Miss Mavis hasn't been there to-day.'

'Oh, it goes on all the same.'

'It goes on?'

'Well, it's too late.'

'Too late?'

'Well, you'll see. There'll be a row.

This was not comforting, but I did not repeat it above. Mrs. Nettlepoint returned early to her cabin, professing herself much tired. I know not what 'went on,' but Grace Mavis continued not to show. I went in late, to bid Mrs. Nettlepoint good-night, and learned from her that the girl had not been to her. She had sent the stewardess to her room for news, to see if she were ill and needed assistance, and the stewardess came back with the information that she was not there. I went above after this; the night was not quite so fair and the deck was almost empty. In a moment Jasper Nettlepoint and our young lady moved past me together. 'I hope you are better!' I called after her; and she replied, over her shoulder—

'Oh, yes, I had a headache; but the air now does me good!'

I went down again—I was the only person there but they, and I wished to not appear to be watching them—and returning to Mrs. Nettlepoint's room found (her door was open into the little passage) that she was still sitting up.

'She's all right!' I said. 'She's on the deck with Jasper.'

The old lady looked up at me from her book. 'I didn't know you called that all right.'

'Well, it's better than something else.'

'Something else?'

'Something I was a little afraid of.' Mrs. Nettlepoint continued to look at me; she asked me what that was. 'I'll tell you when we are ashore,' I said.

The next day I went to see her, at the usual hour of my morning visit, and found her in considerable agitation. 'The scenes have begun,' she said; 'you know I told you I shouldn't get through without them! You made me nervous last night—I haven't the least idea what you meant; but you made me nervous. She came in to see me an hour ago, and I had the courage to say to her, "I don't know why I shouldn't tell you frankly that I have been scolding my son about you." Of course she asked me what I meant by that, and I said—"It seems to me he drags you about the ship too much, for a girl in your position. He has the air of not remembering that you belong to some one else. There is a kind of want of taste and even of want of respect in it." That produced an explosion; she became very violent.'

'Do you mean angry?'

'Not exactly angry, but very hot and excited—at my presuming to think her relations with my son were not the simplest in the world. I might scold him as much as I liked—that was between ourselves; but she didn't see why I should tell her that I had done so. Did I think she allowed him to treat her with disrespect? That idea was not very complimentary to her! He had treated her better and been kinder to her than most other people—there were very few on the ship that hadn't been insulting. She should be glad enough when she got off it, to her own people, to some one whom no one would have a right to say anything about. What was there in her position that was not perfectly natural? what was the idea of making a fuss about her position? Did I mean that she took it too easily—that she didn't think as much as she ought about Mr. Porterfield? Didn't I believe she was attached to him—didn't I believe she was just counting the hours until she saw him? That would be the happiest moment of her life. It showed how little I knew her, if I thought anything else.'

'All that must have been rather fine—I should have liked to hear it,' I said. 'And what did you reply?'

'Oh, I grovelled; I told her that I accused her (as regards my son) of nothing worse than an excess of good nature. She helped him to pass his time—he ought to be immensely obliged. Also that it would be a very happy moment for me too when I should hand her over to Mr. Porterfield.'

'And will you come up to-day?'

'No indeed—she'll do very well now.'

I gave a sigh of relief. 'All's well that ends well!'

Jasper, that day, spent a great deal of time with his mother. She had told me that she really had had no proper opportunity to talk over with him their movements after disembarking. Everything changes a little, the last two or three days of a voyage; the spell is broken and new combinations take place. Grace Mavis was neither on deck nor at dinner, and I drew Mrs. Peck's attention to the extreme propriety with which she now conducted herself. She had spent the day in meditation and she judged it best to continue to meditate.

'Ah, she's afraid,' said my implacable neighbour.

'Afraid of what?'

'Well, that we'll tell tales when we get there.'

'Whom do you mean by "we"?'

'Well, there are plenty, on a ship like this.'

'Well then, we won't.'

'Maybe we won't have the chance,' said the dreadful little woman.

'Oh, at that moment a universal geniality reigns.'

'Well, she's afraid, all the same.'

'So much the better.'

'Yes, so much the better.'

All the next day, too, the girl remained invisible and Mrs. Nettlepoint told me that she had not been in to see her. She had inquired by the stewardess if she would receive her in her own cabin, and Grace Mavis had replied that it was littered up with things and unfit for visitors: she was packing a trunk over. Jasper made up for his devotion to his mother the day before by now spending a great deal of his time in the smoking-room. I wanted to say to him 'This is much better,' but I thought it wiser to hold my tongue. Indeed I had begun to feel the emotion of prospective arrival (I was delighted to be almost back in my dear old Europe again) and had less to spare for other matters. It will doubtless appear to the critical reader that I had already devoted far too much to the little episode of which my story gives an account, but to this I can only reply that the event justified me. We sighted land, the dim yet rich coast of Ireland, about sunset and I leaned on the edge of the ship and looked at it. 'It doesn't look like much, does it?' I heard a voice say, beside me; and, turning, I found Grace Mavis was there. Almost for the first time she had her veil up, and I thought her very pale.

'It will be more to-morrow,' I said.

'Oh yes, a great deal more.'

'The first sight of land, at sea, changes everything,' I went on. 'I always think it's like waking up from a dream. It's a return to reality.'

For a moment she made no response to this; then she said, 'It doesn't look very real yet.'

'No, and meanwhile, this lovely evening, the dream is still present.'

She looked up at the sky, which had a brightness, though the light of the sun had left it and that of the stars had not come out. 'It *is* a lovely evening.'

'Oh yes, with this we shall do.'

She stood there a while longer, while the growing dusk effaced the line of the land more rapidly than our progress made it distinct. She said nothing more, she only looked in front of her; but her very quietness made me want to say something suggestive of sympathy and service. I was unable to think what to say—some things seemed too wide of the mark and others too importunate. At last, unexpectedly, she appeared to give me my chance. Irrelevantly, abruptly she broke out:

'Didn't you tell me that you knew Mr. Porterfield?'

'Dear me, yes—I used to see him. I have often wanted to talk to you about him.'

She turned her face upon me and in the deepened evening I fancied she looked whiter. 'What good would that do?'

'Why, it would be a pleasure,' I replied, rather foolishly.

'Do you mean for you?'

'Well, yes—call it that,' I said, smiling.

'Did you know him so well?'

My smile became a laugh and I said—'You are not easy to make speeches to.'

'I hate speeches!' The words came from her lips with a violence that surprised me; they were loud and hard. But before

I had time to wonder at it she went on—'Shall you know him when you see him?'

'Perfectly, I think.' Her manner was so strange that one had to notice it in some way, and it appeared to me the best way was to notice it jocularly; so I added, 'Shan't you?'

'Oh, perhaps you'll point him out!' And she walked quickly away. As I looked after her I had a singular, a perverse and rather an embarrassed sense of having, during the previous days, and especially in speaking to Jasper Nettlepoint, interfered with her situation to her loss. I had a sort of pang in seeing her move about alone; I felt somehow responsible for it and asked myself why I could not have kept my hands off. I had seen Jasper in the smoking-room more than once that day, as I passed it, and half an hour before this I had observed, through the open door, that he was there. He had been with her so much that without him she had a bereaved, forsaken air. It was better, no doubt, but superficially it made her rather pitiable. Mrs. Peck would have told me that their separation was gammon; they didn't show together on deck and in the saloon, but they made it up elsewhere. The secret places on shipboard are not numerous; Mrs. Peck's 'elsewhere' would have been vague and I know not what license her imagination took. It was distinct that Jasper had fallen off, but of course what had passed between them on this subject was not so and could never be. Later, through his mother, I had *his* version of that, but I may remark that I didn't believe it. Poor Mrs. Nettlepoint did, of course. I was almost capable, after the girl had left me, of going to my young man and saying, 'After all, do return to her a little, just till we get in! It won't make any difference after we land.' And I don't think it was the fear he would tell me I was an idiot that prevented me. At any rate the next time I passed the door of the smoking-room I saw that he had left it. I paid my usual visit to Mrs. Nettlepoint that night, but I troubled her no further about Miss Mavis. She had made up her mind that everything was smooth and settled now, and it seemed to me that I had worried her and that she had worried herself enough. I left her to enjoy the foretaste of arrival, which had taken possession of her mind. Before turning in I went above and found more passengers on deck than I had ever seen so late. Jasper was walking about among them alone, but I forebore to join him. The coast of Ireland had disappeared, but the night and the sea were perfect. On the way to my cabin, when I came down, I met the stewardess in one of the passages and the idea entered my head to say to her—'Do you happen to know where Miss Mavis is?'

'Why, she's in her room, sir, at this hour.'

'Do you suppose I could speak to her?' It had come into my mind to ask her why she had inquired of me whether I should recognise Mr. Porterfield.

'No, sir,' said the stewardess; 'she has gone to bed.'

'That's all right.' And I followed the young lady's excellent example.

The next morning, while I was dressing, the steward of my side of the ship came to me as usual to see what I wanted. But the first thing he said to me was—'Rather a bad job, sir—a passenger missing.'

'A passenger—missing?'

'A lady, sir. I think you knew her. Miss Mavis, sir.'

'*Missing?*' I cried—staring at him, horror-stricken.

'She's not on the ship. They can't find her.'

'Then where to God is she?'

I remember his queer face. 'Well sir, I suppose you know that as well as I.'

'Do you mean she has jumped overboard?'

'Some time in the night, sir—on the quiet. But it's beyond every one, the way she escaped notice. They usually sees 'em, sir. It must have been about half-past two. Lord, but she was clever, sir. She didn't so much as make a splash. They say she *'ad* come against her will, sir.'

I had dropped upon my sofa—I felt faint. The man went on, liking to talk, as persons of his class do when they have something horrible to tell. She usually rang for the stewardess early, but this morning of course there had been no ring. The stewardess had gone in all the same about eight o'clock and found the cabin empty. That was about an hour ago. Her things were there in confusion—the things she usually wore when she went above. The stewardess thought she had been rather strange last night, but she waited a little and then went back. Miss Mavis hadn't turned up—and she didn't turn up. The stewardess began to look for her—she hadn't been seen on deck or in the saloon. Besides, she wasn't dressed—not to show herself; all her clothes were in her room. There was another lady, an old lady, Mrs. Nettlepoint—I would know her—that she was sometimes with, but the stewardess had been with *her* and she knew Miss Mavis had not come near her that morning. She had spoken to *him* and they had taken a quiet look they had hunted everywhere. A ship's a big place, but you do come to the end of it, and if a person ain't there why they ain't. In short an hour had passed and the young lady was not accounted for: from which I might judge if she ever would be. The watch couldn't account for her, but no doubt the fishes in the sea could—poor miserable lady! The stewardess and he, they had of course thought it their duty very soon to speak to the doctor, and the doctor had spoken immediately to the captain. The captain didn't like it—they never did. But he would try to keep it quiet—they always did.

By the time I succeeded in pulling myself together and getting on, after a fashion, the rest of my clothes I had learned that Mrs. Nettlepoint had not yet been informed, unless the stewardess had broken it to her within the previous few minutes. Her son knew, the young gentleman on the other side of the ship (he had the other steward); my man had seen him come out of his cabin and rush above, just before he came in to me. He *had* gone above, my man was sure; he had not gone to the old lady's cabin. I remember a queer vision when the steward told me this—the wild flash of a picture of Jasper Nettlepoint leaping with a mad compunction in his young agility over the side of the ship. I hasten to add that no such incident was destined to contribute its horror to poor Grace Mavis's mysterious tragic act. What followed was miserable enough, but I can only glance at it. When I got to Mrs. Nettlepoint's door she was there in her dressing-gown; the stewardess had just told her and she was rushing out to come to me. I made her go back—I said I would go for Jasper. I went for him but I missed him, partly no doubt because it was really, at first, the captain I was after. I found this personage and found him highly scandalised, but he gave me no hope that we were in error, and his displeasure, expressed with seamanlike plainness, was a definite settlement of the question. From the deck, where I merely turned round and looked, I saw the light of another summer day, the coast of Ireland green and near and the sea a more charming colour than it had been at all. When I came below again Jasper had passed back; he had gone to his cabin and his mother had joined him there. He remained there till we reached Liverpool—I never saw him. His mother, after a little, at his request, left him alone. All the world went above to look at the land and chatter about our tragedy, but the poor lady spent the day, dismally enough, in her room. It seemed to me intolerably long; I was thinking so of vague Porterfield and of my prospect of having to face him on the morrow. Now of course I knew why she had asked me if I should recognise him; she had delegated to me mentally a certain pleasant office. I gave Mrs. Peck and Mrs. Gotch a wide berth—I couldn't talk to them. I could, or at least I did a little, to Mrs. Nettlepoint, but with too many reserves for comfort on either side, for I foresaw that it would not in the least do now to mention Jasper to her. I was obliged to assume by my silence that he had had nothing to do with what had happened; and of course I never really ascertained what he *had* had to do. The secret of what passed between him and the strange girl who would have sacrificed her marriage to him on so short an acquaintance remains shut up in his breast. His mother, I know, went to his door from time to time, but he refused her admission. That evening, to be human at a venture, I requested the steward to go in and ask him if he should care to see me, and the attendant returned with an answer which he candidly transmitted. 'Not in the least!' Jasper apparently was almost as scandalised as the captain.

At Liverpool, at the dock, when we had touched, twenty people came on board and I had already made out Mr. Porterfield at a distance. He was looking up at the side of the great vessel with disappointment written (to my eyes) in his face—disappointment at not seeing the woman he loved lean over it and wave her handkerchief to him. Every one was looking at him, every one but she (his identity flew about in a moment) and I wondered if he did not observe it. He used to be lean, he had grown almost fat. The interval between us diminished—he was on the plank and then on the deck with the jostling officers of the customs—all too soon for my equanimity. I met him instantly however, laid my hand on him and drew him away, though I perceived that he had no impression of having seen me before. It was not till afterwards that I thought this a little stupid of him. I drew him far away (I was conscious of Mrs. Peck and Mrs. Gotch looking at us as we passed) into the empty, stale smoking-room; he remained speechless, and that struck me as like him. I had to speak first, he could not even relieve me by saying 'Is anything the matter?' I told him first that she was ill. It was an odious moment.

The Solution

O H YES, you may write it down—every one's dead." I profited by my old friend's permission and made a note of the story, which, at the time he told it to me, seemed curious and interesting. Will it strike you in the same light? Perhaps not, but I will run the risk and copy it out for you as I reported it, with just a little amplification from memory. Though every one *is* dead, perhaps you had better not let it go further. My old friend is dead himself, and how can I say how I miss him? He had many merits, and not the least of them was that he was always at home. The infirmities of the last years of his life confined him to London and to his own house, and of an afternoon, between five and six o'clock, I often knocked at his door. He is before me now, as he leans back in his chair, with his eyes wandering round the top of his room as if a thousand ghostly pictures were suspended there. Following his profession in many countries, he had seen much of life and knew much of men. This thing dropped from him piece by piece (one wet, windy spring afternoon, when we happened to be uninterrupted), like a painless belated confession. I have only given it continuity.

I.

It was in Rome, a hundred years ago, or as nearly so as it must have been to be an episode of my extreme youth. I was just twenty-three, and attached to our diplomatic agency there; the other secretaries were all my seniors. Is it because I was twenty-three, or because the time and the place were really better, that this period glows in my memory with all sorts of poetic, romantic lights? It seems to me to have consisted of five winters of sunshine without a cloud; of long excursions on the Campagna and in the Alban and Sabine hills; of joyous artists' feasts, spread upon the warm stones of ruined temples and tombs; of splendid Catholic processions and ceremonies; of friendly, familiar evenings, prolonged very late, in the great painted and tapestried saloons of historic palaces. It was the slumberous, pictorial Rome of the Popes, before the Italians had arrived or the local colour departed, and though I have been back there in recent years it is always the early impression that is evoked for me by the name. The yellow steps, where models and beggars lounged in the sun, had a golden tone, and the models and beggars themselves a magnificent brown one, which it looked easy to paint showily. The excavations, in those days, were comparatively few, but the "subjects"—I was an incorrigible sketcher—were many. The carnival lasted a month, the flowers (and even the flower girls) lasted for ever, and the old statues in the villas and the galleries became one's personal friends.

Of course we had other friends than these, and that is what I am coming to. I have lived in places where the society was perhaps better, but I have lived in none where I liked it better, in spite of the fact that it was considerably pervaded by Mrs. Goldie. Mrs. Goldie was an English lady, a widow with three daughters, and her name, accompanied not rarely, I fear, with an irreverent objurgation, was inevitably on our lips. She had a house on the Pincian Hill, from winter to winter; she came early in the season and stayed late, and she formed, with her daughters—Rosina, Veronica and Augusta—an uncompromising feature of every entertainment. As the principal object in any view of Rome is the dome of St. Peter's, so the most prominent figure in the social prospect was always the Honourable Blanche. She was a daughter of Lord Bolitho, and there were several elderly persons among us who remembered her in the years before her marriage, when her maiden designation was jocosely—I forget what the original joke had been—in people's mouths. They reintroduced it, and it became common in speaking of her. There must have been some public occasion when, as a spinster, she had done battle for her precedence and had roared out her luckless title. She was capable of that.

I was so fond of the place that it appeared to be natural every one else should love it, but I afterwards wondered what could have been the source of Mrs. Goldie's interest in it. She didn't know a Raphael from a Caravaggio, and even after many years could not have told you the names of the seven hills. She used to drive her daughters out to sketch, but she would never have done that if she had cared for the dear old ruins. However, it has always been a part of the magic of Rome that the most dissimilar breasts feel its influence; and though it is, or rather it was, the most exquisite place in the world, uncultivated minds have been known to enjoy it as much as students and poets. It has always touched alike the *raffiné* and the barbarian. Mrs. Goldie was a good deal of a barbarian, and she had her reasons for liking the Papal city. Her mind was fixed on tea-parties and the "right people to know." She valued the easy sociability, the picnics, the functions, the frequent opportunities for producing her girls. These opportunities indeed were largely of her own making; for she was highly hospitable, in the simple Roman fashion, and held incessant receptions and *conversazioni*. Dinners she never gave, and when she invited you to lunch, *al fresco*, in the shadow of the aqueducts that stride across the plain, she expected you to bring with you a cold chicken and a bottle of wine. No one, however, in those patriarchal times, was thought the worse of in Rome for being frugal. That was another reason why Mrs. Goldie had elected to live there; it was the capital in Europe where the least money—and she had but little—would go furthest in the way of grandeur. It cost her nothing to produce her girls, in proportion to the impressiveness of the spectacle.

I don't know what we should have done without her house, for the young men of the diplomatic body, as well as many others, treated it almost as a club. It was largely for our benefit that the Misses Goldie were produced. I sometimes wondered, even in those days, if our sense of honour was quite as fine as it might have been, to have permitted us to amuse ourselves at the expense of this innocent and hospitable group. The jokes we made about them were almost as numerous as the cups of tea that we received from the hands of the young ladies; and though I have never thought that youth is delicate (delicacy is an acquired virtue and comes later), there was this excuse for our esoteric mirth, that it was simply contagious. We laughed at the airs of greatness the Honourable Blanche gave herself and at the rough-and-ready usage to which she subjected the foreign tongues. It even seemed to us droll, in a crowd, to see her push and press and make play with her elbows, followed by the compact wedge of Rosina, Veronica and Augusta, whom she had trained to follow up her advantages. We noted the boldness with which she asked for favours when they were not offered and snatched them when they were refused, and we almost admired the perpetual manœuvres and conspiracies, all of the most public and transparent kind, which did not prevent her from honestly believing that she was the most shrinking and disinterested of women. She was always in a front seat, always flushed with the achievement of getting there, and always looking round and grimacing, signalling and telegraphing, pointing to other places for other people, waving her parasol and fan and marshalling and ordering the girls. She was tall and angular, and held her head very high; it was surmounted with wonderful turbans and plumages, and indeed the four ladies were caparisoned altogether in a manner of their own.

The oddest thing in the mother was that she bragged about the fine people and the fine things she had left behind her in England; she protested too much, and if you had listened to her you would have had the gravest doubts of her origin and breeding. They were genuinely "good," however, and her vulgarity was as incontestable as her connections. It is a mistake to suppose it is only the people who would like to be what they are not who are snobs. That class includes equally many of those who are what the others would like to be. I used to think, of old, that Thackeray overdid his ridicule of certain types; but I always did him justice when I remembered Mrs. Goldie. I don't want to finish her off by saying she was good-natured; but she certainly never abused people, and if she was very worldly she was not the only one. She never even thought of the people she didn't like, much less did she speak of them, for all her time was given to talking about her favourites, as she called them, who were usually of princely name (princes in Rome are numerous and *d'un commerce facile*), and her regard for whom was not chilled by the scant pains they sometimes took to encourage it. What was original in her was the candour and, to a certain extent, the brutality with which she played her game.

The girls were not pretty, but they might have been less plain if they had felt less oppressively the responsibility of their looks. You could not say exactly whether they were ugly or only afraid, on every occasion, that their mother would think them so. This expression was naturally the reverse of ornamental. They were good creatures, though they generally had the air of having slept in their clothes in order to be ready in time. Rosina and Augusta were better than Veronica: we had a theory that Veronica had a temper and sometimes "stood up" to her mother. She was the beauty, she had handsome hair, she sang, alas—she quavered out English ditties beneath the Roman *lambris*. She had pretensions individually, in short; the others had not even those that their mother had for them. In general, however, they were bullied and overpowered by their stern parent; all they could do was to follow her like frightened sheep, and they lived with their eyes fixed on her, so as to execute, at a glance from her, the evolutions in which they had been drilled. We were sorry for them, for we were sure that she secretly felt, with rage, that they were not brilliant and sat upon them for it with all her weight, which of course didn't tend to wake them up. None the less we talked of them profanely, and especially of Veronica, who had the habit of addressing us indiscriminately, though so many of us were English, in incomprehensible strange languages.

When I say "we" I must immediately except the young American secretary, with whom we lived much (at least I did, for I liked him, little as the trick I played him may have shown it), and who never was profane about anything: a circumstance to be noticed the more as the conversation of his chief, the representative of the United States *près du Saint-Père* at that time, was apt (though this ancient worthy was not "bearded like the pard," but clean-shaven—once or twice a week) to be full of strange oaths. His name was Henry Wilmerding, he came from some northern State (I am speaking now of the secretary, not of the minister), and he was as fresh and sociable a young fellow as you could wish to see. The minister was the drollest possible type, but we all delighted in him; indeed I think that among his colleagues he was the most popular man in the diplomatic body. He was a product of the Carolinas and always wore a dress-coat and a faded, superannuated neckcloth; his hat and boots were also of a fashion of his own. He talked very slowly, as if he were delivering a public address, used innumerable "sirs," of the forensic, not in the least of the social kind, and always made me feel as if I were the Speaker of the American Congress, though indeed I never should have ventured to call him to order. The curious part of his conversation was that, though it was rich in expletives, it was also extremely sententious: he uttered them with a solemnity which made them patriarchal and scriptural. He used to remind me of the busts of some of the old dry-faced, powerful Roman lawgivers and administrators. He spoke no language but that of his native State, but that mattered little, as we all learned it and practiced it for our amusement. We ended by making constant use of it among ourselves: we talked it to each other in his presence and under his nose. It seems to me, as I look back, that we must have been rare young brutes; but he was an unsuspecting diplomatist. Indeed they were a pair, for I think Wilmerding never knew—he had such a western bloom of his own.

Wilmerding was a gentleman and he was not a fool, but he was not in the least a man of the world. I couldn't fancy in what society he had grown up; I could only see it was something very different from any of our *milieux*. If he had been turned out by one of ours he couldn't have been so innocent without being stupid or so unworldly without being underbred. He was full of natural delicacy, worse luck: if he hadn't been I shouldn't be telling you this little story of my own shame. He once mentioned to me that his ancestors had been Quakers, and though he was not at all what you call a muff (he was a capital rider, and in the exaltation of his ideas of what was due to women a very knight of romance), there was something rather dove-like in his nature, suggestive of drab tints and the smell of lavender. All the Quakers, or people of Quaker origin, of whom I ever heard have been rich, and Wilmerding, happy dog, was not an exception to the rule. I think this was partly the reason why we succumbed to temptation: we should have handled him more tenderly if he had had the same short allowance as ourselves. He never talked of money (I have noticed Americans rarely do—it's a part of their prudery), but he was free-handed and extravagant and evidently had a long purse to draw upon. He used to buy shocking daubs from those of his compatriots who then cultivated "arrt" (they pronounced the word so oddly), in Rome, and I knew a case where he let a fellow have his picture back (it was certainly a small loss), to sell it over again. His family were proprietors of large cotton-mills from which bank-notes appeared to flow in inexhaustible streams. They sent him the handsomest remittances and let him know that the question of supplies was the last he need trouble himself about. There was something so enviable, so ideal in such a situation as this that I daresay it aggravated us a little, in spite of our really having such a kindness for him.

It had that effect especially upon one of our little band—a young French attaché, Guy de Montaut, one of the most de-lightful creatures I have ever known and certainly the French-man I have met in the world whom I have liked best. He had all the qualities of his nation and none of its defects—he was born for human intercourse. He loved a joke as well as I, but his jokes as a general thing were better than mine. It is true that this one I am speaking of, in which he had an equal hand, was bad enough. We were united by a community of debt—we owed money at the same places. Montaut's family was so old that they had long ago spent their substance and were not in the habit of pressing unsolicited drafts upon his acceptance. Neither of us quite understood why the diplomatic career should be open to a young Quaker, or the next thing to it, who was a cotton-spinner into the bargain. At the British es-tablishment, at least, no form of dissent less fashionable than the Catholic was recognised, and altogether it was very clear to me that the ways of the Americans were not as our ways. Montaut, as you may believe, was as little as possible of a Quaker; and if he was considerate of women it was in a very different manner from poor Wilmerding. I don't think he re-spected them much, but he would have insisted that he some-times spared them. I wondered often how Wilmerding had ever come to be a secretary of legation, as at that period, in America (I don't know how much they have changed it), such posts were obtained by being begged for and "worked" for in various crooked ways. It was impossible to go in less for haughtiness; yet with all Wilmerding's mildness, and his being the model of the nice young man, I couldn't have imagined his asking a favour.

He went to Mrs. Goldie's as much as the rest of us, but really no more, I think—no more, certainly, until the summer we all spent at Frascati. During that happy September we were constantly in and out of her house, and it is possible that when the others were out he was sometimes in. I mean that he played backgammon in the loggia of the villa with Rosy and Gussie, and even strolled, or sat, in the dear old Roman garden with them, looking over Veronica's shoulder while her pencil vainly attempted a perspective or a perpendicular. It was a charming, sociable, promiscuous time, and these poor girls were more or less gilded, for all of us, by it. The long, hot Roman summer had driven the strangers away, and the native society had gone into *villeggiatura*. My chief had crossed the Alps, on his annual leave, and the affairs of our house—they were very simple matters, no great international questions—were in the hands of a responsible underling. I forget what had become of Montaut's people; he himself, at any rate, was not to have his holiday till later. We were in the same situation, he and I, save that I had been able to take several bare rooms, for a couple of months, in a rambling old palace in a fold of the Alban hills. The few survivors of our Roman circle were my neighbours there, and I offered hospitality to Montaut, who, as often as he was free, drove out along the Appian Way to stay with me for a day or two at a time. I think he had a little personal tie in Rome which took up a good deal of his time.

The American minister and his lady—she was easily shocked but still more easily reassured—had fled to Switzerland, so that Wilmerding was left to watch over the interests of the United States. He took a furnished villa at Frascati (you could have one for a few *scudi* a month), and gave very pleasant and innocent bachelor parties. If he was often at Mrs. Goldie's she returned his visits with her daughters, and I can live over lovely evenings (oh youth, oh memory!) when tables were set for supper in the garden and lighted by the fireflies, when some of the villagers—such voices as one heard there and such natural art!—came in to sing for us, and when we all walked home in the moonlight with the ladies, singing, ourselves, along the road. I am not sure that Mrs. Goldie herself didn't warble to the southern night. This is a proof of the humanising, poetising conditions in which we lived. Mrs. Goldie had remained near Rome to save money; there was also a social economy in it, as she kept her eye on some of her princesses. Several of these high dames were in residence in our neighbourhood, and we were a happy family together.

I don't quite know why we went to see Mrs. Goldie so much if we didn't like her better, unless it be that my immediate colleagues and I inevitably felt a certain loyalty to the principal English house. Moreover we did like the poor lady better in fact than we did in theory and than the irreverent tone we took about her might have indicated. Wilmerding, all the same, remained her best listener, when she poured forth the exploits and alliances of her family. He listened with exaggerated interest—he held it unpardonable to let one's attention wander from a lady, however great a bore she might be. Mrs. Goldie thought very well of him, on these and other grounds, though as a general thing she and her daughters didn't like strangers unless they were very great people. In that case they recognised their greatness, but thought they would have been much greater if they had been English. Of the greatness of Americans they had but a limited sense, and they never compared them with the English, the French or even the Romans. The most they did was to compare them with each other; and in this respect they had a sort of measure. They thought the rich ones much less small than the others.

The summer I particularly speak of, Mrs. Goldie's was not simply the principal English house but really the only one— that is for the world in general. I knew of another that I had a very different attachment to and was even presumptuous enough to consider that I had an exclusive interest in. It was not exactly a house, however; it was only a big, cool, shabby, frescoed sitting-room in the inn at Albano, a huge, melancholy mansion that had come down in the world. It formed for the time the habitation of a charming woman whom I fondly believed to be more to me than any other human being. This part of my tale is rather fatuous, or it would be if it didn't refer to a hundred years ago. Not that my devotion was of the same order as my friend Montaut's, for the object of it was the most honourable of women, an accomplished English lady. Her name was Mrs. Rushbrook, and I should be capable at this hour of telling you a great deal about her. The description that would be most to the purpose, I confess (it puts the matter in a word), is that I was very far gone about her. I was really very bad, and she was some five years my elder, which, given my age, only made my condition more natural. She had been in Rome, for short visits, three or four times during my period there: her little girl was delicate, and her idea was to make a long stay in a southern climate.

She was the widow of an officer in the navy; she spoke of herself as very poor, but I knew enough of her relations in England to be sure that she would suffer no real inconvenience. Moreover she was extravagant, careless, even slightly capricious. If the "Bohemian" had been invented in those days she might possibly have been one—a very small, fresh, dainty one. She was so pretty that she has remained in my mind *the* pretty woman among those I have known, who, thank heaven, have not been few. She had a lovely head, and her chestnut hair was of a shade I have never seen since. And her figure had such grace and her voice such a charm; she was in short the woman a fellow loves. She was natural and clever and kind, and though she was five years older than I she always struck me as an embodiment of youth—of the golden morning of life. We made such happy discoveries together when first I knew her: we liked the same things, we disliked the same people, we had the same favourite statues in the Vatican, the same secret preferences in regard to views on the Campagna. We loved Italy in the same way and in the same degree; that is with the difference that I cared less for it after I knew her, because I cared so much more for her than for anything else. She painted, she studied Italian, she collected and noted the songs of the people, and she had the wit to pick up certain *bibelots* and curiosities—lucky woman—before other people had thought of them. It was long ago that she passed out of my ken, and yet I feel that she was very modern.

Partly as a new-comer (she had been at Sorrento to give her little girl sea-baths), and partly because she had her own occupations and lived to herself, she was rather out of our circle at Frascati. Mrs. Goldie had gone to see her, however, and she had come over to two or three of our parties. Several times I drove to Albano to fetch her, but I confess that my quest usually ended in my remaining with her. She joined more than one of our picnics (it is ridiculous how many we had), and she was notably present on an important occasion, the last general meeting before our little colony dispersed. This was neither more nor less than a tea-party—a regular five o'clock tea, though the fashion hadn't yet come in—on the summit of Monte Cavo. It sounds very vulgar, but I assure you it was delightful. We went up on foot, on ponies, or donkeys: the animals were for the convenience of the ladies, and our provisions and utensils were easily carried. The great heat had abated; besides, it was late in the day. The Campagna lay beneath us like a haunted sea (if you can imagine that—the ghosts of dead sentries walking on the deep) and the glow of the afternoon was divine. You know it all—the way the Alban mount slopes into the plain and the dome of St. Peter's rises out of it, the colour of the Sabines, which look so near, the old grey villages, the ruins of cities, of nations, that are scattered on the hills.

Wilmerding was of our party, as a matter of course, and Mrs. Goldie and the three girls and Montaut, confound him, with his communicative sense that everything was droll. He hadn't in his composition a grain of respect. Fortunately he didn't need it to make him happy. We had our tea, we looked at the view, we chattered in groups or strolled about in couples: no doubt we desecrated sufficiently a sublime historic spot. We lingered late, but late as it was we perceived, when we gathered ourselves together to descend the little mountain, that Veronica Goldie was missing. So was Henry Wilmerding, it presently appeared; and then it came out that they had been seen moving away together. We looked for them a little; we called for them; we waited for them. We were all there and we talked about them, Mrs. Goldie of course rather more loudly than the rest. She qualified their absence, I remember, as a "most extraordinary performance." Montaut said to me, in a lowered voice: "Diable, diable, diable!" I remember his saying also: "You others are very lucky. What would have been thought if it was I?" We waited in a small, a very small, embarrassment, and before long the young lady turned up with her companion. I forget where they had been; they told us, without confusion: they had apparently a perfectly good conscience. They had not really been away long; but it so happened that we all noticed it and that for a quarter of an hour we thought of it. Besides, the dusk had considerably deepened. As soon as they joined us we started homeward. A little later we all separated, and Montaut and I betook ourselves to our own quarters. He said to me that evening, in relation to this little incident: "In my country, you know, he would have to marry her."

"I don't believe it," I answered.

"Well, *he* would believe it, I'm sure."

"I don't believe that."

"Try him and you'll see. He'll believe anything."

The idea of trying him—such is the levity of youth—took possession of me; but at the time I said nothing. Montaut returned to Rome the next day, and a few days later I followed him—my *villeggiatura* was over. Our afternoon at Monte Cavo had had no consequences that I perceived. When I saw Montaut again in Rome one of the first things he said to me was:

"Well, has Wilmerding proposed?"

"Not that I know of."

"Didn't you tell him he ought?"

"My dear fellow, he'd knock me down."

"Never in the world. He'd thank you for the hint—he's so candid." I burst out laughing at this, and he asked if our friend had come back. When I said I had left him at Frascati he exclaimed: "Why, he's compromising her more!"

I didn't quite understand, and I remember asking: "Do you think he really ought to offer her marriage, as a gentleman?"

"Beyond all doubt, in any civilised society."

"What a queer thing, then, is civilisation! Because I'm sure he has done her no harm."

"How can you be sure? However, call it good if you like. It's a benefit one is supposed to pay for the privilege of conferring."

"He won't see it."

"He will if you open his eyes."

"That's not my business. And there's no one to make him see it," I replied.

"Couldn't the Honourable Blanche make him? It seems to me I would trust her."

"Trust her then and be quiet."

"You're afraid of his knocking you down," Montaut said.

I suppose I replied to this remark with another equally derisive, but I remember saying a moment later: "I'm rather curious to see if he would take such a representation seriously."

"I bet you a louis he will!" Montaut declared; and there was something in his tone that led me to accept the bet.

II.

In Rome, of a Sunday afternoon, every one went over to St. Peter's; I don't know whether the agreeably frivolous habit still prevails: it had little to do, I fear, with the spirit of worship. We went to hear the music—the famous vesper-service of the Papal choir, and also to learn the news, to stroll about and talk and look at each other. If we treated the great church as a public promenade, or rather as a splendid international *salon*, the fault was not wholly our own, and indeed practically there was little profanity in such an attitude. One's attitude was insignificant, and the bright immensity of the place protected conversation and even gossip. It struck one not as a particular temple, but as formed by the very walls of the faith that has no small pruderies to enforce. One early autumn day, in especial, we crossed the Tiber and lifted the ponderous leather curtain of the door to get a general view of the return of our friends to Rome. Half an hour's wandering lighted up the question of who had arrived, as every one, in his degree, went there for a solution of it. At the end of ten minutes I came upon Henry Wilmerding; he was standing still, with his head thrown back and his eyes raised to the far-arching dome as if he had felt its spell for the first time. The body of the church was almost clear of people; the visitors were collected in the chapel where service was held and just outside of it; the splendid chant and the strange high voices of some of the choristers came to us from a great distance. Before Wilmerding saw me I had time to say to him: "I thought you intended to remain at Frascati till the end of the week."

"I did, but I changed my mind."

"You came away suddenly, then?"

"Yes, it was rather sudden."

"Are you going back?" I presently asked.

"There's nothing particular to go back for."

I hesitated a moment. "Was there anything particular to come away for?"

"My dear fellow, not that I know of," he replied, with a slight flush in his cheek—an intimation (not that I needed it), that I had a little the air of challenging his right to go and come as he chose.

"Not in relation to those ladies?"

"Those ladies?"

"Don't be so unnaturally blank. Your dearest friends."

"Do you mean the Goldies?"

"Don't overdo it. Whom on earth should I mean?"

It is difficult to explain, but there was something youthfully bland in poor Wilmerding which operated as a provocation: it made him seem imperturbable, which he really was not. My little discussion with Montaut about the success with which he might be made to take a joke seriously had not, till this moment, borne any fruit in my imagination, but the idea became prolific, or at least it became amusing, as I stood face to face with him on those solemn fields of marble. There was a temptation to see how much he would swallow. He *was* candid, and his candour was like a rather foolish blank page, the gaping, gilt-edged page of an album, presenting itself for the receipt of a quotation or a thought. Why shouldn't one write something on it, to see how it would look? In this case the inscription could only be a covert pleasantry—an impromptu containing a surprise. If Wilmerding was innocent, that, no doubt, ought to have made one kind, and I had not the faintest intention of being cruel. His blandness might have operated to conciliate, and it was only the turn of a hair that it had the other effect. That hair, let me suppose, was simply the intrinsic brutality—or call it the high animal-spirits—of youth. If after the little experiment suggested by Montaut had fixed itself in my fancy I let him off, it would be because I pitied him. But it was absurd to pity Wilmerding—we envied him, as I have hinted, too much. If he was the white album-page seductive to pointed doggerel he was unmistakably gilt-edged.

"Oh, the Goldies," he said in a moment—"I wouldn't have stayed any longer for *them*. I came back because I wanted to—I don't see that it requires so much explanation."

"No more do I!" I laughed. "Come and listen to the singing." I passed my hand into his arm and we strolled toward the choir and the concourse of people assembled before the high doorway. We lingered there a little: till this hour I never can recall without an ache for the old days the way the afternoon light, taking the heavenly music and diffusing it, slants through the golden recesses of the white windows, set obliquely in the walls. Presently we saw Guy de Montaut in the crowd, and he came toward us after having greeted us with a gesture. He looked hard at me, with a smile, as if the sight of us together reminded him of his wager and he wanted to know whether he had lost or won. I let him know with a glance that he was to be quiet or he would spoil everything, and he was as quiet as he knew how to be. This is not saying much, for he always had an itch to play with fire. It was really the desire to keep his hands off Wilmerding that led me to deal with our friend in my own manner. I remember that as we stood there together Montaut made several humorous attempts to treat him as a great conqueror, of which I think Wilmerding honestly failed to perceive the drift. It was Montaut's saying "You ought to bring them back—we miss them too much," that made me prepare to draw our amiable victim away.

"They're not my property," Wilmerding replied, accepting the allusion this time as to the four English ladies.

"Ah, *all* of them, *mon cher*—I never supposed!" the Frenchman cried, with great merriment, as I broke up our colloquy. I laughed, too—the image he presented seemed comical then—and judged that we had better leave the church. I proposed we should take a turn on the Pincian, crossing the Tiber by the primitive ferry which in those days still plied at the marble steps of the Ripetta, just under the back-windows of the Borghese palace.

"Montaut was talking nonsense just then, but *have* they refused you?" I asked as we took our way along the rustic lane that used to wander behind the castle of St. Angelo, skirting the old grassy fortifications and coming down to the Tiber between market-gardens, vineyards and dusty little trellised suburban drinking-shops which had a withered bush over the gate.

"Have *who* refused me?"

"Ah, you keep it up too long!" I answered; and I was silent a little.

"What's the matter with you this afternoon?" he asked. "Why can't you leave the poor Goldies alone?"

"Why can't *you*, my dear fellow—that seems to me the natural inquiry. Excuse my having caught Montaut's tone just now. I don't suppose you proposed for all of them."

"Proposed?—I've proposed for none of them!"

"Do you mean that Mrs. Goldie hasn't seemed to expect it?"

"I don't know what she has seemed to expect."

"Can't you imagine what she would naturally look for? If you can't, it's only another proof of the different way you people see things. Of course you have a right to your own way."

"I don't think I know what you are talking about," said poor Wilmerding.

"My dear fellow, I don't want to be offensive, dotting my i's so. You can so easily tell me it's none of my business."

"It isn't your being plain that would be offensive—it's your kicking up such a dust."

"You're very right," I said; "I've taken a liberty and I beg your pardon. We'll talk about something else."

We talked about nothing, however; we went our way in silence and reached the bank of the river. We waited for the ferryman without further speech, but I was conscious that a bewilderment was working in my companion. As I relate my behaviour to you it strikes me, at this distance of time, as that of a very demon. All I can say is that it seemed to me innocent then: youth and gaiety and reciprocity, and something in the sophisticating Roman air which converted all life into a pleasant comedy, apologised for me as I went. Besides, I had no vision of consequences: my part was to prove, as against the too mocking Montaut, that there would be no consequences at all. I remember the way Wilmerding, as we crossed, sat on the edge of the big flat boat, looking down at the yellow swirl of the Tiber. He didn't meet my eye, and he was serious; which struck me as a promise of further entertainment. From the Ripetta we strolled to the Piazza del Popolo, and then began to mount one of the winding ways that diversify the slope of the Pincian. Before we got to the top Wilmerding said to me: "What do you mean by the different way 'we people' see things? Whom do you mean by us people?"

"You innocent children of the west, most unsophisticated of Yankees. Your ideas, your standards, your measures, your manners are different."

"The ideas and the manners of gentlemen are the same all the world over."

"Yes—I fear I can't gainsay you there," I replied.

"I don't ask for the least allowance on the score of being a child of the west. I don't propose to be a barbarian anywhere."

"You're the best fellow in the world," I continued; "but it's nevertheless true—I have been impressed with it on various occasions—that your countrypeople have, in perfect good faith, a different attitude toward women. They think certain things possible that we Europeans, cynical and corrupt, look at with a suspicious eye."

"What things do you mean?"

"Oh, don't you know them? You have more freedom than we."

"Ah, never!" my companion cried, in a tone of conviction that still rings in my ears.

"What I mean is that you have less," I said, laughing. "Evidently women, *chez vous*, are not so easily compromised. You must live, over there, in a state of Arcadian, or rather of much more than Arcadian innocence. You can do all sorts of things without committing yourselves. With a quarter of them, in this uncomfortable hemisphere, one is up to one's neck in engagements."

"In engagements?"

"One has given pledges that have in honour to be redeemed—unless a fellow chooses to wriggle out of them. There is the question of intentions, and the question of how far, in the eyes of the world, people have really gone. Here it's the fashion to assume, if there is the least colour for it, that they have gone pretty far. I daresay often they haven't. But they get the credit of it. That's what makes them often ask themselves—or each other—why they mayn't as well die for sheep as for lambs."

"I know perfectly well what you mean: that's precisely what makes me so careful," said Wilmerding.

I burst into mirth at this—I liked him even better when he was subtile than when he was simple. "You're a dear fellow and a gentleman to the core, and it's all right, and you have only to trust your instincts. There goes the Boccarossa," I said, as we entered the gardens which crown the hill and which used to be as pleasantly neglected of old as they are regulated and cockneyfied to-day. The lovely afternoon was waning and the good-humoured, *blasé* crowd (it has seen so much, in its time) formed a public to admire the heavy Roman coaches, laden with yellow principessas, which rumbled round the contracted circle. The old statues in the shrubbery, the colour of the sunset, the view of St. Peter's, the pines against the sky on Monte Mario, and all the roofs and towers of Rome between—these things are doubtless a still fresher remembrance with you than with me. I leaned with Wilmerding against the balustrade of one of the terraces and we gave the usual tribute of a gaze to the dome of Michael Angelo. Then my companion broke out, with perfect irrelevance:

"Don't you think I've been careful enough?"

It's needless—it would be odious—to tell you in detail what advantage I took of this. I hated (I told him) the slang of the subject, but I was bound to say he would be generally judged—in any English, in any French circle—to have shown what was called marked interest.

"Marked interest in what? Marked interest in whom? You can't appear to have been attentive to four women at once."

"Certainly not. But isn't there one whom you may be held particularly to have distinguished?"

"One?" Wilmerding stared. "You don't mean the old lady?"

"*Commediante!* Does your conscience say absolutely nothing to you?"

"My conscience? What has that got to do with it?"

"Call it then your sense of the way that—to effete prejudice—the affair may have looked."

"The affair—what affair?"

"Honestly, can't you guess? Surely there is one of the young ladies to whom the proprieties point with a tolerably straight finger."

He hesitated; then he cried: "Heaven help me—you don't mean Veronica?"

The pleading wail with which he uttered this question was almost tragic, and for a moment his fate trembled in the balance. I was on the point of letting him off, as I may say, if he disliked the girl so much as that. It was a revelation—I didn't know how much he did dislike her. But at this moment a carriage stopped near the place where we had rested, and, turning round, I saw it contained two ladies whom I knew. They greeted me and prepared to get out, so that I had to go and help them. But before I did this I said to my companion: "Don't worry, after all. It will all blow over."

"Upon my word, it will have to!" I heard him ejaculate as I left him. He turned back to the view of St. Peter's. My ladies alighted and wished to walk a little, and I spent five minutes with them; after which, when I looked for Wilmerding, he had disappeared. The last words he had spoken had had such a sharp note of impatience that I was reassured. I had ruffled him, but I had won my bet of Montaut.

Late that night (I had just come in—I was never at home in the evening) there was a tinkle of my bell, and my servant informed me that the signorino of the "American embassy" wished to speak to me. Wilmerding was ushered in, very pale, so pale that I thought he had come to demand satisfaction of me for having tried to make a fool of him. But he hadn't, it soon appeared; he hadn't in the least: he wanted explanations, but they were quite of another kind. He only wished to arrive at the truth—to ask me two or three earnest questions. I ought of course to have told him on the spot that I had only been making use of him for a slight psychological experiment. But I didn't, and this omission was my great fault. I can only declare, in extenuation of it, that I had scruples about betraying Montaut. Besides, I did cling a little to my experiment.

There was something that fascinated me in the idea of the supreme sacrifice he was ready to make if it should become patent to him that he had put upon an innocent girl, or upon a confiding mother, a slight, a disappointment even purely conventional. I urged him to let me lay the ghost I had too inconsiderately raised, but at the same time I was curious to see what he would do if the idea of reparation should take possession of him. He would be consistent, and it would be strange to see that. I remember saying to him before he went away: "Have you really a very great objection to Veronica Goldie?" I thought he was going to reply "I loathe her!" But he answered:

"A great objection? I pity her, if I've deceived her."

"Women must have an easy time in your country," I said; and I had an idea the remark would contribute to soothe him.

Nevertheless, the next day, early in the afternoon, being still uneasy, I went to his lodgings. I had had, by a rare chance, a busy morning, and this was the first moment I could spare. Wilmerding had delightful quarters in an old palace with a garden—an old palace with old busts ranged round an old loggia and an old porter in an old cocked hat and a coat that reached to his heels leaning against the *portone*. From this functionary I learned that the signorino had quitted Rome in a two-horse carriage an hour before: he had gone back to Frascati—he had taken a servant and a portmanteau. This news did not confirm my tranquillity in exactly the degree I could have wished, and I stood there looking, and I suppose feeling, rather blank while I considered it. A moment later I was surprised in this attitude by Guy de Montaut, who turned into the court with the step of a man bent on the same errand as myself. We looked at each other—he with a laugh, I with a frown—and then I said: "I don't like it—he's gone."

"Gone?—to America?"

"On the contrary—back to the hills."

Montaut's laugh rang out, and he exclaimed: "Of course you don't like it! Please to hand me over the sum of money that I have had the honour of winning from you."

"Not so fast. What proves to you that you've won it?"

"Why, his going like this—after the talk I had with him this morning."

"What talk had you with him this morning?"

Montaut looked at the old porter, who of course couldn't understand us, but, as if he scented the drift of things, was turning his perceptive Italian eye from one of us to the other. "Come and walk with me, and I'll tell you. The drollest thing!" he went on, as we passed back to the street. "The poor child has been to see me."

"To propose to you a meeting?"

"Not a bit—to ask my advice."

"Your advice?"

"As to how to act in the premises. *Il est impayable.*"

"And what did you say to him?"

"I said Veronica was one of the most charming creatures I had ever seen."

"You ought to be ashamed of yourself."

"*Tudieu, mon cher*, so ought you, if you come to that!" Montaut replied, taking his hand out of my arm.

"It's just what I am. We're a pair of scoundrels."

"Speak for yourself. I wouldn't have missed it for the world."

"You wouldn't have missed what?"

"His visit to me to-day—such an exhibition!"

"What did he exhibit?"

"The desire to be correct—but in a degree! You're a race apart, *vous autres.*"

"Don't lump him and me together," I said: "the immeasurable ocean divides us. Besides, it's you who were stickling for correctness. It was your insistence to me on what he ought to do—on what the family would have a right to expect him to do—that was the origin of the inquiry in which (yesterday, when I met him at St. Peter's,) I so rashly embarked."

"My dear fellow, the beauty of it is that the family have brought no pressure: that's an element I was taking for granted. He has no claim to recognise, because none has been made. He tells me that the Honourable Blanche, after her daughter's escapade with him, didn't open her mouth. *Ces Anglaises!*"

"Perhaps that's the way she made her claim," I suggested. "But why the deuce, then, couldn't *he* be quiet?"

"It's exactly what he thinks—that she may have been quiet out of delicacy. He's inimitable!"

"Fancy, in such a matter, his wanting advice!" I groaned, much troubled. We had stopped outside, under the palace windows; the sly porter, from the doorway, was still looking at us.

"Call it information," said Montaut.

"But I gave him lots, last night. He came to me."

"He wanted more—he wanted to be sure! He wanted an honest impression; he begged me, as a favour to him, to be very frank. Had he definitely, yes or no, according to my idea, excited expectations? I told him, definitely, yes—according to my idea!"

"I shall go after him," I declared; "I shall overtake him—I shall bring him back."

"You'll not play fair, then."

"Play be hanged! The fellow mustn't sacrifice his life."

"Where's the sacrifice?—she's quite as good as he. I don't detest poor Veronica—she has possibilities, and also very pretty hair. What pretensions can *he* have? He's touching, but he's only a cotton-spinner and a blockhead. Besides, it offends an *aimable Français* to see three unmated virgins withering in a row. You people don't mind that sort of thing, but it violates our sense of form—of proper arrangement. Girls marry, *que diable!*"

"I notice they don't marry you!" I cried.

"I don't go and hide in the bushes with them. Let him arrange it—I like to see people act out their character. Don't spoil this—it will be perfect. Such a story to tell!"

"*To tell?* We shall blush for it for ever. Besides, we can tell it even if he does nothing."

"Not I—I shall boast of it. I shall have done a good action, I shall have *assuré un sort* to a portionless girl." Montaut took hold of me again, for I threatened to run after Wilmerding, and he made me walk about with him for half an hour. He took some trouble to persuade me that further interference would be an unwarranted injury to Veronica Goldie. She had apparently got a husband—I had no right to dash him from her lips.

"Getting her a husband was none of my business."

"You did it by accident, and so you can leave it."

"I had no business to try him."

"You believed he would resist."

"I don't find it so amusing as you," I said, gloomily.

"What's amusing is that he has had no equivalent," Montaut broke out.

"No equivalent?"

"He's paying for what he didn't have, I gather, eh? *L'imbécile!* It's a reparation without an injury."

"It's an injury without a provocation!" I answered, breaking away from him.

I went straight to the stables at which I kept my horse—we all kept horses in Rome, in those days, for the Campagna was an incomparable riding-ground—and ordered the animal to be brought immediately to Porta San Giovanni. There was some delay, for I reached this point, even after the time it took me to change my dress, a good while before he came. When he did arrive I sprang into the saddle and dashed out of the gate. I soon got upon the grass and put the good beast to his speed, and I shall never forget that rich afternoon's ride. It seemed to me almost historic, at the time, and I thought of all the celebrated gallops, or those of poetry and fiction, that had been taken to bring good news or bad, to warn of dangers, to save cities, to stay executions. I felt as if staying an execution were now the object of mine. I took the direction of the Appian Way, where so many panting steeds, in the succession of ages, had struck fire from the stones; the ghostly aqueducts watched me as I passed, and these romantic associations gave me a sense of heroism. It was dark when I strained up the hill to Frascati, but there were lights in the windows of Wilmerding's villa, toward which I first pressed my course. I rode straight into the court, and called up to him—there was a window open; and he looked out and asked in unconcealed surprise what had brought me from Rome. "Let me in and I'll tell you," I said; and his servant came down and admitted me, summoning another member of the establishment to look after my horse.

It was very well to say to Wilmerding that I would tell him what had brought me: that was not so easy after I had been introduced into his room. Then I saw that something very important had happened: his whole aspect instantly told me so. He was half undressed—he was preparing for dinner—he was to dine at Mrs. Goldie's. This he explained to me without any question of mine, and it led me to say to him, with, I suspect, a tremor in my voice: "Then you have not yet seen her?"

"On the contrary: I drove to their villa as soon as I got here. I've been there these two hours. I promised them to go back to dine—I only came round here to tidy myself a little." I looked at him hard, and he added: "I'm engaged to be married."

"To which of them?" I asked; and the question seemed to me absurd as soon as I had spoken it.

"Why, to Veronica."

"Any of them would do," I rejoined, though this was not much better. And I turned round and looked out of the window into the dark. The tears rose to my eyes—I had ridden heroically, but I had not saved the city.

"What did you desire to say to me?" Wilmerding went on.

"Only that I wish you all the happiness you deserve," I answered, facing him again.

"Did you gallop out here for *that*?" he inquired.

"I might have done it for less!" I laughed, awkwardly; but he was very mild—he didn't fly at me. They had evidently been very nice to him at the other house—well they might be! Veronica had shaken her hair in his eyes, and for the moment he had accepted his fate.

"You had better come back and dine with me," he said.

"On an occasion so private—so peculiar—when you want them all to yourself? Never in the world."

"What then will you do here—alone?"

"I'll wash and dress first, if you'll lend me some things."

"My man will give you everything you need."

His kindness, his courtesy, his extraordinary subjection to his unnecessary doom filled me with a kind of anguish, and I determined that I would save him even yet. I had a sudden inspiration—it was at least an image of help. "To tell the truth, I didn't ride from Rome at such a rate only to be the first to congratulate you. I've taken you on the way; but a considerable part of my business is to go and see Mrs. Rushbrook."

"Mrs. Rushbrook? Do you call this on your way? She lives at Albano."

"Precisely; and when I've brushed myself up a bit and had a little bread and wine I shall drive over there."

"It will take you a full hour, in the dark."

"I don't care for that—I want to see her. It came over me this afternoon."

Wilmerding looked at me a moment—without any visible irony—and demanded, with positive solemnity: "Do you wish to propose to her?"

"Oh, if she'd marry me it would suit me! But she won't. At least she won't yet. She makes me wait too long. All the same, I want to see her."

"She's very charming," said Wilmerding, simply. He finished dressing and went off to dine with Veronica, while I passed into another room to repair my own disorder. His servant gave me some things that would serve me for the night; for it was my purpose, at Albano, to sleep at the inn. I was so horrified at what I had done, or at what I had not succeeded in undoing, that I hungered for consolation, or at least for advice. Mrs. Rushbrook shone before me in the gloom as a generous dispenser of that sort of comfort.

III.

There was nothing extraordinary in my going to see her, but there was something very extraordinary in my taking such an hour for the purpose. I was supposed to be settled in Rome again, but it was ten o'clock at night when I turned up at the old inn at Albano. Mrs. Rushbrook had not gone to bed, and she greeted me with a certain alarm, though the theory of our intercourse was that she was always glad to see me. I ordered supper and a room for the night, but I couldn't touch the repast before I had been ushered into the vast and vaulted apartment which she used as a parlour, the florid bareness of which would have been vulgar in any country but Italy. She asked me immediately if I had brought bad news, and I replied: "Yes, but only about myself. That's not exactly it," I added; "it's about Henry Wilmerding."

"Henry Wilmerding?" She appeared for the moment not to recognise the name.

"He's going to marry Veronica Goldie."

Mrs. Rushbrook stared. "*Que me contez-vous là?* Have you come all this way to tell me that?"

"But he is—it's all settled—it's awful!" I went on.

"What do I care, and what do you mean?"

"I've got into a mess, and I want you to advise me and to get me out of it," I persisted.

"My poor friend, you must make it a little clearer then," she smiled. "Sit down, please—and have you had your dinner?"

She had been sitting at one end of her faded saloon, where, as the autumn night was fresh at Albano, a fire of faggots was crackling in the big marble-framed cavern of the chimney. Her books, her work, her materials for writing and sketching, were scattered near: the place was a comfortable lamplit corner in the general blankness. There was a piano near at hand, and beyond it were the doors of further chambers, in one of which my hostess's little daughter was asleep. There was always something vaguely annoying to me in these signs of occupation and independence: they seemed to limit the ground on which one could appeal to her for oneself.

"I'm tired and I'm hungry," I said, "but I can't think of my dinner till I've talked to you."

"Have you come all the way from Rome?"

"More than all the way, because I've been at Frascati."

"And how did you get here?"

"I hired a chaise and pair at Frascati—the man drove me over."

"At this hour? You weren't afraid of brigands?"

"Not when it was a question of seeing you. You must do something for me—you must stop it."

"What must I do, and what must I stop?" said Mrs. Rushbrook, sitting down.

"This odious union—it's too unnatural."

"I see, then. Veronica's to marry some one, and you want her for yourself."

"Don't be cruel, and don't torment me—I'm sore enough already. You know well enough whom I want to marry!" I broke out.

"How can I stop anything?" Mrs. Rushbrook asked.

"When I see you this way, at home, between the fire and the lamp, with the empty place beside you—an image of charming domesticity—do you suppose I have any doubt as to what I want?"

She rested her eyes on the fire, as if she were turning my words over as an act of decent courtesy and of pretty form. But immediately afterwards she said: "If you've come out here to make love to me, please say so at once, so that we may have it over on the spot. You will gain nothing whatever by it."

"I'm not such a fool as to have given you such a chance to snub me. That would have been presumptuous, and what is at the bottom of my errand this evening is extreme humility. Don't therefore think you've gained the advantage of putting me in my place. You've done nothing of the sort, for I haven't come out of it—except, indeed, so far as to try a bad joke on Wilmerding. It has turned out even worse than was probable. You're clever, you're sympathetic, you're kind."

"What has Wilmerding to do with that?"

"Try and get him off. That's the sort of thing a woman can do."

"I don't in the least follow you, you know. Who is Wilmerding?"

"Surely you remember him—you've seen him at Frascati, the young American secretary—you saw him a year ago in Rome. The fellow who is always opening the door for you and finding the things you lose."

"The things I lose?"

"I mean the things women lose. He went with us the other day to Monte Cavo."

"And got himself lost with the girl? Oh yes, I recall him," said Mrs. Rushbrook.

"It was the darkest hour of his life—or rather of mine. I told him that after that the only thing he could do was to marry Veronica. And he has believed me."

"Does he believe everything you tell him?" Mrs. Rushbrook asked.

"Don't be impertinent, because I feel very wretched. He loathes Veronica."

"Then why does he marry her?"

"Because I worked upon him. It's comical—yet it's dreadful."

"Is he an idiot—can't he judge for himself?" said Mrs. Rushbrook.

"He's marrying her for good manners. I persuaded him they require it."

"And don't they, then?"

"Not the least in the world!"

"Was that *your* idea of good manners? Why did you do it?"

"I didn't—I backed out, as soon as I saw he believed me. But it was too late. Besides, a friend of mine had a hand in it—he went further than I. I may as well tell you that it's Guy de Montaut, the little Frenchman of the embassy, whom you'll remember—he was of our party at Monte Cavo. Between us, in pure sport and without meaning any harm, we have brought this thing on. And now I'm devoured with remorse—it wasn't a creditable performance."

"What was the beauty of the joke?" Mrs. Rushbrook inquired, with exasperating serenity.

"Don't ask me now—I don't see it! It seems to me hideous."

"And M. de Montaut—has he any compunction?"

"Not a bit—he looks at it from the point of view of the Goldies. Veronica is a *fille sans dot*, and not generally liked; therefore with poor prospects. He has put a husband in her way—a rich, good-natured young man, without encumbrances and of high character. It's a service, where a service was needed, of which he is positively proud."

Mrs. Rushbrook looked at me reflectively, as if she were trying to give me her best attention and to straighten out this odd story.

"Mr. Wilmerding is rich?" she asked in a moment.

"Dear me, yes—very well off."

"And of high character?"

"An excellent fellow—without a fault."

"I don't understand him, then."

"No more do I!"

"Then what can we do? How can we interfere?" my companion went on.

"That's what I want you to tell me. It's a woman's business—that's why I've tumbled in on you here. You must invent something, you must attempt something."

"My dear friend, what on earth do I care for Mr. Wilmerding?"

"You ought to care—he's a knight of romance. Do it for me, then."

"Oh, for you!" my hostess laughed.

"Don't you pity me—doesn't my situation appeal to you?"

"Not a bit! It's grotesque."

"That's because you don't know."

"What is it I don't know?"

"Why, in the first place, what a particularly shabby thing it was to play such a trick on Wilmerding—a gentleman and a man that never injured a fly; and, in the second place, how miserable he'll be and how little comfort he'll have with Veronica."

"What's the matter with Veronica—is she so bad?"

"You know them all—one doesn't want to marry them. Fancy putting oneself deliberately under Mrs. Goldie's heel! The great matter with Veronica is that, left to himself, he would never have dreamed of her. That's enough."

"You say he hasn't a fault," Mrs. Rushbrook replied. "But isn't it rather a fault that he's such a booby?"

"I don't know whether it's because I'm rather exalted, rather morbid, in my reaction against my momentary levity, that he strikes me as so far from being a booby that I really think what he has engaged to do is very fine. If without intending it, and in ignorance of the social perspective of a country not his own, he has appeared to go so far that they have had a right to expect he would go further, he's willing to pay the penalty. Poor fellow, he pays for all of us."

"Surely he's very meek," said Mrs. Rushbrook. "He's what you call a muff."

"*Que voulez-vous?* He's simple—he's generous."

"I see what you mean—I like that."

"You would like him if you knew him. He has acted like a gallant gentleman—from a sense of duty."

"It *is* rather fine," Mrs. Rushbrook murmured.

"He's too good for Veronica," I continued.

"And you want me to tell her so?"

"Well, something of that sort. I want you to arrange it."

"I'm much obliged—that's a fine large order!" my companion laughed.

"Go and see Mrs. Goldie, intercede with her, entreat her to let him go, tell her that they really oughtn't to take advantage of a momentary aberration, an extravagance of magnanimity."

"Don't you think it's *your* place to do all that?"

"Do you imagine it would do any good—that they would release him?" I demanded.

"How can I tell? You could try. Is Veronica very fond of him?" Mrs. Rushbrook pursued.

"I don't think any of them can really be very fond of any one who isn't 'smart.' They want certain things that don't belong to Wilmerding at all—to his nationality or his type. He isn't at all 'smart,' in their sense."

"Oh yes, *their* sense: I know it. It's not a nice sense!" Mrs. Rushbrook exclaimed, with a critical sigh.

"At the same time Veronica is dying to be married, and they are delighted with his money. It makes up for deficiencies," I explained.

"And is there so much of it?"

"Lots and lots. I know by the way he lives."

"An American, you say? One doesn't know Americans."

"How do you mean, one doesn't know them?"

"They're vague to me. One doesn't meet many."

"More's the pity, if they're all like Wilmerding. But they can't be. You must know him—I'm sure you'll like him."

"He comes back to me; I see his face now," said Mrs. Rushbrook. "Isn't he rather good-looking?"

"Well enough; but I'll say he's another Antinous if it will interest you for him."

"What I don't understand is *your* responsibility," my friend remarked after a moment. "If he insists and persists, how is it your fault?"

"Oh, it all comes back to that. I put it into his head—I

perverted his mind. I started him on the fatal course—I administered the primary push."

"Why can't you confess your misdemeanour to him, then?"

"I *have* confessed—that is, almost. I attenuated, I retracted, when I saw how seriously he took it; I did what I could to pull him back. I rode after him to-day and almost killed my horse. But it was no use—he had moved so abominably fast."

"How fast do you mean?"

"I mean that he had proposed to Veronica a few hours after I first spoke to him. He couldn't bear it a moment longer—I mean the construction of his behaviour as shabby."

"He *is* rather a knight!" murmured Mrs. Rushbrook.

"*Il est impayable*, as Montaut says. Montaut practiced upon him without scruple. I really think it was Montaut who settled him."

"Have you told him, then, it was a trick?" my hostess demanded.

I hesitated. "No, not quite that."

"Are you afraid he'll cut your throat?"

"Not in the least. I would give him my throat if it would do any good. But he would cut it and then cut his own. I mean he'd still marry the girl."

"Perhaps he *does* love her," Mrs. Rushbrook suggested.

"I wish I could think it!"

She was silent a moment; then she asked: "Does he love some one else?"

"Not that I know of."

"Well then," said Mrs. Rushbrook, "the only thing for you to do, that I can see, is to take her off his hands."

"To take Veronica off?"

"That would be the only real reparation. Go to Mrs. Goldie to-morrow and tell her your little story. Say: 'I want to prevent the marriage, and I've thought of the most effective thing. If *I* will take her, she will let him go, won't she? Therefore consider that I *will* take her.' "

"I would almost do that; I have really thought of it," I answered. "But Veronica wouldn't take *me*."

"How do you know? It's your duty to try."

"I've no money."

"No, but you're 'smart.' And then you're charming."

"Ah, you're cruel—you're not so sorry for me as I should like!" I returned.

"I thought that what you wanted was that I should be sorry for Mr. Wilmerding. You must bring him to see me," said Mrs. Rushbrook.

"And do you care so little about me that you could be witness of my marrying another woman? I enjoy the way you speak of it!" I cried.

"Wouldn't it all be for your honour? That's what I care about," she laughed.

"I'll bring Wilmerding to see you to-morrow: *he'll* make you serious," I declared.

"Do; I shall be delighted to see him. But go to Mrs. Goldie, too—it *is* your duty."

"Why mine only? Why shouldn't Montaut marry her?"

"You forget that he has no compunction."

"And is that the only thing you can recommend?"

"I'll think it over—I'll tell you to-morrow," Mrs. Rushbrook said. "Meanwhile, I do like your American—he sounds so unusual." I remember her exclaiming further, before we separated: "Your poor Wilmerding—he *is* a knight! But for a diplomatist—fancy!"

It was agreed between us the next day that she should drive over to Frascati with me; and the vehicle which had transported me to Albano and remained the night at the hotel conveyed us, before noon, in the opposite sense, along the side of the hills and the loveliest road in the world—through the groves and gardens, past the monuments and ruins and the brown old villages with feudal and papal gateways that overhang the historic plain. If I begged Mrs. Rushbrook to accompany me there was always reason enough for that in the extreme charm of her society. The day moreover was lovely, and a drive in those regions was always a drive. Besides, I still attached the idea of counsel and aid to Mrs. Rushbrook's presence, in spite of her not having as yet, in regard to my difficulty, any acceptable remedy to propose. She had told me she would try to think of something, and she now assured me she had tried, but the happy idea that would put everything right had not descended upon her. The most she could say was that probably the marriage wouldn't really take place. There was time for accidents; I should get off with my fright; the girl would see how little poor Wilmerding's heart was in it and wouldn't have the ferocity to drag him to the altar. I endeavoured to take that view, but through my magnifying spectacles I could only see Veronica as ferocious, and I remember saying to Mrs. Rushbrook, as we journeyed together: "I wonder if they would take money."

"Whose money—yours?"

"Mine—what money have I? I mean poor Wilmerding's."

"You can always ask them—it's a possibility," my companion answered; from which I saw that she quite took for granted I would intercede with the Honourable Blanche. This was a formidable prospect, a meeting on such delicate ground, but I steeled myself to it in proportion as I seemed to perceive that Mrs. Rushbrook held it to be the least effort I could reputably make. I desired so to remain in her good graces that I was ready to do anything that would strike her as gallant—I didn't want to be so much less of a "knight" than the wretched Wilmerding. What I most hoped for—secretly, however, clinging to the conception of a clever woman's tact as infinite—was that she would speak for me either to Mrs. Goldie or to Veronica herself. She had powers of manipulation and she would manipulate. It was true that she protested against any such expectation, declaring that intercession on her part would be in the worst possible taste and would moreover be attributed to the most absurd motives: how could I fail to embrace a truth so flagrant? If she was still supposed to be trying to think of something, it was something that *I* could do. Fortunately she didn't say again to me that the solution was that I should "take over" Veronica; for I could scarcely have endured that. You may ask why, if she had nothing to suggest and wished to be out of it, if above all she didn't wish, in general, to encourage me, she should have gone with me on this occasion to Frascati. I can only reply that that was her own affair, and I was so far from quarrelling with such a favour that as we rolled together along the avenues of ilex, in the exquisite Roman weather, I was almost happy.

I went straight to Mrs. Goldie's residence, as I should have gone to a duel, and it was agreed that Mrs. Rushbrook should drive on to the Villa Mondragone, where I would rejoin her after the imperfect vindication of my honour. The Villa Mondragone—you probably remember its pompous, painted, faded extent and its magnificent terrace—was open to the public, and any lover of old Rome was grateful for a pretext for strolling in its picturesque, neglected, enchanted grounds. It had been a resource for all of us at Frascati, but Mrs. Rushbrook had not seen so much of it as the rest of us, or as she desired.

I may as well say at once that I shall not attempt to make my encounter with the terrible dowager a vivid scene to you, for to this day I see it only through a blur of embarrassment and confusion, a muddle of difficulties suspended like a sort of enlarging veil before a monstrous Gorgon face. What I had to say to Mrs. Goldie was in truth neither easy nor pleasant, and my story was so abnormal a one that she may well have been excused for staring at me, with a stony refusal to comprehend, while I stammered it forth. I was even rather sorry for her, inasmuch as it was not the kind of appeal that she had reason to expect, and as her imagination had surely never before been led such a dance. I think it glimmered upon her at first, from my strange manner, that I had come to ask for one of the other girls; but that illusion cannot have lasted long. I have no idea of the order or succession of the remarks that we exchanged; I only recall that at a given moment Mrs. Goldie rose, in righteous wrath, to cast me out of her presence. Everything was a part of the general agitation; for the house had been startled by the sudden determination of its mistress to return to Rome. Of this she informed me as soon as I presented myself, and she apprised me in the same breath, you may be sure, of the important cause. Veronica's engagement had altered all their plans; she was to be married immediately, absence and delay being incompatible with dear Henry's official work (I winced at "dear Henry"), and they had no time to lose for conference with dressmakers and shopkeepers. Veronica had gone out for a walk with dear Henry; and the other girls, with one of the maids, had driven to Rome, at an early hour, to see about putting to rights the apartment in Via Babuino. It struck me as characteristic of the Honourable Blanche that *she* had remained on the spot, as if to keep hold of dear Henry.

These announcements gave me, of course, my opening. "Can't you see he is only going through with it as a duty? Do you mean to say you were not very much surprised when he proposed?" I fearlessly demanded.

I maintained that it was *not* a duty—that Wilmerding had a morbid sense of obligation and that at that rate any one of us might be hauled up for the simple sociability, the innocent conviviality of youth. I made a clean breast of it and tried to explain the little history of my unhappy friend's mistake. I am not very proud of any part of my connection with this episode; but though it was a delicate matter to tell a lady that it had been a blunder to offer marriage to her daughter, what I am on the whole least ashamed of is the manner in which I fronted the Honourable Blanche. I was supported by the sense that she was dishonest in pretending that she had not been surprised—that she had regarded our young man as committed to such a step. This was rubbish—her surprise had been at least equal to her satisfaction. I was irritated by her quick assumption, at first, that if I wanted the engagement broken it was because I myself was secretly enamoured of the girl.

Before I went away she put me to the real test, so that I was not able to say afterwards to Mrs. Rushbrook that the opportunity to be fully heroic had not been offered me. She gave me the queerest look I had ever seen a worldly old woman give, and proffered an observation of which the general copious sense was this:

"Come, I do see what you mean, and though you have made a pretty mess with your French monkey-tricks, it may be that if dear Henry's heart isn't in it it simply isn't, and that my sweet, sensitive girl will in the long run have to pay too much for what looks now like a tolerably good match. It isn't so brilliant after all, for what do we really know about him or about his obscure relations in the impossible country to which he may wish to transplant my beloved? He has money, or rather expectations, but he has nothing else, and who knows about American fortunes? Nothing appears to be settled or entailed. Take her yourself and you may have her—I'll engage to make it straight with Mr. Wilmerding. You're impecunious and you're disagreeable, but you're clever and well-connected; you'll rise in your profession—you'll become an ambassador."

All this (it was a good deal), Mrs. Goldie communicated to me in the strange, prolonged, confidential leer with which she suddenly honoured me. It was a good deal, but it was not all, for I understood her still to subjoin: "That will show whether you are sincere or not in wishing to get your friend out of this scrape. It's the only condition on which you can do it. Accept this condition and I will kindly overlook the outrage of your present intrusion and your inexpressible affront to my child."

No, I couldn't tell Mrs. Rushbrook that I had not had my chance to do something fine, for I definitely apprehended this proposition, I looked it well in the face and I sadly shook my head. I wanted to get Wilmerding off, but I didn't want to get him off so much as that.

"Pray, is he aware of your present extraordinary proceeding?" Mrs. Goldie demanded, as she stood there to give me my *congé*.

"He hasn't the faintest suspicion of it."

"And may I take the liberty of inquiring whether it is your design to acquaint him with the scandalous manner in which you have betrayed his confidence?" She was wonderfully majestic and *digne*.

"How can I?" I asked, piteously. "How can I, without uttering words not respectful to the young lady he now stands pledged to marry? Don't you see how that has altered my position?" I wailed.

"Yes, it has given you a delicacy that is wondrous indeed!" cried my hostess, with a laugh of derision which rang in my ears as I withdrew—which rings in my ears at this hour.

I went to the Villa Mondragone, and there, at the end of a quarter of an hour's quest, I saw three persons—two ladies and a gentleman—coming toward me in the distance. I recognised them in a moment as Mrs. Rushbrook, Veronica Goldie, and Wilmerding. The combination amused and even gratified me, as it fell upon my sight, for it immediately suggested that, by the favour of accident, Mrs. Rushbrook would already have had the advantage of judging for herself how little one of her companions was pleased with his bargain, and be proportionately stimulated to come to his rescue. Wilmerding had turned out to spend a perfunctory hour with his betrothed; Mrs. Rushbrook, strolling there and waiting for me, had met them, and she had remained with them on perceiving how glad they were to be relieved of the grimness of their union. I pitied the mismated couple, pitied Veronica almost as much as my more particular victim, and reflected as they came up to me that unfortunately our charming friend would not always be there to render them this delicate service. She seemed pleased, however, with the good turn she had already done them and even disposed to continue the benevolent work. I looked at her hard, with a perceptible headshake, trying to communicate in this way the fact that nothing had come of my attack on Mrs. Goldie; and she smiled back as if to say: "Oh, no matter; I daresay I shall think of something now."

Wilmerding struck me as rather less miserable than I had expected; though of course I knew that he was the man to make an heroic effort not to appear miserable. He immediately proposed that we should all go home with him to luncheon; upon which Veronica said, hesitating with responsibility: "Do you suppose, for me, mamma will mind?" Her intended made no reply to this; his silence was almost a suggestion that if she were in doubt she had perhaps better go home. But Mrs. Rushbrook settled the question by declaring that it was, on the contrary, exactly what mamma would like. Besides, was not she, Mrs. Rushbrook, the most satisfactory of duennas? We walked slowly together to Wilmerding's villa, and I was not surprised at his allowing me complete possession of Veronica. He fell behind us with Mrs. Rushbrook and succeeded, at any rate, in shaking off his gloom sufficiently to manifest the proper elation at her having consented to partake of his hospitality. As I moved beside Veronica I wondered whether she had an incipient sense that it was to me she owed her sudden prospect of a husband. I think she must have wondered to what she owed it. I said nothing to awaken that conjecture: I didn't even allude to her engagement—much less did I utter hollow words of congratulation. She had a

right to expect something of that sort, and my silence disconcerted her and made her stiff. She felt important now, and
she was the kind of girl who likes to show the importance that
she feels. I was sorry for her—it was not *her* fault, poor child—
but I couldn't flatly lie to her, couldn't tell her I was "delighted." I was conscious that she was waiting for me to speak,
and I was even afraid that she would end by asking me if I
didn't know what had happened to her. Her pride, however,
kept her from this, and I continued to be dumb and to pity
her—to pity her the more as I was sure her mystification
would not be cleared up by any revelation in regard to my
visit to her mother. Mrs. Goldie would never tell her of that.

Our extemporised repast at Wilmerding's was almost merry;
our sociability healed my soreness and I forgot for the moment that I had grounds of discomposure. Wilmerding had
always the prettiest courtesy in his own house, with pressing,
preoccupied, literal ways of playing the master, and Mrs.
Rushbrook enjoyed anything that was unexpected and casual.
Our carriage was in waiting, to convey us back to Albano, and
we offered our companions a lift, as it was time for Wilmerding to take Veronica home. We put them down at the gate
of Mrs. Goldie's villa, after I had noticed the double-dyed
sweetness with which Mrs. Rushbrook said to Veronica, as the
carriage stopped: "You must bring him over to Albano to
return my visit." This was spoken in my interest, but even
then the finished feminine hypocrisy of it made me wince a
little. I should have winced still more had I foreseen what was
to follow.

Mrs. Rushbrook was silent during much of the rest of our
drive. She had begun by saying: "Now that I see them together I understand what you mean"; and she had also requested me to tell her all I could about poor Wilmerding—
his situation in life, his character, his family, his history, his
prospects—since, if she were really to go into the matter, she
must have the facts in her hand. When I had told her everything I knew, she sat turning my instructions over in her mind,
as she looked vaguely at the purple Campagna: she was lovely
with that expression. I intimated to her that there was very
little time to lose: every day that we left him in his predicament he would sink deeper and be more difficult to extricate.

"Don't you like him—don't you think he's worthy to marry some woman he's really fond of?" I remember asking.

Her answer was rather short: "Oh yes, he's a good creature." But before we reached Albano she said to me: "And is he really rich?"

"I don't know what you call 'really'—I only wish I had his pocket-money."

"And is he generous—free-handed?"

"Try him and you'll see."

"How can I try him?"

"Well then, ask Mrs. Goldie."

"Perhaps he'd pay to get off," mused Mrs. Rushbrook.

"Oh, they'd ask a fortune!"

"Well, he's perfect to her." And Mrs. Rushbrook repeated that he was a good creature.

That afternoon I rode back to Rome, having reminded my friend at Albano that I gave her *carte-blanche* and that delay would not improve matters. We had a little discussion about this, she maintaining, as a possible view, that if one left the affair alone a rupture would come of itself.

"Why should it come when, as you say, he's perfect?"

"Yes, he's very provoking," said Mrs. Rushbrook: which made me laugh as I got into the saddle.

IV.

In Rome I kept quiet three or four days, hoping to hear from Mrs. Rushbrook; I even removed myself as much as possible from the path of Guy de Montaut. I observed preparations going forward in the house occupied during the winter by Mrs. Goldie, and, in passing, I went so far as to question a servant who was tinkering a flower-stand in the doorway and from whom I learned that the *padrona* was expected at any hour. Wilmerding, however, returned to Rome without her; I perceived it from meeting him in the Corso—he didn't come to see me. This might have been accidental, but I was willing to consider that he avoided me, for it saved me the trouble of avoiding him. I couldn't bear to see him—it made me too uncomfortable; I was always thinking that I ought to say something to him that I couldn't say, or that he would say something to me that he didn't. As I had remarked to Mrs. Goldie, it was impossible for me now to allude in invidious terms to Veronica, and the same license on his side would have been still less becoming. And yet it hardly seemed as if we could go on like that. He couldn't quarrel with me avowedly about his prospective wife, but he might have quarrelled with me ostensibly about something else. Such subtleties however (I began to divine), had no place in his mind, which was presumably occupied with the conscientious effort to like Veronica —as a matter of duty—since he was doomed to spend his life with her. Wilmerding was capable, for a time, of giving himself up to this effort: I don't know how long it would have lasted. Our relations were sensibly changed, inasmuch as after my singular interview with Mrs. Goldie, the day following her daughter's betrothal, I had scruples about presenting myself at her house as if on the old footing.

She came back to town with the girls, immediately showing herself in her old cardinalesque chariot of the former winters, which was now standing half the time before the smart shops in the Corso and Via Condotti. Wilmerding perceived of course that I had suddenly begun to stay away from his future mother-in-law's; but he made no observation about it—a reserve of which I afterwards understood the reason. This was not, I may say at once, any revelation from Mrs. Goldie of my unmannerly appeal to her. Montaut amused himself with again taking up his habits under her roof; the entertainment might surely have seemed mild to a man of his temper, but he let me know that it was richer than it had ever been before—poor Wilmerding showed such a face there. When I answered that it was just his face that I didn't want to see, he declared that I was the best sport of all, with my tergiversations and superstitions. He pronounced Veronica *très-embellie* and said that he was only waiting for her to be married to make love to her himself. I wrote to Mrs. Rushbrook that I couldn't say she had served me very well, and that now the Goldies had quitted her neighbourhood I was in despair of her doing anything. She took no notice of my letter, and I availed myself of the very first Sunday to drive out to Albano and breakfast with her. Riding across the Campagna now suddenly appeared to me too hot and too vain.

"Then what *did* you speak of?"

"Of other things. How you catechise!"

"If I catechise it's because I thought it was all for me."

"For you—and for him. I went to Frascati again," said Mrs. Rushbrook.

"Lord, and what was that for?"

"It was for you," she smiled. "It was a kindness, if they're so uncomfortable together. I relieve them, I know I do!"

"Gracious, you might live with them! Perhaps that's the way out of it."

"We took another walk to Villa Mondragone," my hostess continued. "Augusta Goldie went with us. It went off beautifully."

"Oh, then it's all right," I said, picking up my hat.

Before I took leave of her Mrs. Rushbrook told me that she certainly would move to Rome on the Thursday—or on the Friday. She would give me a sign as soon as she was settled. And she added: "I daresay I shall be able to put my idea into execution. But I shall tell you only if it succeeds."

I don't know why I felt, at this, a slight movement of contrariety; at any rate I replied: "Oh, you had better leave them alone."

On the Wednesday night of that week I found, on coming in to go to bed, Wilmerding's card on my table, with "Good-bye—I'm off to-morrow for a couple of months" scrawled on it. I thought it an odd time for him to be "off"—I wondered whether anything had happened. My servant had not seen him; the card had been transmitted by the porter, and I was obliged to sleep upon my mystification. As soon as possible the next morning I went to his house, where I found a post-chaise, in charge of one of the old *vetturini* and prepared for a journey, drawn up at the door. While I was in the act of asking for him Wilmerding came down, but to my regret, for it was an obstacle to explanations, he was accompanied by his venerable chief. The American Minister had lately come back, and he leaned affectionately on his young secretary's shoulder. He took, or almost took, the explanations off our hands; he was oratorically cheerful, said that his young friend wanted to escape from the Roman past—to breathe a less tainted air, that he had fixed it all right and was going to see him off, to ride

with him a part of the way. The General (have I not mentioned that he was a general?) climbed into the vehicle and
waited, like a sitting Cicero, while Wilmerding gave directions
for the stowage of two or three more parcels. I looked at him
hard as he did this and thought him flushed and excited. Then
he put out his hand to me and I held it, with my eyes still on
his face. We were a little behind the carriage, out of sight of
the General.

"Frankly—what's the matter?" I asked.

"It's all over—they don't want me."

"Don't want you?"

"Veronica can't—she told me yesterday. I mean she can't
marry me," Wilmerding explained, with touching lucidity.
"She doesn't care for me enough."

"Ah, thank God!" I murmured, with great relief, pressing
his hand.

The General put his head out of the chaise. "If there was
a railroad in this queer country I guess we should miss the
train."

"All the same, I'm glad," said Wilmerding.

"I should think you would be."

"I mean I'm glad I did it."

"You're a *preux chevalier*."

"No, I ain't." And, blushing, he got into the carriage,
which rolled away.

Mrs. Rushbrook failed to give me the "sign" she promised,
and two days after this I went, to get news of her, to the small
hotel at which she intended to alight and to which she had
told me, on my last seeing her at Albano, that she had sent
her maid to make arrangements. When I asked if her advent
had been postponed the people of the inn exclaimed that she
was already there—she had been there since the beginning of
the week. Moreover she was at home, and on my sending up
my name she responded that she should be happy to see me.
There was something in her face, when I came in, that I didn't
like, though I was struck with her looking unusually pretty. I
can't tell you now why I should have objected to that. The
first words I said to her savoured, no doubt, of irritation:
"Will you kindly tell me why you have been nearly a week in
Rome without letting me know?"

"Oh, I've been occupied—I've had other things to do."

"You don't keep your promises."

"Don't I? You shouldn't say that," she answered, with an amused air.

"Why haven't I met you out—in this place where people meet every day?"

"I've been busy at home—I haven't been running about."

I looked round me, asked about her little girl, congratulated her on the brightness she imparted to the most *banal* room as soon as she began to live in it, took up her books, fidgeted, waited for her to say something about Henry Wilmerding. For this, however, I waited in vain; so that at last I broke out: "I suppose you know he's gone?"

"Whom are you talking about?"

"Veronica's *promesso sposo*. He quitted Rome yesterday."

She was silent a moment; then she replied—"I didn't know it."

I thought this odd, but I believed what she said, and even now I have no doubt it was true. "It's all off," I went on: "I suppose you know that."

"How do *you* know it?" she smiled.

"From his own lips; he told me, at his door, when I bade him good-bye. Didn't you really know he had gone?" I continued.

"My dear friend, do you accuse me of lying?"

"*Jamais de la vie*—only of joking. I thought you and he had become so intimate."

"Intimate—in three or four days? We've had very little communication."

"How then did you know his marriage was off?"

"How you cross-examine one! I knew it from Veronica."

"And is it *your* work?"

"Ah, mine—call it rather yours: you set me on."

"Is that what you've been so busy with that you couldn't send me a message?" I asked.

"What shall I say? It didn't take long."

"And how did you do it?"

"How shall I tell you—how shall I tell?"

"You said you would tell me. Did you go to Mrs. Goldie?"

"No, I went to the girl herself."

"And what did you say?"

"Don't ask me—it's my secret. Or rather it's hers."

"Ah, but you promised to let me know if you succeeded."

"Who can tell? It's too soon to speak of success."

"Why so—if he's gone away?"

"He may come back."

"What will that matter if she won't take him?"

"Very true—she won't."

"Ah, what did you do to her?" I demanded, very curious.

Mrs. Rushbrook looked at me with strange, smiling eyes. "I played a bold game."

"Did you offer her money?"

"I offered her yours."

"Mine? I have none. The bargain won't hold."

"I offered her mine, then."

"You might be serious—you promised to tell me," I repeated.

"Surely not. All I said was that if my attempt didn't succeed I wouldn't tell you."

"That's an equivocation. If there was no promise and it was so disagreeable, why did you make the attempt?"

"It was disagreeable to me, but it was agreeable to you. And now, though you goaded me on, you don't seem delighted."

"Ah, I'm too curious—I wonder too much!"

"Well, be patient," said Mrs. Rushbrook, "and with time everything will probably be clear to you."

I endeavoured to conform to this injunction, and my patience was so far rewarded that a month later I began to have a suspicion of the note that Mrs. Rushbrook had sounded. I quite gave up Mrs. Goldie's house, but Montaut was in and out of it enough to give me occasional news of *ces dames.* He had been infinitely puzzled by Veronica's retractation and Wilmerding's departure: he took it almost as a personal injury, the postponement of the event that would render it proper for him to make love to the girl. Poor Montaut was destined never to see that attitude legitimated, for Veronica Goldie never married. Mrs. Rushbrook, somewhat to my surprise, accepted on various occasions the hospitality of the Honourable Blanche—she became a frequent visitor at Casa Goldie. I was therefore in a situation not to be ignorant of matters relating to it, the more especially as for many weeks after the conversation I have last related my charming friend was remarkably humane in her treatment of me—kind, communicative, sociable, encouraging me to come and see her and consenting often to some delightful rummaging Roman stroll. But she would never tolerate, on my lips, the slightest argument in favour of a union more systematic; she once said, laughing: "How can we possibly marry when we're so impoverished? Didn't we spend every penny we possess to buy off Veronica?" This was highly fantastic, of course, but there was just a sufficient symbolism in it to minister to my unsatisfied desire to know what had really taken place.

I seemed to make that out a little better when, before the winter had fairly begun, I learned from both of my friends that Mrs. Goldie had decided upon a change of base, a new campaign altogether. She had got some friends to take her house off her hands; she was quitting Rome, embarking on a scheme of foreign travel, going to Naples, proposing to visit the East, to get back to England for the summer, to *promener* her daughters, in short, in regions hitherto inaccessible and unattempted. This news pointed to a considerable augmentation of fortune on the part of the Honourable Blanche, whose conspicuous thrift we all knew to be funded on slender possessions. If she was undertaking expensive journeys it was because she had "come into" money—a reflection that didn't make Mrs. Rushbrook's refusal to enlighten my ignorance a whit less tormenting. When I said to this whimsical woman, as I did several times, that she really oughtn't to leave me so in the dark, her reply was always the same, that the matter was all too delicate—she didn't know how she had done, there were some transactions so tacit, so made up of subtle *sousentendus*, that you couldn't describe them. So I groped for the missing link without finding it—the secret of how it had been possible for Mrs. Rushbrook to put the key of Wilmerding's coffers into Mrs. Goldie's hand.

I was present at the large party the latter lady gave as her leave-taking of her Roman friends, and as soon as I stood face to face with her I recognised that she had had much less "feeling" than I about our meeting again. I might have come at any time. She was good-natured, in her way, she forgot things and was not rancorous: it had now quite escaped her that she had turned me out of the house. The air of prosperity was in the place, the shabby past was sponged out. The tea was potent, the girls had all new frocks, and Mrs. Goldie looked at me with an eye that seemed to say that I might still have Veronica if I wanted. Veronica was now a fortune, but I didn't take it up.

Wilmerding came back to Rome in February, after Casa Goldie, as we had known it, was closed. In his absence I had been at the American Legation on various occasions—no *chancellerie* in Europe was steeped in dustier leisure—and the good General confided to me that he missed his young friend *as* a friend, but so far as missing him as a worker went (there *was* no work), "Uncle Sam" might save his salary. He repeated that he had fixed it all right: Wilmerding had taken three months to cross the Atlantic and see his people. He had doubtless important arrangements to make and copious drafts to explain. They must have been extraordinarily obliging, his people, for Mrs. Goldie (to finish with her), was for the rest of her days able to abjure cheap capitals and follow the chase where it was doubtless keenest—among the lordly herds of her native land. If Veronica never married the other girls did, and Miss Goldie, disencumbered and bedizened, reigned as a beauty, a good deal contested, for a great many years. I think that after her sisters went off she got her mother much under control, and she grew more and more to resemble her. She is dead, poor girl, her mother is dead—I told you every one is dead. Wilmerding is dead—his wife is dead.

The subsequent life of this ingenious woman was short: I doubt whether she liked America as well as she had had an idea she should, or whether it agreed with her. She had put me off my guard that winter, and she put Wilmerding a little off his, too, I think, by going down to Naples just before he came back to Rome. She reappeared there, however, late in the spring—though I don't know how long she stayed. At the end of May, that year, my own residence in Rome terminated. I was assigned to a post in the north of Europe, with orders to proceed to it with speed. I saw them together before I quitted Italy, my two good friends, and then the truth suddenly came over me. As she said herself—for I had it out with her fearfully before I left—I had only myself to thank for it. I had made her think of him, I had made her look at him, I had made her do extraordinary things. You won't be surprised to hear they were married less than two years after the service I had induced her to render me.

Ah, don't ask me what really passed between them—that was their own affair. There are "i's" in the matter that have never been dotted, and in later years, when my soreness had subsided sufficiently to allow me a certain liberty of mind, I often wondered and theorised. I was sore for a long time and I never even thought of marrying another woman: that "i" at least I can dot. It made no difference that she probably never would have had me. She fell in love with him, of course—with the idea of him, secretly, in her heart of hearts—the hour I told her, in my distress, of the *beau trait* of which he had been capable. She didn't know him, hadn't seen him, positively speaking; but she took a fancy to the man who had that sort of sense of conduct. Some women would have despised it, but I was careful to pick out the one to whom it happened most to appeal. I dragged them together, I kept them together. When they met he liked her for the interest he was conscious she already took in him, and it all went as softly as when you tread on velvet. Of course I had myself to thank for it, for I not only shut her up with Wilmerding—I shut her up with Veronica.

What she said to Veronica in this situation was no doubt that it was all a mistake (she appealed to the girl's conscience to justify her there), but that he would pay largely for his mistake. Her warrant for that was simply one of the subtle *sousentendus* of which she spoke to me when I attacked her and which are the medium of communication of people in love. She took upon herself to speak for him—she despoiled him, at a stroke, in advance, so that when she married him she married a man of relatively small fortune. This was disinterested at least. There was no bargain between them, as I read it—it all passed in the air. He divined what she had promised for him and he immediately performed. Fancy how she must have liked him then! Veronica believed, her mother believed, because he had already given them a specimen of his disposition to do the handsome thing. I had arranged it all in perfection. My only consolation was that I had done what I wanted; but do you suppose that was sufficient?

The Pupil

THE POOR young man hesitated and procrastinated: it cost him such an effort to broach the subject of terms, to speak of money to a person who spoke only of feelings and, as it were, of the aristocracy. Yet he was unwilling to take leave, treating his engagement as settled, without some more conventional glance in that direction than he could find an opening for in the manner of the large, affable lady who sat there drawing a pair of soiled *gants de Suède* through a fat, jewelled hand and, at once pressing and gliding, repeated over and over everything but the thing he would have liked to hear. He would have liked to hear the figure of his salary; but just as he was nervously about to sound that note the little boy came back—the little boy Mrs. Moreen had sent out of the room to fetch her fan. He came back without the fan, only with the casual observation that he couldn't find it. As he dropped this cynical confession he looked straight and hard at the candidate for the honour of taking his education in hand. This personage reflected, somewhat grimly, that the first thing he should have to teach his little charge would be to appear to address himself to his mother when he spoke to her —especially not to make her such an improper answer as that.

When Mrs. Moreen bethought herself of this pretext for getting rid of their companion, Pemberton supposed it was precisely to approach the delicate subject of his remuneration. But it had been only to say some things about her son which it was better that a boy of eleven shouldn't catch. They were extravagantly to his advantage, save when she lowered her voice to sigh, tapping her left side familiarly: "And all over-clouded by *this*, you know—all at the mercy of a weakness—!" Pemberton gathered that the weakness was in the region of the heart. He had known the poor child was not robust: this was the basis on which he had been invited to treat, through an English lady, an Oxford acquaintance, then at Nice, who happened to know both his needs and those of the amiable American family looking out for something really superior in the way of a resident tutor.

The young man's impression of his prospective pupil, who had first come into the room, as if to see for himself, as soon as Pemberton was admitted, was not quite the soft solicitation the visitor had taken for granted. Morgan Moreen was, somehow, sickly without being delicate, and that he looked intelligent (it is true Pemberton wouldn't have enjoyed his being stupid), only added to the suggestion that, as with his big mouth and big ears he really couldn't be called pretty, he might be unpleasant. Pemberton was modest—he was even timid, and the chance that his small scholar might prove cleverer than himself had quite figured, to his nervousness, among the dangers of an untried experiment. He reflected, however, that these were risks one had to run when one accepted a position, as it was called, in a private family; when as yet one's University honours had, pecuniarily speaking, remained barren. At any rate, when Mrs. Moreen got up as if to intimate that, since it was understood he would enter upon his duties within the week she would let him off now, he succeeded, in spite of the presence of the child, in squeezing out a phrase about the rate of payment. It was not the fault of the conscious smile which seemed a reference to the lady's expensive identity, if the allusion did not sound rather vulgar. This was exactly because she became still more gracious to reply: "Oh! I can assure you that all that will be quite regular."

Pemberton only wondered, while he took up his hat, what "all that" was to amount to—people had such different ideas. Mrs. Moreen's words, however, seemed to commit the family to a pledge definite enough to elicit from the child a strange little comment, in the shape of the mocking, foreign ejaculation, "Oh, là-là!"

Pemberton, in some confusion, glanced at him as he walked slowly to the window with his back turned, his hands in his pockets and the air in his elderly shoulders of a boy who didn't play. The young man wondered if he could teach him to play, though his mother had said it would never do and that this was why school was impossible. Mrs. Moreen exhibited no discomfiture; she only continued blandly: "Mr. Moreen will be delighted to meet your wishes. As I told you, he has been called to London for a week. As soon as he comes back you shall have it out with him."

This was so frank and friendly that the young man could only reply, laughing as his hostess laughed: "Oh! I don't imagine we shall have much of a battle."

"They'll give you anything you like," the boy remarked unexpectedly, returning from the window. "We don't mind what anything costs—we live awfully well."

"My darling, you're too quaint!" his mother exclaimed, putting out to caress him a practiced but ineffectual hand. He slipped out of it, but looked with intelligent, innocent eyes at Pemberton, who had already had time to notice that from one moment to the other his small satiric face seemed to change its time of life. At this moment it was infantine; yet it appeared also to be under the influence of curious intuitions and knowledges. Pemberton rather disliked precocity, and he was disappointed to find gleams of it in a disciple not yet in his teens. Nevertheless he divined on the spot that Morgan wouldn't prove a bore. He would prove on the contrary a kind of excitement. This idea held the young man, in spite of a certain repulsion.

"You pompous little person! We're not extravagant!" Mrs. Moreen gayly protested, making another unsuccessful attempt to draw the boy to her side. "You must know what to expect," she went on to Pemberton.

"The less you expect the better!" her companion interposed. "But we *are* people of fashion."

"Only so far as *you* make us so!" Mrs. Moreen mocked, tenderly. "Well, then, on Friday—don't tell me you're superstitious—and mind you don't fail us. Then you'll see us all. I'm so sorry the girls are out. I guess you'll like the girls. And, you know, I've another son, quite different from this one."

"He tries to imitate me," said Morgan to Pemberton.

"He tries? Why, he's twenty years old!" cried Mrs. Moreen.

"You're very witty," Pemberton remarked to the child—a proposition that his mother echoed with enthusiasm, declaring that Morgan's sallies were the delight of the house. The boy paid no heed to this; he only inquired abruptly of the visitor, who was surprised afterwards that he hadn't struck him as offensively forward: "Do you *want* very much to come?"

"Can you doubt it, after such a description of what I shall

hear?" Pemberton replied. Yet he didn't want to come at all; he was coming because he had to go somewhere, thanks to the collapse of his fortune at the end of a year abroad, spent on the system of putting his tiny patrimony into a single full wave of experience. He had had his full wave, but he couldn't pay his hotel bill. Moreover, he had caught in the boy's eyes the glimpse of a far-off appeal.

"Well, I'll do the best I can for you," said Morgan; with which he turned away again. He passed out of one of the long windows, Pemberton saw him go and lean on the parapet of the terrace. He remained there while the young man took leave of his mother, who, on Pemberton's looking as if he expected a farewell from him, interposed with: "Leave him, leave him; he's so strange!" Pemberton suspected she was afraid of something he might say. "He's a genius—you'll love him," she added. "He's much the most interesting person in the family." And before he could invent some civility to oppose to this, she wound up with: "But we're all good, you know!"

"He's a genius—you'll love him!" were words that recurred to Pemberton before the Friday, suggesting, among other things that geniuses were not invariably lovable. However, it was all the better if there was an element that would make tutorship absorbing: he had perhaps taken too much for granted that it would be dreary. As he left the villa after his interview, he looked up at the balcony and saw the child leaning over it. "We shall have great larks!" he called up.

Morgan hesitated a moment; then he answered, laughing: "By the time you come back I shall have thought of something witty!"

This made Pemberton say to himself: "After all he's rather nice."

II.

On the Friday he saw them all, as Mrs. Moreen had promised, for her husband had come back and the girls and the other son were at home. Mr. Moreen had a white moustache, a confiding manner and, in his buttonhole, the ribbon of a foreign order—bestowed, as Pemberton eventually learned, for services. For what services he never clearly ascertained: this was a point—one of a large number—that Mr. Moreen's manner never confided. What it emphatically did confide was that he was a man of the world. Ulick, the firstborn, was in visible training for the same profession—under the disadvantage as yet, however, of a buttonhole only feebly floral and a moustache with no pretensions to type. The girls had hair and figures and manners and small fat feet, but had never been out alone. As for Mrs. Moreen, Pemberton saw on a nearer view that her elegance was intermittent and her parts didn't always match. Her husband, as she had promised, met with enthusiasm Pemberton's ideas in regard to a salary. The young man had endeavoured to make them modest, and Mr. Moreen confided to him that *he* found them positively meagre. He further assured him that he aspired to be intimate with his children, to be their best friend, and that he was always looking out for them. That was what he went off for, to London and other places—to look out; and this vigilance was the theory of life, as well as the real occupation, of the whole family. They all looked out, for they were very frank on the subject of its being necessary. They desired it to be understood that they were earnest people, and also that their fortune, though quite adequate for earnest people, required the most careful administration. Mr. Moreen, as the parent bird, sought sustenance for the nest. Ulick found sustenance mainly at the club, where Pemberton guessed that it was usually served on green cloth. The girls used to do up their hair and their frocks themselves, and our young man felt appealed to to be glad, in regard to Morgan's education, that, though it must naturally be of the best, it didn't cost too much. After a little he *was* glad, forgetting at times his own needs in the interest inspired by the child's nature and education and the pleasure of making easy terms for him.

During the first weeks of their acquaintance Morgan had been as puzzling as a page in an unknown language—altogether different from the obvious little Anglo-Saxons who had misrepresented childhood to Pemberton. Indeed the whole mystic volume in which the boy had been bound demanded some practice in translation. To-day, after a considerable in-

terval, there is something phantasmagoric, like a prismatic reflection or a serial novel, in Pemberton's memory of the
queerness of the Moreens. If it were not for a few tangible
tokens—a lock of Morgan's hair, cut by his own hand, and
the half-dozen letters he got from him when they were separated—the whole episode and the figures peopling it would
seem too inconsequent for anything but dream-land. The
queerest thing about them was their success (as it appeared to
him for a while at the time), for he had never seen a family
so brilliantly equipped for failure. Wasn't it success to have
kept him so hatefully long? Wasn't it success to have drawn
him in that first morning at *déjeuner*, the Friday he came—it
was enough to *make* one superstitious—so that he utterly
committed himself, and this not by calculation or a *mot
d'ordre*, but by a happy instinct which made them, like a band
of gipsies, work so neatly together? They amused him as much
as if they had really been a band of gipsies. He was still young
and had not seen much of the world—his English years had
been intensely usual; therefore the reversed conventions of the
Moreens (for they had their standards), struck him as topsy-
turvy. He had encountered nothing like them at Oxford; still
less had any such note been struck to his younger American
ear during the four years at Yale in which he had richly supposed himself to be reacting against Puritanism. The reaction
of the Moreens, at any rate, went ever so much further. He
had thought himself very clever that first day in hitting them
all off in his mind with the term "cosmopolite." Later, it
seemed feeble and colourless enough—confessedly, helplessly
provisional.

However, when he first applied it to them he had a degree
of joy—for an instructor he was still empirical—as if from the
apprehension that to live with them would really be to see
life. Their sociable strangeness was an intimation of that—
their chatter of tongues, their gaiety and good humour, their
infinite dawdling (they were always getting themselves up, but
it took forever, and Pemberton had once found Mr. Moreen
shaving in the drawing-room), their French, their Italian and,
in the spiced fluency, their cold, tough slices of American.
They lived on macaroni and coffee (they had these articles
prepared in perfection), but they knew recipes for a hundred

other dishes. They overflowed with music and song, were always humming and catching each other up, and had a kind of professional acquaintance with continental cities. They talked of "good places" as if they had been strolling players. They had at Nice a villa, a carriage, a piano and a banjo, and they went to official parties. They were a perfect calendar of the "days" of their friends, which Pemberton knew them, when they were indisposed, to get out of bed to go to, and which made the week larger than life when Mrs. Moreen talked of them with Paula and Amy. Their romantic initiations gave their new inmate at first an almost dazzling sense of culture. Mrs. Moreen had translated something, at some former period—an author whom it made Pemberton feel *borné* never to have heard of. They could imitate Venetian and sing Neapolitan, and when they wanted to say something very particular they communicated with each other in an ingenious dialect of their own—a sort of spoken cipher, which Pemberton at first took for Volapuk, but which he learned to understand as he would not have understood Volapuk.

"It's the family language—Ultramoreen," Morgan explained to him drolly enough; but the boy rarely condescended to use it himself, though he attempted colloquial Latin as if he had been a little prelate.

Among all the "days" with which Mrs. Moreen's memory was taxed she managed to squeeze in one of her own, which her friends sometimes forgot. But the house derived a frequented air from the number of fine people who were freely named there and from several mysterious men with foreign titles and English clothes whom Morgan called the princes and who, on sofas with the girls, talked French very loud, as if to show they were saying nothing improper. Pemberton wondered how the princes could ever propose in that tone and so publicly: he took for granted cynically that this was what was desired of them. Then he acknowledged that even for the chance of such an advantage Mrs. Moreen would never allow Paula and Amy to receive alone. These young ladies were not at all timid, but it was just the safeguards that made them so graceful. It was a houseful of Bohemians who wanted tremendously to be Philistines.

In one respect, however, certainly, they achieved no rigour

—they were wonderfully amiable and ecstatic about Morgan. It was a genuine tenderness, an artless admiration, equally strong in each. They even praised his beauty, which was small, and were rather afraid of him, as if they recognised that he was of a finer clay. They called him a little angel and a little prodigy and pitied his want of health effusively. Pemberton feared at first that their extravagance would make him hate the boy, but before this happened he had become extravagant himself. Later, when he had grown rather to hate the others, it was a bribe to patience for him that they were at any rate nice about Morgan, going on tiptoe if they fancied he was showing symptoms, and even giving up somebody's "day" to procure him a pleasure. But mixed with this was the oddest wish to make him independent, as if they felt that they were not good enough for him. They passed him over to Pemberton very much as if they wished to force a constructive adoption on the obliging bachelor and shirk altogether a responsibility. They were delighted when they perceived that Morgan liked his preceptor, and could think of no higher praise for the young man. It was strange how they contrived to reconcile the appearance, and indeed the essential fact, of adoring the child with their eagerness to wash their hands of him. Did they want to get rid of him before he should find them out? Pemberton was finding them out month by month. At any rate, the boy's relations turned their backs with exaggerated delicacy, as if to escape the charge of interfering. Seeing in time how little he had in common with them (it was by *them* he first observed it—they proclaimed it with complete humility), his preceptor was moved to speculate on the mysteries of transmission, the far jumps of heredity. Where his detachment from most of the things they represented had come from was more than an observer could say—it certainly had burrowed under two or three generations.

As for Pemberton's own estimate of his pupil, it was a good while before he got the point of view, so little had he been prepared for it by the smug young barbarians to whom the tradition of tutorship, as hitherto revealed to him, had been adjusted. Morgan was scrappy and surprising, deficient in many properties supposed common to the *genus* and abounding in others that were the portion only of the supernaturally

clever. One day Pemberton made a great stride: it cleared up
the question to perceive that Morgan *was* supernaturally clever
and that, though the formula was temporarily meagre, this
would be the only assumption on which one could successfully
deal with him. He had the general quality of a child for whom
life had not been simplified by school, a kind of homebred
sensibility which might have been bad for himself but was
charming for others, and a whole range of refinement and
perception—little musical vibrations as taking as picked-up
airs—begotten by wandering about Europe at the tail of his
migratory tribe. This might not have been an education to
recommend in advance, but its results with Morgan were as
palpable as a fine texture. At the same time he had in his
composition a sharp spice of stoicism, doubtless the fruit of
having had to begin early to bear pain, which produced the
impression of pluck and made it of less consequence that he
might have been thought at school rather a polyglot little
beast. Pemberton indeed quickly found himself rejoicing that
school was out of the question: in any million of boys it was
probably good for all but one, and Morgan was that millionth.
It would have made him comparative and superior—it might
have made him priggish. Pemberton would try to be school
himself—a bigger seminary than five hundred grazing donkeys; so that, winning no prizes, the boy would remain
unconscious and irresponsible and amusing—amusing, because, though life was already intense in his childish nature,
freshness still made there a strong draught for jokes. It turned
out that even in the still air of Morgan's various disabilities
jokes flourished greatly. He was a pale, lean, acute, undeveloped little cosmopolite, who liked intellectual gymnastics and
who, also, as regards the behaviour of mankind, had noticed
more things than you might suppose, but who nevertheless
had his proper playroom of superstitions, where he smashed
a dozen toys a day.

III.

At Nice once, towards evening, as the pair sat resting in the
open air after a walk, looking over the sea at the pink western

lights, Morgan said suddenly to his companion: "Do you like it—you know, being with us all in this intimate way?"

"My dear fellow, why should I stay if I didn't?"

"How do I know you will stay? I'm almost sure you won't, very long."

"I hope you don't mean to dismiss me," said Pemberton.

Morgan considered a moment, looking at the sunset. "I think if I did right I ought to."

"Well, I know I'm supposed to instruct you in virtue; but in that case don't do right."

"You're very young—fortunately," Morgan went on, turning to him again.

"Oh yes, compared with you!"

"Therefore, it won't matter so much if you do lose a lot of time."

"That's the way to look at it," said Pemberton accommodatingly.

They were silent a minute; after which the boy asked: "Do you like my father and mother very much?"

"Dear me, yes. They're charming people."

Morgan received this with another silence; then, unexpectedly, familiarly, but at the same time affectionately, he remarked: "You're a jolly old humbug!"

For a particular reason the words made Pemberton change colour. The boy noticed in an instant that he had turned red, whereupon he turned red himself and the pupil and the master exchanged a longish glance in which there was a consciousness of many more things than are usually touched upon, even tacitly, in such a relation. It produced for Pemberton an embarrassment; it raised, in a shadowy form, a question (this was the first glimpse of it), which was destined to play as singular and, as he imagined, owing to the altogether peculiar conditions, an unprecedented part in his intercourse with his little companion. Later, when he found himself talking with this small boy in a way in which few small boys could ever have been talked with, he thought of that clumsy moment on the bench at Nice as the dawn of an understanding that had broadened. What had added to the clumsiness then was that he thought it his duty to declare to Morgan that he might abuse him (Pemberton) as much as he liked, but must never abuse his parents. To this Morgan had the easy reply that he hadn't dreamed of abusing them; which appeared to be true: it put Pemberton in the wrong.

"Then why am I a humbug for saying *I* think them charming?" the young man asked, conscious of a certain rashness.

"Well—they're not *your* parents."

"They love you better than anything in the world—never forget that," said Pemberton.

"Is that why you like them so much?"

"They're very kind to me," Pemberton replied, evasively.

"You *are* a humbug!" laughed Morgan, passing an arm into his tutor's. He leaned against him, looking off at the sea again and swinging his long, thin legs.

"Don't kick my shins," said Pemberton, while he reflected: "Hang it, I can't complain of them to the child!"

"There's another reason, too," Morgan went on, keeping his legs still.

"Another reason for what?"

"Besides their not being your parents."

"I don't understand you," said Pemberton.

"Well, you will before long. All right!"

Pemberton did understand, fully, before long; but he made a fight even with himself before he confessed it. He thought it the oddest thing to have a struggle with the child about. He wondered he didn't detest the child for launching him in such a struggle. But by the time it began the resource of detesting the child was closed to him. Morgan was a special case, but to know him was to accept him on his own odd terms. Pemberton had spent his aversion to special cases before arriving at knowledge. When at last he did arrive he felt that he was in an extreme predicament. Against every interest he had attached himself. They would have to meet things together. Before they went home that evening, at Nice, the boy had said, clinging to his arm:

"Well, at any rate you'll hang on to the last."

"To the last?"

"Till you're fairly beaten."

"*You* ought to be fairly beaten!" cried the young man, drawing him closer.

IV.

A year after Pemberton had come to live with them Mr. and
Mrs. Moreen suddenly gave up the villa at Nice. Pemberton
had got used to suddenness, having seen it practiced on a
considerable scale during two jerky little tours—one in Switzerland the first summer, and the other late in the winter,
when they all ran down to Florence and then, at the end of
ten days, liking it much less than they had intended, straggled
back in mysterious depression. They had returned to Nice
"for ever," as they said; but this didn't prevent them from
squeezing, one rainy, muggy May night, into a second-class
railway-carriage—you could never tell by which class they
would travel—where Pemberton helped them to stow away a
wonderful collection of bundles and bags. The explanation of
this manœuvre was that they had determined to spend the
summer "in some bracing place;" but in Paris they dropped
into a small furnished apartment—a fourth floor in a third-
rate avenue, where there was a smell on the staircase and the
portier was hateful—and passed the next four months in blank
indigence.

The better part of this baffled sojourn was for the preceptor
and his pupil, who, visiting the Invalides and Notre Dame,
the Conciergerie and all the museums, took a hundred re-
munerative rambles. They learned to know their Paris, which
was useful, for they came back another year for a longer stay,
the general character of which in Pemberton's memory to-day
mixes pitiably and confusedly with that of the first. He sees
Morgan's shabby knickerbockers—the everlasting pair that
didn't match his blouse and that as he grew longer could only
grow faded. He remembers the particular holes in his three
or four pair of coloured stockings.

Morgan was dear to his mother, but he never was better
dressed than was absolutely necessary—partly, no doubt, by
his own fault, for he was as indifferent to his appearance as a
German philosopher. "My dear fellow, you *are* coming to
pieces," Pemberton would say to him in sceptical remonstrance; to which the child would reply, looking at him serenely up and down: "My dear fellow, so are you! I don't
want to cast you in the shade." Pemberton could have no

rejoinder for this—the assertion so closely represented the fact. If however the deficiencies of his own wardrobe were a chapter by themselves he didn't like his little charge to look too poor. Later he used to say: "Well, if we are poor, why, after all, shouldn't we look it?" and he consoled himself with thinking there was something rather elderly and gentlemanly in Morgan's seediness—it differed from the untidiness of the urchin who plays and spoils his things. He could trace perfectly the degrees by which, in proportion as her little son confined himself to his tutor for society, Mrs. Moreen shrewdly forbore to renew his garments. She did nothing that didn't show, neglected him because he escaped notice, and then, as he illustrated this clever policy, discouraged at home his public appearances. Her position was logical enough—those members of her family who did show had to be showy.

During this period and several others Pemberton was quite aware of how he and his comrade might strike people; wandering languidly through the Jardin des Plantes as if they had nowhere to go, sitting, on the winter days, in the galleries of the Louvre, so splendidly ironical to the homeless, as if for the advantage of the *calorifère*. They joked about it sometimes: it was the sort of joke that was perfectly within the boy's compass. They figured themselves as part of the vast, vague, hand-to-mouth multitude of the enormous city and pretended they were proud of their position in it—it showed them such a lot of life and made them conscious of a sort of democratic brotherhood. If Pemberton could not feel a sympathy in destitution with his small companion (for after all Morgan's fond parents would never have let him really suffer), the boy would at least feel it with him, so it came to the same thing. He used sometimes to wonder what people would think they were—fancy they were looked askance at, as if it might be a suspected case of kidnapping. Morgan wouldn't be taken for a young patrician with a preceptor—he wasn't smart enough; though he might pass for his companion's sickly little brother. Now and then he had a five-franc piece, and except once, when they bought a couple of lovely neckties, one of which he made Pemberton accept, they laid it out scientifically in old books. It was a great day, always spent on the quays, rummaging among the dusty boxes that garnish the parapets. These were occasions that helped them to live, for their books ran low very soon after the beginning of their acquaintance. Pemberton had a good many in England, but he was obliged to write to a friend and ask him kindly to get some fellow to give him something for them.

If the bracing climate was untasted that summer the young man had an idea that at the moment they were about to make a push the cup had been dashed from their lips by a movement of his own. It had been his first blow-out, as he called it, with his patrons; his first successful attempt (though there was little other success about it), to bring them to a consideration of his impossible position. As the ostensible eve of a costly journey the moment struck him as a good one to put in a signal protest—to present an ultimatum. Ridiculous as it sounded he had never yet been able to compass an uninterrupted private interview with the elder pair or with either of them singly. They were always flanked by their elder children, and poor Pemberton usually had his own little charge at his side. He was conscious of its being a house in which the surface of one's delicacy got rather smudged; nevertheless he had kept the bloom of his scruple against announcing to Mr. and Mrs. Moreen with publicity that he couldn't go on longer without a little money. He was still simple enough to suppose Ulick and Paula and Amy might not know that since his arrival he had only had a hundred and forty francs; and he was magnanimous enough to wish not to compromise their parents in their eyes. Mr. Moreen now listened to him, as he listened to every one and to everything, like a man of the world, and seemed to appeal to him—though not of course too grossly—to try and be a little more of one himself. Pemberton recognised the importance of the character from the advantage it gave Mr. Moreen. He was not even confused, whereas poor Pemberton was more so than there was any reason for. Neither was he surprised—at least any more than a gentleman had to be who freely confessed himself a little shocked, though not, strictly, at Pemberton.

"We must go into this, mustn't we, dear?" he said to his wife. He assured his young friend that the matter should have his very best attention; and he melted into space as elusively as if, at the door, he were taking an inevitable but deprecatory

precedence. When, the next moment, Pemberton found himself alone with Mrs. Moreen it was to hear her say: "I see, I
see," stroking the roundness of her chin and looking as if she
were only hesitating between a dozen easy remedies. If they
didn't make their push Mr. Moreen could at least disappear
for several days. During his absence his wife took up the subject again spontaneously, but her contribution to it was merely
that she had thought all the while they were getting on so
beautifully. Pemberton's reply to this revelation was that unless they immediately handed him a substantial sum he would
leave them for ever. He knew she would wonder how he
would get away, and for a moment expected her to inquire.
She didn't, for which he was almost grateful to her, so little
was he in a position to tell.

"You won't, you know you won't—you're too interested,"
she said. "You *are* interested, you know you are, you dear,
kind man!" She laughed, with almost condemnatory archness,
as if it were a reproach (but she wouldn't insist), while she
flirted a soiled pocket-handkerchief at him.

Pemberton's mind was fully made up to quit the house the
following week. This would give him time to get an answer
to a letter he had despatched to England. If he did nothing
of the sort—that is, if he stayed another year and then went
away only for three months—it was not merely because before
the answer to his letter came (most unsatisfactory when it did
arrive), Mr. Moreen generously presented him—again with all
the precautions of a man of the world—three hundred francs.
He was exasperated to find that Mrs. Moreen was right, that
he couldn't bear to leave the child. This stood out clearer for
the very reason that, the night of his desperate appeal to his
patrons, he had seen fully for the first time where he was.
Wasn't it another proof of the success with which those patrons practiced their arts that they had managed to avert for
so long the illuminating flash? It descended upon Pemberton
with a luridness which perhaps would have struck a spectator
as comically excessive, after he had returned to his little servile
room, which looked into a close court where a bare, dirty
opposite wall took, with the sound of shrill clatter, the reflection of lighted back-windows. He had simply given himself
away to a band of adventurers. The idea, the word itself, had

a sort of romantic horror for him—he had always lived on such safe lines. Later it assumed a more interesting, almost a soothing, sense: it pointed a moral, and Pemberton could enjoy a moral. The Moreens were adventurers not merely because they didn't pay their debts, because they lived on society, but because their whole view of life, dim and confused and instinctive, like that of clever colour-blind animals, was speculative and rapacious and mean. Oh! they were "respectable," and that only made them more *immondes*. The young man's analysis of them put it at last very simply—they were adventurers because they were abject snobs. That was the completest account of them—it was the law of their being. Even when this truth became vivid to their ingenious inmate he remained unconscious of how much his mind had been prepared for it by the extraordinary little boy who had now become such a complication in his life. Much less could he then calculate on the information he was still to owe to the extraordinary little boy.

V.

But it was during the ensuing time that the real problem came up—the problem of how far it was excusable to discuss the turpitude of parents with a child of twelve, of thirteen, of fourteen. Absolutely inexcusable and quite impossible it of course at first appeared; and indeed the question didn't press for a while after Pemberton had received his three hundred francs. They produced a sort of lull, a relief from the sharpest pressure. Pemberton frugally amended his wardrobe and even had a few francs in his pocket. He thought the Moreens looked at him as if he were almost too smart, as if they ought to take care not to spoil him. If Mr. Moreen hadn't been such a man of the world he would perhaps have said something to him about his neckties. But Mr. Moreen was always enough a man of the world to let things pass—he had certainly shown that. It was singular how Pemberton guessed that Morgan, though saying nothing about it, knew something had happened. But three hundred francs, especially when one owed money, couldn't last for ever; and when they were gone—the boy knew when they were gone—Morgan did say something.

The party had returned to Nice at the beginning of the winter, but not to the charming villa. They went to an hotel, where they stayed three months, and then they went to another hotel, explaining that they had left the first because they had waited and waited and couldn't get the rooms they wanted. These apartments, the rooms they wanted, were generally very splendid; but fortunately they never *could* get them—fortunately, I mean, for Pemberton, who reflected always that if they had got them there would have been still less for educational expenses. What Morgan said at last was said suddenly, irrelevantly, when the moment came, in the middle of a lesson, and consisted of the apparently unfeeling words: "You ought to *filer*, you know—you really ought."

Pemberton stared. He had learnt enough French slang from Morgan to know that to *filer* meant to go away. "Ah, my dear fellow, don't turn me off!"

Morgan pulled a Greek lexicon toward him (he used a Greek-German), to look out a word, instead of asking it of Pemberton. "You can't go on like this, you know."

"Like what, my boy?"

"You know they don't pay you up," said Morgan, blushing and turning his leaves.

"Don't pay me?" Pemberton stared again and feigned amazement. "What on earth put that into your head?"

"It has been there a long time," the boy replied, continuing his search.

Pemberton was silent, then he went on: "I say, what are you hunting for? They pay me beautifully."

"I'm hunting for the Greek for transparent fiction," Morgan dropped.

"Find that rather for gross impertinence, and disabuse your mind. What do I want of money?"

"Oh, that's another question!"

Pemberton hesitated—he was drawn in different ways. The severely correct thing would have been to tell the boy that such a matter was none of his business and bid him go on with his lines. But they were really too intimate for that; it was not the way he was in the habit of treating him; there had been no reason it should be. On the other hand Morgan had quite lighted on the truth—he really shouldn't be able to keep it up much longer; therefore why not let him know one's real motive for forsaking him? At the same time it wasn't decent to abuse to one's pupil the family of one's pupil; it was better to misrepresent than to do that. So in reply to Morgan's last exclamation he just declared, to dismiss the subject, that he had received several payments.

"I say—I say!" the boy ejaculated, laughing.

"That's all right," Pemberton insisted. "Give me your written rendering."

Morgan pushed a copybook across the table, and his companion began to read the page, but with something running in his head that made it no sense. Looking up after a minute or two he found the child's eyes fixed on him, and he saw something strange in them. Then Morgan said: "I'm not afraid of the reality."

"I haven't yet seen the thing that you *are* afraid of—I'll do you that justice!"

This came out with a jump (it was perfectly true), and evidently gave Morgan pleasure. "I've thought of it a long time," he presently resumed.

"Well, don't think of it any more."

The child appeared to comply, and they had a comfortable and even an amusing hour. They had a theory that they were very thorough, and yet they seemed always to be in the amusing part of lessons, the intervals between the tunnels, where there were waysides and views. Yet the morning was brought to a violent end by Morgan's suddenly leaning his arms on the table, burying his head in them and bursting into tears. Pemberton would have been startled at any rate; but he was doubly startled because, as it then occurred to him, it was the first time he had ever seen the boy cry. It was rather awful.

The next day, after much thought, he took a decision and, believing it to be just, immediately acted upon it. He cornered Mr. and Mrs. Moreen again and informed them that if, on the spot, they didn't pay him all they owed him, he would not only leave their house, but would tell Morgan exactly what had brought him to it.

"Oh, you *haven't* told him?" cried Mrs. Moreen, with a pacifying hand on her well-dressed bosom.

"Without warning you? For what do you take me?"

Mr. and Mrs. Moreen looked at each other, and Pemberton could see both that they were relieved and that there was a certain alarm in their relief. "My dear fellow," Mr. Moreen demanded, "what use *can* you have, leading the quiet life we all do, for such a lot of money?"—an inquiry to which Pemberton made no answer, occupied as he was in perceiving that what passed in the mind of his patrons was something like: "Oh, then, if we've felt that the child, dear little angel, has judged us and how he regards us, and we haven't been betrayed, he must have guessed—and, in short, it's *general*!" an idea that rather stirred up Mr. and Mrs. Moreen, as Pemberton had desired that it should. At the same time, if he had thought that his threat would do something towards bringing them round, he was disappointed to find they had taken for granted (how little they appreciated his delicacy!) that he had already given them away to his pupil. There was a mystic uneasiness in their parental breasts, and that was the way they had accounted for it. None the less his threat did touch them; for if they had escaped it was only to meet a new danger. Mr. Moreen appealed to Pemberton, as usual, as a man of the world; but his wife had recourse, for the first time since the arrival of their inmate, to a fine *hauteur*, reminding him that a devoted mother, with her child, had arts that protected her against gross misrepresentation.

"I should misrepresent you grossly if I accused you of common honesty!" the young man replied; but as he closed the door behind him sharply, thinking he had not done himself much good, while Mr. Moreen lighted another cigarette, he heard Mrs. Moreen shout after him, more touchingly:

"Oh, you do, you *do*, put the knife to one's throat!"

The next morning, very early, she came to his room. He recognised her knock, but he had no hope that she brought him money; as to which he was wrong, for she had fifty francs in her hand. She squeezed forward in her dressing-gown, and he received her in his own, between his bath-tub and his bed. He had been tolerably schooled by this time to the "foreign ways" of his hosts. Mrs. Moreen was zealous, and when she was zealous she didn't care what she did; so she now sat down on his bed, his clothes being on the chairs, and, in her preoccupation, forgot, as she glanced round, to be ashamed of giving him such a nasty room. What Mrs. Moreen was zealous about on this occasion was to persuade him that in the first place she was very good-natured to bring him fifty francs, and, in the second, if he would only see it, he was really too absurd to expect to be *paid*. Wasn't he paid enough, without perpetual money—wasn't he paid by the comfortable, luxurious home that he enjoyed with them all, without a care, an anxiety, a solitary want? Wasn't he sure of his position, and wasn't that everything to a young man like him, quite unknown, with singularly little to show, the ground of whose exorbitant pretensions it was not easy to discover? Wasn't he paid, above all, by the delightful relation he had established with Morgan— quite ideal, as from master to pupil—and by the simple privilege of knowing and living with so amazingly gifted a child, than whom really—she meant literally what she said—there was no better company in Europe? Mrs. Moreen herself took to appealing to him as a man of the world; she said "Voyons, mon cher," and "My dear sir, look here now;" and urged him to be reasonable, putting it before him that it was really a chance for him. She spoke as if, according as he *should* be reasonable, he would prove himself worthy to be her son's tutor and of the extraordinary confidence they had placed in him.

After all, Pemberton reflected, it was only a difference of theory, and the theory didn't matter much. They had hitherto gone on that of remunerated, as now they would go on that of gratuitous, service; but why should they have so many words about it? Mrs. Moreen, however, continued to be convincing; sitting there with her fifty francs she talked and repeated, as women repeat, and bored and irritated him, while he leaned against the wall with his hands in the pockets of his wrapper, drawing it together round his legs and looking over the head of his visitor at the grey negations of his window. She wound up with saying: "You see I bring you a definite proposal."

"A definite proposal?"

"To make our relations regular, as it were—to put them on a comfortable footing."

"I see—it's a system," said Pemberton. "A kind of blackmail."

Mrs. Moreen bounded up, which was what the young man wanted.

"What do you mean by that?"

"You practice on one's fears—one's fears about the child if one should go away."

"And, pray, what would happen to him in that event?" demanded Mrs. Moreen, with majesty.

"Why, he'd be alone with *you*."

"And pray, with whom *should* a child be but with those whom he loves most?"

"If you think that, why don't you dismiss me?"

"Do you pretend that he loves you more than he loves *us*?" cried Mrs. Moreen.

"I think he ought to. I make sacrifices for him. Though I've heard of those *you* make, I don't see them."

Mrs. Moreen stared a moment; then, with emotion, she grasped Pemberton's hand. "*Will* you make it—the sacrifice?"

Pemberton burst out laughing. "I'll see—I'll do what I can—I'll stay a little longer. Your calculation is just—I *do* hate intensely to give him up; I'm fond of him and he interests me deeply, in spite of the inconvenience I suffer. You know my situation perfectly; I haven't a penny in the world, and, occupied as I am with Morgan, I'm unable to earn money."

Mrs. Moreen tapped her undressed arm with her folded bank-note. "Can't you write articles? Can't you translate, as *I* do?"

"I don't know about translating; it's wretchedly paid."

"I am glad to earn what I can," said Mrs. Moreen virtuously, with her head high.

"You ought to tell me who you do it for." Pemberton paused a moment, and she said nothing; so he added: "I've tried to turn off some little sketches, but the magazines won't have them—they're declined with thanks."

"You see then you're not such a phœnix—to have such pretensions," smiled his interlocutress.

"I haven't time to do things properly," Pemberton went on. Then as it came over him that he was almost abjectly good-natured to give these explanations he added: "If I stay on longer it must be on one condition—that Morgan shall know distinctly on what footing I am."

Mrs. Moreen hesitated. "Surely you don't want to show off to a child?"

"To show *you* off, do you mean?"

Again Mrs. Moreen hesitated, but this time it was to produce a still finer flower. "And *you* talk of blackmail!"

"You can easily prevent it," said Pemberton.

"And *you* talk of practicing on fears," Mrs. Moreen continued.

"Yes, there's no doubt I'm a great scoundrel."

His visitor looked at him a moment—it was evident that she was sorely bothered. Then she thrust out her money at him. "Mr. Moreen desired me to give you this on account."

"I'm much obliged to Mr. Moreen; but we have no account."

"You won't take it?"

"That leaves me more free," said Pemberton.

"To poison my darling's mind?" groaned Mrs. Moreen.

"Oh, your darling's mind!" laughed the young man.

She fixed him a moment, and he thought she was going to break out tormentedly, pleadingly. "For God's sake, tell me what *is* in it!" But she checked this impulse—another was stronger. She pocketed the money—the crudity of the alternative was comical—and swept out of the room with the desperate concession: "You may tell him any horror you like!"

VI.

A couple of days after this, during which Pemberton had delayed to profit by Mrs. Moreen's permission to tell her son any horror, the two had been for a quarter of an hour walking together in silence when the boy became sociable again with the remark: "I'll tell you how I know it; I know it through Zénobie."

"Zénobie? Who in the world is *she?*"

"A nurse I used to have—ever so many years ago. A charming woman. I liked her awfully, and she liked me."

"There's no accounting for tastes. What is it you know through her?"

"Why, what their idea is. She went away because they didn't pay her. She did like me awfully, and she stayed two years.

She told me all about it—that at last she could never get her wages. As soon as they saw how much she liked me they stopped giving her anything. They thought she'd stay for nothing, out of devotion. And she did stay ever so long—as long as she could. She was only a poor girl. She used to send money to her mother. At last she couldn't afford it any longer, and she went away in a fearful rage one night—I mean of course in a rage against *them*. She cried over me tremendously, she hugged me nearly to death. She told me all about it," Morgan repeated. "She told me it was their idea. So I guessed, ever so long ago, that they have had the same idea with you."

"Zénobie was very shrewd," said Pemberton. "And she made you so."

"Oh, that wasn't Zénobie; that was nature. And experience!" Morgan laughed.

"Well, Zénobie was a part of your experience."

"Certainly I was a part of hers, poor dear!" the boy exclaimed. "And I'm a part of yours."

"A very important part. But I don't see how you know that I've been treated like Zénobie."

"Do you take me for an idiot?" Morgan asked. "Haven't I been conscious of what we've been through together?"

"What we've been through?"

"Our privations—our dark days."

"Oh, our days have been bright enough."

Morgan went on in silence for a moment. Then he said: "My dear fellow, you're a hero!"

"Well, you're another!" Pemberton retorted.

"No, I'm not; but I'm not a baby. I won't stand it any longer. You must get some occupation that pays. I'm ashamed, I'm ashamed!" quavered the boy in a little passionate voice that was very touching to Pemberton.

"We ought to go off and live somewhere together," said the young man.

"I'll go like a shot if you'll take me."

"I'd get some work that would keep us both afloat," Pemberton continued.

"So would I. Why shouldn't *I* work? I ain't such a *crétin*!"

"The difficulty is that your parents wouldn't hear of it," said Pemberton. "They would never part with you; they worship the ground you tread on. Don't you see the proof of it? They don't dislike me; they wish me no harm; they're very amiable people; but they're perfectly ready to treat me badly for your sake."

The silence in which Morgan received this graceful sophistry struck Pemberton somehow as expressive. After a moment Morgan repeated: "You *are* a hero!" Then he added: "They leave me with you altogether. You've all the responsibility. They put me off on you from morning till night. Why, then, should they object to my taking up with you completely? I'd help you."

"They're not particularly keen about my being helped, and they delight in thinking of you as *theirs*. They're tremendously proud of you."

"I'm not proud of them. But you know *that*," Morgan returned.

"Except for the little matter we speak of they're charming people," said Pemberton, not taking up the imputation of lucidity, but wondering greatly at the child's own, and especially at this fresh reminder of something he had been conscious of from the first—the strangest thing in the boy's large little composition, a temper, a sensibility, even a sort of ideal, which made him privately resent the general quality of his kinsfolk. Morgan had in secret a small loftiness which begot an element of reflection, a domestic scorn not imperceptible to his companion (though they never had any talk about it), and absolutely anomalous in a juvenile nature, especially when one noted that it had not made this nature "old-fashioned," as the word is of children—quaint or wizened or offensive. It was as if he had been a little gentleman and had paid the penalty by discovering that he was the only such person in the family. This comparison didn't make him vain; but it could make him melancholy and a trifle austere. When Pemberton guessed at these young dimnesses he saw him serious and gallant, and was partly drawn on and partly checked, as if with a scruple, by the charm of attempting to sound the little cool shallows which were quickly growing deeper. When he tried to figure to himself the morning twilight of childhood, so as to deal with it safely, he perceived that it was never fixed, never arrested, that ignorance, at the instant one touched it, was already flushing faintly into knowledge, that there was nothing that at a given moment you could say a clever child didn't know. It seemed to him that *he* both knew too much to imagine Morgan's simplicity and too little to disembroil his tangle.

The boy paid no heed to his last remark; he only went on: "I should have spoken to them about their idea, as I call it, long ago, if I hadn't been sure what they would say."

"And what would they say?"

"Just what they said about what poor Zénobie told me—that it was a horrid, dreadful story, that they had paid her every penny they owed her."

"Well, perhaps they had," said Pemberton.

"Perhaps they've paid you!"

"Let us pretend they have, and *n'en parlons plus.*"

"They accused her of lying and cheating," Morgan insisted perversely. "That's why I don't want to speak to them."

"Lest they should accuse me, too?"

To this Morgan made no answer, and his companion, looking down at him (the boy turned his eyes, which had filled, away), saw that he couldn't have trusted himself to utter.

"You're right. Don't squeeze them," Pemberton pursued. "Except for that, they *are* charming people."

"Except for *their* lying and *their* cheating?"

"I say—I say!" cried Pemberton, imitating a little tone of the lad's which was itself an imitation.

"We must be frank, at the last; we *must* come to an understanding," said Morgan, with the importance of the small boy who lets himself think he is arranging great affairs—almost playing at shipwreck or at Indians. "I know all about everything," he added.

"I daresay your father has his reasons," Pemberton observed, too vaguely, as he was aware.

"For lying and cheating?"

"For saving and managing and turning his means to the best account. He has plenty to do with his money. You're an expensive family."

"Yes, I'm very expensive," Morgan rejoined, in a manner which made his preceptor burst out laughing.

"He's saving for *you*," said Pemberton. "They think of you in everything they do."

"He might save a little——" The boy paused. Pemberton waited to hear what. Then Morgan brought out oddly: "A little reputation."

"Oh, there's plenty of that. That's all right!"

"Enough of it for the people they know, no doubt. The people they know are awful."

"Do you mean the princes? We mustn't abuse the princes."

"Why not? They haven't married Paula—they haven't married Amy. They only clean out Ulick."

"You *do* know everything!" Pemberton exclaimed.

"No, I don't, after all. I don't know what they live on, or how they live, or *why* they live! What have they got and how did they get it? Are they rich, are they poor, or have they a *modeste aisance*? Why are they always chiveying about—living one year like ambassadors and the next like paupers? Who are they, any way, and what are they? I've thought of all that— I've thought of a lot of things. They're so beastly worldly. That's what I hate most—oh, I've *seen* it! All they care about is to make an appearance and to pass for something or other. What do they want to pass for? What *do* they, Mr. Pemberton?"

"You pause for a reply," said Pemberton, treating the inquiry as a joke, yet wondering too, and greatly struck with the boy's intense, if imperfect, vision. "I haven't the least idea."

"And what good does it do? Haven't I seen the way people treat them—the "nice" people, the ones they want to know? They'll take anything from them—they'll lie down and be trampled on. The nice ones hate that—they just sicken them. You're the only really nice person we know."

"Are you sure? They don't lie down for me!"

"Well, you shan't lie down for them. You've got to go— that's what you've got to do," said Morgan.

"And what will become of you?"

"Oh, I'm growing up. I shall get off before long. I'll see you later."

"You had better let me finish you," Pemberton urged, lending himself to the child's extraordinarily competent attitude.

Morgan stopped in their walk, looking up at him. He had

to look up much less than a couple of years before—he had grown, in his loose leanness, so long and high. "Finish me?" he echoed.

"There are such a lot of jolly things we can do together yet. I want to turn you out—I want you to do me credit."

Morgan continued to look at him. "To give you credit—do you mean?"

"My dear fellow, you're too clever to live."

"That's just what I'm afraid you think. No, no; it isn't fair—I can't endure it. We'll part next week. The sooner it's over the sooner to sleep."

"If I hear of anything—any other chance, I promise to go," said Pemberton.

Morgan consented to consider this. "But you'll be honest," he demanded; "you won't pretend you haven't heard?"

"I'm much more likely to pretend I have."

"But what can you hear of, this way, stuck in a hole with us? You ought to be on the spot, to go to England—you ought to go to America."

"One would think you were *my* tutor!" said Pemberton.

Morgan walked on, and after a moment he began again: "Well, now that you know that I know and that we look at the facts and keep nothing back—it's much more comfortable, isn't it?"

"My dear boy, it's so amusing, so interesting, that it surely will be quite impossible for me to forego such hours as these."

This made Morgan stop once more. "You *do* keep something back. Oh, you're not straight—I am!"

"Why am I not straight?"

"Oh, you've got your idea!"

"My idea?"

"Why, that I probably sha'n't live, and that you can stick it out till I'm removed."

"You *are* too clever to live!" Pemberton repeated.

"I call it a mean idea," Morgan pursued. "But I shall punish you by the way I hang on."

"Look out or I'll poison you!" Pemberton laughed.

"I'm stronger and better every year. Haven't you noticed that there hasn't been a doctor near me since you came?"

"*I'm* your doctor," said the young man, taking his arm and drawing him on again.

Morgan proceeded, and after a few steps he gave a sigh of mingled weariness and relief. "Ah, now that we look at the facts, it's all right!"

VII.

They looked at the facts a good deal after this; and one of the first consequences of their doing so was that Pemberton stuck it out, as it were, for the purpose. Morgan made the facts so vivid and so droll, and at the same time so bald and so ugly, that there was fascination in talking them over with him, just as there would have been heartlessness in leaving him alone with them. Now that they had such a number of perceptions in common it was useless for the pair to pretend that they didn't judge such people; but the very judgment, and the exchange of perceptions, created another tie. Morgan had never been so interesting as now that he himself was made plainer by the sidelight of these confidences. What came out in it most was the soreness of his characteristic pride. He had plenty of that, Pemberton felt—so much that it was perhaps well it should have had to take some early bruises. He would have liked his people to be gallant, and he had waked up too soon to the sense that they were perpetually swallowing humble-pie. His mother would consume any amount, and his father would consume even more than his mother. He had a theory that Ulick had wriggled out of an "affair" at Nice: there had once been a flurry at home, a regular panic, after which they all went to bed and took medicine, not to be accounted for on any other supposition. Morgan had a romantic imagination, fed by poetry and history, and he would have liked those who "bore his name" (as he used to say to Pemberton with the humour that made his sensitiveness manly), to have a proper spirit. But their one idea was to get in with people who didn't want them and to take snubs as if they were honourable scars. Why people didn't want them more he didn't know—that was people's own affair; after all they were not superficially repulsive—they were a hundred times cleverer than most of the dreary grandees, the "poor swells" they rushed about Europe to catch up with. "After all, they *are* amusing—they are!" Morgan used to say, with the wisdom of the ages. To which Pemberton always replied: "Amusing —the great Moreen troupe? Why, they're altogether delightful; and if it were not for the hitch that you and I (feeble performers!) make in the *ensemble*, they would carry everything before them."

What the boy couldn't get over was that this particular blight seemed, in a tradition of self-respect, so undeserved and so arbitrary. No doubt people had a right to take the line they liked; but why should *his* people have liked the line of pushing and toadying and lying and cheating? What had their forefathers—all decent folk, so far as he knew—done to them, or what had *he* done to them? Who had poisoned their blood with the fifth-rate social ideal, the fixed idea of making smart acquaintances and getting into the *monde chic*, especially when it was foredoomed to failure and exposure? They showed so what they were after; that was what made the people they wanted not want *them*. And never a movement of dignity, never a throb of shame at looking each other in the face, never any independence or resentment or disgust. If his father or his brother would only knock some one down once or twice a year! Clever as they were they never guessed how they appeared. They were good-natured, yes—as good-natured as Jews at the doors of clothing-shops! But was that the model one wanted one's family to follow? Morgan had dim memories of an old grandfather, the maternal, in New York, whom he had been taken across the ocean to see, at the age of five: a gentleman with a high neckcloth and a good deal of pronunciation, who wore a dress-coat in the morning, which made one wonder what he wore in the evening, and had, or was supposed to have, "property" and something to do with the Bible Society. It couldn't have been but that *he* was a good type. Pemberton himself remembered Mrs. Clancy, a widowed sister of Mr. Moreen's, who was as irritating as a moral tale and had paid a fortnight's visit to the family at Nice shortly after he came to live with them. She was "pure and refined," as Amy said, over the banjo, and had the air of not knowing what they meant and of keeping something back. Pemberton judged that what she kept back was an approval of many of their ways; therefore it was to be supposed that she too was of a good type, and that Mr. and Mrs. Moreen and Ulick and Paula and Amy might easily have been better if they would.

But that they wouldn't was more and more perceptible from day to day. They continued to "chivey," as Morgan called it, and in due time became aware of a variety of reasons for proceeding to Venice. They mentioned a great many of them—they were always strikingly frank, and had the brightest friendly chatter, at the late foreign breakfast in especial, before the ladies had made up their faces, when they leaned their arms on the table, had something to follow the *demi-tasse*, and, in the heat of familiar discussion as to what they "really ought" to do, fell inevitably into the languages in which they could *tutoyer*. Even Pemberton liked them, then; he could endure even Ulick when he heard him give his little flat voice for the "sweet sea-city." That was what made him have a sneaking kindness for them—that they were so out of the workaday world and kept him so out of it. The summer had waned when, with cries of ecstasy, they all passed out on the balcony that overhung the Grand Canal; the sunsets were splendid—the Dorringtons had arrived. The Dorringtons were the only reason they had not talked of at breakfast; but the reasons that they didn't talk of at breakfast always came out in the end. The Dorringtons, on the other hand, came out very little; or else, when they did, they stayed—as was natural—for hours, during which periods Mrs. Moreen and the girls sometimes called at their hotel (to see if they had returned) as many as three times running. The gondola was for the ladies; for in Venice too there were "days," which Mrs. Moreen knew in their order an hour after she arrived. She immediately took one herself, to which the Dorringtons never came, though on a certain occasion when Pemberton and his pupil were together at St. Mark's—where, taking the best walks they had ever had and haunting a hundred churches, they spent a great deal of time—they saw the old lord turn up with Mr. Moreen and Ulick, who showed him the dim basilica as if it belonged to them. Pemberton noted how much less, among its curiosities, Lord Dorrington carried himself as a man of the world; wondering too whether, for such services, his companions took a fee from him. The autumn, at any rate, waned, the Dorringtons departed, and Lord Verschoyle, the eldest son, had proposed neither for Amy nor for Paula.

One sad November day, while the wind roared round the old palace and the rain lashed the lagoon, Pemberton, for exercise and even somewhat for warmth (the Moreens were horribly frugal about fires—it was a cause of suffering to their inmate), walked up and down the big bare *sala* with his pupil. The scagliola floor was cold, the high battered casements shook in the storm, and the stately decay of the place was unrelieved by a particle of furniture. Pemberton's spirits were low, and it came over him that the fortune of the Moreens was now even lower. A blast of desolation, a prophecy of disaster and disgrace, seemed to draw through the comfortless hall. Mr. Moreen and Ulick were in the Piazza, looking out for something, strolling drearily, in mackintoshes, under the arcades; but still, in spite of mackintoshes, unmistakable men of the world. Paula and Amy were in bed—it might have been thought they were staying there to keep warm. Pemberton looked askance at the boy at his side, to see to what extent he was conscious of these portents. But Morgan, luckily for him, was now mainly conscious of growing taller and stronger and indeed of being in his fifteenth year. This fact was intensely interesting to him—it was the basis of a private theory (which, however, he had imparted to his tutor) that in a little while he should stand on his own feet. He considered that the situation would change—that, in short, he should be "finished," grown up, producible in the world of affairs and ready to prove himself of sterling ability. Sharply as he was capable, at times, of questioning his circumstances, there were happy hours when he was as superficial as a child; the proof of which was his fundamental assumption that he should presently go to Oxford, to Pemberton's college, and, aided and abetted by Pemberton, do the most wonderful things. It vexed Pemberton to see how little, in such a project, he took account of ways and means: on other matters he was so sceptical about them. Pemberton tried to imagine the Moreens at Oxford, and fortunately failed; yet unless they were to remove there as a family there would be no *modus vivendi* for Morgan. How could he live without an allowance, and where was the allowance to come from? He (Pemberton) might live on Morgan; but how could Morgan live on him? What was to become of him anyhow? Somehow, the fact that he was a big boy now, with better prospects of health, made the question of his future more difficult. So long as he was frail the consideration that he inspired seemed enough of an answer to it. But at the bottom of Pemberton's heart was the recognition of his probably being strong enough to live and not strong enough to thrive. He himself, at any rate, was in a period of natural, boyish rosiness about all this, so that the beating of the tempest seemed to him only the voice of life and the challenge of fate. He had on his shabby little overcoat, with the collar up, but he was enjoying his walk.

It was interrupted at last by the appearance of his mother at the end of the *sala*. She beckoned to Morgan to come to her, and while Pemberton saw him, complacent, pass down the long vista, over the damp false marble, he wondered what was in the air. Mrs. Moreen said a word to the boy and made him go into the room she had quitted. Then, having closed the door after him, she directed her steps swiftly to Pemberton. There *was* something in the air, but his wildest flight of fancy wouldn't have suggested what it proved to be. She signified that she had made a pretext to get Morgan out of the way, and then she inquired—without hesitation—if the young man could lend her sixty francs. While, before bursting into a laugh, he stared at her with surprise, she declared that she was awfully pressed for the money; she was desperate for it—it would save her life.

"Dear lady, *c'est trop fort!*" Pemberton laughed. "Where in the world do you suppose I should get sixty francs, *du train dont vous allez?*"

"I thought you worked—wrote things; don't they pay you?"

"Not a penny."

"Are you such a fool as to work for nothing?"

"You ought surely to know that."

Mrs. Moreen stared an instant, then she coloured a little. Pemberton saw she had quite forgotten the terms—if "terms" they could be called—that he had ended by accepting from herself; they had burdened her memory as little as her

conscience. "Oh, yes, I see what you mean—you have been
very nice about that; but why go back to it so often?" She
had been perfectly urbane with him ever since the rough scene
of explanation in his room, the morning he made her accept
his "terms"—the necessity of his making his case known to
Morgan. She had felt no resentment, after seeing that there
was no danger of Morgan's taking the matter up with her.
Indeed, attributing this immunity to the good taste of his
influence with the boy, she had once said to Pemberton: "My
dear fellow; it's an immense comfort you're a gentleman."
She repeated this, in substance, now. "Of course you're a gentleman—that's a bother the less!" Pemberton reminded her
that he had not "gone back" to anything; and she also repeated her prayer that, somewhere and somehow, he would
find her sixty francs. He took the liberty of declaring that if
he could find them it wouldn't be to lend them to *her*—as to
which he consciously did himself injustice, knowing that if he
had them he would certainly place them in her hand. He accused himself, at bottom and with some truth, of a fantastic,
demoralised sympathy with her. If misery made strange bed-
fellows it also made strange sentiments. It was moreover a part
of the demoralisation and of the general bad effect of living
with such people that one had to make rough retorts, quite
out of the tradition of good manners. "Morgan, Morgan, to
what pass have I come for you?" he privately exclaimed, while
Mrs. Moreen floated voluminously down the *sala* again, to
liberate the boy; groaning, as she went, that everything was
too odious.

Before the boy was liberated there came a thump at the
door communicating with the staircase, followed by the apparition of a dripping youth who poked in his head. Pemberton recognised him as the bearer of a telegram and recognised
the telegram as addressed to himself. Morgan came back as,
after glancing at the signature (that of a friend in London),
he was reading the words: "Found jolly job for you—engagement to coach opulent youth on own terms. Come immediately." The answer, happily, was paid, and the messenger
waited. Morgan, who had drawn near, waited too, and looked
hard at Pemberton; and Pemberton, after a moment, having

met his look, handed him the telegram. It was really by wise looks (they knew each other so well), that, while the telegraph-boy, in his waterproof cape, made a great puddle on the floor, the thing was settled between them. Pemberton wrote the answer with a pencil against the frescoed wall, and the messenger departed. When he had gone Pemberton said to Morgan:

"I'll make a tremendous charge; I'll earn a lot of money in a short time, and we'll live on it."

"Well, I hope the opulent youth will be stupid he probably will—" Morgan parenthesised, "and keep you a long time."

"Of course, the longer he keeps me the more we shall have for our old age."

"But suppose *they* don't pay you!" Morgan awfully suggested.

"Oh, there are not two such—!" Pemberton paused, he was on the point of using an invidious term. Instead of this he said "two such chances."

Morgan flushed—the tears came to his eyes. "*Dites toujours,* two such rascally crews!" Then, in a different tone, he added: "Happy opulent youth!"

"Not if he's stupid!"

"Oh, they're happier then. But you can't have everything, can you?" the boy smiled.

Pemberton held him, his hands on his shoulders. "What will become of *you,* what will you do?" He thought of Mrs. Moreen, desperate for sixty francs.

"I shall turn into a man." And then, as if he recognised all the bearings of Pemberton's allusion: "I shall get on with them better when you're not here."

"Ah, don't say that—it sounds as if I set you against them!"

"You do—the sight of you. It's all right; you know what I mean. I shall be beautiful. I'll take their affairs in hand; I'll marry my sisters."

"You'll marry yourself!" joked Pemberton; as high, rather tense pleasantry would evidently be the right, or the safest, tone for their separation.

It was, however, not purely in this strain that Morgan

suddenly asked: "But I say—how will you get to your jolly job? You'll have to telegraph to the opulent youth for money to come on."

Pemberton bethought himself. "They won't like that, will they?"

"Oh, look out for them!"

Then Pemberton brought out his remedy. "I'll go to the American Consul; I'll borrow some money of him—just for the few days, on the strength of the telegram."

Morgan was hilarious. "Show him the telegram—then stay and keep the money!"

Pemberton entered into the joke enough to reply that, for Morgan, he was really capable of that; but the boy, growing more serious, and to prove that he hadn't meant what he said, not only hurried him off to the Consulate (since he was to start that evening, as he had wired to his friend), but insisted on going with him. They splashed through the tortuous perforations and over the humpbacked bridges, and they passed through the Piazza, where they saw Mr. Moreen and Ulick go into a jeweller's shop. The Consul proved accommodating (Pemberton said it wasn't the letter, but Morgan's grand air), and on their way back they went into St. Mark's for a hushed ten minutes. Later they took up and kept up the fun of it to the very end; and it seemed to Pemberton a part of that fun that Mrs. Moreen, who was very angry when he had announced to her his intention, should charge him, grotesquely and vulgarly, and in reference to the loan she had vainly endeavoured to effect, with bolting lest they should "get something out" of him. On the other hand he had to do Mr. Moreen and Ulick the justice to recognise that when, on coming in, *they* heard the cruel news, they took it like perfect men of the world.

VIII.

When Pemberton got at work with the opulent youth, who was to be taken in hand for Balliol, he found himself unable to say whether he was really an idiot or it was only, on his own part, the long association with an intensely living little mind that made him seem so. From Morgan he heard half-

a-dozen times: the boy wrote charming young letters, a patch-
work of tongues, with indulgent postscripts in the family
Volapuk and, in little squares and rounds and crannies of the
text, the drollest illustrations—letters that he was divided between the impulse to show his present disciple, as a kind of
wasted incentive, and the sense of something in them that was
profanable by publicity. The opulent youth went up, in due
course, and failed to pass; but it seemed to add to the presumption that brilliancy was not expected of him all at once
that his parents, condoning the lapse, which they good-
naturedly treated as little as possible as if were Pemberton's,
should have sounded the rally again, begged the young coach
to keep his pupil in hand another year.

The young coach was now in a position to lend Mrs. Moreen sixty francs, and he sent her a post-office order for the
amount. In return for this favour he received a frantic, scrib-
bled line from her: "Implore you to come back instantly—
Morgan dreadfully ill." They were on the rebound, once more
in Paris—often as Pemberton had seen them depressed he had
never seen them crushed—and communication was therefore
rapid. He wrote to the boy to ascertain the state of his health,
but he received no answer to his letter. Accordingly he took
an abrupt leave of the opulent youth and, crossing the Channel, alighted at the small hotel, in the quarter of the Champs
Elysées, of which Mrs. Moreen had given him the address. A
deep if dumb dissatisfaction with this lady and her companions
bore him company: they couldn't be vulgarly honest, but they
could live at hotels, in velvety *entresols*, amid a smell of burnt
pastilles, in the most expensive city in Europe. When he had
left them, in Venice, it was with an irrepressible suspicion that
something was going to happen; but the only thing that had
happened was that they succeeded in getting away. "How is
he? where is he?" he asked of Mrs. Moreen; but before she
could speak, these questions were answered by the pressure
round his neck of a pair of arms, in shrunken sleeves, which
were perfectly capable of an effusive young foreign squeeze.

"Dreadfully ill—I don't see it!" the young man cried. And
then, to Morgan: "Why on earth didn't you relieve me? Why
didn't you answer my letter?"

Mrs. Moreen declared that when she wrote he was very bad,

and Pemberton learned at the same time from the boy that he had answered every letter he had received. This led to the demonstration that Pemberton's note had been intercepted. Mrs. Moreen was prepared to see the fact exposed, as Pemberton perceived, the moment he faced her, that she was prepared for a good many other things. She was prepared above all to maintain that she had acted from a sense of duty, that she was enchanted she had got him over, whatever they might say; and that it was useless of him to pretend that he didn't *know*, in all his bones, that his place at such a time was with Morgan. He had taken the boy away from them, and now he had no right to abandon him. He had created for himself the gravest responsibilities; he must at least abide by what he had done.

"Taken him away from you?" Pemberton exclaimed indignantly.

"Do it—do it, for pity's sake; that's just what I want. I can't stand *this*—and such scenes. They're treacherous!" These words broke from Morgan, who had intermitted his embrace, in a key which made Pemberton turn quickly to him, to see that he had suddenly seated himself, was breathing with evident difficulty and was very pale.

"*Now* do you say he's not ill—my precious pet?" shouted his mother, dropping on her knees before him with clasped hands, but touching him no more than if he had been a gilded idol. "It will pass—it's only for an instant; but don't say such dreadful things!"

"I'm all right—all right," Morgan panted to Pemberton, whom he sat looking up at with a strange smile, his hands resting on either side on the sofa.

"Now do you pretend I've been treacherous—that I've deceived?" Mrs. Moreen flashed at Pemberton as she got up.

"It isn't *he* says it, it's I!" the boy returned, apparently easier, but sinking back against the wall; while Pemberton, who had sat down beside him, taking his hand, bent over him.

"Darling child, one does what one can; there are so many things to consider," urged Mrs. Moreen. "It's his *place*—his only place. You see *you* think it is now."

"Take me away—take me away," Morgan went on, smiling to Pemberton from his white face.

"Where shall I take you, and how—oh, *how*, my boy?" the young man stammered, thinking of the rude way in which his friends in London held that, for his convenience, and without a pledge of instantaneous return, he had thrown them over; of the just resentment with which they would already have called in a successor, and of the little help as regarded finding fresh employment that resided for him in the flatness of his having failed to pass his pupil.

"Oh, we'll settle that. You used to talk about it," said Morgan. "If we can only go, all the rest's a detail."

"Talk about it as much as you like, but don't think you can attempt it. Mr. Moreen would never consent—it would be so precarious," Pemberton's hostess explained to him. Then to Morgan she explained: "It would destroy our peace, it would break our hearts. Now that he's back it will be all the same again. You'll have your life, your work and your freedom, and we'll all be happy as we used to be. You'll bloom and grow perfectly well, and we won't have any more silly experiments, will we? They're too absurd. It's Mr. Pemberton's place— every one in his place. You in yours, your papa in his, me in mine—*n'est-ce pas, chèri?* We'll all forget how foolish we've been, and we'll have lovely times."

She continued to talk and to surge vaguely about the little draped, stuffy *salon*, while Pemberton sat with the boy, whose colour gradually came back; and she mixed up her reasons, dropping that there were going to be changes, that the other children might scatter (who knew?—Paula had her ideas), and that then it might be fancied how much the poor old parent-birds would want the little nestling. Morgan looked at Pemberton, who wouldn't let him move; and Pemberton knew exactly how he felt at hearing himself called a little nestling. He admitted that he had had one or two bad days, but he protested afresh against the iniquity of his mother's having made them the ground of an appeal to poor Pemberton. Poor Pemberton could laugh now, apart from the comicality of Mrs. Moreen's producing so much philosophy for her defence (she seemed to shake it out of her agitated petticoats, which knocked over the light gilt chairs), so little did the sick boy strike him as qualified to repudiate any advantage.

He himself was in for it, at any rate. He should have

Morgan on his hands again indefinitely; though indeed he saw
the lad had a private theory to produce which would be intended to smooth this down. He was obliged to him for it in
advance; but the suggested amendment didn't keep his heart
from sinking a little, any more than it prevented him from
accepting the prospect on the spot, with some confidence
moreover that he would do so even better if he could have a
little supper. Mrs. Moreen threw out more hints about the
changes that were to be looked for, but she was such a mixture
of smiles and shudders (she confessed she was very nervous),
that he couldn't tell whether she were in high feather or only
in hysterics. If the family were really at last going to pieces
why shouldn't she recognise the necessity of pitching Morgan
into some sort of lifeboat? This presumption was fostered by
the fact that they were established in luxurious quarters in the
capital of pleasure; that was exactly where they naturally *would*
be established in view of going to pieces. Moreover didn't she
mention that Mr. Moreen and the others were enjoying themselves at the opera with Mr. Granger, and wasn't *that* also
precisely where one would look for them on the eve of a
smash? Pemberton gathered that Mr. Granger was a rich, vacant American—a big bill with a flourishy heading and no
items; so that one of Paula's "ideas" was probably that this
time she had really done it, which was indeed an unprecedented blow to the general cohesion. And if the cohesion was
to terminate what was to become of poor Pemberton? He felt
quite enough bound up with them to figure, to his alarm, as
a floating spar in case of a wreck.

It was Morgan who eventually asked if no supper had been
ordered for him; sitting with him below, later, at the dim,
delayed meal, in the presence of a great deal of corded green
plush, a plate of ornamental biscuit and a languor marked on
the part of the waiter. Mrs. Moreen had explained that they
had been obliged to secure a room for the visitor out of the
house; and Morgan's consolation (he offered it while Pemberton reflected on the nastiness of lukewarm sauces), proved
to be, largely, that this circumstance would facilitate their escape. He talked of their escape (recurring to it often afterwards), as if they were making up a "boy's book" together.
But he likewise expressed his sense that there was something

in the air, that the Moreens couldn't keep it up much longer. In point of fact, as Pemberton was to see, they kept it up for five or six months. All the while, however, Morgan's contention was designed to cheer him. Mr. Moreen and Ulick, whom he had met the day after his return, accepted that return like perfect men of the world. If Paula and Amy treated it even with less formality an allowance was to be made for them, inasmuch as Mr. Granger had not come to the opera after all. He had only placed his box at their service, with a bouquet for each of the party; there was even one apiece, embittering the thought of his profusion, for Mr. Moreen and Ulick. "They're all like that," was Morgan's comment; "at the very last, just when we think we've got them fast, we're chucked!"

Morgan's comments, in these days, were more and more free; they even included a large recognition of the extraordinary tenderness with which he had been treated while Pemberton was away. Oh, yes, they couldn't do enough to be nice to him, to show him they had him on their mind and make up for his loss. That was just what made the whole thing so sad, and him so glad, after all, of Pemberton's return—he had to keep thinking of their affection less, had less sense of obligation. Pemberton laughed out at this last reason, and Morgan blushed and said: "You know what I mean." Pemberton knew perfectly what he meant; but there were a good many things it didn't make any clearer. This episode of his second sojourn in Paris stretched itself out wearily, with their resumed readings and wanderings and maunderings, their potterings on the quays, their hauntings of the museums, their occasional lingerings in the Palais Royal, when the first sharp weather came on and there was a comfort in warm emanations, before Chevet's wonderful succulent window. Morgan wanted to hear a great deal about the opulent youth—he took an immense interest in him. Some of the details of his opulence—Pemberton could spare him none of them—evidently intensified the boy's appreciation of all his friend had given up to come back to him; but in addition to the greater reciprocity established by such a renunciation he had always his little brooding theory, in which there was a frivolous gaiety too, that their long probation was drawing to a close. Morgan's conviction that the Moreens couldn't go on much longer kept pace with the unexpended impetus with which, from month to month, they did go on. Three weeks after Pemberton had rejoined them they went on to another hotel, a dingier one than the first; but Morgan rejoiced that his tutor had at least still not sacrificed the advantage of a room outside. He clung to the romantic utility of this when the day, or rather the night, should arrive for their escape.

For the first time, in this complicated connection, Pemberton felt sore and exasperated. It was, as he had said to Mrs. Moreen in Venice, *trop fort*—everything was *trop fort*. He could neither really throw off his blighting burden nor find in it the benefit of a pacified conscience or of a rewarded affection. He had spent all the money that he had earned in England, and he felt that his youth was going and that he was getting nothing back for it. It was all very well for Morgan to seem to consider that he would make up to him for all inconveniences by settling himself upon him permanently— there was an irritating flaw in such a view. He saw what the boy had in his mind; the conception that as his friend had had the generosity to come back to him he must show his gratitude by giving him his life. But the poor friend didn't desire the gift—what could he do with Morgan's life? Of course at the same time that Pemberton was irritated he remembered the reason, which was very honourable to Morgan and which consisted simply of the fact that he was perpetually making one forget that he was after all only a child. If one dealt with him on a different basis one's misadventures were one's own fault. So Pemberton waited in a queer confusion of yearning and alarm for the catastrophe which was held to hang over the house of Moreen, of which he certainly at moments felt the symptoms brush his cheek and as to which he wondered much in what form it would come.

Perhaps it would take the form of dispersal—a frightened *sauve qui peut*, a scuttling into selfish corners. Certainly they were less elastic than of yore; they were evidently looking for something they didn't find. The Dorringtons hadn't reappeared, the princes had scattered; wasn't that the beginning of the end? Mrs. Moreen had lost her reckoning of the famous "days;" her social calendar was blurred—it had turned its face to the wall. Pemberton suspected that the great, the cruel, discomfiture had been the extraordinary behaviour of Mr. Granger, who seemed not to know what he wanted, or, what was much worse, what *they* wanted. He kept sending flowers, as if to bestrew the path of his retreat, which was never the path of return. Flowers were all very well, but—Pemberton could complete the proposition. It was now positively conspicuous that in the long run the Moreens were a failure; so that the young man was almost grateful the run had not been short. Mr. Moreen, indeed, was still occasionally able to get away on business, and, what was more surprising, he was also able to get back. Ulick had no club, but you could not have discovered it from his appearance, which was as much as ever that of a person looking at life from the window of such an institution; therefore Pemberton was doubly astonished at an answer he once heard him make to his mother, in the desperate tone of a man familiar with the worst privations. Her question Pemberton had not quite caught; it appeared to be an appeal for a suggestion as to whom they could get to take Amy. "Let the devil take her!" Ulick snapped, so that Pemberton could see that not only they had lost their amiability, but had ceased to believe in themselves. He could also see that if Mrs. Moreen was trying to get people to take her children she might be regarded as closing the hatches for the storm. But Morgan would be the last she would part with.

One winter afternoon—it was a Sunday—he and the boy walked far together in the Bois de Boulogne. The evening was so splendid, the cold lemon-coloured sunset so clear, the stream of carriages and pedestrians so amusing and the fascination of Paris so great, that they stayed out later than usual and became aware that they would have to hurry home to arrive in time for dinner. They hurried accordingly, arm-in-arm, good-humoured and hungry, agreeing that there was nothing like Paris after all and that after all, too, that had come and gone they were not yet sated with innocent pleasures. When they reached the hotel they found that, though scandalously late, they were in time for all the dinner they were likely to sit down to. Confusion reigned in the apartments of the Moreens (very shabby ones this time, but the best in the house), and before the interrupted service of the table (with objects displaced almost as if there had been a scuffle, and a great wine stain from an overturned bottle), Pemberton could not blink the fact that there had been a scene of proprietary mutiny. The storm had come—they were all seeking refuge. The hatches were down—Paula and Amy were invisible (they had never tried the most casual art upon Pemberton, but he felt that they had enough of an eye to him not to wish to meet him as young ladies whose frocks had been confiscated), and Ulick appeared to have jumped overboard. In a word, the host and his staff had ceased to "go on" at the pace of their guests, and the air of embarrassed detention, thanks to a pile of gaping trunks in the passage, was strangely commingled with the air of indignant withdrawal.

When Morgan took in all this—and he took it in very quickly—he blushed to the roots of his hair. He had walked, from his infancy, among difficulties and dangers, but he had never seen a public exposure. Pemberton noticed, in a second glance at him, that the tears had rushed into his eyes and that they were tears of bitter shame. He wondered for an instant, for the boy's sake, whether he might successfully pretend not to understand. Not successfully, he felt, as Mr. and Mrs. Moreen, dinnerless by their extinguished hearth, rose before him in their little dishonoured *salon*, considering apparently with much intensity what lively capital would be next on their list. They were not prostrate, but they were very pale, and Mrs. Moreen had evidently been crying. Pemberton quickly learned however that her grief was not for the loss of her dinner, much as she usually enjoyed it, but on account of a necessity much more tragic. She lost no time in laying this necessity bare, in telling him how the change had come, the bolt had fallen, and how they would all have to turn themselves about. Therefore cruel as it was to them to part with their darling she must look to him to carry a little further the influence he had so fortunately acquired with the boy—to induce his young charge to follow him into some modest retreat. They depended upon him, in a word, to take their delightful child temporarily under his protection—it would leave Mr. Moreen and herself so much more free to give the proper attention (too little, alas! had been given), to the readjustment of their affairs.

"We trust you—we feel that we can," said Mrs. Moreen,

slowly rubbing her plump white hands and looking, with compunction, hard at Morgan, whose chin, not to take liberties, her husband stroked with a tentative paternal forefinger.

"Oh, yes; we feel that we can. We trust Mr. Pemberton fully, Morgan," Mr. Moreen conceded.

Pemberton wondered again if he might pretend not to understand; but the idea was painfully complicated by the immediate perception that Morgan had understood.

"Do you mean that he may take me to live with him—for ever and ever?" cried the boy. "Away, away, anywhere he likes?"

"For ever and ever? *Comme vous-y-allez!*" Mr. Moreen laughed indulgently. "For as long as Mr. Pemberton may be so good."

"We've struggled, we've suffered," his wife went on; "but you've made him so your own that we've already been through the worst of the sacrifice."

Morgan had turned away from his father—he stood looking at Pemberton with a light in his face. His blush had died out, but something had come that was brighter and more vivid. He had a moment of boyish joy, scarcely mitigated by the reflection that, with this unexpected consecration of his hope—too sudden and too violent; the thing was a good deal less like a boy's book—the "escape" was left on their hands. The boyish joy was there for an instant, and Pemberton was almost frightened at the revelation of gratitude and affection that shone through his humiliation. When Morgan stammered "My dear fellow, what do you say to *that*?" he felt that he should say something enthusiastic. But he was still more frightened at something else that immediately followed and that made the lad sit down quickly on the nearest chair. He had turned very white and had raised his hand to his left side. They were all three looking at him, but Mrs. Moreen was the first to bound forward. "Ah, his darling little heart!" she broke out; and this time, on her knees before him and without respect for the idol, she caught him ardently in her arms. "You walked him too far, you hurried him too fast!" she tossed over her shoulder at Pemberton. The boy made no protest, and the next instant his mother, still holding him, sprang up with her face convulsed and with the terrified cry "Help, help! he's going, he's gone!" Pemberton saw, with equal horror, by Morgan's own stricken face, that he *was* gone. He pulled him half out of his mother's hands, and for a moment, while they held him together, they looked, in their dismay, into each other's eyes. "He couldn't stand it, with his infirmity," said Pemberton—"the shock, the whole scene, the violent emotion."

"But I thought he *wanted* to go to you!" wailed Mrs. Moreen.

"I *told* you he didn't, my dear," argued Mr. Moreen. He was trembling all over, and he was, in his way, as deeply affected as his wife. But, after the first, he took his bereavement like a man of the world.

Brooksmith

WE ARE scattered now, the friends of the late Mr. Oliver Offord; but whenever we chance to meet I think we are conscious of a certain esoteric respect for each other. "Yes, you too have been in Arcadia," we seem not too grumpily to allow. When I pass the house in Mansfield Street I remember that Arcadia was there. I don't know who has it now, and I don't want to know; it's enough to be so sure that if I should ring the bell there would be no such luck for me as that Brooksmith should open the door. Mr. Offord, the most agreeable, the most lovable of bachelors, was a retired diplomatist, living on his pension, confined by his infirmities to his fireside and delighted to be found there any afternoon in the year by such visitors as Brooksmith allowed to come up. Brooksmith was his butler and his most intimate friend, to whom we all stood, or I should say sat, in the same relation in which the subject of the sovereign finds himself to the prime minister. By having been for years, in foreign lands, the most delightful Englishman any one had ever known, Mr. Offord had, in my opinion, rendered signal service to his country. But I suppose he had been too much liked—liked even by those who didn't like *it*—so that as people of that sort never get titles or dotations for the horrid things they have *not* done, his principal reward was simply that we went to see him.

Oh, we went perpetually, and it was not our fault if he was not overwelmed with this particular honour. Any visitor who came once came again—to come merely once was a slight which nobody, I am sure, had ever put upon him. His circle, therefore, was essentially composed of *habitués*, who were *habitués* for each other as well as for him, as those of a happy *salon* should be. I remember vividly every element of the place, down to the intensely Londonish look of the grey opposite houses, in the gap of the white curtains of the high windows, and the exact spot where, on a particular afternoon, I put down my tea-cup for Brooksmith, lingering an instant, to gather it up as if he were plucking a flower. Mr. Offord's

articulate and human. *L'Ecole Anglaise*, Mr. Offord used to call him, laughing, when, later, it happened more than once that we had some conversation about him. But I remember accusing Mr. Offord of not doing him quite ideal justice. That he was not one of the giants of the school, however, my old friend, who really understood him perfectly and was devoted to him, as I shall show, quite admitted; which doubtless poor Brooksmith had himself felt, to his cost, when his value in the market was originally determined. The utility of his class in general is estimated by the foot and the inch, and poor Brooksmith had only about five feet two to put into circulation. He acknowledged the inadequacy of this provision, and I am sure was penetrated with the everlasting fitness of the relation between service and stature. If *he* had been Mr. Offord he certainly would have found Brooksmith wanting, and indeed the laxity of his employer on this score was one of many things which he had had to condone and to which he had at last indulgently adapted himself.

I remember the old man's saying to me: "Oh, my servants, if they can live with me a fortnight they can live with me for ever. But it's the first fortnight that tries 'em." It was in the first fortnight, for instance, that Brooksmith had had to learn that he was exposed to being addressed as "my dear fellow" and "my poor child." Strange and deep must such a probation have been to him, and he doubtless emerged from it tempered and purified. This was written to a certain extent in his appearance; in his spare, brisk little person, in his cloistered white face and extraordinarily polished hair, which told of responsibility, looked as if it were kept up to the same high standard as the plate; in his small, clear, anxious eyes, even in the permitted, though not exactly encouraged tuft on his chin. "He thinks me rather mad, but I've broken him in, and now he likes the place, he likes the company," said the old man. I embraced this fully after I had become aware that Brooksmith's main characteristic was a deep and shy refinement, though I remember I was rather puzzled when, on another occasion, Mr. Offord remarked: "What he likes is the talk—mingling in the conversation." I was conscious that I had never seen Brooksmith permit himself this freedom, but I guessed in a moment that what Mr. Offord alluded to was a

participation more intense than any speech could have represented—that of being perpetually present on a hundred legitimate pretexts, errands, necessities, and breathing the very
atmosphere of criticism, the famous criticism of life. "Quite
an education, sir, isn't it, sir?" he said to me one day at the
foot of the stairs, when he was letting me out; and I have
always remembered the words and the tone as the first sign
of the quickening drama of poor Brooksmith's fate. It was
indeed an education, but to what was this sensitive young man
of thirty-five, of the servile class, being educated?

Practically and inevitably, for the time, to companionship,
to the perpetual, the even exaggerated reference and appeal
of a person brought to dependence by his time of life and his
infirmities and always addicted moreover (this was the exag-
geration) to the art of giving you pleasure by letting you do
things for him. There were certain things Mr. Offord was capable of pretending he liked you to do, even when he didn't,
if he thought *you* liked them. If it happened that you didn't
either (this was rare, but it might be), of course there were
cross-purposes; but Brooksmith was there to prevent their going very far. This was precisely the way he acted as moderator:
he averted misunderstandings or cleared them up. He had
been capable, strange as it may appear, of acquiring for this
purpose an insight into the French tongue, which was often
used at Mr. Offord's; for besides being habitual to most of
the foreigners, and they were many, who haunted the place
or arrived with letters (letters often requiring a little worried
consideration, of which Brooksmith always had cognisance),
it had really become the primary language of the master of
the house. I don't know if all the *malentendus* were in French,
but almost all the explanations were, and this didn't a bit prevent Brooksmith from following them. I know Mr. Offord
used to read passages to him from Montaigne and Saint-
Simon, for he read perpetually when he was alone—when they
were alone, I should say—and Brooksmith was always about.
Perhaps you'll say no wonder Mr. Offord's butler regarded
him as "rather mad." However, if I'm not sure what he
thought about Montaigne I'm convinced he admired Saint-
Simon. A certain feeling for letters must have rubbed off on
him from the mere handling of his master's books, which he

was always carrying to and fro and putting back in their places.

I often noticed that if an anecdote or a quotation, much more a lively discussion, was going forward, he would, if busy with the fire or the curtains, the lamp or the tea, find a pretext for remaining in the room till the point should be reached. If his purpose was to catch it you were not discreet to call him off, and I shall never forget a look, a hard, stony stare (I caught it in its passage), which, one day when there were a good many people in the room, he fastened upon the footman who was helping him in the service and who, in an undertone, had asked him some irrelevant question. It was the only manifestation of harshness that I ever observed on Brooksmith's part, and at first I wondered what was the matter. Then I became conscious that Mr. Offord was relating a very curious anecdote, never before perhaps made so public, and imparted to the narrator by an eye-witness of the fact, bearing upon Lord Byron's life in Italy. Nothing would induce me to reproduce it here; but Brooksmith had been in danger of losing it. If I ever should venture to reproduce it I shall feel how much I lose in not having my fellow-auditor to refer to.

The first day Mr. Offord's door was closed was therefore a dark date in contemporary history. It was raining hard and my umbrella was wet, but Brooksmith took it from me exactly as if this were a preliminary for going upstairs. I observed however that instead of putting it away he held it poised and trickling over the rug, and then I became aware that he was looking at me with deep, acknowledging eyes—his air of universal responsibility. I immediately understood; there was scarcely need of the question and the answer that passed between us. When I did understand that the old man had given up, for the first time, though only for the occasion, I exclaimed dolefully: "What a difference it will make—and to how many people!"

"I shall be one of them, sir!" said Brooksmith; and that was the beginning of the end.

Mr. Offord came down again, but the spell was broken, and the great sign of it was that the conversation was, for the first time, not directed. It wandered and stumbled, a little frightened, like a lost child—it had let go the nurse's hand. "The worst of it is that now we shall talk about my health—*c'est la fin de tout*," Mr. Offord said, when he reappeared; and then I recognised what a sign of change that would be—for he had never tolerated anything so provincial. The talk became ours, in a word—not his; and as ours, even when *he* talked, it could only be inferior. In this form it was a distress to Brooksmith, whose attention now wandered from it altogether: he had so much closer a vision of his master's intimate conditions than our superficialities represented. There were better hours, and he was more in and out of the room, but I could see that he was conscious that the great institution was falling to pieces. He seemed to wish to take counsel with me about it, to feel responsible for its going on in some form or other. When for the second period—the first had lasted several days—he had to tell me that our old friend didn't receive, I half expected to hear him say after a moment: "Do you think I ought to, sir, in his place?"—as he might have asked me, with the return of autumn, if I thought he had better light the drawing-room fire.

He had a resigned philosophic sense of what his guests—our guests, as I came to regard them in our colloquies—would expect. His feeling was that he wouldn't absolutely have approved of himself as a substitute for the host; but he was so saturated with the religion of habit that he would have made, for our friends, the necessary sacrifice to the divinity. He would take them on a little further, till they could look about them. I think I saw him also mentally confronted with the opportunity to deal—for once in his life—with some of his own dumb preferences, his limitations of sympathy, *weeding* a little, in prospect, and returning to a purer tradition. It was not unknown to me that he considered that toward the end of Mr. Offord's career a certain laxity of selection had crept in.

At last it came to be the case that we all found the closed door more often than the open one; but even when it was closed Brooksmith managed a crack for me to squeeze through; so that practically I never turned away without having paid a visit. The difference simply came to be that the visit was to Brooksmith. It took place in the hall, at the familiar foot of the stairs, and we didn't sit down—at least Brooksmith didn't; moreover it was devoted wholly to one topic and always had the air of being already over—beginning, as it were, at the end. But it was always interesting—it always gave me something to think about. It is true that the subject of my meditation was ever the same—ever "It's all very well, but what *will* become of Brooksmith?" Even my private answer to this question left me still unsatisfied. No doubt Mr. Offord would provide for him, but *what* would he provide? that was the great point. He couldn't provide society; and society had become a necessity of Brooksmith's nature. I must add that he never showed a symptom of what I may call sordid solicitude—anxiety on his own account. He was rather livid and intensely grave, as befitted a man before whose eyes the "shade of that which once was great" was passing away. He had the solemnity of a person winding up, under depressing circumstances, a long established and celebrated business; he was a kind of social executor or liquidator. But his manner seemed to testify exclusively to the uncertainty of *our* future. I couldn't in those days have afforded it—I lived in two rooms in Jermyn Street and didn't "keep a man;" but even if my income had permitted I shouldn't have ventured to say to Brooksmith (emulating Mr. Offord), "My dear fellow, I'll take you on." The whole tone of our intercourse was so much more an implication that it was *I* who should now want a lift. Indeed there was a tacit assurance in Brooksmith's whole attitude that he would have me on his mind.

One of the most assiduous members of our circle had been Lady Kenyon, and I remember his telling me one day that her ladyship had, in spite of her own infirmities, lately much aggravated, been in person to inquire. In answer to this I remarked that she would feel it more than any one. Brooksmith was silent a moment; at the end of which he said, in a certain tone (there is no reproducing some of his tones), "I'll go and see her." I went to see her myself, and I learned that he had waited upon her; but when I said to her, in the form of a joke but with a core of earnest, that when all was over some of us ought to combine, to club together to set Brooksmith up on his own account, she replied a trifle disappointingly: "Do you mean in a public-house?" I looked at her in a way that I think Brooksmith himself would have approved, and then I answered: "Yes, the Offord Arms." What I had meant, of course, was that, for the love of art itself, we ought to look to it that such a peculiar faculty and so much acquired experience should not be wasted. I really think that if we had caused a few black-edged cards to be struck off and circulated—"Mr. Brooksmith will continue to receive on the old premises from four to seven; business carried on as usual during the alterations"—the majority of us would have rallied.

Several times he took me upstairs—always by his own proposal—and our dear old friend, in bed, in a curious flowered and brocaded *casaque* which made him, especially as his head was tied up in a handkerchief to match, look, to my imagination, like the dying Voltaire, held for ten minutes a sadly shrunken little *salon*. I felt indeed each time, as if I were attending the last *coucher* of some social sovereign. He was royally whimsical about his sufferings and not at all concerned —quite as if the Constitution provided for the case—about his successor. He glided over *our* sufferings charmingly, and none of his jokes—it was a gallant abstention, some of them would have been so easy—were at our expense. Now and again, I confess, there was one at Brooksmith's, but so pathetically sociable as to make the excellent man look at me in a way that seemed to say: "Do exchange a glance with me, or I sha'n't be able to stand it." What he was not able to stand was not what Mr. Offord said about him, but what he wasn't able to say in return. His notion of conversation, for himself, was giving you the convenience of speaking to him; and when he went to "see" Lady Kenyon, for instance, it was to carry her the tribute of his receptive silence. Where would the speech of his betters have been if proper service had been a manifestation of sound? In that case the fundamental difference would have had to be shown by *their* dumbness, and many of them, poor things, were dumb enough without that provision. Brooksmith took an unfailing interest in the preservation of the fundamental difference; it was the thing he had most on his conscience.

What had become of it, however, when Mr. Offord passed away like any inferior person—was relegated to eternal stillness like a butler upstairs? His aspect for several days after the expected event may be imagined, and the multiplication by

funereal observance of the things he didn't say. When everything was over—it was late the same day—I knocked at the
door of the house of mourning as I so often had done before.
I could never call on Mr. Offord again, but I had come, literally, to call on Brooksmith. I wanted to ask him if there was
anything I could do for him, tainted with vagueness as this
inquiry could only be. My wild dream of taking him into my
own service had died away: my service was not worth his being taken into. My offer to him could only be to help him to
find another place, and yet there was an indelicacy, as it were,
in taking for granted that his thoughts would immediately be
fixed on another. I had a hope that he would be able to give
his life a different form—though certainly not the form, the
frequent result of such bereavements, of his setting up a little
shop. That would have been dreadful; for I should have
wished to further any enterprise that he might embark in, yet
how could I have brought myself to go and pay him shillings
and take back coppers over a counter? My visit then was simply an intended compliment. He took it as such, gratefully
and with all the tact in the world. He knew I really couldn't
help him and that I knew he knew I couldn't; but we discussed the situation—with a good deal of elegant general-
ity—at the foot of the stairs, in the hall already dismantled,
where I had so often discussed other situations with him. The
executors were in possession, as was still more apparent when
he made me pass for a few minutes into the dining-room,
where various objects were muffled up for removal.

Two definite facts, however, he had to communicate; one
being that he was to leave the house for ever that night (servants, for some mysterious reason, seem always to depart by
night), and the other—he mentioned it only at the last, with
hesitation—that he had already been informed his late master
had left him a legacy of eighty pounds. "I'm very glad," I
said, and Brooksmith rejoined: "It was so like him to think
of me." This was all that passed between us on the subject,
and I know nothing of his judgment of Mr. Offord's memento. Eighty pounds are always eighty pounds, and no one
has ever left *me* an equal sum; but, all the same, for Brooksmith, I was disappointed. I don't know what I had ex-

pected—in short I was disappointed. Eighty pounds might stock a little shop—a *very* little shop; but, I repeat, I couldn't bear to think of that. I asked my friend if he had been able to save a little, and he replied: "No, sir; I have had to do things." I didn't inquire what things he had had to do; they were his own affair, and I took his word for them as assentingly as if he had had the greatness of an ancient house to keep up; especially as there was something in his manner that seemed to convey a prospect of further sacrifice.

"I shall have to turn round a bit, sir—I shall have to look about me," he said; and then he added, indulgently, magnanimously: "If you should happen to hear of anything for me——"

I couldn't let him finish; this was, in its essence, too much in the really grand manner. It would be a help to my getting him off my mind to be able to pretend I *could* find the right place, and that help he wished to give me, for it was doubtless painful to him to see me in so false a position. I interposed with a few words to the effect that I was well aware that wherever he should go, whatever he should do, he would miss our old friend terribly—miss him even more than I should, having been with him so much more. This led him to make the speech that I have always remembered as the very text of the whole episode.

"Oh, sir, it's sad for *you*, very sad, indeed, and for a great many gentlemen and ladies; that it is, sir. But for me, sir, it is, if I may say so, still graver even than that: it's just the loss of something that was everything. For me, sir," he went on, with rising tears, "he was just *all*, if you know what I mean, sir. You have others, sir, I daresay—not that I would have you understand me to speak of them as in any way tantamount. But you have the pleasures of society, sir; if it's only in talking about him, sir, as I daresay you do freely—for all his blessed memory has to fear from it—with gentlemen and ladies who have had the same honour. That's not for me, sir, and I have to keep my associations to myself. Mr. Offord was *my* society, and now I have no more. You go back to conversation, sir, after all, and I go back to my place," Brooksmith stammered, without exaggerated irony or dramatic bitterness, but with a

flat, unstudied veracity and his hand on the knob of the street-
door. He turned it to let me out and then he added: "I just
go downstairs, sir, again, and I stay there."

"My poor child," I replied, in my emotion, quite as Mr.
Offord used to speak, "my dear fellow, leave it to me; we'll
look after you, we'll all do something for you."

"Ah, if you could give me some one *like* him! But there
ain't two in the world," said Brooksmith as we parted.

He had given me his address—the place where he would
be to be heard of. For a long time I had no occasion to make
use of the information; for he proved indeed, on trial, a very
difficult case. In a word the people who knew him and had
known Mr. Offord, didn't want to take him, and yet I
couldn't bear to try to thrust him among people who didn't
know him. I spoke to many of our old friends about him, and
I found them all governed by the odd mixture of feelings of
which I myself was conscious, and disposed, further, to entertain a suspicion that he was "spoiled," with which I then
would have nothing to do. In plain terms a certain embarrassment, a sensible awkwardness, when they thought of it,
attached to the idea of using him as a menial: they had met
him so often in society. Many of them would have asked him,
and did ask him, or rather did ask me to ask him, to come
and see them; but a mere visiting-list was not what I wanted
for him. He was too short for people who were very particular; nevertheless I heard of an opening in a diplomatic household which led me to write him a note, though I was looking
much less for something grand than for something human.
Five days later I heard from him. The secretary's wife had
decided, after keeping him waiting till then, that she couldn't
take a servant out of a house in which there had not been a
lady. The note had a P.S.: "It's a good job there wasn't, sir,
such a lady as some."

A week later he came to see me and told me he was
"suited"—committed to some highly respectable people (they
were something very large in the City), who lived on the Bayswater side of the Park. "I daresay it will be rather poor, sir,"
he admitted; "but I've seen the fireworks, haven't I, sir?—it
can't be fireworks *every* night. After Mansfield Street there
ain't much choice." There was a certain amount, however, it

seemed; for the following year, going one day to call on a country cousin, a lady of a certain age who was spending a fortnight in town with some friends of her own, a family unknown to me and resident in Chester Square, the door of the house was opened, to my surprise and gratification, by Brooksmith in person. When I came out I had some conversation with him, from which I gathered that he had found the large City people too dull for endurance, and I guessed, though he didn't say it, that he had found them vulgar as well. I don't know what judgment he would have passed on his actual patrons if my relative had not been their friend; but under the circumstances he abstained from comment.

None was necessary, however, for before the lady in question brought her visit to a close they honoured me with an invitation to dinner, which I accepted. There was a largeish party on the occasion, but I confess I thought of Brooksmith rather more than of the seated company. They required no depth of attention—they were all referable to usual, irredeemable, inevitable types. It was the world of cheerful commonplace and conscious gentility and prosperous density, a full-fed, material, insular world, a world of hideous florid plate and ponderous order and thin conversation. There was not a word said about Byron. Nothing would have induced me to look at Brooksmith in the course of the repast, and I felt sure that not even my overturning the wine would have induced him to meet my eye. We were in intellectual sympathy—we felt, as regards each other, a kind of social responsibility. In short we had been in Arcadia together, and we had both come to *this*! No wonder we were ashamed to be confronted. When he helped on my overcoat, as I was going away, we parted, for the first time since the earliest days in Mansfield Street, in silence. I thought he looked lean and wasted, and I guessed that his new place was not more "human" than his previous one. There was plenty of beef and beer, but there was no reciprocity. The question for him to have asked before accepting the position would have been not "How many footmen are kept?" but "How much imagination?"

The next time I went to the house—I confess it was not very soon—I encountered his successor, a personage who evidently enjoyed the good fortune of never having quitted his natural level. Could any be higher? he seemed to ask—over the heads of three footmen and even of some visitors. He made me feel as if Brooksmith were dead; but I didn't dare to inquire—I couldn't have borne his "I haven't the least idea, sir." I despatched a note to the address Brooksmith had given me after Mr. Offord's death, but I received no answer. Six months later, however, I was favoured with a visit from an elderly, dreary, dingy person, who introduced herself to me as Mr. Brooksmith's aunt and from whom I learned that he was out of place and out of health and had allowed her to come and say to me that if I could spare half-an-hour to look in at him he would take it as a rare honour.

I went the next day—his messenger had given me a new address—and found my friend lodged in a short sordid street in Marylebone, one of those corners of London that wear the last expression of sickly meanness. The room into which I was shown was above the small establishment of a dyer and cleaner who had inflated kid gloves and discoloured shawls in his shop-front. There was a great deal of grimy infant life up and down the place, and there was a hot, moist smell within, as of the "boiling" of dirty linen. Brooksmith sat with a blanket over his legs at a clean little window, where, from behind stiff bluish-white curtains, he could look across at a huckster's and a tinsmith's and a small greasy public-house. He had passed through an illness and was convalescent, and his mother, as well as his aunt, was in attendance on him. I liked the mother, who was bland and intensely humble, but I didn't much fancy the aunt, whom I connected, perhaps unjustly, with the opposite public-house (she seemed somehow to be greasy with the same grease), and whose furtive eye followed every movement of my hand, as if to see if it were not going into my pocket. It didn't take this direction—I couldn't, unsolicited, put myself at that sort of ease with Brooksmith. Several times the door of the room opened, and mysterious old women peeped in and shuffled back again. I don't know who they were; poor Brooksmith seemed encompassed with vague, prying, beery females.

He was vague himself, and evidently weak, and much embarrassed, and not an allusion was made between us to Mansfield Street. The vision of the *salon* of which he had been an

ornament hovered before me, however, by contrast, sufficiently. He assured me that he was really getting better, and
his mother remarked that he would come round if he could
only get his spirits up. The aunt echoed this opinion, and I
became more sure that in her own case she knew where to go
for such a purpose. I'm afraid I was rather weak with my old
friend, for I neglected the opportunity, so exceptionally good,
to rebuke the levity which had led him to throw up honourable positions—fine, stiff, steady berths, with morning prayers,
as I knew, attached to one of them—in Bayswater and Belgravia. Very likely his reasons had been profane and sentimental; he didn't want morning prayers, he wanted to be
somebody's dear fellow; but I couldn't be the person to rebuke him. He shuffled these episodes out of sight—I saw that
he had no wish to discuss them. I perceived further, strangely
enough, that it would probably be a questionable pleasure for
him to see me again: he doubted now even of my power to
condone his aberrations. He didn't wish to have to explain;
and his behaviour, in future, was likely to need explanation.
When I bade him farewell he looked at me a moment with
eyes that said everything: "How can I talk about those exquisite years in this place, before these people, with the old
women poking their heads in? It was very good of you to
come to see me—it wasn't my idea; *she* brought you. We've
said everything; it's over; you'll lose all patience with me, and
I'd rather you shouldn't see the rest." I sent him some money,
in a letter, the next day, but I saw the rest only in the light
of a barren sequel.

A whole year after my visit to him I became aware once, in
dining out, that Brooksmith was one of the several servants
who hovered behind our chairs. He had not opened the door
of the house to me, and I had not recognised him in the
cluster of retainers in the hall. This time I tried to catch his
eye, but he never gave me a chance, and when he handed me
a dish I could only be careful to thank him audibly. Indeed I
partook of two *entrées* of which I had my doubts, subse-
quently converted into certainties, in order not to snub him.
He looked well enough in health, but much older, and wore,
in an exceptionally marked degree, the glazed and expressionless mask of the British domestic *de race*. I saw with dismay

that if I had not known him I should have taken him, on the showing of his countenance, for an extravagant illustration of irresponsive servile gloom. I said to myself that he had become a reactionary, gone over to the Philistines, thrown himself into religion, the religion of his "place," like a foreign lady *sur le retour*. I divined moreover that he was only engaged for the evening—he had become a mere waiter, had joined the band of the white-waistcoated who "go out." There was something pathetic in this fact, and it was a terrible vulgarisation of Brooksmith. It was the mercenary prose of butlerhood; he had given up the struggle for the poetry. If reciprocity was what he had missed, where was the reciprocity now? Only in the bottoms of the wine-glasses and the five shillings (or whatever they get), clapped into his hand by the permanent man. However, I supposed he had taken up a precarious branch of his profession because after all it sent him less downstairs. His relations with London society were more superficial, but they were of course more various. As I went away, on this occasion, I looked out for him eagerly among the four or five attendants whose perpendicular persons, fluting the walls of London passages, are supposed to lubricate the process of departure; but he was not on duty. I asked one of the others if he were not in the house, and received the prompt answer: "Just left, sir. Anything I can do for you, sir?" I wanted to say "Please give him my kind regards;" but I abstained; I didn't want to compromise him, and I never came across him again.

Often and often, in dining out, I looked for him, sometimes accepting invitations on purpose to multiply the chances of my meeting him. But always in vain; so that as I met many other members of the casual class over and over again, I at last adopted the theory that he always procured a list of expected guests beforehand and kept away from the banquets which he thus learned I was to grace. At last I gave up hope, and one day, at the end of three years, I received another visit from his aunt. She was drearier and dingier, almost squalid, and she was in great tribulation and want. Her sister, Mrs. Brooksmith, had been dead a year, and three months later her nephew had disappeared. He had always looked after her a bit—since her troubles; I never knew what her troubles had been—and now she hadn't so much as a petticoat to pawn. She had also a niece, to whom she had been everything, before her troubles, but the niece had treated her most shameful. These were details; the great and romantic fact was Brooksmith's final evasion of his fate. He had gone out to wait one evening, as usual, in a white waistcoat she had done up for him with her own hands, being due at a large party up Kensington way. But he had never come home again, and had never arrived at the large party, or at any party that any one could make out. No trace of him had come to light—no gleam of the white waistcoat had pierced the obscurity of his doom. This news was a sharp shock to me, for I had my ideas about his real destination. His aged relative had promptly, as she said, guessed the worst. Somehow and somewhere he had got out of the way altogether, and now I trust that, with characteristic deliberation, he is changing the plates of the immortal gods. As my depressing visitant also said, he never *had* got his spirits up. I was fortunately able to dismiss her with her own somewhat improved. But the dim ghost of poor Brooksmith is one of those that I see. He had indeed been spoiled.

The Marriages

WON'T YOU stay a little longer?" the hostess said, holding the girl's hand and smiling. "It's too early for every one to go; it's too absurd." Mrs. Churchley inclined her head to one side and looked gracious; she held up to her face, in a vague, protecting, sheltering way, an enormous fan of red feathers. Everything about her, to Adela Chart, was enormous. She had big eyes, big teeth, big shoulders, big hands, big rings and bracelets, big jewels of every sort and many of them. The train of her crimson dress was longer than any other; her house was huge; her drawing-room, especially now that the company had left it, looked vast, and it offered to the girl's eyes a collection of the largest sofas and chairs, pictures, mirrors, and clocks that she had ever beheld. Was Mrs. Churchley's fortune also large, to account for so many immensities? Of this Adela could know nothing, but she reflected, while she smiled sweetly back at their entertainer, that she had better try to find out. Mrs. Churchley had at least a high-hung carriage drawn by the tallest horses, and in the Row she was to be seen perched on a mighty hunter. She was high and expansive herself, though not exactly fat; her bones were big, her limbs were long, and she had a loud, hurrying voice, like the bell of a steamboat. While she spoke to his daughter she had the air of hiding from Colonel Chart, a little shyly, behind the wide ostrich fan. But Colonel Chart was not a man to be either ignored or eluded.

"Of course every one is going on to something else," he said. "I believe there are a lot of things to-night."

"And where are *you* going?" Mrs. Churchley asked, dropping her fan and turning her bright, hard eyes on the Colonel.

"Oh, I don't do that sort of thing!" he replied, in a tone of resentment just perceptible to his daughter. She saw in it that he thought Mrs. Churchley might have done him a little more justice. But what made the honest soul think that she was a person to look to for a perception of fine shades? Indeed the shade was one that it might have been a little difficult to seize—the difference between "going on" and coming to a dinner of twenty people. The pair were in mourning; the second year had not lightened it for Adela, but the Colonel had not objected to dining with Mrs. Churchley, any more than he had objected, at Easter, to going down to the Millwards', where he had met her, and where the girl had her reasons for believing him to have known he should meet her. Adela was not clear about the occasion of their original meeting, to which a certain mystery attached. In Mrs. Churchley's exclamation now there was the fullest concurrence in Colonel Chart's idea; she didn't say, "Ah, yes, dear friend, I understand!" but this was the note of sympathy she plainly wished to sound. It immediately made Adela say to her, "Surely you must be going on somewhere yourself."

"Yes, you must have a lot of places," the Colonel observed, looking at her shining raiment with a sort of invidious directness. Adela could read the tacit implication: "You're not in sorrow, in desolation."

Mrs. Churchley turned away from her at this, waiting just a moment before answering. The red fan was up again, and this time it sheltered her from Adela. "I'll give everything up—for *you*," were the words that issued from behind it. "*Do* stay a little. I always think this is such a nice hour. One can really talk," Mrs. Churchley went on. The Colonel laughed; he said it wasn't fair. But their hostess continued, to Adela, "Do sit down; it's the only time to have any talk." The girl saw her father sit down, but she wandered away, turning her back and pretending to look at a picture. She was so far from agreeing with Mrs. Churchley that it was an hour she particularly disliked. She was conscious of the queerness, the shyness, in London, of the gregarious flight of guests, after a dinner, the general *sauve qui peut* and panic fear of being left with the host and hostess. But personally she always felt the contagion, always conformed to the flurry. Besides, she felt herself turning red now, flushed with a conviction that had come over her and that she wished not to show.

Her father sat down on one of the big sofas with Mrs. Churchley; fortunately he was also a person with a presence that could hold its own. Adela didn't care to sit and watch them while they made love, as she crudely formulated it, and she cared still less to join in their conversation. She wandered

further away, went into another of the bright, "handsome,"
rather nude rooms—they were like women dressed for a
ball—where the displaced chairs, at awkward angles to each
other, seemed to retain the attitudes of bored talkers. Her
heart beat strangely, but she continued to make a pretense of
looking at the pictures on the walls and the ornaments on the
tables, while she hoped that, as she preferred it, it would be
also the course that her father would like best. She hoped
"awfully," as she would have said, that he wouldn't think her
rude. She was a person of courage, and he was a kind, an
intensely good-natured man; nevertheless, she was a good deal
afraid of him. At home it had always been a religion with them
to be nice to the people he liked. How, in the old days, her
mother, her incomparable mother, so clever, so unerring, so
perfect—how in the precious days her mother had practiced
that art! Oh, her mother, her irrecoverable mother! One of
the pictures that she was looking at swam before her eyes.
Mrs. Churchley, in the natural course, would have begun immediately to climb staircases. Adela could see the high bony
shoulders and the long crimson tail and the universal corus-
cating nod wriggle their business-like way through the rest of
the night. Therefore she *must* have had her reasons for de-
taining them. There were mothers who thought every one
wanted to marry their eldest son, and the girl asked herself if
she belonged to the class of daughters who thought every one
wanted to marry their father. Her companions left her alone;
and though she didn't want to be near them, it angered her
that Mrs. Churchley didn't call her. That proved that she was
conscious of the situation. She would have called her, only
Colonel Chart had probably murmured, "Don't." That
proved that he also was conscious. The time was really not
long—ten minutes at the most elapsed—when he cried out,
gayly, pleasantly, as if with a little jocular reproach, "I say,
Adela, we must release this dear lady!" He spoke, of course,
as if it had been Adela's fault that they lingered. When they
took leave she gave Mrs. Churchley, without intention and
without defiance, but from the simple sincerity of her anxiety,
a longer look into the eyes than she had ever given her before.
Mrs. Churchley's onyx pupils reflected the question; they
seemed to say: "Yes, I *am*, if that's what you want to know!"

What made the case worse, what made the girl more sure, was the silence preserved by her companion in the brougham, on their way home. They rolled along in the June darkness from Prince's Gate to Seymour Street, each looking out of a window in conscious dumbness; watching without seeing the hurry of the London night, the flash of lamps, the quick roll on the wood of hansoms and other broughams. Adela had expected that her father would say something about Mrs. Churchley; but when he said nothing, it was, strangely, still more as if he had spoken. In Seymour Street he asked the footman if Mr. Godfrey had come in, to which the servant replied that he had come in early and gone straight to his room. Adela had perceived as much, without saying so, by a lighted window in the third story; but she contributed no remark to the question. At the foot of the stairs her father halted a moment, hesitating, as if he had something on his mind; but what it amounted to, apparently, was only the dry "Good-night" with which he presently ascended. It was the first time since her mother's death that he had bidden her good-night without kissing her. They were a kissing family, and after her mother's death the habit had taken a fresh spring. She had left behind her such a general passion of regret that in kissing each other they seemed to themselves a little to be kissing her. Now, as, standing in the hall, with the stiff watching footman (she could have said to him angrily, "Go away!") planted near her, she looked with unspeakable pain at her father's back while he mounted, the effect was of his having withheld from other and still more sensitive lips the touch of his own.

He was going to his room, and after a moment she heard his door close. Then she said to the servant, "Shut up the house" (she tried to do everything her mother had done, to be a little of what she had been, conscious only of mediocrity), and took her own way upstairs. After she had reached her room she waited, listening, shaken by the apprehension that she should hear her father come out again and go up to Godfrey. He would go up to tell him, to have it over without delay, precisely because it would be so difficult. She asked herself, indeed, why he should tell Godfrey when he had not taken the occasion—their drive home was an occasion—to tell herself. However, she wanted no announcing, no telling; there was such a horrible clearness in her mind that what she now waited for was only to be sure her father wouldn't leave his room. At the end of ten minutes she saw that this particular danger was over, upon which she came out and made her way to Godfrey. Exactly what she wanted to say to him first, if her father counted on the boy's greater indulgence, and before he could say anything, was, "Don't forgive him; don't, don't!"

He was to go up for an examination, poor fellow, and during these weeks his lamp burned till the small hours. It was for the diplomatic service, and there was to be some frightful number of competitors; but Adela had great hopes of him— she believed so in his talents, and she saw, with pity, how hard he worked. This would have made her spare him, not trouble his night, his scanty rest, if anything less dreadful had been at stake. It was a blessing, however, that one could count upon his coolness, young as he was—his bright, good-looking discretion. Moreover he was the one who would care most. If Leonard was the eldest son—he had, as a matter of course, gone into the army and was in India, on the staff, by good luck, of a governor-general—it was exactly this that would make him comparatively indifferent. His life was elsewhere, and his father and he had been in a measure military comrades, so that he would be deterred by a certain delicacy from protesting; he wouldn't have liked his father to protest in an affair of *his*. Beatrice and Muriel would care, but they were too young to speak, and this was just why her own responsibility was so great.

Godfrey was in working-gear—shirt and trousers and slippers and a beautiful silk jacket. His room felt hot, though a window was open to the summer night; the lamp on the table shed its studious light over a formidable heap of text books and papers, and the bed showed that he had flung himself down to think out a problem. As soon as she got in she said to him: "Father's going to marry Mrs. Churchley!"

She saw the poor boy's pink face turn pale. "How do you know?"

"I've seen with my eyes. We've been dining there—we've just come home. He's in love with her—she's in love with him; they'll arrange it."

"Oh, I say!" Godfrey exclaimed, incredulous.

"He will, he will, he will!" cried the girl; and with this she burst into tears.

Godfrey, who had a cigarette in his hand, lighted it at one of the candles on the mantelpiece as if he were embarrassed. As Adela, who had dropped into his arm-chair, continued to sob, he said, after a moment: "He oughtn't to—he oughtn't to."

"Oh, think of mamma—think of mamma!" the girl went on.

"Yes, he ought to think of mamma;" and Godfrey looked at the tip of his cigarette.

"To such a woman as that, after *her*!"

"Dear old mamma!" said Godfrey, smoking.

Adela rose again, drying her eyes. "It's like an insult to her; it's as if he denied her." Now that she spoke of it, she felt herself tremendously exalted. "It's as if he rubbed out at a stroke all the years of their happiness."

"They were awfully happy," said Godfrey.

"Think what she was—think how no one else will ever again be like her!" the girl cried.

"I suppose he's not very happy now," Godfrey continued vaguely.

"Of course he isn't, any more than you and I are; and it's dreadful of him to want to be."

"Well, don't make yourself miserable till you're sure," the young man said.

But his sister showed him confidently that she *was* sure, from the way the pair had behaved together and from her father's attitude on the drive home. If Godfrey had been there he would have seen everything; it couldn't be explained, but he would have felt. When he asked at what moment the girl had first had her suspicion, she replied that it had all come at once, that evening; or that at least she had had no conscious fear till then. There had been signs for two or three weeks, but she hadn't understood them—ever since the day Mrs. Churchley had dined in Seymour Street. Adela had thought it odd then that her father had wished to invite her, in the quiet way they were living; she was a person they knew so little. He had said something about her having been very civil to him, and that evening, already, she had guessed that he had been to Mrs. Churchley's oftener than she had supposed. To-night it had come to her clearly that he had been to see her every day since the day she dined with them; every afternoon, about the hour she thought he was at his club. Mrs. Churchley was his club,—she was just like a club. At this Godfrey laughed; he wanted to know what his sister knew about clubs. She was slightly disappointed in his laugh, slightly wounded by it, but she knew perfectly what she meant: she meant that Mrs. Churchley was public and florid, promiscuous and mannish.

"Oh, I dare say she's all right," said Godfrey, as if he wanted to get on with his work. He looked at the clock on the mantelshelf; he would have to put in another hour.

"All right to come and take darling mamma's place—to sit where *she* used to sit, to lay her horrible hands on *her* things?" Adela was appalled—all the more that she had not expected it—at her brother's apparent acceptance of such a prospect.

He coloured; there was something in her passionate piety that scorched him. She glared at him with her tragic eyes as if he had profaned an altar. "Oh, I mean nothing will come of it."

"Not if we do our duty," said Adela.

"Our duty?"

"You must speak to him—tell him how we feel; that we shall never forgive him, that we can't endure it."

"He'll think I'm cheeky," returned Godfrey, looking down at his papers, with his back to her and his hands in his pockets.

"Cheeky, to plead for *her* memory?"

"He'll say it's none of my business."

"Then you believe he'll do it?" cried the girl.

"Not a bit. Go to bed!"

"*I'll* speak to him," said Adela, as pale as a young priestess.

"Don't cry out till you're hurt; wait till he speaks to *you*."

"He won't, he won't!" the girl declared. "He'll do it without telling us."

Her brother had faced round to her again; he started a little at this, and again, at one of the candles, lighted his cigarette, which had gone out. She looked at him a moment; then he said something that surprised her.

"Is Mrs. Churchley very rich?"

"I haven't the least idea. What has that to do with it?"

Godfrey puffed his cigarette. "Does she live as if she were?"

"She has got a lot of showy things."

"Well, we must keep our eyes open," said Godfrey. "And now you *must* let me get on." He kissed his sister, as if to make up for dismissing her, or for his failure to take fire; and she held him a moment, burying her head on his shoulder. A wave of emotion surged through her; she broke out with a wail:

"Ah, why did she leave us? Why did she leave us?"

"Yes, why indeed?" the young man sighed, disengaging himself with a movement of oppression.

II.

Adela was so far right as that by the end of the week, though she remained certain, her father had not made the announcement she dreaded. What made her certain was the sense of her changed relations with him—of there being between them something unexpressed, something of which she was as conscious as she would have been of an unhealed wound. When she spoke of this to Godfrey, he said the change was of her own making, that she was cruelly unjust to the governor. She suffered even more from her brother's unexpected perversity; she had had so different a theory about him that her disappointment was almost an humiliation and she needed all her fortitude to pitch her faith lower. She wondered what had happened to him and why he had changed. She would have trusted him to feel right about anything, above all about such a matter as this. Their worship of their mother's memory, their recognition of her sacred place in their past, her exquisite influence in their father's life, his fortunes, his career, in the whole history of the family and welfare of the house—accomplished, clever, gentle, good, beautiful and capable as she had been, a woman whose soft distinction was universally proclaimed, so that on her death one of the Princesses, the most august of her friends, had written Adela such a note about her as princesses were understood very seldom to write: their hushed tenderness over all this was a kind of religion, and also a sort of honour, in falling away from which there was a semblance of treachery. This was not the way people usually felt in London, she knew; but, strenuous, ardent, observant girl as she was, with secrecies of sentiment and dim originalities of attitude, she had already made up her mind that London was no place to look for delicacies. Remembrance there was hammered thin, and to be faithful was to be a bore. The patient dead were sacrificed; they had no shrines, for people were literally ashamed of mourning. When they had hustled all sensibility out of their lives, they invented the fiction that they felt too much to utter. Adela said nothing to her sisters; this reticence was part of the virtue it was her system to exercise for them. *She* was to be their mother, a direct deputy and representative. Before the vision of that other woman parading in such a character, she felt capable of ingenuities and subtleties. The foremost of these was tremulously to watch her father. Five days after they had dined together at Mrs. Churchley's he asked her if she had been to see that lady.

"No indeed, why should I?" Adela knew that he knew she had not been, since Mrs. Churchley would have told him.

"Don't you call on people after you dine with them?" said Colonel Chart.

"Yes, in the course of time. I don't rush off within the week."

Her father looked at her, and his eyes were colder than she had ever seen them, which was probably, she reflected, just the way her own appeared to him. "Then you'll please rush off to-morrow. She's to dine with us on the 12th, and I shall expect your sisters to come down."

Adela stared. "To a dinner party?"

"It's not to be a dinner party. I want them to know Mrs. Churchley."

"Is there to be nobody else?"

"Godfrey, of course. A family party."

The girl asked her brother that evening if *that* was not tantamount to an announcement. He looked at her queerly, and then he said, "I've been to see her."

"What on earth did you do that for?"

"Father told me he wished it."

"Then he *has* told you?"

"Told me what?" Godfrey asked, while her heart sank with the sense that he was making difficulties for her.

"That they're engaged, of course. What else can all this mean?"

"He didn't tell me that, but I like her."

"*Like* her!" the girl shrieked.

"She's very kind, very good."

"To thrust herself upon us when we hate her? Is that what you call kind? Is that what you call decent?"

"Oh, *I* don't hate her," Godfrey rejoined, turning away as if his sister bored him.

She went the next day to see Mrs. Churchley, with a vague plan of breaking out to her, appealing to her, saying, "Oh, spare us! have mercy on us! let him alone! go away!" But that was not easy when they were face to face. Mrs. Churchley had every intention of getting, as she would have said—she was perpetually using the expression—into touch; but her good intentions were as depressing as a tailor's misfits. She could never understand that they had no place for her vulgar charity, that their life was filled with a fragrance of perfection for which she had no sense fine enough. She was as undomestic as a shop-front and as out of tune as a parrot. She would make them live in the streets, or bring the streets into their lives— it was the same thing. She had evidently never read a book, and she used intonations that Adela had never heard, as if she had been an Australian or an American. She understood every-thing in a vulgar sense; speaking of Godfrey's visit to her and praising him according to her idea, saying horrid things about him—that he was awfully good-looking, a perfect gentleman, the kind she liked. How could her father, who was after all, in everything else, such a dear, listen to a woman, or endure her, who thought she was pleasing when she called the son of his dead wife a perfect gentleman? What would he have been, pray? Much she knew about what any of them were! When she told Adela she wanted her to like her, the girl thought for an instant her opportunity had come—the chance to plead with her and beg her off. But she presented such an impen-etrable surface that it would have been like giving a message to a varnished door. She wasn't a woman, said Adela; she was an address.

When she dined in Seymour Street, the "children," as the girl called the others, including Godfrey, liked her. Beatrice and Muriel stared shyly and silently at the wonders of her apparel (she was brutally overdressed!) without, of course, guessing the danger that tainted the air. They supposed her, in their innocence, to be amusing, and they didn't know, any more than she did herself, that she patronised them. When she was upstairs with them, after dinner, Adela could see her looking round the room at the things she meant to alter; their mother's things, not a bit like her own and not good enough for her. After a quarter of an hour of this, our young lady felt sure she was deciding that Seymour Street wouldn't do at all, the dear old home that had done for their mother for twenty years. Was she plotting to transport them all to her horrible Prince's Gate? Of one thing, at any rate, Adela was certain: her father, at that moment, alone in the dining-room with Godfrey, pretending to drink another glass of wine to make time, was coming to the point, was telling the news. When they came upstairs, they both, to her eyes, looked strange: the news had been told.

She had it from Godfrey before Mrs. Churchley left the house, when, after a brief interval, he followed her out of the drawing-room on her taking her sisters to bed. She was waiting for him at the door of her room. Her father was then alone with his *fiancée* (the word was grotesque to Adela); it was already as if it were her home.

"What did you say to him?" the girl asked, when her brother had told her.

"I said nothing." Then he added, colouring (the expression of her face was such), "There was nothing to say."

"Is that how it strikes you?" said Adela, staring at the lamp.

"He asked me to speak to her," Godfrey went on.

"To speak to her?"

"To tell her I was glad."

"And did you?" Adela panted.

"I don't know. I said something. She kissed me."

"Oh, how *could* you?" shuddered the girl, covering her face with her hands.

"He says she's very rich," said Godfrey simply.

"Is that why you kissed her?"

"I didn't kiss her. Good-night," and the young man, turning his back upon her, went out.

When her brother was gone Adela locked herself in, as if with the fear that she should be overtaken or invaded, and during a sleepless, feverish, memorable night she took counsel of her uncompromising spirit. She saw things as they were, in all the indignity of life. The levity, the mockery, the infidelity, the ugliness, lay as plain as a map before her; it was a world *pour rire*, but she cried about it, all the same. The morning dawned early, or rather it seemed to her that there had been no night, nothing but a sickly, creeping day. But by the time she heard the house stirring again she had determined what to do. When she came down to the breakfast-room her father was already in his place, with newspapers and letters; and she expected the first words he would utter to be a rebuke to her for having disappeared, the night before, without taking leave of Mrs. Churchley. Then she saw that he wished to be intensely kind, to make every allowance, to conciliate and console her. He knew that she knew from Godfrey, and he got up and kissed her. He told her as quickly as possible, to have it over, stammering a little, with an "I've a piece of news for you that will probably shock you," yet looking even exaggeratedly grave and rather pompous, to inspire the respect he didn't deserve. When he kissed her she melted, she burst into tears. He held her against him, kissing her again and again, saying tenderly, "Yes, yes, I know, I know." But he didn't know, or he could never have done it. Beatrice and Muriel came in, frightened when they saw her crying, and still more scared when she turned to them with words and an air that were terrible in their comfortable little lives: "Papa's going to be married; he's going to marry Mrs. Churchley!" After staring a moment and seeing their father look as strange, on his side, as Adela, though in a different way, the children also began to cry, so that when the servants arrived, with tea and boiled eggs, these functionaries were greatly embarrassed with their burden, not knowing whether to come in or hang back. They all scraped together a decorum, and as soon as the things had been put on the table the Colonel banished the men with a glance. Then he made a little affectionate speech to Beatrice and Muriel, in which he assured them that Mrs. Churchley was the kindest, the most delightful, of women, only wanting to make them happy, only wanting to make him happy, and convinced that he would be if they were and that they would be if he was.

"What do such words mean?" Adela asked herself. She declared privately that they meant nothing, but she was silent, and every one was silent, on account of the advent of Miss Flynn, the governess, before whom Colonel Chart preferred not to discuss the situation. Adela recognized on the spot that, if things were to go as he wished, his children would practically never again be alone with him. He would spend all his time with Mrs. Churchley till they were married, and then Mrs. Churchley would spend all her time with him. Adela was ashamed of him, and that was horrible—all the more that every one else would be, all his other friends, every one who had known her mother. But the public dishonour to that high memory should not be enacted; he should not do as he wished.

After breakfast her father told her that it would give him pleasure if, in a day or two, she would take her sisters to see Mrs. Churchley, and she replied that he should be obeyed. He held her hand a moment, looking at her with an appeal in his eyes which presently hardened into sternness. He wanted to know that she forgave him, but he also wanted to say to her that he expected her to mind what she did, to go straight. She turned away her eyes; she was indeed ashamed of him.

She waited three days, and then she took her sisters to see Mrs. Churchley. That lady was surrounded with callers, as Adela knew she would be; it was her "day" and the occasion the girl preferred. Before this she had spent all her time with her sisters, talking to them about their mother, playing upon their memory of her, making them cry and making them laugh, reminding them of certain hours of their early childhood, telling them anecdotes of her own. None the less she assured them that she believed there was no harm at all in Mrs. Churchley, and that when the time should come she would probably take them out immensely. She saw with smothered irritation that they enjoyed their visit in Prince's

Gate; they had never been at anything so "grown up," nor seen so many smart bonnets and brilliant complexions. Moreover, they were considered with interest, as if, as features of Mrs. Churchley's new life, they had been described in advance and were the heroines of the occasion. There were so many ladies present that Mrs. Churchley didn't talk to them much; but she called them her "chicks" and asked them to hand about teacups and bread and butter. All this was highly agreeable and indeed intensely exciting to Beatrice and Muriel, who had little round red spots in *their* cheeks when they came away. Adela quivered with the sense that her mother's children were now Mrs. Churchley's "chicks" and features of Mrs. Churchley's life.

It was one thing to have made up her mind, however; it was another thing to make her attempt. It was when she learned from Godfrey that the day was fixed, the 20th of July, only six weeks removed, that she felt the importance of prompt action. She learned everything from Godfrey now, having determined that it would be hypocrisy to question her father. Even her silence was hypocritical, but she couldn't weep and wail. Her father showed extreme tact; taking no notice of her detachment, treating her as if it were a moment of *bouderie* which he was bound to allow her and which would pout itself away. She debated much as to whether she should take Godfrey into her confidence; she would have done so without hesitation if he had not disappointed her. He was so strange and so perversely preoccupied that she could explain it only by the high pressure at which he was living, his anxiety about his "exam." He was in a fidget, in a fever, putting on a spurt to come in first; skeptical moreover about his success and cynical about everything else. He appeared to agree to the general axiom that they didn't want a strange woman thrust into their home, but he found Mrs. Churchley "very jolly as a person to know." He had been to see her by himself; he had been to see her three times. He said to his sister that he would make the most of her now; he should probably be so little in Seymour Street after these days. What Adela at last determined to say to him was that the marriage would never take place. When he asked her what she meant and who was to prevent it, she replied that the interesting couple would give it up themselves, or that Mrs. Churchley at least would after a week or two back out of it.

"That will be really horrid then," Godfrey rejoined. "The only respectable thing, at the point they've come to, is to put it through. Charming for poor father to have the air of being 'chucked.'"

This made her hesitate two days more, but she found answers more valid than any objections. The many-voiced answer to everything—it was like the autumn wind around the house—was the backward affront to her mother. Her mother was dead, but it killed her again. So one morning, at eleven o'clock, when Adela knew her father was writing letters, she went out quietly and, stopping the first hansom she met, drove to Prince's Gate. Mrs. Churchley was at home, and she was shown into the drawing-room with the request that she would wait five minutes. She waited, without the sense of breaking down at the last, the impulse to run away, which was what she had expected to have. In the cab and at the door her heart had beat terribly, but now, suddenly, with the game really to play, she found herself lucid and calm. It was a joy to her to feel later that this was the way Mrs. Churchley found her; not confused, not stammering nor prevaricating, only a little amazed at her own courage, conscious of the immense responsibility of her step and wonderfully older than her years. Her hostess fixed her at first with the waiting eyes of a cashier, but after a little, to Adela's surprise, she burst into tears. At this the girl cried herself, but with the secret happiness of believing they were saved. Mrs. Churchley said she would think over what she had been told, and she promised Adela, freely enough and very firmly, not to betray the secret of her visit to the Colonel. They were saved—they were saved: the words sung themselves in the girl's soul as she came downstairs. When the door was opened for her she saw her brother on the step, and they looked at each other in surprise, each finding it on the part of the other an odd hour for Prince's Gate. Godfrey remarked that Mrs. Churchley would have enough of the family, and Adela answered that she would perhaps have too much. None the less the young man went in, while his sister took her way home.

III.

Adela Chart saw nothing of her brother for nearly a week; he had more and more his own time and hours, adjusted to his tremendous responsibilities, and he spent whole days at his crammer's. When she knocked at his door, late in the evening, he was not in his room. It was known in the house that he was greatly worried; he was horribly nervous about his ordeal. It was to begin on the 23d of June, and his father was as worried as himself. The wedding had been arranged in relation to this; they wished poor Godfrey's fate settled first, though it was felt that the nuptials would be darkened if it should not be settled right.

Ten days after her morning visit to Mrs. Churchley Adela began to perceive that there was a difference in the air; but as yet she was afraid to exult. It was not a difference for the better, so that there might be still many hours of pain. Her father, since the announcement of his intended marriage, had been visibly pleased with himself, but that pleasure appeared to have undergone a check. Adela had the impression which the passengers on a great steamer receive when, in the middle of the night, they hear the engines stop. As this impression resolves itself into the general sense that something serious has happened, so the girl asked herself what had happened now. She had expected something serious; but it was as if she couldn't keep still in her cabin—she wanted to go up and see. On the 20th, just before breakfast, her maid brought her a message from her brother. Mr. Godfrey would be obliged if she would speak to him in his room. She went straight up to him, dreading to find him ill, broken down on the eve of his formidable week. This was not the case, however, inasmuch as he appeared to be already at work, to have been at work since dawn. But he was very white, and his eyes had a strange and new expression. Her beautiful young brother looked older; he looked haggard and hard. He met her there as if he had been waiting for her, and he said immediately: "Please to tell me this, Adela: what was the purpose of your visit, the other morning, to Mrs. Churchley—the day I met you at her door?"

She stared—she hesitated. "The purpose? What's the matter? Why do you ask?"

"They've put it off—they've put it off a month."

"Ah, thank God!" said Adela.

"Why do you thank God?" Godfrey exclaimed roughly.

His sister gave a strained, intense smile. "You know I think it's all wrong."

He stood looking at her up and down. "What did you do there? How did you interfere?"

"Who told you I interfered?" she asked, flushing.

"You said something—you did something. I knew you had done it when I saw you come out."

"What I did was my own business."

"Damn your own business!" cried the young man.

She had never in her life been so spoken to, and in advance, if she had been given the choice, she would have said that she would rather die than be so spoken to by Godfrey. But her spirit was high, and for a moment she was as angry as if some one had cut at her with a whip. She escaped the blow, but she felt the insult. "And *your* business, then?" she asked. "I wondered what that was when I saw *you*."

He stood a moment longer frowning at her; then, with the exclamation "You've made a pretty mess!" he turned away from her and sat down to his books.

They had put it off, as he said; her father was dry and stiff and official about it. "I suppose I had better let you know that we have thought it best to postpone our marriage till the end of the summer—Mrs. Churchley has so many arrangements to make:" he was not more expansive than that. She neither knew nor greatly cared whether it was her fancy or a reality that he watched her obliquely, to see how she would take these words. She flattered herself that, thanks to Godfrey's preparation, cruel as the form of it had been, she took them very cleverly. She had a perfectly good conscience, for she was now able to judge what odious elements Mrs. Churchley, whom she had not seen since the morning in Prince's Gate, had already introduced into their relations with each other. She was able to infer that her father had not concurred in the postponement, for he was more restless than before, more absent, and distinctly irritable. There was of course still the question of how much of this condition was to be attributed to his solicitude about Godfrey. That young man took occasion to say a horrible thing to his sister: "If I don't pass it will be your fault." These were dreadful days for the girl, and she asked herself how she could have borne them if the hovering spirit of her mother had not been at her side. Fortunately, she always felt it there, sustaining, commending, sanctifying. Suddenly her father announced to her that he wished her to go immediately, with her sisters, down to Overland, where there was always part of a household and where for a few weeks they would be sufficiently comfortable. The only explanation he gave of this desire was that he wanted them out of the way. "Out of the way of what?" she queried, since, for the time, there were to be no preparations in Seymour Street. She was willing to believe that it was out of the way of his nerves.

She never needed urging, however, to go to Overland, the dearest old house in the world, where the happiest days of her young life had been spent and the silent nearness of her mother always seemed greatest. She was happy again, with Beatrice and Muriel and Miss Flynn, and the air of summer, and the haunted rooms, and her mother's garden, and the talking oaks and the nightingales. She wrote briefly to her father, to give him, as he had requested, an account of things; and he wrote back that, since she was so contented (she didn't remember telling him that), she had better not return to town at all. The rest of the season was not important for her, and he was getting on very well. He mentioned that Godfrey had finished his exam; but, as she knew, there would be a tiresome wait before they could learn the result. Godfrey was going abroad for a month with young Sherard—he had earned a little rest and a little fun. He went abroad without a word to Adela, but in his beautiful little hand he took a chaffing leave of Beatrice. The child showed her sister the letter, of which she was very proud and which contained no message for Adela. This was the worst bitterness of the whole crisis for that young lady—that it exhibited so strangely the creature in the world whom, after her mother, she had loved best.

Colonel Chart had said he would "run down" while his children were at Overland, but they heard no more about it. He only wrote two or three times to Miss Flynn, upon matters in regard to which Adela was surprised that he should not have communicated with herself. Muriel accomplished an upright little letter to Mrs. Churchley—her eldest sister neither fostered nor discouraged the performance—to which Mrs. Churchley replied, after a fortnight, in a meagre and, as Adela thought, illiterate fashion, making no allusion to the approach of any closer tie. Evidently the situation had changed; the question of the marriage was dropped, at any rate for the time. This idea gave the girl a singular and almost intoxicating sense of power; she felt as if she were riding a great wave of responsibility. She had chosen and acted, and the greatest could do no more than that. The grand thing was to see one's results, and what else was she doing? These results were in important and opulent lives; the stage was large on which she moved her figures. Such a vision was exciting, and as they had the use of a couple of ponies at Overland she worked off her excitement by a long gallop. A day or two after this, however, came news of which the effect was to re-kindle it. Godfrey had come back, the list had been published, he had passed first. These happy tidings proceeded from the young man himself; he announced them by a telegram to Beatrice, who had never in her life before received such a missive and was proportionately inflated. Adela reflected that she herself ought to have felt snubbed, but she was too happy. They were free again, they were themselves, the nightmare of the previous weeks was blown away, the unity and dignity of her father's life were restored, and, to round off her sense of success, Godfrey had achieved his first step toward high distinction. She wrote to him the next day, as frankly and affectionately as if there had been no estrangement between them; and besides telling him that she rejoiced in his triumph, she begged him in charity to let them know exactly how the case stood with regard to Mrs. Churchley.

Late in the summer afternoon she walked through the park to the village with her letter, posted it and came back. Suddenly, at one of the turns of the avenue, halfway to the house, she saw a young man looking toward her and waiting for her—a young man who proved to be Godfrey, on his march, on foot, across from the station. He had seen her, as he took his short cut, and if he had come down to Overland it was not, apparently, to avoid her. There was none of the joy of his triumph in his face, however, as he came a very few steps to meet her; and although, stiffly enough, he let her kiss him and say, "I'm so glad—I'm so glad!" she felt that this tolerance was not quite the calmness of the rising diplomatist. He turned toward the house with her and walked on a short distance, while she uttered the hope that he had come to stay some days.

"Only till to-morrow morning. They are sending me straight to Madrid. I came down to say good-by; there's a fellow bringing my portmanteau."

"To Madrid? How awfully nice! And it's awfully nice of you to have come," Adela said, passing her hand into his arm.

The movement made him stop, and, stopping, he turned on her, in a flash, a face of something more than suspicion—of passionate reprobation. "What I really came for—you might as well know without more delay—is to ask you a question."

"A question?" Adela repeated with a beating heart.

They stood there, under the old trees, in the lingering light, and, young and fine and fair as they both were, they were in complete superficial accord with the peaceful English scene. A near view, however, would have shown that Godfrey Chart had not come down to Overland to be superficial. He looked deep into his sister's eyes and demanded: "What was it you said that morning to Mrs. Churchley?"

Adela gazed at the ground a moment; then, raising her eyes: "If she has told you, why do you ask?"

"She has told me nothing. I've seen for myself."

"What have you seen?"

"She has broken it off—everything's over—father's in the depths."

"In the depths?" the girl quavered.

"Did you think it would make him jolly?" asked her brother.

"He'll get over it; he'll be glad."

"That remains to be seen. You interfered, you invented something, you got round her. I insist on knowing what you did."

Adela felt that she could be obstinate if she wished, and that if it should be a question of organizing a defense she should find treasures of perversity under her hand. She stood looking down again a moment, and saying to herself, "I could be dumb and dogged if I chose, but I scorn to be." She was not ashamed of what she had done, but she wanted to be clear. "Are you absolutely certain it's broken off?"

"He is, and she is; so that's as good."

"What reason has she given?"

"None at all—or half a dozen; it's the same thing. She has changed her mind—she mistook her feelings—she can't part with her independence; moreover, he has too many children."

"Did he tell you this?" said Adela.

"Mrs. Churchley told me. She has gone abroad for a year."

"And she didn't tell you what I said to her?"

"Why should I take this trouble if she had?"

"You might have taken it to make me suffer," said Adela. "That appears to be what you want to do."

"No, I leave that to *you*; it's the good turn you've done me!" cried the young man, with hot tears in his eyes.

She stared, aghast with the perception that there was some dreadful thing she didn't know; but he walked on, dropping the question angrily and turning his back to her as if he couldn't trust himself. She read his disgust in his averted face, in the way he squared his shoulders and smote the ground with his stick, and she hurried after him and presently over-took him. She accompanied him for a moment in silence; then she pleaded: "What do you mean? What in the world have I done to you?"

"She would have helped me; she was all ready to do it," said Godfrey.

"Helped you in what?" She wondered what he meant; if he had made debts that he was afraid to confess to his father and—of all horrible things—had been looking to Mrs. Churchley to pay. She turned red with the mere apprehension of this and, on the heels of her guess, exulted again at having perhaps averted such a shame.

"Can't you see that I'm in trouble? Where are your eyes, your senses, your sympathy, that you talk so much about? Haven't you seen these six months that I've a cursed worry in my life?"

She seized his arm, she made him stop, she stood looking

up at him like a frightened little girl. "What's the matter, Godfrey—what *is* the matter?"

"You've vexed me so—I could strangle you!" he growled. This idea added nothing to her dread; her dread was that he had done some wrong, was stained with some guilt. She uttered it to him with clasped hands, begging him to tell her the worst; but, still more passionately, he cut her short with his own cry: "In God's name, satisfy me! What infernal thing did you do?"

"It was not infernal; it was right. I told her mamma had been wretched," said Adela.

"Wretched? You told her such a lie?"

"It was the only way, and she believed me."

"Wretched how—wretched when—wretched where?" the young man stammered.

"I told her papa had made her so, and that *she* ought to know it. I told her the question troubled me unspeakably, but that I had made up my mind it was my duty to initiate her." Adela paused, with the light of bravado in her face, as if, though struck while she phrased it, with the monstrosity of what she had done, she was incapable of abating a jot of it. "I notified her that he had faults and peculiarities that made mamma's life a long worry—a martyrdom that she hid wonderfully from the world, but that we saw and that I had often pitied. I told her what they were, these faults and peculiarities; I put the dots on the *i*'s. I said it wasn't fair to let another person marry him without a warning. I warned her; I satisfied my conscience. She could do as she liked. My responsibility was over."

Godfrey gazed at her; he listened, with parted lips, incredulous and appalled. "You invented such a tissue of falsities and calumnies, and you talk about your conscience? You stand there in your senses and proclaim your crime?"

"I would have committed any crime that would have rescued us."

"You insult and defame your own father?" Godfrey continued.

"He'll never know it; she took a vow she wouldn't tell him."

"I'll be damned if *I* won't tell him!" Godfrey cried.

Adela felt sick at this, but she flamed up to resent the treachery, as it struck her, of such a menace. "I did right—I did right!" she vehemently declared. "I went down on my knees to pray for guidance, and I saved mamma's memory from outrage. But if I hadn't, if I hadn't"—she faltered for an instant—"I'm not worse than you, and I'm not so bad, for you've done something that you're ashamed to tell me."

Godfrey had taken out his watch; he looked at it with quick intensity, as if he were not hearing nor heeding her. Then, glancing up with his calculating eye, he fixed her long enough to exclaim, with unsurpassable horror and contempt: "You raving maniac!" He turned away from her; he bounded down the avenue in the direction from which they had come, and, while she watched him, strode away across the grass, toward the short cut to the station.

IV.

Godfrey's portmanteau, by the time Adela got home, had been brought to the house, but Beatrice and Muriel, who had been informed of this, waited for their brother in vain. Their sister said nothing to them about having seen him, and she accepted, after a little, with a calmness that surprised herself, the idea that he had returned to town to denounce her. She believed that would make no difference now—she had done what she had done. She had somehow a faith in Mrs. Churchley. If Mrs. Churchley had broken off she wouldn't renew. She was a heavy-footed person, incapable of further agility. Adela recognised too that it might well have come over her that there were too many children. Lastly the girl fortified herself with the reflection, grotesque under the circumstances and tending to prove that her sense of humor was not high, that her father, after all, was not a man to be played with. It seemed to her, at any rate, that if she *had* prevented his marriage she could bear anything—bear imprisonment and bread and water, bear lashes and torture, bear even his lifelong reproach. What she could bear least was the wonder of the inconvenience she had inflicted on Godfrey. She had time to turn this over, very vainly, for a succession of days—days more

numerous than she had expected, which passed without bringing her from London any summons to come up and take her
punishment. She sounded the possible, she compared the degrees of the probable; feeling however that, as a cloistered girl
she was poorly equipped for speculation. She tried to imagine
the calamitous things young men might do, and could only
feel that such things would naturally be connected either with
money or with women. She became conscious that after all
she knew almost nothing about either subject. Meanwhile
there was no reverberation from Seymour Street—only a
sultry silence.

At Overland she spent hours in her mother's garden, where
she had grown up, where she considered that she was training
for old age, for she meant not to depend upon whist. She
loved the place as, had she been a good Catholic, she would
have loved the smell of her parish church; and indeed there
was in her passion for flowers something of the respect of a
religion. They seemed to her the only things in the world that
really respected themselves, unless one made an exception for
Nutkins, who had been in command all through her mother's
time, with whom she had had a real friendship, and who had
been affected by their pure example. He was the person left
in the world with whom, on the whole, she could talk most
intimately about her mother. They never had to name her
together—they only said "she;" and Nutkins freely conceded
that she had taught him everything he knew. When Beatrice
and Muriel said "she" they referred to Mrs. Churchley. Adela
had reason to believe that she should never marry, and that
some day she should have about a thousand a year. This made
her see in the far future a little garden of her own, under a
hill, full of rare and exquisite things, where she would spend
most of her old age on her knees, with an apron and stout
gloves, a pair of shears and a trowel, steeped in the comfort
of being thought mad.

One morning, ten days after her scene with Godfrey, upon
coming back into the house shortly before lunch, she was met
by Miss Flynn with the notification that a lady in the drawing-
room had been waiting for her for some minutes. "A lady"
suggested immediately Mrs. Churchley. It came over Adela
that the form in which her penalty was to descend would be

a personal explanation with that misdirected woman. The lady
had not given her name, and Miss Flynn had not seen Mrs.
Churchley; nevertheless the governess was certain that Adela's
surmise was wrong.

"Is she big and dreadful?" the girl asked.

Miss Flynn, who was circumspection itself, hesitated a moment. "She's dreadful, but she's not big." She added that she
was not sure she ought to let Adela go in alone; but this
young lady felt throughout like a heroine, and it was not for
a heroine to shrink from any encounter. Was she not, every
instant, in transcendent contact with her mother? The visitor
might have no connection whatever with the drama of her
father's frustrated marriage; but everything, to-day, to Adela,
was a part of that.

Miss Flynn's description had prepared her for a considerable
shock, but she was not agitated by her first glimpse of the
person who awaited her. A youngish, well-dressed woman
stood there, and silence was between them while they looked
at each other. Before either of them had spoken, however,
Adela began to see what Miss Flynn had intended. In the light
of the drawing-room window the lady was five-and-thirty
years of age and had vivid yellow hair. She also had a blue
cloth suit with brass buttons, a stick-up collar like a gentleman's, a necktie arranged in a sailor's knot, with a golden pin
in the shape of a little lawn-tennis racket, and pearl-grey
gloves with big black stitchings. Adela's second impression
was that she was an actress; her third was that no such person
had ever before crossed that threshold.

"I'll tell you what I've come for," said the apparition. "I've
come to ask you to intercede." She was not an actress; an
actress would have had a nicer voice.

"To intercede?" Adela was too bewildered to ask her to sit
down.

"With your father, you know. He doesn't know, but he'll
have to." Her "have" sounded like " 'ave." She explained,
with many more such sounds, that she was Mrs. Godfrey, that
they had been married seven mortal months. If Godfrey was
going abroad she must go with him, and the only way she
could go with him would be for his father to do something.
He was afraid of his father—that was clear; he was afraid even

to tell him. What she had come down for was to see some other member of the family face to face ("fice to fice" Mrs. Godfrey called it), and try if he couldn't be approached by another side. If no one else would act, then she would just have to act herself. The Colonel would have to do something—that was the only way out of it.

What really happened Adela never quite understood; what seemed to be happening was that the room went round and round. Through the blur of perception accompanying this effect the sharp stabs of her visitor's revelation came to her like the words heard by a patient "going off" under ether. She denied passionately, afterwards, even to herself, that she had done anything so abject as to faint; but there was a lapse in her consciousness in relation to Miss Flynn's intervention. This intervention had evidently been active, for when they talked the matter over, later in the day, with bated breath and infinite dissimulation for the schoolroom quarter, the governess had more information, and still stranger, to impart than to receive. She was at any rate under the impression that she had athletically contended, in the drawing-room, with the yellow hair, after removing Adela from the scene and before inducing Mrs. Godfrey to withdraw. Miss Flynn had never known a more thrilling day, for all the rest of it too was pervaded with agitations and conversations, precautions and alarms. It was given out to Beatrice and Muriel that their sister had been taken suddenly ill, and the governess ministered to her in her room. Indeed Adela had never found herself less at ease; for this time she had received a blow that she couldn't return. There was nothing to do but to take it, to endure the humiliation of her wound.

At first she declined to take it; it was much easier to consider that her visitor was a monstrous masquerader. On the face of the matter, moreover, it was not fair to believe till one heard; and to hear in such a case was to hear Godfrey himself. Whatever his sister had tried to imagine about him she had not arrived at anything so belittling as an idiotic secret marriage with a dyed and painted hag. Adela repeated this last word as if it gave her some comfort; and indeed where everything was so bad fifteen years of seniority made the case little worse. Miss Flynn was portentous, for Miss Flynn had had it out with the wretch. She had cross-questioned her and had not broken her down. This was the most important hour of Miss Flynn's life; for whereas she usually had to content herself with being humbly and gloomily in the right, she could now be magnanimously and showily so. Her only perplexity was as to what she ought to do—write to Colonel Chart or go up to town to see him. She bloomed with alternatives, never having known the like before. Toward evening Adela was obliged to recognise that Godfrey's worry, of which he had spoken to her, had appeared bad enough to consist even of a low wife, and to remember that, so far from its being inconceivable that a young man in his position should clandestinely take one, she had been present, years before, during her mother's lifetime, when Lady Molesley declared gayly, over a cup of tea, that this was precisely what she expected of her eldest son. The next morning it was the worst possibilities that seemed the clearest; the only thing left with a tatter of dusky comfort being the ambiguity of Godfrey's charge that his sister's action had "done" for him. That was a matter by itself, and she racked her brains for a connecting link between Mrs. Churchley and Mrs. Godfrey. At last she made up her mind that they were related by blood; very likely, though differing in fortune, they were cousins or even sisters. But even then what did her brother mean?

Arrested by the unnatural fascination of opportunity, Miss Flynn received before lunch a telegram from Colonel Chart—an order for dinner and a vehicle; he and Godfrey were to arrive at six o'clock. Adela had plenty of occupation for the interval, for she was pitying her father when she was not rejoicing that her mother had gone too soon to know. She flattered herself she discerned the providential reason of that cruelty now. She found time however still to wonder for what purpose, under the circumstances, Godfrey was to be brought down. She was not unconscious, it is true, that she had little general knowledge of what usually was done with young men in that predicament. One talked about the circumstances, but the circumstances were an abyss. She felt this still more when she found, on her father's arrival, that nothing, apparently, was to happen as she had taken for granted it would. There was a kind of inviolable hush over the whole affair, but no tragedy, no publicity, nothing ugly. The tragedy had been in town, and the faces of the two men spoke of it, in spite of themselves; so that at present there was only a family dinner, with Beatrice and Muriel and the governess, and almost a company tone, the result of the desire to avoid publicity. Adela admired her father; she knew what he was feeling, if Mrs. Godfrey had been at him, and yet she saw him positively gallant. He was very gentle, he never looked at his son, and there were moments when he seemed almost sick with sadness. Godfrey was equally inscrutable and therefore wholly different from what he had been as he stood before her in the park. If he was to start on his career (with such a wife!—wouldn't she utterly blight it?) he was already professional enough to know how to wear a mask.

Before they rose from table the girl was wholly bewildered, so little could she perceive the effects of such large causes. She had nerved herself for a great ordeal, but the air was as sweet as an anodyne. It was constantly plain to her that her father was deadly sad—as pathetic as a creature jilted. He was broken, but he showed no resentment; there was a weight on his heart, but he had lightened it by dressing as immaculately as usual for dinner. She asked herself what immensity of a row there could have been in town to have left his anger so spent. He went through everything, even to sitting with his son after dinner. When they came out together he invited Beatrice and Muriel to the billiard-room; and as Miss Flynn discreetly withdrew Adela was left alone with Godfrey, who was completely changed and not in a rage any more. He was broken, too, but he was not so pathetic as his father. He was only very correct and apologetic; he said to his sister, "I'm awfully sorry *you* were annoyed; it was something I never dreamed of."

She couldn't think immediately what he meant; then she grasped the reference to the yellow hair. She was uncertain, however, what tone to take; perhaps his father had arranged with him that they were to make the best of it. But she spoke her own despair in the way she murmured: "O Godfrey, Godfrey, is it true?"

"I've been the most unutterable donkey—you can say what you like to me. You can't say anything worse than I've said to myself."

"My brother, my brother!" his words made her moan. He hushed her with a movement, and she asked, "What has father said?"

Godfrey looked over her head. "He'll give her six hundred a year."

"Ah, the angel!"

"On condition she never comes near me. She has solemnly promised; and she'll probably leave me alone, to get the money. If she doesn't—in diplomacy—I'm lost." The young man had been turning his eyes vaguely about, this way and that, to avoid meeting hers; but after another instant he gave up the effort, and she had the miserable confession of his glance. "I've been living in hell," he said.

"My brother, my brother!" she repeated.

"I'm not an idiot; yet for her I've behaved like one. Don't ask me—you mustn't know. It was all done in a day, and since then, fancy my condition—fancy my work!"

"Thank God you passed!" cried Adela.

"I would have shot myself if I hadn't. I had an awful day yesterday with father; it was late at night before it was over. I leave England next week. He brought me down here for it to look well—so that the children sha'n't know."

"He's wonderful!" she murmured.

"He's wonderful!" said Godfrey.

"Did *she* tell him?" the girl asked.

"She came straight to Seymour Street from here. She saw him alone first; then he called me in. *That* luxury lasted about an hour."

Adela said, "Poor, poor father!" to this; on which her brother remained silent. Then, after he had remarked that it had been the scene he had lived in terror of all through his cramming, and she had stammered her pity and admiration at such a mixture of anxieties and such a triumph of talent, she demanded: "Have you told him?"

"Told him what?"

"What you said you would—what *I* did."

Godfrey turned away as if at present he had very little interest in that inferior tribulation. "I was angry with you, but I cooled off. I held my tongue."

Adela clasped her hands. "You thought of mamma!"

"Oh, don't speak of mamma," said the young man tenderly.

It was indeed not a happy moment; and she murmured: "No; if you *had* thought of her"—

This made Godfrey turn back at her, with a little flare in his eyes. "Oh, *then* it didn't prevent. I thought that woman was good. I believed in her."

"Is she *very* bad?" his sister inquired.

"I shall never mention her to you again," Godfrey answered, with dignity.

"You may believe that *I* won't speak of her. So father doesn't know?" she added.

"Doesn't know what?"

"That I said that to Mrs. Churchley."

"I don't think so, but you must find out for yourself."

"I shall find out," said Adela. "But what had Mrs. Churchley to do with it?"

"With *my* misery? I told her. I had to tell some one."

"Why didn't you tell me?"

Godfrey hesitated. "Oh, you take things so beastly hard—you make such rows." Adela covered her face with her hands, and he went on: "What I wanted was comfort—not to be lashed up. I thought I should go mad. I wanted Mrs. Churchley to break it to father, to intercede for me and help him to meet it. She was awfully kind to me; she listened and she understood; she could fancy how it had happened. Without her I shouldn't have pulled through. She liked me, you know," Godfrey dropped. "She said she would do what she could for me; she was full of sympathy and resource; I really leaned on her. But when you cut in, of course it spoiled everything. That's why I was so angry with you. She couldn't do anything then."

Adela dropped her hands, staring; she felt that she had walked in darkness. "So that he had to meet it alone?"

"*Dame!*" said Godfrey, who had got up his French tremendously.

Muriel came to the door to say papa wished the two others to join them, and the next day Godfrey returned to town. His father remained at Overland, without an intermission, the rest of the summer and the whole of the autumn, and Adela had a chance to find out, as she had said, whether he knew that she had interfered. But in spite of her chance she never found out. He knew that Mrs. Churchley had thrown him over and he knew that his daughter rejoiced in it, but he appeared not to have divined the relation between the two facts. It was strange that one of the matters he was clearest about—Adela's secret triumph—should have been just the thing which, from this time on, justified less and less such a confidence. She was too sorry for him to be consistently glad. She watched his attempts to wind himself up on the subject of shorthorns and drainage, and she favoured to the utmost of her ability his intermittent disposition to make a figure in orchids. She wondered whether they mightn't have a few people at Overland; but when she mentioned the idea her father asked what in the world there would be to attract them. It was a confoundedly stupid house, he remarked, with all respect to *her* cleverness. Beatrice and Muriel were mystified; the prospect of going out immensely had faded so utterly away. They were apparently not to go out at all. Colonel Chart was aimless and bored; he paced up and down and went back to smoking, which was bad for him, and looked drearily out of windows, as if on the bare chance that something might arrive. Did he expect Mrs. Churchley to arrive, to relent? It was Adela's belief that she gave no sign. But the girl thought it really remarkable of her not to have betrayed her ingenious young visitor. Adela's judgment of human nature was perhaps harsh, but she believed that many women, under the circumstances, would not have been so forbearing. This lady's conception of the point of honour presented her as rather a higher type than one might have supposed.

Adela knew her father found the burden of Godfrey's folly very heavy to bear and was incommoded at having to pay the horrible woman six hundred a year. Doubtless he was having dreadful letters from her; doubtless she threatened them all with a hideous exposure. If the matter should be bruited Godfrey's prospects would collapse on the spot. He thought Madrid very charming and curious, but Mrs. Godfrey was in England, so that his father had to face the music. Adela took a dolorous comfort in thinking that her mother was out of *that*—it would have killed her; but this didn't blind her to the fact that the comfort for her father would perhaps have been greater if he had had some one to talk to about his trouble. He never dreamed of doing so to her, and she felt that she couldn't ask him. In the family life he wanted utter silence about it. Early in the winter he went abroad for ten weeks, leaving her with her sisters in the country, where it was not to be denied that at this time existence had very little savour. She half expected that her sister-in-law would descend upon her again; but the fear was not justified, and the quietude of such a personage savoured terribly of expense. There were sure to be extras. Colonel Chart went to Paris and to Monte Carlo and then to Madrid to see his boy. Adela wondered whether he would meet Mrs. Churchley somewhere, since, if she had gone for a year, she would still be on the Continent. If he should meet her perhaps the affair would come on again: she caught herself musing over this. Her father brought back no news of her, and seeing him after an interval, she was struck afresh with his jilted and wasted air. She didn't like it; she resented it. A little more and she would have said that that was no way to treat such a man.

They all went up to town in March, and on one of the first days of April she saw Mrs. Churchley in the park. She herself remained apparently invisible to that lady—she herself and Beatrice and Muriel, who sat with her in their mother's old bottle-green landau. Mrs. Churchley, perched higher than ever, rode by without a recognition; but this didn't prevent Adela from going to her before the month was over. As on her great previous occasion she went in the morning, and she again had the good fortune to be admitted. But this time her visit was shorter, and a week after making it—the week was a desolation—she addressed to her brother at Madrid a letter which contained these words:

"I could endure it no longer—I confessed and retracted; I explained to her as well as I could the falsity of what I said to her ten months ago and the benighted purity of my motives for saying it. I besought her to regard it as unsaid, to forgive me, not to despise me too much, to take pity on poor *perfect* papa and come back to him. She was more good-natured than you might have expected; indeed, she laughed extravagantly. She had never believed me—it was too absurd; she had only, at the time, disliked me. She found me utterly false (she was very frank with me about this), and she told papa that she thought I was horrid. She said she could never live with such a girl, and as I would certainly never marry I must be sent away; in short she quite loathed me. Papa defended me, he refused to sacrifice me, and this led practically to their rupture. Papa gave her up, as it were, for me. Fancy the angel, and fancy what I must try to be to him for the rest of his life! Mrs. Churchley can never come back—she's going to marry Lord Dovedale."

The Chaperon

A N OLD LADY, in a high drawing-room, had had her chair
moved close to the fire, where she sat knitting and
warming her knees. She was dressed in deep mourning; her
face had a faded nobleness, tempered, however, by the somewhat illiberal compression assumed by her lips in obedience
to something that was passing in her mind. She was far from
the lamp, but though her eyes were fixed upon her active
needles she was not looking at them. What she really saw was
quite another train of affairs. The room was spacious and dim;
the thick London fog had oozed into it even through its superior defences. It was full of dusky, massive, valuable things.
The old lady sat motionless save for the regularity of her clicking needles, which seemed as personal to her and as expressive
as prolonged fingers. If she was thinking something out, she
was thinking it thoroughly.

When she looked up, on the entrance of a girl of twenty, it
might have been guessed that the appearance of this young
lady was not an interruption of her meditation, but rather a
contribution to it. The young lady, who was charming to behold, was also in deep mourning, which had a freshness, if
mourning can be fresh, an air of having been lately put on.
She went straight to the bell beside the chimney-piece and
pulled it, while in her other hand she held a sealed and directed letter. Her companion glanced in silence at the letter;
then she looked still harder at her work. The girl hovered near
the fireplace, without speaking, and after a due, a dignified
interval the butler appeared in response to the bell. The time
had been sufficient to make the silence between the ladies
seem long. The younger one asked the butler to see that her
letter should be posted; and after he had gone out she moved
vaguely about the room, as if to give her grandmother—for
such was the elder personage—a chance to begin a colloquy
of which she herself preferred not to strike the first note. As
equally with herself her companion was on the face of it capable of holding out, the tension, though it was already late
in the evening, might have lasted long. But the old lady after

a little appeared to recognise, a trifle ungraciously, the girl's superior resources.

"Have you written to your mother?"

"Yes, but only a few lines, to tell her I shall come and see her in the morning."

"Is that all you've got to say?" asked the grandmother.

"I don't quite know what you want me to say."

"I want you to say that you've made up your mind."

"Yes, I've done that, granny."

"You intend to respect your father's wishes?"

"It depends upon what you mean by respecting them. I do justice to the feelings by which they were dictated."

"What do you mean by justice?" the old lady retorted.

The girl was silent a moment; then she said: "You'll see my idea of it."

"I see it already! You'll go and live with her."

"I shall talk the situation over with her to-morrow and tell her that I think that will be best."

"Best for her, no doubt!"

"What's best for her is best for me."

"And for your brother and sister?" As the girl made no reply to this her grandmother went on: "What's best for them is that you should acknowledge some responsibility in regard to them and, considering how young they are, try and do something for them."

"They must do as I've done—they must act for themselves. They have their means now, and they're free."

"Free? They're mere children."

"Let me remind you that Eric is older than I."

"He doesn't like his mother," said the old lady, as if that were an answer.

"I never said he did. And she adores him."

"Oh, your mother's adorations!"

"Don't abuse her now," the girl rejoined, after a pause.

The old lady forbore to abuse her, but she made up for it the next moment by saying: "It will be dreadful for Edith."

"What will be dreadful?"

"Your desertion of her."

"The desertion's on her side."

"Her consideration for her father does her honour."

"Of course I'm a brute, *n'en parlons plus*," said the girl. "We must go our respective ways," she added, in a tone of extreme wisdom and philosophy.

Her grandmother straightened out her knitting and began to roll it up. "Be so good as to ring for my maid," she said, after a minute. The young lady rang, and there was another wait and another conscious hush. Before the maid came her mistress remarked: "Of course then you'll not come to *me*, you know."

"What do you mean by 'coming' to you?"

"I can't receive you on that footing."

"She'll not come *with* me, if you mean that."

"I don't mean that," said the old lady, getting up as her maid came in. This attendant took her work from her, gave her an arm and helped her out of the room, while Rose Tramore, standing before the fire and looking into it, faced the idea that her grandmother's door would now under all circumstances be closed to her. She lost no time however in brooding over this anomaly: it only added energy to her determination to act. All she could do to-night was to go to bed, for she felt utterly weary. She had been living, in imagination, in a prospective struggle, and it had left her as exhausted as a real fight. Moreover this was the culmination of a crisis, of weeks of suspense, of a long, hard strain. Her father had been laid in his grave five days before, and that morning his will had been read. In the afternoon she had got Edith off to St. Leonard's with their aunt Julia, and then she had had a wretched talk with Eric. Lastly, she had made up her mind to act in opposition to the formidable will, to a clause which embodied if not exactly a provision, a recommendation singularly emphatic. She went to bed and slept the sleep of the just.

"Oh, my dear, how charming! I must take another house!" It was in these words that her mother responded to the announcement Rose had just formally made and with which she had vaguely expected to produce a certain dignity of effect. In the way of emotion there was apparently no effect at all, and the girl was wise enough to know that this was not simply on account of the general line of non-allusion taken by the extremely pretty woman before her, who looked like her elder sister. Mrs. Tramore had never manifested, to her daughter, the slightest consciousness that her position was peculiar; but the recollection of something more than that fine policy was required to explain such a failure to appreciate Rose's sacrifice. It was simply a fresh reminder that she had never appreciated anything, that she was nothing but a tinted and stippled surface. Her situation was peculiar indeed. She had been the heroine of a scandal which had grown dim only because, in the eyes of the London world, it paled in the lurid light of the contemporaneous. That attention had been fixed on it for several days, fifteen years before; there had been a high relish of the vivid evidence as to his wife's misconduct with which, in the divorce-court, Charles Tramore had judged well to regale a cynical public. The case was pronounced awfully bad, and he obtained his decree. The folly of the wife had been inconceivable, in spite of other examples: she had quitted her children, she had followed the "other fellow" abroad. The other fellow hadn't married her, not having had time: he had lost his life in the Mediterranean by the capsizing of a boat, before the prohibitory term had expired.

Mrs. Tramore had striven to extract from this accident something of the austerity of widowhood; but her mourning only made her deviation more public, she was a widow whose husband was awkwardly alive. She had not prowled about the Continent on the classic lines; she had come back to London to take her chance. But London would give her no chance, would have nothing to say to her; as many persons had remarked, you could never tell how London would behave. It would not receive Mrs. Tramore again on any terms, and when she was spoken of, which now was not often, it was inveterately said of her that she went nowhere. Apparently she had not the qualities for which London compounds; though in the cases in which it does compound you may often wonder what these qualities are. She had not at any rate been successful: her lover was dead, her husband was liked and her children were pitied, for in payment for a topic London will parenthetically pity. It was thought interesting and magnanimous that Charles Tramore had not married again. The disadvantage to his children of the miserable story was thus left uncorrected, and this, rather oddly, was counted as *his* sacrifice. His mother, whose arrangements were elaborate, looked after them a great deal, and they enjoyed a mixture of laxity and discipline under the roof of their aunt, Miss Tramore, who was independent, having, for reasons that the two ladies had exhaustively discussed, determined to lead her own life. She had set up a home at St. Leonard's, and that contracted shore had played a considerable part in the upbringing of the little Tramores. They knew about their mother, as the phrase was, but they didn't know her; which was naturally deemed more pathetic for them than for her. She had a house in Chester Square and an income and a victoria—it served all purposes, as she never went out in the evening—and flowers on her window-sills, and a remarkable appearance of youth. The income was supposed to be in part the result of a bequest from the man for whose sake she had committed the error of her life, and in the appearance of youth there was a slightly impertinent implication that it was a sort of afterglow of the same connection.

Her children, as they grew older, fortunately showed signs of some individuality of disposition. Edith, the second girl, clung to her aunt Julia; Eric, the son, clung frantically to polo; while Rose, the elder daughter, appeared to cling mainly to herself. Collectively, of course, they clung to their father, whose attitude in the family group, however, was casual and intermittent. He was charming and vague; he was like a clever actor who often didn't come to rehearsal. Fortune, which but for that one stroke had been generous to him, had provided him with deputies and trouble-takers, as well as with whimsical opinions, and a reputation for excellent taste, and whist at his club, and perpetual cigars on morocco sofas, and a beautiful absence of purpose. Nature had thrown in a remarkably fine hand, which he sometimes passed over his children's heads when they were glossy from the nursery brush. On Rose's eighteenth birthday he said to her that she might go to see her mother, on condition that her visits should be limited to an hour each time and to four in the year. She was to go alone; the other children were not included in the arrangement. This was the result of a visit that he himself had paid his repudiated wife at her urgent request, their only encounter during the fifteen years. The girl knew as much as this from her aunt Julia, who was full of tell-tale secrecies. She availed herself eagerly of the license, and in course of the period that elapsed before her father's death she spent with Mrs. Tramore exactly eight hours by the watch. Her father, who was as inconsistent and disappointing as he was amiable, spoke to her of her mother only once afterwards. This occasion had been the sequel of her first visit, and he had made no use of it to ask what she thought of the personality in Chester Square or how she liked it. He had only said "Did she take you out?" and when Rose answered "Yes, she put me straight into a carriage and drove me up and down Bond Street," had rejoined sharply "See that that never occurs again." It never did, but once was enough, every one they knew having happened to be in Bond Street at that particular hour.

After this the periodical interview took place in private, in Mrs. Tramore's beautiful little wasted drawing-room. Rose knew that, rare as these occasions were, her mother would not have kept her "all to herself" had there been anybody she could have shown her to. But in the poor lady's social void there was no one; she had after all her own correctness and she consistently preferred isolation to inferior contacts. So her daughter was subjected only to the maternal; it was not necessary to be definite in qualifying that. The girl had by this time a collection of ideas, gathered by impenetrable processes; she had tasted, in the ostracism of her ambiguous parent, of the acrid fruit of the tree of knowledge. She not only had an approximate vision of what every one had done, but she had a private judgment for each case. She had a particular vision of her father, which did not interfere with his being dear to her, but which was directly concerned in her resolution, after his death, to do the special thing he had expressed the wish she should not do. In the general estimate her grandmother and her grandmother's money had their place, and the strong probability that any enjoyment of the latter commodity would now be withheld from her. It included Edith's marked inclination to receive the law, and doubtless eventually a more substantial memento, from Miss Tramore, and opened the question whether her own course might not contribute to make her sister's appear heartless. The answer to this question however would depend on the success that might attend her own, which would very possibly be small. Eric's attitude was eminently simple; he didn't care to know people who didn't know *his* people. If his mother should ever get back into society perhaps he would take her up. Rose Tramore had decided to do what she could to bring this consummation about; and strangely enough—so mixed were her superstitions and her heresies—a large part of her motive lay in the value she attached to such a consecration.

Of her mother intrinsically she thought very little now, and if her eyes were fixed on a special achievement it was much more for the sake of that achievement and to satisfy a latent energy that was in her than because her heart was wrung by this sufferer. Her heart had not been wrung at all, though she had quite held it out for the experience. Her purpose was a pious game, but it was still essentially a game. Among the ideas I have mentioned she had her idea of triumph. She had caught the inevitable note, the pitch, on her very first visit to Chester Square. She had arrived there in intense excitement, and her excitement was left on her hands in a manner that reminded her of a difficult air she had once heard sung at the opera when no one applauded the performer. That flatness had made her sick, and so did this, in another way. A part of her agitation proceeded from the fact that her aunt Julia had told her, in the manner of a burst of confidence, something she was not to repeat, that she was in appearance the very image of the lady in Chester Square. The motive that prompted this declaration was between aunt Julia and her conscience; but it was a great emotion to the girl to find her entertainer so beautiful. She was tall and exquisitely slim; she had hair more exactly to Rose Tramore's taste than any other she had ever seen, even to every detail in the way it was dressed, and a complexion and a figure of the kind that are always spoken of as "lovely." Her eyes were irresistible, and so were her clothes, though the clothes were perhaps a little more precisely the right thing than the eyes. Her appearance was marked to her daughter's sense by the highest distinction; though it may be mentioned that this had never been the opinion of all the world. It was a revelation to Rose that she herself might look a little like that. She knew however that aunt Julia had not seen her deposed sister-in-law for a long time, and she had a general impression that Mrs. Tramore was to-day a more complete production—for instance as regarded her air of youth—than she had ever been. There was no excitement on her side—that was all her visitor's; there was no emotion—that was excluded by the plan, to say nothing of conditions more primal. Rose had from the first a glimpse of her mother's plan. It was to mention nothing and imply nothing, neither to acknowledge, to explain nor to extenuate. She would leave everything to her child; with her child she was secure. She only wanted to get back into society; she would leave even that to her child, whom she treated not as a high-strung and heroic daughter, a creature of exaltation, of devotion, but as a new, charming, clever, useful friend, a little younger than herself. Already on that first day she had talked about dressmakers. Of course, poor thing, it was to be remembered that in her circumstances there were not many things she *could* talk about. "She wants to go out again; that's the only thing in the wide world she wants," Rose had promptly, compendiously said to herself. There had been a sequel to this observation, uttered, in intense engrossment, in her own room half an hour before she had, on the important evening, made known her decision to her grandmother: "Then I'll *take* her out!"

"She'll drag you down, she'll drag you down!" Julia Tramore permitted herself to remark to her niece, the next day, in a tone of feverish prophecy.

As the girl's own theory was that all the dragging there might be would be upward, and moreover administered by herself, she could look at her aunt with a cold and inscrutable eye.

"Very well, then, I shall be out of your sight, from the pinnacle you occupy, and I sha'n't trouble you."

"Do you reproach me for my disinterested exertions, for the way I've toiled over you, the way I've lived for you?" Miss Tramore demanded.

"Don't reproach *me* for being kind to my mother and I won't reproach you for anything."

"She'll keep you out of everything—she'll make you miss everything," Miss Tramore continued.

"Then she'll make me miss a great deal that's odious," said the girl.

"You're too young for such extravagances," her aunt declared.

"And yet Edith, who is younger than I, seems to be too old for them: how do you arrange that? My mother's society will make me older," Rose replied.

"Don't speak to me of your mother; you *have* no mother."

"Then if I'm an orphan I must settle things for myself."

"Do you justify her, do you approve of her?" cried Miss Tramore, who was inferior to her niece in capacity for retort and whose limitations made the girl appear pert.

Rose looked at her a moment in silence; then she said, turning away: "I think she's charming."

"And do you propose to become charming in the same manner?"

"Her manner is perfect; it would be an excellent model. But I can't discuss my mother with you."

"You'll have to discuss her with some other people!" Miss Tramore proclaimed, going out of the room.

Rose wondered whether this were a general or a particular vaticination. There was something her aunt might have meant by it, but her aunt rarely meant the best thing she might have meant. Miss Tramore had come up from St. Leonard's in response to a telegram from her own parent, for an occasion like the present brought with it, for a few hours, a certain relaxation of their dissent. "Do what you can to stop her," the old lady had said; but her daughter found that the most she could do was not much. They both had a baffled sense that Rose had thought the question out a good deal further than they; and this was particularly irritating to Mrs. Tramore, as consciously the cleverer of the two. A question thought out as far as *she* could think it had always appeared to her to have performed its human uses; she had never encountered a ghost emerging from that extinction. Their great contention was that Rose would cut herself off; and certainly if she wasn't afraid of that she wasn't afraid of anything. Julia Tramore could only tell her mother how little the girl was afraid. She was already prepared to leave the house, taking with her the possessions, or her share of them, that had accumulated there during her father's illness. There had been a going and coming of her maid, a thumping about of boxes, an ordering of four-wheelers; it appeared to old Mrs. Tramore that something of the objectionableness, the indecency, of her granddaughter's prospective connection had already gathered about the place. It was a violation of the decorum of bereavement which was still fresh there, and from the indignant gloom of the mistress of the house you might have inferred not so much that the daughter was about to depart as that the mother was about to arrive. There had been no conversation on the dreadful subject at luncheon; for at luncheon at Mrs. Tramore's (her son never came to it) there were always, even after funerals and other miseries, stray guests of both sexes whose policy it was to be cheerful and superficial. Rose had sat down as if nothing had happened—nothing worse, that is, than her father's death; but no one had spoken of anything that any one else was thinking of.

Before she left the house a servant brought her a message from her grandmother—the old lady desired to see her in the drawing-room. She had on her bonnet, and she went down as if she were about to step into her cab. Mrs. Tramore sat there with her eternal knitting, from which she forebore even to raise her eyes as, after a silence that seemed to express the fulness of her reprobation, while Rose stood motionless, she began: "I wonder if you really understand what you're doing."

"I think so. I'm not so stupid."

"I never thought you were; but I don't know what to make of you now. You're giving up everything."

The girl was tempted to inquire whether her grandmother called herself "everything"; but she checked this question, answering instead that she knew she was giving up much.

"You're taking a step of which you will feel the effect to the end of your days," Mrs. Tramore went on.

"In a good conscience, I heartily hope," said Rose.

"Your father's conscience was good enough for his mother; it ought to be good enough for his daughter."

Rose sat down—she could afford to—as if she wished to be very attentive and were still accessible to argument. But this demonstration only ushered in, after a moment, the surprising words "I don't think papa had any conscience."

"What in the name of all that's unnatural do you mean?" Mrs. Tramore cried, over her glasses. "The dearest and best creature that ever lived!"

"He was kind, he had charming impulses, he was delightful. But he never reflected."

Mrs. Tramore stared, as if at a language she had never heard, a farrago, a *galimatias*. Her life was made up of items, but she had never had to deal, intellectually, with a fine shade. Then while her needles, which had paused an instant, began to fly again, she rejoined: "Do you know what you are, my dear? You're a dreadful little prig. Where do you pick up such talk?"

"Of course I don't mean to judge between them," Rose pursued. "I can only judge between my mother and myself. Papa couldn't judge for me." And with this she got up.

"One would think you were horrid. I never thought so before."

"Thank you for that."

"You're embarking on a struggle with society," continued Mrs. Tramore, indulging in an unusual flight of oratory. "Society will put you in your place."

"Hasn't it too many other things to do?" asked the girl.

This question had an ingenuity which led her grandmother to meet it with a merely provisional and somewhat sketchy answer. "Your ignorance would be melancholy if your behaviour were not so insane."

"Oh, no; I know perfectly what she'll do!" Rose replied, almost gaily. "She'll drag me down."

"She won't even do that," the old lady declared contradictiously. "She'll keep you forever in the same dull hole."

"I shall come and see *you*, granny, when I want something more lively."

"You may come if you like, but you'll come no further than the door. If you leave this house now you don't enter it again."

Rose hesitated a moment. "Do you really mean that?"

"You may judge whether I choose such a time to joke."

"Good-bye, then," said the girl.

"Good-bye."

Rose quitted the room successfully enough; but on the other side of the door, on the landing, she sank into a chair and buried her face in her hands. She had burst into tears, and she sobbed there for a moment, trying hard to recover herself, so as to go downstairs without showing any traces of emotion, passing before the servants and again perhaps before aunt Julia. Mrs. Tramore was too old to cry; she could only drop her knitting and, for a long time, sit with her head bowed and her eyes closed.

Rose had reckoned justly with her aunt Julia; there were no footmen, but this vigilant virgin was posted at the foot of the stairs. She offered no challenge however; she only said: "There's some one in the parlour who wants to see you." The girl demanded a name, but Miss Tramore only mouthed inaudibly and winked and waved. Rose instantly reflected that there was only one man in the world her aunt would look such deep things about. "Captain Jay?" her own eyes asked, while Miss Tramore's were those of a conspirator: they were, for a moment, the only embarrassed eyes Rose had encountered that day. They contributed to make aunt Julia's further response evasive, after her niece inquired if she had communicated in advance with this visitor. Miss Tramore merely said that he had been upstairs with her mother—hadn't she mentioned it?—and had been waiting for her. She thought herself acute in not putting the question of the girl's seeing him before her as a favour to him or to herself; she presented it as a duty, and wound up with the proposition: "It's not fair to him, it's not kind, not to let him speak to you before you go."

"What does he want to say?" Rose demanded.

"Go in and find out."

She really knew, for she had found out before; but after standing uncertain an instant she went in. "The parlour" was the name that had always been borne by a spacious sitting-room downstairs, an apartment occupied by her father during his frequent phases of residence in Hill Street—episodes increasingly frequent after his house in the country had, in consequence, as Rose perfectly knew, of his spending too much money, been disposed of at a sacrifice which he always char-

acterised as horrid. He had been left with the place in Hertfordshire and his mother with the London house, on the
general understanding that they would change about; but
during the last years the community had grown more rigid,
mainly at his mother's expense. The parlour was full of his
memory and his habits and his things—his books and pictures
and *bibelots*, objects that belonged now to Eric. Rose had sat
in it for hours since his death; it was the place in which she
could still be nearest to him. But she felt far from him as
Captain Jay rose erect on her opening the door. This was a
very different presence. He had not liked Captain Jay. She
herself had, but not enough to make a great complication of
her father's coldness. This afternoon however she foresaw
complications. At the very outset for instance she was not
pleased with his having arranged such a surprise for her with
her grandmother and her aunt. It was probably aunt Julia who
had sent for him; her grandmother wouldn't have done it. It
placed him immediately on their side, and Rose was almost as
disappointed at this as if she had not known it was quite where
he would naturally be. He had never paid her a special visit,
but if that was what he wished to do why shouldn't he have
waited till she should be under her mother's roof? She knew
the reason, but she had an angry prospect of enjoyment in
making him express it. She liked him enough, after all, if it
were measured by the idea of what she could make him do.

In Bertram Jay the elements were surprisingly mingled; you
would have gone astray, in reading him, if you had counted
on finding the complements of some of his qualities. He
would not however have struck you in the least as incomplete,
for in every case in which you didn't find the complement you
would have found the contradiction. He was in the Royal Engineers, and was tall, lean and high-shouldered. He looked
every inch a soldier, yet there were people who considered
that he had missed his vocation in not becoming a parson. He
took a public interest in the spiritual life of the army. Other
persons still, on closer observation, would have felt that his
most appropriate field was neither the army nor the church,
but simply the world—the social, successful, worldly world. If
he had a sword in one hand and a Bible in the other he had
a Court Guide concealed somewhere about his person. His

profile was hard and handsome, his eyes were both cold and kind, his dark straight hair was imperturbably smooth and prematurely streaked with grey. There was nothing in existence that he didn't take seriously. He had a first-rate power of work and an ambition as minutely organised as a German plan of invasion. His only real recreation was to go to church, but he went to parties when he had time. If he was in love with Rose Tramore this was distracting to him only in the same sense as his religion, and it was included in that department of his extremely sub-divided life. His religion indeed was of an encroaching, annexing sort. Seen from in front he looked diffident and blank, but he was capable of exposing himself in a way (to speak only of the paths of peace) wholly inconsistent with shyness. He had a passion for instance for open-air speaking, but was not thought on the whole to excel in it unless he could help himself out with a hymn. In conversation he kept his eyes on you with a kind of colourless candour, as if he had not understood what you were saying and, in a fashion that made many people turn red, waited before answering. This was only because he was considering their remarks in more relations than they had intended. He had in his face no expression whatever save the one just mentioned, and was, in his profession, already very distinguished.

He had seen Rose Tramore for the first time on a Sunday of the previous March, at a house in the country at which she was staying with her father, and five weeks later he had made her, by letter, an offer of marriage. She showed her father the letter of course, and he told her that it would give him great pleasure that she should send Captain Jay about his business. "My dear child," he said, "we must really have some one who will be better fun than that." Rose had declined the honour, very considerately and kindly, but not simply because her father wished it. She didn't herself wish to detach this flower from the stem, though when the young man wrote again, to express the hope that he *might* hope—so long was he willing to wait—and ask if he might not still sometimes see her, she answered even more indulgently than at first. She had shown her father her former letter, but she didn't show him this one; she only told him what it contained, submitting to him also that of her correspondent. Captain Jay moreover wrote to Mr.

Tramore, who replied sociably, but so vaguely that he almost neglected the subject under discussion—a communication that made poor Bertram ponder long. He could never get to the bottom of the superficial, and all the proprieties and conventions of life were profound to him. Fortunately for him old Mrs. Tramore liked him, he was satisfactory to her long-sightedness; so that a relation was established under cover of which he still occasionally presented himself in Hill Street—presented himself nominally to the mistress of the house. He had had scruples about the veracity of his visits, but he had disposed of them; he had scruples about so many things that he had had to invent a general way, to dig a central drain. Julia Tramore happened to meet him when she came up to town, and she took a view of him more benevolent than her usual estimate of people encouraged by her mother. The fear of agreeing with that lady was a motive, but there was a stronger one, in this particular case, in the fear of agreeing with her niece, who had rejected him. His situation might be held to have improved when Mr. Tramore was taken so gravely ill that with regard to his recovery those about him left their eyes to speak for their lips; and in the light of the poor gentleman's recent death it was doubtless better than it had ever been.

He was only a quarter of an hour with the girl, but this gave him time to take the measure of it. After he had spoken to her about her bereavement, very much as an especially mild missionary might have spoken to a beautiful Polynesian, he let her know that he had learned from her companions the very strong step she was about to take. This led to their spending together ten minutes which, to her mind, threw more light on his character than anything that had ever passed between them. She had always felt with him as if she were standing on an edge, looking down into something decidedly deep. To-day the impression of the perpendicular shaft was there, but it was rather an abyss of confusion and disorder than the large bright space in which she had figured everything as ranged and pigeon-holed, presenting the appearance of the labelled shelves and drawers at a chemist's. He discussed without an invitation to discuss, he appealed without a right to appeal. He was nothing but a suitor tolerated after dismissal, but he took strangely for granted a participation in her affairs. He assumed all sorts of things that made her draw back. He implied that there was everything now to assist them in arriving at an agreement, since she had never informed him that he was positively objectionable; but that this symmetry would be spoiled if she should not be willing to take a little longer to think of certain consequences. She was greatly disconcerted when she saw what consequences he meant and at his reminding her of them. What on earth was the use of a lover if he was to speak only like one's grandmother and one's aunt? He struck her as much in love with her and as particularly careful at the same time as to what he might say. He never mentioned her mother; he only alluded, indirectly but earnestly, to the "step." He disapproved of it altogether, took an unexpectedly prudent, politic view of it. He evidently also believed that she would be dragged down; in other words that she would not be asked out. It was his idea that her mother would contaminate her, so that he should find himself interested in a young person discredited and virtually unmarriageable. All this was more obvious to him than the consideration that a daughter should be merciful. Where was his religion if he understood mercy so little, and where were his talent and his courage if he were so miserably afraid of trumpery social penalties? Rose's heart sank when she reflected that a man supposed to be first-rate hadn't guessed that rather than not do what she could for her mother she would give up all the Engineers in the world. She became aware that she probably would have been moved to place her hand in his on the spot if he had come to her saying "Your idea is the right one; put it through at every cost." She couldn't discuss this with him, though he impressed her as having too much at stake for her to treat him with mere disdain. She sickened at the revelation that a gentleman could see so much in mere vulgarities of opinion, and though she uttered as few words as possible, conversing only in sad smiles and headshakes and in intercepted movements toward the door, she happened, in some unguarded lapse from her reticence, to use the expression that she was disappointed in him. He caught at it and, seeming to drop his field-glass, pressed upon her with nearer, tenderer eyes.

"Can I be so happy as to believe, then, that you had thought of me with some confidence, with some faith?"

"If you didn't suppose so, what is the sense of this visit?" Rose asked.

"One can be faithful without reciprocity," said the young man. "I regard you in a light which makes me want to protect you even if I have nothing to gain by it."

"Yet you speak as if you thought you might keep me for yourself."

"For *yourself.* I don't want you to suffer."

"Nor to suffer yourself by my doing so," said Rose, looking down.

"Ah, if you would only marry me next month!" he broke out inconsequently.

"And give up going to mamma?" Rose waited to see if he would say "What need that matter? Can't your mother come to us?" But he said nothing of the sort; he only answered—

"She surely would be sorry to interfere with the exercise of any other affection which I might have the bliss of believing that you are now free, in however small a degree, to entertain."

Rose knew that her mother wouldn't be sorry at all; but she contented herself with rejoining, her hand on the door: "Good-bye. I sha'n't suffer. I'm not afraid."

"You don't know how terrible, how cruel, the world can be."

"Yes, I do know. I know everything!"

The declaration sprang from her lips in a tone which made him look at her as he had never looked before, as if he saw something new in her face, as if he had never yet known her. He hadn't displeased her so much but that she would like to give him that impression, and since she felt that she was doing so she lingered an instant for the purpose. It enabled her to see, further, that he turned red; then to become aware that a carriage had stopped at the door. Captain Jay's eyes, from where he stood, fell upon this arrival, and the nature of their glance made Rose step forward to look. Her mother sat there, brilliant, conspicuous, in the eternal victoria, and the footman was already sounding the knocker. It had been no part of the arrangement that she should come to fetch her; it had been out of the question—a stroke in such bad taste as would have put Rose in the wrong. The girl had never dreamed of it, but somehow, suddenly, perversely, she was glad of it now; she even hoped that her grandmother and her aunt were looking out upstairs.

"My mother has come for me. Good-bye," she repeated; but this time her visitor had got between her and the door.

"Listen to me before you go. I will give you a life's devotion," the young man pleaded. He really barred the way.

She wondered whether her grandmother had told him that if her flight were not prevented she would forfeit money. Then, vividly, it came over her that this would be what he was occupied with. "I shall never think of you—let me go!" she cried, with passion.

Captain Jay opened the door, but Rose didn't see his face, and in a moment she was out of the house. Aunt Julia, who was sure to have been hovering, had taken flight before the profanity of the knock.

"Heavens, dear, where did you get your mourning?" the lady in the victoria asked of her daughter as they drove away.

II.

Lady Maresfield had given her boy a push in his plump back and had said to him, "Go and speak to her now; it's your chance." She had for a long time wanted this scion to make himself audible to Rose Tramore, but the opportunity was not easy to come by. The case was complicated. Lady Maresfield had four daughters, of whom only one was married. It so happened moreover that this one, Mrs. Vaughan-Vesey, the only person in the world her mother was afraid of, was the most to be reckoned with. The Honourable Guy was in appearance all his mother's child, though he was really a simpler soul. He was large and pink; large, that is, as to everything but the eyes, which were diminishing points, and pink as to everything but the hair, which was comparable, faintly, to the hue of the richer rose. He had also, it must be conceded, very small neat teeth, which made his smile look like a young lady's. He had no wish to resemble any such person, but he was perpetually smiling, and he smiled more than ever as he approached Rose Tramore, who, looking altogether, to his mind, as a pretty girl should, and wearing a soft white opera-cloak over a softer black dress, leaned alone against the wall of the vestibule at Covent Garden while, a few paces off, an old gentleman engaged her mother in conversation. Madame Patti had been singing, and they were all waiting for their carriages. To their ears at present came a vociferation of names and a rattle of wheels. The air, through banging doors, entered in damp, warm gusts, heavy with the stale, slightly sweet taste of the London season when the London season is overripe and spoiling.

Guy Mangler had only three minutes to reëstablish an interrupted acquaintance with our young lady. He reminded her that he had danced with her the year before, and he mentioned that he knew her brother. His mother had lately been to see old Mrs. Tramore, but this he did not mention, not being aware of it. That visit had produced, on Lady Maresfield's part, a private crisis, engendered ideas. One of them was that the grandmother in Hill Street had really forgiven the wilful girl much more than she admitted. Another was that there would still be some money for Rose when the others should come into theirs. Still another was that the others would come into theirs at no distant date; the old lady was so visibly going to pieces. There were several more besides, as for instance that Rose had already fifteen hundred a year from her father. The figure had been betrayed in Hill Street; it was part of the proof of Mrs. Tramore's decrepitude. Then there was an equal amount that her mother had to dispose of and on which the girl could absolutely count, though of course it might involve much waiting, as the mother, a person of gross insensibility, evidently wouldn't die of cold-shouldering. Equally definite, to do it justice, was the conception that Rose was in truth remarkably good looking, and that what she had undertaken to do showed, and would show even should it fail, cleverness of the right sort. Cleverness of the right sort was exactly the quality that Lady Maresfield prefigured as indispensable in a young lady to whom she should marry her second son, over whose own deficiencies she flung the veil of a maternal theory that *his* cleverness was of a sort that was wrong. Those who knew him less well were content to wish that he might not conceal it for such a scruple. This enumeration of his mother's views does not exhaust the list, and it was in obedience to one too profound to be uttered even by the historian that, after a very brief delay, she decided to move across the crowded lobby. Her daughter Bessie was the only one with her; Maggie was dining with the Vaughan-Veseys, and Fanny was not of an age. Mrs. Tramore the younger showed only an admirable back—her face was to her old gentleman—and Bessie had drifted to some other people; so that it was comparatively easy for Lady Maresfield to say to Rose, in a moment: "My dear child, are you never coming to see us?"

"We shall be delighted to come if you'll ask us," Rose smiled.

Lady Maresfield had been prepared for the plural number, and she was a woman whom it took many plurals to disconcert. "I'm sure Guy is longing for another dance with you," she rejoined, with the most unblinking irrelevance.

"I'm afraid we're not dancing again quite yet," said Rose, glancing at her mother's exposed shoulders, but speaking as if they were muffled in crape.

Lady Maresfield leaned her head on one side and seemed almost wistful. "Not even at my sister's ball? She's to have something next week. She'll write to you."

Rose Tramore, on the spot, looking bright but vague, turned three or four things over in her mind. She remembered that the sister of her interlocutress was the proverbially rich Mrs. Bray, a bankeress or a breweress or a builderess, who had so big a house that she couldn't fill it unless she opened her doors, or her mouth, very wide. Rose had learnt more about London society during these lonely months with her mother than she had ever picked up in Hill Street. The younger Mrs. Tramore was a mine of *commérages*, and she had no need to go out to bring home the latest intelligence. At any rate Mrs. Bray might serve as the end of a wedge. "Oh, I dare say we might think of that," Rose said. "It would be very kind of your sister."

"Guy'll think of it, won't you, Guy?" asked Lady Maresfield.

"Rather!" Guy responded, with an intonation as fine as if

he had learnt it at a music hall; while at the same moment the name of his mother's carriage was bawled through the place. Mrs. Tramore had parted with her old gentleman; she turned again to her daughter. Nothing occurred but what always occurred, which was exactly this absence of everything—a universal lapse. She didn't exist, even for a second, to any recognising eye. The people who looked at her—of course there were plenty of those—were only the people who didn't exist for hers. Lady Maresfield surged away on her son's arm.

It was this noble matron herself who wrote, the next day, inclosing a card of invitation from Mrs. Bray and expressing the hope that Rose would come and dine and let her ladyship take her. She should have only one of her own girls; Gwendolen Vesey was to take the other. Rose handed both the note and the card in silence to her mother; the latter exhibited only the name of Miss Tramore. "You had much better go, dear," her mother said; in answer to which Miss Tramore slowly tore up the documents, looking with clear, meditative eyes out of the window. Her mother always said "You had better go"—there had been other incidents—and Rose had never even once taken account of the observation. She would make no first advances, only plenty of second ones, and, condoning no discrimination, would treat no omission as venial. She would keep all concessions till afterwards; then she would make them one by one. Fighting society was quite as hard as her grandmother had said it would be; but there was a tension in it which made the dreariness vibrate—the dreariness of such a winter as she had just passed. Her companion had cried at the end of it, and she had cried all through; only her tears had been private, while her mother's had fallen once for all, at luncheon on the bleak Easter Monday—produced by the way a silent survey of the deadly square brought home to her that every creature but themselves was out of town and having tremendous fun. Rose felt that it was useless to attempt to explain simply by her mourning this severity of solitude; for if people didn't go to parties (at least a few didn't) for six months after their father died, this was the very time other people took for coming to see them. It was not too much to say that during this first winter of Rose's period with her mother she had no communication whatever with the world.

It had the effect of making her take to reading the new American books: she wanted to see how girls got on by themselves. She had never read so much before, and there was a legitimate indifference in it when topics failed with her mother. They often failed after the first days, and then, while she bent over instructive volumes, this lady, dressed as if for an impending function, sat on the sofa and watched her. Rose was not embarrassed by such an appearance, for she could reflect that, a little before, her companion had not even a girl who had taken refuge in queer researches to look at. She was moreover used to her mother's attitude by this time. She had her own description of it: it was the attitude of waiting for the carriage. If they didn't go out it was not that Mrs. Tramore was not ready in time, and Rose had even an alarmed prevision of their some day always arriving first. Mrs. Tramore's conversation at such moments was abrupt, inconsequent and personal. She sat on the edge of sofas and chairs and glanced occasionally at the fit of her gloves (she was perpetually gloved, and the fit was a thing it was melancholy to see wasted), as people do who are expecting guests to dinner. Rose used almost to fancy herself at times a perfunctory husband on the other side of the fire.

What she was not yet used to—there was still a charm in it—was her mother's extraordinary tact. During the years they lived together they never had a discussion; a circumstance all the more remarkable since if the girl had a reason for sparing her companion (that of being sorry for her) Mrs. Tramore had none for sparing her child. She only showed in doing so a happy instinct—the happiest thing about her. She took in perfection a course which represented everything and covered everything; she utterly abjured all authority. She testified to her abjuration in hourly ingenious, touching ways. In this manner nothing had to be talked over, which was a mercy all round. The tears on Easter Monday were merely a nervous gust, to help show she was not a Christmas doll from the Burlington Arcade; and there was no lifting up of the repentant Magdalen, no uttered remorse for the former abandonment of children. Of the way she could treat her children her demeanour to this one was an example; it was an uninterrupted appeal to her eldest daughter for direction. She took

the law from Rose in every circumstance, and if you had noticed these ladies without knowing their history you would
have wondered what tie was fine enough to make maturity so
respectful to youth. No mother was ever so filial as Mrs. Tramore, and there had never been such a difference of position
between sisters. Not that the elder one fawned, which would
have been fearful; she only renounced—whatever she had to
renounce. If the amount was not much she at any rate made
no scene over it. Her hand was so light that Rose said of her
secretly, in vague glances at the past, "No wonder people liked
her!" She never characterised the old element of interference
with her mother's respectability more definitely than as "people." They were people, it was true, for whom gentleness
must have been everything and who didn't demand a variety
of interests. The desire to "go out" was the one passion that
even a closer acquaintance with her parent revealed to Rose
Tramore. She marvelled at its strength, in the light of the poor
lady's history: there was comedy enough in this unquenchable
flame on the part of a woman who had known such misery.
She had drunk deep of every dishonour, but the bitter cup
had left her with a taste for lighted candles, for squeezing up
staircases and hooking herself to the human elbow. Rose had
a vision of the future years in which this taste would grow
with restored exercise—of her mother, in a long-tailed dress,
jogging on and on and on, jogging further and further from
her sins, through a century of the "Morning Post" and down
the fashionable avenue of time. She herself would then be very
old—she herself would be dead. Mrs. Tramore would cover a
span of life for which such an allowance of sin was small. The
girl could laugh indeed now at that theory of her being
dragged down. If one thing were more present to her than
another it was the very desolation of their propriety. As she
glanced at her companion, it sometimes seemed to her that if
she had been a bad woman she would have been worse than
that. There were compensations for being "cut" which Mrs.
Tramore too much neglected.

The lonely old lady in Hill Street—Rose thought of her that
way now—was the one person to whom she was ready to say
that she would come to her on any terms. She wrote this to
her three times over, and she knocked still oftener at her door.

But the old lady answered no letters; if Rose had remained in
Hill Street it would have been her own function to answer
them; and at the door, the butler, whom the girl had known
for ten years, considered her, when he told her his mistress
was not at home, quite as he might have considered a young
person who had come about a place and of whose eligibility
he took a negative view. That was Rose's one pang, that she
probably appeared rather heartless. Her aunt Julia had gone
to Florence with Edith for the winter, on purpose to make
her appear more so; for Miss Tramore was still the person
most scandalised by her secession. Edith and she, doubtless,
often talked over in Florence the destitution of the aged victim in Hill Street. Eric never came to see his sister, because,
being full both of family and of personal feeling, he thought
she really ought to have stayed with his grandmother. If she
had had such an appurtenance all to herself she might have
done what she liked with it; but he couldn't forgive such a
want of consideration for anything of his. There were moments when Rose would have been ready to take her hand
from the plough and insist upon reintegration, if only the
fierce voice of the old house had allowed people to look her
up. But she read, ever so clearly, that her grandmother had
made this a question of loyalty to seventy years of virtue. Mrs.
Tramore's forlornness didn't prevent her drawing-room from
being a very public place, in which Rose could hear certain
words reverberate: "Leave her alone; it's the only way to see
how long she'll hold out." The old woman's visitors were
people who didn't wish to quarrel, and the girl was conscious
that if they had not let her alone—that is if they had come to
her from her grandmother—she might perhaps not have held
out. She had no friends quite of her own; she had not been
brought up to have them, and it would not have been easy in
a house which two such persons as her father and his mother
divided between them. Her father disapproved of crude intimacies, and all the intimacies of youth were crude. He had
married at five-and-twenty and could testify to such a truth.
Rose felt that she shared even Captain Jay with her grandmother; she had seen what *he* was worth. Moreover, she had
spoken to him at that last moment in Hill Street in a way
which, taken with her former refusal, made it impossible that

he should come near her again. She hoped he went to see his protectress: he could be a kind of substitute and administer comfort.

It so happened, however, that the day after she threw Lady Maresfield's invitation into the wastepaper basket she received a visit from a certain Mrs. Donovan, whom she had occasionally seen in Hill Street. She vaguely knew this lady for a busybody, but she was in a situation which even busybodies might alleviate. Mrs. Donovan was poor, but honest—so scrupulously honest that she was perpetually returning visits she had never received. She was always clad in weather-beaten sealskin, and had an odd air of being prepared for the worst, which was borne out by her denying that she was Irish. She was of the English Donovans.

"Dear child, won't you go out with me?" she asked.

Rose looked at her a moment and then rang the bell. She spoke of something else, without answering the question, and when the servant came she said: "Please tell Mrs. Tramore that Mrs. Donovan has come to see her."

"Oh, that'll be delightful; only you mustn't tell your grandmother!" the visitor exclaimed.

"Tell her what?"

"That I come to see your mamma."

"You don't," said Rose.

"Sure I hoped you'd introduce me!" cried Mrs. Donovan, compromising herself in her embarrassment.

"It's not necessary; you knew her once."

"Indeed and I've known every one once," the visitor confessed.

Mrs. Tramore, when she came in, was charming and exactly right; she greeted Mrs. Donovan as if she had met her the week before last, giving her daughter such a new illustration of her tact that Rose again had the idea that it was no wonder "people" had liked her. The girl grudged Mrs. Donovan so fresh a morsel as a description of her mother at home, rejoicing that she would be inconvenienced by having to keep the story out of Hill Street. Her mother went away before Mrs. Donovan departed, and Rose was touched by guessing her reason—the thought that since even this circuitous personage had been moved to come, the two might, if left together, invent some remedy. Rose waited to see what Mrs. Donovan had in fact invented.

"You won't come out with me then?"

"Come out with you?"

"My daughters are married. You know I'm a lone woman. It would be an immense pleasure to me to have so charming a creature as yourself to present to the world."

"I go out with my mother," said Rose, after a moment.

"Yes, but sometimes when she's not inclined?"

"She goes everywhere she wants to go," Rose continued, uttering the biggest fib of her life and only regretting it should be wasted on Mrs. Donovan.

"Ah, but do you go everywhere *you* want?" the lady asked sociably.

"One goes even to places one hates. Every one does that."

"Oh, what *I* go through!" this social martyr cried. Then she laid a persuasive hand on the girl's arm. "Let me show you at a few places first, and then we'll see. I'll bring them all here."

"I don't think I understand you," replied Rose, though in Mrs. Donovan's words she perfectly saw her own theory of the case reflected. For a quarter of a minute she asked herself whether she might not, after all, do so much evil that good might come. Mrs. Donovan would take her out the next day, and be thankful enough to annex such an attraction as a pretty girl. Various consequences would ensue and the long delay would be shortened; her mother's drawing-room would re-sound with the clatter of teacups.

"Mrs. Bray's having some big thing next week; come with me there and I'll show you what I mane," Mrs. Donovan pleaded.

"I see what you mane," Rose answered, brushing away her temptation and getting up. "I'm much obliged to you."

"You know you're wrong, my dear," said her interlocutress, with angry little eyes.

"I'm not going to Mrs. Bray's."

"I'll get you a kyard; it'll only cost me a penny stamp."

"I've got one," said the girl, smiling.

"Do you mean a penny stamp?" Mrs. Donovan, especially

at departure, always observed all the forms of amity. "You can't do it alone, my darling," she declared.

"Shall they call you a cab?" Rose asked.

"I'll pick one up. I choose my horse. You know you require your start," her visitor went on.

"Excuse my mother," was Rose's only reply.

"Don't mention it. Come to me when you need me. You'll find me in the Red Book."

"It's awfully kind of you."

Mrs. Donovan lingered a moment on the threshold. "Who will you *have* now, my child?" she appealed.

"I won't have any one!" Rose turned away, blushing for her. "She came on speculation," she said afterwards to Mrs. Tramore.

Her mother looked at her a moment in silence. "You can do it if you like, you know."

Rose made no direct answer to this observation; she remarked instead: "See what our quiet life allows us to escape."

"We don't escape it. She has been here an hour."

"Once in twenty years! We might meet her three times a day."

"Oh, I'd take her with the rest!" sighed Mrs. Tramore; while her daughter recognised that what her companion wanted to do was just what Mrs. Donovan was doing. Mrs. Donovan's life was her ideal.

On a Sunday, ten days later, Rose went to see one of her old governesses, of whom she had lost sight for some time and who had written to her that she was in London, unoccupied and ill. This was just the sort of relation into which she could throw herself now with inordinate zeal; the idea of it, however, not preventing a foretaste of the queer expression in the excellent lady's face when she should mention with whom she was living. While she smiled at this picture she threw in another joke, asking herself if Miss Hack could be held in any degree to constitute the nucleus of a circle. She would come to see her, in any event—come the more the further she was dragged down. Sunday was always a difficult day with the two ladies—the afternoons made it so apparent that they were not frequented. Her mother, it is true, was comprised in the habits of two or three old gentlemen—she had for a long time avoided male friends of less than seventy—who disliked each other enough to make the room, when they were there at once, crack with pressure. Rose sat for a long time with Miss Hack, doing conscientious justice to the conception that there could be troubles in the world worse than her own; and when she came back her mother was alone, but with a story to tell of a long visit from Mr. Guy Mangler, who had waited and waited for her return. "He's in love with you; he's coming again on Tuesday," Mrs. Tramore announced.

"Did he say so?"

"That he's coming back on Tuesday?"

"No, that he's in love with me."

"He didn't need, when he stayed two hours."

"With you? It's you he's in love with, mamma!"

"That will do as well," laughed Mrs. Tramore. "For all the use we shall make of him!" she added in a moment.

"We shall make great use of him. His mother sent him."

"Oh, she'll never come!"

"Then *he* sha'n't," said Rose. Yet he was admitted on the Tuesday, and after she had given him his tea Mrs. Tramore left the young people alone. Rose wished she hadn't—she herself had another view. At any rate she disliked her mother's view, which she had easily guessed. Mr. Mangler did nothing but say how charming he thought his hostess of the Sunday, and what a tremendously jolly visit he had had. He didn't remark in so many words "I had no idea your mother was such a good sort"; but this was the spirit of his simple discourse. Rose liked it at first—a little of it gratified her; then she thought there was too much of it for good taste. She had to reflect that one does what one can and that Mr. Mangler probably thought he was delicate. He wished to convey that he desired to make up to her for the injustice of society. Why shouldn't her mother receive gracefully, she asked (not audibly) and who had ever said she didn't? Mr. Mangler had a great deal to say about the disappointment of his own parent over Miss Tramore's not having come to dine with them the night of his aunt's ball.

"Lady Maresfield knows why I didn't come," Rose answered at last.

"Ah, now, but *I* don't, you know; can't you tell *me*?" asked the young man.

"It doesn't matter, if your mother's clear about it."

"Oh, but why make such an awful mystery of it, when I'm dying to know?"

He talked about this, he chaffed her about it for the rest of his visit: he had at last found a topic after his own heart. If her mother considered that he might be the emblem of their redemption he was an engine of the most primitive construction. He stayed and stayed; he struck Rose as on the point of bringing out something for which he had not quite, as he would have said, the cheek. Sometimes she thought he was going to begin: "By the way, my mother told me to propose to you." At other moments he seemed charged with the admission: "I say, of course I really know what you're trying to do for her," nodding at the door: "therefore hadn't we better speak of it frankly, so that I can help you with my mother, and more particularly with my sister Gwendolen, who's the difficult one? The fact is, you see, they won't do anything for nothing. If you'll accept me they'll call, but they won't call without something 'down.'" Mr. Mangler departed without their speaking frankly, and Rose Tramore had a hot hour during which she almost entertained, vindictively, the project of "accepting" the limpid youth until after she should have got her mother into circulation. The cream of the vision was that she might break with him later. She could read that this was what her mother would have liked, but the next time he came the door was closed to him, and the next and the next.

In August there was nothing to do but to go abroad, with the sense on Rose's part that the battle was still all to fight; for a round of country visits was not in prospect, and English watering-places constituted one of the few subjects on which the girl had heard her mother express herself with disgust. Continental autumns had been indeed for years, one of the various forms of Mrs. Tramore's atonement, but Rose could only infer that such fruit as they had borne was bitter. The stony stare of Belgravia could be practised at Homburg; and somehow it was inveterately only gentlemen who sat next to

her at the *table d'hôte* at Cadenabbia. Gentlemen had never
been of any use to Mrs. Tramore for getting back into society;
they had only helped her effectually to get out of it. She once
dropped, to her daughter, in a moralising mood, the remark
that it was astonishing how many of them one could know
without its doing one any good. Fifty of them—even very
clever ones—represented a value inferior to that of one stupid
woman. Rose wondered at the offhand way in which her
mother could talk of fifty clever men; it seemed to her that
the whole world couldn't contain such a number. She had a
sombre sense that mankind must be dull and mean. These
cogitations took place in a cold hotel, in an eternal Swiss rain,
and they had a flat echo in the transalpine valleys, as the lonely
ladies went vaguely down to the Italian lakes and cities. Rose
guided their course, at moments, with a kind of aimless ferocity; she moved abruptly, feeling vulgar and hating their life,
though destitute of any definite vision of another life that
would have been open to her. She had set herself a task and
she clung to it; but she appeared to herself despicably idle.
She had succeeded in not going to Homburg waters, where
London was trying to wash away some of its stains; that would
be too staring an advertisement of their situation. The main
difference in situations to her now was the difference of being
more or less pitied, at the best an intolerable danger; so that
the places she preferred were the unsuspicious ones. She
wanted to triumph with contempt, not with submission.

One morning in September, coming with her mother out
of the marble church at Milan, she perceived that a gentleman
who had just passed her on his way into the cathedral and
whose face she had not noticed, had quickly raised his hat,
with a suppressed ejaculation. She involuntarily glanced back;
the gentleman had paused, again uncovering, and Captain Jay
stood saluting her in the Italian sunshine. "Oh, good-morning!" she said, and walked on, pursuing her course; her
mother was a little in front. She overtook her in a moment,
with an unreasonable sense, like a gust of cold air, that men
were worse than ever, for Captain Jay had apparently moved
into the church. Her mother turned as they met, and suddenly, as she looked back, an expression of peculiar sweetness came into this lady's eyes. It made Rose's take the same

direction and rest a second time on Captain Jay, who was planted just where he had stood a minute before. He immediately came forward, asking Rose with great gravity if he might speak to her a moment, while Mrs. Tramore went her way again. He had the expression of a man who wished to say something very important; yet his next words were simple enough and consisted of the remark that he had not seen her for a year.

"Is it really so much as that?" asked Rose.

"Very nearly. I would have looked you up, but in the first place I have been very little in London, and in the second I believed it wouldn't have done any good."

"You should have put that first," said the girl. "It wouldn't have done any good."

He was silent over this a moment, in his customary deciphering way; but the view he took of it did not prevent him from inquiring, as she slowly followed her mother, if he mightn't walk with her now. She answered with a laugh that it wouldn't do any good but that he might do as he liked. He replied without the slightest manifestation of levity that it would do more good than if he didn't, and they strolled together, with Mrs. Tramore well before them, across the big, amusing piazza, where the front of the cathedral makes a sort of builded light. He asked a question or two and he explained his own presence: having a month's holiday, the first clear time for several years, he had just popped over the Alps. He inquired if Rose had recent news of the old lady in Hill Street, and it was the only tortuous thing she had ever heard him say.

"I have had no communication of any kind from her since I parted with you under her roof. Hasn't she mentioned that?" said Rose.

"I haven't seen her."

"I thought you were such great friends."

Bertram Jay hesitated a moment. "Well, not so much now."

"What has she done to you?" Rose demanded.

He fidgeted a little, as if he were thinking of something that made him unconscious of her question; then, with mild violence, he brought out the inquiry: "Miss Tramore, are you happy?"

She was startled by the words, for she on her side had been
reflecting—reflecting that he had broken with her grandmother and that this pointed to a reason. It suggested at least
that he wouldn't now be so much like a mouthpiece for that
cold ancestral tone. She turned off his question—said it never
was a fair one, as you gave yourself away however you answered it. When he repeated "You give yourself away?" as if
he didn't understand, she remembered that he had not read
the funny American books. This brought them to a silence,
for she had enlightened him only by another laugh, and he
was evidently preparing another question, which he wished
carefully to disconnect from the former. Presently, just as they
were coming near Mrs. Tramore, it arrived in the words "Is
this lady your mother?" On Rose's assenting, with the addition that she was travelling with her, he said: "Will you be so
kind as to introduce me to her?" They were so close to Mrs.
Tramore that she probably heard, but she floated away with
a single stroke of her paddle and an inattentive poise of her
head. It was a striking exhibition of the famous tact, for Rose
delayed to answer, which was exactly what might have made
her mother wish to turn; and indeed when at last the girl
spoke she only said to her companion: "Why do you ask me
that?"

"Because I desire the pleasure of making her acquaintance."

Rose had stopped, and in the middle of the square they
stood looking at each other. "Do you remember what you
said to me the last time I saw you?"

"Oh, don't speak of that!"

"It's better to speak of it now than to speak of it later."

Bertram Jay looked round him, as if to see whether any one
would hear; but the bright foreignness gave him a sense of
safety, and he unexpectedly exclaimed: "Miss Tramore, I love
you more than ever!"

"Then you ought to have come to see us," declared the
girl, quickly walking on.

"You treated me the last time as if I were positively offensive to you."

"So I did, but you know my reason."

"Because I protested against the course you were taking? I

did, I did!" the young man rang out, as if he still, a little, stuck to that.

His tone made Rose say gaily: "Perhaps you do so yet?"

"I can't tell till I've seen more of your circumstances," he replied with eminent honesty.

The girl stared; her light laugh filled the air. "And it's in order to see more of them and judge that you wish to make my mother's acquaintance?"

He coloured at this and he evaded; then he broke out with a confused "Miss Tramore, let me stay with you a little!" which made her stop again.

"Your company will do us great honour, but there must be a rigid condition attached to our acceptance of it."

"Kindly mention it," said Captain Jay, staring at the façade of the cathedral.

"You don't take us on trial."

"On trial?"

"You don't make an observation to me—not a single one, ever, ever!—on the matter that, in Hill Street, we had our last words about."

Captain Jay appeared to be counting the thousand pinnacles of the church. "I think you really must be right," he remarked at last.

"There you are!" cried Rose Tramore, and walked rapidly away.

He caught up with her, he laid his hand upon her arm to stay her. "If you're going to Venice, let me go to Venice with you!"

"You don't even understand my condition."

"I'm sure you're right, then: you must be right about everything."

"That's not in the least true, and I don't care a fig whether you're sure or not. Please let me go."

He had barred her way, he kept her longer. "I'll go and speak to your mother myself!"

Even in the midst of another emotion she was amused at the air of audacity accompanying this declaration. Poor Captain Jay might have been on the point of marching up to a battery. She looked at him a moment; then she said: "You'll be disappointed!"

"Disappointed?"

"She's much more proper than grandmamma, because she's much more amiable."

"Dear Miss Tramore—dear Miss Tramore!" the young man murmured helplessly.

"You'll see for yourself. Only there's another condition," Rose went on.

"Another?" he cried, with discouragement and alarm.

"You must understand thoroughly, before you throw in your lot with us even for a few days, what our position really is."

"Is it very bad?" asked Bertram Jay artlessly.

"No one has anything to do with us, no one speaks to us, no one looks at us."

"Really?" stared the young man.

"We've no social existence, we're utterly despised."

"Oh, Miss Tramore!" Captain Jay interposed. He added quickly, vaguely, and with a want of presence of mind of which he as quickly felt ashamed: "Do none of your family—?" The question collapsed; the brilliant girl was looking at him.

"We're extraordinarily happy," she threw out.

"Now that's all I wanted to know!" he exclaimed, with a kind of exaggerated cheery reproach, walking on with her briskly to overtake her mother.

He was not dining at their inn, but he insisted on coming that evening to their *table d'hôte*. He sat next Mrs. Tramore, and in the evening he accompanied them gallantly to the opera, at a third-rate theatre where they were almost the only ladies in the boxes. The next day they went together by rail to the Charterhouse of Pavia, and while he strolled with the girl, as they waited for the homeward train, he said to her candidly: "Your mother's remarkably pretty." She remembered the words and the feeling they gave her: they were the first note of new era. The feeling was somewhat that of an anxious, gratified matron who has "presented" her child and is thinking of the matrimonial market. Men might be of no use, as Mrs. Tramore said, yet it was from this moment Rose dated the rosy dawn of her confidence that her *protégée* would go off; and when later, in crowded assemblies, the phrase, or something like it behind a hat or a fan, fell repeatedly on her anxious ear, "Your mother *is* in beauty!" or "I've never seen her look better!" she had a faint vision of the yellow sunshine and the afternoon shadows on the dusty Italian platform.

Mrs. Tramore's behaviour at this period was a revelation of her native understanding of delicate situations. She needed no account of this one from her daughter—it was one of the things for which she had a scent; and there was a kind of loyalty to the rules of a game in the silent sweetness with which she smoothed the path of Bertram Jay. It was clear that she was in her element in fostering the exercise of the affections, and if she ever spoke without thinking twice it is probable that she would have exclaimed, with some gaiety, "Oh, I know all about *love*!" Rose could see that she thought their companion would be a help, in spite of his being no dispenser of patronage. The key to the gates of fashion had not been placed in his hand, and no one had ever heard of the ladies of his family, who lived in some vague hollow of the Yorkshire moors; but none the less he might administer a muscular push. Yes indeed, men in general were broken reeds, but Captain Jay was peculiarly representative. Respectability was the woman's maximum, as honour was the man's, but this distinguished young soldier inspired more than one kind of confidence. Rose had a great deal of attention for the use to which his respectability was put; and there mingled with this attention some amusement and much compassion. She saw that after a couple of days he decidedly liked her mother, and that he was yet not in the least aware of it. He took for granted that he believed in her but little; notwithstanding which he would have trusted her with anything except Rose herself. His trusting her with Rose would come very soon. He never spoke to her daughter about her qualities of character, but two or three of them (and indeed these were all the poor lady had, and they made the best show) were what he had in mind in praising her appearance. When he remarked: "What attention Mrs. Tramore seems to attract everywhere!" he meant: "What a beautifully simple nature it is!" and when he said: "There's something extraordinarily harmonious in the colours she wears," it signified: "Upon my word, I never saw such a sweet temper in my life!" She lost one of her boxes at Verona, and made the prettiest joke of it to Captain Jay. When Rose saw this she said to herself, "Next season we shall have only to choose." Rose knew what was in the box.

By the time they reached Venice (they had stopped at half a dozen little old romantic cities in the most frolicsome aesthetic way) she liked their companion better than she had ever liked him before. She did him the justice to recognise that if he was not quite honest with himself he was at least wholly honest with *her*. She reckoned up everything he had been since he joined them, and put upon it all an interpretation so favourable to his devotion that, catching herself in the act of glossing over one or two episodes that had not struck her at the time as disinterested she exclaimed, beneath her breath, "Look out—you're falling in love!" But if he liked correctness wasn't he quite right? Could any one possibly like it more than *she* did? And if he had protested against her throwing in her lot with her mother, this was not because of the benefit conferred but because of the injury received. He exaggerated that injury, but this was the privilege of a lover perfectly willing to be selfish on behalf of his mistress. He might have wanted her grandmother's money for her, but if he had given her up on first discovering that she was throwing away her chance of it (oh, this was *her* doing too!) he had given up her grandmother as much: not keeping well with the old woman, as some men would have done; not waiting to see how the perverse experiment would turn out and appeasing her, if it should promise tolerably, with a view to future operations. He had had a simple-minded, evangelical, lurid view of what the girl he loved would find herself in for. She could see this now—she could see it from his present bewilderment and mystification, and she liked him and pitied him, with the kindest smile, for the original *naïveté* as well as for the actual meekness. No wonder he hadn't known what she was in for, since he now didn't even know what he was in for himself. Were there not moments when he thought his companions almost unnaturally good, almost suspiciously safe? He had lost all power to verify that sketch of their isolation and *déclassement* to which she had treated him on the great square at Milan. The last thing he noticed was that they were neglected, and he had never, for himself, had such an impression of society.

It could scarcely be enhanced even by the apparition of a large, fair, hot, red-haired young man, carrying a lady's fan in his hand, who suddenly stood before their little party as, on the third evening after their arrival in Venice, it partook of ices at one of the tables before the celebrated Café Florian. The lamplit Venetian dusk appeared to have revealed them to this gentleman as he sat with other friends at a neighbouring table, and he had sprung up, with unsophisticated glee, to shake hands with Mrs. Tramore and her daughter. Rose recalled him to her mother, who looked at first as though she didn't remember him but presently bestowed a sufficiently gracious smile on Mr. Guy Mangler. He gave with youthful candour the history of his movements and indicated the whereabouts of his family: he was with his mother and sisters; they had met the Bob Veseys, who had taken Lord Whiteroy's yacht and were going to Constantinople. His mother and the girls, poor things, were at the Grand Hotel, but he was on the yacht with the Veseys, where they had Lord Whiteroy's cook. Wasn't the food in Venice filthy, and wouldn't they come and look at the yacht? She wasn't very fast, but she was awfully jolly. His mother might have come if she would, but she wouldn't at first, and now, when she wanted to, there were other people, who naturally wouldn't turn out for her. Mr. Mangler sat down; he alluded with artless resentment to the way, in July, the door of his friends had been closed to him. He was going to Constantinople, but he didn't care—if *they* were going anywhere; meanwhile his mother hoped awfully they would look her up.

Lady Maresfield, if she had given her son any such message, which Rose disbelieved, entertained her hope in a manner compatible with her sitting for half an hour, surrounded by her little retinue, without glancing in the direction of Mrs. Tramore. The girl, however, was aware that this was not a good enough instance of their humiliation; inasmuch as it was rather she who, on the occasion of their last contact, had held off from Lady Maresfield. She was a little ashamed now of not having answered the note in which this affable personage ignored her mother. She couldn't help perceiving indeed a dim movement on the part of some of the other members of the group; she made out an attitude of observation in the high-plumed head of Mrs. Vaughan-Vesey. Mrs. Vesey, perhaps, might have been looking at Captain Jay, for as this gentleman walked back to the hotel with our young lady (they were at the "Britannia," and young Mangler, who clung to them, went in front with Mrs. Tramore) he revealed to Rose that he had some acquaintance with Lady Maresfield's eldest daughter, though he didn't know and didn't particularly want to know, her ladyship. He expressed himself with more acerbity than she had ever heard him use (Christian charity so generally governed his speech) about the young donkey who had been prattling to them. They separated at the door of the hotel. Mrs. Tramore had got rid of Mr. Mangler, and Bertram Jay was in other quarters.

"If you know Mrs. Vesey, why didn't you go and speak to her? I'm sure she saw you," Rose said.

Captain Jay replied even more circumspectly than usual. "Because I didn't want to leave you."

"Well, you can go now; you're free," Rose rejoined.

"Thank you. I shall never go again."

"That won't be civil," said Rose.

"I don't care to be civil. I don't like her."

"Why don't you like her?"

"You ask too many questions."

"I know I do," the girl acknowledged.

Captain Jay had already shaken hands with her, but at this he put out his hand again. "She's too worldly," he murmured, while he held Rose Tramore's a moment.

"Ah, you dear!" Rose exclaimed almost audibly as, with her mother, she turned away.

The next morning, upon the Grand Canal, the gondola of our three friends encountered a stately barge which, though it contained several persons, seemed pervaded mainly by one majestic presence. During the instant the gondolas were passing each other it was impossible either for Rose Tramore or for her companions not to become conscious that this distinguished identity had markedly inclined itself—a circumstance commemorated the next moment, almost within earshot of the other boat, by the most spontaneous cry that had issued for many a day from the lips of Mrs. Tramore. "Fancy, my dear, Lady Maresfield has bowed to us!"

"We ought to have returned it," Rose answered; but she looked at Bertram Jay, who was opposite to her. He blushed, and she blushed, and during this moment was born a deeper understanding than had yet existed between these associated spirits. It had something to do with their going together that afternoon, without her mother, to look at certain out-of-the-way pictures as to which Ruskin had inspired her with a desire to see sincerely. Mrs. Tramore expressed the wish to stay at home, and the motive of this wish—a finer shade than any that even Ruskin had ever found a phrase for—was not translated into misrepresenting words by either the mother or the daughter. At San Giovanni in Bragora the girl and her companion came upon Mrs. Vaughan-Vesey, who, with one of her sisters, was also endeavouring to do the earnest thing. She did it to Rose, she did it to Captain Jay, as well as to Gianbellini; she was a handsome, long-necked, aquiline person, of a different type from the rest of her family, and she did it remarkably well. She secured our friends—it was her own expression—for luncheon, on the morrow, on the yacht, and she made it public to Rose that she would come that afternoon to invite her mother. When the girl returned to the hotel, Mrs. Tramore mentioned, before Captain Jay, who had come up to their sitting-room, that Lady Maresfield had called. "She stayed a long time—at least it seemed long!" laughed Mrs. Tramore.

The poor lady could laugh freely now; yet there was some grimness in a colloquy that she had with her daughter after Bertram Jay had departed. Before this happened Mrs. Vesey's card, scrawled over in pencil and referring to the morrow's luncheon, was brought up to Mrs. Tramore.

"They mean it all as a bribe," said the principal recipient of these civilities.

"As a bribe?" Rose repeated.

"She wants to marry you to that boy; they've seen Captain Jay and they're frightened."

"Well, dear mamma, I can't take Mr. Mangler for a husband."

"Of course not. But oughtn't we to go to the luncheon?"

"Certainly we'll go to the luncheon," Rose said; and when the affair took place, on the morrow, she could feel for the first time that she was taking her mother out. This appearance was somehow brought home to every one else, and it was really the agent of her success. For it is of the essence of this simple history that, in the first place, that success dated from Mrs. Vesey's Venetian *déjeuner*, and in the second reposed, by a subtle social logic, on the very anomaly that had made it dubious. There is always a chance in things, and Rose Tramore's chance was in the fact that Gwendolen Vesey was, as some one had said, awfully modern, an immense improvement on the exploded science of her mother, and capable of seeing what a "draw" there would be in the comedy, if properly brought out, of the reversed positions of Mrs. Tramore and Mrs. Tramore's diplomatic daughter. With a first-rate managerial eye she perceived that people would flock into any room—and all the more into one of hers—to see Rose bring in her dreadful mother. She treated the cream of English society to this thrilling spectacle later in the autumn, when she once more "secured" both the performers for a week at Brimble. It made a hit on the spot, the very first evening—the girl was felt to play her part so well. The rumour of the performance spread; every one wanted to see it. It was an entertainment of which, that winter in the country, and the next season in town, persons of taste desired to give their friends the freshness. The thing was to make the Tramores come late, after every one had arrived. They were engaged for a fixed hour, like the American imitator and the Patagonian contralto. Mrs. Vesey had been the first to say the girl was awfully original, but that became the general view.

Gwendolen Vesey had with her mother one of the few quarrels in which Lady Maresfield had really stood up to such an antagonist (the elder woman had to recognise in general in whose veins it was that the blood of the Manglers flowed) on account of this very circumstance of her attaching more importance to Miss Tramore's originality ("Her originality be hanged!" her ladyship had gone so far as unintelligently to exclaim) than to the prospects of the unfortunate Guy. Mrs. Vesey actually lost sight of these pressing problems in her admiration of the way the mother and the daughter, or rather the daughter and the mother (it was slightly confusing) "drew." It was Lady Maresfield's version of the case that the brazen girl (she was shockingly coarse) had treated poor Guy abominably. At any rate it was made known, just after Easter, that Miss Tramore was to be married to Captain Jay. The marriage was not to take place till the summer; but Rose felt that before this the field would practically be won. There had been some bad moments, there had been several warm corners and a certain number of cold shoulders and closed doors and stony stares; but the breach was effectually made—the rest was only a question of time. Mrs. Tramore could be trusted to keep what she had gained, and it was the dowagers, the old dragons with prominent fangs and glittering scales, whom the trick had already mainly caught. By this time there were several houses into which the liberated lady had crept alone. Her daughter had been expected with her, but they couldn't turn her out because the girl had stayed behind, and she was fast acquiring a new identity, that of a parental connection with the heroine of such a romantic story. She was at least the next best thing to her daughter, and Rose foresaw the day when she would be valued principally as a memento of one of the prettiest episodes in the annals of London. At a big official party, in June, Rose had the joy of introducing Eric to his mother. She was a little sorry it was an official party—there were some other such queer people there; but Eric called, observing the shade, the next day but one.

No observer, probably, would have been acute enough to fix exactly the moment at which the girl ceased to take out her mother and began to be taken out by her. A later phase was more distinguishable—that at which Rose forbore to inflict on her companion a duality that might become oppressive. She began to economise her force, she went only when the particular effect was required. Her marriage was delayed by the period of mourning consequent upon the death of her grandmother, who, the younger Mrs. Tramore averred, was killed by the rumour of her own new birth. She was the only one of the dragons who had not been tamed. Julia Tramore knew the truth about this—she was determined such things should not kill *her*. She would live to do something—she hardly knew what. The provisions of her mother's will were published in the "Illustrated News"; from which it appeared that everything that was not to go to Eric and to Julia was to go to the fortunate Edith. Miss Tramore makes no secret of her own intentions as regards this favourite. Edith is not pretty, but Lady Maresfield is waiting for her; she is determined Gwendolen Vesey shall not get hold of her. Mrs. Vesey however takes no interest in her at all. She is whimsical, as befits a woman of her fashion; but there are two persons she is still very fond of, the delightful Bertram Jays. The fondness of this pair, it must be added, is not wholly expended in return. They are extremely united, but their life is more domestic than might have been expected from the preliminary signs. It owes a portion of its concentration to the fact that Mrs. Tramore has now so many places to go to that she has almost no time to come to her daughter's. She is, under her son-in-law's roof, a brilliant but a rare apparition, and the other day he remarked upon the circumstance to his wife.

"If it hadn't been for you," she replied, smiling, "she might have had her regular place at our fireside."

"Good heavens, how did I prevent it?" cried Captain Jay, with all the consciousness of virtue.

"You ordered it otherwise, you goose!" And she says, in the same spirit, whenever her husband commends her (which he does, sometimes, extravagantly) for the way she launched her mother: "Nonsense, my dear—practically it was *you*!"

Sir Edmund Orme

T HE STATEMENT appears to have been written, though the fragment is undated, long after the death of his wife, whom I take to have been one of the persons referred to. There is, however, nothing in the strange story to establish this point, which is, perhaps, not of importance. When I took possession of his effects I found these pages, in a locked drawer, among papers relating to the unfortunate lady's too brief career (she died in childbirth a year after her marriage), letters, memoranda, accounts, faded photographs, cards of invitation. That is the only connection I can point to, and you may easily and will probably say that the tale is too extravagant to have had a demonstrable origin. I cannot, I admit, vouch for his having intended it as a report of real occurrence—I can only vouch for his general veracity. In any case it was written for himself, not for others. I offer it to others—having full option—precisely because it is so singular. Let them, in respect to the form of the thing, bear in mind that it was written quite for himself. I have altered nothing but the names.

If there's a story in the matter I recognise the exact moment at which it began. This was on a soft, still Sunday noon in November, just after church, on the sunny Parade. Brighton was full of people; it was the height of the season, and the day was even more respectable than lovely—which helped to account for the multitude of walkers. The blue sea itself was decorous; it seemed to doze, with a gentle snore (if that *be* decorum), as if nature were preaching a sermon. After writing letters all the morning I had come out to take a look at it before luncheon. I was leaning over the rail which separates the King's Road from the beach, and I think I was smoking a cigarette, when I became conscious of an intended joke in the shape of a light walking-stick laid across my shoulders. The idea, I found, had been thrown off by Teddy Bostwick, of the Rifles and was intended as a contribution to talk. Our talk came off as we strolled together—he always took your arm to show you he forgave your obtuseness about his humour—and looked at the people, and bowed to some of them, and wondered who others were, and differed in opinion as to the prettiness of the girls. About Charlotte Marden we agreed, however, as we saw her coming toward us with her mother; and there surely could have been no one who wouldn't have agreed with us. The Brighton air, of old, used to make plain girls pretty and pretty girls prettier still—I don't know whether it works the spell now. The place, at any rate, was rare for complexions, and Miss Marden's was one that made people turn round. It made *us* stop, heaven knows—at least, it was one of the things, for we already knew the ladies.

We turned with them, we joined them, we went where they were going. They were only going to the end and back—they had just come out of church. It was another manifestation of Teddy's humour that he got immediate possession of Charlotte, leaving me to walk with her mother. However, I was not unhappy; the girl was before me and I had her to talk about. We prolonged our walk, Mrs. Marden kept me, and presently she said she was tired and must sit down. We found a place on a sheltered bench—we gossiped as the people passed. It had already struck me, in this pair, that the resemblance between the mother and the daughter was wonderful even among such resemblances—the more so that it took so little account of a difference of nature. One often hears mature mothers spoken of as warnings—signposts, more or less discouraging, of the way daughters may go. But there was nothing deterrent in the idea that Charlotte, at fifty-five, should be as beautiful, even though it were conditioned on her being as pale and preoccupied, as Mrs. Marden. At twenty-two she had a kind of rosy blankness and she was admirably handsome. Her head had the charming shape of her mother's, and her features the same fine order. Then there were looks and movements and tones (moments when you could scarcely say whether it were aspect or sound), which, between the two personalities, were a reflection, a recall.

These ladies had a small fortune and a cheerful little house at Brighton, full of portraits and tokens and trophies (stuffed animals on the top of bookcases, and sallow, varnished fish under glass), to which Mrs. Marden professed herself attached by pious memories. Her husband had been "ordered" there in ill-health, to spend the last years of his life, and she had already mentioned to me that it was a place in which she felt herself still under the protection of his goodness. His goodness appeared to have been great, and she sometimes had the air of defending it against mysterious imputations. Some sense of protection, of an influence invoked and cherished, was evidently necessary to her; she had a dim wistfulness, a longing for security. She wanted friends and she had a good many. She was kind to me on our first meeting, and I never suspected her of the vulgar purpose of "making up" to me—a suspicion, of course, unduly frequent in conceited young men. It never struck me that she wanted me for her daughter, nor yet, like some unnatural mammas, for herself. It was as if they had had a common deep, shy need and had been ready to say: "Oh, be friendly to us and be trustful! Don't be afraid, you won't be expected to marry us." "Of course there's something about mamma; that's really what makes her such a dear!" Charlotte said to me, confidentially, at an early stage of our acquaintance. She worshipped her mother's appearance. It was the only thing she was vain of; she accepted the raised eyebrows as a charming ultimate fact. "She looks as if she were waiting for the doctor, dear mamma," she said on another occasion. "Perhaps *you're* the doctor; do you think you are?" It appeared in the event that I had some healing power. At any rate when I learned, for she once dropped the remark, that Mrs. Marden also thought there was something "awfully strange" about Charlotte, the relation between the two ladies became extremely interesting. It was happy enough, at bottom; each had the other so much on her mind.

On the Parade the stream of strollers held its course, and Charlotte presently went by with Teddy Bostwick. She smiled and nodded and continued, but when she came back she stopped and spoke to us. Captain Bostwick positively declined to go in, he said the occasion was too jolly: might they therefore take another turn? Her mother dropped a "Do as you like," and the girl gave me an impertinent smile over her shoulder as they quitted us. Teddy looked at me with his glass

in one eye; but I didn't mind that; it was only of Miss Marden
I was thinking as I observed to my companion, laughing:

"She's a bit of a coquette, you know."

"Don't say that—don't say that!" Mrs. Marden murmured.

"The nicest girls always are—just a little," I was magnanimous enough to plead.

"Then why are they always punished?"

The intensity of the question startled me—it had come out
in such a vivid flash. Therefore I had to think a moment before I inquired: "What do you know about it?"

"I was a bad girl myself."

"And were you punished?"

"I carry it through life," said Mrs. Marden, looking away
from me. "Ah!" she suddenly panted, in the next breath, rising to her feet and staring at her daughter, who had reappeared again with Captain Bostwick. She stood a few seconds,
with the queerest expression in her face; then she sank
upon the seat again and I saw that she had blushed crimson.
Charlotte, who had observed her movement, came straight up
to her and, taking her hand with quick tenderness, seated herself on the other side of her. The girl had turned pale—she
gave her mother a fixed, frightened look. Mrs. Marden, who
had had some shock which escaped our detection, recovered
herself; that is she sat quiet and inexpressive, gazing at the
indifferent crowd, the sunny air, the slumbering sea. My eye
happened to fall, however, on the interlocked hands of the
two ladies, and I quickly guessed that the grasp of the elder
one was violent. Bostwick stood before them, wondering what
was the matter and asking me from his little vacant disk if *I*
knew; which led Charlotte to say to him after a moment, with
a certain irritation:

"Don't stand there that way, Captain Bostwick; go
away—*please* go away."

I got up at this, hoping that Mrs. Marden wasn't ill; but
she immediately begged that we would *not* go away, that we
would particularly stay and that we would presently come
home to lunch. She drew me down beside her and for a moment I felt her hand pressing my arm in a way that might have
been an involuntary betrayal of distress and might have been
a private signal. What she might have wished to point out to

me I couldn't divine: perhaps she had seen somebody or something abnormal in the crowd. She explained to us in a few minutes that she was all right; that she was only liable to palpitations—they came as quickly as they went. It was time to move, and we moved. The incident was felt to be closed. Bostwick and I lunched with our sociable friends, and when I walked away with him he declared that he had never seen such dear kind creatures.

Mrs. Marden had made us promise to come back the next day to tea, and had exhorted us in general to come as often as we could. Yet the next day, when at five o'clock I knocked at the door of the pretty house, it was to learn that the ladies had gone up to town. They had left a message for us with the butler: he was to say that they had suddenly been called—were very sorry. They would be absent a few days. This was all I could extract from the dumb domestic. I went again three days later, but they were still away; and it was not till the end of a week that I got a note from Mrs. Marden, saying "We are back; do come and forgive us." It was on this occasion, I remember (the occasion of my going just after getting the note), that she told me she had intuitions. I don't know how many people there were in England at that time in that predicament, but there were very few who would have mentioned it; so that the announcement struck me as original, especially as her point was that some of these uncanny promptings were connected with me. There were other people present—idle Brighton folk, old women with frightened eyes and irrelevant interjections—and I had but a few minutes' talk with Charlotte; but the day after this I met them both at dinner and had the satisfaction of sitting next to Miss Marden. I recall that hour as the hour on which it first completely came over me that she was a beautiful, liberal creature. I had seen her personality in patches and gleams, like a song sung in snatches, but now it was before me in a large rosy glow, as if it had been a full volume of sound—I heard the whole of the air. It was sweet, fresh music—I was often to hum it over.

After dinner I had a few words with Mrs. Marden; it was at the moment, late in the evening, when tea was handed about. A servant passed near us with a tray, I asked her if she would have a cup, and, on her assenting, took one and handed it to her. She put out her hand for it and I gave it to her, safely as I supposed; but as she was in the act of receiving it she started and faltered, so that the cup and saucer dropped with a crash of porcelain and without, on the part of my interlocutress, the usual woman's movement to save her dress. I stooped to pick up the fragments and when I raised myself Mrs. Marden was looking across the room at her daughter, who looked back at her smiling, but with an anxious light in her eyes. "Dear mamma, what on earth *is* the matter with you?" the silent question seemed to say. Mrs. Marden coloured, just as she had done after her strange movement on the Parade the other week, and I was therefore surprised when she said to me with unexpected assurance: "You should really have a steadier hand!" I had begun to stammer a defence of my hand when I became aware that she had fixed her eyes upon me with an intense appeal. It was ambiguous at first and only added to my confusion; then suddenly I understood, as plainly as if she had murmured "Make believe it was you—make believe it was you." The servant came back to take the morsels of the cup and wipe up the spilt tea, and while I was in the midst of making believe Mrs. Marden abruptly brushed away from me and from her daughter's attention and went into another room. I noticed that she gave no heed to the state of her dress.

I saw nothing more of either of them that evening, but the next morning, in the King's Road, I met Miss Marden with a roll of music in her muff. She told me she had been a little way alone, to practice duets with a friend, and I asked her if she would go a little way further in company. She gave me leave to attend her to her door, and as we stood before it I inquired if I might go in. "No, not to-day—I don't want you," she said, candidly, though not roughly; while the words caused me to direct a wistful, disconcerted gaze at one of the windows of the house. It fell upon the white face of Mrs. Marden, who was looking out at us from the drawing-room. She stood there long enough for me to see that it *was* she and not an apparition, as I had thought for a second, and then she vanished before her daughter had observed her. The girl, during our walk, had said nothing about her. As I had been told they didn't want me I left them alone a little, after which circumstances supervened that kept us still longer apart. I finally went up to London, and while there I received a pressing invitation to come immediately down to Tranton, a pretty old place in Sussex belonging to a couple whose acquaintance I had lately made.

I went to Tranton from town, and on arriving found the Mardens, with a dozen other people, in the house. The first thing Mrs. Marden said was: "Will you forgive me?" and when I asked what I had to forgive she answered: "My throwing my tea over you." I replied that it had gone over herself; whereupon she said: "At any rate I was very rude; but some day I think you'll understand, and then you'll make allowances for me." The first day I was there she dropped two or three of these references (she had already indulged in more than one), to the mystic initiation that was in store for me; so that I began, as the phrase is, to chaff her about it, to say I would rather it were less wonderful and take it out at once. She answered that when it should come to me I would have to take it out—there would be little enough option. That it *would* come was privately clear to her, a deep presentiment, which was the only reason she had ever mentioned the matter. Didn't I remember she had told me she had intuitions? From the first time of her seeing me she had been sure there were things I should not escape knowing. Meanwhile there was nothing to do but wait and keep cool, not to be precipitate. She particularly wished not to be any more nervous than she was. And I was above all not to be nervous myself—one got used to everything. I declared that though I couldn't make out what she was talking about I was terribly frightened; the absence of a clue gave such a range to one's imagination. I exaggerated on purpose; for if Mrs. Marden was mystifying I can scarcely say she was alarming. I couldn't imagine what she meant, but I wondered more than I shuddered. I might have said to myself that she was a little wrong in the upper story; but that never occurred to me. She struck me as hopelessly right.

There were other girls in the house, but Charlotte Marden was the most charming; which was so generally felt to be the case that she really interfered with the slaughter of ground game. There were two or three men, and I was of the number, who actually preferred her to the society of the beaters. In short she was recognised as a form of sport superior and exquisite. She was kind to all of us—she made us go out late and come in early. I don't know whether she flirted, but several other members of the party thought *they* did. Indeed, as regards himself, Teddy Bostwick, who had come over from Brighton, was visibly sure.

The third day I was at Tranton was a Sunday, and there was a very pretty walk to morning service over the fields. It was grey, windless weather, and the bell of the little old church that nestled in the hollow of the Sussex down sounded near and domestic. We were a straggling procession, in the mild damp air (which, as always at that season, gave one the feeling that after the trees were bare there was more of it—a larger sky), and I managed to fall a good way behind with Miss Marden. I remember entertaining, as we moved together over the turf, a strong impulse to say something intensely personal, something violent and important—important for *me*, such as that I had never seen her so lovely, or that that particular moment was the sweetest of my life. But always, in youth, such words have been on the lips many times before they are spoken; and I had the sense, not that I didn't know her well enough (I cared little for that), but that she didn't know *me* well enough. In the church, where there were old Tranton tombs and brasses, the big Tranton pew was full. Several of us were scattered, and I found a seat for Miss Marden, and another for myself beside it, at a distance from her mother and from most of our friends. There were two or three decent rustics on the bench, who moved in further to make room for us, and I took my place first, to cut off my companion from our neighbours. After she was seated there was still a space left, which remained empty till service was about half over.

This at least was the moment at which I became aware that another person had entered and had taken the seat. When I noticed him he had apparently been for some minutes in the pew, for he had settled himself and put down his hat beside him, and, with his hands crossed on the nob of his cane, was gazing before him at the altar. He was a pale young man in black, with the air of a gentleman. I was slightly startled on perceiving him, for Miss Marden had not attracted my attention to his entrance by moving to make room for him. After a few minutes, observing that he had no prayer-book, I reached across my neighbour and placed mine before him, on the ledge of the pew; a manœuvre the motive of which was not unconnected with the possibility that, in my own destitution, Miss Marden would give me one side of *her* velvet volume to hold. The pretext, however, was destined to fail, for at the moment I offered him the book the intruder—whose intrusion I had so condoned—rose from his place without thanking me, stepped noiselessly out of the pew (it had no door), and, so discreetly as to attract no attention, passed down the centre of the church. A few minutes had sufficed for his devotions. His behaviour was unbecoming, his early departure even more than his late arrival; but he managed so quietly that we were not incommoded, and I perceived, on turning a little to glance after him, that nobody was disturbed by his withdrawal. I only noticed, and with surprise, that Mrs. Marden had been so affected by it as to rise, involuntarily, an instant, in her place. She stared at him as he passed, but he passed very quickly, and she as quickly dropped down again, though not too soon to catch my eye across the church. Five minutes later I asked Miss Marden, in a low voice, if she would kindly pass me back my prayer-book—I had waited to see if she would spontaneously perform the act. She restored this aid to devotion, but had been so far from troubling herself about it that she could say to me as she did so: "Why on earth did you put it there?" I was on the point of answering her when she dropped on her knees, and I held my tongue. I had only been going to say: "To be decently civil."

After the benediction, as we were leaving our places, I was slightly surprised, again, to see that Mrs. Marden, instead of going out with her companions, had come up the aisle to join us, having apparently something to say to her daughter. She said it, but in an instant I observed that it was only a pretext—her real business was with me. She pushed Charlotte forward and suddenly murmured to me: "Did you see him?"

"The gentleman who sat down here? How could I help seeing him?"

"Hush!" she said, with the intensest excitement; "don't *speak* to her—don't tell her!" She slipped her hand into my arm, to keep me near her, to keep me, it seemed, away from her daughter. The precaution was unnecessary, for Teddy Bostwick had already taken possession of Miss Marden, and as they passed out of church in front of me I saw one of the other men close up on her other hand. It appeared to be considered that I had had my turn. Mrs. Marden withdrew her hand from my arm as soon as we got out, but not before I felt that she had really needed the support. "Don't speak to any one—don't tell any one!" she went on.

"I don't understand. Tell them what?"

"Why, that you saw him."

"Surely they saw him for themselves."

"Not one of them, not one of them." She spoke in a tone of such passionate decision that I glanced at her—she was staring straight before her. But she felt the challenge of my eyes and she stopped short, in the old brown timber porch of the church, with the others well in advance of us, and said, looking at me now and in a quite extraordinary manner: "You're the only person, the only person in the world."

"But *you*, dear madam?"

"Oh me—of course. That's my curse!" And with this she moved rapidly away from me to join the body of the party. I hovered on its outskirts on the way home, for I had food for rumination. Whom had I seen and why was the apparition— it rose before my mind's eye very vividly again—invisible to the others? If an exception had been made for Mrs. Marden, why did it constitute a curse, and why was I to share so questionable an advantage? This inquiry, carried on in my own locked breast, kept me doubtless silent enough during luncheon. After luncheon I went out on the old terrace to smoke a cigarette, but I had only taken a couple of turns when I perceived Mrs. Marden's moulded mask at the window of one of the rooms which opened on the crooked flags. It re- minded me of the same flitting presence at the window at Brighton the day I met Charlotte and walked home with her. But this time my ambiguous friend didn't vanish; she tapped on the pane and motioned me to come in. She was in a queer little apartment, one of the many reception-rooms of which the ground-floor at Tranton consisted; it was known as the Indian room and had a decoration vaguely Oriental—

bamboo lounges, lacquered screens, lanterns with long fringes and strange idols in cabinets, objects not held to conduce to sociability. The place was little used, and when I went round to her we had it to ourselves. As soon as I entered she said to me: "Please tell me this; are you in love with my daughter?"

I hesitated a moment. "Before I answer your question will you kindly tell me what gives you the idea? I don't consider that I have been very forward."

Mrs. Marden, contradicting me with her beautiful anxious eyes, gave me no satisfaction on the point I mentioned; she only went on strenuously:

"Did you say nothing to her on the way to church?"

"What makes you think I said anything?"

"The fact that you saw him."

"Saw whom, dear Mrs. Marden?"

"Oh, you know," she answered, gravely, even a little reproachfully, as if I were trying to humiliate her by making her phrase the unphraseable.

"Do you mean the gentleman who formed the subject of your strange statement in church—the one who came into the pew?"

"You saw him, you saw him!" Mrs. Marden panted, with a strange mixture of dismay and relief.

"Of course I saw him; and so did you."

"It didn't follow. Did you feel it to be inevitable?"

I was puzzled again. "Inevitable?"

"That you *should* see him?"

"Certainly, since I'm not blind."

"You might have been; every one else is." I was wonderfully at sea, and I frankly confessed it to my interlocutress; but the case was not made clearer by her presently exclaiming: "I knew you would, from the moment you should be really in love with her! I knew it would be the test—what do I mean?—the proof."

"Are there such strange bewilderments attached to that high state?" I asked, smiling.

"You perceive there are. You see him, you see him!" Mrs. Marden announced, with tremendous exaltation. "You'll see him again."

"I've no objection; but I shall take more interest in him if you'll kindly tell me who he is."

She hesitated, looking down a moment; then she said, raising her eyes: "I'll tell you if you'll tell me first what you said to her on the way to church."

"Has she told you I said anything?"

"Do I need that?" smiled Mrs. Marden.

"Oh yes, I remember—your intuitions! But I'm sorry to see they're at fault this time; because I really said nothing to your daughter that was the least out of the way."

"Are you very sure?"

"On my honour, Mrs. Marden."

"Then you consider that you're not in love with her?"

"That's another affair!" I laughed.

"You are—you *are*! You wouldn't have seen him if you hadn't been."

"Who the deuce *is* he, then, madam?" I inquired with some irritation.

She would still only answer me with another question. "Didn't you at least *want* to say something to her—didn't you come very near it?"

The question was much to the point; it justified the famous intuitions. "Very near it—it was the turn of a hair. I don't know what kept me quiet."

"That was quite enough," said Mrs. Marden. "It isn't what you say that determines it; it's what you feel. *That's* what he goes by."

I was annoyed, at last, by her reiterated reference to an identity yet to be established, and I clasped my hands with an air of supplication which covered much real impatience, a sharper curiosity and even the first short throbs of a certain sacred dread. "I entreat you to tell me whom you're talking about."

She threw up her arms, looking away from me, as if to shake off both reserve and responsibility. "Sir Edmund Orme."

"And who is Sir Edmund Orme?"

At the moment I spoke she gave a start. "Hush, here they come." Then as, following the direction of her eyes, I saw Charlotte Marden on the terrace, at the window, she added, with an intensity of warning: "Don't notice him—*never!*"

Charlotte, who had had her hands beside her eyes, peering into the room and smiling, made a sign that she was to be admitted, on which I went and opened the long window. Her mother turned away, and the girl came in with a laughing challenge: "What plot, in the world are you two hatching here?" Some plan—I forget what—was in prospect for the afternoon, as to which Mrs. Marden's participation or consent was solicited—*my* adhesion was taken for granted—and she had been half over the place in her quest. I was flurried, because I saw that Mrs. Marden was flurried (when she turned round to meet her daughter she covered it by a kind of extravagance, throwing herself on the girl's neck and embracing her), and to pass it off I said, fancifully, to Charlotte:

"I've been asking your mother for your hand."

"Oh, indeed, and has she given it?" Miss Marden answered, gayly.

"She was just going to when you appeared there."

"Well, it's only for a moment—I'll leave you free."

"Do you like him, Charlotte?" Mrs. Marden asked, with a candour I scarcely expected.

"It's difficult to say it *before* him isn't it?" the girl replied, entering into the humour of the thing, but looking at me as if she didn't like me.

She would have had to say it before another person as well, for at that moment there stepped into the room from the terrace (the window had been left open), a gentleman who had come into sight, at least into mine, only within the instant. Mrs. Marden had said "Here *they* come," but he appeared to have followed her daughter at a certain distance. I immediately recognised him as the personage who had sat beside us in church. This time I saw him better, saw that his face and his whole air were strange. I speak of him as a personage, because one felt, indescribably, as if a reigning prince had come into the room. He held himself with a kind of habitual majesty, as if he were different from us. Yet he looked fixedly and gravely at me, till I wondered what he expected of me. Did he consider that I should bend my knee or kiss his hand? He turned his eyes in the same way on Mrs. Marden, but she knew what to do. After the first agitation produced by his approach she took no notice of him whatever; it made me remember her passionate adjuration to me. I had to achieve a great effort to imitate her, for though I knew nothing about him but that he was Sir Edmund Orme I felt his presence as a strong appeal, almost as an oppression. He stood there without speaking—young, pale, handsome, clean-shaven, decorous, with extraordinary light blue eyes and something old-fashioned, like a portrait of years ago, in his head, his manner of wearing his hair. He was in complete mourning (one immediately felt that he was very well dressed), and he carried his hat in his hand. He looked again strangely hard at me, harder than any one in the world had ever looked before; and I remember feeling rather cold and wishing he would say something. No silence had ever seemed to me so soundless. All this was of course an impression intensely rapid; but that it had consumed some instants was proved to me suddenly by the aspect of Charlotte Marden, who stared from her mother to me and back again (he never looked at her, and she had no appearance of looking at him), and then broke out with: "What on earth is the matter with you? You've such odd faces!" I felt the colour come back to mine, and when she went on in the same tone: "One would think you had seen a ghost!" I was conscious that I had turned very red. Sir Edmund Orme never blushed, and I could see that he had no capacity for embarrassment. One had met people of that sort, but never any one with such a grand indifference.

"Don't be impertinent; and go and tell them all that I'll join them," said Mrs. Marden with much dignity, but with a quaver in her voice.

"And will you come—*you?*" the girl asked, turning away. I made no answer, taking the question, somehow, as meant for her companion. But he was more silent than I, and when she reached the door (she was going out that way), she stopped, with her hand on the knob, and looked at me, repeating it. I assented, springing forward to open the door for her, and as she passed out she exclaimed to me mockingly: "You haven't got your wits about you—you sha'n't have my hand!"

I closed the door and turned round to find that Sir Edmund Orme had during the moment my back was presented to him retired by the window. Mrs. Marden stood there and we looked at each other long. It had only then—as the girl flitted away—come home to me that her daughter was unconscious of what had happened. It was *that*, oddly enough, that gave me a sudden, sharp shake, and not my own perception of our visitor, which appeared perfectly natural. It made the fact vivid to me that she had been equally unaware of him in church, and the two facts together—now that they were over—set my heart more sensibly beating. I wiped my forehead, and Mrs. Marden broke out with a low distressful wail: "Now you know my life—now you know my life!"

"In God's name who is he—*what* is he?"

"He's a man I wronged."

"How did you wrong him?"

"Oh, awfully—years ago."

"Years ago? Why, he's very young."

"Young—young?" cried Mrs. Marden. "He was born before *I* was!"

"Then why does he look so?"

She came nearer to me, she laid her hand on my arm, and there was something in her face that made me shrink a little. "Don't you understand—don't you *feel?*" she murmured, reproachfully.

"I feel very queer!" I laughed; and I was conscious that my laugh betrayed it.

"He's dead!" said Mrs. Marden, from her white face.

"Dead?" I panted. "Then that gentleman was—?" I couldn't even say the word.

"Call him what you like—there are twenty vulgar names. He's a perfect presence."

"He's a splendid presence!" I cried. "The place is haunted—*haunted!*" I exulted in the word as if it represented the fulfilment of my dearest dream.

"It isn't the place—more's the pity! That has nothing to do with it!"

"Then it's you, dear lady?" I said, as if this were still better.

"No, nor me either—I wish it were!"

"Perhaps it's me," I suggested with a sickly smile.

"It's nobody but my child—my innocent, innocent child!" And with this Mrs. Marden broke down—she dropped into a chair and burst into tears. I stammered some question—I pressed on her some bewildered appeal, but she waved me off, unexpectedly and passionately. I persisted—couldn't I help her, couldn't I intervene? "You *have* intervened," she sobbed; "you're *in* it, you're *in* it."

"I'm very glad to be in anything so curious," I boldly declared.

"Glad or not, you can't get out of it."

"I don't want to get out of it—it's too interesting."

"I'm glad you like it. Go away."

"But I want to know more about it."

"You'll see all you want—go away!"

"But I want to understand what I see."

"How can you—when I don't understand myself?"

"We'll do so together—we'll make it out."

At this she got up, doing what she could to obliterate her tears. "Yes, it will be better together—that's why I've liked you."

"Oh, we'll see it through!" I declared.

"Then you must control yourself better."

"I will, I will—with practice."

"You'll get used to it," said Mrs. Marden, in a tone I never forgot. "But go and join them—I'll come in a moment."

I passed out to the terrace and I felt that I had a part to play. So far from dreading another encounter with the "perfect presence," as Mrs. Marden called it, I was filled with an excitement that was positively joyous. I desired a renewal of the sensation—I opened myself wide to the impression, I went round the house as quickly as if I expected to overtake Sir Edmund Orme. I didn't overtake him just then, but the day was not to close without my recognising that, as Mrs. Marden had said, I should see all I wanted of him.

We took, or most of us took, the collective sociable walk which, in the English country-house, is the consecrated pastime on Sunday afternoons. We were restricted to such a regulated ramble as the ladies were good for; the afternoons, moreover, were short, and by five o'clock we were restored to the fireside in the hall, with a sense, on my part at least, that we might have done a little more for our tea. Mrs. Marden had said she would join us, but she had not appeared; her daughter, who had seen her again before we went out, only explained that she was tired. She remained invisible all the afternoon, but this was a detail to which I gave as little heed as I had given to the circumstance of my not having Miss Marden to myself during all our walk. I was too much taken up with another emotion to care; I felt beneath my feet the threshold of the strange door, in my life, which had suddenly been thrown open and out of which unspeakable vibrations played up through me like a fountain. I had heard all my days of apparitions, but it was a different thing to have seen one and to know that I should in all probability see it familiarly, as it were, again. I was on the look-out for it, as a pilot for the flash of a revolving light, and I was ready to generalise on the sinister subject, to declare that ghosts were much less alarming and much more amusing than was commonly supposed. There is no doubt that I was extremely nervous. I couldn't get over the distinction conferred upon me—the exception (in the way of mystic enlargement of vision), made in my favour. At the same time I think I did justice to Mrs. Marden's absence; it was a commentary on what she had said to me—"Now you know my life." She had probably been seeing Sir Edmund Orme for years, and, not having my firm fibre, she had broken down under him. Her nerve was gone, though she had also been able to attest that, in a degree, one got used to him. She had got used to breaking down.

Afternoon tea, when the dusk fell early, was a friendly hour at Tranton; the firelight played into the wide, white last-century hall; sympathies almost confessed themselves, lingering together, before dressing, on deep sofas, in muddy boots, for last words, after walks; and even solitary absorption in the third volume of a novel that was wanted by some one else seemed a form of geniality. I watched my moment and went over to Charlotte Marden when I saw she was about to withdraw. The ladies had left the place one by one, and after I had addressed myself particularly to Miss Marden the three men who were near her gradually dispersed. We had a little vague talk—she appeared preoccupied, and heaven knows *I* was—after which she said she must go: she should be late for dinner. I proved to her by book that she had plenty of time, and she objected that she must at any rate go up to see her mother: she was afraid she was unwell.

"On the contrary, she's better than she has been for a long

time—I'll guarantee that," I said. "She has found out that she can have confidence in me, and that has done her good." Miss Marden had dropped into her chair again. I was standing before her, and she looked up at me without a smile—with a dim distress in her beautiful eyes; not exactly as if I were hurting her, but as if she were no longer disposed to treat as a joke what had passed (whatever it was, it was at the same time difficult to be serious about it), between her mother and myself. But I could answer her inquiry in all kindness and candour, for I was really conscious that the poor lady had put off a part of her burden on me and was proportionately relieved and eased. "I'm sure she has slept all the afternoon as she hasn't slept for years," I went on. "You have only to ask her."

Charlotte got up again. "You make yourself out very useful."

"You've a good quarter of an hour," I said. "Haven't I a right to talk to you a little this way, alone, when your mother has given me your hand?"

"And is it *your* mother who has given me yours? I'm much obliged to her, but I don't want it. I think our hands are not our mothers'—they happen to be our own!" laughed the girl.

"Sit down, sit down and let me tell you!" I pleaded.

I still stood before her, urgently, to see if she wouldn't oblige me. She hesitated a moment, looking vaguely this way and that, as if under a compulsion that was slightly painful. The empty hall was quiet—we heard the loud ticking of the great clock. Then she slowly sank down and I drew a chair close to her. This made me face round to the fire again, and with the movement I perceived, disconcertedly, that we were not alone. The next instant, more strangely than I can say, my discomposure, instead of increasing, dropped, for the person before the fire was Sir Edmund Orme. He stood there as I had seen him in the Indian room, looking at me with the expressionless attention which borrowed its sternness from his sombre distinction. I knew so much more about him now that I had to check a movement of recognition, an acknowledgment of his presence. When once I was aware of it, and that it lasted, the sense that we had company, Charlotte and I, quitted me; it was impressed on me on the contrary that I was more intensely alone with Miss Marden. She evidently saw nothing to look at, and I made a tremendous and very nearly successful effort to conceal from her that my own situation was different. I say "very nearly," because she watched me an instant—while my words were arrested—in a way that made me fear she was going to say again, as she had said in the Indian room: "What on earth is the matter with you?"

What the matter with me was I quickly told her, for the full knowledge of it rolled over me with the touching spectacle of her unconsciousness. It was touching that she became, in the presence of this extraordinary portent. What was portended, danger or sorrow, bliss or bane, was a minor question; all I saw, as she sat there, was that, innocent and charming, she was close to a horror, as she might have thought it, that happened to be veiled from her but that might at any moment be disclosed. I didn't mind it now, as I found, but nothing was more possible than she should, and if it wasn't curious and interesting it might easily be very dreadful. If I didn't mind it for myself, as I afterwards saw, this was largely because I was so taken up with the idea of protecting *her*. My heart beat high with this idea, on the spot; I determined to do everything I could to keep her sense sealed. What I could do might have been very obscure to me if I had not, in all this, become more aware than of anything else that I loved her. The way to save her was to love her, and the way to love her was to tell her, now and here, that I did so. Sir Edmund Orme didn't prevent me, especially as after a moment he turned his back to us and stood looking discreetly at the fire. At the end of another moment he leaned his head on his arm, against the chimneypiece, with an air of gradual dejection, like a spirit still more weary than discreet. Charlotte Marden was startled by what I said to her, and she jumped up to escape it; but she took no offence—my tenderness was too real. She only moved about the room with a deprecating murmur, and I was so busy following up any little advantage that I might have obtained that I didn't notice in what manner Sir Edmund Orme disappeared. I only observed presently that he had gone. This made no difference—he had been so small a hindrance; I only remember being struck, suddenly, with something inexorable in the slow, sweet, sad headshake that Miss Marden gave me.

"I don't ask for an answer now," I said; "I only want you to be sure—to know how much depends on it."

"Oh, I don't want to give it to you, now or ever!" she replied. "I hate the subject, please—I wish one could be let alone." And then, as if I might have found something harsh in this irrepressible, artless cry of beauty beset, she added quickly, vaguely, kindly, as she left the room: "Thank you, thank you—thank you so much!"

At dinner I could be generous enough to be glad, for her, that I was placed on the same side of the table with her, where she couldn't see me. Her mother was nearly opposite to me, and just after we had sat down Mrs. Marden gave me one long, deep look, in which all our strange communion was expressed. It meant of course "She has told me," but it meant other things beside. At any rate I know what my answering look to her conveyed: "I've seen him again—I've seen him again!" This didn't prevent Mrs. Marden from treating her neighbours with her usual scrupulous blandness. After dinner, when, in the drawing-room, the men joined the ladies and I went straight up to her to tell her how I wished we could have some private conversation, she said immediately, in a low tone, looking down at her fan while she opened and shut it:

"He's here—he's here."

"Here?" I looked round the room, but I was disappointed.

"Look where *she* is," said Mrs. Marden, with just the faintest asperity. Charlotte was in fact not in the main saloon, but in an apartment into which it opened and which was known as the morning-room. I took a few steps and saw her, through a doorway, upright in the middle of the room, talking with three gentlemen whose backs were practically turned to me. For a moment my quest seemed vain; then I recognised that one of the gentlemen—the middle one—was Sir Edmund Orme. This time it *was* surprising that the others didn't see him. Charlotte seemed to be looking straight at him, addressing her conversation to him. She saw me after an instant, however, and immediately turned her eyes away. I went back to her mother with an annoyed sense that the girl would think I was watching *her*, which would be unjust. Mrs. Marden had found a small sofa—a little apart—and I sat down beside her. There were some questions I had so wanted to go into that I wished we were once more in the Indian room. I presently gathered, however, that our privacy was all-sufficient. We communicated so closely and completely now, and with such silent reciprocities, that it would in every circumstance be adequate.

"Oh, yes, he's there," I said; "and at about a quarter-past seven he was in the hall."

"I knew it at the time, and I was so glad!"

"So glad?"

"That it was your affair, this time, and not mine. It's a rest for me."

"Did you sleep all the afternoon?" I asked.

"As I haven't done for months. But how did you know that?"

"As *you* knew, I take it, that Sir Edmund was in the hall. We shall evidently each of us know things now—where the other is concerned."

"Where *he* is concerned," Mrs. Marden amended. "It's a blessing, the way you take it," she added, with a long, mild sigh.

"I take it as a man who's in love with your daughter."

"Of course—of course." Intense as I now felt my desire for the girl to be, I couldn't help laughing a little at the tone of these words; and it led my companion immediately to say: "Otherwise you wouldn't have seen him."

"But every one doesn't see him who's in love with her, or there would be dozens."

"They're not in love with her as you are."

"I can, of course, only speak for myself; and I found a moment, before dinner, to do so."

"She told me immediately."

"And have I any hope—any chance?"

"That's what *I* long for, what I pray for."

"Ah, how can I thank you enough?" I murmured.

"I believe it will all pass—if she loves you," Mrs. Marden continued.

"It will all pass?"

"We shall never see him again."

"Oh, if she loves me I don't care how often I see him!"

"Ah, you take it better than I could," said my companion. "You have the happiness not to know—not to understand."

"I don't indeed. What on earth does he want?"

"He wants to make me suffer." She turned her wan face upon me with this, and I saw now for the first time, fully, how perfectly, if this had been Sir Edmund Orme's purpose, he had succeeded. "For what I did to him," Mrs. Marden explained.

"And what did you do to him?"

She looked at me a moment. "I killed him." As I had seen him fifty yards away only five minutes before the words gave me a start. "Yes, I make you jump; be careful. He's there still, but he killed himself. I broke his heart—he thought me awfully bad. We were to have been married, but I broke it off—just at the last. I saw some one I liked better; I had no reason but that. It wasn't for interest, or money, or position, or anything of that sort. All *those* things were his. It was simply that I fell in love with Captain Marden. When I saw him I felt that I couldn't marry any one else. I wasn't in love with Edmund Orme—my mother, my elder sister had brought it about. But he did love me. I told him I didn't care—that I couldn't, that I *wouldn't*. I threw him over, and he took something, some abominable drug or draught that proved fatal. It was dreadful, it was horrible, he was found that way—he died in agony. I married Captain Marden, but not for five years. I was happy, perfectly happy; time obliterates. But when my husband died I began to see him."

I had listened intently, but I wondered. "To see your husband?"

"Never, never *that* way, thank God! To see *him*, with Chartie—always with Chartie. The first time it nearly killed me—about seven years ago, when she first came out. Never when I'm by myself—only with her. Sometimes not for months, then every day for a week. I've tried everything to break the spell—doctors and *régimes* and climates; I've prayed to God on my knees. That day at Brighton, on the Parade with you, when you thought I was ill, that was the first for an age. And then, in the evening, when I knocked my tea over you, and the day you were at the door with Charlotte and I saw you from the window—each time he was there."

"I see, I see." I was more thrilled than I could say.

"It's an apparition like another."

"Like another? Have you ever seen another?"

"No, I mean the sort of thing one has heard of. It's tremendously interesting to encounter a case."

"Do you call me a 'case'?" Mrs. Marden asked, with exquisite resentment.

"I mean myself."

"Oh, you're the right one!" she exclaimed. "I was right when I trusted you."

"I'm devoutly grateful you did; but what made you do it?"

"I had thought the whole thing out—I had had time to in those dreadful years, while he was punishing me in my daughter."

"Hardly that," I objected, "if she never knew."

"That has been my terror, that she *will*, from one occasion to another. I've an unspeakable dread of the effect on her."

"She sha'n't, she sha'n't!" I declared, so loud that several people looked round. Mrs. Marden made me get up, and I had no more talk with her that evening. The next day I told her I must take my departure from Tranton—it was neither comfortable nor considerate to remain as a rejected suitor. She was disconcerted, but she accepted my reasons, only saying to me out of her mournful eyes: "You'll leave me alone then with my burden?" It was of course understood between us that for many weeks to come there would be no discretion in "worrying poor Charlotte": such were the terms in which, with odd feminine and maternal inconsistency, she alluded to an attitude on my part that she favoured. I was prepared to be heroically considerate, but it seemed to me that even this delicacy permitted me to say a word to Miss Marden before I went. I begged her, after breakfast, to take a turn with me on the terrace, and as she hesitated, looking at me distantly, I informed her that it was only to ask her a question and to say good-bye—I was leaving Tranton for *her.*

She came out with me, and we passed slowly round the house three or four times. Nothing is finer than this great airy platform, from which every look is a sweep of the country, with the sea on the furthest edge. It might have been that as we passed the windows we were conspicuous to our friends in the house, who would divine, sarcastically, why I was so significantly bolting. But I didn't care; I only wondered whether they wouldn't really this time make out Sir Edmund Orme, who joined us on one of our turns and strolled slowly on the other side of my companion. Of what transcendent essence he was composed I knew not; I have no theory about him (leaving that to others), any more than I have one about such or such another of my fellow-mortals whom I have elbowed in life. He was as positive, as individual, as ultimate a fact as any of these. Above all he was as respectable, as sensitive a fact; so that I should no more have thought of taking a liberty, of practicing an experiment with him, of touching him, for instance, or speaking to him, since he set the example of silence, than I should have thought of committing any other social grossness. He had always, as I saw more fully later, the perfect propriety of his position—had always the appearance of being dressed and, in attitude and aspect, of comporting himself, as the occasion demanded. He looked strange, incontestably, but somehow he always looked *right*. I very soon came to attach an idea of beauty to his unmentionable presence, the beauty of an old story of love and pain. What I ended by feeling was that he was on my side, that he was watching over my interest, that he was looking to it that my heart shouldn't be broken. Oh, he had taken it seriously, his own catastrophe—he had certainly proved that in his day. If poor Mrs. Marden, as she told me, had thought it out, I also subjected the case to the finest analysis of which my intellect was capable. It was a case of retributive justice. The mother was to pay, in suffering, for the suffering she had inflicted, and as the disposition to jilt a lover might have been transmitted to the daughter, the daughter was to be watched, so that *she* might be made to suffer should she do an equal wrong. She might reproduce her mother in character as vividly as she did in face. On the day she should transgress, in other words, her eyes would be opened suddenly and unpitiedly to the "perfect presence," which she would have to work as she could into her conception of a young lady's universe. I had no great fear for her, because I didn't believe she was, in any cruel degree, a coquette. We should have a good deal of ground to get over before I, at least, should be in a position to be sacrificed by her. She couldn't throw me over before she had made a little more of me.

The question I asked her on the terrace that morning was whether I might continue, during the winter, to come to Mrs. Marden's house. I promised not to come too often and not to speak to her for three months of the question I had raised the day before. She replied that I might do as I liked, and on this we parted.

I carried out the vow I had made her; I held my tongue for my three months. Unexpectedly to myself there were moments of this time when she struck me as capable of playing with a man. I wanted so to make her like me that I became subtle and ingenious, wonderfully alert, patiently diplomatic. Sometimes I thought I had earned my reward, brought her to the point of saying: "Well, well, you're the best of them all—you may speak to me now." Then there was a greater blankness than ever in her beauty, and on certain days a mocking light in her eyes, of which the meaning seemed to be: "If you don't take care, I *will* accept you, to have done with you the more effectually." Mrs. Marden was a great help to me simply by believing in me, and I valued her faith all the more that it continued even though there was a sudden intermission of the miracle that had been wrought for me. After our visit to Tranton Sir Edmund Orme gave us a holiday, and I confess it was at first a disappointment to me. I felt less designated, less connected with Charlotte. "Oh, don't cry till you're out of the wood," her mother said; "he has let me off sometimes for six months. He'll break out again when you least expect it—he knows what he's about." For her these weeks were happy, and she was wise enough not to talk about me to the girl. She was so good as to assure me that I was taking the right way, that I looked as if I felt secure and that in the long run women give way to that. She had known them do it even when the man was a fool for looking so—or was a fool on any terms. For herself she felt it to be a good time, a sort of St. Martin's summer of the soul. She was better than she had been for years, and she had me to thank for it. The sense of visitation was light upon her—she wasn't in anguish every time she looked round. Charlotte contradicted me very often, but she contradicted herself still more. That winter was a wonder of mildness, and we often sat out in the sun. I walked up and down with Charlotte, and Mrs. Marden, sometimes on a bench, sometimes in a bath-chair, waited for us and smiled at us as we passed. I always looked out for a sign in her face—"He's with you, he's with you" (she would see him before I should), but nothing came; the season had brought us also a sort of spiritual softness. Toward the end of April the air was so like June that, meeting my two friends one night at some Brighton sociability—an evening party with amateur music— I drew Miss Marden unresistingly out upon a balcony to which a window in one of the rooms stood open. The night was close and thick, the stars were dim, and below us, under the cliff, we heard the regular rumble of the sea. We listened to it a little and we heard mixed with it, from within the house, the sound of a violin accompanied by a piano—a performance which had been our pretext for passing out.

"Do you like me a little better?" I asked, abruptly, after a minute. "Could you listen to me again?"

I had no sooner spoken than she laid her hand quickly, with a certain force, on my arm. "Hush!—isn't there some one there?" She was looking into the gloom of the far end of the balcony. This balcony ran the whole width of the house, a width very great in the best of the old houses at Brighton. We were lighted a little by the open window behind us, but the other windows, curtained within, left the darkness undiminished, so that I made out but dimly the figure of a gentleman standing there and looking at us. He was in evening dress, like a guest—I saw the vague shine of his white shirt and the pale oval of his face—and he might perfectly have been a guest who had stepped out in advance of us to take the air. Miss Marden took him for one at first—then evidently, even in a few seconds, she saw that the intensity of his gaze was unconventional. What else she saw I couldn't determine; I was too taken up with my own impression to do more than feel the quick contact of her uneasiness. My own impression was in fact the strongest of sensations, a sensation of horror; for what could the thing mean but that the girl at last *saw*? I heard her give a sudden, gasping "Ah!" and move quickly into the house. It was only afterwards that I knew that I myself had had a totally new emotion—my horror passing into anger, and my anger into a stride along the balcony with a gesture of reprobation. The case was simplified to the vision of a frightened girl whom I loved. I advanced to vindicate her security, but I found nothing there to meet me. It was either all a mistake or Sir Edmund Orme had vanished.

I followed Miss Marden immediately, but there were symptoms of confusion in the drawing-room when I passed in. A lady had fainted, the music had stopped; there was a shuffling of chairs and a pressing forward. The lady was not Charlotte, as I feared, but Mrs. Marden, who had suddenly been taken ill. I remember the relief with which I learned this, for to see Charlotte stricken would have been anguish, and her mother's condition gave a channel to her agitation. It was of course all a matter for the people of the house and for the ladies, and I could have no share in attending to my friends or in conducting them to their carriage. Mrs. Marden revived and insisted on going home, after which I uneasily withdrew.

I called the next morning to ask about her and was informed that she was better, but when I asked if Miss Marden would see me the message sent down was that it was impossible. There was nothing for me to do all day but to roam about with a beating heart. But toward evening I received a line in pencil, brought by hand—"Please come; mother wishes you." Five minutes afterward I was at the door again and ushered into the drawing-room. Mrs. Marden lay upon the sofa, and as soon as I looked at her I saw the shadow of death in her face. But the first thing she said was that she was better, ever so much better; her poor old heart had been behaving queerly again, but now it was quiet. She gave me her hand and I bent over her with my eyes in hers, and in this way I was able to read what she didn't speak—"I'm really very ill, but appear to take what I say exactly as I say it." Charlotte stood there beside her, looking not frightened now, but intensely grave, and not meeting my eyes. "She has told me—she has told me!" her mother went on.

"She has told you?" I stared from one of them to the other, wondering if Mrs. Marden meant that the girl had spoken to her of the circumstances on the balcony.

"That you spoke to her again—that you're admirably faithful."

I felt a thrill of joy at this; it showed me that that memory had been uppermost, and also that Charlotte had wished to say the thing that would soothe her mother most, not the thing that would alarm her. Yet I now knew, myself, as well as if Mrs. Marden had told me, that she knew and had known at the moment what her daughter had seen. "I spoke—I spoke, but she gave me no answer," I said.

"She will now, won't you, Chartie? I want it so, I want it!" the poor lady murmured, with ineffable wistfulness.

"You're very good to me," Charlotte said to me, seriously and sweetly, looking fixedly on the carpet. There was something different in her, different from all the past. She had recognised something, she felt a coercion. I could see that she was trembling.

"Ah, if you would let me show you *how* good I can be!" I exclaimed, holding out my hands to her. As I uttered the words I was touched with the knowledge that something had happened. A form had constituted itself on the other side of the bed, and the form leaned over Mrs. Marden. My whole being went forth into a mute prayer that Charlotte shouldn't see it and that I should be able to betray nothing. The impulse to glance toward Mrs. Marden was even stronger than the involuntary movement of taking in Sir Edmund Orme; but I could resist even that, and Mrs. Marden was perfectly still. Charlotte got up to give me her hand, and with the definite act she saw. She gave, with a shriek, one stare of dismay, and another sound, like a wail of one of the lost, fell at the same instant on my ear. But I had already sprung toward the girl to cover her, to veil her face. She had already thrown herself into my arms. I held her there a moment—bending over her, given up to her, feeling each of her throbs with my own and not knowing which was which; then, all of a sudden, coldly, I gathered that we were alone. She released herself. The figure beside the sofa had vanished; but Mrs. Marden lay in her place with closed eyes, with something in her stillness that gave us both another terror. Charlotte expressed it in the cry of "Mother, mother!" with which she flung herself down. I fell on my knees beside her. Mrs. Marden had passed away.

Was the sound I heard when Chartie shrieked—the other and still more tragic sound I mean—the despairing cry of the poor lady's death-shock or the articulate sob (it was like a waft from a great tempest), of the exercised and pacified spirit? Possibly the latter, for that was, mercifully, the last of Sir Edmund Orme.

CHRONOLOGY

NOTE ON THE TEXTS

NOTES

Chronology

1843 Born April 15 at 21 Washington Place, New York City, the second child (after William, born January 11, 1842, N.Y.C.) of Henry James of Albany and Mary Robertson Walsh of New York. Father lives on inheritance of $10,000 a year, his share of litigated $3,000,000 fortune of his Albany father, William James, an Irish immigrant who came to the U.S. immediately after the Revolution.

1843–45 Accompanied by mother's sister, Catharine Walsh, and servants, the James parents take infant children to England and later to France. Reside at Windsor, where father has nervous collapse ("vastation") and experiences spiritual illumination. He becomes a Swedenborgian (May 1844), devoting his time to lecturing and religious-philosophical writings. James later claimed his earliest memory was a glimpse, during his second year, of the Place Vendôme in Paris with its Napoleonic column.

1845–47 Family returns to New York. Garth Wilkinson James (Wilky) born July 21, 1845. Family moves to Albany at 50 N. Pearl St., a few doors from grandmother Catharine Barber James. Robertson James (Bob or Rob) born August 29, 1846.

1847–55 Family moves to a large house at 58 W. 14th St., New York. Alice James born August 7, 1848. Relatives and father's friends and acquaintances—Horace Greeley, George Ripley, Charles Anderson Dana, William Cullen Bryant, Bronson Alcott, and Ralph Waldo Emerson ("I knew he was great, greater than any of our friends")—are frequent visitors. Thackeray calls during his lecture tour on the English humorists. Summers at New Brighton on Staten Island and Fort Hamilton on Long Island's south shore. On steamboat to Fort Hamilton August 1850, hears Washington Irving tell his father of Margaret Fuller's drowning in shipwreck off Fire Island. Frequently visits Barnum's American Museum on free days. Taken to art shows and theaters; writes and draws stage scenes. Described by father as "a devourer of libraries." Taught in assorted private schools and by tutors in lower Broadway and Greenwich Village. But father claims in 1848 that American schooling fails to provide "sensuous education" for his children and plans to take them to Europe.

1855–58   Family (with Aunt Kate) sails for Liverpool, June 27. James is intermittently sick with malarial fever as they travel to Paris, Lyon, and Geneva. After Swiss summer, leaves for London where Robert Thomson (later Robert Louis Stevenson's tutor) is engaged. Early summer 1856, family moves to Paris. Another tutor engaged and children attend experimental Fourierist school. Acquires fluency in French. Family goes to Boulogne-sur-mer in summer, where James contracts typhoid. Spends late October in Paris, but American crash of 1857 returns family to Boulogne where they can live more cheaply. Attends public school (fellow classmate is Coquelin, the future French actor).

1858–59   Family returns to America and settles in Newport, Rhode Island. Goes boating, fishing, and riding. Attends the Reverend W. C. Leverett's Berkeley Institute, and forms friendship with classmate Thomas Sergeant Perry. Takes long walks and sketches with the painter John La Farge.

1859–60   Father, still dissatisfied with American education, returns family to Geneva in October. James attends a pre-engineering school, Institution Rochette, because parents, with "a flattering misconception of my aptitudes," feel he might benefit from less reading and more mathematics. After a few months withdraws from all classes except French, German, and Latin, and joins William as a special student at the Academy (later the University of Geneva) where he attends lectures on literary subjects. Studies German in Bonn during summer 1860.

1860–62   Family returns to Newport in September where William studies with William Morris Hunt, and James sits in on his classes. La Farge introduces him to works of Balzac, Merimée, Musset, and Browning. Wilky and Bob attend Frank Sanborn's experimental school in Concord with children of Hawthorne and Emerson and John Brown's daughter. Early in 1861, orphaned Temple cousins come to live in Newport. Develops close friendship with cousin

Mary (Minnie) Temple. Goes on a week's walking tour in July in New Hampshire with Perry. William abandons art in autumn 1861 and enters Lawrence Scientific School at Harvard. James suffers back injury in a stable fire while serving as a volunteer fireman. Reads Hawthorne ("an American could be an artist, one of the finest").

1862–63 Enters Harvard Law School (Dane Hall). Wilky enlists in the Massachusetts 44th Regiment, and later in Colonel Robert Gould Shaw's 54th, one of the first black regiments. Summer 1863, Bob joins the Massachusetts 55th, another black regiment, under Colonel Hollowell. James withdraws from law studies to try writing. Sends unsigned stories to magazines. Wilky is badly wounded and brought home to Newport in August.

1864 Family moves from Newport to 13 Ashburton Place, Boston. First tale, "A Tragedy of Error" (unsigned), published in *Continental Monthly* (Feb. 1864). Stays in Northampton, Massachusetts, early August–November. Begins writing book reviews for *North American Review* and forms friendship with its editor, Charles Eliot Norton, and his family, including his sister Grace (with whom he maintains a long-lasting correspondence). Wilky returns to his regiment.

1865 First signed tale, "The Story of a Year," published in *Atlantic Monthly* (March 1865). Begins to write reviews for the newly founded *Nation* and publishes anonymously in it during next fifteen years. William sails on a scientific expedition with Louis Agassiz to the Amazon. During summer James vacations in the White Mountains with Minnie Temple and her family; joined by Oliver Wendell Holmes Jr. and John Chipman Gray, both recently demobilized. Father subsidizes plantation for Wilky and Bob in Florida with black hired workers. (The idealistic but impractical venture fails in 1870.)

1866–68 Continues to publish reviews and tales in Boston and New York journals. William returns from Brazil and resumes medical education. James has recurrence of back ailment and spends summer in Swampscott, Massachusetts. Begins friendship with William Dean Howells. Family moves to 20 Quincy St., Cambridge. William, suffering from nervous ailments, goes to Germany in spring 1867. "Poor Richard," James's longest story to date, published in *Atlantic Monthly* (June–Aug. 1867). William begins intermittent criticism of Henry's story-telling and style (which will continue throughout their careers). Momentary meeting with Charles Dickens at Norton's house. Vacations in Jefferson, New Hampshire, summer 1868. William returns from Europe.

1869–70   Sails in February for European tour. Visits English towns and cathedrals. Through Nortons meets Leslie Stephen, William Morris, Dante Gabriel Rossetti, Edward Burne-Jones, John Ruskin, Charles Darwin, and George Eliot (the "one marvel" of his stay in London). Goes to Paris in May, then travels in Switzerland in summer and hikes into Italy in autumn, where he stays in Milan, Venice (Sept.), Florence, and Rome (Oct. 30–Dec. 28). Returns to England to drink the waters at Malvern health spa in Worcestershire because of digestive troubles. Stays in Paris en route and has first experience of Comédie Française. Learns that his beloved cousin, Minnie Temple, has died of tuberculosis.

1870–72   Returns to Cambridge in May. Travels to Rhode Island, Vermont, and New York to write travel sketches for *The Nation*. Spends a few days with Emerson in Concord. Meets Bret Harte at Howells' home April 1871. *Watch and Ward*, his first novel, published in *Atlantic Monthly* (Aug.–Dec. 1871). Serves as occasional art reviewer for the *Atlantic* January–March 1872.

1872–74   Accompanies Aunt Kate and sister Alice on tour of England, France, Switzerland, Italy, Austria, and Germany from May through October. Writes travel sketches for *The Nation*. Spends autumn in Paris, becoming friends with James Russell Lowell. Escorts Emerson through the Louvre. (Later, on Emerson's return from Egypt, will show him the Vatican.) Goes to Florence in December and from there to Rome, where he becomes friends with actress Fanny Kemble, her daughter Sarah Butler Wister, and William Wetmore Story and his family. In Italy sees old family friend Francis Boott and his daughter Elizabeth (Lizzie), expatriates who have lived for many years in Florentine villa on Bellosguardo. Takes up horseback riding on the Campagna. Encounters Matthew Arnold in April 1873 at Story's. Moves from Rome hotel to rooms of his own. Continues writing and now earns enough to support himself. Leaves Rome in June, spends summer in Bad Homburg. In October goes to Florence, where William joins him. They also visit Rome, William returning to America in March. In Baden-Baden June–August and returns to America September 4, with *Roderick Hudson* all but finished.

1875   *Roderick Hudson* serialized in *Atlantic Monthly* from January (published by Osgood at the end of the year). First book, *A Passionate Pilgrim and Other Tales*, published January 31. Tries living and writing in New York, in rooms at 111 E. 25th Street. Earns $200 a month from novel installments and continued reviewing, but finds New York too expensive. *Transatlantic Sketches*, published in April, sells almost 1,000 copies in three months. In Cambridge in July decides to return to Europe; arranges with John Hay, assistant to the publisher, to write Paris letters for the *New York Tribune*.

1875–76   Arriving in Paris in November, he takes rooms at 29 Rue de Luxembourg (since renamed Cambon). Becomes friend of Ivan Turgenev and is introduced by him to Gustave Flaubert's Sunday parties. Meets Edmond de Goncourt, Émile Zola, G. Charpentier (the publisher), Catulle Mendès, Alphonse Daudet, Guy de Maupassant, Ernest Renan, Gustave Doré. Makes friends with Charles Sanders Peirce, who is in Paris. Reviews (unfavorably) the early Impressionists at the Durand-Ruel gallery. By midsummer has received $400 for *Tribune* pieces, but editor asks for more Parisian gossip and James resigns. Travels in France during July, visiting Normandy and the Midi, and in September crosses to San Sebastian, Spain, to see a bullfight ("I thought the bull, in any case, a finer fellow than any of his tormentors"). Moves to London in December, taking rooms at 3 Bolton Street, Piccadilly, where he will live for the next decade.

1877   *The American* published. Meets Robert Browning and George du Maurier. Leaves London in midsummer for visit to Paris and then goes to Italy. In Rome rides again in Campagna and hears of an episode that inspires "Daisy

Miller." Back in England, spends Christmas at Stratford with Fanny Kemble.

1878 Publishes first book in England, *French Poets and Novelists* (Macmillan). Appearance of "Daisy Miller" in *Cornhill Magazine*, edited by Leslie Stephen, is international success, but by publishing it abroad loses American copyright and story is pirated in U.S. *Cornhill* also prints "An International Episode." *The Europeans* is serialized in *Atlantic*. Now a celebrity, he dines out often, visits country houses, gains weight, takes long walks, fences, and does weight-lifting to reduce. Elected to Reform Club. Meets Tennyson, George Meredith, and James McNeill Whistler. William marries Alice Howe Gibbens.

1879 Immersed in London society (". . . dined out during the past winter 107 times!"). Meets Edmund Gosse and Robert Louis Stevenson, who will later become his close friends. Sees much of Henry Adams and his wife, Marian (Clover), in London and later in Paris. Takes rooms in Paris, September–December. *Confidence* is serialized in *Scribner's* and published by Chatto & Windus. *Hawthorne* appears in Macmillan's "English Men of Letters" series.

1880–81 Stays in Florence March–May to work on *The Portrait of a Lady*. Meets Constance Fenimore Woolson, American novelist and grandniece of James Fenimore Cooper. Returns to Bolton Street in June, where William visits him. *Washington Square* serialized in *Cornhill Magazine* and published in U.S. by Harper & Brothers (Dec. 1880). *The Portrait of a Lady* serialized in *Macmillan's Magazine* (Oct. 1880–Nov. 1881) and *Atlantic Monthly*; published by Macmillan and Houghton, Mifflin (Nov. 1881). Publication both in United States and in England yields him the then-large income of $500 a month, though book sales are disappointing. Leaves London in February for Paris, the south of France, the Italian Riviera, and Venice, and returns home in July. Sister Alice comes to London with her friend Katharine Loring. James goes to Scotland in September.

1881–83 In November revisits America after absence of six years. Lionized in New York. Returns to Quincy Street for Christmas and sees ailing brother Wilky for the first time in ten years. In January visits Washington and the Henry Adamses and meets President Chester A. Arthur. Summoned to Cambridge by mother's death January 29 ("the sweetest, gentlest, most beneficent human being I have ever known"). All four brothers are together for the first time in fifteen years at her funeral. Alice and father move from Cambridge to Boston. Prepares a stage version of "Daisy Miller" and returns to England in May. William, now a Harvard professor, comes to Europe in September. Proposed by Leslie Stephen, James becomes member, without the usual red tape, of the Atheneum Club. Travels in France in October to write *A Little Tour in France* (published 1884) and has last visit with Turgenev, who is dying. Returns to England in December and learns of father's illness. Sails for America but Henry James Sr. dies December 18, 1882, before his arrival. Made executor of father's will. Visits brothers Wilky and Bob in Milwaukee in January. Quarrels with William over division of property—James wants to restore Wilky's share. Macmillan publishes a collected pocket edition of James's novels and tales in fourteen volumes. *Siege of London* and *Portraits of Places* published. Returns to Bolton Street in September. Wilky dies in November. Constance Fenimore Woolson comes to London for the winter.

1884–86 Goes to Paris in February and visits Daudet, Zola, and Goncourt. Again impressed with their intense concern with "art, form, manner" but calls them "mandarins." Misses Turgenev, who had died a few months before. Meets John Singer Sargent and persuades him to settle in London. Returns to Bolton Street. Sargent introduces him to young Paul Bourget. During country visits encounters many British political and social figures, including W. E. Gladstone, John Bright, and Charles Dilke. Alice, suffering from nervous ailment, arrives in England for visit in November but is too ill to travel and settles near her brother. *Tales of Three Cities* ("The Impressions of a Cousin," "Lady Barberina," "A New England Winter") and "The Art of Fiction" published 1884. Alice goes to Bournemouth in late January. James joins her in May and becomes an intimate of Robert Louis Stevenson, who resides nearby. Spends August at Dover and is visited by Paul Bourget. Stays in Paris for the next two months. Moves into a flat at 34 De Vere Gardens in Kensington early in March 1886. Alice takes rooms in London. *The Bostonians* serialized in *Century* (Feb. 1885–Feb. 1886; published 1886), *The Princess Casamassima* serialized in *Atlantic Monthly* (Sept. 1885–Oct. 1886; published 1886).

1886–87   Leaves for Italy in December for extended stay, mainly in Florence and Venice. Sees much of Constance Fenimore Woolson and stays in her villa. Writes "The Aspern Papers" and other tales. Returns to De Vere Gardens in July and begins work on *The Tragic Muse*. Pays several country visits. Dines out less often ("I know it all—all that one sees by 'going out'—today, as if I had made it. But if I had, I would have made it better!").

1888   *The Reverberator, The Aspern Papers, Louisa Pallant, The Modern Warning*, and *Partial Portraits* published. Elizabeth Boott Duveneck dies. Robert Louis Stevenson leaves for the South Seas. Engages fencing teacher to combat "symptoms of a portentous corpulence." Goes abroad in October to Geneva (where he visits Woolson), Genoa, Monte Carlo, and Paris.

1889–90   Catharine Walsh (Aunt Kate) dies March 1889. William comes to England to visit Alice in August. James goes to Dover in September and then to Paris for five weeks. Writes account of Robert Browning's funeral in Westminster Abbey. Dramatizes *The American* for the Compton Comedy Company. Meets and becomes close friends with American journalist William Morton Fullerton and young American publisher Wolcott Balestier. Goes to Italy for the summer, staying in Venice and Florence, and takes a brief walking tour in Tuscany with W. W. Baldwin, an American physician practicing in Florence. Miss Woolson moves to Cheltenham, England, to be near James. *Atlantic Monthly* rejects his story "The Pupil," but it appears in England. Writes series of drawing-room comedies for theater. Meets Rudyard Kipling. *The Tragic Muse* serialized in *Atlantic Monthly* (Jan. 1889–May 1890; published 1890). *A London Life* (including "The Patagonia," "The Liar," "Mrs. Temperly") published 1889.

1891   *The American* produced at Southport is a success during road tour. After residence in Leamington, Alice returns to London, cared for by Katharine Loring. Doctors discover she has breast cancer. James circulates comedies (*Mrs. Vibert*, later called *Tenants*, and *Mrs. Jasper*, later named *Disengaged*) among theater managers who are cool to his work. Unimpressed at first by Ibsen, writes an appreciative review after seeing a performance of *Hedda Gabler* with Elizabeth Robins, a young Kentucky actress; persuades her to take the part of Mme. de Cintré in the London production of *The American*. Recuperates from flu in Ireland. James Russell Lowell dies. *The American* opens in London, September 26, and runs for seventy nights. Wolcott Balestier dies, and James attends his funeral in Dresden in December.

1892   Alice James dies March 6. James travels to Siena to be near the Paul Bourgets, and Venice, June–July, to visit the Daniel Curtises, then to Lausanne to meet William and his family, who have come abroad for sabbatical. Attends funeral of Tennyson at Westminster Abbey. Augustin Daly agrees to produce *Mrs. Jasper*. *The American* continues to be performed on the road by the Compton Company. *The Lesson of the Master* (with a collection of stories including "The Marriages," "The Pupil," "Brooksmith," "The Solution," and "Sir Edmund Orme") published.

1893   Fanny Kemble dies in January. Continues to write unproduced plays. In March goes to Paris for two months. Sends Edward Compton first act and scenario for *Guy Domville*. Meets William and family in Lucerne and stays a month, returning to London in June. Spends July completing *Guy Domville* in Ramsgate. George Alexander, actor-manager, agrees to produce the play. Daly stages first reading of *Mrs. Jasper*, and James withdraws it, calling the rehearsal a mockery. *The Real Thing and Other Tales* (including "The Wheel of Time," "Lord Beaupré," "The Visit") published.

1894   Constance Fenimore Woolson dies in Venice, January. Shocked and upset, James prepares to attend funeral in Rome but changes his mind on learning she is a suicide. Goes to Venice in April to help her family settle her affairs. Receives one of four copies, privately printed by Miss Loring, of Alice's diary. Finds it impressive but is concerned that so much gossip he told Alice in private has been included (later burns his copy). Robert Louis Ste venson dies in the South Pacific. *Guy Domville* goes into rehearsal. *Theatricals: Two Comedies* and *Theatricals: Second Series* published.

1895   *Guy Domville* opens January 5 at St. James's Theatre. At play's end James is greeted by a fifteen-minute roar of boos, catcalls, and applause. Horrified and depressed, abandons the theater. Play earns him $1,300 after five-week run. Feels he can salvage something useful from playwriting for his fiction ("a key that, working in the same *general* way fits the complicated chambers of *both* the dramatic and the narrative lock"). Writes scenario for *The Spoils of Poynton*. Visits Lord Wolseley and Lord Houghton in Ireland. In the summer goes to Torquay in Devonshire and stays until November while electricity is being installed in De Vere Gardens flat. Friendship with W. E. Norris, who resides at Torquay. Writes a one-act play ("Mrs. Gracedew") at request of Ellen Terry. *Terminations* (containing "The Death of the Lion," "The Coxon Fund," "The Middle Years," "The Altar of the Dead") published.

1896–97   Finishes *The Spoils of Poynton* (serialized in *Atlantic Monthly* April–Oct. 1896 as *The Old Things*, published 1897). *Embarrassments* ("The Figure in the Carpet," "Glasses," "The Next Time," "The Way It Came") published. Takes a house on Point Hill, Playden, opposite the old town of Rye, Sussex, August–September. Ford Madox Hueffer (later Ford Madox Ford) visits him. Converts play *The Other House* into novel and works on *What Maisie Knew* (published Sept. 1897). George du Maurier dies early in October. Because of increasing pain in wrist, hires stenographer William MacAlpine in February and then purchases a typewriter; soon begins direct dictation to MacAlpine at the machine. Invites Joseph Conrad to lunch at De Vere Gardens and begins their friendship. Goes to Bournemouth in July. Serves on jury in London before going to Dunwich, Suffolk, to spend time with Temple-Emmet cousins. In late September 1897 signs a twenty-one-year lease for Lamb House in Rye for £70 a year ($350). Takes on extra work to pay for setting up his house—the life of William Wetmore Story ($1,250 advance) and will furnish an "American Letter" for new magazine *Literature* (precursor of *Times Literary Supplement*) for $200 a month. Howells visits.

1898   "The Turn of the Screw" (serialized in *Collier's* Jan.–April;
        published with "Covering End" under the title *The Two
        Magics*) proves his most popular work since "Daisy
        Miller." Sleeps in Lamb House for first time June 28. Soon
        after is visited by William's son, Henry James Jr. (Harry),
        followed by a stream of visitors: future Justice Oliver
        Wendell Holmes, Mrs. J. T. Fields, Sarah Orne Jewett, the
        Paul Bourgets, the Edward Warrens, the Daniel Curtises,
        the Edmund Gosses, and Howard Sturgis. His witty
        friend Jonathan Sturges, a young, crippled New Yorker,
        stays for two months during autumn. *In the Cage* pub-
        lished. Meets neighbors Stephen Crane and H. G. Wells.

1899   Finishes *The Awkward Age* and plans trip to the Conti-
        nent. Fire in Lamb House delays departure. To Paris in
        March and then visits the Paul Bourgets at Hyères. Stays
        with the Curtises in their Venice palazzo, where he meets
        and becomes friends with Jessie Allen. In Rome meets
        young American-Norwegian sculptor Hendrik C. Ander-
        sen; buys one of his busts. Returns to England in July and
        Andersen comes for three days in August. William, his
        wife, Alice, and daughter, Peggy, arrive at Lamb House
        in October. First meeting of brothers in six years. William
        now has confirmed heart condition. James B. Pinker be-
        comes literary agent and for first time James's professional
        relations are systematically organized; he reviews copy-
        rights, finds new publishers, and obtains better prices for
        work ("the germ of a new career"). Purchases Lamb
        House for $10,000 with an easy mortgage.

1900   Unhappy at whiteness of beard which he has worn since
        the Civil War, he shaves it off. Alternates between Rye
        and London. Works on *The Sacred Fount*. Works on and
        then sets aside *The Sense of the Past* (never finished). Be-
        gins *The Ambassadors*. *The Soft Side*, a collection of twelve
        tales, published. Niece Peggy comes to Lamb House for
        Christmas.

1901   Obtains permanent room at the Reform Club for London
        visits and spends eight weeks in town. Sees funeral of
        Queen Victoria. Decides to employ a typist, Mary Weld,
        to replace the more expensive overqualified shorthand ste-
        nographer, MacAlpine. Completes *The Ambassadors* and
        begins *The Wings of the Dove*. *The Sacred Fount* published.

Has meeting with George Gissing. William James, much improved, returns home after two years in Europe. Young Cambridge admirer Percy Lubbock visits. Discharges his alcoholic servants of sixteen years (the Smiths). Mrs. Paddington is new housekeeper.

1902	In London for the winter but gout and stomach disorder force him home earlier. Finishes *The Wings of the Dove* (published in August). William James Jr. (Billy) visits in October and becomes a favorite nephew. Writes "The Beast in the Jungle" and "The Birthplace."

1903	*The Ambassadors, The Better Sort* (a collection of eleven tales), and *William Wetmore Story and His Friends* published. After another spell in town, returns to Lamb House in May and begins work on *The Golden Bowl*. Meets and establishes close friendship with Dudley Jocelyn Persse, a nephew of Lady Gregory. First meeting with Edith Wharton in December.

1904–05	Completes *The Golden Bowl* (published Nov. 1904). Rents Lamb House for six months, and sails in August for America after twenty-year absence. Sees new Manhattan skyline from New Jersey on arrival and stays with Colonel George Harvey, president of Harper's, in Jersey shore house with Mark Twain as fellow guest. Goes to William's country house at Chocorua in the White Mountains, New Hampshire. Re-explores Cambridge, Boston, Salem, Newport, and Concord, where he visits brother Bob. In October stays with Edith Wharton in the Berkshires and motors with her through Massachusetts and New York. Later visits New York, Philadelphia (where he delivers lecture "The Lesson of Balzac"), and then Washington, D.C., as a guest in Henry Adams' house. Meets (and is critical of) President Theodore Roosevelt. Returns to Philadelphia to lecture at Bryn Mawr. Travels to Richmond, Charleston, Jacksonville, Palm Beach, and St. Augustine. Then lectures in St. Louis, Chicago, South Bend, Indianapolis, Los Angeles (with a short vacation at Coronado Beach near San Diego), San Francisco, Portland, and Seattle. Returns to explore New York City ("the terrible town"), May–June. Lectures on "The Question of Our Speech" at Bryn Mawr commencement. Elected to newly founded American Academy of Arts and Letters

(William declines). Returns to England in July; lectures had more than covered expenses of his trip. Begins revision of novels for the New York Edition.

1906–08 Writes "The Jolly Corner" and *The American Scene* (published 1907). Writes eighteen prefaces for the New York Edition (twenty-four volumes published 1907–09). Visits Paris and Edith Wharton in spring 1907 and motors with her in Midi. Travels to Italy for the last time, visiting Hendrik Andersen in Rome, and goes on to Florence and Venice. Engages Theodora Bosanquet as his typist in autumn. Again visits Edith Wharton in Paris, spring 1908. William comes to England to give a series of lectures at Oxford and receives an honorary Doctor of Science degree. James goes to Edinburgh in March to see a tryout by the Forbes-Robertsons of his play *The High Bid*, a rewrite in three acts of the one-act play originally written for Ellen Terry (revised earlier as the story "Covering End"). Play gets only five special matinees in London. Shocked by slim royalties from sales of the New York Edition.

1909 Growing acquaintance with young writers and artists of Bloomsbury, including Virginia and Vanessa Stephen and others. Meets and befriends young Hugh Walpole in February. Goes to Cambridge in June as guest of admiring dons and undergraduates and meets John Maynard Keynes. Feels unwell and sees doctors about what he believes may be heart trouble. They reassure him. Late in year burns forty years of his letters and papers at Rye. Suffers severe attacks of gout. *Italian Hours* published.

1910 Very ill in January ("food-loathing") and spends much time in bed. Nephew Harry comes to be with him in February. In March is examined by Sir William Osler, who finds nothing physically wrong. James begins to realize that he has had "a sort of nervous breakdown." William, in spite of now severe heart trouble, and his wife, Alice, come to England to give him support. Brothers and Alice go to Bad Nauheim for cure, then travel to Zurich, Lucerne, and Geneva, where they learn Robertson (Bob) James has died in America of heart attack. James's health begins to improve but William is failing. Sails with William and Alice for America in August. William dies at Chocorua soon after arrival, and James remains with the family for the winter. *The Finer Grain* and *The Outcry* published.

1911   Honorary degree from Harvard in spring. Visits with Howells and Grace Norton. Sails for England July 30. On return to Lamb House, decides he will be too lonely there and starts search for a London flat. Theodora Bosanquet obtains two work rooms adjoining her flat in Chelsea and he begins autobiography, *A Small Boy and Others.* Continues to reside at the Reform Club.

1912   Delivers "The Novel in *The Ring and the Book*," on the 100th anniversary of Browning's birth, to the Royal Society of Literature. Honorary Doctor of Letters from Oxford University June 26. Spends summer at Lamb House. Sees much of Edith Wharton ("the Firebird"), who spends summer in England. (She secretly arranges to have Scribner's put $8,000 into James's account.) Takes 21 Carlyle Mansions, in Cheyne Walk, Chelsea, as London quarters. Writes a long admiring letter for William Dean Howells' seventy-fifth birthday. Meets André Gide. Contracts bad case of shingles and is ill four months, much of the time not able to leave bed.

1913   Moves into Cheyne Walk flat. Two hundred and seventy friends and admirers subscribe for seventieth birthday portrait by Sargent and present also a silver-gilt Charles II porringer and dish ("golden bowl"). Sargent turns over his payment to young sculptor Derwent Wood, who does a bust of James. Autobiography *A Small Boy and Others* published. Goes with niece Peggy to Lamb House for the summer.

1914   *Notes of a Son and Brother* published. Works on "The Ivory Tower." Returns to Lamb House in July. Niece Peggy joins him. Horrified by the war ("this crash of our civilisation," "a nightmare from which there is no waking"). In London in September participates in Belgian Relief, visits wounded in St. Bartholomew's and other hospitals; feels less "finished and useless and doddering" and recalls Walt Whitman and his Civil War hospital visits. Accepts chairmanship of American Volunteer Motor Ambulance Corps in France. *Notes on Novelists* (essays on Balzac, Flaubert, Zola) published.

1915–16   Continues work with the wounded and war relief. Has
occasional lunches with Prime Minister Asquith and family, and meets Winston Churchill and other war leaders.
Discovers that he is considered an alien and has to report
to police before going to coastal Rye. Decides to become
a British national and asks Asquith to be one of his spon-
sors. Receives Certificate of Naturalization on July 26.
H. G. Wells satirizes him in *Boon* ("leviathan retrieving
pebbles") and James, in the correspondence that follows,
writes: "Art *makes* life, makes interest, makes importance."
Burns more papers and photographs at Lamb House in
autumn. Has a stroke December 2 in his flat, followed by
another two days later. Develops pneumonia and during
delirium gives his last confused dictation (dealing with the
Napoleonic legend) to Theodora Bosanquet, who types it
on the familiar typewriter. Mrs. William James arrives December 13 to care for him. On New Year's Day, George V
confers the Order of Merit. Dies February 28. Funeral services held at the Chelsea Old Church. The body is cre-
mated and the ashes are buried in Cambridge Cemetery
family plot.

Note on the Texts

This volume, one of five collecting the complete stories of Henry James, presents in the approximate order of their composition 17 stories that were first published between 1884 and 1891. All of these stories were published in periodicals and later collected, with revisions, in book form. For all but three of the stories, the first English and American book versions were published by the same firm, Macmillan and Company, from the same typesetting. In the cases of "Georgina's Reasons," "A New England Winter," and "The Path of Duty," James had different publishers in England and America, with resulting variation between the English and American versions of the stories; James was living in England at the time, and the English book printings contain James' latest authorial revisions. The texts printed in this volume are taken from their first English book editions.

The following list gives the first periodical, first American, and first English book publications of the stories included in this volume. (James later included 11 of the stories in the 1907–9 New York Edition of his collected works: "Louisa Pallant," "The Liar," "The Aspern Papers," "A London Life," "The Lesson of the Master," "The Patagonia," "The Pupil," "Brooksmith," "The Marriages," "The Chaperon," and "Sir Edmund Orme.")

"Georgina's Reasons." *New York Sun*, July 20 and 27, August 3, 1884. Collected in *The Author of Beltraffio* (Boston: James R. Osgood, 1885) and in *Stories Revived* (London: Macmillan, 1885).

"A New England Winter." *Century Magazine*, August–September 1884. Collected in *Tales of Three Cities* (Boston: James R. Osgood, 1884), and in *Tales of Three Cities* (London: Macmillan, 1884).

"The Path of Duty." *English Illustrated Magazine*, December 1884. Collected in *The Author of Beltraffio* (Boston: James R. Osgood, 1885) and in *Stories Revived* (London: Macmillan, 1885).

"Mrs. Temperly." *Harper's Weekly*, August 6, 13, and 20, 1887, with the title "Cousin Maria." Collected in *A London Life, The Patagonia, The Liar, Mrs. Temperly* (London and New York: Macmillan, 1889).

"Louisa Pallant." *Harper's New Monthly*, February 1888. Collected in *The Aspern Papers, Louisa Pallant, The Modern Warning* (London and New York: Macmillan, 1888).

"The Aspern Papers." *Atlantic Monthly*, March–May 1888. Collected in *The Aspern Papers, Louisa Pallant, The Modern Warning* (London and New York: Macmillan, 1888).

"The Liar." *Century Magazine*, May–June 1888. Collected in *A London Life, The Patagonia, The Liar, Mrs. Temperly* (London and New York: Macmillan, 1889).

"The Modern Warning." *Harper's New Monthly*, June 1888, with the title "Two Countries." Collected in *The Aspern Papers, Louisa Pallant, The Modern Warning* (London and New York: Macmillan, 1888).

"A London Life." *Scribner's Magazine*, June, July–September 1888. Collected in *A London Life, The Patagonia, The Liar, Mrs. Temperly* (London and New York: Macmillan, 1889).

"The Lesson of the Master." *Universal Review*, July–August 1888. Collected in *The Lesson of the Master* (London and New York: Macmillan, 1892).

"The Patagonia." *English Illustrated Magazine*, August–September 1888. Collected in *A London Life, The Patagonia, The Liar, Mrs. Temperly* (London and New York: Macmillan, 1889).

"The Solution." *New Review*, February 1889. Collected in *The Lesson of the Master* (London and New York: Macmillan, 1892).

"The Pupil." *Longman's Magazine*, March–April 1891. Collected in *The Lesson of the Master* (London and New York: Macmillan, 1892).

"Brooksmith." *Harper's Weekly*, May 2, 1891, and *Black and White*, May 2, 1891. Collected in *The Lesson of the Master* (London and New York: Macmillan, 1892).

"The Marriages." *Atlantic Monthly*, August 1891. Collected in *The Lesson of the Master* (London and New York: Macmillan, 1892).

"The Chaperon." *Atlantic Monthly*, November–December 1891. Collected in *The Real Thing and Other Tales* (London and New York: Macmillan, 1893).

"Sir Edmund Orme." *Black and White*, November 25, 1891. Collected in *The Lesson of the Master* (London and New York: Macmillan, 1892).

This volume presents the texts of the printings chosen for inclusion here but does not attempt to reproduce features of their typographic design. Spelling, punctuation, and capitalization often are expressive features, and they are not altered, even when inconsistent or irregular. The following is a list of typographical errors corrected, cited by page and line number: 221.8, you?; 235.29, Does'nt; 257.33, poem's; 269.13, Aspern's!; 328.22, 'the likes'; 329.3, too; 377.4, M.P.; 380.17, Grice.'; 391.21, movement; 397.1, nonenity; 414.10, that; 455.2, this she; 520.25, heattempted; 590.40, then; 759.8, its.

Notes

In the notes below, the reference numbers denote page and line of this volume (the line count includes titles and headings). No note is made for material included in standard desk-reference books such as Webster's *Collegiate, Biographical,* and *Geographical* dictionaries. Quotations from Shakespeare are keyed to *The Riverside Shakespeare,* ed. G. Blakemore Evans (Boston: Houghton Mifflin, 1974). For further background than is provided in the notes, see *Henry James Letters,* ed. Leon Edel (Cambridge: The Belknap Press of Harvard University Press, Vol. I—1843–1875 [1974]; Vol. II—1875–1883 [1975]; Vol III—1883–1895 [1980]; Vol. IV—1895–1916 [1984]) and *The Complete Notebooks of Henry James,* ed. Leon Edel and Lyall H. Powers (New York and Oxford: Oxford University Press, 1987).

25.38 contadina] Peasant woman.

29.4 *poverina*] Poor little girl.

35.13 lazzarone] Beggar; vagabond.

45.10 scagliola] Plaster.

52.9 Pisana] Native of Pisa.

66.18–19 *appartement de garçon*] Bachelor apartment.

67.15 *froissé*] Offended.

82.34–36 famous dragon . . . to be sacrificed] The Minotaur.

83.1 Appleton Brown] John Appleton Brown (1844–1902), American painter.

83.12 Germans] Dancing parties at which the German cotillion was the chief dance.

86.25–26 *bonnes d'enfants*] Nursery maids.

98.18 *enfoncée*] Ensconced.

104.2–3 *Boisson fade, écœurante*] Tasteless, nauseating drink.

109.15 *de votre façon*] In your style.

109.31–32 *Jamais de la vie*] Not on your life.

110.4–5 *Qu'est-ce qui vous prend, ma mère?*] What's the matter with you, mother?

113.3   *dans le monde*] In society.

120.23   *entrée en matière*] Preamble.

134.11–12 *les convenances*] Propriety.

137.34   *arrière-pensée*] Ulterior motive.

142.22   *boutade*] Witticism.

150.6   *lambris*] Ceiling panels.

165.7   *predella*] Altar step.

166.18   *Murray*] One of a series of popular travel guides to the Continent, published by John Murray in London beginning in 1820 and continuing throughout the century.

167.3   *à la portée*] Within the grasp.

170.25   *toilette de jeune fille*] Young girl's outfit.

171.5   Bastien-Lepage] Jules Bastien-Lepage (1848–84), French painter.

173.26   *Mais j'espère bien*] I should hope so.

173.28–29 *Je m'en rapporte à*] I will go along with.

174.22   *empressement*] Alacrity.

176.26   *succès de bonté*] Triumph of virtue (lit., success of goodness).

179.26   *bal blanc . . . jeunes filles*] Ball for young girls.

182.2–3   *femme forte*] Strong woman.

182.15   Gobelins] Tapestries made at Gobelins, the state factory of tapestry in Paris, or imitations of these; damasks used for upholstery.

182.15   *Ces dames*] These women.

182.26   *sergents de ville*] Police constables.

182.28   *beaux quartiers*] Elegant neighborhoods.

183.32   *en fin de compte*] When all is said and done.

184.19–20 'Décidément, ma bonne . . . perfection——'] "Decidedly, my dear, there is no one like you! It's perfection——"

187.18–19 'Que voulez-vous? . . . mère!'] "What do you expect? She adores her mother!"

190.16   *succès de bonté*] See note 176.26.

192.9   Kursaal] The main building of a health spa.

201.1   *Wirthschaften*] Country inn.

215.8   *en pension*] As boarders.

215.34   *Votre siège est fait*]   You've taken your position.

219.23   *parti*]   Match.

233.5   *quartier perdu*]   Godforsaken neighborhood.

233.23   *felze*]   Cabin of a gondola.

235.26   *padrona*]   Landlady.

236.1   scagliola]   See note 45.10.

240.17   *C'est la moindre des choses*]   It's the least of things.

242.16   *comme il faut*]   Elegant.

247.24   *forestieri*]   Foreigners.

247.31   *quartiere*]   Lodgings.

258.10   *contadina . . . pifferaro*]   Peasant woman . . . fife-player.

264.24   *arrière-pensée*]   See note 137.34.

264.36   *passeggio*]   Promenade.

265.11   *avvocato*]   Lawyer.

265.14   *capo d'anno*]   New Year's Day.

276.20   *giro*]   Stroll.

286.37   *padrona di casa*]   Mistress of the house.

298.20   *comme il faut*]   See note 242.16.

305.23–24   *la vecchia*]   The old woman.

305.31   passeggio]   Promenade.

305.31–32   Poveretta!]   Poor little girl!

308.13   the Giorgione at Castelfranco]   Altar piece in the Venetian Castelfranco, commissioned in 1504 or 1505, depicting Mary enthroned between St. Francis and a knight.

315.25   *'Dove commanda?'*]   "Where to?"

318.22   fondamentas]   Footings.

321.22   'goody']   Sentimental.

323.36   to *aborder*]   To take on.

328.5   *contadina*]   See note 25.38.

328.19–25   Werther's Charlotte . . . Newcome]   Characters in Goethe's *Die Leiden des jungen Werthers* (*The Sorrows of Young Werther*, 1774) and W.M. Thackeray's *The Newcomes* (1855).

339.31   *que voulez-vous?*]   What do you expect?

353.8   Moroni]   *The Tailor*, by Giovanni Battista Moroni (c. 1525–78), Italian portraitist.

357.3   *Jamais de la vie!*]   See note 109.31–32.

357.23   *toupet*]   Nerve.

365.31   *bavardise*]   Talkativeness.

369.34–35   *n'en parlons plus*]   Let's drop it.

393.33   *qui vaut bien la vôtre*]   Who is just as good as yours.

419.13   *sur le vif*]   From life.

421.2   *visé*]   Countersignature.

442.2   *larmoyer*]   Weep.

442.12   *c'est de naissance*]   It's inborn.

443.26   *Nous verrons cela*]   We'll see to that.

445.17   *Ce n'est pas pour vous blesser*]   I don't want to upset you.

445.40   *pour me renseigner*]   To inform myself.

459.17   *cabotin*]   Graceless; boorish.

459.32   *ces dames*]   See note 182.15.

478.4   Lecky]   W.E.H. Lecky (1838–1903), Irish historian, author of *History of Rationalism in Europe* (1865) and *History of European Morals from Augustus to Charlemagne* (1869).

488.18   Mr. John Timbs]   Prolific popular writer (1801–75) of such works as *Things Not Generally Known, Familiarly Explained* (1857), *Hints for the Table* (1859), *School Days of Eminent Men* (1864), *English Eccentricities and Eccentrics* (1866), and *Clubs and Club Life in London* (1872).

492.2   *imprévu*]   Unforeseen.

512.19–20   Meyerbeer's *Huguenots*]   *Les Huguenots*, by Gustave Meyerbeer, first performed at the Paris Opera in 1836.

526.19   Voyons un peu!]   Let me see.

528.29   Vous faisiez votre cour]   You paid court to her.

538.6   *éclaircissement*]   Exposure.

540.22   the 'Bradshaw']   Railroad schedule.

550.2   *Il s'attache à ses pas*]   He follows her everywhere.

558.19   *à fleur de peau*]   Superficially.

561.40   *mot*] Remark.

569.13   *Cela s'est passé comme ça?*] That's the way it happened?

570.39   *jamais de la vie*] See note 109.31–32.

573.19   *mornes*] Dismal.

577.11–12   *C'est d'un trouvé*] He's a find.

584.22–23   *il ne manquerait plus que ça*] That's all we'd need.

587.19   *carton-pierre*] Pasteboard.

587.21   Lincrusta-Walton] A decorative embossed wall covering simulating carved plaster or wood, invented in 1877.

589.18   *n'en parlons plus*] See note 369.34–35.

621.34–35   *jeunesse des écoles*] Students.

625.15   *Elle ne sait pas se conduire*] She doesn't know how to behave.

625.34   *cœur de mère*] . Mother's heart.

628.18   *C'est toujours ça*] There's always that.

637.12   *Ohne Hast, ohne Rast*] Without haste, without rest.

650.14–15   *Voyez-vous ça?*] You see?

654.11   *n'en parlons plus*] See note 369.34–35.

667.34–35   *d'un commerce facile*] Of easy access.

668.10   *lambris*] See note 150.6.

668.28   *près du Saint-Père*] At the Vatican.

668.29–30   "bearded like the pard,"] Shakespeare, *As You Like It*, II.vii.150.

669.27   muff] One who is generally inept or deficient in practical sense.

671.13   *villeggiatura*] Rural retreat.

683.22   *portone*] Front gate.

684.11   *Il est impayable.*] He is priceless.

684.25   *vous autres*] You people.

685.33   *assuré un sort*] Guaranteed a provision.

689.6   *Que me contez-vous là?*] What are you telling me?

691.27   *fille sans dot*] Girl without a dowry.

692.36   muff] See note 669.27.

692.37   *Que voulez-vous?*] See note 339.31.

694.13   *Il est impayable*] See note 684.11.

699.21   *congé*] Goodbye.

699.26   *digne*] Dignified.

702.31   *padrona*] See note 235.26.

706.31   *vetturini*] Coachmen.

707.23   *preux chevalier*] Gallant knight.

708.15   *promesso sposo*] Fiancé.

708.26   *Jamais de la vie*] See note 109.31–32.

709.32   *ces dames*] See note 182.15.

710.20   *promener*] Show off.

710.32–33   *sousentendus*] Innuendoes.

714.9   *gants de Suède*] Suede gloves.

719.14–15   *mot d'ordre*] Command.

720.13   *borné*] Limited.

726.21   *calorifère*] Heating system.

729.9   *immondes*] Disgusting.

733.17–18   "Voyons, mon cher,"] "Look here, my dear."

739.14   *modeste aisance*] Comfortable living.

743.15   *tutoyer*] Speak familiarly.

745.29–31   *c'est trop fort . . . dont vous allez?*] It's too much . . . at the rate you're going?

747.20–21   *Dites toujours*] Go ahead and say it.

754.34   *sauve qui peut*] Stampede; free for all.

757.12   *Comme vous-y-allez!*] How you go on!

759.23   dotations] Endowments.

762.1   *L'Ecole Anglaise*] The English School.

763.30   *malentendus*] Misunderstandings.

765.1–2   *c'est la fin de tout*] It's all over.

773.40   *de race*] Pure bred.

774.6   *sur le retour*]   Past her prime.

777.31   *sauve qui peut*]   See note 754.34.

787.10   *pour rire*]   To make one laugh.

789.23   *bouderie*]   Sulking.

805.35   *"Dame!"*]   "Well!"

811.1   *n'en parlons plus*]   See note 369.34–35.

828.33   *commérages*]   Gossip.

844.36–37   *déclassement*]   Loss of social position.

875.31   St. Martin's summer]   Second or autumnal summer, from late
October to late November.

Library of Congress Cataloging-in-Publication Data

James, Henry, 1843–1916.
  [Short stories. Selections]
  Complete stories, 1884–1891 / Henry James.
    p. cm. — (Library of America ; 107)
  ISBN 1–883011–64–7
  I. Title. II. Series.
PS2112 1999b
813′.4—dc21   98–19250
                            CIP

THE LIBRARY OF AMERICA SERIES

This book is set in 10 point Linotron Galliard,
a face designed for photocomposition by Matthew Carter
and based on the sixteenth-century face Granjon. The paper is
acid-free Ecusta Nyalite and meets the requirements for permanence
of the American National Standards Institute. The binding
material is Brillianta, a woven rayon cloth made by
Van Heek-Scholco Textielfabrieken, Holland.
The composition is by The Clarinda
Company. Printing and binding by
R.R.Donnelley & Sons Company.
Designed by Bruce Campbell.